Illustrated by

E. BROOKS
DAVID CHARLES
FRANK CLIFFORD
HILARY EVANS
CHARLES GORHAM
DONALD GREEN
DAVID HUGHES
STAN MARTIN
DAVE NASH
FREDA NICHOLS
HAZEL POPE
CHRISTOPHER REYNOLDS
BRUCE ROBINSON
SHIREEN NATHOO

JUNIOR

PEARS

ENCYCLOPAEDIA

TWENTY-SIXTH EDITION

EDITED BY EDWARD BLISHEN

This edition first published 1986
by Pelham Books Ltd.
27 Wrights Lane
Kensington
London W8 5TZ

All enquiries to be addressed to
Pelham Books Ltd.,
27 Wrights Lane, Kensington,
London W8 5TZ

ISBN 0 7207 1666 7

Printed and bound in Great Britain
by Richard Clay (The Chaucer Press) Ltd., Bungay, Suffolk

ABOUT THIS BOOK

One of the most exhausting tasks in which I find myself engaged from time to time is that of giving away school prizes. For this you have to be extremely fit: able to stand for long periods, handling great quantities of sometimes very heavy books and transferring them into the hands of prizewinners: and, of course, shaking those hands. I've shaken over two hundred hands on a single occasion: an exercise that deprives you of the use of the prize-giving arm for days afterwards. And now and then I discover I'm in the odd position of handing over copies of JUNIOR PEARS. I feel very tempted to say to a recipient: '*You* are particularly lucky!—this is an amazingly good book! And *astonishingly well-edited*! A first-class choice!' And so on. I don't say it, of course. But I always hope that some day a prizewinner will identify me as the editor. The trouble is that, on the whole, you don't notice who's edited a book. It's not a glamorous function. I actually once met a child who believed this encyclopaedia was edited by someone called Junior Pear. Though it turned out she suspected he might, in private life, have a title: she thought he was probably Professor Junior Pear.

What I'm also tempted to do on those prize-giving platforms is to explain what JUNIOR PEARS is—this single, annual, much-compressed volume, into which for over a quarter of a century the contributors and I have stuffed as many of the current facts of things as we could.

Properly speaking, of course, an encyclopaedia, being a volume or set of volumes that tells you everything about everything, ought to provide an answer to any question whatever. But the days when a book, or even a row of books, could do that (if ever they existed) are long since over. Today most encyclopaedias have to be much more modest.

This, in fact, is a specialised encyclopaedia, for a particular audience. It's for young people, and is intended to provide information on the main topics in which, as we judge, young people are likely to be interested. Partly we hope it will be found a helpful handbook by students: thus the sections on history, geography, and so on. But no young reader is simply a schoolboy, or a schoolgirl, or a student: and though we hope your schooling is so wide-based that sections on sport and ships, and railways and music, may often have some bearing on what you're studying, still these and other similar sections are there mainly to supply information about out-of-school or out-of-college activities.

But if our basic purpose is to provide information, we've never wanted the book to be merely a bulging collection of facts. We've tried to make it pleasant to read as well as easy to consult: here, for example, are all the main facts about motor-cars, but imbedded in a history of the motor-car, and an account of the workings and makings of the motor-car, that form, we hope, more than a dry assemblage of information.

Nevertheless, we've tried to bear in mind that you ought to be able to track down as quickly as possible any single piece of information for which you have some desperate need: therefore each section is arranged so that it yields any particular fact as easily as possible. The list of contents on the title-pages of some sections will be found useful; and other sections, which lend themselves to such treatment, are in dictionary form.

But, of course, a single-volume encyclopaedia is not and could not be a substitute for deeper reading. You can learn from JUNIOR PEARS that nine hundred years ago, in 1086, the Domesday Book was completed: but to discover what the Domesday Book was (actually it was a survey of the land and wealth of England: and if it had an editor, *his* name, too, is forgotten), and why the Normans who'd conquered England set out to make such a survey, you must look to the historians. This is one kind of book—aiming to give the gleaming bare bones of information. For the flesh you must look to other sorts of book to which we provide pointers here and there in our lists of 'Further Reading'.

Now and then, alas, a reader fails to find the bone he is after, or finds something amiss with the bone itself. If this happens to you, write to me about it. Complaints or comments of any kind—addressed to 27 Wrights Lane, Kensington, London W8 5TZ—will be taken into account in next year's revision.

Behind certain changes in this 26th edition lie the very helpful suggestions made by many readers. On the whole, I'd be glad if you wouldn't ask me to carry out extensive research on some subject or other: I'd have to be twenty men to provide such a service. And now and then I've had the mean suspicion that I was being asked to do someone's homework. ('Please tell me everything about the French Revolution and let me have it, with maps, diagrams and time-charts, by next Monday at the latest.') But simpler inquiries, and certainly any criticism you wish to make, will be most welcome. A book like this ought to be shaped not only by a body of contributors but also by a body of readers, and all of us who are responsible for JUNIOR PEARS will welcome your collaboration.

It may be worth giving our usual warning that this section has been found so useful by some parents that the true owners of the book have been deprived of it. Keep it in a safe place.

CONTENTS

THE WORLD

1: ITS HISTORY

A DIARY OF WORLD EVENTS

The story of man, who first appeared on the Earth a little less than a million years ago, can be traced back only about 6,000 years. For earlier times there are no written records (nor have archaeologists made discoveries) to help the historian to form an accurate or detailed picture of human activity.

This diary is planned not only to be referred to if you are hurriedly searching for a particular event (or revising a particular period) but also to be read as a story. And a hair-raising story it is, with its empires rising and falling, its barbarian Franks and Goths and Vandals becoming the French and Germans and Italians of today, and the uneasy groupings of nations against one another becoming the enormous anxious grouping of our own time. Read the diary through, and consider what a tiny pinch of time these 6,000 years are when measured against the total life of our planet. And remember, as you read, that the diary doesn't cease to be written simply because we have had to break off at 1986 to put it in this book. This diary is now your diary; History is your history.

The first reference to any historical figure in this account is printed in black type. So that if you are interested in, say, Napoleon, and come across his name in ordinary type, you will know that you are somewhere in the middle of his story, and must look back to **Napoleon** in order to find its beginning. The names of battles are printed in small capitals, like this: WATERLOO.

Some of the most important events of all, the passing of great Acts of Parliament and achievements of exploration and discovery, are omitted because they are dealt with separately elsewhere in this section.

For Britain, the present year's outstanding anniversary is that of the completion, exactly 900 years ago, of the Domesday Book.

B.C.

4000–3000 First settlements in the river valleys of the Nile in Egypt, the Tigris and Euphrates in Mesopotamia, the Indus in India and the Yellow River in China.

By 2000 Chinese civilisation, oldest in the world, covers practically the whole of China.

In the Indus valley the Dravidians have established an orderly system of government; they are often invaded, but out of the give and take of ideas between conquerors and conquered, Hinduism begins to emerge. In Mesopotamia the Sumerians have invented a form of writing (cuneiform), divided the circle into 360°, a degree into 60 minutes and a minute into 60 seconds, and discovered how to extract copper and make bronze. Their knowledge lives on despite their absorption into the Babylonian Empire, whose best-known king, **Hammurabi**, extends the authority of Babylon as far as Syria and codifies his country's laws.

The Great Pyramids

In the Nile valley the Egyptians have already built the Great Pyramids at Gizeh and the Sphinx (2600) and divided time into solar years.

The spread of knowledge from Egypt has helped to create the Minoan civilisation in Crete (named after the legendary king **Minos** (see DICTIONARY OF MYTHOLOGY), whose magnificent palace at Knossos was discovered in 1900).

In Britain the great stone circles at Stonehenge and Avebury are still used for religious worship.

1800–1700 First use in Egypt of papyrus, an early form of paper. Nile valley overrun by Hyksos ('princes of the desert').

The Babylonian empire is overrun by the Hittites; but there is conflict, lasting several centuries, between these and other invading tribes based on Babylon, Nineveh and other cities.

1580 Hyksos driven out of Egypt. Founding of the 'New Kingdom', under which Egypt is to be at her greatest.

1400 Moses leads the Israelites out of Egypt. Knossos destroyed by earthquake or enemies, and Cretan civilisation at an end.

1300–1200 Hittites, now controlling all Mesopotamia, discover how to smelt iron, equip their troops with iron weapons, and clash with Egypt. Neither wins, and both empires begin to crumble.

1180 Siege of Troy: one of the wars by which the ancestors of the ancient Greeks settled themselves round the Aegean, and the only one of which an account survives (in Homer's *Iliad*).

c. **1060–***c.* **970** David king of Israel.

c. **970–***c.* **940** Solomon king of Israel. He uses his enormous wealth, gained through trade, to build the Temple at Jerusalem.

800 The Phoenicians, whose cities of Tyre and Sidon are nearly 1,000 years old, found Carthage.

776 First Olympiad.

753 Rome founded.

750–550 Greek city states emerge on Greek mainland and around the coasts of Mediterranean and Black Sea.

691 Assyrians (already lords of Mesopotamia, Syria, Palestine, Arabia) conquer Egypt.

660 First Mikado in Japan.

612 Chaldeans conquer Assyrians and establish second Babylonian Empire.

597 Nebuchadnezzar, mightiest Chaldean emperor, captures Jerusalem and carries off the Jews into captivity.

594 Solon lays the foundations of Athenian democracy.

560 Buddha born.

551 Confucius born.

539–525 Cyrus, king of Persia, makes himself master of Asia Minor, captures Babylon, founds the Persian empire and allows the Jews to return to Jerusalem.

525 Cambyses, Cyrus's successor, conquers Egypt.

510 Rome becomes a republic.

490 Athens has helped Greek cities on the coast of Asia Minor to revolt—unsuccessfully—against their Persian overlords, **Darius I** of Persia lands a force in Greece to punish Athens; is beaten at MARATHON.

480 Xerxes makes a second attempt to crush Greece; exterminates a Spartan army under **Leonidas** at THERMOPYLAE and occupies Athens; but the Persian fleet is destroyed at SALAMIS.

479 Persians defeated at PLAETAEA.

461 Pericles becomes the most important person in Athenian politics. Under his leadership Greek civilisation, free of the Persian menace, has its 'golden age'; it is now that the Parthenon is built (447–438). But removal of the Persian danger leads to quarrelling among the Greek city states.

431–404 Peloponnesian War between Athens and Sparta, ending with capture of Athens.

The Parthenon

390 Gauls capture Rome except for the Capitol, but Romans regain the city by paying huge ransom.

359 Philip becomes king of Macedonia; sets out to make himself overlord of quarrelsome Greek cities.

338 Philip defeats combined armies of Athens and Thebes, becomes master of Greece.

336 Philip assassinated; succeeded by his son, **Alexander the Great**.

333 Alexander defeats **Darius III** of Persia and conquers Egypt, where he founds Alexandria.

327 Alexander extends his empire as far as the Indus.

323 Alexander dies; his empire is divided among his generals.

280 Pyrrhus, king of Epirus, aids Greek cities in S. Italy against Rome; defeats the Romans twice but himself suffers heavy losses (hence the term 'Pyrrhic victories', meaning victories won at great cost).

275 Defeating Pyrrhus, Rome becomes mistress of S. Italy, and thus comes into conflict with Carthage.

264 First Punic War between Rome and Carthage for control of Sicily.

The Roman Empire at its furthest extent

260 Roman sea victory at MYLAE.

256 Roman landing near Carthage repulsed.

246 Great Wall of China built.

241 Remainder of Carthaginian fleet defeated; Carthage sues for peace and loses control of Sicily.

238 Carthage sets out to create new empire in Spain.

225 Gauls invade Roman territory and are defeated. To prevent this happening again, Rome extends her frontiers northwards by conquering Cisalpine Gaul (modern Lombardy); is now mistress of all Italy.

219 Second Punic War. A 26-year-old Carthaginian general, **Hannibal**, crosses the Alps into Italy, where he is unbeaten for 15 years.

217 Hannibal destroys a Roman army at LAKE TRASIMENE.

216 Hannibal destroys a second Roman army at CANNAE, but is unable to capture Rome itself.

210–206 Roman army wipes out Carthaginian forces in Spain and conquers the country.

204 Romans cross from Spain to Africa.

202 Hannibal returns to Africa to save Carthage, but is defeated at ZAMA.

201 Carthage surrenders her fleet and hands Spain over to Rome.

166 Tartar invasion of China.

149 Third Punic War. Uneasy at the steady recovery of Carthage, Rome resolves to destroy her rival.

146 Carthage destroyed.

102 **Marius** drives back invading German tribes.

91 Revolt of Italian cities belonging to Rome but with no say in government.

89 All Italians become Roman citizens.

88 Civil war in Rome between plebeians (people's party), led by Marius, and patricians (nobles), under **Sulla.** Sulla wins and Marius escapes to Africa.

87 While Sulla is fighting in Greece, Marius seizes power in Rome.

86 Marius dies.

82 Sulla returns, massacres his enemies, strengthens the power of the Senate, becomes dictator.

78 Sulla dies.

73 **Spartacus** leads revolt of 60,000 slaves.

71 **Crassus** crushes Spartacus revolt.

70 Crassus and **Pompey** reduce power of the Senate.

66–62 Pompey captures Jerusalem, conquers Syria and advances to the Euphrates.

60 Pompey, Crassus and **Caesar** divide the government of Rome's dominions, becoming the First Triumvirate (rule of three men). Caesar begins conquest of Gaul.

55 Caesar's first visit to Britain.

53 Crassus defeated and killed by Parthians.

51 Caesar completes conquest of Gaul.

49 Caesar crosses the Rubicon, boundary of his own command, to overthrow Pompey, now his only rival.

48 Caesar defeats Pompey at PHARSALUS. Pompey escapes to Egypt and is murdered.

44 Caesar is murdered.

43 **Octavian**, Caesar's nephew, **Antony** and **Lepidus** form Second Triumvirate.

42 Octavian and Antony defeat **Brutus** and **Cassius**, chief plotters against Caesar. The government of Rome's dominions is divided, Octavian taking the West, Antony the East (which he rules from Egypt with **Cleopatra**) and Lepidus, Carthaginian Africa.

31 Octavian defeats Antony and Cleopatra at ACTIUM.

30 Deaths of Antony and Cleopatra.

27 Octavian, now known as Augustus, becomes first Roman emperor.

4 True date of birth of **Jesus**.

A.D.

14 Augustus dies.

30 Jesus crucified.

43 Emperor **Claudius** sends force to conquer Britain. The South is soon subdued, despite resistance from **Caractacus**, who is captured and sent to Rome. The Romans work their way northwards.

61 **Boadicea**, queen of the Iceni, revolts against Romans, burns their settlement at London; but her army is annihilated and she takes poison.

68 **Nero**, last emperor of the house of Augustus, commits suicide.

70 Emperor **Titus** captures and destroys Jerusalem, drives the Jews from the Holy Land.

79 Pompeii and Herculaneum destroyed in eruption of Vesuvius.

82 **Agricola**, governor of Britain, attempts conquest of Scotland.

93 **Trajan** adds Dacia (modern Rumania) and Mesopotamia to Roman empire, now at its largest.

117 **Hadrian** tries to keep barbarians out of Roman territories by building permanent fortifications, including 70-mile-long wall (Hadrian's Wall) from Tyne to Solway.

164–80 Plagues ravage Roman and Chinese empires.

180 Century of war and disorder begins for Rome, during which a succession of generals, many not even Roman by birth, are made emperors by troops in their pay. Perpetual invasions by Franks, Goths, Parthians, Vandals and Huns.

226 **Artaxerxes** founds new dynasty in Persia.

284 **Diocletian**, last Roman emperor to persecute Christians, re-organises the empire with two joint emperors and two subordinate emperors.

312 **Constantine** defeats his joint emperor, **Maxentius**, and becomes sole emperor in West.

313 Constantine legalises Christianity; later makes it State religion.

324 Constantine defeats emperor in the East, becomes sole ruler of Roman world.

328 To celebrate victory, Constantine founds 'new Rome' by enlarging ancient Greek city of Byzantium, calls it Constantinople.

330 Constantine moves capital to Constantinople.

337 Constantine dies, and empire is again ruled by succession of joint (and rival) emperors.

379 **Theodosius the Great**, emperor in the East, drives Goths from Greece and Italy.

382 Theodosius makes peace with Goths.

394 Theodosius becomes last sole emperor of Roman world.

395 Theodosius dies; division of empire into West and East becomes final.

407 As barbarians pour into Western empire, Roman legions are withdrawn from Britain in last attempt to defend Rome. Britain is left easy prey to Angles and Saxons.

410 Visigoths under **Alaric** plunder Rome. Waves of barbarians sweep into Spain, Portugal, Italy, Gaul and North Africa.

434 **Attila** becomes king of the Huns, Mongolians whose invasion of Europe is death-blow for Western empire.

449 **Hengist** and **Horsa**, Jutish chiefs, invade England, set up kingdom in Kent.

451 Invading Gaul, Attila is defeated by army of Goths and Romans at CHALONS.

452 Attila invades Italy; is persuaded by **Pope Leo I** to spare Rome.

453 Attila dies.

455 Vandals sack Rome. In next twenty years ten different emperors rule.

476 Last Roman emperor deposed; Western empire ends.

482 **Clovis**, king of Salian Franks, makes himself first king of Frankland (France), with Paris as his capital.

496 Clovis baptised; Franks become Christians.

527 **Justinian**, whose codification of Roman law is basis for much later Western law, becomes emperor in Constantinople. Attempting re-conquest of Western Empire, he recovers North Africa, S.E. Spain and Italy.

536 Belisarius, Justinian's famous general, captures Rome.

565 Justinian dies.

568 Lombards invade Italy, settle in the north.

570 Birth of **Mohammed**.

590 Gregory the Great becomes Pope; declares Rome supreme centre of the Church.

597 St Augustine lands in England, baptises **Ethelbert**, king of Kent.

601 St Augustine becomes first archbishop of Canterbury.

c. **616** Mohammed proclaims himself the apostle of Allah.

618 Great T'ang dynasty founded in China.

628 Mohammed writes to all rulers of the earth, demanding that they acknowledge the One True God, Allah, and serve Him.

632 Mohammed dies; his friend **Abu Bakr**, first Caliph ('successor'), leads Arabs out of the desert to achieve Mohammed's aim of making the world submit to Islam.

637 Arabs defeat Persians at KARDESSIA. Soon after, Mesopotamia, Syria, Palestine and Egypt fall to them.

638 Jerusalem surrenders to Arabs.

641 Arabs capture Alexandria. Its famous library is destroyed.

643 The Arabs defeat armies of the Eastern empire at YARMAK.

669 Arabs unsuccessfully attack Constantinople from sea.

711 Having conquered East and North Africa, Arabs cross into Spain.

720 Spain subdued, the Arabs (with the Moors) invade France.

732 Charles Martel drives Arabs out of France.

751 Pepin, son of Charles Martel, crowned King of the Franks, founding Carolingian dynasty.

762 Baghdad founded; becomes capital of Arab empire.

768 Pepin dies; his kingdom divided between his son Charles (later known as **Charlemagne**) and **Carloman**.

771 Carloman dies and Charlemagne takes possession of his lands. From then onwards Charlemagne enlarges his dominions until his power reaches from the Pyrenees to the river Elbe in Germany, and from the Atlantic to the Danube and Tiber.

786 Haroun-al-Raschid becomes Caliph at Baghdad; under him Arab empire is at its greatest.

800 Charlemagne crowned in Rome emperor of the Holy Roman Empire.

802 Egbert king of Wessex, one of seven Anglo-Saxon kingdoms fighting for supremacy in England. Others are Northumbria, Mercia, Kent, Sussex, Essex and E. Anglia.

809 Haroun-al-Raschid dies; beginning of 200 years of chaos and civil war in Arab empire.

814 Charlemagne dies.

829 Egbert unites England for first time under one king.

840 Frankish empire is divided between Charlemagne's sons and grandsons, whose quarrels lead to its breaking up.

871 **Alfred the Great** king of Wessex, practically the only part of England not in Danish hands.

878 Alfred defeats Danes, compels them by Treaty of Wedmore to stay in their settlements in N.E. England and become Christians.

900 Alfred dies.

919 **Henry I** king of Germany; completes the separation of the Frankish empire into Germany and France.

987 **Louis V**, last Carolingian king of France, dies, and is succeeded by **Hugh Capet**, first modern French king.

1013 **Sweyn** of Denmark conquers England, is accepted as king.

1015 **Canute**, Sweyn's son, defeats **Edmund Ironside**, son of last Anglo-Saxon king, and divides realm with him.

1016 Edmund dies; Canute becomes sole king.

Viking Ship

1042 Edward the Confessor returns to England as king from Normandy, where he has been living at the court of the Norman duke. Leaves government to **Earl Godwin**, devotes himself to religion.

1054 Eastern Orthodox Church breaks with Church of Rome.

1065 Westminster Abbey, rebuilt by Edward the Confessor, consecrated.

1066 Edward the Confessor dies; **Harold**, son of Earl Godwin, elected king. **William** of Normandy invades England and kills Harold at HASTINGS.

1071 Seljuk Turks, having seized Baghdad, sweep across Asia Minor and take fortress of Niceaea opposite Constantinople.

1075 Turks take Jerusalem and Holy Places.

1086 Domesday Book, a survey of England, completed.

1095 Pope Urban II summons Christian nations to First Crusade.

1098 Crusaders take Antioch.

1099 Crusaders take Jerusalem.

1135 England plunged in civil war when **Stephen**, grandson of William the Conqueror, allows himself to be elected king although he had previously recognised **Mathilda**, Henry I's daughter, as heir to throne.

1149 Second Crusade ends in failure.

1153 Stephen acknowledges Mathilda's son as his heir.

1164 Henry II tries to bring English clergy into the power of the royal courts and clashes with **Thomas à Becket**, his chancellor and Archbishop of Canterbury, who flees to France.

1170 Becket returns, but the quarrel breaks out afresh, and he is murdered in Canterbury Cathedral.

1174 Saladin proclaimed caliph; launches a holy war of all Muslims against Christians.

1187 Saladin recaptures Jerusalem.

1189 Third Crusade, under **Philip Augustus** of France and **Richard I**, fails to retake Jerusalem. Siege of Acre.

1191 Crusaders capture ACRE.

1192 Richard concludes armistice with Saladin.

1202 Fourth Crusade; Constantinople captured.

1206 Mogul empire founded in India.

1215 King John is forced at Runnymede to accept Magna Carta, which lays it down that no freeman may be imprisoned or punished except by law of the land.

1218–21 Fifth Crusade captures Damietta, in Egypt, but loses it again.

1228–29 Sixth Crusade recovers Jerusalem by negotiation.

1264 Henry III, whose misrule has caused barons to revolt, is taken prisoner at LEWES by **Simon de Montfort**.

1265 De Montfort summons first Parliament in which towns are represented; is defeated and killed at EVESHAM.

1273 Rudolf of Hapsburg, founder of dynasty that is to reign in Austria until 1918, elected Holy Roman Emperor.

1280 Kublai Khan emperor of China; encourages trade and teaches religious tolerance. Visited by **Marco Polo**.

1282 Edward I completes conquest of Wales.

1291 Acre, last Christian stronghold in Syria, is lost.

1295 Edward I summons Model Parliament, so called because for the first time King, Lords and Commons meet.

1296 Edward I attempts to annex Scotland.

1297 Sir William Wallace defeats Edward at STIRLING.

1298 Edward defeats Wallace at FALKIRK.

1301 Edward makes his son Prince of Wales.

1304 Wallace captured and executed, but **Robert Bruce** raises another revolt against Edward.

1306 Robert Bruce crowned king of Scotland.

1309 Papacy falls into French control; residence of the Popes moved to Avignon.

1314 Edward II defeated at BANNOCKBURN by Robert Bruce.

1328 Robert Bruce recognised by England as king of Scotland.

1337 Outbreak of 'Hundred Years' War' between England and France. Causes: a conflict of commercial interests and Edward III's claim to French throne.

1340 English defeat French by sea at SLUYS.

1346 Edward III defeats French at CRECY.

1347 Edward captures Calais.

1348–49 Black Death, the bubonic plague, reaches England, killing nearly one half of the population, and causing acute shortage of labour and social unrest.

1356 Edward, the Black Prince, defeats French at POITIERS.

1369 French renew the war; reconquer province after province.

1372 English fleet destroyed. Impoverished by war, weakened by quarrels between Black Prince and his brother, **John of Gaunt**, England loses French possessions except Bordeaux and Calais.

1378 Rival Popes elected in Rome and Avignon.

1381 Heavily taxed, tied to the land as serfs, the peasants revolt under **Wat Tyler**. Tyler is murdered and the rising crushed, but from this time serfdom gradually declines.

1384 Death of **John Wycliffe**, who has attacked abuses in the Church of Rome and ordered a translation of the Bible into English.

1385 Scots invade England; **Richard II** takes Edinburgh.

1388 Scots again invade; are victorious at OTTERBURN.

1397 Richard II executes or banishes leaders of the barons. Among those banished is **Henry, Duke of Hereford**, John of Gaunt's son and heir.

1399 John of Gaunt dies; Richard II confiscates his estates. Henry, Duke of Hereford, returns to England to lead revolt of the nobles. Parliament deposes Richard and accepts Henry as king—the first to speak English (grown out of Norman French and Anglo-Saxon) as his mother-tongue.

1400 Welsh revolt under **Owen Glendower**.

1403 Scots defeated at HOMILDON HILL. Henry IV crushes revolt at SHREWSBURY.

1415 **Henry V** renews war against France, captures HARFLEUR and is victorious at AGINCOURT.

1420 Henry V recognised by French king as his heir; marries French princess.

1422 Henry dies. French refuse to recognise his one-year-old son, **Henry VI**, as king of France; Henry V's brother continues war.

1429 English overcome all French resistance except in ORLEANS; they besiege the town, but are driven off by an army led by **Joan of Arc**.

1431 Joan of Arc, captured by the English, is burned at the stake; but French advance continues.

1445 **Johann Gutenberg**, first European printer, sets up business in Mainz.

1453 The Eastern empire is at an end when Constantinople falls to the Ottoman Turks, who sweep into Greece and across to the Danube.

1455 Disastrous end of Hundred Years' War has made the English government unpopular, and the **Duke of York** (white rose) claims the throne from Henry VI, a Lancastrian (red rose). So begin Wars of the Roses. Yorkists win at ST ALBANS, but are then defeated; York flees to Ireland.

1460 York returns, is victorious at NORTHAMPTON, but is defeated and killed at WAKEFIELD.

1461 Edward, York's son, proclaimed king in London as **Edward IV**. Defeats the Lancastrians at TOWTON; Henry VI is captured and imprisoned.

1464 Lancastrians defeated at HEXHAM.

1470 Yorkist **Earl of Warwick**, the 'Kingmaker', quarrels with Edward IV, frees Henry VI. Edward flees to Flanders.

1471 Edward returns, defeats and kills Warwick at BARNET and routs Lancastrians at TEWKESBURY.

1476 **Caxton** sets up as printer.

1478 Inquisition begins in Spain.

1483 Edward IV succeeded by 12-year-old son, **Edward V**. Richard, Duke of Gloucester, Protector of the Realm, has himself proclaimed king as **Richard III**. Edward V and his brother are murdered in the Tower.

1485 Henry Tudor, Earl of Richmond, lands in England and defeats Richard III at BOSWORTH. As **Henry VII**, he founds the line of Tudors, breaks the power of the nobles and establishes strong central government.

1492 **Ferdinand** of Aragon and **Isabella** of Castile, whose marriage unites Spain for the first time, finally free the country from the Moors by capturing GRANADA.

1513 **James IV** of Scotland invades England, is defeated at FLODDEN.

1517 **Martin Luther**, founder of Protestantism, nails to church door at Wittenberg his condemnation of many practices of the Church of Rome.

1519 **Cortes** conquers Mexico.

1520 Luther publicly burns the Papal Bull excommunicating him, and refuses to go back on his teachings. Protestantism spreads; is adopted in Sweden in 1527, in Denmark in 1536. In Switzerland it is established by **Calvin**, whose followers in France, the Huguenots, wage bitter wars with the Catholics between 1562 and 1598. In Scotland the Reformation, as this great movement is called, triumphs by 1560, largely owing to teaching of Calvin's disciple, **John Knox**.

1526 **Baber**, Moslem warrior king, captures Delhi.

1528 Conquest of Peru.

The *Santa Maria* 1492

1529 The Ottoman Sultan, **Suleiman** the Magnificent, having taken Belgrade, the island of Rhodes and Budapest, attempts to storm Vienna but is beaten back.

Cardinal Wolsey, Henry VIII's chief minister, fails to persuade the Pope to grant Henry a divorce from **Catherine of Aragon**, and Henry dismisses him.

1533 Archbishop Cranmer dissolves Henry's marriage and crowns **Anne Boleyn** as queen.

1534 Henry VIII, though no Protestant, repudiates authority of the Pope, proclaims himself head of the Church and dissolves the monasteries, confiscating their wealth.

1536 Death of Catherine of Aragon; execution of Anne Boleyn. Henry marries **Jane Seymour**.

1538 Henry VIII excommunicated.

1540 Henry marries **Anne of Cleves**; later in the year marries **Catherine Howard**.

1542 Catherine Howard executed; Henry marries **Catherine Parr**.

The Tower of London

1547 Ten-year-old **Edward VI** succeeds Henry VIII.

1549 & 1553 First Prayer Books in English are issued by Cranmer.

1553 Mary, Henry VIII's daughter and a Catholic, becomes Queen. **Lady Jane Grey**, to whom Edward VI had bequeathed the crown to avoid return to Catholicism, is also proclaimed Queen, but is arrested and executed. Cranmer is burnt at the stake and succeeded by a Catholic Archbishop of Canterbury. Supremacy of Pope again acknowledged. Persecution of Protestants marking Mary's reign wins her the nickname of 'Bloody Mary'.

1558 Calais, last French possession still in English hands, falls.

Elizabeth succeeds Mary and repudiates authority of the Pope. To spare England the bitter religious wars with which Europe is being ravaged, she begins working out a religious compromise, in which the Protestant doctrines of the Church of England are mixed with many Catholic elements in its ritual.

1568 Mary Queen of Scots, Catholic and heir to Elizabeth, forced to flee to England; imprisoned by Elizabeth.

1571 Fleet of the Christian League, led by Spain, defeats Turkish fleet at LEPANTO and destroys Moslem sea power in Mediterranean.

1585 Elizabeth lands English army in Netherlands to support Dutch in their revolt against Spanish rule, and this brings into the open the undeclared war England has been fighting with **Philip of Spain** as a result of trade rivalry and religious differences.

1586 Battle of ZUTPHEN; **Sir Philip Sidney** slain.

1587 Mary Queen of Scots executed.

    Drake attacks Cadiz.

1588 Philip of Spain sends Great Armada against England; it is destroyed by the English fleet under **Howard of Effingham**, Drake, **Hawkins** and **Frobisher**.

1603 Elizabeth dies; James VI of Scotland becomes king as **James I**. His High Church views displease the Puritans, and the powerful new merchant class is offended by his insistence on the Divine Right of Kings.

1605 Gunpowder Plot, a Catholic conspiracy to blow up James and his Parliament, is discovered.

1609 Holland frees herself from Spain; is soon to be a great power, leading the world in trade, art and science and founding an empire in East and West Indies.

1618 Outbreak of the Thirty Years' War, last attempt of the Catholics to stamp out the Reformation in Europe. The Catholics are at first successful, but the tide turns against them when in 1629 **Gustavus Adolphus** of Sweden comes in on the Protestant side.

1620 Pilgrim Fathers sail from Plymouth in the *Mayflower* to found the first colony in New England.

The *Mayflower* 1620

1628 Parliament refuse to vote **Charles I** any money until he has accepted their Petition of Right, which declares taxation without consent of Parliament and imprisonment without trial illegal.

1629 Charles dissolves Parliament, imprisoning its leaders. He reigns without Parliament for the next eleven years, raising money by means regarded as illegal, and suppressing all opposition by special royal courts.

1632 Gustavus Adolphus wins the battle of LUTZEN but is slain.

1640 England invaded by Scots; Charles I obliged to recall Parliament to raise money for the war. The 'Short' Parliament insists on airing its grievances before voting money, and is dismissed. Charles has to summon new Parliament and this (the 'Long' Parliament lasting until 1660) sets out to make personal government by a monarch impossible.

1641 Irish rebel against English.

1642 Charles I goes to House of Commons to arrest his enemies, finds them gone. Slips out of London and the Civil War begins. First battle, at EDGEHILL, is indecisive.

1644 Royalists defeated at MARSTON MOOR by **Cromwell**.

1645 Cromwell wins decisive victory at NASEBY.

1646 Charles surrenders to Scots.

1647 The Scots, having made alliance with Parliamentarians, hand Charles over.

1648 Scots, uneasy about their alliance and encouraged by Charles, invade England, are defeated by Cromwell at PRESTON. Thirty Years' War ends without victor.

1649 Charles I executed. England, calling itself a Commonwealth, becomes a republic. Cromwell ruthlessly restores English rule in Ireland.

1650 Charles I's son, later **Charles II**, lands in Scotland, is crowned King of Scotland.

1651 Prince Charles invades England, is defeated by Cromwell at WORCESTER, and escapes to the continent.

1652–54 Trade rivalry between English and Dutch leads to war. Cromwell's navy, commanded by admirals like **Robert Blake**, holds its own against the mighty Dutch fleet.

1653 Cromwell becomes Lord Protector.

1655 Cromwell seizes Jamaica from Spain.

1658 Cromwell dies; is succeeded by his son, **Richard Cromwell**.

1659 Richard Cromwell resigns.

A Royalist   A Parliamentarian

1660 General Monk, Commonwealth commander in Scotland, occupies London and invites Princes Charles to return as Charles II.

1664 War between Britain and Holland; British capture New Amsterdam and rename it New York.

1665 Great Plague of London.

1666 Great Fire of London.

1667 Dutch fleet sails up the Medway and destroys British squadron. Britain makes peace but keeps New York.

1670 Charles II makes secret Treaty of Dover with **Louis XIV** of France, promising to declare himself a Catholic, restore Catholicism in England and support Louis against the Dutch; in return Louis agrees to help Charles with money and, if necessary, troops.

1672 Charles suspends all laws against Catholics, and joins with France in attacking Holland. The Dutch, under **William of Orange**, hold up the French by piercing the dykes; the Dutch admiral **De Ruyter** puts the Anglo-French fleet out of action in SOUTHWOLD BAY.

1673 Charles II forced to summon Parliament to ask for money; is compelled to accept Test Act excluding all Catholics from office and to end war with Holland.

1678 Titus Oates announces 'Popish plot' to restore Catholicism in England. Attempt is made to exclude from the succession Charles's brother, **James**, a Catholic convert.

1681 William Penn establishes colony of Pennsylvania as refuge for persecuted Quakers.

1683 Turks make final effort to carry Islam into the heart of Europe; are defeated at VIENNA.

1685 Charles II dies; James, though a Catholic, becomes king as James II. **Monmouth**, illegitimate son of Charles II and a Protestant, tries to seize the throne, but is defeated at SEDGEMOOR and executed.

1688 William of Orange, married to **Mary**, James's Protestant daughter, is invited to come over with an army to save the English constitution and Church. William lands at Torbay, and James II flees to France.

1689 The Crown is accepted by William and Mary after they have agreed to the Bill of Rights, limiting royal power. James II lands in Ireland to lead an Irish rising.

1690 William defeats James and the Irish at the battle of the BOYNE.

1701 Parliament passes the Act of Settlement confining the succession to Protestants.

Louis XIV uses a dispute over the succession to the Spanish throne to resume his plan to make France strongest European power. William forms Britain, Holland and Austria into 'Grand Alliance' to stop him.

1702 William dies; succeeded by **Anne**.

1704 Marlborough's victory at BLENHEIM saves Vienna from the French.

1704 Admiral Rooke captures Gibraltar.

1706 Marlborough defeats French at RAMILLIES.

1707 Act of Union between England and Scotland.

1708 Marlborough defeats French at OUDENARDE.

1709 Marlborough victorious at MALPLAQUET.

1710 Replacement of Whigs by Tories, who want to end the war, leads to Marlborough's downfall.

1713 War ends. Britain receives Newfoundland and Hudson Bay territory from France; Gibraltar and Minorca from Spain.

1714 Anne dies and Elector of Hanover becomes king as **George I**. He cannot speak English and has no interest in English affairs; his reign helps to make Parliament even more powerful, leads to the modern pattern of government by a cabinet of ministers.

1715 The 'Old Pretender', son of James II, lands in Scotland to find his supporters have already been defeated.

1720 A financial crisis, the 'South Sea Bubble', produced by wild speculation, ruins thousands.

   Sir Robert Walpole becomes first Prime Minister.

1739 Walpole, though anxious to preserve peace, is forced into war with Spain (the 'War of Jenkins' Ear').

1740 Hapsburg emperor, **Charles VI**, dies. The European powers have agreed to accept his daughter, **Maria Theresa**, as his heir; but France, Spain and Prussia ignore the arrangement. Prussia attacks Austria; France invades Germany. Britain and Holland enter this War of the Austrian Succession on Maria Theresa's side.

1743 **George II** defeats French at DETTINGEN—the last time a British king is personally in command in a battle.

1745 French defeat Austro-English army at FONTENOY. **Prince Charles Edward**, the 'Young Pretender', lands in Scotland and wins victory at PRESTONPANS. He invades England, but finds little support; his army returns to Scotland.

1746 The Jacobites (Charles Edward's followers) defeated at CULLODEN; the 'Young Pretender' escapes to the continent.

1748 War of the Austrian Succession ends. Prussia under **Frederick the Great** has emerged as the strongest power in N. Germany; Britain has proved herself superior at sea over the French, with whom she continues a struggle for supremacy in India and America.

1756 Seven Years' War breaks out. Maria Theresa, helped by France and Russia, seeks to win back Silesia from Frederick of Prussia, who is supported by Britain under the elder **Pitt**. **The Nawab of Bengal** captures Calcutta; locks 140 British men and women into small military guardroom—the 'Black Hole of Calcutta'—where most suffocate. In America French capture Fort Oswego, main British trading centre on Great Lakes.

1757 **Clive** defeats Nawab of Bengal at PLASSEY.

1758 Fort Oswego recaptured; British take Fort Duquesne, renaming it Pittsburgh in honour of Pitt.

1759 French defeated at MINDEN; in America **General Wolfe** is slain capturing QUEBEC. There are British naval victories at LAGOS and QUIBERON BAY.

1760 French defeated in India, leaving British supreme. George

II succeeded by his grandson, **George III**, first Hanoverian king to speak English and to regard himself as king of England rather than Elector of Hanover.

1761 George brings about downfall of Pitt.

1763 Seven Years' War ends, leaving Britain with her conquests in India and America.

1773 'Boston Tea Party' brings to a head the long quarrel between George III and American colonists. Colonists maintain they should not be taxed without their consent. When Britain imposes tax on tea, a group of colonists, disguised as Indians, board ships in Boston and throw their cargoes into the harbour.

1775 First shots exchanged between colonists and British troops at Lexington. **George Washington** made American Commander-in-Chief.

1776 The 13 American colonies issue Declaration of Independence (July 4).

1777 **General Burgoyne**, marching from Canada to New York, forced to surrender at SARATOGA. France and Spain declare war on Britain.

1781 British army under **General Cornwallis** forced to surrender at YORKTOWN, Virginia.

1783 Britain recognises American independence.

1788 Founding Fathers draw up American constitution.

1789 George Washington first US President. French Revolution breaks out. Faced with bankruptcy, **Louis XVI** is compelled to summon the States-General (French Parliament) for first time since 1614. States-General turns itself into National Assembly, determined to abolish absolute power of king, and proclaims principles of Liberty, Equality, Fraternity. Louis calls in soldiers; people of Paris retaliate by storming Bastille prison (July 14).

1791 Louis XVI flees, but is caught and brought back to Paris.

1792 Austria and Prussia, wishing to restore Louis, make war on France; Louis is deposed and imprisoned, France becoming republic. Extreme revolutionaries (the Jacobins) gain control.

1793 French occupy Austrian Netherlands (now Belgium); Britain joins in war against France with Holland, Spain, Austria and Prussia. Louis XVI is executed; Reign of Terror begins. In Britain the government, afraid that revolutionary ideas will spread, suppresses all societies in favour of reform.

1794 Execution of **Robespierre** ends Reign of Terror.

1795 Prussia has withdrawn from war, Holland been conquered and Spain defeated; only Austria and Britain are left. **Napoleon Bonaparte** becomes French C.-in-C. in Italy, where he rapidly masters the Austrians. Britain takes Cape of Good Hope, formerly Dutch.

1797 Napoleon threatens Vienna; Austria makes peace. **Jarvis** and **Nelson** defeat Spanish fleet at CAPE ST VINCENT; **Duncan** the Dutch fleet at CAMPERDOWN.

1798 Bonaparte eludes a British fleet under Nelson, lands in Egypt and defeats Mameluke Turks in BATTLE OF THE PYRAMIDS. Nelson destroys French fleet anchored in Aboukir Bay, in BATTLE OF THE NILE. Bonaparte advances into Syria, is stopped by **Sir Sidney Smith** at ACRE.

1799 Britain, Turkey, Austria and Russia combine against France. Bonaparte abandons army in Egypt and returns to France, where he makes himself First Consul.

1800 Bonaparte defeats Austrians at MARENGO. Ireland made part of United Kingdom.

Early Watt's Pumping Engine

The *Victory*, Nelson's flagship

1801 Austria sues for peace. Russia has withdrawn from war and, with Denmark, Sweden and Prussia, has taken measures against Britain for searching neutral ships to ensure that they do not carry cargoes useful to France. Nelson smashes Danish fleet at COPENHAGEN.

1802 Peace returns for a time. Britain restores Cape of Good Hope to Dutch, but keeps Ceylon (formerly Dutch) and Trinidad (formerly Spanish). Bonaparte made First Consul for life.

1803 War between Britain and France renewed, with Spain on France's side. Bonaparte sells Louisiana to the USA.

1804 Bonaparte becomes Emperor Napoleon.

1805 Younger **Pitt** builds alliance against Napoleon with Austria and Russia. Napoleon gathers army at Boulogne to invade England. Nelson defeats French and Spanish fleets at TRAFALGAR.

Napoleon defeats Austrians and Russians at AUSTERLITZ. Pitt dies.

1806 Australia again sues for peace; **Francis II** drops title of Holy Roman Emperor, becomes Emperor of Austria. Napoleon crushes Prussia at JENA; is master of Germany.

1807 Napoleon defeats Russians at EYLAU and FRIEDLAND; forms an alliance with Russia at Tilsit. Britain now his only enemy; he seeks to ruin her by excluding British goods from Europe. Britain replies by blockading all countries under Napoleon's control; forces surrender of the Danish fleet by bombardment of Copenhagen. Napoleon occupies Portugal, which has thriving trade with Britain.

1808 Napoleon makes brother Joseph king of Spain. Spain and Portugal revolt; Peninsular War begins.

1809 Sir Arthur Wellesley (later Duke of Wellington) defeats French at TALAVERA. Austria re-enters war; is defeated at WAGRAM and again sues for peace.

1812 Napoleon invades Russia; occupies Moscow after battle of BORODINO, but the Russians burn the city and he is forced to retreat in winter, his 'Grande Armée' being destroyed. Wellington defeats French at SALAMANCA; occupies Madrid.

Dispute arising out of Britain's insistence on searching neutral ships leads to war between Britain and US. Britain occupies and burns Washington.

1813 Prussia and Austria drive Napoleon from Germany. Wellington defeats French at VITORIA; drives them out of Spain.

1814 Britain and America make peace.

Austria, Russia and Prussia invade France, occupy Paris; Wellington marches into S. France. Napoleon abdicates, is banished to Elba. Bourbon dynasty restored.

1815 Napoleon escapes, resumes power, but is defeated at WATERLOO. Banished to St Helena. **Louis XVIII** returns to Paris.

1819 At 'Peterloo Massacre' in Manchester cavalry charge an open-air meeting of supporters of parliamentary reform.

1821 Greeks revolt against Turkish rule. Death of Napoleon.

1822 The poet **Lord Byron** is among many volunteers who go to Greece to help her in her war of independence.

1823 Spain tries to regain her American colonies; Britain recognises their independence, threatens to use British navy to prevent interference from Spain. **President Monroe** of the USA issues what is known as the 'Monroe Doctrine', saying that any interference by European powers on the American continent would be regarded as unfriendly to the USA.

1827 British, French and Russian fleets destroy the Turkish fleet at NAVARINO, making it impossible for the Turks to put down the Greeks.

1829 Greece becomes independent kingdom.

1830 **Charles X** of France, who has tried to re-establish absolute monarchy, is driven from the throne and replaced by **Louis-Philippe**. Belgians revolt against Dutch rule and become independent. Unrest in Italy and Germany; in Britain the struggle for parliamentary reform becomes intense.

1832 Great Reform Bill is passed (see HISTORIC ACTS OF PARLIAMENT).

1833 Slavery abolished throughout British Empire.

1835–36 Boers undertake their 'Great Trek' to escape from British rule in the Cape; set up republic in Transvaal.

1837 **Queen Victoria** ascends the throne.

1846 Faced with famine in Ireland, **Sir Robert Peel** repeals Corn Laws (see HISTORIC ACTS OF PARLIAMENT).

1848 A year of unrest: revolt against Austrian rule by Hungarians, Czechs and Italians; Rome declared a republic; Sicily and Naples rise against their King. All these revolts suppressed. The crown of a unified Germany offered to **Frederick William IV** of Prussia, but as a believer in Divine Right of Kings he refuses because crown is offered by representatives of the people. He is forced to give his own subjects a constitution. Louis-Philippe of France deposed; republic proclaimed. In Britain the Chartists demand the vote for all.

1851 Great Exhibition in London.

1852 **Louis-Napoleon** makes himself French emperor as Napoleon III.

1853 Britain, seeing her position in India threatened by Russian ambitions, and France, under Napoleon III, who wants to strengthen his power by military triumphs, declare war on Russia. Anglo-French and Turkish force landed in the Crimea to capture Sevastopol. In the battles of BALACLAVA and INKERMANN, the Russians fail to drive out allied force. The harsh winter exposes the inefficiency of the British army, especially of its medical services, which **Florence Nightingale** does her best to remedy.

Paxton's Crystal Palace, home of the Great Exhibition

1855 Sardinia, wanting French and British support in the struggle to unite all Italy, joins war against Russia. Russians abandon SEVASTOPOL.

1856 Crimean War ends.

1857 Indian Mutiny breaks out. Delhi seized by rebels, besieged and captured by the British; Lucknow defended by British garrison. Last Mogul emperor is deposed and British Crown takes over administration of India from East India Company.

1859 Sardinia, under **Victor Emmanuel II**, and France declare war on Austria; defeat her at MAGENTA and SOLFERINO. Sardinia receives Lombardy, gives Nice and Savoy to France.

1860 Garibaldi overthrows Kingdom of the Two Sicilies (Naples and Sicily), which, with four remaining Italian duchies, are annexed by Sardinia.

  Araham Lincoln elected US President. Eleven southern states, wishing to maintain State rights against the central government, particularly on the issue of Negro slavery, claim the right to break away from the Union. Lincoln denies this right; American Civil War breaks out.

1861 Victor Emmanuel proclaimed first king of a United Italy.

1862 Bismarck, foreign minister of Prussia, sets out to unify Germany.

1863 General Robert E. Lee, commander of Southern forces in the American Civil War, defeated at GETTYSBURG. Lincoln proclaims abolition of slavery.

1864 Maximilian of Hapsburg made emperor of Mexico by

Napoleon III. Mexican republicans, under **Juarez**, bitterly oppose him.

1865 General Lee surrenders to **General Grant** and American Civil War is over. Abraham Lincoln assassinated.

1866 USA insists that French troops be withdrawn from Mexico. Maximilian shot.

In brief campaign against Austria, ending in overwhelming victory at SADOWA, Prussia smashes Austria's influence over Germany and insists that Venetia be handed over to Italy.

1867 Canada becomes Dominion.

1869 Suez Canal opened.

1870 Napoleon III declares war on Prussia. French army surrounded at METZ and another, with Napoleon in command, surrenders at SEDAN. Napoleon's Empire collapses; is followed by Third Republic.

1871 United Germany proclaimed with king of Prussia as Emperor. France forced to give Alsace-Lorraine to Germany.

1872 Voting becomes secret in Britain.

1875 **Disraeli** wins control of Suez Canal for Britain by buying shares of the Khedive of Egypt. The Khedive's misrule has made Egypt bankrupt, and Britain and France have to pour money into the country to save it from collapse.

1877 Queen Victoria becomes Empress of India. Russia comes to aid of Serbs, Montenegrans, Rumanians and Bulgarians, risen against Turkish rule. Turks defeated; only under threat from Britain and Austria does Russia stop the war.

1878 Bulgaria established as a separate principality under Turkey; Serbia and Montenegro become independent kingdoms; and Bosnia and Herzogovina, both with largely Serbian populations, pass into Austrian hands, thus causing bad blood between Serbia and Austria. Britain receives Cyprus.

1881 At MAJUBA HILL Boers defeat British force trying to occupy Transvaal. Transvaal is recognised as independent republic under British authority.

France occupies Tunis as part of her policy of creating an empire for herself in Africa and Indo-China. Following discovery of the interior of Africa by **Livingstone** and others, 'scramble for Africa' becomes intense.

1882 Britain occupies Egypt and is drawn into the affairs of the Sudan, where **Mohammed Ahmed** has proclaimed himself

Mahdi (Messiah) and declared a holy war against Egypt and all non-Moslems.

1884 Germany joins in 'scramble for Africa', acquiring S.W. Africa, Cameroons, Togoland and Tanganyika.

1885 General Gordon, sent to evacuate British and Egyptian garrisons in the Sudan, killed in Khartoum by Mahdi's forces.

1886 Royal Niger Company formed to open up interior of Nigeria.

1888 British Africa Company secures what is now Kenya and takes over Uganda.

William II becomes German emperor.

1890 Cecil Rhodes, founder of Rhodesia, who hopes to see British territory extend from the Cape to Cairo, becomes Prime Minister of Cape Colony.

In Germany William II drops Bismarck as Chancellor; the German drive to 'win a place in the sun' becomes fiercer.

1896 Jameson's raid into the Transvaal in support of the British there, whose lives the Boers are making difficult, is a failure. Rhodes, suspected of backing Jameson, has to resign as Prime Minister of Cape Colony.

Italy, having established herself in Eritrea as part of the 'scramble for Africa', tries to conquer Ethiopia; is defeated at ADOWA.

1898 British General **Kitchener**, having defeated the Mahdi's forces at OMDURMAN and recaptured Khartoum, encounters a French force at Fashoda. The 'Fashoda incident' brings Britain and France close to war; but France, fearing the growing strength of Germany, gives in.

Grievances of British settlers in the Boer republic lead to the Boer War, beginning with a series of British defeats.

1900 Lord Roberts wipes out main Boer forces, but Boer guerilla units continue war.

Failure of the Boxer rising in China (a revolt against European and Japanese interference in Chinese affairs) speeds the collapse of Chinese imperial rule.

1901 Queen Victoria dies.

Australia becomes self-governing dominion.

1902 Boer War ends; Boer republics annexed by British Crown.

1904 'Entente Cordiale' ('warm understanding') established between Britain and France.

Russia which, after completion of the Trans-Siberian Railway, has extended her influence into Manchuria and Korea, clashes with Japan, which is trying to secure for herself as much of the decaying Chinese empire as she can. Japan declares war on Russia, and in a series of brilliant land and sea victories crushes Russia's Far Eastern forces.

1905 Russia forced to make peace and evacuate Manchuria.

1906 In Britain Liberals win great electoral victory and embark on sweeping programme of social reform.

1907 New Zealand becomes dominion.

Alliance between Britain and France extended to include Russia. There are now two great power blocs in Europe—Germany and Austria on one hand, Britain, France and Russia on the other. Tension increases, and the powers begin an armaments race.

1908 Austria annexes Bosnia and Herzogovina, offending Serbia and Russia, since both provinces have largely Serb (or Slav) populations.

1910 Union of S. Africa formed of Cape of Good Hope, Natal, Orange Free State and Transvaal; becomes a dominion.

1911 In Britain the powers of the House of Lords are sharply cut.

Italy, seeking colonies, makes war on Turkey in order to seize Tripoli.

Germany tries to prevent French penetration of Morocco by sending a warship to Agadir. Backed by Britain, France refuses to give way.

Wright Brothers' biplane 1907–8

1912–13 Two Balkan wars result in the expulsion of Turkey from Europe.

British government introduces an Irish Home Rule Bill which nearly leads to civil war in Ireland.

Tripoli is yielded to Italy.

1914 Assassination of the heir to the Austrian throne at Sarajevo triggers off First World War.

The Germans sweep through neutral Belgium; are halted only a few miles from Paris. The Allies force the Germans back in the battle of the MARNE; by October the struggle has settled down into trench warfare. Russians invade East Prussia, are stopped by **Hindenburg**'s victory at TANNENBERG.

1915 Both sides make costly attempts to break through, without success.

On the eastern front the Germans push the Russians further back.

Turkey, fighting on Germany's side, tries to cut the Suez Canal, but fails. The British fail to open communications with Russia through the Black Sea by forcing the Dardanelles and landing troops on the Gallipoli peninsula.

Italy enters the war on the Allied side. Germans announce that their U-boats will sink all merchant ships in British waters.

1916 Trench warfare continues; huge losses on both sides. British and German fleets meet off JUTLAND; the Germans are so battered that they remain in port for the rest of the war.

Following the sinking of the *Lusitania* with many Americans on board, the Germans are forced to abandon their unrestricted submarine campaign. The Arabs, aided by **T. E. Lawrence**, revolt against Turkish rule. In Britain **Lloyd George** becomes Prime Minister.

1917 Anti-war feeling in Russia leads to overthrow of the Czar; but the provisional government's attempt to continue the war enables **Lenin** and the Bolsheviks to seize power.

The Germans renew unrestricted submarine warfare, and in April the USA declares war.

British and French troops are sent to Italy after the Germans and Austrians have broken through the Italian front at CAPORETTO.

General Allenby captures Jerusalem.

1918 Germans launch their final offensive, but fail to break through. Allies counter-attack under **Marshal Foch** and force Germans to sue for armistice in November. William II, the Kaiser, abdicates; Germany becomes republic. Hapsburg monarchy in Austria comes to an end.

1919 Under peace treaties France regains Alsace-Lorraine; Germany loses the 'Polish Corridor' to the new Polish republic; Austria and Hungary are separated; Serbia is enlarged and becomes Yugoslavia; Czechoslovakia is created; the Ottoman empire is broken up, leaving only Turkey itself, which becomes a republic; a League of Nations is created, but its founder, **President Wilson**, fails to persuade his own country, the USA, to become a member; Germany's colonies become League of Nation's mandates; and Germany has limits set on the size of her armed forces.

1921 Ireland, with the exception of Northern Ireland, which remains linked to the UK, is made a dominion after nearly three years of disturbances.

1922 **Kemal Ataturk** seizes power in Turkey, sets out to modernise his country.

Mussolini becomes head of the Italian government, establishes Fascism.

1924 Lenin, having established Communist rule in Russia despite famine and foreign intervention, dies; **Stalin** emerges as his successor and sets out to make Russia a great industrial power.

In Britain **Ramsay MacDonald** forms the short-lived first Labour government.

1926 General Strike in Britain collapses after six weeks.

1929 World-wide economic crisis causes millions to be thrown out of work in the USA and Europe. In Germany **Hitler**'s National Socialist ('Nazi') party makes large gains.

1931 In Britain the second Labour government is replaced by a largely conservative National Government.

In Spain the monarchy collapses and a republic is established.

Japan invades China, sets up a puppet regime in Manchuria. China appeals unsuccessfully to the League of Nations, from which Japan resigns.

1933 **Franklin D. Roosevelt** becomes US President and launches his 'New Deal' of social and economic reform to help America out of the Great Depression. Hitler is appointed Chancellor and makes himself dictator of Germany.

1935 Hitler denounces the terms of the Versailles Treaty limiting the size of the German armed forces.

Mussolini invades and conquers Ethiopia, which appeals in vain to the League of Nations. Mussolini leaves the League.

1936 Military rising against the left-wing government in Spain leads to the outbreak of the Spanish Civil War. Germans and Italians fight openly on Franco's side, and the government receives aid from Russia.

1938 Hitler occupies Austria and claims the Sudetenland in Czechoslovakia. Under the Munich Agreement, signed by Britain, France, Germany and Italy, the Sudetenland is given to Germany; the new frontiers of Czechoslovakia are guaranteed.

1939 The Spanish Civil War ends with the surrender of Madrid; Fascist dictatorship established under **General Franco**. Hitler seizes the rest of Czechoslovakia. Mussolini seizes Albania.

Hitler makes a pact with Stalin and invades and crushes Poland, which is divided between Germany and Russia. Britain and France declare war; the Second World War has begun.

Russia makes war on Finland (in order to bring the approaches to Leningrad under her control), but her armies are beaten in the winter campaign.

1940 Russians break through; Finland sues for peace. Hitler occupies Norway and Denmark. In Britain **Chamberlain** is brought down, and **Winston Churchill** forms a coalition government. Sweeping through Holland, Belgium and Luxembourg, Hitler crushes France, which sues for armistice. Free French under **General de Gaulle** continue to fight from Britain. Britain, having extricated her army from France at Dunkirk, fights on alone. Hitler's plan to invade Britain collapses when his air force (the Luftwaffe) fails to win control of the air in the Battle of Britain; but the Luftwaffe continues its effort to smash Britain by 'blitz' bombing.

Italy enters war on German side, attacks Greece. British troops begin the capture of Italian colonies in E. Africa; reconquer Ethiopia.

1941 Hitler conquers Yugoslavia and Greece; in June, attacks Russia. Germans sweep to gates of Moscow and Leningrad, are caught by the winter. German force under **Rommel** arrives to strengthen Italians in N. Africa and becomes a dangerous threat to Egypt, the Suez Canal and Britain's position in the Middle East.

In December Japan attacks the US Pacific Fleet at Pearl Harbor, bringing the USA into the war, and invades Malaya, Siam, the Philippines, Burma and Indonesia. Hong Kong falls.

1942 In Russia the Germans conquer the Ukraine and penetrate deep into the Caucasus, but winter sets in again, and a German army of over 300,000 is trapped and wiped out at STALINGRAD.

In Africa Rommel defeats the British and gets within 60 miles of Alexandria, but in the battle of ALAMEIN **Montgomery** defeats him decisively. An Anglo-American force under **Eisenhower** takes French N. Africa. Singapore falls, and by May the Japanese are masters of S.E. Asia, but their advance in the Central and S.W. Pacific is halted by American naval and air victories in the CORAL SEA and off MIDWAY.

The Americans begin to roll back the Japanese across the Pacific, capturing Guadalcanal in 1943, the Gilbert, Marshall and Mariana Islands in 1943 and 1944, the Philippines in 1944 and Iwo-Jima and Okinawa in 1945.

1943 German forces sent against Eisenhower in Africa, together with what remains of Rommel's force—altogether over a quarter of a million men—are forced to surrender.

The Allies invade Italy, but the Germans put up stiff resistance, and the Allied advance becomes a long, bitter push up the mountainous Italian peninsula, lasting until the end of the war. Mussolini is deposed and imprisoned; Italy joins the Allies. With Hitler's help, Mussolini escapes.

1944 Russians push Germans out of Russia and advance into Europe.

The Western allies, under Eisenhower, land in Normandy and sweep across France almost to the Rhine. A group of German officers attempt to assassinate Hitler, without success.

The British foil a Japanese attempt to invade India from Burma and launch a drive for the reconquest of Burma, Malaya and Singapore: completed successfully in 1945.

1945 The Allies cross the Rhine; the Russians invade Germany from the East. Hitler commits suicide as the Russians take Berlin. Germany surrenders. Japan surrenders after atom bombs have been dropped on Hiroshima and Nagasaki.

In Britain the Labour party wins an overwhelming victory

and sets out on a programme of social reforms designed to produce the 'welfare state' and to give self-government to non-white colonial peoples.

The United Nations organisation is formed.

1947 India, Pakistan, Burma and Ceylon become independent. **General Marshall**, US Secretary of State, pledges American aid for Europe's recovery provided the European nations unite in a co-operative effort. With help given under this Marshall Plan living standards in nearly the whole of Western Europe rise within three years well above those of before the war. Russia and countries under her control boycott the Plan.

1948 Communists take over government in Czechoslovakia. There is now an 'iron curtain' between east and west. The Russians try to squeeze the Western Allies out of Berlin by cutting road and rail communications. The Allies supply Berlin by airlift until the blockade is lifted.

The state of Israel is proclaimed.

1949 The USA, Canada, Britain, France and eight other W. European countries join together for mutual defence in the North Atlantic Treaty Organisation (NATO). Chinese Nationalists, under **Chiang-Kai-Shek**, are driven from Chinese mainland and take refuge in Formosa; Communist Chinese People's Republic is set up in China.

1950 N. Korea, under communist control, invades S. Korea. United Nations Security Council (from which the Russian delegate happens to be absent) calls upon its members to stop the aggressor; and American, British and other UN forces land just in time to save Korea from being overrun. The communists are driven back into N. Korea, but as they near the Chinese frontiers the Chinese intervene to drive the UN forces back into S. Korea.

1951 In Britain the Conservatives under Churchill defeat Labour.

1952 In Egypt **King Farouk** is forced to abdicate by **General Neguib**.

Elizabeth II succeeds her father, **George VI**.

1953 General Eisenhower becomes first Republican president for twenty years.

Stalin dies; there is a struggle for power inside Russia.

In Egypt Neguib is replaced by **Nasser**.

Korean War ends.

1954 After seven years of war between French and communists

United Nations Building, New York

in French Indo-China, an armistice is arranged. At the Geneva Conference, French rule in Indo-China is ended, and Laos, Cambodia and Vietnam become independent; but N. Vietnam is left under communist control.

1955 Heads of government of the USA, Russia, Britain and France hold a 'summit' meeting at Geneva, and tension is temporarily eased.

1956 Kruschev denounces Stalin's methods in a speech at the 20th Congress of the Soviet Communist party. His speech causes the downfall of the Stalinist government in Poland; and in Hungary it leads to a popular uprising, put down by Russian tanks.

In Egypt Nasser seizes the Suez Canal. Goaded by the aggressive attitude of the Arabs, who refuse to recognise her, Israel invades Egypt and advances on the Suez Canal. Britain and France demand an immediate cease-fire and, when their demand is disregarded, land at Port Said. Their action is condemned by the United Nations, who order the Anglo-French forces to withdraw. This they do.

1957 Ghana and Malaya become independent.

Russia launches into space the first man-made satellite, Sputnik I.

1958 In France, on the brink of civil war as a result of the dis-
obedience of the Algerian settlers and sections of the army, de
Gaulle is returned to power, remodels the constitution, and
gives independence within the French community to France's
colonies.

1959 Macmillan visits Kruschev in Moscow, and Kruschev
becomes the first Soviet head of government to visit the USA.

In Cuba **Fidel Castro** ends the **Batista** regime.

1960 Belgian Congo given independence; sinks almost immediately into chaos. UN intervenes, but disagreement between the
great powers and the African nations hampers its work.

Nigeria becomes independent.

1961 John F. Kennedy, the youngest candidate ever to be elected
to the White House, is installed as President of the USA.

Man's first flight into space is made by **Major Yuri Gagarin**,
Soviet airman, who circles the earth at 25,000 miles an hour
before landing safely in Russia.

South Africa leaves the Commonwealth because of the opposition of the African and Asian Commonwealth countries to
her racial policies. Sierra Leone and Tanganyika become
independent. Cyprus joins the Commonwealth.

In Algeria extremists among the European settlers and French
Army make two attempts to seize power, but President de Gaulle
reasserts his authority on both occasions and continues his
efforts to reach a settlement with the Algerian Arabs. The extremists form a Secret Army (the OAS) and launch a terrorist
campaign in Algeria and France.

World tension mounts when the Communist East German
authorities build a wall across Berlin to stop the flow of East
German refugees to West Berlin.

Dag Hammarskjoeld, the UN Secretary-General, is killed in
an air crash in Africa, and is succeeded by a Burmese, **U Thant**.

Britain applies to join the European Common Market.

1962 Colonel John Glenn, American astronaut, successfully
circles the earth three times in his Mercury space capsule.

Two Russian astronauts, **Major Nicolaev** and **Colonel
Popovich**, are launched into space, the former orbiting the earth
for 94½ hours and the second for 71 hours.

France and the Algerian Arabs sign a cease-fire, and Algeria
becomes an independent country.

Jamaica and Trinidad become independent. Tanganyika declares itself a republic but stays within the Commonwealth.

The world's first communications satellite, Telstar, is launched.

Three thousand Cardinals and Bishops of the Roman Catholic Church meet in Rome to discuss Church problems and Christian unity under **Pope John XXIII**.

The Soviet Union establishes atomic missile bases in Fidel Castro's Cuba, President Kennedy orders Cuba to be blockaded, and the world seems to be on the brink of nuclear war. War is avoided, and tension eases, when Kruschev orders the dismantling of the Soviet missile bases.

1963 President de Gaulle objects to Britain's proposed entry into the Common Market, and the negotiations between Britain and the Common Market 'Six' are broken off.

UN military forces seize the main towns in Katanga, **President Tshombe's** secessionist province in the Congo, thus breaking the power of the biggest of the many separatist governments which have been defying the authority of the Central Congolese Government since independence in 1960.

Valentina Tereshkova, of Russia, becomes first woman in space.

Signing of Test Ban Treaty in Moscow between USA, Russia and Britain marks easing of East–West tension.

Pope John XXIII dies. His successor is **Pope Paul VI**. New state of Malaysia, comprising Malaya, Singapore, Sarawak and parts of Borneo, is set up despite strong opposition of **President Soekarno** of Indonesia. Kenya and Zanzibar become independent members of Commonwealth.

Harold Macmillan resigns for health reasons and is succeeded by Lord Home who relinquishes his peerage to become **Sir Alec Douglas-Home**.

President Kennedy is assassinated. His Vice-President, **Lyndon B. Johnson**, takes over.

1964 In Zanzibar the Sultan is expelled and Zanzibar unites with Tanganyika to form the new state of Tanzania.

Kruschev falls from power. As Secretary General of the Russian Communist Party he is succeeded by **Brezhnev** and as Chairman of the Soviet Council of Ministers by **Kosygin**.

Labour Party narrowly defeats Conservatives in General

Election. **Harold Wilson** becomes Prime Minister.

Lyndon B. Johnson, the Democratic candidate, wins a landslide victory in US presidential election over **Senator Barry Goldwater**, the Republican candidate.

1965 Sir Winston Churchill dies and is given a State funeral.

Russian **Colonel Leonov** becomes first man to 'walk' in space, American **Major White** the second.

Fighting breaks out between India and Pakistan over Kashmir. A cease-fire is arranged after three weeks.

The Government of **Mr Smith** in Rhodesia, a British colony, declares independence without Britain's consent, and is condemned as 'illegal'.

Singapore leaves Malaysia to become independent state within Commonwealth.

1966 Mrs Gandhi, Nehru's daughter, becomes India's first woman Prime Minister after **Mr Shastri**'s death.

Nigeria's unity is shaken by a series of military coups in which many of the country's leaders are killed. A colonel in his thirties, **Yakubu Gowon**, emerges as Head of State.

President Nkrumah of Ghana is deposed by a military coup while on a visit to China.

The fighting in Vietnam between the Communist Vietcong supported by the North Vietnamese, and the South Vietnamese supported by the Americans, becomes fiercer.

Mr Wilson and Labour Party win substantial victory in General Election.

England wins World Cup in football.

Dr Erhard's Christian Democrat Government in West Germany collapses. Christian Democrats under a new leader, **Herr Kiesinger**, form a coalition government with the main opposition party, the Social Democrats.

1967 Britain applies for membership of the Common Market for the second time but again General de Gaulle says no.

A military junta seizes power in Greece.

Israel routs the armed forces of Egypt, Jordan and Syria in six days but, despite a hurriedly arranged cease-fire, there is no relaxation of tension in the Middle East.

Civil war rages in Nigeria between the Federal Nigerian Government and the breakaway state of Biafra.

1968 In Czechoslovakia **President Novotny**, a 'Stalinist hardliner', is ousted by **Alexander Dubcek** and other Communist 'liberals' who introduce political, social and economic reforms. The Russians invade and occupy Czechoslovakia and arrest Dubcek and many of his followers, but when they fail to find any Czechoslovak Communist willing to run the country for them they are forced to reinstate Dubcek. But Dubcek's powers of government are drastically reduced.

Britain announces her intention to withdraw from all her bases East of Suez by 1971 (with the exception of Hong Kong).

France is brought virtually to a standstill by violent student riots and strikes by more than 8 million workers, and it is several weeks before General de Gaulle restores his authority.

Peace talks to end the Vietnam War begin in Paris.

Dr Martin Luther King, the American Negro leader, and **Senator Robert Kennedy**, the late President Kennedy's brother, are assassinated.

Three American astronauts, **Frank Borman**, **Bill Anders** and **Jim Lovell**, become the first men to circle round the moon.

1969 **Richard M. Nixon**, a Republican and President Eisenhower's Vice-President, is installed as US President. He begins withdrawal of American troops from Vietnam.

Alexander Dubcek is ousted as First Secretary of Czechoslovak Communist Party and replaced by **Dr Husak**. 'Hardline' Communists tighten their control in Czechoslovakia.

American astronauts **Neil Armstrong** and **Edwin Aldrin** become the first men to walk on the moon.

General de Gaulle, defeated in a referendum on local regional reform, retires from public life.

After general elections in West Germany, the Social Democrats become the dominant partners in a coalition government for the first time since the foundation of the West German Federal Republic, with **Willy Brandt** as Chancellor.

Greece withdraws from Council of Europe to avoid being expelled because of the undemocratic and repressive nature of its military regime.

1970 The Nigerian civil war ends with the capitulation of Biafra. A treaty, limiting spread of nuclear armaments, comes into force after ratification by 43 states, including Britain, the USA and the Soviet Union, but excluding France and Communist China.

In Britain the Conservatives, led by **Edward Heath**, defeat Labour.

Britain, for the third time, begins negotiations to join the Common Market.

President Nasser of Egypt dies and is succeeded by **Anwar Sadat**.

Serious riots in the Polish ports on the Baltic, sparked off by large increases in food prices, cause downfall of **Gomulka** and his replacement by **Gierek**.

1971 Commonwealth Prime Ministers' Conference meets in Singapore, the first ever to be held in Asia.

In East Pakistan, the Awami League, victorious in the previous year's elections, demands first autonomy for the eastern province and then independence as the Republic of Bangladesh. **President Yahya Khan** treats this demand as sedition. The Awami League's leader, **Sheik Mujibur Rahman**, is arrested and flown to West Pakistan. West Pakistani troops are flown to East Pakistan to suppress all support for independence. Millions of refugees flood across the border into India. India intervenes with its armed forces. In East Pakistan the West Pakistani forces surrender, and Bangladesh is proclaimed. In the West of the Indian sub-continent, a cease-fire is arranged between India and Pakistan. Yahya Khan resigns and hands over the presidency to **Zulfikar Ali Bhutto**.

Britain reaches agreement on the main points in her negotiations for joining the Common Market, and Parliament votes in favour of the principle of Britain becoming a member.

Communist China replaces Chiang-Kai-Shek's government as the official representative of China in the UN.

Kurt Waldheim, an Austrian diplomat, is elected fourth Secretary-General of the UN in succession to U Thant.

1972 President Bhutto releases Sheik Mujibur Rahman who becomes Prime Minister of Bangladesh.

Pakistan leaves the Commonwealth when some Commonwealth countries recognise Bangladesh as an independent state.

Britain signs a Treaty of Accession to the Common Market. Eire, Denmark and Norway sign similar treaties.

President Nixon visits Peking at the invitation of the Chinese Communist Government, and later Moscow at the invitation of the Soviet Government.

Edward Heath's Conservative Government takes over direct rule of Northern Ireland, suspending the powers of the Northern Irish Government and Parliament.

West German Parliament ratifies treaties of reconciliation between West Germany on the one hand and on the other the Soviet Union, Poland and East Germany.

Elizabeth II becomes the first British monarch to visit a Communist country when she pays a State visit to Yugoslavia.

Willy Brandt calls for a general election in West Germany and wins a majority for his Social Democrats and his coalition partners, the Free Democrats (Liberals).

The British Parliament ratifies the Treaty of Accession to the European Economic Community. Eire and Denmark vote in favour of joining but Norway votes against.

President Amin of Uganda expels tens of thousands of Asians from his country in pursuit of his policy of 'Africanisation'. Britain receives nearly 30,000 Ugandan Asians.

1973 Britain, Eire and Denmark become full members of the enlarged European Economic Community.

President Nixon is sworn in for a second term of office after his sweeping victory over **Senator George McGovern**.

Cease-fire agreement in Vietnamese war is signed between US, North Vietnam, South Vietnam and Vietcong.

President Nixon is suspected of being involved in the attempt, during the 1972 Presidential campaign, to break into the headquarters of his political opponents in a building called Watergate, and several of his top assistants resign.

Vice-President **Spiro Agnew**, after pleading guilty to tax evasion, resigns his office.

Dr Henry Kissinger is appointed US Secretary of State, the first non-US-born citizen to be appointed to this office.

Leonid Brezhnev, General Secretary of the Soviet Communist Party, visits the United States and stresses the importance of détente between the super-powers.

The Conference on European Security and Co-operation opens in Geneva; and talks begin in Vienna between East and West on the reduction of forces in Central Europe.

Elections for a new local assembly are held in Northern Ireland; a 12-man executive is created, and the setting-up of a Council of Ireland is agreed.

In Argentina, **Juan Peron** returns to power.

In Chile, **President Allende's** Marxist government is overthrown by a military junta. Allende is killed.

In Greece, **President Papadopoulos**, having deposed **King Constantine** and the monarchy and declared his country a republic, is overthrown by a rival military junta.

Egypt and Syria attack Israel on Yom Kippur, the Jewish Day of Atonement, and, after initial successes, are fought to a standstill. The United States and the USSR agree to bring the fighting to an end to prevent a world-wide conflagration. The Soviet–US agreement is approved by the UN Security Council; but before the fighting is stopped, a second cease-fire agreement has to be negotiated. On Dr Kissinger's initiative, a Middle East peace conference convenes in Geneva.

The oil-producing states of Kuwait, Saudi Arabia, Algeria, Abu Dhabi and Libya cut back oil deliveries to countries declared to be pro-Israel. The use of the 'oil weapon' causes an acute energy crisis—made worse in Britain by the overtime ban imposed by miners and railway drivers.

1974 The British Government announces that the working week for most of British industry has to be cut to three days. The miners vote in favour of a national coal strike.

The US government convenes a conference of oil-consuming countries to discuss the world energy crisis.

Edward Heath calls an election on the issue 'Who governs

Britain?' Harold Wilson takes power at the head of a minority Labour Government. The miners accept a settlement of over £100,000,000.

Harold Wilson calls a second election in the autumn and wins a narrow majority over all other parties. The British government presses ahead with re-negotiating the terms of British membership of the European Economic Community.

High oil prices cause the economies of many industrial countries, including Britain, to slow down.

President Nixon is forced to resign because of his involvement in the Watergate break-in and the manoeuvres to cover it up—the first President in US history to resign his office.

President Makarios is forced to leave Cyprus after a coup organised by Greek Cypriots who support union with Greece (*Enosis*), encouraged in their action by the military junta in Athens. The Turks invade Cyprus and occupy the northern part of the island. The Turkish invasion leads to the collapse of the military junta in Athens. The Greeks vote in favour of remaining a republic. President Makarios returns but the Turks continue to occupy the north.

In Portugal, 50 years of dictatorship are ended when **Dr Caetano** is ousted. The new government moves rapidly to give Portugal's African colonies – Guinea-Bissau, Mozambique and Angola—their independence.

The approach of African rule in Mozambique and Angola changes the balance of power in southern Africa, and, under pressure from **Mr Vorster**, the South African Prime Minister, Mr Ian Smith, the Rhodesian leader, releases two black leaders of the banned African Nationalist parties and allows them to fly to Lusaka in Zambia for talks with the leaders of other African states. Negotiations between the black and white leaders of Rhodesia soon become bogged down.

President Pompidou of France dies and **Giscard d'Estaing** is elected in his place.

Emperor Haile Selassie of Ethiopia is deposed by radical elements in his army.

Willy Brandt, West Germany's first Social Democratic Chancellor, resigns when it is revealed that an alleged East German spy has been working in his office.

The IRA extends its terrorist activities to Britain.

1975 Sheik Mujibur Rahman, Prime Minister of Bangladesh, changes his country's constitution: makes himself President.

In a referendum to decide whether Britain is to stay in the European Economic Community, more than 17 million vote for staying in and more than 8 million against.

The British Government decides to halt work on the Channel Tunnel because of rapidly rising construction costs.

Mrs Margaret Thatcher is elected leader of the Conservative Party, replacing Edward Heath.

In Lebanon the Muslims become the largest community in the country, a position previously held by Christians. Fighting breaks out between extremist factions in the two communities. The situation is made worse by the presence in Lebanon of tens of thousands of Palestinian refugees, many of them members of the Palestinian Liberation Army. The country slides into civil war.

King Feisal of Saudi Arabia is assassinated.

The deposed Emperor Haile Selassie dies in detention.

President Anwar Sadat re-opens Suez Canal and, with the agreement of Israel, the first ships pass through the Canal since its closure after the 1967 war.

In Helsinki, the leaders of 35 countries sign a document intended to reduce tension between East and West—the result of three years work by the Conference on European Security and Co-operation. The document fails to receive universal acclaim, especially in the West.

In Britain, the Government and the trade unions agree to a £6 limit on pay increases for the next 12 months.

In Nigeria General Gowon is removed as Head of State by a military coup.

In Indo-China the longest war in the 20th century, lasting 30 years, comes to an end. In South Vietnam, Communist forces capture Saigon, the capital, and rename it Ho Chi Minh City. In Cambodia the Communist Khmer Rouge occupy the capital, Phnom Penh, and **Prince Sihanouk**, ousted in 1970, returns from exile as Head of State. Laos falls to the pro-Communist Pathet Lao after an almost bloodless coup.

In Portugal, more moderate political elements begin to assert themselves. In Mozambique, Portugal hands over power peacefully and smoothly; but in Angola, after 500 years of colonial rule, the last Commissioner-General can find no one to whom to hand over power. Three rival liberation movements are left fighting for control.

President Sheik Mujibur Rahman of Bangladesh and his family are assassinated in a military coup.

In Northern Ireland the number of civilians killed since 1969 passes the 1,000 mark. In Britain the IRA terror campaign is stepped up.

In Spain, General Franco dies at the age of 82, and **Prince Juan Carlos** is sworn in as King and Head of State.

In India, Mrs Indira Gandhi declares a state of emergency.

British oil starts flowing ashore from the North Sea. Britain is expected to be self-sufficient in oil by 1980.

1976 Chou-En-Lai, Chinese Prime Minister, **Mao-Tse-Tung**'s right hand man for 40 years and the architect of China's policy of rapprochement towards the United States and the West, dies at the age of 77.

The world's first commercial passenger supersonic aircraft, the Anglo-French Concorde, goes into regular service.

Unemployment in Britain passes the $1\frac{1}{2}$ million mark, and the pound falls below \$2 for the first time in history.

Harold Wilson resigns as Prime Minister and **James Callaghan** takes his place.

In Portugal the Socialists emerge as the largest single party but without an overall majority.

The Americans carry out man's deepest probe into space by launching two unmanned spacecraft, Viking I and Viking II, and landing them safely more than 200 million miles from earth, on Mars. The spacecraft beam back pictures, but the answer to the question, whether or not there is life on Mars, remains unsolved.

In Sweden, the Social Democrats lose power after 44 years.

In West Germany **Helmut Schmidt**, the leader of the Social Democratic–Free Democrat (Liberal) Coalition Government, narrowly defeats the Christian Democrats.

The Cod War between Iceland and Britain ends and British trawlers withdraw from the 200-mile fishing limits declared by Iceland.

The EEC, the USA and the Soviet Union declare 200-mile fishing zones around their territories.

Ian Smith agrees, under pressure from the South African Prime Minister, to proposals for majority rule within 2 years in Rhodesia.

In South Africa, the independence of Transkei, the first of the Bantustans, the separate homelands for black South Africans, is proclaimed. The UN General Assembly refuses to recognise Transkei.

Chairman Mao Tse-Tung dies and is succeeded as Chairman by the moderate **Hua Kuo-feng**. After a brief power struggle, Mao's widow and her alleged 'radical' supporters (the 'Gang of Four') are arrested.

In Britain the Devolution Bill is laid before Parliament but is defeated by a vote in the House of Commons.

In Lebanon the Syrian army, with the approval of Egypt and Saudi Arabia, imposes a truce on the warring factions of Maronite Christians and Muslims after 19 months of civil war in which more than 50,000 people have been killed and Beirut, once the business and financial centre of the Middle East, reduced to rubble.

1977 **Jimmy Carter**, Democrat, is installed as 39th President of the USA.

The new Race Relations Bill in Britain strengthens the law on racial discrimination.

The Labour Government in Britain is kept in power by the making of a formal pact between itself and the Liberals.

In Israel, Labour, the dominant party since 1948, is defeated, and **Menahem Begin** forms a coalition cabinet.

The Soviet Union and the USA reach agreement on co-operation in exploration and the use of outer space.

British proposals for an interim government leading to majority rule are rejected outright by Ian Smith, Rhodesia's Prime Minister, who wins a general election.

Steve Biko, founder and first president of the South African Students Association, dies while under arrest, and the post mortem finds 'extensive brain damage'. At the inquiry which follows world-wide expressions of horror, the police are exonerated from blame for Biko's death.

Three Baader-Meinhof terrorists commit suicide in Stammheim Prison, in West Germany, following the rescue of 86 hostages on board a hi-jacked Boeing 737.

President Sadat, in an attempt to resolve the conflict in the Middle East, is the first Egyptian leader to visit Israel.

1978 In Britain, for the first time in six years, there is a balance of payments surplus, and at one time the inflation rate falls to under 8%. The radio broadcasting of Parliamentary business begins. The Lib-Lab pact is ended, but the Government survives.

Rebels crossing from Angola into Zaire enter the mining town of Kolwezi and massacre nearly 130 European miners and their families.

The first baby ever conceived outside its mother is born in Manchester.

Pope Paul VI dies and is succeeded by **John Paul I**, who dies of a heart attack 33 days after his election. **Cardinal Karol Wojtala**, Archbishop of Cracow, becomes the 265th Pope and the first non-Italian to be elected for four and a half centuries. He takes the title of **John Paul II**.

A summit meeting between President Sadat and Prime Minister Begin, arranged by President Carter at Camp David, ends hopefully, but afterwards many differences prevent the signing of a peace treaty.

Ian Smith agrees to majority rule in Rhodesia, but the Patriotic Front continues to wage guerrilla warfare and a form of martial law is proclaimed.

Vietnam and Cambodia fight, and boatloads of Vietnamese refugees of Chinese extraction seek asylum.

The USA announces that diplomatic relations with Communist China will begin in January, and those with Nationalist China (Taiwan) will cease.

1979 In Britain, there are stoppages and strikes in revolt against the Government's policy of a 5% pay rise and no more. The BBC is affected; and ITV is off the air for nearly three months. *The Times* and its subsidiaries remain unpublished for nearly a year.

The Iranian people bring about the fall of the Shah. His enemy, the **Ayatollah Khomeini**, returns from exile and sets up an Islamic Republic.

President Sadat and Prime Minister Begin sign a peace treaty and the 30-year war between Egypt and Israel is ended. The first Israeli ship for 25 years enters the Suez Canal.

The British Embassy in the Hague is bombed and the Ambassador killed. **Airey Neave**, MP, and **Lord Mountbatten** together with members of his family, are among victims of the IRA.

The pound rises to its highest level for nearly four years, but by the end of the year inflation has reached over 16%.

Tanzania invades Uganda and Idi Amin flees.

Margaret Thatcher becomes Britain's first woman Prime Minister when the Conservatives win the General Election.

The Salt II strategic arms limitation treaty is signed by the US and the USSR.

The European Parliament has its first session in Strasbourg.

Freak storms drown 17 yachtsmen taking part in the Fastnet race.

The American Embassy in Teheran is seized by students and 52 hostages are held; the students demand the return to Iran for trial of the Shah, receiving medical treatment in the US.

In Rhodesia there is an overwhelming vote for the establishment of majority rule. **Bishop Muzorewa** becomes the first black Prime Minister. Final agreement is reached at Lancaster House in London; a ceasefire is proclaimed, the state of UDI ends and Lord Soames arrives as British Governor.

Russian troops invade Afghanistan in support of the Communist Government.

1980 Pierre Trudeau is returned to power in Canada.

In India, three years after defeat, Mrs Gandhi wins an overwhelming victory in a general election.

After elections, **Robert Mugabe** becomes Prime Minister and Southern Rhodesia achieves independence as Zimbabwe.

The House of Commons' vote to support a boycott of the Olympic Games in Moscow as a protest against the Russian occupation of Afghanistan is ignored by the British Olympic Association.

26 people are taken hostage at the Iranian Embassy in London, but a successful rescue bid is made by the Special Air Service Regiment.

President Tito of Yugoslavia dies, aged 87.

The annual rate of inflation in Britain increases to nearly 22% and unemployment reaches 2,000,000—the highest since the 1930s.

The exiled Shah of Iran dies in Cairo.

Jerusalem, by Israeli law, becomes the capital city of the country.

In Poland, the Gdansk strikers win the right to form trade unions and to strike and the promise of greater freedom of speech. The Silesian mine and steel workers demand similar concessions, granted when they return to work. Polish radio begins to transmit Sunday Mass for the first time in forty years. Further strikes break out when the Polish Government fails to honour its promises and more areas demand similar concessions. Fears of Russian intervention mount.

Iraq and Iran drift into an indecisive war over border and territorial rights.

Prison officers start disruptive action and, in certain prisons, troops are called in. An Emergency Bill is introduced into Parliament to ease the accommodation crisis in prisons.

Ronald Reagan, Republican, former Governor of California and film star, is elected President of the USA.

Michael Foot is elected Leader of the Labour Party.

Jiang Qing, Mao's widow, is tried for alleged persecution of the people and responsibility for the death of 30,000 workers.

The Pope visits France, Africa and Brazil.

Iranian students surrender responsibility for the 52 hostages to the Iranian government, which makes four demands from America before agreeing to release them. Various efforts to release the hostages, including an abortive attack by US aircraft and commandos, prove fruitless.

Over 6,000 people are killed and missing and over a quarter of a million made homeless by earthquakes that rock the villages around Naples. **John Lennon**, erstwhile Beatle, is shot dead in New York.

1981 Immediately after President Reagan is inaugurated as the 40th President of the United States, the American hostages in Iran are released.

In Peking, a suspended death sentence is passed on Jiang Qing.

The Pope visits Tokyo.

A new political party, the Social Democratic Party, is formed by Labour rebels.

An unsuccessful attempt is made on the life of President Reagan.

Tension in Poland grows as the free trade union movement Solidarity continues to press for increased rights.

Throughout the spring and summer in Britain, there is rioting in major cities.

The rate of inflation rises to 12·6%; and the worst spring weather for years brings freak blizzards that cause havoc to travel, livestock and power supplies.

Twenty-three years of right-wing rule in France end when **François Mitterand**, the socialist candidate, is elected President.

Pope John Paul II and two women are shot and seriously wounded in St Peter's Square by a Turkish gunman.

The Queen, riding from Buckingham Palace to the Horse Guards Parade for the Trooping of the Colour, has five blanks fired at her by a youth in the crowd.

The Humber Bridge, nearly a mile and a half long and the world's longest single-span bridge, is formally opened.

The Prince of Wales marries **Lady Diana Spencer** in St Paul's Cathedral.

The first crossing of the English Channel by a solar-powered balloon is made in 75 minutes.

Unemployment in the UK continues to rise to nearly 3 million, only just below the highest ever recorded in 1933.

Russian gold from the wreck of the cruiser HMS *Edinburgh*, sunk in 1942, is salvaged by British divers.

An IRA hunger-strike at the Maze Prison in Ireland is abandoned after nearly eight months and a number of deaths.

President Sadat of Egypt is assassinated while watching a military parade in Cairo.

Bombs explode in London. One kills the disposal expert attempting to defuse it; and a woman and a boy are killed and forty people injured when another explodes as a coachload of Irish Guardsmen is about to enter a barracks in Chelsea.

There is increasing dissension between left and right in the Labour Party. Polls and by-elections point to strong support for the newly-formed Social Democratic Party, to which a number of Labour MPs defect, and which forms an alliance with the Liberal Party. **Mrs Shirley Williams** wins the first parliamentary seat for the alliance.

The Polish Government announces martial law to break strikes throughout the country organised by Solidarity. Solidarity's leader, **Lech Walesa**, is placed under house arrest.

1982 Unemployment in Britain rises to over three million.

A third satellite of the planet Neptune is noted by American astronomers.

Though some of the last settlers have to be removed by force, Israel evacuates the Sinai and hands it back to Egypt.

The Falkland Islands, territories dependent upon Britain, whose sovereignty has been frequently discussed between Britain and Argentina, are annexed, together with South Georgia, by Argentinian forces. The British Foreign Secretary, **Lord Carrington**, resigns and is succeeded by **Francis Pym**. After a turbulent special session of Parliament, a naval task force is assembled and sets sail for the South Atlantic. Attempts at mediation by the American Secretary of State fail, and America calls on Argentina to respond to a United Nations resolution requiring her to withdraw her forces from the Falklands. Britain declares a 200-mile exclusion zone round the islands. South Georgia is reoccupied by a force of British marines. The EEC, the United States and others announce economic sanctions against Argentina. In appalling winter weather, the Argentine cruiser, *General Belgrano*, is torpedoed by a submarine and sinks with the loss of 368 lives. The British destroyer *HMS Sheffield* is lost as the result of an air-launched missile attack, and 30 of her crew are killed. After seven sets of peace proposals are considered Mrs Thatcher tells Parliament that she has grave doubts of the seriousness of the Argentine response to these plans. An attempt to recapture the islands begins with the establishment of a British bridgehead at Port San Carlos in East Falklands with serious loss on both sides, among British ships and Argentine aircraft flying on missions from mainland bases. Six of Britain's partners in the EEC agree to trade sanctions against Argentina for an indefinite period.

This follows a serious crisis in the EEC itself, caused by a vote bypassing the British veto on proposed new agricultural prices.

After six days, the British task force fans out from San Carlos towards Port Darwin and Goose Green, both of which are quickly taken. The advance continues and, twenty-four days after the first landing, British troops enter Stanley, the capital of the islands. The Argentinian forces surrender on June 15. British casualties are assessed at nearly 300; Argentinian casualties at 700.

President Galtieri of Argentina is deposed and the newly-formed government announces it will not formally declare an end to hostilities. The EEC drops its trade embargoes against Argentina, but promises to reintroduce them should hostilities break out again.

Prisoners-of-war are shipped back to Argentina, the British Civil Administrator returns to the islands, and a 3,000-strong defence force is based there. An inquiry is set up into the origins of the war. A report argues that the Falklands economy is in need of a £100-million boost. Some 830 awards are made for gallantry, including two VCs. Later, it is announced that the campaign has cost £700 million.

During the campaign, the Pope visits both Britain and Argentina.

A Palestinian group claims responsibility for the shooting and wounding of the Israeli ambassador to Britain. Three days later, Israeli troops march into Lebanon and take Palestinian strongholds. They continue to advance to within fifteen miles of Beirut, ignoring a UN order for a ceasefire and withdrawal. Beirut, where the PLO is entrenched, comes under gunfire and aerial attack, with heavy military and civilian losses on both sides. After protracted and confused negotiations, Israel agrees to a ceasefire, and an internationally supervised evacuation of Palestinian and Syrian forces follows. Hundreds of men, women and children are massacred by Christian Phalangist militiamen, and there is worldwide condemnation of Israel for allowing this to happen. A crowd of nearly half a million demonstrate in Tel Aviv, calling for the resignation of Prime Minister Begin and Defence Minister **Sharon**.

In Poland, **General Jaruzelski** lifts some restrictions imposed under martial law, but Lech Walesa is not released. The cost of living rises by 125%, and on the second anniversary of the founding of Solidarity, thousands of protesters clash with the authorities. Walesa is released, but is temporarily held again to stop him talking to shipyard workers in Gdansk. Most internees are freed and martial law ends.

For eight months, National Health Service workers and nurses take action in protest against pay offers; but with an offer of 6–7½%, action is suspended.

The London Underground is halted when drivers refuse to

work new timetables. A national rail strike is averted with a vote to return to work while demands are referred to a tribunal, but train drivers belonging to ASLEF begin their own strike. British Rail announces it will close the whole system down unless agreement is reached. Following the intervention of the TUC, the strike is called off.

An overtime ban by miners in support of their pay claim is called off: strike action is not authorised, and the National Coal Board's offer of an increase of just over 8% is accepted.

Roy Jenkins, a founder member of the Social Democratic Party, is elected its first leader; Shirley Williams becomes its president.

The IRA claim the killing of 11 people and the injury of over 50 when bombs explode in London's Hyde Park and Regents Park. Seventeen are killed and over 60 injured when the Irish National Liberation Army explode a bomb in a public house in Co. Londonderry.

Helmut Schmidt's coalition government in West Germany falls.

The 'Mary Rose', Henry VIII's flagship, is successfully raised from the seabed and taken into Portsmouth Harbour.

The Thames anti-flooding barrier becomes operational after nine years' work and an expenditure of £435 million.

In a tunnel through the Salang Pass, near Kabul, Soviet soldiers and Afghans are asphyxiated and injured after an accident between a petrol tanker and a military vehicle.

President Brezhnev of the Soviet Union dies and is succeeded by **Yuri Andropov**, a former head of the KGB.

Security measures at Buckingham Palace are questioned when an intruder chats with the Queen after breaking into her bedroom.

The frontier between Gibraltar and Spain is re-opened, but only to Britons resident in Gibraltar.

Throughout the year, anti-nuclear movements grow stronger in America and Europe.

1983 The report of the Franks Commission on the Falklands War concludes that the invasion could not have been anticipated.

The death sentence on Chairman Mao's widow, Jiang Qing, is rescinded, and she receives a life sentence instead.

Klaus Barbie, an alleged Nazi war criminal, is arrested in

Bolivia and extradited to France to await trial.

In Britain, the wearing of front seat belts is made mandatory for motorists.

The Campaign for Nuclear Disarmament has an estimated 100,000 demonstrators lining the 15 miles between Greenham Common missile site and the Burghfield Ordnance Factory. Similar protests take place all over Europe.

A massive charge of explosive blasts the American Embassy in Beirut, killing over 50 people and injuring over 100 others.

In June, the Conservatives win the General Election and Mrs Thatcher is Prime Minister for a second term of office. The Conservatives win 44% of the vote and 61% of the seats in the House of Commons; the Labour Party win 28% of the vote and 32% of the seats; the Alliance win 26% of the vote and 4% of the seats.

Michael Foot, resigns as leader of the Labour Party and **Neil Kinnock** is elected in his place. **Dr David Owen** is elected leader of the SDP.

The Commons rejects the restoration of the death penalty, but the Home Secretary announces that the murderers of police officers, prison officers and children, and terrorists and robbers who murder, will receive minimum sentences of 20 years.

After the Pope visits Poland, the Polish government declares an amnesty for political prisoners, but Solidarity remains outlawed. Lech Walesa is awarded the Nobel Peace Prize.

A heatwave in the middle states of America kills over 180. In England, the month of July is the hottest for over 300 years.

In riots in Sri Lanka between Sinhalese and the Tamil minority, 350 die. Many Tamils flee the country before order is restored.

The National Union of Teachers criticise the Government's Act to allow parents to decide if their children should be exempt or not from corporal punishment in schools.

Menachem Begin resigns as Prime Minister of Israel and is succeeded by **Yitzhak Shamir** as a serious financial crisis overtakes the country.

Two hundred and sixty-nine civilians on board a Jumbo jet die when their plane is shot down by Soviet fighters over the island of Sakhalin. The International Civil Aviation Organisation's inquiry finds that human error in computer programming caused the aircraft to stray over Russian territory.

Anti-nuclear demonstrations are held throughout Europe in protest against the siting of American cruise and Pershing II missiles. The Soviet Union walks out of the Geneva nuclear disarmament conference and warns that unless these weapons are withdrawn, America will be threatened by Soviet missiles from 'ocean areas and seas.'

In Grenada, the army sets up a 'revolutionary and military council' after seizing control. Against the advice of the British Government, American troops invade the island. President Reagan claims that a take-over by Cuba has been forestalled. Within a week, hostilities have ceased and US troops begin to withdraw. The nine members of the Organisation of Eastern Caribbean States form an interim government and take over control.

British assets, frozen in Argentina since the Falklands War, are released. Argentina elects a civilian government and, following the discovery of hundreds of bodies buried near the capital, former military leaders are arrested and charged. Both Britain and Argentina make reconciliatory overtures.

On the Saturday before Christmas, an IRA car bomb explodes outside Harrods department store. Six people are killed, and 90 injured.

1984 In protest against meat imports, French farmers blockade British lorries carrying lamb at French ports. Later, they block roads and railway tracks in protest at the go-slow by French and Italian customs at the ends of the Mont Blanc tunnel. Over 300 British lorries are trapped in the blockade, which spreads to Austria and Germany.

The right to trade union membership is withdrawn from employees at Government Communication Headquarters in Cheltenham, on the grounds that it could lead to breaches of security and disruption of nationally vital work. The High Court rules that the ban is unlawful; but a Court of Appeal rules against this, and the unions concerned decide to appeal to the House of Lords.

After being Prime Minister of Canada for 16 years, Pierre Trudeau resigns.

Iran claims that nearly 1,000 of its soldiers are affected by skin-burning gas fired by Iraqi guns. Neutral sources confirm that wounds appear to be caused by such chemicals.

Captain Bruce McCandless becomes the first man to walk in space without a safety line; and **Svetlana Savitskaya** is the first woman to space-walk.

President Yuri Andropov of the USSR dies, and is succeeded by **Konstantin Chernenko**.

Yorkshire miners are called out on strike in protest at the closing of two pits at Barnsley and Rotherham. The chairman of the National Coal Board, **Ian MacGregor**, confirms the intention to close some 20 more 'uneconomic' pits in the following year. This marks the beginning of a long, bitter and sometimes violent dispute between the NCB and the National Union of Mineworkers, led by their President, **Arthur Scargill**. A majority of miners come out on strike, though the Nottinghamshire men, their demand for a national pithead ballot refused, remain largely at work. Neither side will make concessions on the NCB's principle that pits it defines as uneconomic must close.

Government plans to cancel elections for the Greater London Council, due to be abolished, are rejected by the House of Lords, and a backbench revolt in the Commons leaves the Government with only a small majority. The Government approves a stay of execution for the GLC until 1986.

WPC Yvonne Fletcher is killed when shots are fired from the Libyan People's Bureau in London into a crowd of demonstrators. The Bureau is put under siege and diplomats inside the building are given seven days to leave the country. The British Embassy staff are ordered to leave Tripoli.

The USSR withdraws from the Olympic Games in Los Angeles because of alleged anti-Soviet hysteria. Other Communist countries follow suit.

The Thames flood barrier is officially opened by the Queen.

In India, Sikhs in Amritsar, demanding recognition as a nation, are besieged in the Golden Temple by national troops.

Norman Willis is elected General Secretary of the TUC.

The 2,500-year-old body of a man, the first prehistoric man to be discovered in Britain with hair and skin intact, is displayed in the British Museum.

The 6,000,000 population of Ethiopia is pronounced to be on the verge of famine due to drought. Massive international rescue operations are launched.

An IRA bomb explodes at the Grand Hotel in Brighton, where

the Prime Minister and members of the Cabinet are staying during the annual Conservative Party Conference. Five people are killed; and over 30 are injured, including **Norman Tebbitt**, the Secretary of State for Trade and Industry.

In New Delhi, Indira Gandhi, Prime Minister of India, is assassinated by Sikh members of her bodyguard. **Rajiv Gandhi**, her son, is sworn in to replace her and is later elected Prime Minister in her place. Many Sikhs are murdered and have their homes and businesses wrecked.

Ronald Reagan is re-elected as President of the United States, winning all states but one.

A natural gas plant explodes in a suburb of Mexico City, killing 600 people and injuring 3,000. At least 2,500 people are killed and many more injured when toxic gas seeps from an underground storage tank at a pesticide plant near Bhopal in India.

British Telecom goes private.

Margaret Thatcher and **Deng Xiaping** sign a joint pact in Peking on the future of Hong Kong, which will pass into Chinese sovereignty in 1997.

1985 Soviet–US arms talks begin in Geneva; it is agreed to enter at a future date into negotiations on nuclear arms and 'war games'.

The House of Lords is televised for the first time.

The day before the first anniversary of the strike, the longest in British history, a special delegate conference of the National Union of Mineworkers votes for a return to work without a settlement of the dispute with the National Coal Board.

Konstantin Chernenko, President of the USSR for only fifteen months, dies. **Mikhail Gorbachev**, aged 54, becomes the new leader.

A stand at Bradford City's football ground catches fire: 55 people burn to death, and 200 are injured.

Liverpool football fans fight supporters of the Italian team Juventus in Brussels before the European Cup Final. Thirty-eight people are killed and over 430 injured. FIFA imposes a world-wide ban on English football clubs.

Bombing and the hijacking of aircraft and ships are used increasingly by political extremists in the attempt to gain their ends. Brussels, Frankfurt, Paris, Rome, Vienna, Tokyo, Madrid and Athens are among the cities affected. An Italian cruise ship, the 'Achille Lauro', spends two days in the hands of Palestinian Liberation Front guerillas demanding the release of prisoners by Israel.

The oldest bones ever found in North America, those of a 225-million-year-old dinosaur, are discovered in the Painted Desert in Arizona.

15,000 people die after a 45-foot tidal wave descends on Bangladesh.

The British Government announces that London's third major airport will be at Stansted, in Essex.

Throughout the year teachers carry out selective strikes and other forms of protest following their claim for a pay rise and the authorities' very much smaller counter-proposals. **Sir Keith Joseph**, the Secretary of State for Education, refuses to make more government money available, or to abandon the demand that a pay rise should be associated with re-negotiated conditions of employment.

Just before setting out to lead a protest fleet to Mururoa Atoll, the French nuclear testing site in the Pacific, the Greenpeace ship 'Rainbow Warrior' is wrecked by explosives and sinks in Auckland Harbour, New Zealand. A member of the crew is killed. Those responsible are quickly proved to be French secret service agents: and Paris admits as much. Two agents are sentenced to ten years' imprisonment for their part in the affair.

President Reagan undergoes a successful operation for a cancerous growth in the colon.

The pop singer, **Bob Geldof**, organises a rock concert that raises over £50 million for famine relief.

Over 500 passengers and crew die when a Japanese Boeing 747 crashes into mountains near Tokyo. It is the worst aircraft accident ever involving a single plane. This is also the worst year ever for air disasters: over 2,000 deaths occur, mainly in Spain, Japan, at Manchester Airport and in Newfoundland. One of the worst incidents, the destruction of an Air India 747 off the coast of Ireland on its way from Canada, is judged by experts to be the result of a bomb exploding in the luggage compartment.

It is announced that the wreck of the 'unsinkable' ship 'Titanic', which hit an iceberg and sank with the loss of 1,513 lives in 1912, has been found at a depth of 13,000 feet off the Newfoundland coast. There are plans for raising it, though some argue that out of respect to those who died in it, the ship should remain where it is.

An earthquake overtakes Mexico City, killing nearly 5,000 people and injuring over 30,000.

When a black woman is accidentally shot by a policeman, riots break out in Brixton, London. Shops are looted and burned and a police station is attacked. Riots occur also in Peckham, London, and Toxteth, Liverpool; and when a woman collapses and dies as her home in Tottenham, in North London, is being searched by police, there is serious rioting in the course of which a policeman is killed. There is argument about the possible use of plastic bullets in future riots in mainland Britain.

The Queen tours Portugal and the Caribbean.

The struggle against apartheid in South Africa grows more fierce. Soweto and other black townships where emergency regulations are in force closed to Press and TV. Cries increase for the release of **Nelson Mandela**, the black African leader imprisoned for nearly a quarter of a century. His wife, **Winnie**, defies orders restricting her movements and right to speak.

The Nevada del Ruz, a volcano in Columbia, erupts and some 25,000 people are buried under snow and mud in the town of Armero and three villages.

By 275 votes to 263, MPs block the televising of proceedings in the House of Commons.

The first summit conference for six years takes place between President Reagan and the Soviet leader, Mikhail Gorbachev. It concludes with a joint statement declaring a new start between the two countries. Later the two leaders promise, in simultaneous broadcasts, to work for peace, trust and the reduction of nuclear armaments.

An Argentinian resolution, requesting the start of talks between Argentina and the UK to resolve their differences over the Falkland Islands, is adopted by the UN General Assembly.

An agreement is signed between the British and Irish governments, allowing for participation by the Republic in the affairs of Northern Ireland. The Ulster Unionists MPs resign in protest and submit themselves for re-election: which, in the New Year, all achieve but one.

The British Government's withdrawal from UNESCO is confirmed.

The Employment Conditions Abroad Agency declares Britain to be one of the cheapest countries in which to live. The cost of a miscellaneous selection of essentials in seventy countries is found to be greater in 64 of them than in Britain.

1986 Rupert Murdoch, owner of Times Newspapers, transfers much of the operation from Fleet Street to new buildings in Wapping, which are heavily defended with barbed wire and in other ways. Most of the journalists concerned agree to make the move, but 5,000 printers and other workers belonging to the print unions go on strike, and are sacked. It turns out that a much smaller staff of electricians are ready to operate the new printing technology: this leads to serious conflict between the electricians' union and the TUC.

Michael Heseltine, Defence Secretary, resigns from the Government in the middle of a Cabinet meeting, and claims that there has been improper prevention of discussion in Cabinet of the affairs of the ailing helicopter company, Westland. He alleges also that there has been an attempt to ensure the take-over of the company by the American firm, Sikorksy, instead of by a European consortium favoured by Mr Heseltine on defence grounds. As a result of the claims and counter-claims that follow, and of the leak of a letter from the Attorney-General, **Mr Leon Brittan**, Trade and Industry Secretary, also resigns. The Government is seen to be in crisis.

The space shuttle Challenger, seconds after its launch from Cape Canaveral, explodes in a ball of fire. Among the crew was a teacher, **Mrs Christa McAuliffe**, chosen from thousands of applicants to be the first civilian to go into space. While there it was intended that she should broadcast television lessons on space travel to American schools.

Mrs Thatcher and President Mitterand agree at a meeting at Lille that a rail-only Channel Tunnel should be built.

The National Resistance Army of Uganda enters Kampala, the capital, and its leader, **Yoweri Museveni**, is sworn in as the country's new president.

After some weeks of popular unrest, **President Jean-Claude Duvalier** flees from Haiti.

President Botha of South Africa announces that the pass

system, used to control the movement of black people, is to be abolished from July, 1986. Violent unrest continues throughout the country.

After claiming to have defeated **Corazon Aquino** in presidential election, amid allegations of electoral fraud, **President Ferdinand Marcos** and his entourage are airlifted out of the presidential palace in Manila, capital of the Philippines, he goes into exile. Mrs Aquino is formally declared to have won the election.

Olaf Palme, Prime Minister of Sweden, is shot dead by an unknown assailant on his way home from a cinema in Stockholm.

Following American deaths in terrorist acts in Europe, American aircraft bomb targets in Tripoli, the Libyan capital, causing a number of civilian deaths and casualties: among the dead is the adopted baby daughter of the country's leader, **Colonel Qadhafi**. The United States claims that it has evidence that Libya is behind the acts of terrorism, and that it is acting under an article of the United Nations Charter which permits military action in self-defence. Outside America, the action is widely condemned, and the claim that the raid was covered by the provisions of the UN Charter is rejected. In Britain, opinion polls show that a majority disapprove of the Governments decision to allow American aircraft taking part in the raid to fly from bases in Britain. The Western allies agree to sanctions against Libya.

A major accident to a nuclear reactor in a power station at Chernobyl, in the Ukraine, is first made known to the outside world two days later, when Sweden detects high levels of radiation in the atmosphere. Meltdown is prevented and the release of radiation limited by dropping sand and other materials on the reactor from helicopters. A radioactive cloud is blown by winds back and forth over Europe and beyond: there is widespread alarm about the possible effect on rainwater, milk and dairy products.

HISTORIC ACTS OF PARLIAMENT

Act	Date	What it did
Catholic Emancipation Act	1829	Gave full civic rights to Catholics.
Combination Acts	1799 & 1800	Made trade unions and meetings of men to discuss wages and hours illegal. Repealed, 1824. Trade Unions made legal, 1871.
Conventicle Act	1664	Made it illegal for more than five people to meet for religious worship. An anti-Catholic measure.
Corn Laws	1815	Prohibited import of foreign corn till wheat reached famine prices. Repealed, 1846.
Corporation Act	1661	Required that anyone taking up a municipal office should receive communion according to the rites of the Anglican Church and should declare it unlawful on any grounds to take up arms against the king. An anti-Presbyterian measure.
Education Act	1870	Introduced elementary education for all.
Education Act	1944	Introduced secondary education for all.
Factory Acts	Throughout 19th century	Regulated conditions of work. The Act of 1833 provided for the appointment of factory inspectors; the Act of 1847 limited the working day to 10 hours.
Government, Act	1657	Made Cromwell's rule legal, and enabled him to name his successor.
Habeas Corpus	1679	Made it illegal to hold a man in prison without trial.
Heresy, Statute of	1401	Provided that all heretics (people whose beliefs were not those of the Church) were to be imprisoned and, if they refused to give up their heresy, to be burned alive. Repealed, 1548.

Act	Date	What it did
Indemnity, Bill of	1660	First measure passed after restoration of Charles II; pardoned all offences committed during the Cromwellian period.
Kilkenny, Statute of	1366	Forbade the mixing of the English in Ireland with the Irish people.
Labourers, Statute of	1349	Passed during the labour shortage that followed the Black Death; bound a labourer to serve under anyone requiring him to do so for wages current two years before the plague began.
Libel Act	1791	Made the decision as to what was libellous a matter for the jury and not the judge.
Mines Act	1842	Prohibited the employment in mines of women, girls and boys under 10.
National Insurance Act	1916	First introduced compulsory national health contributions and a scheme of insurance against unemployment.
Navigation Act	1652	Prohibited the importation in foreign ships of any but products of the countries to which the ships belonged. Aimed at the Dutch.
Old Age Pensions Act	1908	Introduced old age pensions for the first time.
Parliament Acts	1911 & 1949	Limited the powers of the House of Lords.
Poor Laws	1562–1601	Placed on local authorities the responsibility for settling and supporting the poor.
Poyning's Act	1494	Forbade the Parliament of the Pale in Ireland to deal with matters not first approved of by the English king and his Council. Repealed, 1779.
Public Health Act	1848	Set up the first Central Board of Health.
Reform Bill	1832	Took away the right to elect MPs from 56 'rotten boroughs', gave the seats to counties or large

Act	Date	What it did
		towns hitherto unrepresented in Parliament, and gave the vote to £10 householders. Followed by the Act of 1867, which extended the vote to working people in towns; the Act of 1884, which gave the vote to country labourers; and the Acts of 1918 and 1928, which gave the vote to women.
Rights, Bill of	1689	Established the right of the people, through their representatives in Parliament, to depose the king and set on the throne whomever they chose.
Security, Act of	1706	Required the sovereign to swear to support the Presbyterian Church.
Settlement, Act of	1701	Confined the succession to the throne to Protestants and settled it on the House of Hanover.
Six Articles, Act of the	1539	An anti-Protestant measure, establishing the celibacy of the clergy, monastic vows and private masses. Repealed, 1548.
Stamp Act	1765	Imposed a tax on all legal documents issued within the colonies. Repealed, 1766.
Succession, Act of	1534	Required an oath to be taken by all acknowledging that Henry VIII's marriage with Catherine of Aragon was invalid.
Supremacy, Act of	1534	Ordered that the king 'shall be taken, accepted and reputed the only supreme head on earth of the Church of England'.
Test Act	1563	First anti-Catholic Act, exacting from all office-holders an oath of allegiance to Queen Elizabeth and a declaration that the Pope had no authority. A similar act was passed in 1673, and set aside in 1686.

Act	Date	What it did
Toleration Act	1689	Established freedom of worship.
Treaty of Accession to European Communities, Act	1972	It made Britain a full member as from 1 Jan 1973, of the three European Communities, i.e. the Economic Community, the Coal and Steel Community and of Euratom.
Triennial Bill	1641	Enforced the assembly of the House of Commons every three years.
Uniformity, Act of	1559	Restored the English Prayer Book and enforced its use on the clergy.
Union, Act of	1707	United England and Scotland.
Union with Ireland, Act of	1800	United England and Ireland.
Winchester, Statute of	1285	Bound every man to serve the king in case of invasion or revolt and to pursue felons when the hue and cry was raised against them.

EXPLORATIONS AND DISCOVERIES

Date	Explorer	Nationality	Exploration or Discovery
982	Eric the Red	Viking	Discovered Greenland
c. 1000	Leif Ericsson	Viking	Reached N. America
1255	Nicolo and Maffeo Polo	Venetian	Travelled to Peking
1271–94	Marco Polo	Venetian	Journeyed through China, India and other parts of Asia
14th century	João Zarco, Tristão Vas and others	Portuguese	Discovered Madeira and the Azores
1487–88	Bartholomew Diaz	Portuguese	Rounded Cape of Good Hope

Date	Explorer	Nationality	Exploration or Discovery
1492	Christopher Columbus	Italian in Spanish service	Discovered San Salvador (now Watling Island), the Bahamas, Cuba and Haiti
1493–96	Christopher Columbus	Italian in Spanish service	Discovered Guadeloupe, Montserrat, Antigua, Puerto Rico and Jamaica
1497	John Cabot	Genoese in English service	Discovered Cape Breton Island, Newfoundland and Nova Scotia
1497–1503	Amerigo Vespucci	Florentine	Explored Mexico, part of E. coast of America and S. American coast
1498	Vasco da Gama	Portuguese	Discovered sea-route from Europe to India
1498	Christopher Columbus	Italian in Spanish service	Landed on mainland of S. America
1501–16	Various	Portuguese	Discovered Ceylon, Goa, Malacca, Canton, Japan and E. Indies
1502–4	Christopher Columbus	Italian in Spanish service	Discovered Trinidad
1509	Sebastian Cabot	Genoese in English service	Explored American coast as far as Florida, Brazilian coast and mouth of R. Plate
1519–22	Ferdinand Magellan	Portuguese in Spanish service	First to sail round the world; discovered the Magellan Strait, reached the Philippines and named the Pacific
1534–36	Jacques Cartier	French	Discovered Canada, explored the St Lawrence and named Mount Royal (Montreal)

Date	Explorer	Nationality	Exploration or Discovery
1539	De Soto	Spanish	Discovered Florida, Georgia and the R. Mississippi
1554	Sir Hugh Willoughby and Richard Chancellor	English	Discovered the White Sea and the ocean route to Russia
1576	Martin Frobisher	English	Began search for N.W. Passage
	John Davis	English	Discovered Davis Strait between Atlantic and Arctic Oceans
1577–80	Sir Francis Drake	English	Sailed round the world in the *Golden Hind*
1606	William Janszoon	Dutch	Discovered Australia
1606	Capt. John Smith and a party of colonists	English	Explored Chesapeake Bay, discovered Potomac and Susquehannah
1611	Henry Hudson	English	Sought N.E. and N.W. Passages; discovered Hudson River, Strait and Bay
1642	Abel Tasman	Dutch	Discovered Tasmania, New Zealand, the Tonga and Fiji islands
1700	William Dampier	English	Explored W. Coast of Australia
1728	Vitus Bering	Danish in Russian service	Discovered Bering Strait between Asia and America
1740–44	George, Lord Anson	English	Sailed round the world in the *Centurion*
1767	Capt. Wallis	English	Discovered Tahiti
1768–71	Capt. James Cook	English	Sailed round the world in the *Endeavour*; charted New Zealand coasts and surveyed E. Coast of Australia, naming New South Wales and Botany Bay

Date	Explorer	Nationality	Exploration or Discovery
1772	Capt. James Cook	English	Discovered Easter Island, New Caledonia and Norfolk Island
1776	Capt. James Cook	English	Discovered several of the Cook (or Hervey) islands. Rediscovered Sandwich (now Hawaiian) islands
1776	Mungo Park	Scottish	Explored the course of R. Niger
1831	Sir James Clark Ross and Rear-Admiral Sir John Ross	English	Located the magnetic pole
1839–43	Sir James Clark Ross	English	Discovered Victoria Land, Mounts Erebus and Terror, the Ross ice barrier
1847	Rear-Admiral Sir John Franklin	English	Lost in Arctic Ocean while seeking N.W. Passage
1852–73	David Livingstone	Scottish	Discovered the course of the Zambesi, the Victoria Falls and Lake Nyasa
1856	Capt. John Speke	English	Discovered Lake Tanganyika
1858	Capt. John Speke	English	Discovered Lake Victoria Nyanza
1862	Capt. John Speke and Lt.-Col. J. A. Grant	English	Discovered source of White Nile
1901	Capt. R. F. Scott	English	Discovered King Edward VII Land
1903–6	Capt. Roald Amundsen	Norwegian	First navigation of the N.W. Passage
1908–9	Sir Ernest Shackleton	English	Reached within 100 miles of South Pole

Date	Explorer	Nationality	Exploration or Discovery
1909	Rear-Admiral Robert Peary	American	Reached North Pole
1911	Capt. Roald Amundsen	Norwegian	First reached South Pole (December 14)
1912	Capt. R. F. Scott	English	Reached South Pole (January 18)
1929	Admiral R. Byrd	American	First flight over South Pole
1957–58	Sir Vivian Fuchs and Sir Edmund Hillary	English and New Zealander	First crossing of the Antarctic Continent
1961–62	Major Yuri Gagarin, Major Gherman Titov, Commander Alan Shepard, Capt. Virgil Grissom and Col. John Glenn	Russian and American	First journeys into space
1963	Valentina Tereshkova	Russian	First woman in space
1965	Col. Leonov, Major White	Russian and American	First men to 'walk' in space
1968	Frank Borman, Bill Anders, and Jim Lovell	American	First men to circle moon
1969	Neil Armstrong and Edwin Aldrin	American	First men to step on the moon
	Charles Conrad and Alan Bean	American	Second pair to step on the moon

BRITISH PRIME MINISTERS

REIGN OF GEORGE I

Sir Robert Walpole (*Whig*)   1721–27

REIGN OF GEORGE II

Sir Robert Walpole (*Whig*)	1727–42
Earl of Wilmington (*Whig*)	1742–43
Henry Pelham (*Whig*)	1743–46
Henry Pelham (*Whig*)	1746–54
Duke of Newcastle (*Whig*)	1754–56
Duke of Devonshire (*Whig*)	1756–57
Duke of Newcastle (*Whig*)	1757–60

REIGN OF GEORGE III

Duke of Newcastle (*Whig*)	1760–62
Earl of Bute (*Tory*)	1762–63
George Grenville (*Whig*)	1763–65
Marquess of Rockingham (*Whig*)	1765–66
Earl of Chatham (*Whig*)	1766–67
Duke of Grafton (*Whig*)	1767–70
Lord North (*Tory*)	1770–82
Marquess of Rockingham (*Whig*)	1782
Earl of Shelburne (*Whig*)	1782–83
Duke of Portland (*Coalition*)	1783
William Pitt (*Tory*)	1783–1801
Henry Addington (*Tory*)	1801–4
William Pitt (*Tory*)	1804–6
Lord Grenville (*Whig*)	1806–7
Duke of Portland (*Tory*)	1807–9
Spencer Perceval (*Tory*)	1809–12
Earl of Liverpool (*Tory*)	1812–20

REIGN OF GEORGE IV

Earl of Liverpool (*Tory*)	1820–27
George Canning (*Tory*)	1827
Viscount Goderich (*Tory*)	1827–28
Duke of Wellington (*Tory*)	1828–30

REIGN OF WILLIAM IV

Earl Grey (*Whig*)	1830–34
Viscount Melbourne (*Whig*)	1834
Sir Robert Peel (*Tory*)	1834–35
Viscount Melbourne (*Whig*)	1835–37

REIGN OF VICTORIA

Viscount Melbourne (*Whig*)	1837–41
Sir Robert Peel (*Tory*)	1841–46
Lord John Russell (*Whig*)	1846–52
Earl of Derby (*Tory*)	1852
Earl of Aberdeen (*Peelite*)	1852–55
Viscount Palmerston (*Liberal*)	1855–58
Earl of Derby (*Conservative*)	1858
Viscount Palmerston (*Liberal*)	1858–65
Earl Russell (*Liberal*)	1865–66
Earl of Derby (*Conservative*)	1866–68
Benjamin Disraeli (*Conservative*)	1868
W. E. Gladstone (*Liberal*)	1868–74
Benjamin Disraeli (*Conservative*)	1874–80
W. E. Gladstone (*Liberal*)	1880–85
Marquess of Salisbury (*Conservative*)	1885–86
W. E. Gladstone (*Liberal*)	1886
Marquess of Salisbury (*Conservative*)	1886–92
W. E. Gladstone (*Liberal*)	1892–94
Earl of Rosebery (*Liberal*)	1894–95
Marquess of Salisbury (*Conservative*)	1895–1902

REIGN OF EDWARD VII

A. J. Balfour (*Conservative*)	1902–5
Sir Henry Campbell-Bannerman (*Liberal*)	1905–8
Herbert H. Asquith (*Liberal*)	1908–10

REIGN OF GEORGE V

H. H. Asquith (*Liberal*)	1910–15
H. H. Asquith (*Coalition*)	1915–16
D. Lloyd George (*Coalition*)	1916–22
A. Bonar Law (*Conservative*)	1922–23
Stanley Baldwin (*Conservative*)	1923–24
J. Ramsay MacDonald (*Labour*)	1924
Stanley Baldwin (*Conservative*)	1924–29
J. Ramsay MacDonald (*Labour*)	1929–31
J. Ramsay MacDonald (*National Government*)	1931–35
Stanley Baldwin (*National Government*)	1935–36

REIGN OF EDWARD VIII

Stanley Baldwin (*National Government*)   1936

REIGN OF GEORGE VI

Stanley Baldwin (*National Government*)	1936–37
Neville Chamberlain (*National Government*)	1937–40
Winston S. Churchill (*Coalition*)	1940–45
Clement R. Attlee (*Labour*)	1945–51
Winston S. Churchill (*Conservative*)	1951–52

REIGN OF ELIZABETH II

Sir Winston S. Churchill (*Conservative*)	1952–55
Sir Anthony Eden (*Conservative*)	1955–57
Harold Macmillan (*Conservative*)	1957–63
Sir Alec Douglas-Home (*Conservative*)	1963–64
Harold Wilson (*Labour*)	1964–70
Edward Heath (*Conservative*)	1970–74
Harold Wilson (*Labour*)	1974–76
James Callaghan (*Labour*)	1976–79
Margaret Thatcher (*Conservative*)	1979–

LIST OF KINGS AND QUEENS OF SCOTLAND

ALPINES

Kenneth I, 843–60
Donald I, 860–63
Constantine I, 863–77
Aedh, 877–78
Eocha, 878–89
Donald II, 889–900
Constantine II, 900–43
Malcolm I, 943–54
Indulf, 954–62
Duff, 962–67
Colin, 967–71
Kenneth II, 971–95
Constantine III, 995–97
Kenneth III, 997–1005
Malcolm II, 1005–34
Duncan I, 1034–40
Macbeth, 1040–57
Malcolm III, 1057–93
Donald Bane, 6 months in 1093
Duncan II, 6 months in 1094
Donald Bane again, 1094–97
Edgar, 1097–1107
Alexander I, 1107–24
David I, 1124–53
Malcolm IV (The Maiden),
    1153–65

William I (The Lion), 1165–1214
Alexander II, 1214–49
Alexander III, 1249–86
Margaret, 1286–90
No king, 1290–92
John Baliol, 1292–96
No king, 1296–1306

BRUCES

Robert I, 1306–29
David II, 1329–71

STUARTS

Robert II, 1371–90
Robert III, 1390–1406
Regent Albany, 1406–19
Regent Murdoch, 1419–24
James I, 1424–37
James II, 1437–60
James III, 1460–88
James IV, 1488–1513
James V, 1513–42
Mary, 1542–67
James VI, 1567–1625

Until 1603 James VI reigned over Scotland only; in 1603 he
became King of England and Ireland. From 1603 onwards the
kings of Scotland are the same as the kings of England.

THE ENGLISH LINE OF SUCCESSION

ALFRED the GREAT 871–899

EDWARD the ELDER 901–924

ATHELSTAN 924–940   EDMUND the ELDER 940–946   EDRED 946–955

EDWY 955–959   EDGAR 959–975

EDWARD the MARTYR 975–978   ETHELRED 978–1016

EDWARD the CONFESSOR 1042–1066   EDMUND IRONSIDE 1016   CANUTE 1016–1035
                                                                          HAROLD I 1035–10

WILLIAM the CONQUEROR 1066–1087   Edward   HARDICANUTE 1040–10
m. Matilda of Flanders   Margaret
                                          m. Malcolm III of Scotland

WILLIAM II   HENRY I 1100–1135   m.   Matilda
1087–1100
                    Matilda
Adela   m. Geoffrey of Anjou

STEPHEN 1135–1154   HENRY II 1154–1189
                    m. Eleanor of Aquitaine

RICHARD I 1189–1199   JOHN 1199–1216
                             m. Isabella of Angouleme

                             HENRY III 1216–1272
                             m. Eleanor of Provence

                             EDWARD I 1272–1307
                             m. Eleanor of Castille

                             EDWARD II 1307–1327
                             m. Isabella of France

                             EDWARD III 1327–1377
                             m. Philippa of Hainault

Edward the Black Prince   John of Gaunt   Edmund of York
                                      m.
RICHARD II   1 Blanche of Lancaster 2 Katherine Swynford   Richard of York
1377–1399   m. Anne Mortimer

                                                                         Richard of York
                                                                         m. Cicely Neville

          HENRY IV   John Beaufort
          1399–1413
          m. Mary Bahun   John Beaufort   EDWARD IV 1461–1483   RICHARD
                                                        m. Elizabeth Woodville   1483–148
          HENRY V 1413–1422   Margaret
          m. Katherine of France   m. Edmund Tudor

          HENRY VI   HENRY VII   m.   Elizabeth   EDWARD
          1422–1461   1485–1509   1483
                                                                             m. Anne Nev

Margaret
m. James IV of Scotland

HENRY VIII 1509–1547

James V of Scotland
m. Mary of Guise

EDWARD VI   MARY I   ELIZABETH I
1547–1553   1553–1558   1558–1603

Mary Queen of Scots
m. Henry, Lord Darnley

JAMES I of ENGLAND 1603–1625
m. Anne of Denmark

CHARLES I 1625–1649
m. Henrietta Maria of France

Elizabeth
m. Frederick V Elector Palatine

CHARLES II   Mary   JAMES II 1685–1688
1660–1685   m. William II   m.
m. Katherine of   of Orange
Braganza   1 Anne Hyde

2 Mary of
Modena

Sophia of Hanover
m. Ernest Augustus of Hanover

GEORGE I 1714–1727
m. Dorothea of Zelt

WILLIAM III m. MARY II   ANNE
1689–1702 1689–1694 1702–1714
m. George of
Denmark

James, the
Old Pretender

GEORGE II 1727–1760
m. Caroline of Brandenburg-Auspach

Charles, the
Young Pretender

Maria   m. Frederick V. m.   Louisa
of Brunswick

Frederick
m. Augusta of Saxe Gotha

Louisa
of Denmark

Frederick
of Denmark

GEORGE III 1760–1820
m. Charlotte of Mecklenburg Strelitz

Louisa
of Hesse Cassel

Charlotte

Christian IX   m.

Louisa
of Hesse Cassel

GEORGE IV WILLIAM IV
1820–1830 1830–1837
m. Caroline
of Brunswick
Wolfenbuttell

Edward
m. Victoria of Saxe-
Coburg-Gotha

Adolfus

Marie
m. Francis
of Teck

William became George I, King of Hellenes

Louisa
of Hesse Cassel

VICTORIA 1837–1901
m. Albert of Saxe-
Coburg-Gotha

Andrew, Prince of Greece
m. Alice

Alice
m. Louis of Hesse

EDWARD VII 1901–1910
m. Alexandra of Denmark

Victoria
m. Louis of Battenberg
(Mountbatten)

GEORGE V
1910–1936

m. Mary of Teck

Mary Henry George

Philip m. ELIZABETH II
1952

EDWARD VIII
1936
m. Wallis Simpson

GEORGE VI
1936–1952
m. Elizabeth Bowes-Lyon

Margaret
m. Antony Armstrong-Jones

Charles   Ann   Andrew   Edward
1. Lady Diana Spencer m. Mark Phillips m. Sarah Ferguson

David   Sarah

William   Henry   Peter   Zara

UNITED STATES PRESIDENTS

George Washington (*Federalist*)	1789–97
John Adams (*Federalist*)	1797–1801
Thomas Jefferson (*Republican*)	1801–9
James Madison (*Republican*)	1809–17
James Monroe (*Republican*)	1817–25
John Quincy Adams (*Republican*)	1825–29
Andrew Jackson (*Democrat*)	1829–37
Martin Van Buren (*Democrat*)	1837–41
William Henry Harrison (*Whig*)	1841
John Tyler (*Whig*)	1841–45
James Knox Polk (*Democrat*)	1845–49
Zachary Taylor (*Whig*)	1849–50
Millard Fillmore (*Whig*)	1850–53
Franklin Pierce (*Democrat*)	1853–57
James Buchanan (*Democrat*)	1857–61
Abraham Lincoln (*Republican*)	1861–65
Andrew Johnson (*Republican*)	1865–69
Ulysses Simpson Grant (*Republican*)	1869–77
Rutherford Birchard Hayes (*Republican*)	1877–81
James Abram Garfield (*Republican*)	1881
Chester Alan Arthur (*Republican*)	1881–85
Grover Cleveland (*Democrat*)	1885–89
Benjamin Harrison (*Republican*)	1889–93
Grover Cleveland (*Democrat*)	1893–97
William McKinley (*Republican*)	1897–1901
Theodore Roosevelt (*Republican*)	1901–9
William Howard Taft (*Republican*)	1909–13
Woodrow Wilson (*Democrat*)	1913–21
Warren Gamaliel Harding (*Republican*)	1921–23
Calvin Coolidge (*Republican*)	1923–29
Herbert C. Hoover (*Republican*)	1929–33
Franklin Delano Roosevelt (*Democrat*)	1933–45
Harry S. Truman (*Democrat*)	1945–53
Dwight D. Eisenhower (*Republican*)	1953–61
John F. Kennedy (*Democrat*)	1961–63
Lyndon B. Johnson (*Democrat*)	1963–69
Richard M. Nixon (*Republican*)	1969–74
Gerald Ford (*Republican*)	1974–77
Jimmy Carter (*Democrat*)	1977–81
Ronald Reagan (*Republican*)	1981–

GOVERNMENT IN BRITAIN: LOCAL AFFAIRS

The management of local affairs is left to local authorities subject to supervision—largely exercised through financial control—by the central Government in London.

In a drastic reorganisation in 1974, the 1,400 local authorities formerly existing in England and Wales (County Councils, County Borough Councils, Municipal Boroughs, Rural Districts, Urban Districts, Parish Councils and Meetings) were replaced by:

6 Metropolitan counties —large conurbations— West Midlands, Merseyside, West Yorkshire, South Yorkshire, Tyne and Wear, Greater Manchester—responsible for education and personal social services.	52 new counties responsible for planning, transport, education and personal social services.	some 375 new district authorities responsible for housing, refuse collection, play- and sportsgrounds etc.

The 430 local authorities formerly existing in Scotland (counties, counties of cities, town councils and district councils) were in 1975 replaced by:

8 regional authorities responsible for major planning, transport, education and personal social services.	47 district authorities responsible for housing, refuse collection, parks and sports grounds.

Under the Local Government Act of 1985, which came into force on April 1, 1986, the Greater London Council, which in the reorganisation of 1974 took over the administration of London from the London County Council, was abolished together with the six Metropolitan county councils, and most of their functions became the responsibility of the existing borough and district councils. The running of the fire service in London and the fire, police and public transport services in the Metropolitan counties was taken over by new joint authorities, composed of borough and district councillors. Education in Inner London was made the responsibility of a new Inner London Education Authority, directly elected.

GOVERNMENT IN BRITAIN

THE QUEEN

The Queen reigns; she does not rule. All of Britain's business is officially done in her name, but in practice Parliament makes the laws, the Prime Minister and the Cabinet govern the country, and the law courts administer justice.

LEGISLATURE

Parliament
Consists of two Houses. (House of Commons predominates.)

Civil Cour

England   Scotland

House of Lords
2 Archbishops; 24 Church of England bishops; Hereditary Peers (Dukes, Marquesses, Earls, Viscounts, Barons), Life Peers.

House of Commons
650 Members of Parliament (M.P.s) elected by universal suffrage.

Court of Appeal (Civil)   Court of Ses

High Court (3 divisions)   Court of Ses (Outer Hou

County Court   Sheriff Co

EXECUTIVE

Prime Minister (who retains power only as long as in command of a majority in the House of Commons) and ministers, the more important of whom belong to the Cabinet.

Lord Chancellor's Office   Treasury   Foreign Office (incorporating Commonwealth Office)   Defence   Lord President of the Council's Office   Northe Irelan

Overseas Development   Royal Navy   Army   Royal Air Force

Chancellor of the Duchy of Lancaster

Attorney-General Solicitor-General   Paymaster-General's Office   Posts & Tele-communications   Health & Social Security

Note that there is *no* upward line of appeal from the Scottish High Court of Justiciary to the House of Lords.

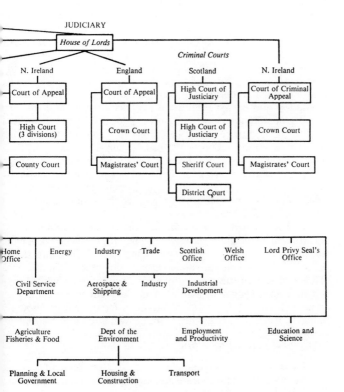

JUDICIARY

House of Lords

Criminal Courts

N. Ireland	England	Scotland	N. Ireland
Court of Appeal	Court of Appeal	High Court of Justiciary	Court of Criminal Appeal
High Court (3 divisions)	Crown Court	High Court of Justiciary	Crown Court
County Court	Magistrates' Court	Sheriff Court	Magistrates' Court
		District Court	

Home Office · Energy · Industry · Trade · Scottish Office · Welsh Office · Lord Privy Seal's Office

Civil Service Department · Aerospace & Shipping · Industry · Industrial Development

Agriculture Fisheries & Food · Dept of the Environment · Employment and Productivity · Education and Science

Planning & Local Government · Housing & Construction · Transport

THE COMMONWEALTH

The Commonwealth grew out of the British Empire. All the states, nations and territories which belong to it today were once governed by men sent out from England who received their orders from London.

The transformation from dependence to independent nationhood usually followed this broad pattern:

Once British power was firmly established, the British Government would try to draw local notabilities into the business of running the country, consulting them on important matters, and even appointing them to be his official advisers; in due course he would set up a legislative Council or Parliament, but he would make certain of being able to get his way in the last resort by allowing only a minority of its members to be elected by the local population and by appointing the majority himself; later on he would gradually increase the number of locally elected members until in the end there would be no officially appointed members left; at that stage London would usually surrender its powers to run the affairs of the country concerned, the leader of the majority in the Legislative Council or Parliament would become Prime Minister, the Governor would cease to play an active part in politics and, like the Queen in Britain, would be able to act only as advised by the Prime Minister.

The first countries to reach the top of the ladder of self-government were those settled by people of British or European stock. They were known as 'Dominions', and in defining their relationship to one another and to Britain, the Imperial Conference of 1926 described them as 'autonomous communities within the British Empire, equal in status, in no way subordinate one to another in any aspect of their domestic or foreign affairs, though united by a common allegiance to the Crown, and freely associated as members of the British Commonwealth of Nations.'

They were—apart from Britain—five in number:

Australia   Canada   New Zealand
Newfoundland (after a referendum joined Canada as a Pro-
      vince in 1949 and ceased being an independent Dom-
      inion)
South Africa (left the Commonwealth in 1961).

After the Second World War the number of countries which attained independent nationhood increased rapidly and, since many of them had populations which were not predominantly of British or European descent, it became customary to refer to the Commonwealth and not the British Commonwealth.

In January 1986 the following were fully independent members of the Commonwealth, in addition to those listed above:

Antigua and Barbuda	Jamaica	Seychelles
Bahamas	Kenya	Sierra Leone
Bangladesh	Kiribati[3]	Singapore
Barbados	Lesotho[4]	Solomon Islands
Belize	Malawi[5]	Sri Lanka
Botswana[1]	Malaysia	Swaziland
Brunei	Malta	Tanzania
Cyprus	Maldives (The)	Tonga
Dominica	Mauritius	Trinidad and Tobago
Fiji	Nauru	Tuvalu
Gambia (The)	Nigeria	Uganda[6]
Ghana	Papua New Guinea	Vanuatu[7]
Grenada	Saint Kitts-Nevis	Western Samoa
Guyana[2]	Saint Lucia	Zambia[8]
India	St Vincent and the Grenadines	Zimbabwe[9]

(Burma became independent in 1948 but decided to leave the Commonwealth. Pakistan left the Commonwealth in January 1971.)

There are altogether 49 independent countries within the Commonwealth (including Britain). They form an association of countries. They are not a state or even a federation. There is no single parliament or government, no central defence force or executive power. They are no longer 'united by a common allegiance to the Crown'. For example, twenty-five member countries are republics although all recognise the Queen as Head of the Commonwealth. And there is no common foreign policy. Britain, Canada, Australia and New Zealand belong to military alliances designed to stop the spread of Communism; India, Sri Lanka, Ghana and Tanzania are 'uncommitted'. Four countries, The Maldives, Nauru, St Vincent and Tuvalu, are special members, with the right of participation in all functional Commonwealth

Former names: [1]Bechuanaland. [2]Brit. Guiana. [3]Gilbert Islands. [4]Basutoland. [5]Nyasaland. [6]Tanganyika and Zanzibar. [7]New Hebrides. [8]N. Rhodesia. [9]S. Rhodesia.

meetings and activities, but not of attendance at meetings of Commonwealth Heads of Government.

The essence of the Commonwealth relationship is consultation, and the most important forms of consultation are the Commonwealth Prime Ministers' Conferences which, whenever possible, are held in London at least once every two years and now have a permanent home in Marlborough House.

Other Commonwealth bonds:

Constant consultation between the Commonwealth delegations at the United Nations in New York.

Commercial ties and Imperial preferences.

Language (Many Commonwealth leaders with multilingual populations find that English is the only language in which they can talk to all their people.)

Common political traditions and habits of thought.

Education (Many Commonwealth universities are linked to British universities in order to ensure high academic standards. Moreover, many Commonwealth countries continue to have their doctors, scientists, engineers, administrators and soldiers trained in Britain.)

Sport (Cricket and cricketing language are familiar in countries like Britain, Australia, New Zealand and the West Indies, but hardly outside the Commonwealth.)

Despite the rapid increase since the end of the Second World War in the number of independent countries within the Commonwealth, there still remain territories which continue to be dependent on Britain. Some are well advanced in self-government; others are little more than small island communities, fortresses, anchorages or former coaling stations which may have difficulty in surviving as independent states. The still dependent territories are:

In the Atlantic: Bermuda, Falkland Islands, St Helena

In the Caribbean: Leeward Islands, Windward Islands

Four of the larger islands units in these two groups—Antigua, Grenada, Dominica, St Lucia and the island group of St Kitts—Nevis and Anguilla—were in 1967 granted the new status of 'Associated States', i.e. complete self-government except in foreign and defence policy. St Vincent joined the group in 1969. Grenada, Dominica, St

Lucia, St Vincent, St Kitts-Nevis and Antigua ceased to be associated states when they became independent.

In the Mediterranean: Gibraltar
In and around the Indian Ocean: Aldabra Is.
In the Far East: Brunei, Hong Kong
In the Pacific: Ellice Islands, Pitcairn Islands

Total population of the Commonwealth: about 1,200 million, or a quarter of the world's total.

THE UNITED NATIONS

The United Nations came into existence on October 24, 1945, and every year October 24 is celebrated as United Nations' Day throughout the world.

The aims of the United Nations are set out in its Charter in these words: 'to save succeeding generations from the scourge of war ... to reaffirm faith in fundamental human rights, in the dignity and worth of the human person, in the equal rights of men and women and of nations large and small, and to establish conditions under which justice and respect for the obligations arising from treaties and other sources of international law can be maintained, and to employ international machinery for the promotion of the economic and social advancement of all peoples'.

Members of the UN in 1945: 51 countries.
Members of the UN in 1986: 159 countries.

The principal organ of the UN is the General Assembly. Around it are grouped the other five main organs of the UN:

General Assembly All other UN bodies report to it. It controls the UN budget and assesses each country's contribution. It elects new members on the recommendation of the Security Council. On 'important' questions, i.e., questions affecting the world's peace and security or the election of new members or the budget, a two-thirds majority of those present and voting is essential before any action can be taken. It meets every year in regular session beginning on the third Tuesday in September.

Security Council It is primarily responsible for keeping international peace and security. Any nation—whether a member

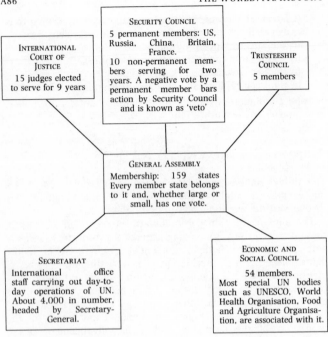

SECURITY COUNCIL
5 permanent members: US, Russia, China, Britain, France.
10 non-permanent members serving for two years. A negative vote by a permanent member bars action by Security Council and is known as 'veto'

INTERNATIONAL COURT OF JUSTICE
15 judges elected to serve for 9 years

TRUSTEESHIP COUNCIL
5 members

GENERAL ASSEMBLY
Membership: 159 states
Every member state belongs to it and, whether large or small, has one vote.

SECRETARIAT
International office staff carrying out day-to-day operations of UN. About 4,000 in number, headed by Secretary-General.

ECONOMIC AND SOCIAL COUNCIL
54 members.
Most special UN bodies such as UNESCO, World Health Organisation, Food and Agriculture Organisation, are associated with it.

of the UN or not—may bring a dispute or threat to peace to its attention and ask it to take action. Any of the five permanent members can block action by voting 'No'. This is known as the veto. Its ten non-permanent members are elected by the General Assembly.

International Court of Justice Its 15 judges are elected by the General Assembly on the recommendation of the Security Council. They consider legal disputes brought before them by nations which cannot agree between themselves. They also give advice on international law when asked to by the General Assembly, the Security Council or other UN bodies.

Trusteeship Council It looks after the interests of non-self-governing territories in different parts of the world which have been placed under the trusteeship of the UN. Its aim is to help

these territories towards full self-government as quickly as possible.

Secretariat It consists of international civil servants who, while
they belong to it, must forget their national loyalties and work
only for the best interests of the UN. The head of the Secretariat
is the Secretary-General, who is appointed by the General
Assembly on the recommendation of the Security Council,
usually for a five-year term.

The UN has had four Secretaries-General:

1. Trygve Lie, of Norway (1945–1953).
2. Dag Hammarskjoeld, of Sweden (1953–1961. Killed in an
   air crash in Africa).
3. U Thant, of Burma (1961–1971).
4. Kurt Waldheim, of Austria (1972–1982).
5. Javier Perez de Cuellar of Peru (1982–).

Economic and Social Council (ECOSOC) Its aim is to establish
lasting world peace by helping the poor, the sick, the hungry,
the illiterate in all parts of the globe. It is responsible for assisting
under-developed countries and promotes health and education
schemes. In a broad sense it supervises the work of many special
UN bodies like the UN Educational, Scientific and Cultural
Organisation (UNESCO), the International Bank for Re-
construction and Development, the International Labour
Organisation (ILO), the Food and Agriculture Organisation
(FAO), the UN International Children's Emergency Fund
(UNICEF) and the International Atomic Energy Agency which
seeks to help countries by encouraging and supporting the use
of atomic energy for peaceful development purposes.

Location of UN Headquarters: New York.

Official languages in which the UN conducts its business:
Chinese, English, French, Russian, Spanish.

THE EUROPEAN COMMUNITY

The European Economic Community (EEC), also known as the
Common Market, was set up by the Treaty of Rome in 1958.
There were then six full members—Belgium, France, Holland,
Italy, Luxembourg and West Germany. Britain had taken part in
the negotiations, but took another point of view on several issues:

it was, for example, opposed to free trade in agricultural products. As a result, Britain joined with six other countries—Austria, Denmark, Norway, Portugal, Sweden and Switzerland—in forming the European Free Trade Area (EFTA). Britain acceded as a full member in 1973, with two of her partners in EFTA—Ireland and Denmark.

The EEC forms a common market: there are no tariffs or trade controls within it, and there is a Common External Tariff. There is also a Common Agricultural Policy (CAP): and free movement within the Community of capital and labour.

The **Commission** is able to set Community action going, mediates between member governments and is the guardian of the various treaties involved. The **Council of Ministers** considers proposals submitted to it by the Commission, and makes decisions on them. The **European Parliament** (with 198 members nominated by their national Parliaments) has to be consulted in all major matters: it has the right to dismiss the Commission through a vote of censure: and it has some control over the annual budget of the Community. The **European Court of Justice** safeguards the law when it comes to interpreting and applying the Community treaties: decides on whether or not decisions of the Council of Ministers or the Commission are legal: and judges cases where a violation of the Treaties is alleged. Cases may be brought to it by the member States, any of the institutions of the community, firms or individuals. Its decisions are binding. The **European Investment Bank** (EIB) makes long-term loans to public authorities, financial institutions and enterprises of various kinds, for the financing of schemes and projects designed to aid the development of less advanced regions or the renewal of ageing industries.

Greece signed the Treaty of Accession in 1979 to become the tenth member. Portugal and Spain became the eleventh and twelfth members of the Community in 1986.

A GLOSSARY OF POLITICAL TERMS

Absolutism or Absolute Monarchy A system of government where the hereditary ruler, usually a king, has complete power to decide a country's internal and external policy without having to consult anyone. The French Revolution heralded the end of absolutism, and in the nineteenth century absolute monarchies everywhere gave place to constitutional monarchies or republics.

Amnesty An act granting forgiveness (literally, forgetfulness) to political and other offenders.

Anarchism Anarchists (from the Greek word *anarchia*, non-rule) believe that every form of government is evil. Towards the end of the last century anarchists assassinated Czar Alexander of Russia and other political leaders in order to draw attention to their theories. There was a strong anarchist movement in Spain during the 1930s.

Aristocracy From the Greek, meaning government by the best. It has come to mean the best by birth. The government of Britain can be said to have been aristocratic up to the Great Reform Bill of 1832 in the sense that both Houses of Parliament were virtually controlled by members of the great landed aristocratic families.

Autocracy Absolute rule by one man.

Authoritarian A term denoting a dictatorial system of government.

Autonomy A word of Greek origin meaning 'self-government'.

Balance of Payments The balance between the cost of a country's imports and the receipts for its exports. Britain is said to pass through a balance-of-payments crisis whenever the value of her imports exceeds the value of her exports.

Balance of Power The theory that the strength of one group of powers on the European continent should be equal to the strength of the other group, thus preventing any one group from becoming dominant.

Bi-partisan Foreign Policy A foreign policy on which both the government and opposition parties are agreed.

Bourgeoisie French for 'citizen class'. A term used by Marxist socialists to denote manufacturers, merchants and people with a business of their own, as opposed to the 'proletariat', who earn a living only by selling their labour.

Buffer State A small state established or preserved between two greater states to prevent direct clashes between them.

Communism The theory, as expounded by Marx and Engels, which aims at the creation of a society in which the private ownership of land, factories, banks, trading houses, etc., is abolished, and everyone receives what he needs and works according to his capacity. Communists believe that revolution and the use of force are justified to bring about the creation of such a society.

Constitution Document or set of documents which set out how a country is to be governed. Britain is said to have an 'unwritten constitution' because, although there are many documents, such as the Great Reform Bill of 1832 or the Parliament Act of 1911, which deal with constitutional matters, there is no single document which sets out the constitutional machinery of Britain, and such written documents as the Great Reform Bill make sense only against the background of the unwritten customs and traditions which have grown up in Britain over the centuries. By contrast, countries such as the USA, France and Germany are all said to have 'written constitutions' because there is a single document or set of documents to which one can refer.

Constitutional Monarchy A system of government where the king's political power is limited by the constitution: real power usually resting with an elected parliament.

Coup d'état A seizure of power and the machinery of government by force.

Democracy From Greek words meaning 'government by the people'. Democracy may be either direct, as practised in some city-states in Ancient Greece where all the adult citizens met in the market-place to discuss and decide on all questions of policy, or indirect, as practised in modern times when the people elect representatives to some kind of parliament. A democracy can be either a monarchy if its head of State is a king or queen as in Britain, or a republic if its head of State is a president as in the USA and France.

démarche a move or some procedure (especially diplomatic) to achieve some end.

détente This is a French word, meaning an easing of tensions between people or, in the political sense, between nations. The commonest use of the word at the moment is to describe the sequence of acts, events and negotiations designed to bring about less tense relations between the Soviet Union and the West. This has led to the partial nuclear test-ban treaty, signed in 1963 between Britain, the USA and the USSR; the 1967 treaty to prevent the spread of nuclear weapons; the seabed treaty of 1971, banning nuclear weapons from the seabed; the treaty of 1973 which banned the future production of biological weapons and required the destruction of existing stockpiles; the Helsinki agreement on human rights and co-operation in various fields; and the Strategic Arms Limitation Talks (SALT), which began in 1969. The policy of détente has suffered setbacks in recent years, especially following the Russian invasion of Afghanistan, but the outlook seems brighter since the 1985 summit meeting between President Reagan and President Gorbachev (see A61).

Dictatorship Rule by one man who, in deciding what to do about the internal or external affairs of the country he controls, does not have to consider or consult anyone but himself.

Fascism An authoritarian extreme right-wing nationalist movement which denies the individual all rights in his relations with the state. In Italy Fascism was led by Mussolini, who held power from 1922 to 1943, and there were strong Fascist movements in many other countries between the two world wars. The German version was Hitler's National Socialism. Fascism derives from the Latin word *fasces*, the name for the axe encased in a bundle of rods which was carried in procession before the chief magistrates in Ancient Rome as a symbol of their power over the life and liberty of ordinary citizens.

Federation A union of states or provinces under a common central government to which they surrender some but not all their powers of government. A federal form of government is usually found in countries which cover a vast area such as the USA, Canada and Australia, but in Europe Switzerland is a federation, and its component states, called cantons, enjoy a large measure of autonomy.

Free Trade A policy of allowing goods to move freely between countries without imposing tariffs or customs duties. Adam Smith in 1776 set out the classic case for Free Trade in his *Wealth of Nations*. Britain's superiority as a manufacturing country in the Victorian era made her favour Free Trade, but as other countries became industralised towards the end of the nineteenth century and her superiority vanished, the demand for 'Protection', i.e. tariffs and customs duties to 'protect' goods manufactured in Britain from foreign competition, grew. All countries today are partially 'protected', but many countries, such as Britain and the USA, are working towards making industrial trade as free as possible.

Imperialism In its original sense, the system of government by an emperor. It has come to be used of any policy of political, military or economic expansion carried out at the expense of weaker people. British imperialism saw its heyday in the latter part of the nineteenth century, its leading exponents being Disraeli, Lord Rosebery and Joseph Chamberlain; but since then the tendency within the Commonwealth has been to give colonial people self-government and independence as soon as and wherever possible.

Industrial Revolution Term applied to the economic developments which between the 1750s and the 1830s transformed Britain from a primarily agricultural to a primarily industrial country.

Isolation A refusal to enter into firm commitments and alliances with other powers.

Laisser-Faire The theory that the state should refrain from all interference in economic affairs. From a phrase coined by eighteenth-century French economists, 'laisser-faire et laisser-passer', 'to let go and pass', i.e. to leave the individual alone and let commodities circulate freely. A reaction against laisser-faire set in during the nineteenth century, inspired by a revulsion against the social conditions created by the Industrial Revolution, and found expression, for example, in the Factory Acts regulating working conditions. The twentieth century has seen an ever-increasing degree of state intervention for social and economic reasons.

Liberalism The body of political and social ideas associated with the Liberal Party in Britain and similar parties elsewhere. The British Liberal Party, which developed out of the Whig Party in the nineteenth century, stood for parliamentary reform, individual liberty, freedom of speech, of the press and of worship, for laisser-faire, i.e. a minimum of state interference in economic affairs, and for international free trade. Towards the end of the century, the Liberal Party modified its views on laisser-faire to ensure minimum living standards for the working class, and, inspired by Lloyd George, the Liberal governments of 1906–14 laid the foundation of what we call today the Welfare State. Since the First World War the influence of the Liberals has declined everywhere, their place as the party of social reform being taken by the Socialists.

Nationalism Term for movements which aim at the strengthening of national feeling and at the unification of a nation or its liberation from foreign rule. Modern nationalism was born in the French Revolution, and under the impact of that event nationalism became a potent factor in European politics in the nineteenth century and helped to bring about the unification of Germany and Italy. In the twentieth century nationalism became a powerful force in Asia and Africa.

National Socialism A German authoritarian extreme right-wing nationalist movement which denied the individual all rights in his relations with the state, personified by Hitler as the Fuehrer ('Leader').

Neutral Term used to describe the condition of a country which in war refrains from hostilities and maintains a strictly impartial attitude towards the belligerents, and in peace stands aloof from the quarrels of other countries and refuses to enter into military alliances. Example: Switzerland and Sweden.

Neutralist Term which has come into use since the Second World War to describe countries which are unwilling to become involved in the Cold War disputes between the Communist and Western power blocs. Example: India.

Nuclear Test Ban Treaty The agreement signed by the Soviet Union, the USA and Britain in Moscow in July, 1963, by which the signatories bound themselves not to test nuclear weapons of any sort by exploding them either under water or in the atmosphere, including outer space. The purpose of the Treaty was to stop the further pollution of the world by radio-active debris. The conclusion of the Treaty led to a dramatic lessening of tension (*détente*) between the Western and Communist powers.

Plebiscite A direct vote by the voters of a country or district on a specific question. In the usual election the people vote for or against the government on all the policies for which it stands; in a plebiscite or referendum they vote only on one particular question, as in Britain in 1975 when they were asked to vote on whether they wanted Britain to stay in the Common Market or not.

Radical A person seeking political, social or economic reform 'from the root'. Term used to describe the wing of the Liberal party which was most forward in its demands for reform. Radicalism lost much of its popular support with the rise of Socialism in this century.

Reactionary In politics, a person who wants to prevent or undo reforms.

Republic A country where the head of state is a president and not a king.

Responsible Government A country is said to have responsible government where the government is responsible to Parliament for everything it does, and where it must resign if it loses the 'confidence' of Parliament. In this sense Britain has responsible government, but the USA has not, because there the President, elected by the whole country for a term of four years, continues in office whether he has the approval of Congress (Parliament) or not. Both countries are, of course, democracies, despite this difference in their constitutions.

Socialism The political, social and economic theories which aim at the establishment of a classless society, through the substitution of common for private ownership of the means of production (land, factories), distribution (shops, transport), and exchange (banks). The Communists believe that all means, including revolution and oppression, are justified in the pursuit of their aims. The Socialists in Britain, Western Europe and most of the African and Asian countries of the Commonwealth are Social Democrats, i.e. they want to bring about a Socialist society by means such as elections and through democratic institutions such as Parliament. Some Social Democrats want a *'mixed economy'*, i.e. one in which not all the means of production, distribution and exchange pass into public ownership, but a large proportion remains in private hands.

Tory Name given to the forerunner of the present Conservative party. Traditionally the Tories were the party of the squire and the parson, as opposed to the *Whigs*, the forerunners of the Liberals, who, though led by a group of great land-owning families, drew their support mainly from the business classes and Nonconformists.

White House The official residence of the President of the USA in Washington. It was partially burnt when the British occupied Washington briefly during the 1812–14 war with the USA, and afterwards painted white to hide the scars left by the fire. Hence the name. The term 'The White House' is often used to mean 'the American government', e.g. 'The White House reviews its Far Eastern policy.'

THE WORLD

2: ITS GEOGRAPHY

THE WORLD

The word Geography comes from the two Greek words *geo* and *graphos* and literally means 'writing about the earth'. It is the science that describes and explains the features and patterns of the earth's surface, both those of the physical and natural world and those of the human or man-made world. In particular, Geography studies the links between the physical and human worlds, that is, the relationships between man and land. In its study of the physical world, Geography looks at landforms such as mountains, rivers, seas and plains, and also at climate, vegetation and soils. This brings it close to the borders of other subjects such as Geology, Meteorology (a branch of Physics), Biology and Pedology (the study of soils). In dealing with the human world, Geography looks at population, settlements, agriculture and industry, countries, trade and communications. This brings it close to subjects like History, Economics, Politics and Anthropology. But though the subject is divided into physical and human parts, the real role of Geography is to study the influence of nature on man and man on nature.

THE EARTH: *Some facts and figures*

The earth is one of the nine planets in the solar system which revolves around the sun. The others are Mercury, Venus, Mars, Jupiter, Saturn, Uranus, Neptune and Pluto. The earth is the fifth largest of these planets and the third in distance from the sun— about 149,700,000 kilometres (93,000,000 miles). The earth is a sphere, like a ball, but it is slightly flattened at the North and South Poles and bulges a little at the Equator. The earth's path around the sun is known as its orbit; and it takes a year for the orbit, whose path is an ellipse, to be completed.

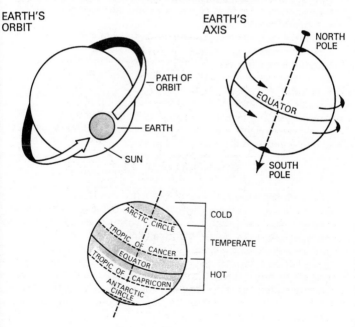

As well as revolving around the sun, the earth also spins on its axis, which is like an imaginary rod passing through the earth's centre from pole to pole. The angle of the axis always stays the same and one complete spin takes about twenty four hours. This spinning, with reference to the light from the sun, produces night and day. The earth's orbit around the sun, together with the angle at which the earth is tilted, is responsible for the seasons. This relationship to the sun causes the earth's major climate and vegetation zones.

The earth can be divided into three main types of climatic regions. The cold regions lie around the North and South Poles, within the Arctic and Antarctic Circles. The tropics are the hot regions north and south of the Equator; their outer boundaries being marked by the Tropic of Cancer in the north and the Tropic of Capricorn in the south. Between these hot and cold regions lie the temperate regions, where climates vary greatly.

Polar diameter (i.e. from pole to pole through the earth's centre), 12,700 km (7,900 miles).

Equatorial diameter (between points on the Equator exactly opposite one another), 12,756·5 km (7,926·5 miles).

Equatorial circumference, 40,076 km (24,901·8 miles).

Total surface area, 510,098,530 sq km (196,950,000 sq miles).

Area of land, 148,437,500 sq km (57,312,000 sq miles).

Area of sea, 361,661,020 sq km (139,638,000 sq miles).

Total mass (weight), about 6,694,000,000,000,000,000,000 (i.e. 6,694 million million million) tonnes.

THE EARTH'S STRUCTURE

The earth is made up of a number of concentric layers of material, like the bulb of an onion. The main layers are the core, the mantle and the crust, and each has its own chemical composition and physical properties. Some 4,500 million years ago the earth's surface was molten rock, but as it cooled and hardened the heavier materials sank towards the earth's centre, whilst the lighter (less dense) materials stayed near the surface. During this process, cooling steam was released which condensed to form the oceans and seas. Gases were also given off, and these formed a kind of atmosphere.

EARTH'S STRUCTURE

The solid crust of the earth, which supports the oceans, the continents and all forms of life, is about as thick in relation to the earth as the shell is to an egg or the skin to an apple. Below the crust, like the flesh of an apple, is the mantle, a section of great thickness and composed of many different layers of material. The mantle is partly fluid. At the earth's centre is the core, and scientists believe that its inner section is solid.

OCEANS AND SEAS

About seven-tenths of the earth's crust is covered with water, forming the main oceans and seas. The other three-tenths is land, and occupies the continents and innumerable islands. If, from outer space, the world was viewed from its Pacific side, hardly any land would be visible at all. All the oceans form one vast and continuous mass of water which, for convenience, is divided into the Pacific, the Atlantic, the Indian and the Arctic Oceans. Some atlases also refer to the Antarctic Ocean; but this is really made up of the southern portions of the Pacific, Atlantic and Indian Oceans.

The seas are smaller, more self-contained areas of the oceans: such as the Mediterranean Sea, the Baltic Sea and the Caribbean Sea. Some of the world's large water bodies are entirely surrounded by land, and are known either as inland seas, such as the Caspian and Aral seas in central Asia, or as lakes: e.g. the Great Lakes on the borders of Canada and the United States, and Lake Victoria in East Africa.

Like the world's land masses, the floors of the oceans have many ridges and depressions. They are made up of shelves, slopes and deeps. The continental shelf is the relatively shallow part of the oceans and seas adjoining the continents. The ocean floor gradually slopes away from the continental shelf to the ocean deeps, where submarine plains and trenches are found. The deeps off the coast of the Philippines reach down to 11,033 metres (36,198 feet). This is about a mile more than the greatest land height (Mount Everest, 8,848 metres or 29,028 feet).

Within the oceans there are also huge mountain ranges, such as the Mid-Atlantic Ridge. These mountains were formed in the same way as mountains on land. The average depth of the oceans (3,795 metres or 12,451 feet) is much greater than the average height of land above sea level. The Mid-Atlantic Ridge marks the boundary of two important *plates* (see B7) in the earth's surface.

You won't find the Malay Sea on an atlas map. It consists of the following seas: Sulu, Celebes, Molucca, Halmahera, Ceram,

OCEANS AND MAIN SEAS: Their Areas

Ocean or sea	Area (sq km.)	Area (sq miles)
Pacific	165,245,700	63,801,668
Atlantic	82,463,500	31,839,306
Indian	73,442,500	28,356,276
Arctic	14,090,100	5,440,197
Seas		
Malay	8,143,100	3,144,056
Caribbean Sea	2,754,000	1,063,340
Mediterranean Sea	2,503,900	966,757
Bering Sea	2,268,200	875,753
Gulf of Mexico	1,543,000	595,760
Sea of Okhotsk	1,527,600	589,807
East China Sea	1,249,200	482,317
Hudson Bay	1,232,200	475,762
Sea of Japan	1,007,700	389,074
Andaman Sea	797,600	307,954
North Sea	575,300	222,124
Black Sea	462,000	178,378
Red Sea	437,900	169,073
Baltic Sea	422,300	163,059

The Mid-Atlantic Ridge

The Average Height of Land Compared with the Average Depth of Ocean

OCEANS AND MAIN SEAS: Their Depths

Ocean or sea	Average depth in metres	Average depth in feet	Greatest depth in metres	Greatest depth in feet
Pacific	4,280	14,048	11,033	36,198
Atlantic	3,926	12,880	9,219	30,246
Indian	3,963	13,002	8,047	26,400
Arctic	1,205	3,953	5,441	17,850
Seas				
Malay Sea	1,212	3,976	6,505	21,342
Caribbean Sea	2,491	8,172	7,239	23,748
Mediterranean Sea	1,487	4,878	4,400	14,435
Bering Sea	2,351	7,714	4,091	13,422
Gulf of Mexico	1,512	4,961	3,885	12,744
Sea of Okhotsk	838	2,749	3,400	11,154
East China Sea	188	617	3,200	10,500
Hudson Bay	128	420	457	1,500
Sea of Japan	1,350	4,429	3,742	12,276
Andaman Sea	870	2,854	3,777	12,392
North Sea	94	308	609	1,998
Black Sea	963	3,160	2,092	6,864
Red Sea	491	1,611	2,211	7,254
Baltic Sea	58	189	421	1,380

Banda, Arafura, Timor, Flores, Bali, Java, Savu and South China; the following gulfs: Thailand, Tomini and Boni; and the following straits: Malacca, Singapore and Macassar.

Because of waves, currents and tides, the water of oceans and seas is constantly moving. Waves are surface movements of water and are caused by winds. Ocean currents can be either cold or warm and have important effects on the earth's climate. For example, the North Atlantic Drift, of which the Gulf Stream is a part, is a warm current that keeps the harbours of north-west Europe ice-free in winter.

Tides are regular rises and falls of the seas and oceans and are related to the attraction (or gravity pull) of the moon and, to a lesser extent, the sun. Tides ebb and flow twice in every 24 hours 50 minutes, which is the time it takes for the moon to orbit the earth. The highest tides, the Spring Tides, occur when the gravitational pull of the moon and sun act together. The lowest or Neap Tides occur when the gravitational pull of the moon and sun are out of phase with each other.

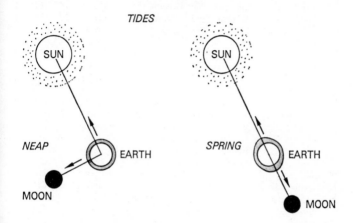

TIDES

THE CONTINENTS

The land surface of the earth is made up of immense land masses which are divided into continental areas and a great number of islands. A huge land mass, largely in the eastern hemisphere, consists of the continents of Asia, Europe and Africa. The Americas in the western hemisphere are divided between the continents of North America and South America. The two island continents in the southern hemisphere are Australia and Antarctica. Generally, islands are regarded as belonging to the nearest continents. The far-flung islands of the Pacific, however, are usually grouped with Australia, New Zealand and New Guinea in the continental area of Oceania.

Although the ice that forms over it in winter makes it a solid mass, the Arctic is a sea, not a continent. Antarctica, however, is a land mass covered by ice and snow (see B41–42).

The largest of the world's seven continents is Asia. It covers an

THE LARGEST ISLANDS

Island	Ocean	Continent	Area (sq km)	Area (sq miles)
Australia	Indian-Pacific	Oceania	7,636,240	2,948,366
Greenland	Atlantic-Arctic	N. America	2,175,030	839,782
New Guinea	Pacific	Oceania	820,670	316,861
Borneo	Pacific	Asia	738,150	285,000
Baffin Is.	Arctic	N. America	611,240	236,000
Malagasy	Indian	Africa	589,840	227,737
Sumatra	Indian	Asia	418,570	161,612
Honshu	Pacific	Asia	230,300	88,919
Great Britain	Atlantic	Europe	218,040	84,186
Victoria Is.	Arctic	N. America	208,360	80,450
Celebes	Indian	Asia	189,480	73,160
South Is. N.Z.	Pacific	Oceania	150,460	58,093
Java	Indian	Asia	125,700	48,534
North Is.N.Z.	Pacific	Oceania	114,690	44,281
Cuba	Atlantic	N. America	114,490	44,206
Newfoundland	Atlantic	N. America	110,680	42,734
Ellesmere Is.	Arctic	N. America	106,190	41,000
Luzon	Pacific	Asia	104,690	40,420
Iceland	Atlantic	Europe	102,970	39,758
Mindanao	Pacific	Asia	94,630	36,537
Hokkaido	Pacific	Asia	88,770	34,276
Novaya Zemlya	Arctic	Asia	82,880	32,000
Ireland	Atlantic	Europe	82,460	31,839
Hispaniola	Atlantic	N. America	76,500	29,536
Tasmania	Pacific	Oceania	67,900	26,215

area of about 17,000,000 sq miles (43,000,000 sq km). The next largest is Africa with about 12,000,000 sq miles (30,000,000 sq km). North America has an area of 9,400,000 sq miles (24,000,000 sq km), while South America covers 6,800,000 sq miles (17,800,000 sq km).

The continent of Europe has a long land boundary with Asia which partly follows the Ural Mountains. Europe's area, including one-quarter of the U.S.S.R., covers 4,000,000 sq miles (10,400,000 sq km). Antarctica is bigger, with an area of 5,500,000 sq miles (14,200,000 sq km). The smallest continent is Australia which combines with the islands mentioned above to form Oceania, covering an area of 3,200,000 sq miles (8,510,000 sq km).

ORIGIN AND STRUCTURE OF THE CONTINENTS

Scientists believe there was originally only one large land mass, which they call Pangaea. This split into a northern mass, Laurasia, and a southern one, Gondwanaland. Out of these land masses the continents gradually drifted to where they are today, and movement is still going on. One of the main arguments offered as proof of *continental drift* is that the shores of the continents, particularly South America and Africa, fit together fairly well, like pieces of a jig-saw.

The crust of the earth is made up of several rigid, but slowly moving, plates on which the continents sit. They might be said to 'float' like rafts on the denser material of the earth's mantle. The

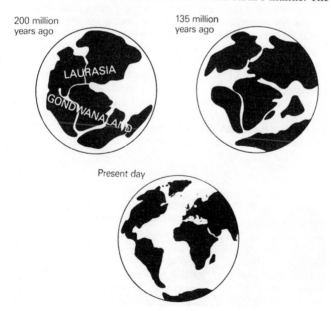

200 million years ago

135 million years ago

Present day

continents split up and drifted apart because, at the edges of the plates, new material came up from the earth's mantle and forced the plates apart. Such movement causes great structural cracks called faults (see B54) and, as land masses push against each other, rock layers are forced up and folded. An upfold of rock strata (layers) is called an *anticline* and a downfold a *syncline*.

In the process of time the *weathering* and *erosion* of the surface folds produces the rugged scenery of the earth's great mountain ranges: for example, the Rockies, the Andes, the Himalayas and the Alps. Some of the world's mountains are considerably older than others, but most of the highest mountains occur in 'younger' folded ranges.

Weathering and erosion by agents such as temperature changes, running water, moving ice, wind and sea action begin as soon as land forms. Rivers are important etchers of land, as are glaciers (see B56). Large parts of the earth have been shaped by past ice action, and similar processes continue today in high mountain regions and around the Poles.

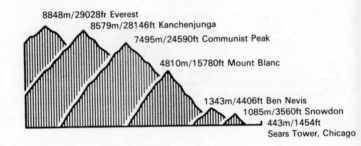

THE WORLD'S HIGHEST MOUNTAINS

Peak	Location	Height (metres)	Height (ft)
Everest	Nepal-Tibet	8,848	29,028
Godwin Austen (K-2)	Pakistan	8,611	28,250
Kanchenjunga	Nepal-Sikkim	8,579	28,146
Makalu	Nepal-Tibet	8,481	27,824
Dhaulagari	Nepal	8,172	26,811
Nanga Parbat	N.W. Kashmir	8,117	26,629
Nanda Devi	Tibet, nr. India	7,817	25,645
Kamet	India-Tibet	7,756	25,447
Minya Konka	Sinkiang (China)	7,590	24,900
Communist Peak	U.S.S.R.	7,495	24,590

HIGHEST POINTS IN EACH CONTINENT

Continent	Highest point	Height (metres)	Height (ft)
Europe	Mt. Elbrus, U.S.S.R.	5,633	18,481
Asia	Mt. Everest, Nepal-Tibet	8,848	29,028
Africa	Mt. Kilimanjaro (Kibo Peak), Tanzania	5,889	19,321
N. America	Mt. McKinley, Alaska, U.S.A.	6,194	20,320
S. America	Mt. Aconcagua, Argentina-Chile	6,960	22,835
Oceania	Mt. Carstenztoppen, New Guinea	5,000	16,404
Antarctica	Vinson Range	5,140	16,864

Wind action also shapes the land, especially in desert areas where material is transported and deposited as high dune ridges. The sea, too, wears land away and builds it up. Bays, cliffs and caves result from marine erosion. Beaches, sandbars and spits are products of marine deposition (See Dictionary section).

LOWEST POINTS IN EACH CONTINENT

Continent	Lowest point	Depth (metres)	Depth (ft)
Europe	Polders, Netherlands	3·7–4·6	12–15
Asia	Dead Sea, Jordan-Israel	392	1,286
Africa	Qattara Depression, Egypt	133	436
N. America	Death Valley, U.S.A.	86	282
S. America	Rio Negro, Argentina	30	98
Oceania	Lake Eyre, South Australia	11·6	38
Antarctica	Interior	2,499	8,200 (ice-filled)

EARTHQUAKES AND VOLCANOES

Earthquakes and volcanic eruptions occur at the edges of the plates in the earth's crust. When plates are forced to move and grind against each other, a series of violent jerks and shudders occur. Like the waves which spread from the centre when a stone is thrown into a pond, the vibrations of an earthquake travel out from a centre called a focus. The surface of the earth above the focus is called the epicentre. Earthquakes cause great damage and can start landslides and floods. The Richter Scale is used to measure the strength of the shock waves.

Volcanoes are the earth's most spectacular displays of energy. Volcanic eruptions of molten rock (lava), ashes, dust and gases can, like earthquakes, lead to major loss of life. Sometimes the lava reaches the surface through great cracks and flows over large areas to form volcanic plateaus. Other eruptions produce characteristic volcanic cones with vents that link the earth's surface with reservoirs of molten rock below (see B55). Volcanoes that have not erupted for long periods are called quiescent or dormant. Many other volcanoes are now extinct.

Earthquakes and volcanic eruptions occur in well-defined areas which lie at the edges of the earth's plates. For example, the largest belt is called the 'Fiery Girdle' and extends around the shores of the Pacific Ocean. A second belt runs through the Mediterranean to the Himalayas and south-east Asia. A third belt follows the Mid-Atlantic Ridge from Iceland in the north to Tristan da Cunha in the south. There are about 430 volcanoes in all with recorded eruptions—275 in the northern hemisphere and 155 in the southern. Some of the world's countries that have experienced disastrous earthquakes in recent times include Turkey, Iran, Greece, Italy, Morocco and Mexico.

Chief earthquake and volcanic zones

THE WORLD'S POPULATION

Of all the species that inhabit the earth's surface, man has been the most inventive and successful, but also the most destructive. In 1986 the world's population was estimated as being 4,900 million. Every five days this figure is said to increase by 1 million. One of the major problems facing the world is that of providing food and resources for this huge population explosion. Many parts of the world are at starvation level, and food production in many countries has been greatly affected by disastrous droughts.

THE PRINCIPAL VOLCANOES OF THE WORLD

I. Active

Volcano	Height (metres)	Height (ft)	Volcano	Height (metres)	Height (ft)
Cotopaxi (Ecuador)	5,978	19,613	Colima (Mexico)	3,850	12,631
Popocatepetl (Mexico)	5,452	17,887	Fuego (Guatemala)	3,835	12,582
Sangay (Ecuador)	5,410	17,749	Kerinti (Indonesia)	3,805	12,484
Tungurahua (Ecuador)	5,033	16,512	Santa Maria (Guatemala)	3,768	12,362
Cotacachi (Ecuador)	4,937	16,197	Rindjani (Indonesia)	3,726	12,225
Klyuchevskaya (USSR)	4,850	15,912	Semeru (Indonesia)	3,676	12,060
Purace (Columbia)	4,756	15,604	Ichinskaya (USSR)	3,607	11,834
Wrangell (Alaska, USA)	4,269	14,005	Atitlan (Guatemala)	3,525	11,565
Tajmulco (Guatemala)	4,210	13,812	Nyiregongo (Congo)	3,470	11,384
Mauna Loa (Hawaii, USA)	4,168	13,675	Irazu (Costa Rica)	3,432	11,260
Cameroons (Nigeria)	4,069	13,350	Slamat (Indonesia)	3,428	11,247
Tacana (Guatemala)	4,064	13,333	Spurr (Alaska, USA)	3,374	11,070
Erebus (Antarctica)	4,023	13,200	Raung (Indonesia)	3,332	10,932
Acatenango (Guatemala)	3,960	12,992	Etna (Sicily)	3,287	10,784

II. Quiescent

Volcano	Height (metres)	Height (ft)	Volcano	Height (metres)	Height (ft)
Kilimanjaro (Tanzania)	5,889	19,321	Sundoro (Indonesia)	3,135	10,285
Misti (Peru)	5,801	19,031	Balbi (Solomon Is.)	3,100	10,171
Pichincha (Ecuador)	4,789	15,712	Apo (Philippine Is.)	2,954	9,690
Kronotskaya (USSR)	3,730	12,238	Marapi (Indonesia)	2,911	9,551
Lassen (USA)	3,190	10,466	Tambora (Indonesia)	2,851	9,353
Welirang (Indonesia)	3,156	10,354	Paricutin (Mexico)	2,774	9,100

III. Believed Extinct

Volcano	Height (metres)	Height (ft)
Aconcagua (Argentine–Chile)	6,960	22,835
Chimborazo (Ecuador)	6,282	20,610
Orizaba (Mexico)	5,700	18,701
Elbrus (USSR)	5,647	18,526

Volcano	Height (metres)	Height (ft)
Demavend (Iran)	5,366	17,604
Karisimbi (Congo)	4,578	15,020
Mikeno (Congo)	4,505	14,780
Fujiyama (Japan)	3,778	12,395

PRINCIPAL LAKES, RIVERS AND WATERFALLS OF THE WORLD

LAKES OF THE WORLD*

Lake	Location	Area (sq km)	Area (sq miles)	Length (km)	Length (miles)	Salt or fresh
Caspian Sea[1]	USSR–Iran (Asia-Europe)	440,300	170,000	1,094	680	Salt
Superior	USA–Canada	82,410	31,820	616	383	Fresh
Victoria	Uganda–Kenya–Tanzania	67,860	26,200	322	200	Fresh
Aral Sea[1]	Kazakhstan Republic, USSR	67,770	26,166	426	265	Salt
Huron	USA–Canada	59,600	23,010	398	247	Fresh
Michigan	USA	58,020	22,400	494	307	Fresh
Baikal	USSR	34,180	13,197	620	385	Fresh
Tanganyika	Congo–Zambia, Tanzania–Burundi	32,890	12,700	676	420	Fresh
Great Bear	Canada	31,080	12,000	314	195	Fresh
Great Slave	Canada	28,930	11,170	523	325	Fresh
Nyasa	Malawi–Tanzania–Mozambique	28,490	11,000	563	350	Fresh
Erie	USA–Canada	25,750	9,940	388	241	Fresh
Winnipeg	Canada	24,340	9,398	418	260	Fresh
Ontario	USA–Canada	19,530	7,540	311	193	Fresh
Chad[2]	Niger–Chad–Cameroun–Nigeria	18,650	7,200	—	—	Fresh

[1] Classified as lakes, despite their names, as they are completely landlocked (See B6).
[2] In flood, Lake Chad becomes the world's largest fresh-water lake, covering 129,500 sq km (50,000 sq miles).
* Some of these lakes are subject to seasonal variations in area.

PRINCIPAL RIVERS OF THE WORLD

River	Continent	Approx length (km)	Approx length (miles)	Flow (cu m/sec) where known	Flow (cu ft/sec) where known	Outflow into:
Nile	Africa	6,680	4,150	11,900	420,000	Mediterranean Sea
Amazon	S. America	6,280	3,900	203,900	7,200,000	Atlantic Ocean
Missouri–Mississippi	N. America	6,120	3,800	14,500	513,000	Mississippi River
Yangtze Kiang	Asia	5,470	3,400	21,800	770,000	Pacific Ocean
Ob–Irtish	Asia	5,150	3,200	—	—	Gulf of Ob/Pacific
Hwang Ho (Yellow)	Asia	4,670	2,900	3,300	116,000	Yellow Sea (Pacific)
Congo	Africa	4,670	2,900	56,600	2,000,000	Atlantic Ocean
Amur	Asia	4,510	2,800	—	—	Gulf of Tartary
Lena	Asia	4,510	2,800	17,000	600,000	Arctic Ocean
Mekong	Asia	4,510	2,800	—	—	South China Sea
Niger	Africa	4,180	2,600	—	—	Atlantic Ocean
Yenisei	Asia	4,100	2,550	—	—	Arctic Ocean
MacKenzie	N. America	4,020	2,500	12,700	450,000	Arctic Ocean
La Plata Parana	S. America	3,700	2,300	79,300	2,800,000	Atlantic Ocean
Volga	Europe	3,700	2,300	9,900	350,000	Caspian Sea
Yukon	N. America	3,220	2,000	—	—	Bering Sea
St Lawrence	N. America	2,900	1,800	11,300	400,000	Atlantic Ocean
Rio Grande	N. America	2,900	1,800	150	5,180	Gulf of Mexico

THE WORLD'S GREAT WATERFALLS

In Order of Height (Single Leaps Only)

Waterfall	Country	River	Height (metres)	Height (ft)
Angel Falls	Venezuela	Tributary of Caroni River	979	3,212
Ribbon Falls	California, USA	Tributary of Yosemite River	491	1,612
King George VI	Guyana	Utshi River	488	1,600
Upper Yosemite	California, USA	Yosemite Creek	436	1,430
Gavarnie	Pyrenees, France	Gave de Pau	422	1,385
Tugela (highest fall)	Natal, Republic of S. Africa	Tugela River	412	1,350
Wollomombi	New South Wales, Australia	Wollomombi River	335	1,100
Takakkaw	British Columbia, Canada	Tributary of Yoho River	305	1,100
Staubbach	Switzerland	Pletschen River	299	980
Mardola	Norway	Elkesdals Lake	297	974
Chirombo	Zambia	Ieisa River	268	880
Vettisfoss	Norway	Utla River	261	856
King Edward VIII	Guyana	Semang River	256	840
Gersoppa	India	Sharavati River	253	830
Sutherland	New Zealand	Arthur River	248	815

In Order of Volume

Waterfall	Country	River	Height (metres)	Height (ft)	Average annual flow (cu m/sec)	Average annual flow (cu ft/sec)
Guaira or Sete Quedas	Brazil-Paraguay	Alto Parana River	40	130	13,310	470,000
Khon	Laos-Khmer	Mekong River	21	70	11,610	410,000
Niagara	USA-Canada	Niagara River	51	167	6,000	212,000
Paolo Afonse	Brazil	Sao Francisco River	59	192	2,830	100,000
Urubupunga	Brazil	Alto Parana River	12	40	2,750	97,000
Iguazu	Argentina–Brazil	Iguazu River	72	237	1,750	61,660
Patos-Maribondo	Brazil	Rio Grande	35	115	1,500	53,000
Victoria	Zambia and Zimbabwe	Zambesi River	108	354	1,100	38,430
Grand	Labrador	Hamilton River	75	245	990	35,000
Kaieteur	Guyana	Potaro River	226	741	660	23,400

■ 10 million people

(This map shows the sizes of countries according to their populations
rather than their areas. On this basis, China and India are larger
than the USSR and the USA).

Ethiopia and Sudan, for example, are countries experiencing acute hunger, and millions of people have died from the lack of food. Similar conditions occur throughout the whole of Africa's Sahel—the dry countries that border the southern regions of the Sahara desert.

If average population densities are taken, there are about 30 people to every square kilometre. But land, climate and vegetation all influence the distribution of the world's population, which is very uneven. Some large areas are too cold, too dry or too forested to support high population densities. On the other hand, where land is fertile and the climate favourable, many people are crowded together. Manufacturing industry and commerce are also responsible for high population densities, especially in Western European countries and in North America. The world's ten most populated countries are listed in the following table:

Country	Population
China	1,024,000,000 (1984)
India	730,000,000 (1984)
Soviet Union	273,843,000 (1984)
United States	233,982,000 (1983)
Indonesia	157,000,000 (1983)
Brazil	129,660,000 (1983)
Japan	118,390,690 (1984)
Bangladesh	94,650,000 (1983)
Pakistan	89,730,000 (1983)
Nigeria	88,600,000 (1983)

Added together, the populations of China, India, Indonesia, Brazil, Bangladesh, Pakistan, Nigeria and Mexico (the last being the world's eleventh most populated country with 72,920,000 in 1982) account for one-half of the world's total population.

The map on B20 shows the sizes of countries according to their populations rather than their areas. The countries mentioned in the above table all appear as large shapes. Yet many of the world's smaller countries have very high population densities: for example, West Germany, the United Kingdom, Italy and France. At the same time many countries that are large in terms of area have very small populations. Australia has less than two persons per square kilometre: two-thirds of the country being practically empty because of its dryness. More than half of all Australians live in the four cities of Sydney, Melbourne, Brisbane and Adelaide.

THE WORLD'S GREAT CITIES

In spite of the importance of farming in feeding the world's ever-increasing population, more and more people are leaving the countryside for the towns and cities.

In the richer countries, where agriculture has become mechanised, fewer people are needed to work the land. The towns and cities offer alternative employment, often better-paid jobs and many social amenities: sporting, entertainment and shopping facilities.

In the world's poorer or developing countries, cities are also growing at an extremely rapid rate. Thousands of people flock to them every year, attempting to escape from the poverty of the countryside. Yet poverty, slums and unemployment are found in the cities, too, and crime rates are high. Whether in rich or poor countries, dwellers in larger cities face similar problems such as air

WORLD'S LARGEST CITIES AND URBAN AREAS (IN THOUSANDS)

Mexico City (Mexico)	16,700	Chicago (USA)	7,150
Sao Paolo (Brazil)	> 14,800	Jakarta (Indonesia)	> 7,028
Shanghai (China)	11,859	Tehran (Iran)	7,000
Tokyo (Japan)	11,807	Chunking (China)	> 6,200
London (Greater, UK)	> 11,000	Delhi (India)	6,200
		Hong Kong (Hong Kong)	6,100
Cairo (Egypt)	> 11,000	Bangkok (Thailand)	> 6,000
Buenos Aires (Argentina)	11,000	Karachi (Pakistan)	5,500
		Ruhrstadt (W. Germany)	5,350
Paris (France)	> 10,740	Canton (China)	> 5,000
Calcutta (India)	> 10,000	Guangzhou (China)	> 5,000
Seoul (S. Korea)	9,455	Istanbul (Turkey)	> 5,000
Peking (China)	9,231	Lima (Peru)	> 5,000
New York (USA)	9,120	Bogota (Columbia)	5,000
Rio de Janeiro (Brazil)	9,000	Leningrad (USSR)	4,832
Moscow (USSR)	8,546	Philadelphia (USA)	4,750
Bombay (India)	8,300	Lagos (Nigeria)	4,500
Manila (Philippines)	> 8,000	Santiago (Chile)	4,500
Osaka (Japan)	7,800	Shenyang (China)	4,500
Tientsin (China)	7,700	Detroit (USA)	4,354
Los Angeles (USA)	7,500	Madras (India)	4,300

Note: > in excess of

pollution, traffic congestion, lack of land for building, and noise. Many countries encourage people to return to the countryside or to new towns, built to attract people away from the overcrowded cities.

The table on B22 lists the world's forty largest urban areas. Many are made up of one or more major city, together with smaller centres and numerous residential and manufacturing suburbs. Such complexes are called *conurbations* or *metropolitan areas*. Tokyo, for example, is the centre of the Kei Hin conurbation, which in 1985 had a population of over 28 million. London is the centre of a huge urban region of at least 11 million. In West Germany, the urban and industrial area of Ruhrstadt includes the cities of Essen, Duisburg, Dortmund and Bochum.

RACE, LANGUAGE AND RELIGION

As well as varying in density from one part of the world to another, the world's population is divided by factors such as race, language and religion. Scientists describe modern man as *Homo sapiens*, but divide mankind into three sub-groups or races: **Caucasoids**, **Mongoloids** and **Negroids**.

Most Europeans, and many Asian and North African peoples, belong to the **Caucasoid** race, the largest of the sub-groups. As a result of exploration and migration, European Caucasoids have settled in many parts of the world, particularly in the Americas, Australasia and Africa.

Mongoloid peoples form the second largest racial group. The Chinese, Japanese, Koreans, Malays, Mongols and, as a result of early migrations, the American Indians and Eskimos, all belong to the Mongoloid race.

The **Negroid** races belong mainly to central and north Africa, but slavery transferred many Negroids to North and South America. Some of the world's tallest people (the Nilotes of the White Nile region) and also the shortest (the Negrillos or pygmies of central Africa) belong to the Negroid race.

There are probably over 2,700 languages spoken in the world today. Nobody knows the exact number, since many are spoken only by small groups and tribes and have never been recorded on paper. About two-thirds of the world's population speak twelve principal languages, and another ten important languages account for about half of the remaining population. Differences in language can lead to suspicion, rivalry and conflict between peoples. This is also true of religion. The principal languages and religions of the world are given in the following tables:

LANGUAGE

Language	Speakers (millions)	Language	Speakers (millions)
Chinese	920	French	90
English	390	Bantu (Middle and	
Spanish	250	South Africa)	80
Hindi	245	Italian	60
Russian	145	Javanese (Indonesia)	55
Arabic	140	Korean	55
Portuguese	140	Telugu (India)	54
Bengali (India and		Tamil (India and	
Bangladesh)	130	Sri Lanka)	54
German	120	Swaheli (East and	
Japanese	117	Central Africa)	50
Sudanese	100	Punjabi (India and	
		Pakistan)	50

RELIGION
Followers in thousands

Christianity		
Catholicism	794,380 ⎫	
Protestantism	341,000 ⎬ 1,248,380	
Orthodoxy	100,000	
Others	13,000 ⎭	
Islam		
Sunnis	400,000 ⎫	
Shi'ites	90,000 ⎬ 605,580	
Others	115,580 ⎭	
Judaism	16,821	
Asiatic religions		
Confucianism	310,000	
Taoism	31,243	
Buddhism	900,000	
Hinduism	518,794	
Shintoism	61,156	
Sikhs	10,000	
Zoroastrianism	271	

COUNTRIES OF THE WORLD

The world is further divided into political areas called countries, nations or states. These are by far the most important divisions. The world is made up of over 200 countries and political areas: some very small like Monaco (2 sq km) and the Vatican (0·4 sq km), and others exceptionally large. The world's largest countries in terms of area (but not necessarily in terms of population—see page B20) are:

Country	Area in sq km
Soviet Union	22,402,200
Canada	9,976,139
China	9,561,000
United States	9,363,123
Brazil	8,511,965
Australia	7,686,848
India	3,287,590
Argentina	2,776,889
Sudan	2,505,800
Algeria	2,381,741
Zaire	2,345,409
Greenland	2,175,030
Saudi Arabia	2,150,000
Mexico	1,972,000
Indonesia	1,919,443
Libya	1,759,540
Iran	1,648,000
Mongolia	1,565,000
Peru	1,285,216
Chad	1,284,000

Political ideas play an important part in dividing mankind. One of the chief divisions of the world today is between communist and non-communist countries. But such groups are by no means united among themselves.

The world's nations are also grouped into rich and poor countries. These are also known as the *developed countries* (the 'haves') and the *developing countries* (the 'have-nots'). Developing countries are often referred to as *Third World* countries to distinguish them from Second World communist countries and First World developed and non-communist countries (see map on B26).

Countries often combine with one another to form larger units. This might be for economic or military reasons or because they

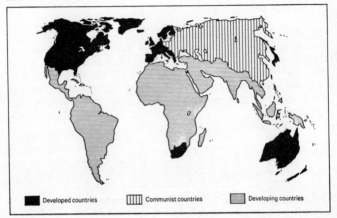

Developed countries   Communist countries   Developing countries

share some common history or identity. The *Commonwealth of Nations* is a very large grouping of countries (see A82). In 1981 its combined area was 28,443,279 square kilometres and its population was 1,069,144,290.

Another important group of countries to which Britain belongs are those which make up the *European Economic Community* (the *Common Market*). Brussels is the seat of the Common Market Commission, and Strasbourg the seat of the European parliament.

Some of the world's most powerful states have formed unions in which they dominate the affairs of other countries. The Soviet Union does this through the Warsaw Pact, and the United States through the Organisation of American States. There is also the Organisation of African Unity; and in the Middle East, the Arab countries have founded the Arab League.

Groups of countries combine with each other for purely military reasons, as in NATO (North Atlantic Treaty Organisation).

By far the largest of the world organisations is the United Nations (see A85).

The following tables give the areas and populations of all the world's countries and the names and populations of their capital cities. The number of people in any country is constantly changing so only approximate figures, based on the latest counts (or censuses), can be given.

EUROPE AND THE MEDITERRANEAN

Country	Area (sq km)	Area (sq miles)	Population	Capital	Population of Capital
Albania	28,748	11,100	2,900,000	Tirana	210,000
Andorra	453	175	41,600	Andorra La Vella	15,300
Austria	83,853	32,376	7,552,000	Vienna	1,529,500
Belgium	30,513	11,781	9,863,374	Brussels	993,005
Bulgaria	110,912	42,823	8,970,000	Sofia	1,115,700
Cyprus	9,251	3,572	660,000	Nicosia	233,600
Czechoslovakia	127,869	49,370	15,500,000	Prague	1,193,135
Denmark	43,075	16,631	5,116,464	Copenhagen	1,372,019
Finland	338,127	130,551	4,845,000	Helsinki	880,000
France	547,026	211,207	54,500,000	Paris	10,073,000
Germany: West	248,678	96,015	61,335,000	Bonn	292,500
East	108,181	43,446	16,735,000	E. Berlin	1,173,208
Gibraltar	6·5	2·5	28,700	Gibraltar	28,700
Greece	131,944	50,944	9,800,000	Athens	3,355,000
Hungary	93,032	35,920	10,750,000	Budapest	2,093,000
Iceland	103,829	39,702	238,000	Reykjavik	126,000
Irish Republic	70,283	27,136	3,480,000	Dublin	700,000
Italy	301,252	116,313	56,850,000	Rome	2,830,569
Liechtenstein	160	62	26,520	Vaduz	4,896
Luxembourg	2,586	998	366,000	Luxembourg	80,000
Malta, Gozo	316	122	370,000	Valetta	14,042
Monaco	1·95	0·75	28,000	Monaco-ville	1,445

Country	Area (sq km)	Area (sq miles)	Population	Capital	Population of Capital
Netherlands	41,548	15,770	14,405,000	Amsterdam	1,002,022
Norway	324,219	125,181	4,168,000	Oslo	697,018
Poland	312,683	120,727	36,610,000	Warsaw	1,615,000
Portugal	92,082	35,553	10,235,000	Lisbon	2,100,000
Romania	237,500	91,699	22,710,000	Bucharest	1,961,000
San Marino	61	23	22,000	San Marino	4,700
Spain	504,782	194,896	38,500,000	Madrid	3,322,000
Sweden	449,964	173,731	8,327,484	Stockholm	1,535,600
Switzerland	41,293	15,943	6,425,500	Berne	286,903
Turkey (in Europe)	23,623	9,121	5,267,000	Ankara *	3,200,000
United Kingdom of Great Britain and Northern Ireland	244,046	94,226	56,340,000	London	11,000,000
USSR. (in Eur.)	17,075,400	6,592,818	214,397,000		
RSFSR. (Eur.)	603,700	233,089	142,108,000	Moscow	8,546,000
Ukraine	207,600	80,154	50,681,000	Kiev	2,400,000
Byelorussia	65,200	25,174	9,878,000	Minsk	1,445,000
Lithuania	63,700	24,594	3,539,000	Vilnius	540,000
Latvia	45,100	17,413	2,589,000	Riga	880,000
Estonia	33,700	13,011	1,519,000	Tallinn	460,000
Moldavia	44 hectares	109 acres	4,083,000	Kishinev	610,000
Vatican City			1,000	Vatican City	1,000
Yugoslavia	255,804	98,766	23,000,000	Belgrade	1,455,046

* In Asiatic Turkey.

ASIA

Country	Area (sq km)	Area (sq miles)	Population	Capital	Population of Capital
Afghanistan	647,497	249,999	17,500,000	Kabul	1,200,000
Bahrain	622	240	375,000	Manama	122,000
Bangladesh	143,998	55,598	94,650,000	Dacca	3,460,000
Bhutan	47,000	18,147	1,380,000	Thimpu	20,000
Brunei	5,765	2,226	260,000	Bandam Seri Begawan	58,000
Burma	676,552	261,217	35,855,000	Rangoon	2,500,000
Cambodia	181,035	69,898	6,650,000	Phnom Penh	300,000
China					
Mainland	9,560,779	3,691,420	1,024,000,000	Peking	9,231,000
Taiwan (Formosa)	36,182	13,970	18,547,000	Taipei	4,200,000
Macau	16	6	450,000	Macau	300,000
Hong Kong	1,045	403	6,100,000	Victoria	1,000,000
India	3,287,590	1,269,340	730,000,000	Delhi	6,200,000
Indonesia	1,919,443	741,098	157,000,000	Jakarta	7,028,000
Iran (Persia)	1,648,000	636,293	41,030,000	Tehran	7,000,000
Iraq	438,446	169,284	14,260,000	Baghdad	3,500,000
Israel	20,770	8,019	4,078,000	Jerusalem	450,000
Japan	372,313	143,750	118,390,000	Tokyo	11,807,000
Jordan	97,740	37,737	3,501,000	Amman	1,250,000
Kashmir	88,000	33,977	1,350,000	Muzzafarabad	15,000
Korea: North	120,538	46,540	18,900,000	Pyongyang	1,700,000
South	98,484	38,025	40,867,000	Seoul	9,455,000
Kuwait	17,818	6,880	1,790,000	Kuwait	700,000

Country	Area (sq km)	Area (sq miles)	Population	Capital	Population of Capital
Laos	236,800	91,428	3,700,000	Vientiane	200,000
Lebanon	10,400	4,015	2,700,000	Beirut	600,000
Malaysia	333,403	128,727	15,100,000	Kuala Lumpur	1,100,000
Maldive Islands	298	115	165,700	Malé	45,000
Mongolia (Outer)	1,565,000	604,247	1,821,000	Ulan Bator	435,000
Nepal	140,797	54,361	16,000,000	Katmandu	800,000
Oman	212,457	82,030	1,080,000	Muscat	100,000
Pakistan	803,943	310,403	89,730,000	Islamabad	240,000
Philippines	300,000	115,830	51,960,000	Manila	8,000,000
Qatar	11,000	4,247	265,000	Doha	209,000
Saudi Arabia	2,149,690	829,996	9,730,000	Riyadh	1,250,000
Singapore	581	224	2,505,000	Singapore	2,505,000
Sri Lanka	65,610	25,332	15,450,000	Colombo	1,000,000
Syria	185,180	71,498	10,500,000	Damascus	1,250,000
Thailand (Siam)	514,000	198,456	50,136,000	Bangkok	6,000,000
Turkey (in Asia)	756,953	292,260	47,500,000	Ankara	3,200,000
United Arab Emirates	83,600	32,278	1,300,000	Abu Dhabi	350,000
USSR (in Asia)					
R.S.F.S.R.	see Europe	see Europe	59,446,000	Alma Ata	1,050,000
Kazakhstan	2,715,100	1,048,301	15,654,000	Ashkahabad	350,000
Turkmenistan	488,100	188,456	3,123,000	Tashkent	2,000,000
Uzbekistan	449,600	173,591	17,496,000		

Country	Area (sq km)	Area (sq miles)	Population	Capital	Population of Capital
Kirghizia	198,500	76,641	3,875,000	Frunze	600,000
Tadzhikistan	143,100	52,251	4,366,000	Dushanbe	550,000
Georgia	69,700	26,911	5,171,000	Tbilisi	1,150,000
Azerbaijan	86,600	33,436	6,498,000	Baku	1,690,000
Armenia	29,800	11,506	3,263,000	Erevan	1,115,000
Vietnam	332,556	128,400	60,000,000	Hanoi	2,570,909
Yemen	195,000	75,290	7,100,000	Sana'a	500,000
Yemen PDR	332,968	128,559	2,100,000	Aden	343,000

Note The map of the world above is based on a projection called the Mercator. Map projections are a means of representing the earth's spherical shape on a flat surface. This results in distortion, either of distance or of area. In Mercator's Projection, the world is shown as a rectangle based on lines of longitude that are parallel rather than meeting at the poles. Also, all lines of latitude are made equal in length to the Equator, whereas on a globe they decrease in size in the direction of the poles. This produces a distortion of area which becomes greater, the further away from the Equator. Greenland, for example, is shown to be larger in area than Australia when, in fact, Australia is 3·5 times the greater. Maps in atlases make use of a variety of projections according to the area depicted. A globe is the best way of showing the world's land and countries.

AFRICA

Country	Area (sq km)	Area (sq miles)	Population	Capital	Population of Capital
Algeria	2,381,743	919,592	20,900,000	Algiers	3,000,000
Angola	1,246,700	481,351	8,200,000	Luanda	1,170,000
Benin	112,622	43,483	3,800,000	Porto Novo	131,989
Botswana	600,372	231,804	940,000	Gaborone	65,000
Burkina-Faso	274,200	105,869	7,200,000	Ouagadougou	300,000
Burundi	27,834	10,747	4,500,000	Bujumbura	171,000
Cameroun	475,442	183,568	9,160,000	Yaounde	600,000
Cape Verde Islands	4,033	1,557	340,000	Praia	40,000
Central African Rep.	622,984	240,534	2,575,000	Bangui	400,000
Chad	1,284,000	495,753	4,700,000	Ndjaména	300,000
Congo	342,000	132,046	2,000,000	Brazzaville	425,000
Comores Islands	1,797	694	380,000	Moroni	16,000
Djibouti	22,000	8,494	420,000	Djibouti	200,000
Egypt	1,001,449	386,660	46,000,000	Cairo	11,000,000
Equatorial Guinea	28,051	10,830	380,000	Malabo	80,000
Ethiopia	1,221,900	471,776	33,600,000	Addis Ababa	1,500,000
Gabon	267,667	103,346	1,253,000	Libreville	350,000
Gambia	11,295	4,361	696,000	Banjul	50,000
Ghana	238,537	92,099	13,100,000	Accra	1,080,000
Guinea	245,857	94,925	6,110,000	Conakry	750,000
Guinea Bissau	36,125	13,948	863,000	Bissau	120,000
Ivory Coast	322,463	124,503	8,900,000	Abidjan	2,000,000
Kenya	582,646	224,960	18,500,000	Nairobi	1,000,000
Lesotho	30,355	11,720	1,490,000	Maseru	196,000
Liberia	111,369	43,000	2,190,000	Monrovia	350,000
Libya	1,759,540	679,359	3,300,000	Tripoli	1,100,000

Country	Area (sq km)	Area (sq miles)	Population	Capital	Population of Capital
Madagascar	587,041	226,657	9,930,000	Antananarivo	820,000
Malawi	118,484	45,747	6,650,000	Lilongwe	110,000
Mali	1,240,142	478,819	7,700,000	Bamako	660,000
Mauritania	1,030,700	397,954	1,800,000	Nouakchott	210,000
Mauritius, etc.	2,045	790	990,000	Port Louis	148,000
Morocco	458,730	177,116	22,000,000	Rabat	850,000
Mozambique	799,380	308,641	13,000,000	Maputo	848,000
Niger	1,267,000	489,189	5,730,000	Niamey	365,000
Nigeria	923,768	356,667	88,600,000	Lagos	4,500,000
Réunion	2,510	969	520,000	St Denis	110,000
Rwanda	26,338	10,169	5,200,000	Kigali	160,000
Sahara, Western	266,000	102,703	139,000	El Alaiun	20,000
St Helena	122	47	5,500	Jamestown	1,576
Ascension Is.	88	34	1,438	Georgetown	—
Tristan da Cunha	209	81	300	Edinburgh	—
S. Tomé and Principé	964	372	110,000	São Tomé	20,000
Sénégal	196,192	75,750	6,000,000	Dakar	1,100,000
Seychelles	404	156	70,000	Victoria	25,000
Sierra Leone	71,740	27,699	3,700,000	Freetown	316,000
Somalia	637,657	246,200	5,300,000	Mogadishu	611,000
South Africa	1,216,265	469,600	32,000,000	Pretoria	740,000
				Cape Town	1,500,000
S.W. Africa (Namibia)	823,168	317,825	1,200,000	Windhoek	88,700
Spanish Presidios:					
Ceuta	19	7	67,000	—	—
Melilla	12	5	65,000	—	—
Sudan	2,505,813	967,495	19,600,000	Khartoum	1,688,000

Country	Area (sq km)	Area (sq miles)	Population	Capital	Population of Capital
Swaziland	17,363	6,704	623,000	Mbabane	31,000
Tanzania	945,087	364,898	20,110,000	Dar es Salaam	1,000,000
Togo	56,000	21,622	2,925,000	Lomé	350,000
Tunisia	164,150	63,378	6,812,000	Tunis	1,250,000
Uganda	236,036	91,133	14,200,000	Kampala	477,000
Zaïre	2,345,409	905,563	31,060,000	Kinshasa	4,000,000
Zambia	752,614	290,584	6,316,000	Lusaka	650,000
Zimbabwe	390,622	150,819	7,900,000	Harare	690,000

NORTH AND CENTRAL AMERICA AND THE WEST INDIES

Country	Area (sq km)	Area (sq miles)	Population	Capital	Population of Capital
Anguilla	88	34	7,100	—	—
Antigua and Barbuda	452	175	78,810	St John's	35,000
Bahamas	13,935	5,380	237,100	Nassau	140,000
Barbados	431	166	270,000	Bridgetown	102,000
Belize	22,962	8,866	163,000	Belmopan	4,000
Bermuda	53.5	20.7	58,000	Hamilton	3,000
Canada	9,976,139	3,851,791	24,928,000	Ottawa	717,978
Cayman Islands	259	100	18,750	George Town	8,210
Costa Rica	50,700	19,575	2,505,000	San José	820,000
Cuba	114,524	44,218	10,000,000	Havana	2,000,000
Dominica	.751	290	82,000	Roseau	20,000

Country	Area (sq km)	Area (sq miles)	Population	Capital	Population of Capital
Dominican Rep.	48,734	18,816	6,680,000	Santo Domingo	1,600,000
Grenada	344	133	110,500	St George's	30,800
Guadeloupe	1,779	687	330,000	Basse-Terre	15,780
Guatemala	108,889	42,042	7,860,000	Guatemala	1,550,000
Haiti	27,750	10,714	6,010,500	Pt-au-Prince	800,000
Honduras	112,088	43,277	4,097,000	Tegucigalpa	535,000
Jamaica	10,991	4,244	2,491,000	Kingston	766,000
Martinique	1,102	425	330,000	Fort-de-France	101,000
Mexico	1,972,547	761,601	72,920,000	Mexico City	16,700,000
Monserrat	106	41	12,073	Plymouth	3,500
Netherlands Antilles	993	383	257,000	Willemstad	155,000
Nicaragua	130,000	50,193	3,000,000	Managua	653,000
Panama	75,650	29,208	2,126,000	Panama City	570,000
Panama Canal Zone	1,676	647	41,800	Balboa Heights	6,000
Puerto Rico	8,897	3,435	3,203,000	San Juan	1,100,000
St Kitts-Nevis	262	101	60,000	Basseterre	14,725
St Pierre and Miquelon	242	93	6,041	St Pierre	5,415
St Lucia	616	238	127,000	Castries	50,300
St Vincent	389	150	128,000	Kingstown	23,650
El Salvador	21,041	8,124	5,300,000	San Salvador	902,600
Trinidad and Tobago	5,128	1,980	1,179,000	Port-of-Spain	260,000
Turks and Caicos Is.	430	166	7,436	Grand Turk	3,150
United States	9,363,123	3,615,105	233,982,000	Washington, D.C.	3,060,922

Country	Area (sq km)	Area (sq miles)	Population	Capital	Population of Capital
Virgin Islands:					
British	153	59	11,500	Road Town	3,500
US	344	133	95,214	Charlotte Amalie	12,372

SOUTH AMERICA

Country	Area (sq km)	Area (sq miles)	Population	Capital	Population of Capital
Argentina	2,776,889	1,072,158	29,900,000	Buenos Aires	11,000,000
Bolivia	1,098,581	424,162	6,200,000	La Paz	1,800,000
Brazil	8,511,965	3,286,473	129,660,000	Brasilia	1,300,500
Chile	756,945	292,257	11,760,000	Santiago	4,500,000
Colombia	1,138,914	439,735	28,500,000	Bogotá	5,000,000
Ecuador	283,561	109,483	9,494,000	Quito	1,010,730
Falkland Is.	16,263	6,279	1,813	Stanley	1,079
Guiana, French	91,000	35,135	74,000	Cayenne	38,135
Guyana	214,969	83,000	910,000	Georgetown	185,000
Paraguay	406,752	157,047	3,500,000	Asuncion	729,000
Peru	1,285,216	496,222	19,000,000	Lima	5,000,000
Surinam	163,265	63,037	421,000	Paramaribo	150,000
Uruguay	177,508	68,536	2,991,700	Montevideo	1,350,000
Venezuela	912,050	352,143	15,200,000	Caracas	4,160,000

OCEANIA

Country	Area (sq km)	Area (sq miles)	Population	Capital	Population of Capital
Australia	7,686,240	2,967,660	15,451,900	Canberra	255,000
New South Wales	801,600	309,498	5,360,400	Sydney†	3,342,000
Queensland	1,727,200	666,872	2,471,600	Brisbane†	1,135,000
South Australia	984,000	379,923	1,340,400	Adelaide	970,000
Tasmania	67,800	26,178	433,300	Hobart†	178,800
Victoria	227,600	87,876	4,034,600	Melbourne†	2,840,000
Western Australia	2,525,500	975,096	1,363,200	Perth	969,300
Northern Territory	1,346,200	519,768	134,000	Darwin†	46,658
Norfolk Island	36	14	1,800	Kingston†	800
Fiji	18,272	7,055	680,000	Suva†	120,000
French Polynesia	3,941	1,522	150,000	Papeete†	65,000
Kiribati	886	342	61,300	Tarawa	22,000
Guam	549	212	106,200	Agaña	2,119
Mariana, Caroline and Marshall Islands*	2,156	832	160,010	Saipan	—
Nauru	21	8	7,254	Yaren†	—
New Caledonia	19,103	7,376	145,000	Noumea†	80,000

*Trust Territory of the Pacific Islands.   † Seaport.

Country	Area (sq km)	Area (sq miles)	Population	Capital	Population of Capital
New Zealand	268,676	103,736	3,230,000	Wellington†	343,200
Cook Islands	510	197	19,000	Avarua	—
Niue	10	3·9	3,578	Aolfi	3,000
Tokelau			1,572	Fakaofo	—
Papua New Guinea	461,691	178,259	3,250,000	Port Moresby†	140,000
Samoa					
Eastern	197	76	32,400	Pago Pago†	2,451
Western	2,842	1,097	160,000	Apia†	33,800
Solomon Islands	28,446	10,983	255,000	Honiara	18,346
Tonga, etc.	699	270	100,000	Nuku'alofa†	20,600
Tuvalu	25	9·5	9,000	Funajuti	2,120
Vanuaatu	14,763	5,700	125,000	Vila	15,759

† Seaport.

ANTARCTICA

Antarctica is the world's seventh continent surrounding the South Pole. It was the last to be discovered (after 1819) and explored. Even today it has no permanent settlements, although many nations are interested in the strategic value of the continent and the marketable resources it might contain—oil, perhaps, and other minerals. Rich fishing grounds also surround its coasts. By the Treaty of Antarctica, signed in December 1959, the following countries agreed to freeze all their claims to Antarctic territory for thirty years, without giving them up: Australia, Argentina, Belgium, Chile,

France, Britain, Japan, New Zealand, Norway, the Republic of South Africa, the USA and the USSR. The aim of the treaty was to allow the research and peaceful co-operation that had started during the International Geophysical Year to continue in this scientifically important area. The main claims and dependencies are shown on the map. Britain has been involved in Antarctic territory since the days of Captain Cook, but now both Argentina and Chile lay claim to much of British territory. What the future holds for Antarctica when the treaty comes to an end remains, as yet, undecided.

TRANSPORT AND COMMUNICATIONS

Transportation and communications are vital to the functioning of individual countries and to the world as a whole. There are three types of transport: land, water and air transport. Developed countries have good transport systems, and goods and passengers are moved swiftly from one place to another. In many developing countries, animal transport is still important: but the main forms of land transport today are railways, roads and pipelines, the latter being used for carrying oil, gas and water across country. Inland water transport relies on lakes, navigable rivers and canals. The world has important sea canals, as well as inland canals that link rivers.

The oceans and seas are essential to transportation, trade and communications. Today the countries with the largest shipping fleets are Liberia, the United Kingdom, the USA, Norway, Japan and the USSR (*see* K7).

Air transport is the fastest form of movement from place to place today, and the time it takes to travel tends to have become more important than actual distances.

RAILWAYS
Countries with Longest Networks

	length in km		length in km
United States	288,073	Australia	40,753
Soviet Union	142,800	Argentina	40,113
India	60,301	France	34,318
Canada	59,240	Brazil	33,000
China	48,000	West Germany	28,517

Countries with Densest Passenger Traffic		Countries with Densest Cargo Traffic	
	Passenger-km (millions)		Tonne-km (millions)
Soviet Union	347,856	Soviet Union	3,464,484
Japan	314,840	United States	1,168,152
India	220,572	China	663,444
China	177,336	Canada	200,844
France	56,856	India	174,372
Poland	50,148	Poland	118,032
Italy	40,020	South Africa	82,032
West Germany	36,828	Romania	73,740
United Kingdom	27,780	Czechoslovakia	71,580
Romania	22,812	France	61,200

WORLD'S BUSIEST SEAPORTS (1982)

Seaport	Country	Goods (in million tonnes)
Ras Tamira*	Saudi Arabia	377·1 (1979)
Rotterdam	Netherlands	237·8
Kharg*	Iran	190·3 (1979)
New Orleans	USA	166·1
Chiba	Japan	134·8
Kobe	Japan	132·8 (1979)
Yokohama	Japan	111·8
Nagoya	Japan	103·0
Singapore	Singapore	101·0
Marseille	France	91·8
Kawasaki	Japan	91·6 (1979)
Aruba-Curaçao*	Netherland Antilles	87·0 (1979)
Macapa	Brazil	86·9 (1979)
Osaka	Japan	84·9
Antwerp	Belgium	84·2
Hampton Roads	USA	62·1
Tokyo	Japan	61·9
Hamburg	West Germany	61·6
Houston	USA	58·9 (1979)
London	UK	46·9

* denotes oil port

GREAT SHIP CANALS OF THE WORLD

Canal	Year opened	Length (km)	Length (miles)	Depth (metres)	Depth (feet)	Width (metres)	Width (feet)
Amsterdam (Netherlands)	1876	26·6	16·5	7	23	26·8	88
Corinth (Greece)	1893	6·4	4	8	26·25	22	72
Elbe and Trave (Germany)	1900	66	41	3	10	22	72
Gota (Sweden)	1832	185·1	115	3	10	14·3	47
Kiel (Germany)	1895	98·2	61	13·7	45	45·7	150
Manchester (England)	1894	57·1	35·5	8·5–9·1	28–30	36·6	120
Panama (U.S.A.)	1914	81·3	50·5	13·7	45	91·4	300
Princess Juliana (Netherlands)	1935	32·2	20	4·9	16	15·8	52
Saulte Ste. Marie (U.S.A.)	1855	2·6	1·6	6·7	22	30·5	100
Saulte Ste. Marie (Canada)	1895	1·8	1·11	6·8–7·6	22–25	43·3	142
Suez (Egypt)	1869	161	100	10·4	34	60	197
Welland (Canada)	1887	43·1	26·75	7·6	25	61	200

WORLD'S BUSIEST AIRPORTS (1982)

Airport	Country	Passengers (in thousands)
Chicago (O'Hare)	USA	37,744
Atlanta	USA	34,702
Los Angeles (International)	USA	32,383
New York (Kennedy)	USA	26,453
London (Heathrow)*	UK	26,406
Dallas-Fort Worth	USA	24,767
Denver	USA	24,553
Tokyo (Haneda)	Japan	21,929
San Francisco (International)	USA	21,029
Miami	USA	19,388
New York (La Guardia)	USA	18,517
Frankfurt (Rhein-Main)	W. Germany	16,493
Paris (Orly)	France	16,062
Osaka	Japan	16,049
Boston	USA	15,868

* N.B. Heathrow is the world's busiest international airport

UNITED KINGDOM OF GREAT BRITAIN AND NORTHERN IRELAND

The UK comprises the island of Great Britain (which includes England, Wales and Scotland) and Northern Ireland (the north-east part of the island of Ireland, also known as Ulster). The UK's total land area is 244,104 square kilometres, of which England covers 130,441 sq km, Scotland 78,775 sq km, Wales 20,768 sq km, and Northern Ireland 14,120 sq km.

There are other countries which, though independent, are attached to the British Crown. The Isle of Man has been a separate state for a thousand years, but the UK is responsible for its defence and external relations. The same applies to the autonomous Channel Islands of Jersey and Guernsey. Guernsey, too, has its dependencies in the islands of Alderney, Sark, Herm, and Jethou.

The UK's population in 1981 was 55,880,000, of which England had 46,395,000, Scotland 5,166,000, Wales 2,774,500 and Northern Ireland 1,544,500. The population of the Isle of Man was 65,000; and of the Channel Islands, 130,000.

After April 1974, when the provisions of the Local Government Act, 1972, came into force, some old county divisions were brought to an end, or their areas and boundaries rearranged. England was given 39 non-metropolitan counties and six metropolitan counties (in addition to Greater London), though the latter were disbanded in Spring 1986. Wales had eight counties, Scotland had twelve regions and Northern Ireland had twenty-six districts. For this edition of the book the former populations and areas of England's six metropolitan counties are given, though in effect (administratively, if not functionally) they have reverted to the pre-1974 arrangement. The following table lists the counties and regions with their areas and populations. The former metropolitan regions are in italic.

ENGLAND
National Capital: London (6,745,891)

County or Shire	Administrative Headquarters	Area (sq km)	Area (sq miles)	Population
Avon	Bristol	1,346	520	934,000
Bedford	Bedford	1,235	477	514,500
Berkshire	Reading	1,255	485	715,400
Buckinghamshire	Aylesbury	1,882	727	599,400
Cambridgeshire	Cambridge	3,409	1,316	617,095
Cheshire	Chester	2,328	899	948,300
Cleveland	Middlesbrough	583	225	563,900
Cornwall	Truro	3,546	1,369	433,700
Cumbria	Carlisle	6,886	2,659	482,500
Derbyshire	Matlock	2,631	1,016	912,500
Devonshire	Exeter	6,711	2,591	970,200
Dorset	Dorchester	2,688	1,038	614,200
Durham	Durham	2,436	941	606,150
Essex	Chelmsford	3,674	1,419	1,498,600
Gloucester	Gloucester	2,642	1,020	508,400
Greater Manchester	Manchester	1,289	498	2,595,700
Hampshire	Winchester	3,774	1,457	1,497,000
Hereford & Worcester	Worcester	3,926	1,516	643,000
Hertford	Hertford	1,634	631	970,400
Humberside	Kingston-upon-Hull	3,512	1,356	857,500
Isle of Wight	Newport	380	147	120,400
Kent	Maidstone	3,732	1,441	1,494,200
Lancashire	Preston	3,039	1,174	1,388,300
Leicestershire	Leicester	2,553	986	865,800
Lincoln	Lincoln	5,885	2,272	556,900
Greater London	S.E.1.	1,579	610	6,745,891
Merseyside	Liverpool	646	250	1,489,200
Norfolk	Norwich	5,355	2,067	713,400
Northampton	Northampton	2,367	914	542,930
Northumberland	Newcastle-upon-Tyne	5,033	1,943	301,400
Nottinghamshire	Nottingham	2,164	836	991,400

County or Shire	Administrative Headquarters	Area (sq km)	Area (sq miles)	Population
Oxfordshire	Oxford	2,611	1,008	554,600
Shropshire	Shrewsbury	3,490	1,348	386,600
Somerset	Taunton	3,458	1,335	437,400
Staffordshire	Stafford	2,716	1,048	1,020,500
Suffolk	Ipswich	3,807	1,470	618,800
Surrey	Kingston-upon-Thames	1,679	648	1,023,300
Sussex, East	Lewes	1,795	693	677,600
Sussex West	Chichester	1,991	769	681,600
Tyne & Wear	Newcastle	540	208	1,142,515
Warwick	Warwick	1,981	765	480,500
West Midlands	Birmingham	899	347	2,654,000
Wight, Isle of	Newport I.O.W.	381	147	120,400
Wiltshire	Trowbridge	3,481	1,344	532,800
Yorkshire North	Northallerton	8,316	3,211	683,000
Yorkshire South	Barnsley	1,561	603	1,311,600
Yorkshire West	Wakefield	2,039	787	2,065,000

WALES
National Capital: Cardiff (279,800)

Region	Administrative Headquarters	Area (sq km)	Area (sq miles)	Population
Clwyd	Mold	2,426	937	394,500
Dyfed	Carmarthen	5,765	2,226	336,100
Gwent	Cwmbran	1,376	531	439,100
Gwynedd	Caernarvon	3,866	1,493	323,400
Mid Glamorgan	Cardiff	1,019	393	541,800
Powys	Llandrindod Wells	5,077	1,960	112,000
South Glamorgan	Cardiff	416	161	391,600
West Glamorgan	Swansea	815	315	365,700

SCOTLAND
National Capital: Edinburgh (419,200)*

	Administrative Headquarters	Area (sq km)	Area (sq miles)	Population
Borders	Newton St Boswells	4,671	1,804	100,953
Central	Stirling	2,631	1,016	272,662
Dumfries and Galloway	Dumfries	6,371	2,460	146,156
Fife	Cupar	1,305	504	342,826
Grampian	Aberdeen	8,705	3,361	494,491
Highlands	Inverness	25,416	9,813	196,079
Lothian	Edinburgh	1,756	678	744,802
Orkney	Kirkwall	975	376	19,239
Shetland	Lerwick	1,426	551	23,454
Strathclyde	Glasgow	13,850	5,348	2,338,077
Tayside	Dundee	7,665	2,960	394,895
Western Isles	Stornoway, Lewis	2,901	1,210	31,519

*Glasgow, Aberdeen and Dundee are other principal Scottish cities. Glasgow (747,486) being the country's largest urban centre.

Administrative
Districts of
Northern
Ireland

NORTHERN IRELAND
National Capital: Belfast (372,600)

District	Area (sq km)	Area (sq miles)	Population	Map ref.
Antrim	562	217	45,500	1
Ards	361	139	59,700	2
Armagh	674	260	49,900	3
Ballymena	634	245	55,400	4
Ballymoney	417	161	24,400	5
Banbridge	445	172	30,600	6
Belfast	115	44	322,600	7
Carrickfergus	77	30	28,400	8
Castlereagh	84	32	59,800	9
Coleraine	484	187	47,400	10
Cookstown	610	235	29,300	11
Craigavon	388	150	73,400	12
Down	645	250	54,000	13
Dungannon	779	301	45,700	14
Fermanagh	1,875	724	51,600	15
Larne	338	130	29,300	16
Limavady	589	227	28,000	17
Lisburn	446	172	87,900	18
Londonderry	386	145	96,100	19
Magerafelt	562	217	34,200	20
Moyle	494	190	14,500	21
Newry-Mourne	909	350	83,400	22
Newtonabbey	139	54	71,900	23
North Down	73	28	66,800	24
Omagh	1,124	433	46,900	25
Strabane	861	332	37,000	26

OTHER BRITISH ISLES

Island	Capital or chief town	Area (sq km)	Area (sq miles)	Population
Isle of Man	Douglas	588	227	64,679
Channel Islands				
Jersey	St. Helier	116	45	76,050
Guernsey	St. Peter Port	63	24	54,380
Alderney	St. Anne's	8	3	2,000
Sark	—	5	2	604
Isles of Scilly	St. Mary's	16	6	1,850

BRITAIN'S LARGEST CITIES

London	6,745,891	Manchester	457,500	Leicester	283,000
Birming-		Bradford	454,200	Newcastle	283,000
ham	1,011,000	Edinburgh	419,200	Cardiff	279,800
Glasgow	747,486	Bristol	399,600	Nottingham	277,800
Leeds	716,100	Belfast	322,600	Kingston	
Sheffield	546,700	Coventry	314,120	upon Hull	271,100
Liverpool	497,300				

BRITAIN'S HIGHEST MOUNTAINS AND LARGEST LAKES

Peak	Height (m)	Height (ft)	Lake	Area (sq km)	Area (sq miles)
England					
Scafell Pike (Cumbria)	978·4	3,210	Windermere (Cumbria Lancs)	26	10
Wales					
Snowdon (Gwynedd)	1,085	3,560	Bala (Gwynedd)	10·4	4
Scotland					
Ben Nevis (Inverness)	1,343	4,406	Loch Lomond (Central Strathclyde)	70	27
Northern Ireland					
Slieve Donard (Down)	852·2	2,796	Lough Neagh (Antrim–Londonderry–Tyrone–Armagh)	388·5	150

IMPORTANT RIVERS OF BRITAIN

River	Length (km)	Length (miles)	Rises in:	Flows to:
Severn	354	220	Plynlimmon, Dyfed	Bristol Channel
Thames	336	209	Cotswold Hills, nr Cirencester	North Sea
Trent	274	170	N. Staffordshire	Joins Ouse to form R. Humber
Great Ouse	251	156	Northants.	The Wash
Wye	209	130	Plynlimmon	Severn, nr Chepstow
Tay	188	117	Grampian Mts, N. Argyll	Firth of Tay
Spey	177	110	Grampians Mts, Inverness	Moray Firth
Clyde	171	106	S. Lanark (union of Daer and Potrail Water)	Firth of Clyde

Tweed	156	97	Tweedsmuir Hills, S. Peebles	North Sea, at Scot-Eng border
Dee	140	87	Cairngorm Mts, W. Aberdeenshire	North Sea (at Aberdeen)
Ribble	121	75	Pennine Chain, W. Yorkshire	Irish Sea (nr Southport)
Dee	113	70	Gwynedd, N. Wales	Irish Sea
Mersey	113	70	Pennine Chain (union of Goyt and Tame at Stockport)	Irish Sea (at Liverpool)
Tees	113	70	Cross Fell, Cumbria	North Sea
Forth	106	66	S. Perth	Firth of Forth
Towy	106	66	Hills between Cardigan and Radnor	Carmarthen Bay
Eden	105	65	Pennine Chain (Cumbria-Yorks.)	Solway Firth (Irish Sea)
Wear	105	65	Pennine Chain (W. Durham)	North Sea
Derwent	97	60	N. of the Peak (Derby)	Trent
Ouse	97	60	Yorks (union of Swale and Ure)	Joins Trent to form R. Humber
Tamar	97	60	Devonian Hills	English Channel (at Plymouth)
Derwent	92	57	Yorkshire moors	Ouse (between Selby and Goole)
Exe	87	54	Exmoor (N. Devon)	English Channel (Exeter)
Teifi	85	53	Llyn Teifi, N.E. Dyfyd	Cardigan Bay (at Cardigan)
Tyne	72	45	Northumberland (union of N. and S. Tyne)	North Sea (at Tynemouth)

A DICTIONARY OF GEOGRAPHICAL TERMS

Alluvium The fine sand, silt and mud material deposited by rivers to form plains and *deltas*.

Archipelago A sea containing many islands: e.g. Aegean Archipelago between mainland Greece and Turkey. The term is also used to mean any group of islands.

Atoll A low-lying coral island, shaped like a ring or horseshoe around a lagoon. Atolls are typical of the Pacific Ocean.

Avalanche A large mass of snow and ice at high altitudes which crashes down a mountainside under its own weight. Spring, when snow starts to melt, is a common time for avalanches.

Bar A collection of gravel, sand and mud deposited along some coasts, particularly across the mouth of a river or bay.

Basin An area of land drained by a river and its tributaries. The boundary between one river basin and another is known as a *watershed*.

Bay A wide indentation along a coast formed by the sea. Large lakes can also have bays.

Beach An area of sand, pebbles or mud where the land borders the sea. A raised beach is the former sea shore now at a higher level because of a fall in sea level or a rise in the land.

Blow-hole A hole in the roof of a coastal *cave* through which sea spray is blown at high tide.

Bore A tidal wave arising in the estuaries of certain rivers: e.g. the Severn. It is usually associated with spring tides and is also called an eagre.

Butte An isolated, flat-topped and steep-sided hill. It is similar to the larger *mesa* and is part of the remains of old *plateaux* surfaces.

Caldera A large, steep-sided *crater* at the top of a volcano which often contains a lake. Crater Lake, Oregon, is an example.

Canyon A deep, narrow, steep-sided gorge, cut by a river, usually in arid regions: e.g. Grand Canyon of the Colorado River, USA.

Cape This is another name for headland, an area of (usually) resistant land that projects into the sea. It is also known as a promontory.

Cataract A waterfall or series of waterfalls along a river. The term is sometimes used for rapids: e.g. the cataracts along the river Nile.

Cave A hollow beneath the surface of the land produced by river or sea erosion, or volcanic activity. Some of the largest caves and *caverns* are found in limestone regions. These caves often have *stalactites* (giant icicle-like columns of calcium carbonate hanging from their roofs) and *stalagmites* (similar columns, but rising from the floor). See *pothole*.

Col A depression or *pass* in a range of hills or mountains.

Coral Reef A low ridge in the sea formed from the skeletons of vast numbers of dead coral polyps. Fringing and barrier are names given to such reefs. See *atolls*.

Crater A funnel-shaped hollow at the top of a volcanic cone from which gases and lava are ejected. A cone and crater often rise from the centre of a *caldera*. Another type of crater is formed when meteorites strike the earth's surface.

Crevasse A deep crack in the surface of a *glacier*, especially where the ice broadens out or flows over a steep slope.

Delta A low-lying area of deposits (see *alluvium*) found where a river reaches the sea or a lake. Some deltas are fan-shaped (e.g. the Nile Delta), others are called bird's-foot (e.g. the Mississippi) deltas.

Desert Barren areas of the earth's surface where few plants grow on account of aridity (e.g. the tropical and sub-tropical desert) or intense cold (e.g. the Arctic and Antarctic, which can be regarded as cold deserts).

Drumlins A series of low egg-shaped hills formed by the deposition and moulding of material by an ice-sheet or *glacier*.

Dry Valley A valley which once contained a river or stream, but is now dry. Such a valley is a common feature of the chalklands of southern England.

Earthquake A movement or tremor in the earth's crust caused either by volcanic activity or by the existence of a *fault*.

Erosion The wearing away of the land by natural forces such as *weathering*, rivers, winds, seas, glaciers and ice-sheets.

Estuary The part of a river's mouth that is affected by tides, so that river and sea-water mix. Many estuaries are the lower reaches of river valleys that have been flooded by the sea. See *ria*.

Fault A break or fracture in rocks in the earth's crust along which movement has taken place, so that the layers of rock no longer match.

Fjord A deep, steep-sided and long inlet of the sea. Fjords are flooded valleys that were eroded by glaciers.

THE WORLD: ITS GEOGRAPHY

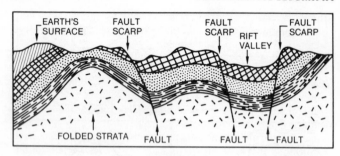

Flood plains These occur when rivers are in their 'old age' stage. They consist of sediment spread over the land during periodic flooding. *Meanders*, *ox-bow lakes* and *levees* are features of flood plains.

Fold A bend in rock layers (strata) caused by earth movements. The arch of a fold is known as an anticline. The trough of a fold is known as a syncline. Heavy folding often leads to fractures and *faults*.

Geysers Hot springs which shoot jets of hot water and steam into the air at various intervals. Some of the best-known geysers are those of Iceland, New Zealand and Yellowstone National Park, USA. The famous 'Old Faithful' geyser of Yellowstone used to erupt every 66·5 minutes, but is not now so regular in its activity.

Glacier Masses of ice that move very slowly down a valley under the force of gravity. They carry rock material and are major agents of erosion. Glaciers start in a snowfield and end where the rate of melting equals the supply of up-slope ice.

Gorge A deep narrow valley often having almost vertical sides. The Cheddar Gorge in the Mendip Hills is formed in carboniferous limestone.

Hanging valleys These are found in glaciated regions. When glaciers deepen a main valley into a V-shape, tributary valleys are left hanging above the U-shape trough. Water from hanging valleys descends as rapids or waterfalls.

Island Any area of land surrounded by water. Geographers, however, distinguish between islands and continents. See page B10 for the world's largest islands.

Isthmus A relatively narrow stretch of land joining two large land areas or joining a peninsula to the mainland: e.g. isthmuses of Panama, Suez.

Lake An inland body of water. Some of the world's largest lakes are called seas: e.g. Caspian Sea, Dead Sea.

Levee An embankment along a river which forms when the river overflows and deposits material along its banks. Levees can also be man-made to prevent flooding. See *meander*.

Meander Bends in the channel of a river occurring in the river's mature and old stages. Meanders grow in size as the river undercuts the bank on the outside of the bend and deposits *alluvium* on the inside of the bend. See *ox-bow lakes*.

Mesa (the Spanish word for a table) is a flat-topped upland. The hard rocks which cap mesas are parts of the original land surface that has been eroded. Smaller features are *buttes*. See *plateau*.

Mirage An optical illusion, caused when light rays are refracted (bent) as they pass through layers of air with differing densities. In hot deserts, light rays often give the impression that they are coming off a sheet of water. In polar areas the images of ships or icebergs can appear upside down.

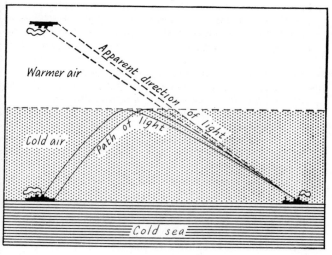

Mirage

Moraine Fragments of eroded rock carried and finally dumped by glaciers and ice-sheets. At the snout of a glacier (that is, where the glacier melts) this material is dumped in ridges called terminal moraine.

Ox-bow lakes These form when the river cuts through a narrow bend of a meander. The old meander is then abandoned as a lake.

Peninsula An area of land almost surrounded by water.

Plateau A large, level or mainly level area of highland. In areas of horizontal rocks, plateaus are often cut by *canyons*. This river *erosion* can lead to the formation of *buttes* or *mesas*.

Polder Land claimed from the sea or lake. In the Low Countries, polders are protected by artificial dykes or sea walls. They are also artificially drained by canals. The greater part of the former Zuider Zee has been transformed into polders.

Pothole A hole worn in solid rock, usually at the foot of a waterfall, by the constant grinding of stones kept in motion by the force of the water. The term is also another name for a swallow hole, commonly found in limestone districts. Swallow holes can lead to underground *caves* and caverns.

Ria A narrow inlet of the sea that is in fact a drowned river *estuary*. Rias may be caused by the downward sinking of the coast or by a rise in sea level. Carrick Roads and the Fal estuary in Cornwall form an example of a ria coastline, as does the coast of South-west Ireland.

Rift valley This forms when a block of land sinks down between long *faults* in the earth's crust: e.g. Great African Rift Valley.

River Terraces Platforms of land lying above the level of the valley floor. They are the remains of earlier valley floors and have been formed by a river's renewed vertical *erosion*.

Scree This is another name for 'talus'—a pile of loose rocks that collect at the foot of mountains or cliffs. Screes are the result of rock weathering and form very unstable slopes.

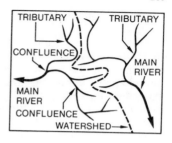

Spit A low ridge of sand and gravel which projects from the land into the sea. It is built up by waves and currents from material transported from another part of the coast. See *bar*.

Strait A narrow stretch of water connecting two large water areas: e.g. the Straits of Gibraltar, connecting the Atlantic and Mediterranean.

Tor An isolated rocky hill often weathered into strange shapes: e.g. the granite tors of Dartmoor.

Tributary A stream or smaller river which joins the main river. The point at which one stream or river joins another is called the confluence.

U-shaped valley A steep-sided trough eroded from an old river valley by a glacier. The *tributaries* often meet the main valleys as *waterfalls* to form *hanging valleys*. See *V-shaped valley*.

Volcano A vent in the earth's surface through which lava, steam and gas are ejected from below the surface. Many volcanoes give rise to conical peaks. See *caldera* and *crater*.

V-shaped valley A valley eroded downwards by a river, but whose slopes have been broadened into a V-shape by weathering. Compare *U-shaped valley* and *canyon*.

Waterfall A vertical fall of river water which often occurs where resistant rocks overlie softer rocks. See *cataract*, *hanging valley*.

Watershed Also known as a divide, a watershed is the boundary between the drainage area of one river (and *tributaries*) and another. See *basin*.

Weathering The decay and break-up of surface rocks. It can be caused by physical (mechanical) action such as temperature changes, or by chemical action.

THE ATMOSPHERE, CLIMATE AND WEATHER

The earth is surrounded by a layer of air which is known as the *atmosphere*. It provides the gases needed for human, animal and plant life, and also acts as a shield which protects us from the sun's harmful ultraviolet rays. The three main gases of the atmosphere (making up 99·97 per cent of the total) are nitrogen (78·09 per cent), oxygen (20·95 per cent) and argon (0·93 per cent). The remaining 0·03 per cent is made up of minute amounts of other gases including carbon dioxide which is used by plants for photosynthesis. The atmosphere also contains water vapour and specks of dust and salt, the latter coming from sea spray.

Layers of the atmosphere

The atmosphere is divided into four main layers. The lowest zone is known as the *troposphere* which extends to about 18 kilometres over the equator, 10–11 kilometres over the middle latitudes and 8 kilometres over the poles. Most of the air and water vapour in the atmosphere are in the troposphere, which ends in what is known as the *tropopause*.

The *stratosphere* extends from the tropopause to about 80 kilometres above the earth's surface. It contains an important layer of ozone which absorbs harmful radiation from the sun. Strong air currents, moving at more than 60 kilometres an hour, are found in the upper troposphere and lower stratosphere. These so-called *jet-streams* are important to pilots of jet aircraft that fly in these zones.

The *ionosphere* extends for some 80–500 kilometres above the earth. Here the air is extremely rarefied and beyond it is the *exosphere*, where the earth's atmosphere gradually merges into space. Many satellites orbit the earth in the iconosphere.

Other interesting phenomena found in the upper layers of the atmosphere are *meteors* and *aurorae*. Also called shooting stars, meteors consist of large lumps of rocks or metal that sometimes enter the earth's atmosphere, becoming white-hot and glowing. Some leave a trail which is visible for several minutes. The largest known meteorite, estimated to weigh 59 tons, was found in 1920 at Hoba West in Namibia.

Aurorae are lights and colours that occur in the iconosphere and are the result of electrical discharges. They can be seen at night at high latitudes and are particularly common in polar regions. The *aurora borealis* (Northern Lights) occurs in the northern hemisphere and the *aurora australis* in the southern hemisphere.

The circulation of the atmosphere

Weather is the day-to-day conditions of the atmosphere, although most of the features that govern the earth's weather occur in the troposphere. Here the atmosphere is constantly on the move, the chief reason being the heat from the sun. The amount of heat absorbed by the earth's surface varies from place to place. In high latitudes the sun's rays have to pass through a greater thickness of atmosphere and they are also spread out over a larger area (see diagram). It is at the equator that the sun's rays are most concentrated. Here the heated air expands and rises, creating a low-pressure area into which *trade winds* blow from north and south. The *doldrums* is the name given to the area of low pressure around the equator. It is marked by calms: sailing ships tried to avoid the doldrums because they might be stationary for days at a time.

As it rises and spreads north and south, the warm air from the equator cools. Around latitudes 30 degrees north and 30

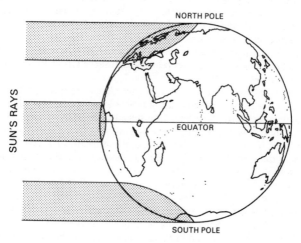

The amount of heat absorbed at the earth's surface

WESTERLIES   TRADES   POLAR EASTERLIES

World's major wind belts

degrees south (the *Horse Latitudes*), it finally sinks back to form an area of high pressure. From the Horse Latitudes some of the air flows back to the equator, and some flows towards the poles as winds known as the *westerlies*. These relatively warm westerlies finally meet cold, dense air flowing from the north and south poles. In these ways the winds redistribute heat around the earth's surface.

As the map of the world's major wind belts shows, the air currents do not flow in a north-to-south direction. Instead, they are deflected by the *Coriolis Force*, caused by the earth's rotation on its axis from west to east. This has the effect that winds (and ocean currents) in the northern hemisphere are deflected to the right of the direction in which they are moving. The opposite occurs in the southern hemisphere. The Coriolis Force, therefore, is responsible for the *north-east* and *south-east trade winds*, the *north-westerlies* and *south-westerlies* and the *polar easterlies*.

Air masses

This general pattern of wind systems is greatly complicated by a number of factors, not least the presence of high mountain ranges that deflect the general direction of global winds. Equally important is the distribution of large land and water bodies, for land areas heat up and cool down more quickly than the oceans and seas. These, and other factors, give rise to air masses, which are bodies of air whose physical characteristics are roughly the same over large areas. Air masses over land differ from air masses over the oceans in the same latitudes. For example, in the tropical zone, *tropical maritime* air masses are cooler and wetter than *tropical continental* air masses. Also, in the polar regions, *polar maritime* air masses differ from the colder and drier *polar maritime* air masses. The temperature differences between land and water bodies are very important and give rise to pressure differences where winds are drawn to relatively low pressure areas from high pressure areas.

A region of high pressure is known as an *anticyclone*, the highest pressure occurring in the centre. In anticyclones, weather conditions are fairly stable and winds circulate in a clockwise direction in the northern hemisphere and in an anti-clockwise direction in the southern hemisphere. A *depression* is an area of low air pressure, associated with unsettled, often stormy weather. Where air masses of differing characteristics meet, a *front* is formed which marks the boundary between the two air masses.

In depressions, the *warm front* is the advancing edge of the warm, lighter air at ground level. The *cold front* behind it is the advancing edge of the colder, denser air. Where the cold front

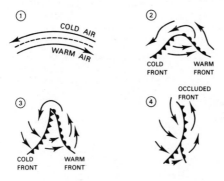

Stages in the development of a depression

overtakes the warm front, the warm air is pushed above ground level, forming an *occluded front* or *occlusion*. Cloudy, rainy weather is associated with the passage of cold and warm fronts and cloud and rain persist for a time along occlusions.

CLOUDS

The passage of a depression or, indeed, most aspects of a daily weather sequence can be interpreted from cloud types and formations. A cloud is a mass of small water drops or ice crystals, formed by the condensation of water vapour in the atmosphere. This condensation usually occurs at great heights above the earth's surface. The water vapour is the result of evaporation of surface water—oceans, lakes and rivers etc.

Although clouds have a large number of shapes, the three principal formations can be recognised from the translations of their Latin names: *stratus*, a flat layer; *cumulus*, a heap, pile or pack; and *cirrus*, meaning a curl or lock of hair. These frequently combine in other formations. It is helpful to remember that *alto* means high and *nimbo* or *nimbus* means rain.

The internationally agreed classification of clouds is more detailed and describes ten main forms. According to their approximate height above the earth's surface these 10 forms are subdivided as low clouds (up to 2000 metres), medium clouds (2000–6000 metres) and high clouds (6000–12,000 metres). (See following table.)

Types of Cloud		
Type	*Usual range of height of base in m/ft*	*Description*
Cumulus	300–450 (1,000–1,500)	Flat base, high rounded tops. Small, white, scattered puffs mean fair weather, but heavy, deep clouds often become cumulonimbus.

Type	Usual range of height of base in m/ft	Description
Stratus	Up to 150–600 (500–2,000)	Unbroken grey layer; looks like fog that has lifted from the ground.
Stratocumulus	300–1,400 (1,000–4,500)	Broad layer arranged in round masses or rolls, often so close together that their edges join.
Nimbostratus	Near surface to 6,000 (20,000)	Dark grey with a base that is the same throughout. Often gives continuous rain or snow; if these do not reach the ground the cloud appears to trail.
Cumulonimbus	Up to 600–1,500 (2,000–5,000)	Heavy, dark, very tall—as high as 3 miles. Tops often spread out in anvil-shape. Thunderstorm cloud; gives showers of rain, snow, hail, etc.
Altocumulus	2,000–6,096 (6,500–20,000)	Small, thin rounded patches, resembling cumulus, sometimes so close together their edges meet.
Altostratus	2,005–6,096 (6,580–20,000)	Sheet or veil, sometimes thin, but sometimes so thick it blocks out the moon or even the sun, when it normally indicates continuous rain.
Cirrus	6,096–12,192 (20,000–40,000)	Detached pieces, delicate and feathery ('mares' tails').
Cirrocumulus	6,096–12,192 (20,000–40,000)	Small flakes or rolls in groups or lines ('mackerel sky'). Made up of ice crystals.
Cirrostratus	6,096–12,192 (20,000–40,000)	Thin, milky veil producing a ring of light round the moon.

THE ELEMENTS OF WEATHER

When applied to weather, precipitation is the deposit of water (in either liquid or solid form) on the earth's surface from the atmosphere. It includes not only rain, but also sleet, snow and hail, which fall from clouds, and dew and hoar frost.

Rain is the main form of precipitation. It falls when water vapour in clouds condenses, the water droplets fusing together to become raindrops. Rain differs from *drizzle* by the size of its water droplets. Raindrops have a diameter greater than 0.5 mm; the diameter of drizzle droplets is 0·2–0·5 mm.

To understand how and why rain falls, it is necessary to understand *dew point*, which is the temperature at which the air is completely saturated by water vapour. When the temperature falls below dew point, *condensation* occurs and water vapour is changed into water droplets. The temperature of dew point varies because warm air can hold more water vapour than cold air.

The three types of rain are known as *orographic, convectional* and *cyclonic*. *Orographic* rain is caused by mountains standing in the path of moisture-laden air. The mountains force the air to rise and when it cools to less than dew point, rain is deposited. *Convectional* rain is caused when the surface layers of the atmosphere are heated, and moisture-laden air rises in a convection current. The air is cooled to below dew point and heavy rain is often deposited. *Cyclonic* rain is associated with the passage of depressions (see page B63). Warm moist air moves upwards over colder, denser air, and when the warm air is cooled to below dew point, rainfall occurs.

Snow falls when the temperature of the atmosphere at cloud level is below freezing; it falls either as individual ice-crystals (always six-sided) or as snow-flakes composed of several ice crystals joined together. Only one-third of the earth's surface experiences snowfalls. Except on high mountain areas, the temperature of the tropics is too warm for snow. On average, 10 centimetres of snow is the equivalent of one centimetre of rain.

Sleet is a mixture of snow and rain. It occurs when the snow has partly melted during its fall to the earth's surface.

Hail consists of ice pellets which fall from clouds, often during thunderstorms. They are caused by the rapid ascent of moist air; the water drops freeze, and the size of the pellets increases as more water vapour freezes onto their surfaces. When they are heavy enough to resist the upward-moving air currents, they fall to the earth's surface.

Dew is moisture deposited by condensation on such things as blades of grass and stones, the moisture coming from water vapour in the air. It occurs at night when the ground surface releases the heat it has stored up during the day, and the air on or immediately above it becomes cooler.

Hoar Frost consists of tiny ice crystals, a kind of frozen dew.

Fog is a mass of small water droplets in the lower air, resulting from air cooling below dew point and water vapour condensing. Fog is, therefore, similar to cloud, except that it occurs near the ground. In some large cities and industrial areas, fog mixes with soot, smoke and gases to produce *smog*, which is harmful to plants, animals and people. Fog is defined as a visibility of less than one kilometre.

Mist is a thinner version of fog where visibility is more than one kilometre, but less than 2 kilometres.

Thunder and lightning These elements are associated with violent storms. Strong upward currents of air form cumulonimbus clouds, and these give rise to heavy rain and sometimes hail. Flashes of lightning are the result of the build-up of static electricity in the clouds, and thunder is produced by the expansion of air, due to the tremendous heat of lightning flashes. Thunderstorms are most numerous in equatorial regions which experience convectional rainfall (page B66).

Wind is an air current, moving with speed in any direction. As well as currents of air that flow across the earth's surface (page B62), there are also upward and downward currents of air. A variety of conditions give rise to local winds, particularly land and sea breezes, which affect coastal and lakeside areas. These breezes are the result of the different rates at which land and water bodies heat up and cool down. This produces local pressure changes, and these determine the direction of the winds.

Wind has an important effect on air temperatures. This is known as the *chill factor*, for wind makes the air feel colder than the thermometer would indicate. As a general rule, subtract 1° C from the temperature for every 3 km per hour wind speed (1° F for every 1 mph). So a strong breeze of 48 km/h (30 mph) in an air temperature of about 15° C (60° F) will feel as cold as if there were no wind and the temperature was about −1° C (30° F).

SOME VIOLENT KINDS OF WEATHER

Typhoons and **hurricanes** are caused by tropical cyclones. These
cyclones occur where the pressure of the atmosphere has sunk
very much lower than that of the surrounding air. Around its
calm centre—known as the 'eye' of the storm—winds of hur-
ricane force (that is, of speeds greater than 121 km (75 mph))
blow continuously. Cyclones cause immense damage in the
tropics. They occur most often in the seas of China (typhoons),
but nearly as often in the West Indies (hurricanes).

Whirlwinds are like cyclones, having an area of low pressure at
their centres, but they are very much smaller, consisting of
columns of air whirling very rapidly round an axis that is
vertical or nearly so. In the desert they can cause **sandstorms**.

A **tornado** is an extremely violent whirlwind.

A **waterspout** is a tornado occurring at sea; a portion of cloud
looking like an upside-down cone reaches down from the base
of a thunder-cloud to where it meets a cone of spray raised
from the sea to form a continuous column or spout between

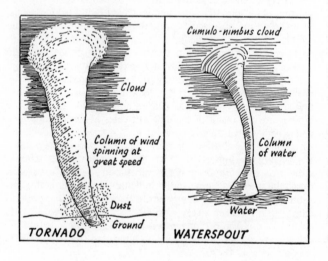

sea and cloud. In the days of sailing-ships waterspouts were
known to tear ships to pieces.

Floods and **droughts** are other examples of the devastating effects
of weather and climate.

WORLD WEATHER RECORDS

Record	Degree or amount	Where recorded	When recorded
Highest shade temperature	57·8° C (136° F)	San Louis, Mexico	1933
Lowest temperature	−89·2° C (−128° F)	Vostok, Antarctica	21.7.83
Maximum rainfall (24 hours)	1,870 mm (73·62 in)	Cilaos, Ile de Réunion	1952
Maximum rainfall (one month)	9,299 mm (366·14 in)	Cherrapunji, India	1861
Greatest annual total rainfall	26,461 mm (1,042 in)	also at Cherrapunji	1861
Heaviest recorded snowfall in one year	31,102 mm (1,224·5 in)	Mount Ranier Washington State US	1971–2
Largest recorded hailstone	750 grams (11·67 lbs)	Kansas US	1970

BRITISH WEATHER RECORDS

Highest temperature	37° C (98° F)	Raunds, Northants; Epsom, Surrey and Canterbury, Kent	1911
Lowest temperature	−27·2° C (−17° F)	Braemar, Scotland	1895 and 1982
Maximum rainfall (24 hours)	2·79 mm (11 in)	Martinstown, nr Dorchester	1955
Maximum annual rainfall	6,527 mm (257 in)	Sprinkling Tarn, Cumberland	1954

Further Reading

A Dictionary of Geography, by W. G. Moore (Penguin)
Standard Encyclopaedia of the World's Oceans and Islands, ed.
    Anthony Huxley (Weidenfeld & Nicolson)
The Observer's Book of The Weather (Warne)
Our Planet Earth (Ward Lock)
Encyclopaedia of the World (Hamlyn)
The Children's World Atlas (Longmans)
The Physical Earth (Mitchell Beazley)
The Modern World (Mitchell Beazley)

THE WORLD

3: ITS FAMOUS PEOPLE
(*Actual and Mythical*)

In *A Dictionary of Famous People* are to be found short biographies of the great men and women of both the distant and the recent past. In *Names in the News* short notes are given about celebrated persons now living. Those in *A Dictionary of Mythology* were, of course, never alive at all, in any ordinary sense—they are the gods and goddesses found in the myths and legends of ancient peoples.

A DICTIONARY OF FAMOUS PEOPLE

When the story of a man's life, his biography, is told very briefly it is called a potted biography. The biographies in this section have been potted and then potted again. They are meant to answer the following questions: 'Who was he?' 'When did he live?' 'Where did he come from?' 'What did he do?' For fuller details you should, of course, consult either a separate biography of your man (or woman) or one of the big encyclopaedias that are devoted entirely to telling the stories of famous lives. (For famous Britishers the best source of all is the *Dictionary of National Biography*.)

Left out of this section are most of those people whose achievements are mentioned elsewhere; for example,

Kings and Queens of England and Scotland (HISTORY);
British writers (THE ENGLISH LANGUAGE);
Explorers and discoverers (HISTORY);
Painters, sculptors and architects (THE ARTS).

In the case of other historical figures, dates of birth and death are given and you are advised to 'see HISTORY'—which usually means the DIARY OF WORLD EVENTS. In some instances people who appear elsewhere in the book are treated fully here (e.g. Captain Scott); this is because there is something important to add that has not been said in the other section where the mention occurs.

The letter *c.* before a date (e.g. *c.* 450 B.C.) is short for the Latin *circa*, 'about', and means that the date is not certainly known.

Aeschylus (*c.* 525–456 B.C.), Greek tragic dramatist.

Akbar, Jalal-ud-din Mohammed (1542–1605), greatest of the Mogul emperors.

Alaric 1st (376–410), King of the Visigoths, who sacked Rome.

Alban, St, lived in the last part of the 3rd century; served as soldier in Rome, was converted to Christianity and, returning to Britain to preach, was martyrised.

Alcibiades (*c.* 450–404 B.C.), Athenian statesman and general, pupil of Socrates.

Alcott, Louisa May (1832–88), American writer, author of *Little Women*.

Alexander II (1818–81), Czar of Russia who emancipated the serfs; assassinated by Nihilists.

Alexander the Great (356–323 B.C.), see HISTORY.

Alfred the Great (849–99), see HISTORY.

Ampère, André Marie (1775–1836), French mathematician, the first to propound the electro-dynamic theory.

Andersen, Hans Christian (1805–75), Danish storyteller and poet; author of famous fairy tales.

Andrew, St, one of Jesus' disciples, and patron saint of Scotland; commemorated on 30 November.

Anselm, St (1033–1109), Archbishop of Canterbury; quarrelled with William Rufus about the authority of the Pope, but regained his position under Henry I.

Antonius Marcus (Mark Antony) (c. 83–30 B.C.), see HISTORY.

Aquinas, Thomas, St (c. 1225–74), Italian religious teacher and philosopher.

Archimedes (c. 287–212 B.C.), Greek mathematician, physicist and inventor; made many discoveries in mechanics (notably the lever) and invented the Archimedean screw. Killed during siege of Syracuse by Romans.

Aristophanes (c. 450–c. 385 B.C.), Greek comic dramatist.

Aristotle (384–322 B.C.), Greek philosopher and pupil of Plato; took the whole field of knowledge as his subject.

Arkwright, Sir Richard (1732–92), pioneer of British cotton industry.

Arne, Thomas (1710–78), English composer.

Arnold, Thomas (1795–1842), headmaster of Rugby; regarded as the creator of the modern Public School system. The original of the headmaster in *Tom Brown's Schooldays*.

Arthur (c. 600), Celtic warrior about whom a great deal of legend has collected.

Atatürk, Kemal (1881–1938), creator of modern Turkey.

Attila (c. 406–53), king of the Huns, see HISTORY.

Attlee, 1st Earl (1883–1967), Deputy Prime Minister, 1942–5; Prime Minister, 1945–51.

Augustine, St (354–430), religious philosopher and teacher.

Augustine, St, missionary monk sent to Britain in 597; first Archbishop of Canterbury. Died in 604.

Augustus Caesar (63 B.C.–A.D. 14), first Emperor of Rome; see HISTORY.

Bach, Johann Sebastian (1685–1750), great German composer.

Bacon, Francis, Lord Verulam (1561–1626), English philosopher and statesman; Attorney-General under Elizabeth, Lord Chancellor under James I; author of *Novum Organum* and *Essays*.

Bacon, Roger (*c.* 1214–94), Franciscan friar, the first man in modern times to insist on the importance of experiment in science.

Baden–Powell, Lord (1857–1941), famous for his defence of Mafeking during Boer War; founded Boy Scouts (1908) and Girl Guides (1910).

Baird, John Logie (1888–1946), pioneer of television.

Bakewell, Robert (1725–95), pioneer of modern agriculture.

Ball, John (d. 1381), English priest who was a leader of the Peasants' Revolt.

Balzac, Honoré de (1799–1850), great French novelist; author of 80 novels with the general title of *La Comédie Humaine*.

Banks, Sir Joseph (1744–1820), English botanist and 'father of Australia'.

Barnado, Dr Thomas (1845–1905), devoted his life to the welfare of homeless children; founder of the homes named after him.

Baudelaire, Charles (1821–67), French poet, whose work has had an immense influence on modern poetry.

Becket, St Thomas à (1118–70), see HISTORY.

Bede, 'The Venerable' (*c.* 673–735), monk and historian, 'the father of English history'.

Beethoven, Ludwig van (1770–1827), great German composer.

Bell, Alexander Graham (1847–1922), inventor of the telephone.

Benedict, St (*c.* 480–544), founded the Order of Benedictine monks.

Bentham, Jeremy (1748–1832), radical writer and thinker; helped develop the Utilitarian philosophy that the aim of politics should be 'the greatest happiness of the greatest number'.

Berlioz, Hector (1803–69), French composer.

Bernard, St (923–1008), Cistercian monk, patron saint of mountaineers.

Bernhardt, Sarah (1845–1923), famous French tragic actress.

Bismarck, Prince Otto (1815–98), see HISTORY.

Blake, Robert (1599–1657), Parliamentary general in the Civil War; admiral in the wars against Holland and Spain.

Blériot, Louis (1872–1936), French inventor and aviator; first to fly the English Channel, 1909.

Blondin, Charles (1824–97), French tight-rope walker famous for his crossing of the Niagara Falls.

Boadicea (d. A.D. 62), see HISTORY.

Boccaccio, Giovanni (1313–75), Italian novelist and poet.

Bolivar, Simon (1783–1830), 'the Liberator'; revolutionary who broke Spanish power in South America; first president of Venezuela and Dictator of Peru.

Boone, Daniel (1734–1820), American explorer and settler.

Booth, William (1829–1912), founder and first general of the Salvation Army.

Borgia, Cesar (1476–1507), son of Pope Alexander VI, made himself ruler of Romagna by murdering those who stood in his way. Banished by Pope Julius II and died in the invasion of Castile.

Botha, General Louis (1862–1919), Boer general who became first Premier of South Africa.

Boyle, Robert (1627–91), English scientist; the first man to distinguish between a mixture and a compound. Author of Boyle's Law (see DICTIONARY OF SCIENCE AND MATHEMATICS).

Bragg, Sir William (1862–1942), English scientist who received the 1915 Nobel Prize with his son, **Sir Lawrence Bragg** (b. 1890), for their work on X-rays and crystal structures.

Brahms, Johannes (1833–97), German composer.

Brecht, Bertolt (1898–1959), German dramatist and poet.

Bright, John (1811–89), famous Radical statesman, one of those responsible for the introduction of Free Trade.

Britten, Benjamin (1913–1976), English composer.

Brown, Sir Arthur Whitten (1886–1948), made the first transatlantic flight in 1919 with Sir John Alcock.

Brown, John (1800–1859), fanatical opponent of slavery in America. He was hanged for having incited slaves to rebel, and his death was a signal for the outbreak of the Civil War.

Bruce, Robert (1274–1329), see HISTORY.

Brummell, George (1778–1840), 'Beau Brummell', leader of fashion in English society when George IV was Prince Regent.

Brunel, Isambard Kingdom (1806–59), engineer and steamship-designer: constructed Clifton Suspension Bridge and much of the G.W. Railway.

Brunel, Sir Mark Isambard (1769–1849), father of Isambard, and constructor of the Thames tunnel.

Brutus, Marcus (85–42 B.C.), see HISTORY.

Buddha (Sidharta Gautama), the founder of Buddhism in the 6th century B.C.

Burghley, William Cecil, Lord (1520–1598), principal adviser to Queen Elizabeth for 40 years.

Burke, Edmund (1729–97), political philosopher, statesman and orator: most famous for his attacks on the French Revolution.

Byrd, William (1543–1623), English composer.

Cabot, John (*c*. 1455–*c*. 1498), see EXPLORATIONS AND DISCOVERIES.

Cabot, Sebastian (*c*. 1493–1557), see EXPLORATIONS AND DIS-COVERIES.

Caesar, Caius Julius (*c*. 101–44 B.C.), see HISTORY.

Calvin, John (1509–64), French religious reformer who preached his severe doctrine (Calvinism), in Geneva, where he created a Protestant republic.

Campbell, Sir Malcolm (1885–1948), racing driver who held land and water speed records.

Canute the Great (995–1035), see HISTORY.

Carnegie, Andrew (1835–1919), son of poor Scottish weaver who became American multi-millionaire; gave away most of his money to benefit the public, especially the founding of libraries.

Cartier, Jaques (1491–1557), see EXPLORATIONS AND DISCOVERIES.

Casabianca, Louis de (*c*. 1754–98), captain of a French warship at the Battle of the Nile; he and his 10-year-old son refused to leave the burning ship and died together.

Cassius, Caius (d. 42 B.C.), see HISTORY.

Catherine the Great (1729–96), Empress of Russia; came to the throne by deposing and murdering her husband, the weak Peter; carried Russia's frontiers by conquest to the Black Sea and the borders of Germany.

Cato, Marcus Porcius (234–149 B.C.), Roman statesman, soldier and writer; opposed the luxurious living of his times.

Cavell, Edith (1865–1915), British nurse shot by the Germans for helping wounded British soldiers to escape from Belgium.

Cavour, Count Camillo de (1810–61), one of the founders of modern Italy.

Caxton, William (*c*. 1422–91), founder of the first English printing press.

Cecilia, Saint, the patron saint of music: martyrised *c.* A.D. 176.

Cervantes, Saavedra, Miguel de (1547–1616), Spanish novelist, author of *Don Quixote*.

Chaplin, Sir Charles Spencer (1889–1977), the most famous of all film comedians.

Charlemagne (742–814), see HISTORY.

Charles V (1510–58), Holy Roman Emperor who ruled Austria, the Netherlands and Spain.

Chatham, William Pitt, Earl of (1708–78), statesman and Parliamentarian, in control of English policy during Seven Years War.

Chekhov, Anton (1860–1904), great Russian dramatist and short-story writer; author of *The Cherry Orchard*, etc.

Chippendale, Thomas (*c.* 1717–79), famous furniture designer.

Chopin, Frédéric (1810–49), Polish composer and pianist.

Churchill, Sir Winston (1874–1965), British statesman and author: Prime Minister 1940–45 and 1951–55.

Cicero, Marcus Tullius (106–43 B.C.), most eloquent of the Roman orators.

Cierva, Juan de la (1895–1936), Spanish engineer who invented the autogiro.

Claudius I (10 B.C.–A.D. 54), Roman Emperor; erected many great buildings; visited Britain; murdered by his wife Agrippina.

Clemens, Samuel Langhorne ('Mark Twain') (1835–1910), American writer and humorist, author of *Tom Sawyer* and *Huckleberry Finn*.

Cleopatra (69–30 B.C.), see HISTORY.

Clive, Robert, Lord (1725–74), English general, victor of Plassey, who laid the foundations of the British empire in India.

Cobbett, William (1762–1835), politician, social reformer and writer, author of *Rural Rides*.

Cobden, Richard (1804–1865), statesman, economist and advocate of Free Trade.

Cody, Samuel (1861–1913), the first man to fly in Britain, 1908.

Cody, William (1846–1917), American plainsman and showman known as 'Buffalo Bill'.

Coke, Sir Edward (1552–1634), great English jurist.

Coke, Thomas William (1752–1842), pioneer of scientific farming.

Columbus, Christopher (1451–1506), see EXPLORATIONS AND DISCOVERIES.

Confucius (*c.* 551–479 B.C.), the most celebrated of the Chinese philosophers.

Cook, Capt. James (1728–79), see EXPLORATIONS AND DISCOVERIES.

Copernicus, Nicholas (1743–1543), Polish founder of modern astronomy; author of the Copernican theory that the planets revolve round the sun.

Corneille, Pierre (1606–84), French tragic dramatist.

Cortes, Hernando (1485–1547), Spanish conqueror of Mexico.

Cranmer, Thomas (1489–1556), first Protestant Archbishop of Canterbury; see HISTORY.

Crispin, St (3rd century), patron of shoemakers: commemorated on 25 October.

Croesus (d. *c.* 546 B.C.), last king of Lydia (part of modern Turkey), celebrated for his fabulous wealth.

Crockett, Davy (1786–1836), American frontiersman; fought in Congress for a fair deal for the Red Indians; killed at the Battle of Alamo.

Cromwell, Oliver (1599–1658), see HISTORY.

Cruikshank, George (1792–1878), famous book illustrator and caricaturist.

Cunard, Sir Samuel (1787–1861), founder of the shipping company which became the Cunard Line.

Curie, Pierre (1859–1906) and **Marie** (1867–1934), pioneers of the science of radioactivity, and first to isolate radium.

Daguerre, Louis (1789–1851), French inventor of the earliest photographic process (the daguerrotype).

Daimler, Gottlieb (1834–90), German inventor with N. A. Otto of the Otto gas engine, and also of the motor-car named after him (see CARS).

Dalton, John (1766–1844), English scientist who discovered atomic theory.

Damien, Father Joseph (1840–89), Belgian missionary who volunteered to look after lepers in Honolulu, and himself died of the disease.

Dante, Alighieri (1265–1321), greatest of the Italian poets, author of the *Divine Comedy*.

Danton, Georges (1759–94), President of the Committee of Public Safety during the first French Revolution; supplanted by Robespierre and guillotined.

Darius I (548–485 B.C.), see HISTORY.

Darling, Grace (1815–42), English lighthouse-keeper's daughter famous for saving a shipwrecked crew by putting out with her father in a small boat.

Darnley, Earl of (1545–67), Mary Queen of Scots' second husband, murdered after Mary had entered into an intrigue with Bothwell.

Darwin, Charles (1809–82), English naturalist whose *Origin of the Species* first set out the theory of evolution by means of natural selection.

David (1038–970 B.C.), king who united Israelites in Canaan.

David, St (6th century), patron saint of Wales.

Davis, Jefferson (1808–89), President of the Confederate States during the American Civil War.

Davy, Sir Humphrey (1778–1829), scientist who invented miners' lamp.

Debussy, Claude (1862–1918), French composer.

De Gaulle, General Charles (1890–1970), led Free French in Second World War; President of France, 1958–69.

De Havilland, Sir Geoffrey (1882–1965), a pioneer of civil and military aviation.

Democritus (*c.* 460–357 B.C.), Greek philosopher to whom the conception of the atomic theory is attributed.

Demosthenes (385–322 B.C.), most famous of the Athenian orators; he roused the Athenians to resist Philip of Macedon.

Descartes, René (1596–1650), French philosopher and mathematician.

Diaghilev, Sergei (1872–1929), Russian ballet impresario and founder of the Ballets Russes.

Diocletian (245–313), Roman Emperor under whom the Christians were ruthlessly persecuted; see HISTORY.

Diogenes (412–322 B.C.), Greek philosopher who scorned wealth and social conventions and is said to have lived in a tub.

Disraeli, Benjamin (Earl of Beaconsfield) (1804–81), see HISTORY.

Dominic, St (1170–1221), founder of the Order of Dominicans, or Black Friars.

Dostoevsky, Feodor (1821–81), one of the greatest Russian novelists, author of *Crime and Punishment*.

Drake, Sir Francis (*c.* 1540–96), see HISTORY.

Dumas, Alexandre (1802–70), prolific French novelist and dramatist, author of *The Count of Monte Cristo* and *The Three Musketeers*.

Dunstan, St (909–88), famous Abbot of Glastonbury and Archbishop of Canterbury, who lived through seven reigns.

Duval, Claude (1643–70), notorious French-born highwayman, hanged at Tyburn.

Dvorak, Antonin (1841–1904), Czech composer.

Edison, Thomas Alva (1847–1931), inventor of electric lighting and the gramophone.

Eiffel, Alexandre (1832–1923), French engineer who built the Eiffel Tower and the locks on the Panama Canal.

Einstein, Albert (1879–1955), German mathematical physicist and one of the greatest of all men of science; author of the theory of relativity.

Elgar, Sir Edward (1857–1934), English composer.

Emmet, Robert (1778–1803), Irish patriot; he led a rebellion in 1803, and was executed for high treason.

Empedocles (c. 500–c. 430 B.C.), Greek philosopher, founder of a school of medicine which regarded the heart as the seat of life.

Epicurus (342–270 B.C.), Greek philosopher who taught that pleasure was the chief good of man and was to be attained through the practice of virtue.

Erasmus, Desiderius (1466–1536), Dutch scholar and philosopher, one of the great figures of the Renaissance.

Essex, Robert Devereux, Earl of (1567–1601), Queen Elizabeth's favourite; he conspired against her and was executed.

Euclid (c. 330–c. 260 B.C.), Greek mathematician who laid the foundations of modern geometry.

Euripides (480–406 B.C.), great Athenian tragic dramatist.

Evelyn, John (1620–1706), famous for his diaries, and one of the founders of the Royal Society.

Fabius Maximus ('Cunctator') (d. 203 B.C.), the Roman dictator who saved Rome from Hannibal by deliberately avoiding battle. From this policy comes the term 'Fabian tactics'.

Fabre, Jean (1823–1915), French naturalist, life-long observer of the habits of insects.

Fahrenheit, Gabriel (1686–1736), German physicist, inventor of the method of grading a thermometer which bears his name.

Faraday, Michael (1791–1867), English physicist and chemist, founder of the science of electro-magnetism.

Fawkes, Guy (1570–1606), a Yorkshire Catholic, one of the conspirators in the Gunpowder Plot; he was captured in the cellar of Parliament House, tried and executed.

Ferdinand of Spain (1452–1516) and **Isabella** (1451–1504), see HISTORY.

Flaubert, Gustave (1821–80), one of the greatest French novelists.

Fleming, Sir Alexander (1881–1955), discoverer of penicillin.

Fokker, Anthony (1860–1939), famous Dutch airman and aeronautical engineer.

Ford, Henry (1863–1947), founder of the Ford Motor Co. and pioneer of the cheap motor-car.

Forester, Cecil Scott (1899–1966), author, creator of Hornblower.

Fox, Charles James (1749–1806), Whig statesman who favoured American independence and opposed the war with France.

Fox, George (1624–91), founder of the Society of Friends (the Quakers).

Francis of Assisi, St (1182–1226), founder of the Franciscan Order of monks; lover of flowers, animals and birds.

Franco, General Don Francisco (1892–1975), Head of Spanish State, 1936–75.

Franklin, Benjamin (1706–90), American statesman, philosopher and scientist; played an important part in framing the constitution of the U.S.A.; invented the lightning conductor.

Frederick I (*c.* 1123–90), Holy Roman Emperor and German national hero; drowned on his way to the Third Crusade.

Frederick II (the Great) (1712–86), King of Prussia; see HISTORY.

Freud, Sigmund (1856–1939), Austrian psychiatrist and founder of psycho-analysis.

Frost, Robert (1874–1963), distinguished American poet.

Fry, Elizabeth (1780–1845), Quaker prison reformer.

Galen, Claudius (131–201), Greek physician, who made important discoveries in anatomy.

Galileo (1564–1642), great Italian mathematician, physicist and astronomer.

Galton, Sir Francis (1822–1911), founder of eugenics and inventor of the device of finger-print identification.

Galvani, Luigi (1737–98), Italian physicist and doctor, who demonstrated the principle of animal electricity.

Gandhi, Mohandas Karamchand (1869–1948), great Indian patriot, social reformer and teacher, driving spirit of the movement for national independence.

Garibaldi, Giuseppe (1807–82), Italian patriot who fought for the unification of Italy.

Garrick, David (1717–79), the leading tragic actor of his day.

George, St, patron saint of England; believed to have been a champion of Christianity during the days of Diocletian, and to have been martyrised in A.D. 303.

Gershwin, George (1898–1937), American jazz pianist and composer; wrote *Rhapsody in Blue* and the Negro opera, *Porgy and Bess*.

Gibbons, Grinling (1648–1720), celebrated wood-carver and sculptor.

Gilbert, Sir William Schwenck (1836–1911), English humorist and playwright, best remembered for the famous Savoy operas, in which he collaborated with Sir Arthur Sullivan.

Gladstone, William Ewart (1809–98), see HISTORY.

Glendower, Owen (1359–1415), Welsh chieftain who opposed Henry IV.

Gluck, Christoph von (1714–87), composer, born in Bohemia.

Goethe, Johann Wolfgang von (1749–1832), the most celebrated German writer; novelist, poet, philosopher and scientist.

Gordon, Charles, General (1833–85), see HISTORY.

Gordon, Lord George (1751–93), instigator of the Anti-Popery riots of 1780.

Gorki, Maxim (1868–1936), Russian novelist.

Grace, Dr William (1845–1915), famous cricketer who dominated the game for over 40 years. Altogether he scored 54,896 runs, including 126 centuries, and took 2,876 wickets.

Grahame-White, Claude (1879–1959), the first Englishman to be granted a British certificate of proficiency in aviation, 1909.

Grant, Ulysses Simpson (1822–85), the most famous American general of the Civil War; twice President of the U.S.A.

Gregory, St (257–336), founder of the Armenian Church; his festival is 9 March.

Gregory the Great, St (*c.* 540–604), one of the most important of the Popes, 590–604.

Gregory XIII (1502–85), Pope who introduced the Gregorian calendar.

Grenville, Sir Richard (1541–91), Elizabethan sea-captain who, with his one ship, the *Revenge*, fought a fleet of Spanish warships in 1591 and died on the deck of the *San Pablo*.

Grieg, Edvard (*c.* 1843–1907), Norwegian composer.

Grey, Lady Jane (1537–54), see HISTORY.

Grimaldi, Joseph (1779–1837), great English clown.

Grimm, the brothers **Jakob** (1785–1863) and **Wilhelm** (1786–1859), German philologists and folk-lorists who collected the famous fairy-tales.

Gustavus Adolphus (1594–1632), King of Sweden; see HISTORY.

Gwynn, Nell (1650–87), the dancer and actress who became mistress to Charles II.

Hadrian (76–138), see HISTORY.

Hakluyt, Richard (*c.* 1552–1616), geographer; first of the English naval historians.

Halley, Edmund (1656–1742), Astronomer Royal; made first magnetic survey of the oceans, and discovered the comet named after him.

Hampden, John (1594–1643), one of the leaders in Parliament's quarrel with Charles I.

Handel, George Frederick (1685–1759), composer.

Hannibal (247–183 B.C.), see HISTORY.

Hardicanute (1019–42), son of Canute the Great, and the last Danish king of England; imposed the tax known as Danegeld.

Hardie, James Keir (1856–1915), first Socialist M.P. (1892).

Hargreaves, James (d. 1778), inventor and pioneer of modern wool industry.

Haroun-al-Rashid (763–809), the most famous Caliph of Baghdad; hero of the *Arabian Nights*.

Harris, Joel Chandler (1848–1908), American author of the Uncle Remus stories.

Harte, Francis Bret (1839–1902), American poet and author, famous for his stories of Californian mining life.

Harvey, William (1578–1657), English doctor who discovered circulation of the blood.

Hastings, Warren (1732–1818), first Governor-General of India; impeached on charges of cruelty and corruption and acquitted after a trial stretching over 7 years.

Havelock, Sir Henry (1795–1857), hero of the relief of Cawnpore and Lucknow in the Indian Mutiny.

Hawke, Edward, Lord (1705–81), victorious admiral in the battle of Quiberon, fought against the French in a storm, 1759.

Hawkins, Sir John (1532–95), Elizabethan naval officer, vice-admiral in the battle with the Spanish Armada.

Hawthorne, Nathaniel (1804–64), American novelist, author of *The Scarlet Letter*.

Haydn, Franz Joseph (1732–1809), Austrian composer.

Heine, Heinrich (1797–1856), German lyric poet.

Hemingway, Ernest (1898–1961), American novelist, author of *A Farewell to Arms* and *For Whom the Bell Tolls*.

Henry the Navigator (1394–1460), Portuguese prince who inspired many voyages of exploration down the Atlantic coast of Africa.

Hepplewhite, George (d. 1786), one of the four great 18th-century cabinet-makers (the others were Chippendale, Robert Adam and Sheraton).

Hereward the Wake, the last of the Saxon chiefs to hold out against the Normans.

Herod the Great (*c*. 73–4 B.C.), King of Judea under the Romans; to him is attributed the massacre of the innocents.

Herodotus (*c*. 485–425 B.C.), Greek historian, called 'the father of history'.

Herschel, Sir John (1792–1871), celebrated astronomer.

Herschel, Sir William (1738–1822), father of the last-named; discoverer of the planet Uranus and the satellites of Saturn.

Hill, Sir Rowland (1795–1879), originator of the penny post.

Hippocrates (*c*. 460–*c*. 370 B.C.), Greek physician: the 'father of medicine'. Rules of conduct for doctors are still based on his Hippocratic Oath.

Hitler, Adolf (1889–1945), see HISTORY.

Hobbes, Thomas (1588–1679), English philosopher, advocate of strong government, author of *Leviathan*.

Homer (*c*. 700 B.C.), most famous of all epic poets, and regarded as the author of the *Iliad* and the *Odyssey*; seven Greek towns vie for the honour of having been his birthplace.

Hood, Samuel, Lord (1724–1816), British admiral who captured Toulon and Corsica, 1793.

Hopkins, Sir Frederick Gowland (1861–1947), English biochemist noted for his work on proteins and vitamins.

Horace (65–8 B.C.), great Roman satirist and poet.

Houdini, Harry (1873–1926), American locksmith who went on the stage as an expert in escaping from handcuffs, locked rooms, etc.

Howard, John (1726–90), prison reformer.

Howe, Richard, Earl (1726–99), British admiral who won a famous victory ('the Glorious First of June') over the French in 1794 off Brest.

Hugo, Victor (1802–85), great French poet, dramatist and novelist, author of *Les Misérables* and *The Hunchback of Notre Dame*.

Hume, David (1711–76), Scottish historian and philosopher.

Hunter, the brothers **William** (1718–83) and **John** (1728–93), both famous Scottish physicians, who made many discoveries in anatomy. John is regarded as the founder of modern surgery.

Huss, John (1369–1415), Bohemian religious reformer, whose death by burning alive led to a half century of civil war.

Huxley, Thomas Henry (1825–95), English naturalist and ardent supporter of the theory of evolution of Charles Darwin (*q.v.*).

Ibsen, Henrik (1828–1906), Norwegian writer, one of the world's greatest dramatists.

Innocent III (1160–1216), powerful Pope who initiated the 4th Crusade.

Irving, Sir Henry (1838–1905), great English actor, and the first to be knighted.

Ivan the Terrible (1530–84), first Czar of Russia, who earned his name by his cruel treatment of his subjects.

Jackson, Andrew (1767–1845), American general, twice President of the U.S.A.

Jackson, Thomas (1824–63), most successful general on the Southern side in the American Civil War; known as 'Stonewall' Jackson for the dogged fight he put up at the First Battle of Bull Run.

James, Henry (1843–1916), great Anglo-American novelist.

Jefferson, Thomas (1743–1826), drew up the American Declaration of Independence; twice U.S. President.

Jeffreys, George, Lord (1648–89), judge notorious for his harsh judgements, especially during the so-called 'Bloody Assize', held to try the followers of the Duke of Monmouth who had rebelled against James II.

Jenghiz Khan (1162–1227), Mogul ruler who twice conquered China and drove the Turks back into Europe.

Jenner, Edward (1749–1823), English country doctor who discovered vaccination as a means of preventing smallpox.

Jerome, Jerome K. (1859–1927), humorous writer, author of *Three Men in a Boat*.

Jesus Christ (*c.* 4 B.C.–A.D. 30 or 33), the founder of Christianity; born at Bethlehem, the first-born of His mother Mary. According to Matthew, His birth was miraculous and Joseph was His foster-father. He learned His father's trade of carpentry at Nazareth, and began His mission when He was about thirty. A summary of His teaching is found in the Sermon on the Mount.

Joan of Arc, St (1412–31), see HISTORY.

John, St, the Baptist (executed A.D. 28), the forerunner of Jesus Christ.

Johnson, Amy (1904–41), first woman aviator to fly solo from England to Australia.

Jones, John Paul (1747–92), Scottish mariner who commanded the American fleet during the War of Independence.

Josephine, Empress (1763–1814), wife of Napoleon I until he divorced her and married Marie-Louise.

Julian the Apostate (331–63), Roman Emperor who professed Christianity until the last two years of his life, when he tried to re-establish paganism.

Jung, Carl (1875–1961), Swiss psychiatrist.

Justinian I (*c.* 483–565), see HISTORY.

Kant, Immanuel (1724–1804), German scientist and philosopher.

Kean, Edmund (1787–1833), one of the greatest English tragic actors.

Kelvin, William Thomson, Lord (1824–1907), scientist and inventor; made important discoveries in the field of thermodynamics (the branch of physics dealing with heat).

Kemble, Frances ('Fanny') (1809–93), noted actress, and member of a famous theatrical family, which included her father, **Charles Kemble** (1775–1854), her uncle **John Philip Kemble**, a famous tragic actor, and her aunt Mrs Siddons (*q.v.*).

Kennedy, John Fitzgerald (1917–63), President of the United States from 1961 until his assassination at Dallas, Texas, in November 1963.

Kepler, Johann (1571–1630), German astronomer who worked out the laws of planetary motion.

Khayyam, Omar (11th century), Persian poet and mathematician, whose *Rubaiyat* was translated by the English poet, Edward Fitzgerald.

Kidd, Captain William (c. 1645–1701), famous pirate whose crimes were committed under cover of the British flag. Hanged at Execution Dock in London.

Kitchener, Horatio, Lord (1850–1916), reconquered the Sudan (1897); Commander-in-Chief in the Boer War; Secretary of State for War, 1914–16. Drowned when the troopship *Hampshire* was sunk by a mine.

Knox, John (1505–72), see HISTORY.

Kruger, Paul (1825–1904), President of the Transvaal who was leader of the Boers in the bitter quarrel with the British that led to the Boer War.

Kruschev, Nikita Sergeyevich (1894–1971), Russian Prime Minister, 1958–64. See HISTORY.

Kublai Khan (1216–94), Mogul Emperor, grandson of Jenghiz Khan; he greatly extended the empire and lived in extraordinary splendour.

Lafayette, Marie-Joseph, Marquis de (1757–1834), French statesman and general, who took an active part in the American War of Independence.

La Fontaine, Jean de (1621–95), French poet and fablewriter.

Lamarck, Jean Baptiste, Chevalier de (1744–1829), French naturalist, author of a theory of the evolution of animals, known as Lamarckism.

Landseer, Sir Edwin (1802–73), most famous English animal painter of his day; designed the lions which are part of the Nelson Monument in Trafalgar Square.

Lanfranc (c. 1005–89), Archbishop of Canterbury in the time of William the Conqueror.

Langton, Stephen (1151–1228), Archbishop of Canterbury; one of the leaders of the group that compelled King John to sign the Magna Carta.

Lasker, Emmanuel (1868–1941), world chess champion, 1894–1921.

Latimer, Hugh (c. 1485–1555), Bishop of Worcester, one of the founders of English Protestantism; burned at the stake in Oxford.

Laud, William (1573–1645), Archbishop of Canterbury; favourite and chief minister of Charles I; tried for treason and executed under the Long Parliament.

Lavoisier, Antoine (1743–94), French chemist who gave oxygen its name and was the first to establish that combustion is a form of chemical action; guillotined during the French Revolution.

Lawrence, John, Lord (1811–79), marched to the relief of Delhi in the Indian Mutiny.

Lawrence, Thomas Edward ('Lawrence of Arabia') (1888–1935), British soldier and archaeologist; led the Arabs against the Turks in the First World War; described his campaign in *Seven Pillars of Wisdom.*

Leacock, Stephen (1869–1944), Canadian economist and humorous writer.

Lee, Robert Edward (1807–70), Commander-in-Chief of the Southern forces in the American Civil War.

Leibnitz, Gottfried (1646–1716), discovered, independently of Newton, the differential calculus.

Leicester, Robert Dudley, Earl of (1531–88), favourite of Queen Elizabeth and leader of the English forces in the Low Countries, 1585–7.

Lenin, Vladimir Ilyich (1870–1924), see HISTORY.

Leonidas, King of Sparta when Greece was invaded by Xerxes, 480 B.C.; killed leading the defence of the Pass of Thermopylae.

Lesseps, Ferdinand, Vicomte de (1805–94), French engineer responsible for building the Suez Canal.

Lilburne, John (1614–57), English politician and pamphleteer, leader of the Levellers during the English Revolution.

Lincoln, Abraham (1809–65), President of the United States whose pronouncement against slavery led to the outbreak of the Civil War. Soon after the victory of the North, he was assassinated while at the theatre by a fanatical anti-abolitionist, John Wilkes Booth.

Linnaeus, Carl (1707–78), Swedish naturalist, founder of modern botany; he devised a system for naming and classifying plants and animals (see NATURAL HISTORY).

Lister, Joseph, Lord (1827–1912), English surgeon who first established the need for antiseptics in surgical operations.

Liszt, Franz (1811–86), Hungarian composer and pianist.

Livy (59 B.C.–A.D. 17), great Roman historian.

Lloyd George, David, Earl of Dwyfor (1865–1945), see HISTORY.

Locke, John (1632–1704), English philosopher and founder of empiricism, which is the doctrine that all knowledge is derived from experience.

London, John ('Jack') (1876–1916), American novelist, author of *White Fang, Call of the Wild*.

Longfellow, Henry Wadsorth (1807–82), American poet, author of *Hiawatha*.

Lonsdale, Earl of (1857–1944), distinguished sportsman who presented the Lonsdale belts for boxing.

Lope de Vega, Felix (1562–1615), Spanish dramatist and author of more than 2,000 plays.

Louis XIV (1638–1715), King of France for 72 years; called *le grande monarque* (the great king), he gave expression to the idea of absolute monarchy, in which the king claims complete power over his subjects. See HISTORY.

Louis XVI (1754–93), see HISTORY.

Loyola, St Ignatius (1491–1556), founder of the Order of Jesuits.

Luther, Martin (1483–1546), see HISTORY.

Macadam, John (1756–1836), inventor of the Macadam process of road-making.

Macaulay, Thomas Babington, Lord (1800–59), celebrated historian and poet, author of *History of England* and the *Lays of Ancient Rome*.

Macbeth, King of Scotland immortalised by Shakespeare; he reigned from 1040 to 1057.

Macdonald, Flora (1722–90), Scottish Jacobite who sheltered Prince Charles Edward after his defeat at Culloden Moor, 1746.

Machiavelli, Niccolo (1469–1527), Florentine statesman and historian; author of *The Prince*, which describes how a ruler may build up his power.

Macready, William Charles (1793–1873), the greatest tragic actor of his day.

Magellan, Ferdinand (*c.* 1480–1521), Portuguese navigator; see EXPLORATIONS AND DISCOVERIES.

Malory, Sir Thomas (*c.* 1430–70), compiled the *Morte D'Arthur*, which tells the story of King Arthur and his Knights of the Round Table.

Malthus, Thomas Robert (1766–1834), English economist, who regarded the growth of the population as a danger, and proposed that marriage should be discouraged.

Mao Tse-Tung (1893–1976), Chairman of the Chinese Communist Party from 1936 until his death.

Marat, Jean-Paul (1743–93), one of the leading figures in the Reign of Terror during the French Revolution; assassinated by Charlotte Corday.

Marconi, Guglielmo, Marchese (1874–1937), inventor of the first practical method of wireless telegraphy.

Marco Polo (see **Polo, Marco**).

Marcus Aurelius (121–180), Roman Emperor who drove off the barbarians, and was famous for his wisdom and his taste for philosophy and literature.

Maria Theresa (1717–80), Empress of Austria, Queen of Bohemia and Hungary; see HISTORY.

Marie Antoinette (1755–93), daughter of Maria Theresa, and wife of Louis XVI of France; see HISTORY.

Mark Antony (see **Antonius, Marcus**).

Marlborough, John Churchill, Duke of (1650–1722), perhaps the greatest of all British soldiers; see HISTORY.

Marx, Karl (1818–83), German philosopher and economist, on whose teaching and writings Communism is based.

Masaryk, Thomas (1850–1937), founder and first President of Czechoslovakia.

Maupassant, Guy de (1850–93), famous French novelist and short-story writer.

Maxim, Sir Hiram (1840–1916), inventor of the automatic quick-firing gun named after him.

Maxwell, James Clerk (1831–79), Scottish physicist who formulated the electro-magnetic theory of light; his work made wireless possible.

Mazzini, Giuseppe (1805–72), Italian patriot who worked for the independence and unification of his country.

Mendel, Gregor (1822–84), Austrian botanist and monk whose study of the common garden pea resulted in the law of heredity known as the Mendelian law.

Mendelssohn, Jakob Ludwig Felix (1809–47), German composer.

Mercator, Gerhardus (1512–94), Flemish geographer who simplified navigation by inventing a system of projection in which the longitudes are represented by equidistant parallel lines and the degrees of latitude by perpendicular lines parallel to the meridian.

Mesmer, Friedrich (1733–1815), German doctor who developed the system of animal magnetism known as 'mesmerism'.

Metternich, Prince (1773–1859), Austrian statesman who led the conservative resistance to the ideas of progress spread by the French Revolution.

Mill, John Stuart (1806–73), writer on politics, economics and philosophy, and one of the founders of modern liberalism.

Millikan, Robert Andrew (1868–1953), American physicist who discovered cosmic rays.

Miltiades (d. 489 B.C.), one of the leaders of the Athenians against the Persians at Marathon.

Mithridates (c. 132–63 B.C.), King of Pontius from 120 to 63 B.C., implacable enemy of the Romans; he spoke 22 languages and, surrounded by enemies, was said to have made himself immune from all poisons.

Mohammed (c. 570–632), the founder of the Moslem religion; see HISTORY.

Molière (Jean Baptiste Poquelin) (1622–73), the greatest of the French comic dramatists.

Monk, George, Duke of Albemarle (1608–69), general and admiral who fought in the Anglo-Dutch wars; having fought on Cromwell's side against the Royalists, he later helped to restore Charles II to the throne.

Montaigne, Michel de (1533–92), great French essayist.

Montcalm, General Louis, Marquis de (1712–59), French commander in Canada, defeated by Wolfe.

Monteverdi, Claudio (1568–1643), Italian composer.

Montezuma II (1466–1520), last Aztec ruler of Mexico, Emperor when Cortes invaded the country.

Montfort, Simon de, Earl of Leicester (1208–65), powerful baron who forced Henry III to grant the first English Parliament; see HISTORY.

Montgolfier, Joseph (1640–1810) and **Jacques** (1745–99), French brothers who made many ascents in balloons inflated by heated air.

Montrose, James Graham, Marquess of (1612–50), general who raised the Highlands in support of Charles I and II.

Moore, Sir John (1761–1809), British general killed during retreat to Corunna in the Peninsular War.

More, Sir Thomas (1478–1535), Lord Chancellor under Henry VIII who was executed for refusing to take the Oath of Supremacy; wrote *Utopia*.

Morgan, Sir Henry (*c.* 1635–88), Welsh buccaneer who preyed on the Spaniards in the Caribbean; captured Panama in 1671.

Mountevans, Admiral Lord (1881–1957), British sailor and explorer known as 'Evans of the Broke'; wrote *South with Scott*.

Mozart, Wolfgang Amadeus (1756–91), great Austrian composer.

Mussolini, Benito (1883–1945), Fascist dictator of Italy, 1922–43; see HISTORY.

Nansen, Fridtjof (1862–1930), Norwegian explorer and organiser of relief for victims of the First World War.

Napoleon I (Bonaparte) (1769–1821), see HISTORY.

Nasser, Gamel Abdel (1819–70), President of the United Arab Republic, 1958–70.

Napoleon III (1808–73), see HISTORY.

Nelson, Horatio, Viscount (1758–1805), England's greatest naval commander; see HISTORY.

Nero, Claudius Caesar (37–68), Roman Emperor whose reign is notorious for his cruelty and wild living.

Newton, Sir Isaac (1642–1727), probably the greatest of all scientists; famous for his work on the nature of white light the calculus and gravitation; wrote the *Principia*.

Ney, Marshal (1769–1815), one of Napoleon's generals.

Nicholas II, Czar of Russia (1868–1918); shot with his family by the revolutionaries, 16 July 1918.

Nicholas, St (4th century), patron saint of Russia; associated (as Santa Claus) with Christmas.

Nietzsche, Friedrich (1844–1900), German philosopher, who believed that the mass of people must be led by the few Supermen.

Nightingale, Florence (1820–1910), creator of modern nursing and hospital reformer; the 'lady with the lamp' of the Crimean War.

Nijinsky, Vaslav (1890–1950), great Russian ballet dancer, Polish-born.

Nobel, Dr Alfred (1833–96), Swedish inventor of dynamite; in his will he left money for the annual prizes named after him (for work done for the benefit of mankind in physics, chemistry, physiology and medicine, literature and peace).

Northcliffe, Lord (1865–1922), pioneer of modern journalism.

Nostradamus (Michel de Notre Dame) (1503–66), French astrologer.

Nuffield, Lord, William Richard Morris (1877–1963), pioneer motor-car manufacturer and philanthropist.

Oates, Captain L. E. G. (1880–1912), British explorer who was in the sledge party that accompanied Captain Scott in his dash for the South Pole. On the return journey the party became storm-bound, and Oates, badly frostbitten, walked out to his death in a blizzard rather than be a burden to his comrades.

Oates, Titus (1649–1705), informer against Roman Catholics in Charles II's reign.

O'Casey, Sean (1883–1964), Irish dramatist, author of *Juno and the Paycock*.

Offa, King of Mercia, reigned from *c.* 757 to 796; built an embankment from the Dee to the Wye, called Offa's Dyke.

Ohm, Georg (1787–1854), discoverer of a law of electric current known as Ohm's Law; see SCIENCE.

Otto, Nikolaus (1832–91), German engineer, inventor of the four-stroke cycle named after him; see CARS.

Ovid (43 B.C.–A.D. 18), Roman poet.

Owen, Robert (1771–1858), social reformer and factory owner; inspired the earliest Factory Acts, trade unionism and co-operative trading.

Paganini, Niccolo (1782–1840), Italian violinist whose virtuosity has become a legend.

Paine, Thomas (1737–1809), English revolutionary writer; after the publication of his *Rights of Man* he was forced to flee to France.

Palestrina, Giovanni de (1525–94), Italian composer.

Palmerston, Viscount (1784–1865), Whig Foreign Secretary, 1830–46; supported liberal uprisings throughout Europe; twice Prime Minister.

Pancras, St (3rd century), patron saint of children; martyrised at the age of fourteen.

Pankhurst, Emmeline (1858–1928), leader of movement for votes for women with her daughters **Dame Christabel** and **Sylvia**.

Paracelsus, Philippus (1493–1541), Swiss mystic and alchemist.

Parnell, Charles Stewart (1846–91), leader of the Irish National Party.

Pascal, Blaise (1623–62), French philosopher and mathematician; constructed the first calculating machine.

Pasteur, Louis (1822–95), French chemist and founder of the sciences of bacteriology and immunology; first to show that infectious diseases are caused by germs; devised the process of pasteurisation by which milk can be prevented from going bad.

Patrick, St (c. 389–c. 461), patron saint of Ireland.

Pavlov, Ivan (1849–1936), Russian physiologist; made many discoveries concerning the digestive system and the brain and nervous system.

Pavlova, Anna (1885–1931), great Russian ballet dancer.

Peel, Sir Robert (1788–1850), British statesman, founder of the modern police service; see HISTORY.

Penn, William (1644–1718), Quaker who founded Pennsylvania.

Pepys, Samuel (1633–1703), naval administrator and famous diarist.

Pericles (c. 490–429 B.C.), greatest of the Athenian statesmen; see HISTORY.

Pétain, Marshal Henri Philippe (1856–1951), hero of the defence of Verdun by the French in 1916; in 1940 signed armistice with the Germans, and in 1945 was condemned to death for treason; the sentence was commuted to life imprisonment.

Peter (the Great) (1672–1725), Czar of Russia who did much to modernise his kingdom; founded St Petersburg (now Leningrad).

Peter the Hermit (d. 1115), French monk who raised the army for the disastrous First Crusade.

Petrarch, Francesco (1304–74), Italian poet and scholar, creator of the sonnet.

Petrie, Sir Flinders (1953–1942), British Egyptologist.

Philip II of Macedonia (382–336 B.C.), conqueror of Greece and father of Alexander the Great; see HISTORY.

Philip II of Spain (1527–98), see HISTORY.

Piccard, Auguste (1884–1962), Swiss physicist; ascended into stratosphere in a balloon, 1931 and 1932, and later explored the ocean in his bathysphere.

Pindar (522–443 B.C.), Greek lyric poet.

Pitman, Sir Isaac (1813–97), founder of the Pitman system of shorthand.

Pitt, William (1759–1806), British Prime Minister (at twenty-four, the youngest) throughout the period of the French Revolution and much of the war with France; see HISTORY.

Pizarro, Francisco (c. 1471–1541), Spaniard who conquered Peru with great cruelty; killed by his own soldiers.

Planck, Professor Max (1858–1947), German physicist whose law of radiation laid the foundation of the quantum theory.

Plato (427–347 B.C.), great Athenian philosopher, pupil of Socrates, teacher of Aristotle.

Plimsoll, Samuel (1824–96), M.P. who secured the passing of an Act of Parliament which defined a line (the Plimsoll Mark) above which the water must not rise when a ship is loaded. (See SHIPS.)

Plutarch (c. 46–210), Greek historian, author of *The Lives of Great Men of Greece and Rome.*

Poe, Edgar Allan (1809–49), American poet and short-story writer; wrote *Tales of Mystery and Imagination*, one of which, *The Murders in the Rue Morgue*, is among the earliest detective stories.

Polo, Marco (1254–1324), Venetian explorer; see EXPLORATIONS AND DISCOVERIES.

Pompey the Great (106–48 B.C.), Roman general; see HISTORY.

Priestley, Joseph (1733–1804), discovered and identified many of the common gases: discovered oxygen.

Proust, Marcel (1871–1922), French novelist; author of 15 novels with the general title, *A la Recherche du Temps Perdu* (*In Search of Lost Time*).

Ptolemy, Claudius (c. 90–168), Greek astronomer and geographer, born in Alexandria; according to the Ptolemaic system, the earth was the centre of the universe and the heavenly bodies revolved around it. (See COPERNICUS).

Purcell, Henry (c. 1659–95), English composer.

Pushkin, Alexander (1799–1837), great Russian poet, author of *Eugene Onegin.*

Pym, John (1584–1643), Puritan statesman who led the campaign in the House of Commons against Charles I.

Pythagoras (c. 582–c. 507 B.C.), Greek scientist and mathematician; to him is attributed the discovery of the multiplication table, the decimal system and the square on the hypotenuse.

Rabelais, François (c. 1494–1553), French monk and satirical writer, author of *Gargantua* and *Pantagruel.*

Rachmaninov, Serge (1873–1943), Russian composer.

Racine, Jean (1639–99), French tragic dramatist.

Raffles, Sir Thomas Stamford (1781–1826), founder of Singapore, 1819; also of the Zoological Society of London.

Raleigh, Sir Walter (1552–1618), English statesman, poet, sailor and explorer; favourite of Queen Elizabeth; founded the colony of Virginia; was imprisoned in the Tower for 12 years, and there wrote a *History of the World*. Set free in 1615 to lead an expedition to Guiana in search of gold, he was unsuccessful; and on his return was executed.

Rasputin, Grigori (1871–1916), Russian monk who became all-powerful at the court of the last Russian Czar, Nicholas II.

Réamur, René (1683–1757), French chemist; inventor of the thermometer that bears his name.

Rhodes, Cecil (1853–1902), see HISTORY.

Richelieu, Cardinal Duc de (1585–1642), one of the greatest of French statesmen; Prime Minister to Louis XIII.

Ridley, Nicholas (1500–55), Bishop of London, burned at the stake with Latimer.

Rienzi, Cola di (1313–54), Roman patriot who led a popular rebellion in 1347.

Rilke, Rainer Marie (1872–1926), German lyric poet.

Rimbaud, Jean (1854–91), important modern French poet; all his poems were written between his 16th and 19th years.

Rizzio, David (*c.* 1540–66), Italian musician, favourite of Mary Queen of Scots; stabbed to death in her presence by the jealous Darnley.

Roberts, Field-Marshal Earl (1832–1914), English general who distinguished himself in the Afghanistan campaign; led the campaign against the Boers.

Robespierre, Maximilien (1758–94), French lawyer who was president of the Committee of Public Safety during the Reign of Terror; sent many people to the guillotine, but was himself overthrown and guillotined.

Rob Roy (Robert McGregor) (1671–1734), Scottish highlander noted for his brigandage.

Rockefeller, John Davison (1839–1937), oil magnate who was said to have been the richest man in the world.

Rodney, Lord (1719–92), English admiral, victor in two great battles in the wars with France and Spain, 1780 and 1782.

Roland, Madame (1754–93), one of the leading figures of the French Revolution; she was guillotined, and died pronouncing the famous words, 'Oh liberty, what crimes are committed in thy name!'

Rommel, Field-Marshal (1891–1944), German general; see HISTORY.

Roosevelt, Franklin Delano (1882–1945), four times U.S. President; see HISTORY.

Ross, Sir Ronald (1857–1932), discoverer of the parasite that causes malaria.

Rouget de Lisle, Claude Joseph (1760–1836), French poet who wrote the words and music of the *Marseillaise*.

Rousseau, Jean-Jacques (1712–78), French writer who urged a return to nature and argued that man was naturally good; his ideas had a great influence on the events of his time.

Rupert, Prince (1619–82), Royalist admiral and general; fought for his uncle, Charles I, against Cromwell's troops, and at sea for Charles II against the Dutch.

Russell, Bertrand (Earl Russell) (1872–1970), English philosopher and mathematician.

Rutherford, Lord (1871–1937), New Zealand-born scientist, author of the nuclear theory of the atom and the first man to split the atom.

Saladin (1137–93), Sultan of Egypt and Syria and Moslem hero of the Third Crusade; see HISTORY.

Santos-Dumont, Alberto (1873–1932), famous Brazilian airman, one of the pioneers of modern aviation.

Sappho (*c.* 611–*c.* 592 B.C.), the most famous poetess of the ancient world; a native of the Greek island of Lesbos.

Savonarola, Girolamo (1452–98), Florentine friar who denounced the corruption of his day and was burned at the stake.

Schiller, Johann Friedrich von (1759–1805), one of the greatest German dramatists and poets.

Schliemann, Heinrich (1822–90), German archaeologist who discovered the ruins of ancient Troy.

Schubert, Franz (1797–1828), Austrian composer.

Schumann, Robert (1810–56), German composer.

Schweitzer, Albert (1875–1965), famous musician and organist who became a doctor of medicine in order to devote his life to the work of a medical missionary in Equatorial Africa.

Scipio, Publius (Scipio Africanus the Elder) (*c.* 232–183 B.C.), Roman general who distinguished himself in the Second Punic War.

Scott, Captain Robert Falcon (1868–1912), polar explorer who commanded the Antarctic expeditions of 1901–4 and 1910. With a small party he reached the South Pole on 18 January 1912, only to find that Amundsen had reached it before him. On the return journey the party were storm-bound, and all perished only 11 miles from their next depot.

Scott-Paine, Hubert (1891–1954), pioneer in the construction of flying-boats and high-speed motor-boats.

Selfridge, Harry Gordon (1858–1947), American whose famous shop in Oxford Street (opened in 1909) was the model for the modern British department store.

Shaftesbury, Anthony Ashley Cooper, Earl of (1801–85), the greatest social reformer of the 19th century; inspired changes in the treatment of lunatics, took part in the campaign against slavery and was largely responsible for the Factory Acts that forbade women and children to work underground in the mines and limited working hours.

Sheraton, Thomas (1751–1806), great English cabinet maker.

Sherman, General William (1820–91), great American soldier and leader of the famous 300-mile march across Georgia during the Civil War.

Shostakovich, Dmitri (1906–1975), Russian composer.

Sibelius, Jean (1865–1957), Finnish composer.

Siddons, Sarah (1755–1831), the greatest English tragic actress of her day.

Sidney, Sir Philip (1554–86), poet and soldier, one of Queen Elizabeth's favourites; killed fighting against the Spaniards at Zutphen.

Simpson, Sir James (1811–70), Scottish surgeon; first to use chloroform as an anaesthetic.

Smeaton, John (1724–92), rebuilder of the Eddystone lighthouse after its destruction by fire.

Smith, Adam (1723–90), political economist and first important advocate of free trade; author of *Wealth of Nations*.

Smuts, Field-Marshal Jan (1870–1950), South African soldier, who fought against the British in the Boer War, but afterwards worked for friendship with Britain. Prime Minister of South Africa, 1912–24 and 1939–48.

Sobieski, John (1629–96), King of Poland who freed Vienna from the Turks, 1683; see HISTORY.

Socrates (470–399 B.C.), Greek philosopher, whose teachings are known from the writings of his pupils, Xenophon and Plato. He taught people to think carefully and logically. Charged with corrupting the morals of the young, he was condemned to die by drinking hemlock.

Solomon (10th c. B.C.), son of David, ruler of Israel and Judah.

Solon (638–558 B.C.), great Athenian law-giver.

Somerset, Duke of (1506–52), Protector of England in early days of Edward VI's reign; later deposed and executed.

Sophocles (495–406 B.C.), popular Athenian dramatist; author of *Antigone, Electra, Oedipus.*

Soult, Marshal Nicholas (1769–1851), one of the most successful of Napoleon's marshals, and Wellington's opponent in the Peninsular War.

Spinoza, Benedict (1632–77), Dutch philosopher.

Stalin, Joseph (1879–1953), Soviet dictator from 1923 until his death; see HISTORY.

Stanley, Sir Henry Morton (1841–1904), explorer of Central Africa; in 1867, as a newspaper correspondent, he sought and found the missing David Livingstone.

Stendhal (Marie Henry Beyle) (1783–1842), French novelist.

Stephenson, George (1781–1848), English engineer, inventor of the first successful railway locomotive (see RAILWAYS).

Stephenson, Robert (1772–1850), lighthouse builder who invented the 'flashing' system of throwing light at sea.

Stowe, Harriet Beecher (1811–96), American author of *Uncle Tom's Cabin,* which helped to create strong feeling against slavery.

Stradivari, Antonio (1644–1730), Italian who was the greatest of all violin-makers.

Strafford, Thomas, Earl of (1593–1641), supporter of the authority of Charles I; abandoned by the King, he was impeached and executed.

Strauss, Johann (1825–99), Austrian composer.

Strauss, Richard (1864–1949), German composer.

Stravinsky, Igor (1882–1971), Russian-born American composer.

Strindberg, August (1849–1912), Swedish dramatist and novelist.

Sullivan, Sir Arthur (1842–1900), English composer; collaborator with W. S. Gilbert (*q.v.*) in the Savoy operas.

Sun Yat Sen, Dr (1867–1925), one of the leaders of the Chinese Revolution of 1911; President of the Chinese Republic, 1921–25.

Suvarov, Alexander (1730–1800), great Russian General.

Swedenborg, Emanuel (1688–1772), Swedish philosopher.

Tacitus, Caius (55–*c.* 120), Roman historian.

Tagore, Sir Rabindranath (1861–1941), Indian poet and philosopher.

Talleyrand-Périgord, Charles-Maurice de (1754–1838), Napoleon's Foreign Minister, 1797–1807.

Tamerlane (Timur the Lame) (1335–1405), founder of the Mogul dynasty in India; brutal conqueror of Turkestan, Persia and Syria.

Tarquin Superbus, the last king of Rome; banished 510 B.C.

Tasso, Torquato (1544–95), great Italian poet.

Tchaikovsky, Peter Ilyitch (1840–93), Russian composer.

Telford, Thomas (1757–1834), Scottish road-maker and builder of canals and bridges, including the Menai Suspension Bridge.

Tell, William (14th century), legendary hero of the Swiss struggle for freedom against the Austrians.

Teresa, St (1515–82), Spanish nun famous for her austere life and her vision.

Terry, Dame Ellen (1848–1928), great English actress, long associated with Sir Henry Irving (*q.v.*).

Thales of Miletus (*c.* 624–565 B.C.), Greek philosopher who believed that water was the principal element.

Themistocles (*c.* 514–449 B.C.), Athenian soldier and statesman who defeated the Persian fleet at Salamis, 480 B.C.

Thomson, Sir Joseph (1856–1940), physicist and mathematician, discoverer of the electron.

Thoreau, Henry David (1817–62), nature-worshipping American philosopher; author of *Walden*.

Thucydides (*c.* 460–399 B.C.), greatest of the Greek historians.

Tito, (Josip Broz) (1892–1980), leader of the Yugoslav partisans in the Second World War and President of Yugoslavia until 1980.

Titus (40–81), Roman emperor, son of Vespasian; did much for the welfare of the Roman people, completed the Colosseum; see HISTORY.

Tolstoy, Count Leo (1828–1910), great Russian novelist; author of *War and Peace*, generally regarded as the greatest novel ever written.

Torquemada, Tomas de (1420–98), Inquisitor-General during Spanish Inquisition.

Toussaint L'Ouverture (1743–1803), Negro ex-slave who freed Santo Domingo (the Dominican Republic) from the French.

Trajan (*c.* 52–117), Roman emperor; did much to consolidate the Empire—work that was continued by his successor, Hadrian; see HISTORY.

Trotsky, Leon (1879–1940), one of the leaders of the Russian Revolution; in 1925 was driven into exile in Mexico, where he was later assassinated.

Turgenev, Ivan (1818–83), Russian novelist.

Tussaud, Madame Marie (1760–1850), Swiss who escaped from Paris at the time of the French Revolution and set up her exhibition of wax figures in London.

Tut-ankh-amen (*c.* 1350 B.C.), Egyptian Pharaoh whose tomb was discovered in 1922, with the mummy and the gold sarcophagus intact.

Twain, Mark (see **Clemens, Samuel**).

Tyler, Wat (d. 1381), leader of the Peasants' Revolt; see HISTORY.

Tyndale, William (*c.* 1492–1536), translator of the Bible; put to death for heresy.

Valentine, St, martyrised *c.* 273. The habit of sending Valentines is of pre-Christian origin, and is not connected with the saint.

Vaughan Williams, Ralph (1872–1958), English composer.

Verdi, Giuseppe (1813–1901), Italian composer.

Verlaine, Paul (1844–1896), French poet.

Verne, Jules (1828–1905), French writer of early science fiction, author of *Twenty Thousand Leagues under the Sea*, *Round the World in Eighty Days*.

Vernier, Pierre (1580–1637), inventor of the sliding scale.

Vespasian (A.D. 9–79), Roman emperor; at one time commander of the Roman Army in Britain.

Vespucci, Amerigo (1451–1512), Italian navigator; the first map-makers gave his name to America.

Villeneuve, Pierre (1763–1806), commanded the French fleet against Nelson at Trafalgar.

Villon, François (1431–*c.* 1489), French poet.

Virgil (Publius Vergilius Maro) (70–19 B.C.), great Roman epic poet, author of the *Aeneid*.

Vitus, St (4th century), Roman Catholic saint and martyr; the custom of dancing before his shrine on his commemoration day, 15 June, gave rise to the name, St Vitus Dance, given to a nervous ailment.

Voltaire, François-Marie Arouet de (1694–1778), great and influential French philosopher and writer, author of *Candide*.

Wagner, Richard (1813–83), German opera composer.

Wallace, Alfred Russel (1823–1913), English traveller and naturalist; one of the founders of zoological geography; author of *Travels on the Amazon*.

Wallace, Sir William (c. 1270–1305), Scottish patriot; see HISTORY.

Warbeck, Perkin (1474–99), Pretender to the English Crown; claimed to be one of the princes murdered in the Tower; provided with an army by the French and the Scots, he invaded England in 1497, but was defeated and hanged.

Warwick, Richard Neville, Earl of (c. 1428–71), 'The Kingmaker'; see HISTORY.

Washington, George (1732–99), first President of the American Republic, 1789; see HISTORY.

Watt, James (1736–1819), great British engineer, designer of first efficient steam-engine.

Wedgwood, Josiah (1730–95), most famous of the English potters.

Wellington, Arthur Wellesley, Duke of (1769–1852), 'the Iron Duke'; see HISTORY.

Wesley, Charles (1708–88), hymn-writer, brother of John.

Wesley, John (1703–91), founder of Methodism.

Whitman, Walt (1819–92), American poet, author of *Leaves of Grass*.

Whittington, Richard (c. 1358–c. 1423), London apprentice who became four times Lord Mayor of London.

Whymper, Edward (1840–1911), first mountaineer to reach the summit of the Matterhorn.

Wilberforce, William (1759–1833), leading spirit of the successful campaign against the Slave Trade.

Wilkes, John (1727–97), popular Whig politician; expelled from the House of Commons, he was three times elected M.P. for

Middlesex, being again expelled each time. In the end his opponents gave way and he was able to take his seat.

William I of Prussia (1797–1888), first German Emperor; see HISTORY.

William II (1859–1941), Emperor of Germany; see HISTORY.

William the Silent (1533–80), Prince of Orange who attempted to free Holland from the grip of Spain; assassinated; see HISTORY.

Wingate, Major-General Orde (1903–44), leader of the Chindit forces that operated behind Japanese lines in Burma during the Second World War. Killed in air crash.

Wolfe, General James (1727–59), British commander at the siege of Quebec, in which he was killed.

Wolsey, Cardinal Thomas (1471–1530), Archbishop of York and Chancellor to Henry VIII; see HISTORY.

Wright, Sir Almroth (1861–1947), discovered the system of inoculation against typhoid.

Wycliff, John (c. 1324–84), religious reformer; translator of the Bible.

Xenophon (430–355 B.C.), Greek historian and general, pupil of Socrates.

Xerxes (c. 519–465 B.C.), King of Persia; see HISTORY.

Ximenes, Francisco (1436–1517), succeeded Torquemada (q.v.) as Inquisitor-General in the Spanish Inquisition.

Young, Brigham (1801–77), Mormon leader and head of the Latter Day Saints of Salt Lake City.

Zeppelin, Ferdinand, Graf von (1838–1917), German inventor of the airship bearing his name.

Zola, Emile (1840–1902), great French novelist.

NAMES IN THE NEWS

At any one moment, thousands of our fellow men and women are 'names in the news'—enjoying the secure fame of, say, a great living composer, or the fleeting celebrity of a popular actor or a sportsman at the height of his career. Out of these thousands we have picked two or three hundred that we believe might be of special interest to readers of JUNIOR PEARS.

Of most of them, we can safely say that they are actors, or musicians, or writers, or whatever it may be: but there is at least one field in which what a man or woman actually *does* may change overnight—making hundreds of encyclopaedias for the moment, and in this respect, out-of-date. This is the field of politics, where a general election can turn all the members of the Government into members of the Opposition, or a cabinet reshuffle can lose half a dozen Ministers their jobs. Foreign Presidents and Prime Ministers present the same difficulty. So we must say of all political figures mentioned here that the positions they are said to hold were those they held towards the beginning of 1986, when this book was prepared for the printer.

A number of British and Commonwealth politicians have the title 'Rt. Hon.' (short for Right Honourable). This title is given to members of the Privy Council, a body that gives advice to the Queen.

Some Chinese names may puzzle us a little at the moment, because from January 1, 1979, there have been two ways of rendering these names into our roman alphabet. According to the older system, the name of the Chinese Vice-Premier is Teng Hsiao-p'ing: according to the new system, it is Deng Xiaping. The new version is intended to make it easier for us to pronounce the Chinese names correctly. Eight familiar names will keep the old spelling: Mao Tse-tung, Sun Yat-sen, Chou-En-lai, Peking, Tibet, Inner Mongolia, Canton and China itself—which is an entirely different word in Chinese and should be written Zhongguo, which means the Middle Kingdom.

Aga Khan (IV) (b. 1936), Imam of the Ismaili Moslems.
Amis, Kingsley (b. 1922), poet and novelist.
Andrews, Julie (b. 1935), actress.
Arlott, John (b. 1914), writer and former broadcaster on cricket.

Armstrong, Neil (b. 1930), U.S. astronaut; first man to set foot on the moon.

Arnold, Malcolm (b. 1921), British composer.

Ashcroft, Dame Peggy (b. 1907), actress.

Ashton, Sir Frederick (b. 1906), principal choreographer, Royal Ballet.

Attenborough, Sir David (b. 1926), maker of zoological films.

Attenborough, Sir Richard (b. 1923), producer and actor.

Ayckbourn, Alan (b. 1940), British playwright.

Baker, Dame Janet (b. 1933), singer.

Banda, Dr Hastings (b. 1905), President of Malawi since 1966; Prime Minister, 1963–66.

Bannister, Dr Roger (b. 1929), first man to run mile inside 4 minutes.

Barenboim, Daniel (b. 1942), pianist and conductor.

Barker, Ronnie (b. 1929), British comedian.

Barkworth, Peter (b. 1929), actor.

Beckett, Samuel (b. 1906), novelist and playwright.

Bellamy, David (b. 1942), biologist.

Benn, Tony (b. 1925), Secretary of State for Energy, 1975–9.

Bennett, Richard Rodney (b. 1936), British composer.

Biffen, John (b. 1931), Lord Privy Seal and Leader of the House of Commons.

Bondi, Sir Hermann (b. 1919), British mathematician and astronomer.

Bonington, Chris (b. 1934), mountaineer.

Borg, Björn (b. 1956), Swedish tennis player, five times Wimbledon champion.

Botha, Pieter (b. 1916), Prime Minister of South Africa.

Botham, Ian (b. 1955), England cricketer.

Boulez, Pierre (b. 1925), French composer and conductor.

Bowie, David (b. 1947), British pop singer.

Bradman, Sir Donald (b. 1908), Australian cricketer who during his career (1927–48) scored 28,067 runs in 338 innings, with 117 centuries and an average of 95·14.

Bragg, Melvyn (b. 1939), novelist and broadcaster.

Brandt, Willy (b. 1913), Chancellor of W. Germany, 1969–74.

Brook, Peter (b. 1925), producer, co-director of the Royal Shakespeare Theatre.

Bush, George (b. 1924), Vice-President of the United States.

Callaghan, Rt. Hon. James (b. 1912), Prime Minister, 1976–9.

Carrington, Lord (b. 1919), Secretary-General, N.A.T.O.

Castro, Dr. Fidel (b. 1927), Prime Minister of Cuba since 1959.

Ceausescu, Nicolae (b. 1918), President of Rumania since 1967.

Channon, Rt. Hon. Paul (b. 1935), Secretary of State for Trade and Industry.

Cheshire, Group Captain Geoffrey, V.C. (b. 1917), famous pilot of Second World War; founder of Cheshire Homes for the Sick.

Clapton, Eric (b. 1945), British rock guitarist.

Cleese, John (b. 1939), comedian.

Cockerell, Sir Christopher (b. 1910), inventor of the hovercraft.

Connery, Sean (b. 1930), actor.

Cook, Peter (b. 1937), comedian.

Cousteau, Jacques-Yves (b. 1910), French underwater explorer.

Copland, Aaron (b. 1900), American composer.

Corbett, Ronnie (b. 1932), comedian.

Crawford, Michael (b. 1942), actor.

Dali, Salvador (b. 1904), Spanish surrealist painter.

Day, Sir Robin (b. 1932), television interviewer.

de Valois, Dame Ninette (b. 1898), founder of the Royal Ballet.

Dench, Judi (b. 1934), British actress.

Deng, Xiaping (b. 1904), Vice-Premier of China.

Dietrich, Marlene (b. 1904), German-born actress.

Dimbleby, David (b. 1938), broadcaster.

Dowell, Anthony (b. 1943), Director, Royal Ballet.

Drabble, Margaret (b. 1939), English novelist.

Du Maurier, Dame Daphne (b. 1907), author.

Dylan, Bob (b. 1941), American singer and guitarist.

Eddington, Paul (b. 1927), actor.

Edwards, Nicholas (b. 1934), Secretary of State for Wales.

Evans, Sir Geraint (b. 1922), singer.

Finney, Albert (b. 1936), British actor.

Fitzgerald, Dr Garrett (b. 1926), Taoiseach (Head of Government) of Republic of Ireland.

Fonteyn, Dame Margot (b. 1919), former prima ballerina, Royal Ballet.

Fowler, Norman (b. 1938), Secretary of State for Social Services.

Fraser, Antonia (b. 1932), novelist, historian.

Frink, Dame Elisabeth (b. 1930), English sculptor.

Frost, David (b. 1939), British TV personality.

Fuchs, Sir Vivian (b. 1908), Director of British Antarctic Survey, 1958–73; led Commonwealth Trans-Antarctic Expedition, 1955–58.

Galway, James (b. 1939), flautist.

Gandhi, Rajiv (b. 1945), Prime Minister of India.

Garbo, Greta (b. 1905), Swedish-born film actress.

Geldof, Bob (b. 1954), rock singer and fund-raiser for famine victims (Band Aid, etc); given honorary knighthood 1986.

Gielgud, Sir John (b. 1904), actor.

Gonzalez, Felipe (b. 1942), Prime Minister of Spain.

Gorbachev, Mikhail (b. 1932), First Secretary of the Communist Party of the Soviet Union Central Committee.

Grass, Günter (b. 1927), German novelist.

Greene, Graham (b. 1904), novelist.

Guinness, Sir Alec (b. 1914), actor.

Hailsham, Lord (b. 1907), Lord Chancellor.

Hall, Sir Peter (b. 1930), Director of the National Theatre.

Harrison, George (b. 1943), song writer and performer.

Hattersley, Roy (b. 1933), deputy-leader, Labour Party.

Havers, Sir Michael (b. 1923), Attorney-General.

Hawke, Bob (b. 1930), Prime Minister of Australia.

Hawthorne, Nigel (b. 1929), actor.

Healey, Rt. Hon. Denis (b. 1917), Chancellor of the Exchequer, 1974–79.

Heath, Rt. Hon. Edward (b. 1916), Leader of the Conservative Party, 1964–75; Prime Minister, 1970–74.

Helpmann, Sir Robert (b. 1909), dancer, choreographer, actor.

Heyerdahl, Thor (b. 1914), author and ethnologist, leader of Kon-Tiki expedition, 1947.

Hillary, Sir Edmund (b. 1919), mountaineer; with Sherpa Tensing, first to reach the summit of Everest, 1953.

Hirohito (b. 1901), Emperor of Japan.

Hoffman, Dustin (b. 1937), American film actor.

Howe, Sir Geoffrey (b. 1926), Foreign Secretary.

Howerd, Frankie (b. 1921), comedian.

Hoyle, Professor Sir Fred (b. 1915), mathematician, astronomer and writer.

Hu Yaobang (b. 1915), Chairman of Communist Party of China.

Hughes, Ted (b. 1930), Poet Laureate.

Hume, Cardinal Basil (b. 1923), Archbishop of Westminster.

Hunt, Lord (b. 1910), soldier and mountaineer; leader of the successful 1953 Mt. Everest expedition.

Hurd, Rt. Hon. Douglas (b. 1930), Home Secretary.

Hussein Ibn Talal (b. 1935), King of Jordan.

Hutton, Sir Leonard (b. 1916), first professional cricketer to captain England.

Innes, Hammond (b. 1913), writer.

Jackson, Glenda (b. 1936), actress.

Jacobi, Derek (b. 1938), actor.

Jenkin, Patrick (b. 1926), Secretary of State for the Environment.

Jenkins, Rt. Hon. Roy (b. 1920), former President, Common Market Commission; a founder of the Social Democratic Party.

John, Elton (b. 1947), British rock singer.

John Paul II (b. 1920), elected Pope in 1978.

Jopling, Michael (b. 1930), Minister of Agriculture.

Juan Carlos I (b. 1938), King of Spain.

Kaunda, Kenneth (b. 1924), President of Zambia.

Kendal, Felicity (b. 1946), actress.

Khomeini, Ayatollah Ruhollah (b. 1902), leader of the Islam revolution in Iran, 1979.

King, Thomas (b. 1933), Secretary of State for Northern Ireland.

Kohl, Dr. Helmut (b. 1930), West German Chancellor.

Kyprianou, Spyros (b. 1932), President of Cyprus.

Lange, David (b. 1942), Prime Minister of New Zealand.

Lawson, Nigel (b. 1936), Chancellor of the Exchequer.

Loach, Ken (b. 1936), British film director.

Lloyd Webber, Andrew (b. 1948), British composer.

Lovell, Professor Sir Bernard (b. 1913), Director of Jodrell Bank Experimental Station, Cheshire.

Luce, Rt. Hon. Richard (b. 1937), Minister for the Arts.

Lyttleton, Humphrey (b. 1921), English jazz musician.

Maclean, Alastair (b. 1922), novelist.

Mandela, Nelson (b. 1923), South African lawyer and politician. National organiser of the African National Council when sentenced to life imprisonment in 1964.

Matthews, Sir Stanley (b. 1915), former professional footballer: first played for England 1934.

McCartney, Paul (b. 1942), British song writer and performer.

McCowen, Alec (b. 1925), British actor.

McEnroe, John (b. 1959), tennis star.

McKellen, Ian (b. 1935), British actor.

Menuhin, Yehudi (b. 1916), American violinist.

Miles, Lord (Bernard) (b. 1907), actor, founder of the Mermaid Theatre.

Miller, Dr Jonathan (b. 1934), British stage and film director and physician.

Milligan, Spike (b. 1918), comedian, writer.

Mills, Sir John (b. 1908), actor and producer.

Milne, Alasdair (b. 1930), Director-General, B.B.C.

Mintoff, Dom (b. 1916), Prime Minister of Malta.

Mitterand, François (b. 1916), President of France.

Moi, Daniel Arap (b. 1924), President of Kenya.

Moore, Dudley (b. 1935), British comedian.

Moore, Henry (b. 1898), sculptor.

Mubarak, Hosni (b. 1928), President of Egypt.

Mugabe, Robert (b. 1925), Prime Minister of Zimbabwe.

Muggeridge, Malcolm (b. 1903), journalist and broadcaster.

Mulroney, Brian (b. 1939), Prime Minister of Canada.

Murdoch, Iris (b. 1919), novelist.

Murdoch, Rupert (b. 1937), newspaper proprietor.

Mwinyi, Ali Hassan, President of Tanzania.

Naipaul, V. S. (b. 1932), Trinidad-born novelist.

Nixon, Richard Milhous (b. 1913), President of the United States, 1969–74. See HISTORY.

Nunn, Trevor (b. 1940), Director, Royal Shakespeare Company.

Nureyev, Rudolf (b. 1938), ballet dancer.

Nyerere, Julius (b. 1922), President of Tanzania 1964–85.

Olivier, Lord (Laurence Olivier) (b. 1907), actor, Director of the National Theatre, 1962–73, now Associate Director.

Osborne, John (b. 1929), playwright and actor.

O'Toole, Peter (b. 1934), actor.

Owen, Dr David (b. 1938), leader, Social Democratic Party.

Park, Merle (b. 1937), principal dancer, Royal Ballet; Director, Royal Ballet School.

Pavarotti, Luciano (b. 1935), Italian opera singer.

Peres, Shimin (b. 1923), Prime Minister of Israel, 1984–6.

Perez du Cuellar, Dr (b. 1930), Secretary-General of the United Nations since 1982.

Pinter, Harold (b. 1930), actor and playwright.

Powell, Rt. Hon. Enoch (b. 1912), Minister of Health, 1960–63;

Ulster Unionist M.P. for South Down.

Previn, André (b. 1929), composer and conductor.

Qadhafi, Col. Muammar (b. 1942), Leader of the Revolution, Libya.

Ramphal, Sir Shridath (b. 1928), Secretary-General of the Commonwealth.

Reagan, Ronald (b. 1911), President of the United States since 1981.

Redgrave, Vanessa (b. 1937), actress; daughter of Sir Michael Redgrave.

Reid, Sir Robert (b. 1930), Chairman, British Railways Board.

Richard, Cliff (b. 1940), British pop singer.

Ridley, Rt. Hon. Nicholas (b. 1929), Secretary of State for the Environment.

Rose, Sir Alec (b. 1908), sailed solo round the world, 1967–68.

Rostropovich, Mstislav (b. 1927), Russian cellist and conductor.

Runcie, Most Rev. and Rt. Hon. Robert (b. 1921), Archbishop of Canterbury.

Ryle, Sir Martin (b. 1918), Astronomer Royal.

Scargill, Arthur (b. 1936), President, National Union of Mineworkers.

Schwarzkopf, Elisabeth (b. 1915), opera and concert singer.

Scofield, Paul (b. 1922), actor.

Scott, Sir Peter (b. 1909), artist, writer and naturalist; son of the explorer, Captain Scott.

Searle, Ronald (b. 1920), artist and cartoonist.

Secombe, Sir Harry (b. 1921), singer and comedian.

Segovia, Andres (b. 1894), Spanish guitarist.

Shamir, Yitzhak (b. 1915), Prime Minister of Israel.

Shankar, Ravi (b. 1920), Indian sitar player and composer.

Sheppard, Rt. Rev. David (b. 1929), Bishop of Liverpool: former English cricket captain.

Shevardnadze, Edvard (b. 1928), Soviet Foreign Minister.

Shultz, George (b. 1920), United States Secretary of State.

Sillitoe, Alan (b. 1928), English novelist.

Simenon, Georges (b. 1903), Belgian novelist, creator of the French detective, Maigret.

Sinatra, Frank (b. 1917), American singer and actor.

Sinden, Donald (b. 1923), actor.

Solzhenitsyn, Alexander (b. 1918), Russian novelist.

Spender, Sir Stephen (b. 1909), poet.

Starr, Ringo (b. 1940), British entertainer; member of The Beatles.

Steel, David (b. 1938), leader of the Liberal Party.

Stockhausen, Karlheinz (b. 1928), German composer.

Stockton, Earl of (b. 1894), Prime Minister, as Harold Macmillan, 1957–63.

Sutherland, Dame Joan (b. 1926), Australian-born opera singer.

Taylor, Alan John Percivale (b. 1906), historian.

Tebbitt, Norman (b. 1931), Chancellor of the Duchy of Lancaster; Chairman, Conservative Party.

Te Kanawa, Dame Kiri (b. 1944), New Zealand opera singer.

Thatcher, Rt. Hon. Margaret (b. 1925), British Prime Minister from 1979; the first woman to occupy the position.

Theodorakis, Mikis (b. 1925), Greek composer.

Tippett, Sir Michael (b. 1905), composer.

Tutin, Dorothy (b. 1931), actress.

Ustinov, Peter (b. 1921), actor, dramatist, producer.

Walesa, Lech (b. 1943), leader of Solidarity, the Polish free trade union movement; Nobel Peace Prize, 1983.

Walker, Peter (b. 1932), Secretary of State for Energy.

Wedgwood, Dame Cicely Veronica (b. 1910), historian.

Whitelaw, Viscount (b. 1918), Lord President of the Council and deputy Prime Minister.

Whitney, John (b. 1931), Director-General of the Independent Broadcasting Authority (I.B.A.).

Whittle, Air Commodore Sir Frank (b. 1907), developed gas turbine for jet propulsion.

Williams, Shirley (b. 1930), a founder and Chairman of the Social Democratic Party.

Williamson, Malcolm (b. 1931), composer and Master of the Queen's Musick.

Willis, Norman (b. 1933), General Secretary of the Trades Union Congress.

Wilson, Lord (b. 1916), Prime Minister, as Harold Wilson, 1964–70; and from February 1974 until his resignation in April 1976.

Wise, Ernie (b. 1926), comedian.

Yamani, Shaikh Ahmad Zaki, Minister of Petroleum and Mineral Resources, Saudi Arabia.

Young, Lord (b. 1932), Secretary of State for Employment.

Younger, George (b. 1931), Secretary of State for Scotland.

A DICTIONARY OF MYTHOLOGY

The majority of the gods, goddesses and other mythological characters who appear in this list are Greek or Roman. Some, however, are Egyptian or Norse; and it is important to remember that, though the Greek and Roman myths are the most familiar to us, the Babylonians, the Hebrews, the Chinese, Japanese, Indians and many other peoples built mythical stories, and invented mythical characters, on the basis of their religious beliefs.

The fact that the Romans borrowed many of their myths from the Greeks, giving their own names to the gods, leads often to confusion. The following table shows, side by side, the Greek and Roman names of the principal gods and goddesses.

Greek	*Roman*
Aphrodite (goddess of love)	**Venus**
Apollo (god of light and the arts)	**Phoebus Apollo**
Ares (god of war)	**Mars**
Artemis (huntress)	**Diana**
Athene (goddess of wisdom)	**Minerva**
Cronus (father of Zeus)	**Saturn**
Demeter (goddess of corn)	**Ceres**
Dionysus (god of wine and revelry)	**Bacchus**
Eros (god of love)	**Cupid**
Hera (mother of the gods and goddess of marriage)	**Juno**
Hermes (messenger of the gods)	**Mercury**
Hestia (goddess of the hearth)	**Vesta**
Pan (god of the flocks)	**Faunus**
Poseidon (god of the sea)	**Neptune**
Zeus (father of the gods)	**Jupiter**

The printing of a name in small capital letters (e.g. VENUS) means that the mythical person named is the subject of a separate entry.

Achilles, King of the Myrmidons, most famous of the Greek heroes of the Trojan War.

Adonis, Greek god: a young man of great beauty, wounded by a boar and changed by APHRODITE into an anemone.

Aeneas, Trojan prince, hero of Virgil's *Aeneid*; the mythical ancestor of the Romans.

Aeolus, wind-god, who unchained the tempests.

Aesculapius, god of medicine.

Agamemnon, King of Mycenae, leader of the Greeks against Troy.

Ajax, Greek warrior at the siege of Troy.

Amazons, mythical race of war-like women.

Amphitrite, sea-goddess and wife of POSEIDON.

Ammon, Egyptian god.

Andromeda, daughter of the king of Ethiopia who, by claiming to be as beautiful as the NEREIDS, roused the anger of POSEIDON, and was condemned to be devoured by a sea monster. She was saved by PERSEUS, who married her.

Antigone, daughter of OEDIPUS. When the king of Thebes forbade the burial of her brother, Polynices, she defied his order, and was buried alive in a cave; there she hanged herself.

Aphrodite, Greek goddess of love; she was said to have sprung from the foam of the sea.

Apollo, Greek and Roman god of light, the arts and divination; also called Phoebus.

Aquilo, the north wind.

Ares, the Greek god of war.

Argonauts, the fifty Greek heroes who, with JASON, sought the Golden Fleece in their ship the *Argo*.

Ariadne, daughter of MINOS of Crete; gave THESEUS the thread which enabled him to find his way out of the Labyrinth.

Artemis, Greek goddess and huntress.

Atalanta, Greek princess who declared she would marry only the man who could beat her at running; she was outrun by Milanion, who dropped three golden apples one after another to tempt Atalanta and slow her down.

Athene or **Pallas**, Greek goddess of wisdom.

Atlas, King of Mauretania who, for warring against ZEUS, was condemned to support the sky on his shoulders.

Bacchus, Roman god of wine.

Baldur, most beautiful of the Norse gods.

Bellerophon, Greek hero who caught PEGASUS, the winged horse, and killed the CHIMAERA.

Boreas, the north wind.

Calypso, nymph who delayed ODYSSEUS for seven years on his way home from Troy.

Cassandra, Trojan princess; she had the gift of prophecy, but was fated never to be believed.

Castor and Pollux, sons of ZEUS and Leda; they were transported to the heavens and became the constellation known as the Twins.

Centaurs, creatures, half-horse and half-man, living on Mt Pelion in Thessaly.

Cerberus, three-headed dog who guarded the gates of HADES.

Ceres, Roman corn goddess.

Charon, boatman who ferried the dead across the STYX.

Chimaera, fire-breathing monster, a mixture of lion, dragon and goat; slain by BELLEROPHON.

Circe, enchantress who turned ODYSSEUS' companions into swine.

Cronus, Greek name for SATURN.

Cupid, Roman name for EROS, the god of love.

Cybele, the 'great mother', goddess of nature.

Cyclops, one-eyed giants who forged ZEUS's thunderbolts.

Danae, daughter of the king of Argos, visited by ZEUS in a shower of gold; mother of PERSEUS.

Daphne, nymph who was changed into a laurel-bush to save her from APOLLO.

Demeter, Greek goddess of the corn.

Diana, Roman goddess and huntress.

Dido, mythical queen who founded Carthage.

Dionysus, Greek god of wine and revelry.

Dryads, Greek goddesses of the forest.

Echo, nymph who, having displeased HERA, was changed into a rock and condemned to repeat the last words of those who spoke to her.

Electra, sister of ORESTES.

Elysium, or **the Elysian fields**, the Greek and Roman paradise.

Endymion, beautiful youth who was loved by the moon.

Erebus, the dark subterranean region below which was HADES.

Eros, the god of love.

Euphrosyne, one of the three GRACES.

Eurydice, wife of ORPHEUS.

Eurus, the south-east wind.

Fates, the three goddesses, Clotho, Lachesis and Atropos, who were in charge of human destinies; they weaved the web of each man's life, which ended when Atropos cut the thread.

Fauns, Roman gods of the fields.

Flora, goddess of flowers and gardens.

Freya, Norse goddess of love.

Furies or **Eumenides,** goddesses whose mission was to punish human crimes.

Gorgons, three sisters, MEDUSA, Euryale and Stheno, who had the power to change into stone all who looked at them.

Graces, the three goddesses, EUPHROSYNE, Aglaia and Thalia, who were regarded as the bestowers of beauty and charm.

Hades, the Greek god of the infernal regions; also the infernal regions themselves.

Harpies, winged monsters with women's faces and long claws.

Hector, most valiant of the defenders of Troy: killed by ACHILLES.

Hecuba, wife of PRIAM, King of Troy; nineteen of her children were killed during the siege.

Helen, Greek princess of great beauty; her removal to Troy by PARIS was the cause of the Trojan War.

Helicon, Greek mountain consecrated to the MUSES.

Hera, wife of ZEUS and goddess of marriage.

Heracles, Greek demi-god.

Hercules, Roman name for HERACLES.

Hermes, Greek messenger of the gods.

Hesperides, daughters of ATLAS, guardians of the golden apples stolen by HERCULES.

Hestia, Greek goddess of the hearth, known to the Romans as Vesta.

Horus, falcon-headed Egyptian god.

Hygieia, Greek goddess of health.

Hymen, god of marriage.

Icarus, son of Daedalus; his father made for them both wings fastened with wax. Icarus flew too near the sun; the wax fastenings melted, and he fell into the sea and was drowned.

Irene, Greek goddess of peace.

Iris, the rainbow, a messenger of the gods.

Isis, Egyptian goddess of medicine, marriage and agriculture.

Ixion, thrown into Hell by ZEUS and condemned to be bound to a flaming wheel everlastingly revolving.

Janus, Roman god of beginnings (hence *Januarius*, the first month of the year); he was able to see both the future and the post and is always represented with two heads.

Jason, Greek hero and leader of the ARGONAUTS, who won the Golden Fleece.

Juno, wife of JUPITER and goddess of marriage.

Jupiter, Roman name for the father of the gods and king of heaven.

Lethe, one of the rivers of Hell; all who drank its waters became forgetful of the past.

Mars, Roman god of war.

Medea, witch who married JASON and, when he left her, took her revenge by devouring their children.

Medusa, one of the three GORGONS. She offended MINERVA, who turned her hair into serpents. PERSEUS cut off her head and carried it with him to turn his enemies into stone.

Menelaus, King of Sparta and husband of HELEN of Troy.

Mercury, messenger of the gods.

Midas, King of Phrygia to whom the favour was granted that everything he touched turned into gold. When this happened even to his food, he prayed for the power to be taken away.

Minerva, Roman goddess of wisdom and the arts.

Minos, King of Crete who demanded an annual tribute of young men and women from Athens; they were sent into the Labyrinth and devoured by the Minotaur.

Mnemosyne, goddess of memory and mother of the MUSES.

Muses, nine goddesses who presided over the arts: Clio (History), Euterpe (music), Thalia (comedy), Melpomene (tragedy), Terpsichore (dancing), Erata (elegaic poetry), Polymnia (lyric poetry), Urania (astronomy), Calliope (eloquence and epic poetry).

Naiads, nymphs presiding over rivers and springs.

Narcissus, beautiful youth who pined away for love of his own reflection and was turned into a flower.

Nemesis, Greek goddess of vengeance and retribution.

Neptune, Roman god of the sea.

Nereids, nymphs of the Mediterranean.

Notus, the south wind.

Oceanides, nymphs of the sea.

Oceanus, Greek god of the sea.

Odin, or **Wotan**, father of the Norse gods.

Odysseus, King of Ithaca, one of the heroes of the siege of Troy, whose many adventures on his return home are described in Homer's *Odyssey*. The Romans called him ULYSSES.

Oedipus, King of Thebes, who, discovering that he had unwittingly killed his father and married his mother, blinded himself.

Orestes, son of AGAMEMNON and Clytemnestra. When Agamemnon was killed by Clytemnestra, Orestes was saved by his sister ELECTRA, who then drove him to kill his mother in revenge.

Orion, giant hunter; killed by ARTEMIS, he became one of the constellations.

Orpheus, great musician of Greek myth; went into Hades in search of his dead wife, EURYDICE, and so charmed the infernal spirits with his music that they returned Eurydice to him on condition that he should not look behind him until he had left the lower world. He broke this condition and was torn to pieces.

Osiris, Egyptian god, protector of the dead.

Pales, Roman goddess of flocks and shepherds.

Pan, goat-footed Greek god who presided over the flocks.

Pandora, the first woman to be created. ATHENE made her wise; ZEUS gave her a box full of evil things. On earth she married Epimetheus, the first man; then opened the box and so released all the ills from which men suffer.

Paris, Trojan prince who took HELEN from her husband and so caused the Trojan War. Appointed to choose the most beautiful of the three goddesses, HERA, ATHENE and APHRODITE, he chose the last, thus bringing down on Troy the hatred of the other two.

Parnassus, Greek mountain sacred to the MUSES.

Pegasus, winged horse that sprang from the blood of MEDUSA.

Penelope, wife of ODYSSEUS. During his long absence she was pressed to choose a new husband, and promised to do so when she had finished weaving a tapestry; but every night she undid the work she had done that day.

Perseus, son of ZEUS and DANAE. He and his mother were cast adrift and came to the country of King Polydectes. The king, hoping to get rid of Perseus, sent him to bring back MEDUSA's head.

Phaethon, son of the Sun-God, whose father allowed him to drive the sun-chariot for one day only; he was unable to manage the horses, and ZEUS, angered, struck him dead.

Pleiades, the seven daughters of ATLAS who killed themselves into despair and were turned into stars.

Pluto, King of HADES and god of the dead.

Polyphemus, the most famous of the CYCLOPS; he imprisoned ODYSSEUS, who escaped by blinding him.

Pomona, goddess of fruits and gardens.

Poseidon, god of the sea.

Priam, the last King of Troy, killed in the sack of the city.

Procrustes, robber who fitted his victims to a bed, stretching them or lopping their limbs to do so. Slain by THESEUS.

Prometheus, the god of fire. Having formed the first man of clay, he stole fire from heaven to bring him to life. ZEUS had him chained to a mountain, where his liver was devoured every day by a vulture, but grew again every night. He was freed by HERACLES.

Proserpina, wife of PLUTO and mother of the FURIES.

Proteus, sea god who could change his shape at will.

Psyche ('the soul'), beautiful maiden loved by CUPID.

Pygmalion, King of Cyprus who fell in love with a statue of a woman he had made himself.

Remus, brother of ROMULUS.

Romulus, thrown with his brother REMUS into the Tiber at birth; washed ashore and adopted by a she-wolf. Romulus founded Rome (the traditional date is 753 B.C.).

Saturn, husband of CYBELE and father of JUPITER. A promise made to Titan forced him to eat his children when they were born. Cybele saved Jupiter by putting a stone in his place. Jupiter dethroned his father and Saturn took refuge in Latium, where he showed men how to cultivate the land.

Satyrs, the companions of BACCHUS.

Sirens, monsters, half-woman and half-bird, who lived on the rocks between the isle of Capri and the coast of Italy. By the sweetness of their singing they lured sailors to destruction.

Sisyphus, founder of Corinth, who for his greed and dishonesty was condemned after death to roll a stone for ever uphill; as soon as it got to the top it rolled down again.

Styx, the river flowing round HADES, over which CHARON ferried the dead.

Tantalus, King of Lydia condemned for ever to hunger and thirst.

Tartarus, the lowest region of HADES.

Telemachus, son of ODYSSEUS who set out in search of his father.

Theseus, Greek hero who, among his many adventures, killed the Minotaur (see MINOS).

Themis, goddess of justice.

Thor, the Norse god of war.

Titans, sons of the Heaven and the Earth. Rebelling against the gods, they attempted to climb to Heaven by piling mountain upon mountain; but they were destroyed by JUPITER's thunderbolts.

Triton, one of the sea-gods.

Ulysses, Roman name for ODYSSEUS.

Venus, the Roman goddess of beauty and love.

Vulcan, Roman god of fire.

Zephyrus, the west wind.

Zeus, Greek name for the father of the gods.

A DICTIONARY OF SCIENCE AND MATHEMATICS

Abacus A digital computing device of ancient origin consisting of counters strung on wires, one wire for each digital position.

Aberration Deviation from perfect image formation in an optical or equivalent system.

Absolute Temperature A temperature scale originally based on *Charles's Law* (q.v.) of the expansion of gases. This law suggests that if a gas could be cooled down to about $-273°$ C it would occupy zero volume. In fact all gases liquefy before reaching such a low temperature, but there does exist a minimum possible temperature, $-273·5°$ C, below which matter cannot be cooled. This temperature is called *absolute zero* and is itself unattainable, although temperatures within one millionth of a degree of it have been reached using special cooling techniques. The Absolute (or Kelvin) Temperature scale measures temperatures from absolute zero in degrees kelvin, the degree kelvin being of the same magnitude as the degree Celsius/centigrade. To convert an absolute temperature to a Celsius/centigrade temperature it is necessary simply to add $273·15$ (in the table the $0·15$ has been omitted for simplicity). The importance of the absolute scale is that it is always absolute temperatures which appear in the equations of *Thermodynamics* (q.v.) e.g. the *gas laws* (q.v.). See *thermometer*.

Temperature conversions		
Fahrenheit	*Celsius/Centigrade*	*Absolute or Kelvin* (K)
$-459·4$	$-273·0$	0
$-148·0$	$-100·0$	173
$-112·0$	$-80·0$	193
$-76·0$	$-60·0$	213
$-40·0$	$-40·0$	233
$-4·0$	$-20·0$	253
0	$-17·8$	$255·2$
$32·0$	0	273
$50·0$	10	283
$68·0$	20	293
$86·0$	30	303

Fahrenheit	Celsius/Centigrade	Absolute or Kelvin (K)
104·0	40	313
122·0	50	323
140·0	60	333
158·0	70	343
176·0	80	353
194·0	90	363
212·0	100	373
1,292·0	700	973
1,472·0	800	1,073
1,832·0	1,000	1,273
2,192·0	1,200	1,473
2,732·0	1,500	1,773

Acceleration The rate of change of velocity, expressed in metres per second per second, or feet per second per second, etc. Negative acceleration = retardation.

Accumulator A type of electric *cell* (q.v.) or battery that can be recharged. The commonest sort (as used for car batteries) has positive plates of lead peroxide and negative plates of spongy lead with dilute sulphuric acid as the electrolyte.

Acid Acids are a very important group of chemical compounds. Examples of inorganic acids are hydrochloric acid (HCl), nitric acid (HNO_3), and sulphuric acid (H_2SO_4). Organic acids such as acetic acid ($CH_3 \cdot COOH$) usually contain the *carboxyl* group, COOH. All acids contain *replaceable* (or *acidic*) hydrogen in their molecules (though in organic acids, only the hydrogen in COOH is acidic), and the most characteristic reaction of acids is for this hydrogen to be replaced by a metal to form a *salt* (q.v.). Some metals react directly with acids to give a salt and hydrogen gas while another example of this kind of reaction is the neutralisation of an acid by a *base* (q.v.) to give a salt and water. E.g. Potassium hydroxide (a base) reacts with dilute nitric acid to give potassium nitrate (a salt) and water. Here the potassium replaces the acidic hydrogen which goes into making the water. The reason why acids so readily lose their acidic hydrogen is that in solutions of acids to a great extent the hydrogen is already separate from the rest of the molecule in the form of positive hydrogen ions.

Acids have a sour taste and when concentrated can be very corrosive and dangerous to handle. *Indicators* (q.v.) can be used to test whether a solution is acidic or not: e.g. in the presence of an acid, blue litmus turns red.

Acoustics The study of *sound*. See RADIO and TELEVISION.

Adsorption The taking-up of a gas by a solid in such a way that a layer of gas only one molecule thick is held firmly in the surface of the solid. Adsorption is an essential part of some chemical phenomena, including *catalysis* (q.v.).

Alkali A *base* (q.v.) that is soluble in water, e.g. the hydroxides of sodium and potassium (caustic soda and caustic potash). Alkalis can be identified in solution by means of *indicators* (q.v.).

Alpha Radiation (Alpha Rays, α-Rays) This is a stream of particles that are the nuclei of helium atoms. They are emitted from radioactive substances. Some emitters of alpha rays are: uranium, radium, plutonium. Alpha rays have such little penetrating power that a sheet of paper will stop them, but where they do penetrate they have intense effects.

Alternating Current See RADIO AND TELEVISION.

Altimeter An instrument used to measure height above the earth.

Amino-acid An organic compound of the form $H_2N–CHR–COOH$ where R represents a univalent side-chain. Glycine is the simplest amino-acid in which R is a hydrogen atom. A large number of different amino-acids are possible, but the 20 or so that are the building blocks for *proteins* (q.v.) are particularly important.

In proteins, amino-acids link together by forming a *peptide bond* between the carboxyl group ($–COOH$) of one amino-acid and the amino group ($H_2N–$) of the next, with the elimination of a water molecule. This process can be repeated to give chains of great length.

Ampere (A) The SI unit of electric *current* (q.v.).

Analog Computer A computer in which numerical quantities are presented by physical quantities, e.g. the numbers between 1 and 2 may be represented by the corresponding voltages between 1 volt and 2 volts. Another example of an analog computer is the slide rule in which numbers are represented by lengths.

Angle Formed when two lines meet at a point. If straight lines *AB* and *BC* meet at the point B, the angle so formed is denoted by $\angle ABC$ or $A\hat{B}C$. Alternatively, a particular angle may be referred to by a symbol, commonly a Greek letter such as θ (theta) or φ (phi). Angles are measured either (*a*) in degrees, there being 360 degrees (360°) to the full circle,

or (*b*) in circular measure, in which case the unit is the *radian*
(q.v.).

Angular Velocity The rate of motion through an angle about an
axis. Measured in degrees, revolutions or *radians* (q.v.) per unit
time. The angular velocity of a point in radians/unit time can
be calculated by dividing its linear velocity perpendicular to the
line joining it to the axis by the length of the line. In the diagram, the angular velocity of *A* (which has linear velocity *v*)
about *C* is *v/r* radians/sec. *Angular acceleration* is the rate of
change of angular velocity.

Angstrom (Å) Unit of length. 1 angstrom $= 10^{-10}$ m $= 10^{-8}$
cm $= 3·9 \times 10^{-9}$ inches. 1 inch $= 2·54 \times 10^{8}$ Å. Used in
atomic physics e.g. to measure the wavelengths of X-rays (0·1
Å to 10 Å) or the distance between atoms in molecules and
crystals (q.v.) (the distance between neighbouring copper atoms
in copper metal is 3·4 Å).

Anion A negatively charged atom or *radical* (q.v.).

Anode Positive electrode. See *Electrolysis*.

Antibody Antibodies are a very important class of *proteins* (q.v.)
found in the blood of higher animals. They play a vital role in
the defence against harmful foreign molecules and organisms
(e.g. poisons, *viruses* (q.v.) and *bacteria* (q.v.)) which may have
entered the body. Each antibody is able to recognise a specific
foreign molecule (in the same way as a key is able only to open
one lock). When this happens, other parts of the defence system
(or *immune system*) are able to break down or inactivate the
invading foreign molecule or organism.

  Antibodies against a particular organism are not present in
an animal until the animal has been infected at least once with
that organism. In other words, the body learns how to make
antibodies against an infectious agent only after it has been in

contact with that agent. If the animal is infected a second time by the same agent, antibodies against it will already exist and the agent can be destroyed before it can cause noticeable illness. This is why many illnesses are only had once in life (often in childhood); after the first attack, the body becomes *immune* to the illness. *Vaccination* is an artificial way of making someone immune to a disease (e.g. smallpox, cholera or influenza). Attenuated or dead infectious organisms are injected into the body. These do not cause the disease but stimulate the body to make antibodies against the organism. The body is thus prepared in advance and can defend itself in the event of a real infection.

Anti-matter Particles like electrons, protons and neutrons all have corresponding anti-particles: anti-electrons (called *positrons*), anti-protons and anti-neutrons. It is possible that somewhere in the universe there exists anti-matter composed entirely of anti-particles (e.g. an anti-hydrogen atom would have an anti-proton as nucleus and one orbiting positron), but this has never been detected. If anti-matter were to meet ordinary matter both would be annihilated and much energy released.

Archimedes Principle This states that when a body is partially or totally immersed in a fluid (i.e. a liquid or gas) its apparent loss of weight is equal to the weight of fluid displaced: i.e. the body experiences an upthrust equal to the weight of fluid displaced.

Area The amount of space covered as a flat expanse, for the calculation of which two dimensions are necessary. Units are square metres, square inches ($\square$), square yards, etc. Units for land measurement are the hectare (metric system) and acre.

Areas of common shapes

Figure	Area
Rectangle, sides a and b	ab
Triangle, sides a, b, c, vertical height h.	$\frac{1}{2}bh$
$\quad s = \frac{1}{2}(a + b + c)$	$\sqrt{s(s - a)(s - b)(s - c)}$
Trapezoid, parallel sides a and c	$\frac{1}{2}h(a + c)$
Parallelogram, sides x and y, $\quad \theta$ = angle between sides	$xy \sin \theta$
Circle, radius r	πr^2
Sector of circle, radius r, θ = angle between radii boundaries	$\dfrac{r^2\theta}{2}$
	(θ in radians)

Segment of circle	$\dfrac{r^2}{2}(\theta - \sin\theta)$ (θ in radians)
Ellipse, semi-axes a and b	πab
Surface of sphere, radius r	$4\pi r^2$
Surface of cylinder, height h, radius r	(1) $2\pi rh$ (curved surface only) (2) $2\pi r(h + r)$ (total surface)
Surface of cone, slant height l, radius r	(1) πrl (curved surface) (2) $\pi r(l + r)$ (total surface)

Arithmetical Progression Series of quantities in which each term differs from the preceding by a constant *common difference*. An A.P. in which the first term is a, the common difference d, the number of terms n and the sum of n terms S has:

$$S = a + (a + d) + (a + 2d) + (a + 3d) + \ldots$$
$$+ (a + (n - 1)d)$$
$$= \frac{n}{2}\{2a + (n - 1)d\}$$

Armature The coil or coils—usually rotating—of an electric motor or dynamo.

Atmosphere Normal or Standard. Unit of pressure = pressure which will support a column of mercury 760 mm or 29·92 in high at 0° C, sea-level at Lat. 45°. 1 Normal atmosphere = 1·0132 Bars = 14·72 lb/sq in = 101,320 N/sq m.

Atom The smallest particle of an *element* (q.v.) still retaining the chemical properties of that element.

It consists of a positively charged heavy nucleus surrounded by negatively charged electrons, which move in orbits very similar to the way in which planets move round the sun. The positive charge on the nucleus exactly balances the total negative charge of all the surrounding electrons when the atom is neutral.

The nucleus consists of two types of particle very strongly held together—protons and neutrons. A proton carries one unit of positive charge. A neutron has no charge. The mass of a neutron is very slightly more than the mass of a proton.

The chemical properties of the atom are determined by the electrons, which in number, of course, are equivalent to the

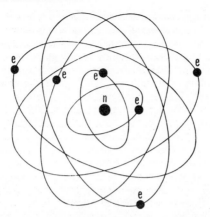

Carbon atom

Schematic diagram, 6 planetary electrons, 2 on inner orbits, 4 on outer orbits. These four are the valency electrons. The nucleus has 6 protons and 6 neutrons all very close together in the one body, which carries almost all the mass of the atom.

proton charge in the nucleus. So if a proton is removed from (or added to) the nucleus of an atom it is no longer the same element. The addition or subtraction of neutrons, however, makes no difference to the chemical properties.

The number of protons (and the corresponding number of electrons) determines the element. An atom of carbon, for example, has six planetary electrons, an atom of copper twenty-nine, an atom of uranium ninety-two. The simplest atom is that of hydrogen, whose nucleus is one proton and which has one planetary electron.

Atomic Number A number that tells the number of protons in the nucleus of an atom and therefore the number of planetary electrons. A list of elements starts with hydrogen of atomic number 1 and continues in series 1, 2, 3, 4, etc. See *element.*

Atomic Pile Original name for a *nuclear reactor* (q.v.).

Atomic Weight A number showing how heavy the atom of an element is compared with the isotope carbon 12 taken as 12·0000. Owing to the facts that when atomic nuclei fuse to make another element energy is given out, and therefore mass lost, and many elements are mixtures of isotopes of different weights, the atomic weight is rarely a whole number.

Avogadro's Law Equal volumes of all gases under the same conditions of temperature and pressure contain equal numbers of molecules.

Bacterium (pl.: **bacteria**) Microscopic single-celled living organisms, more complicated than *viruses* (q.v.) but simpler than animal or plant *cells* (q.v.). Bacteria are found everywhere and are important in causing the decay of organic matter; in making atmospheric nitrogen available for use by plants; and in causing many diseases (such as typhoid, cholera and food poisoning).

Base A chemical substance which reacts with an *acid* (q.v.) to give a *salt* (q.v.) and water only. Bases may be insoluble (e.g. copper II oxide) or soluble (see *Alkali*).

Battery A number of electric *cells* (q.v.) joined together to give a bigger electromotive force. Thus three dry cells, each $1 \cdot 5$ V, in series give $4 \cdot 5$ V.

Beta Radiation (Beta Rays, β-Rays) A stream of very fast electrons emitted by some radioactive substances. These electrons come from the nucleus by breakdown of neutrons, not from the planetary electrons. Beta rays are more penetrating than *alpha rays* (q.v.), the most energetic of them being capable of penetrating 1 mm of lead. Because of their penetrating power they are used for the measurement of thickness in industry, e.g. the thickness of the tin layer on iron in tinplate.

Big Bang Theory The currently favoured theory of the origin of the universe. According to the theory, the universe originally existed in a state of extreme compression, sometimes called the primordial fireball. About ten billion ($10^{10} = 10,000,000,000$) years ago it exploded in a 'big bang', and since then has been continuously expanding at great speed. This expansion of the universe is observed today in the rapidity with which galaxies (distinct groups of many millions of stars) are flying apart from each other. It is possible that the expansion of the universe will slow down and change to a contraction in the future. The universe would then return to its fireball state. However, recent evidence supports the idea that the universe will continue to expand for ever.

Binary numbers A system of numbers in which the only digits used are 0 and 1. In the familiar decimal system the number 268 can be read as $2 \times 10^2 + 6 \times 10^1 + 8 \times 10^0 = 200 + 60 + 8$ $= 268$. In the binary system powers of 2 are used instead of powers of 10. Thus $1101 = 1 \times 2^3 + 1 \times 2^2 + 0 \times 2^1 + 1 \times 2^0 = 8 + 4 + 0 + 1 = 13$. The numbers up to 15 are:

1	0001	6	0110	11	1011
2	0010	7	0111	12	1100
3	0011	8	1000	13	1101
4	0100	9	1001	14	1110
5	0101	10	1010	15	1111

Binary numbers are used in digital computers since an electrical circuit can represent a 0 or a 1 depending on whether it is off or on.

Binomial Theorem One of the most important theorems in algebra, leading to many sorts of *series* (q.v.). It states that the expression $1 + x$ raised to the power of n (i.e. $(1 + x)^n$) can be written in the form $(1 + x)^n = 1 + nx + \dfrac{n(n-1)x^2}{1.2} + \dfrac{n(n-1)(n-2)x^3}{1.2.3} + $ etc.

If n is a positive integer (i.e. a positive whole number) this expansion is valid for any x, and the series ends after $n + 1$ terms. If x is between -1 and 1, the binomial expansion is valid for all n (positive or negative, integer or fraction). In this case the expansion is an infinite series which however adds up to a finite number.

Black hole The term used to describe immensely dense stars with gravitational fields so powerful that no radiation can escape from them.

Bond The method of binding together of atoms to form molecules.

Electrovalent bond

The sodium, less one electron, is positive. The chlorine with an extra electron is negative.

Three types of bond account for most compounds. They are:

(*a*) Electrovalent bond (ionic, polar);

(*b*) Covalent bond (non-polar, homopolar);

(*c*) Dative bond (co-ordinate, semipolar).

The *electrovalent bond* exists in simple compounds where one atom needs an electron and the other gives it. Thus a sodium ion is positively charged when giving an electron and a chlorine ion is negatively charged when it accepts an electron. In solution these ions exist separately, but in the solid the positive binds to the negative to form a *crystal* (q.v.).

The *covalent bond* works differently. It is created by the giving of an electron from each atom in such a way that each shares the pair of electrons thus formed. This accounts for the binding of atoms that are not ionised in solution and atoms that are the same. For example, it is a covalent bond that makes a molecule of hydrogen from two atoms. It is a covalent bond that holds together the two hydrogen atoms and one oxygen atom in a molecule of water.

The *dative bond* also depends on the sharing of a pair of electrons, but in this case one atom supplies both. This bond is that found in many complex compounds in which some of the atoms remain together as a group even when the compound

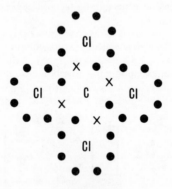

Covalent bond

The seven electrons of chlorine are shown as dots, the four electrons of carbon as x's.

Dative bond

The arrows indicate the giving of electrons by chlorine to aluminium.
These arrowed lines show dative bonds, the ordinary lines covalent bonds.

itself is ionised in solution. For example, potassium ferrocyanide
ionises in water to form positive potassium ions and negative
'ferrocyanide' ions.

Boyle's Law This states that if a fixed mass of gas is compressed
or expanded without change in temperature the product of
volume and pressure remains constant. If P is pressure and V is
volume the law is usually expressed thus:

$$PV = K \text{ (where } K \text{ is a constant)}$$

Calculus The branch of mathematics dealing with the two operations, differentiation and integration.

Calorie The amount of heat required to raise 1 gram of water
through $1°$ C. Now replaced by the *joule* (q.v.) as the unit of
heat energy, though still used to express the energy content of
foodstuffs. 1 calorie = $4·187$ joules.

Catalysis A process in which a chemical reaction is speeded up,
sometimes tremendously, by the presence of an extra substance,
called the catalyst, that is the same chemically at the end of the
reaction as it is at the beginning. Many industrial processes
depend on catalysis. A simple example is the quick combination
of hydrogen and oxygen into water where platinum is present.
It is believed that the catalysis in this case is due to *adsorption*
(q.v.) on the surface of the platinum.

Cation A positively charged atom or *radical* (q.v.).

Cell (a) A source of *electromotive force* (q.v.) caused by chemical
action. A primary cell is one that cannot be recharged once its
electrolyte or electrodes are used up. A simple primary cell
consists of zinc and copper in dilute sulphuric acid. The copper
is the positive electrode and the zinc the negative. This is the
simple voltaic cell. It is of no use for practical work. A dry cell
of the normal type consists of zinc as the negative pole or

electrode, in the form of the container, with a jelly of ammonium chloride as the electrolyte and central carbon rod as the positive pole or electrode. This gives $1 \cdot 5$ V. Many other dry cells have been developed for use in rockets and satellites. A fuel cell is one in which primary fuels or derivatives of them are used. A solar cell is not really chemical. It consists of a special substance that generates electricity when light shines on it. A secondary cell can be recharged. See *Accumulator*. (b) In biology, the cell is the basic structural unit of most living things. Some small organisms such as *bacteria* (q.v.) and the amoeba (a simple animal) consist of only one cell. Higher plants and animals are *multi-cellular*, being composed of many cells fulfilling different functions. A human being consists of approximately 10^{15} cells.

Centripetal force The force acting on a body constrained to move in a curved path. For a body of mass m travelling in a circle of radius r at velocity v the force is $m \cdot v^2/r$ and directed towards the centre of the circle.

Charles's Law The law that determines the effect of heat on a gas when the pressure is kept constant. It states that the volume of a gas (*any* gas) increases by a certain fixed amount ($\frac{1}{273}$ of its volume at $0°$ C) for every degree Centigrade rise in temperature. Another way of stating this is to say that if the pressure is constant, the volume of a fixed mass of any gas is directly proportional to its *absolute temperature* (q.v.).

Coefficient In mathematics this means the number that indicates how many of a thing there are. For example, $2x$ means 2 of the thing called x, and 2 is the coefficient of x. In physics and technology the word coefficient is used to indicate a constant value of importance. For example, the coefficient of linear expansion for a material, the coefficient of friction between two chosen substances, etc.

Colloid A material that does not dissolve in a liquid is usually deposited on the bottom if the particles are big enough. If the particles are small enough, however, they remain in suspension though individually invisible, kept up by the random movements of the molecules of solvent. Particles as small as this are said to be colloidal, and the suspension they form is a colloidal solution. The range of size of colloidal particles is between $0 \cdot 0000001$ and $0 \cdot 00005$ cm (between 1 and 500 nanometres).

Colour The sensation when the eye receives certain wavelengths of light. Ordinary 'white' light consists of electromagnetic radiation of many different wavelengths from about 4,000 angstroms to about 7,000 angstroms. If these are spread out as in a spectrum so that only a portion enters the eye at a time, then as the eye moves along the spectrum from the short-wavelength end to the long-wavelength end colour is seen, going from violet to red through a series usually given as seven, namely, violet, indigo, blue, green, yellow, orange, red. These are the colours of the rainbow. Actually this is a very rough-and-ready description. If tiny separate parts of the spectrum are exposed one at a time hundreds of different hues can be seen.

The colours of everyday objects are caused by selective absorption of parts of the spectrum of white light.

Complex Numbers Algebraic expression such as $x + iy$ where x and y are real, and i is the square root of -1. The real part is x and iy is the imaginary part of the number. In equations involving complex numbers the real and imaginary parts are equated separately, otherwise operations are normal.

Compound A substance that consists of chemical elements bonded together. Examples: the elements sodium and chlorine when combined together chemically make sodium chloride (common salt), a compound.

Conductor An electrical conductor is a material that conducts electricity easily, such as the metals. The best conductor is silver and the next best copper.

Conversion Table

1 cm = 0·3937 in	1 yd = 0·9144018 m
1 m = 39·37 in	1 sq in = 6·451626 sq cm
1 sq cm = 0·1549997 sq in	1 sq yd = 0·8361307 sq m
1 sq m = 1·195985 sq yd	1 acre = 0·404687 hectare
1 hectare = 2·7104 acres	1 cu yd = 0·7645594 cu m
1 cu m = 1·3079428 cu yd	1 gal = 4·5434 litres
1 litre = 0·22009 gal or 0·88036 quarts	1 quart = 1·1358 litres
	1 bushel = 36·37 litres
1 kg = 2·204622341 lbs, Avoirdupois	1 lb, Avoirdupois = 0·4535924277 kg
1 in = 2·54005 cm	

These figures are very exact. Quick, very rough answers can be obtained by the methods below:

To Turn

Metres into feet multiply by $3\frac{1}{4}$

Feet into metres multiply by 3 and divide by 10
Metres into yards add $\frac{1}{10}$
Yards into metres subtract $\frac{1}{10}$
Kilometres into miles multiply by 5 and divide by 8
Miles into kilometres add $\frac{3}{5}$ of the number of miles
Square metres into square yards add $\frac{1}{5}$
Square yards into square metres subtract $\frac{1}{5}$
Square kilometres into square miles multiply by 2 and divide by 5
Square miles into square kilometres multiply by $2\frac{3}{5}$
Cubic metres into cubic yards add $\frac{1}{3}$
Cubic yards into cubic metres subtract $\frac{1}{4}$
Kilogrammes into pounds (Avoirdupois) add $\frac{1}{10}$ and multiply by 2
Pounds into kilogrammes subtract $\frac{1}{10}$ and divide by 2
Litres into pints add $\frac{3}{4}$
Pints into litres multiply by 3 and divide by 5

Cosine In trigonometry the cosine of an angle (other than the right angle) in a right-angled triangle is the ratio of the side next to the angle to the hypotenuse. Cos $90° = 0$, cos $60° = 0.5$, cos $45° = 0.707$, cos $30° = 0.866$. See *trigonometry*.

Cosmic Rays are very energetic charged particles which penetrate the earth's atmosphere from outer space, although their ultimate origin is still uncertain. They consist chiefly of protons with some electrons, alpha-particles and heavier nuclei. Cosmic rays that collide with gas particles in the atmosphere can produce a variety of *elementary particles* (q.v.) which may be detected using equipment carried by balloons, rockets or satellites. Several elementary particles were first discovered in this way.

Cosmology The study of the origin, evolution and structure of the universe, nowadays carried out using satellite-borne X-ray and ultra-violet telescopes as well as earth-bound optical, infra-red and radio telescopes. See *Big Bang Theory*.

Cryogenics The science of producing and maintaining very low temperatures and the study of properties of matter at those temperatures. Modern cryogenics dates from 1908 when helium, the gas with the lowest boiling point at atmospheric pressure ($-269°$ C), was first liquefied. Since then many remarkable effects have been discovered: e.g. *superconductivity* (q.v.).

Crystal A solid composed of a group of atoms or molecules which is repeated in space to form a very regular structure, e.g. common salt, sugar, diamond and ice. Each grain of salt is a small crystal of sodium chloride which is composed of positively charged sodium ions (Na^+) and negatively charged chlorine ions (Cl^-) held together by electrostatic *bonds* (q.v.). The crystal consists of millions of tiny cubes stacked together with the Na$^+$ and Cl$^-$ ions arranged alternately at the corners of each cube. The beautiful hexagonal shapes of snowflakes (which are ice crystals) are due to the very ordered arrangement of the innumerable water molecules (H_2O) in them. However most *metals* (q.v.) are also crystalline even though they do not appear especially regular. Non-crystalline solids (e.g. wood and glass) are called *amorphous* which means without regular structure.

Crystallography The science that investigates the regular structure of *crystals* (q.v.), often by the technique of *X-ray diffraction* (q.v.).

Current Electric current is the rate of flow of electric charge. In a metallic conductor this flow is due to electrons, which drift along between the metal atoms. As electrons are negatively charged, they are going in the opposite direction to the direction of current usually accepted. A current of 1 A is approximately 6 million billion electrons per second.

Decibel See RADIO AND TELEVISION.

Relative densities of common substances

Metals		Liquids at 15°C	
Steel . . .	7·6–7·8	Acetone. . .	0·79
Brass . . .	8·4–8·7	Alcohol . . .	0·79
Aluminium . .	2·70	Ether . . .	0·74
Copper . . .	8·89	Glycerine . .	1·26
Lead . . .	11·34	Oil (lubricating) .	0·9–0·92
Titanium . .	4·5	Turpentine . .	0·87
Mercury . .	13·6	Blood . . .	1·04–1·067
		Water at 4° C .	1·00
Miscellaneous Solids		*Gases at NTP*	
Celluloid . .	1·4	Air . . .	0·00129
Glass . . .	2·4–2·8	Argon . . .	0·00178
Ice. . . .	0·92	Carbon dioxide .	0·00198
Paraffin Wax. .	0·9	Helium . . .	0·000179
Brick . . .	2·1	Hydrogen . .	0·00009
Coal (soft) . .	1·3	Methane . .	0·000717
Diamond . .	3·5	Oxygen . . .	0·00143
Rubber . . .	0·97–0·99		
Balsa wood . .	0·12–0·2		
Ebony . . .	1·19		
Lignum vitae. .	1·25		
Oak . . .	0·74		
Boxwood . .	0·93		
Cork . . .	0·24		

Density The mass per unit volume of a substance. It can be expressed in kilograms/cubic metre, tons/cubic yard, pounds/cubic foot, etc. The density of a substance varies with temperature. Often the *relative density* or *specific gravity* is used. This is the ratio of the density of a substance to that of water at 4° C and is therefore simply a number. The density of water at 4° C is 1,000 kg/m³ or 1 gm/cc. The two densest substances are osmium and iridium.

Deoxyribonucleic acid (DNA) The molecule found in the nucleus of nearly all living cells which carries the genetic code responsible for determining the organism's structure. See *Proteins, DNA*.

Diffraction An important property of light and other *waves* (q.v.). For most everyday purposes light can be assumed to travel in straight lines, although it may undergo *reflection* (q.v.) or *refraction* (q.v.) at the boundary of different media. But because light is a wave motion it can also be spread into secondary waves by objects in its path. This process is known as diffraction and is closely connected with the phenomenon of *interference* (q.v.). Diffraction effects are most marked when the obstacles in the path of the light are roughly of the same size as the wavelength of the light. This is the case in *X-ray diffraction* (q.v.) by *crystals* (q.v.).

Digital computer Any device which performs calculations on numbers represented digitally.

Direct Current (DC) A current passing in the same direction all the time round a circuit. It can vary in size, but not in direction.

Dispersion The name given to the splitting-up of light into the spectrum by a prism or lens.

Dissociation The reversible splitting-up of a chemical compound into parts. *Thermal dissociation* may occur when a compound is heated: e.g. ammonium chloride dissociates into the gases ammonia and hydrogen chloride on heating. *Electrolytic dissociation* into charged ions may occur when a compound is dissolved in water: e.g. hydrogen chloride gas dissolves in water to give hydrochloric acid which is dissociated into positive hydrogen ions and negative chloride ions.

DNA (Deoxyribonucleic acid) A very important biological *polymer* (q.v.) which is the genetic material of most living organisms. It contains four different kinds of chemical units called *bases* or *nucleotides*. These can be joined together in any order to form extremely long chains of many thousands of bases. DNA is usually found in a double helical structure, that is with two chains winding around each other. An important feature of this structure, which was first described by Watson and Crick in 1953, is that the two strands of the double-helix are not identical but *complementary*. This means that the sequence of bases in one strand automatically determines the sequence in the other strand and therefore one strand can be used as a template to reconstruct the other.

In plants and animals, the DNA is packed in structures known as *chromosomes* which are found in the nuclei of *cells* (q.v.). The importance of DNA is that it contains the information required by a cell to make the *proteins* (q.v.) necessary for the cell's proper functioning. This *genetic information* is contained in the particular sequence of bases along the DNA chain according to the *genetic code* (q.v.). Before cells divide, the DNA in them is duplicated so that each of the daughter cells has a copy and can therefore produce its own proteins. In this way the characteristics of living things are transmitted from one generation to the next, a process known as *heredity*. The duplication of DNA depends on the fact (mentioned above) that one strand of the double helix can be used to make the other strand.

Dyne See *Force* and *Newton*.

Electrode The name given to the part by means of which electricity is led into or away from a gas or liquid. The negative electrode is the cathode and the positive one the anode.

Electrolyte A compound which, when molten or dissolved in solution, *dissociates* (q.v.) into oppositely charged *ions* (q.v.) and can thus carry an electric current.

Compounds formed by electrovalent *bonds* (q.v.), such as *salts* (q.v.), are commonly electrolytes. For example, sodium chloride consists of distinct Na^+ and Cl^- ions, but when solid the ions are held rigidly together in a crystal structure which does not conduct electricity. When molten or dissolved in water, the ions are not held together so strongly and are able to move under the influence of an electric potential. Thus an electrolyte can conduct electricity (see *Electrolysis*).

Electrolysis The movement of ions to form an electric current in an electrolyte, usually as the result of an applied electric potential. Negative ions move towards the anode and positive ions towards the cathode. As a result, gases may be liberated or metal deposited. When metal is deposited on the cathode the process is called electroplating.

Electron Elementary particle with small mass and unit negative electric charge. Electrons orbit the nucleus of an atom much as the planets orbit the sun.

Electromagnetic Waves Waves that consist of varying electrical and magnetic quantities travelling along at the speed of light. Light, radio waves, X-rays, gamma rays, are all electromagnetic radiation. (See RADIO AND TELEVISION.)

Electromotive Force (e.m.f.) The electrical pressure developed by a cell, battery or generator which enables them to produce an electric current in a circuit. Measured in volts.

The elements

Atomic number	Name	Symbol	Atomic weight	Relative densities (gases at NTP)
1	Hydrogen	H	1·008	0·0000899
2	Helium	He	4·003	0·0001785
3	Lithium	Li	6·939	0·534
4	Beryllium	Be	9·012	1·85
5	Boron	B	10·811	2·34
6	Carbon	C	12·011	Diamond 3·52 / Graphite 2·25 / Amorphous 0·5–1·0
7	Nitrogen	N	14·007	0·0012506
8	Oxygen	O	15·999	0·0014290
9	Fluorine	F	18·998	0·0016970
10	Neon	Ne	20·183	0·008999
11	Sodium	Na	22·990	0·97
12	Magnesium	Mg	24·312	1·75
13	Aluminium	Al	26·982	2·70
14	Silicon	Si	28·086	2·33
15	Phosphorus	P	30·974	Yellow 1·82 / Red 2·20
16	Sulphur	S	32·064	Monoclinic 1·96 / Rhombic 2·07
17	Chlorine	Cl	35·453	0·00321
18	Argon	Ar	39·948	0·0017837
19	Potassium	K	39·102	0·862
20	Calcium	Ca	40·08	1·55

Atomic number	Name	Symbol	Atomic weight	Relative densities (gases at NTP)
21	Scandium	Sc	44·956	3·0
22	Titanium	Ti	47·90	4·54
23	Vanadium	V	50·94	6·11
24	Chromium	Cr	52·00	7·18
25	Manganese	Mn	54·94	7·21
26	Iron	Fe	55·85	7·87
27	Cobalt	Co	58·93	8·9
28	Nickel	Ni	58·71	8·9
29	Copper	Cu	63·54	8·95
30	Zinc	Zn	65·37	7·14
31	Gallium	Ga	69·72	5·90
32	Germanium	Ge	72·59	5·32
33	Arsenic	As	74·92	5·73
34	Selenium	Se	78·96	{ Red 4·45 Grey 4·80
35	Bromine	Br	79·909	3·12
36	Krypton	Kr	83·80	0·003733
37	Rubidium	Rb	85·47	1·53
38	Strontium	Sr	87·62	2·55
39	Yttrium	Y	88·905	4·46
40	Zirconium	Zr	91·22	6·5
41	Niobium	Nb	92·906	8·57
42	Molybdenum	Mo	95·94	10·2
43	Technetium	Tc	99	—
44	Ruthenium	Ru	101·07	12·2
45	Rhodium	Rh	102·91	12·4
46	Palladium	Pd	106·4	12·0
47	Silver	Ag	107·87	10·5
48	Cadmium	Cd	112·40	8·65
49	Indium	In	114·82	7·31
50	Tin	Sn	118·69	7·31
51	Antimony	Sb	121·75	6·69
52	Tellurium	Te	127·60	6·25
53	Iodine	I	126·904	4·94
54	Xenon	Xe	131·30	0·005887
55	Caesium	Cs	132·905	1·90
56	Barium	Ba	137·34	3·5
57	Lanthanum	La	138·91	6·15
58	Cerium	Ce	140·12	6·77
59	Praseodymium	Pr	140·907	6·77
60	Neodymium	Nd	144·24	7·00
61	Prometheum	Pm	147	—

Atomic number	Name	Symbol	Atomic weight	Relative densities (gases at NTP)
62	Samarium	Sm	150·35	7·54
63	Europium	Eu	151·96	5·25
64	Gadolinium	Gd	157·25	7·90
65	Terbium	Tb	158·92	8·23
66	Dysprosium	Dy	162·50	8·54
67	Holmium	Ho	164·93	8·78
68	Erbium	Er	167·26	9·05
69	Thulium	Tm	168·93	9·31
70	Ytterbium	Yb	173·04	6·97
71	Lutecium	Lu	174·97	9·84
72	Hafnium	Hf	178·49	13·3
73	Tantalum	Ta	180·95	16·6
74	Wolfram	W	183·85	19·3
75	Rhenium	Re	186·2	21·0
76	Osmium	Os	190·2	22·5
77	Iridium	Ir	192·2	22·4
78	Platinum	Pt	195·09	21·4
79	Gold	Au	196·97	19·3
80	Mercury	Hg	200·59	13·55
81	Thallium	Tl	204·37	11·85
82	Lead	Pb	207·19	11·34
83	Bismuth	Bi	208·98	9·75
84	Polonium	Po	210	9·32
85	Astatine	At	211	—
86	Radon	Rn	222	0·009725
87	Francium	Fr	223	—
88	Radium	Ra	226·05	5·0
89	Actinium	Ac	227·05	—
90	Thorium	Th	232·15	11·7
91	Protactinium	Pa	231·05	15·37
92	Uranium	U	238·07	18·95
93*	Neptunium	Np	237	20·25
94*	Plutonium	Pu	239	19·84
95*	Americium	Am	241	13·67
96*	Curium	Cm	242	—
97*	Berkelium	Bk	243–250	—
98*	Californium	Cf	251	—
99*	Einsteinium	Es	246, 247, 249, 251–256	—
100*	Fermium	Fm	250, 252–256	—
101*	Mendelevium	Md	256	—

Atomic number	Name	Symbol	Atomic weight	Relative densities (*gases at NTP*)
102*	Nobelium	No	254	—
103*	Lawrencium	Lr	257	—
104*	Kurchatovium(?)	Ku	—	—
105*	Hahnium(?)	—	—	—

*These are called transuranic elements. They have all been artificially created, often in negligibly small amounts, by means of nuclear reactors or machines such as cyclotrons.

Elements The chemical units of which compounds are made. There are 92 naturally occurring chemical elements, though some have never been prepared, and a number have been made artificially (transuranic elements) to extend the list to 103 or more.

Elementary Particle Electrons, protons and neutrons are the familiar elementary particles that make up atoms and nuclei. However, many other particles smaller than atoms are now known to exist, though high energy *particle accelerators* (q.v.) are usually needed to create them. Many of these fundamental or elementary particles are very short-lived and decay into more stable particles or gamma rays in a minute fraction of a second. Examples of these elementary particles are the *neutrino* (a particle with no mass and no charge), the *π-mesons* (which help to explain how the protons and neutrons in a nucleus stay together) and heavier particles like the Σ (*sigma*) and the Ω− (*omega minus*). The list of elementary particles keeps growing as accelerators of higher and higher energy are built. Recent discoveries have been the psi (1974) and upsilon (1977) particles.

Philosophers and scientists have always wondered what are the fundamental building blocks of matter. Now it is believed that all the elementary particles so far discovered fall into two classes called *leptons* (q.v.) and *hadrons* (q.v.). Leptons (e.g. the electron and neutrino) behave as if they are pointlike and indivisible. Hadrons (of which there are well over a hundred e.g. proton, neutron, mesons, Σ, psi) however are thought to be made up of a small number of yet more fundamental particles called *quarks* (q.v.).

Energy The capacity of a body or substance for doing work. It can exist in a number of forms, e.g. mechanical, potential, heat, chemical, electrical, radiant and nuclear energy. The law of conservation of energy states that energy is never lost or gained but only changes from one form to another.

In driving a car to the top of a hill, work is done against the force of gravity and the car gains *potential* energy. This is converted into *kinetic* energy of motion as the car freewheels down the hill. Friction at the moving parts causes wastage of energy as *heat* energy and the car would slow down without the engine which converts *chemical* energy stored in the petrol into kinetic energy.

Einstein showed that matter is a form of energy. In nuclear fission and fusion, matter is converted into energy according to the formula $E = m.c^2$ (m = mass, c = speed of light). This is the origin of the energy released in nuclear bombs and in the sun. The sun's energy reaches the earth in the form of *radiant* energy (heat and light rays).

All forms of energy are now measured in *joules* (q.v.). Calories were formally used to measure heat energy. The c.g.s. unit of energy is the *erg* $= 10^{-7}$ joules.

Useful formulae:

Kinetic energy $= m.v^2/2$ (m = mass of body, v = velocity of body).

Change in potential energy $= m.g.h$ (m = mass, g = gravitational acceleration, h = change in vertical height).

Electrical energy $= V.I.t$ (V = voltage, I = current, t = time).

Change in heat content $= m.s.(T_2 - T_1)$ (m = mass, s = specific heat, T_2 = final temperature, T_1 = initial temperature).

Enzyme A *catalyst* (q.v.) made by living organisms for the speeding up of biochemical reactions. Enzymes are generally *proteins* (q.v.).

Equivalent Weight The equivalent weight of an element is the number of units by weight of it that will combine with, or displace, 1 unit of hydrogen or 8 units of oxygen. It is therefore equal to the atomic weight divided by the valency. The equivalent weight of an acid is the weight of acid containing unit weight of replaceable hydrogen (see *Acid*), and that of a base is the weight of base required to neutralise the equivalent weight of an acid.

Erg See *Energy*.

Expansion Most substances expand on being heated, and each has its own capacity for such expansion. The coefficient of linear expansion is the figure that is used for finding how much a substance expands in one direction

$$l_2 = l_1 (1 + \alpha t)$$

Where l_1 is the length at the first temperature, t is the rise in temperature in degrees Centigrade, α is the coefficient of linear expansion and l_2 is the length at the second temperature.

A similar relationship exists for volume expansion. If $V_1 =$ volume at first temperature, $t =$ rise in temperature in degrees Centigrade, β is the coefficient of cubical expansion and $V_2 =$ the volume at the second temperature

$$V_2 = V_1 (1 + \beta t)$$

For solids $\beta = 3\alpha$ approximately.

Factorial The factorial of a positive whole number n is the product $n \times (n - 1) \times (n - 2) \times \ldots \times 2 \times 1$ and is written n!. E.g. $4! = 4 \times 3 \times 2 \times 1 = 24$.

Fission The splitting of a thing into two more or less equal parts. In nuclear fission, the nucleus of an atom splits into two parts accompanied by the release of nuclear energy and one or more neutrons. Fission may occur spontaneously or by the nucleus being hit by a neutron, but only occurs readily in certain *fissile* materials such as uranium 235 and plutonium 239. It is possible that the neutrons released during fission can hit other nuclei and bring about further fission. This process can be repeated and result in a runaway *chain reaction* with an enormous build-up of energy. However, a chain reaction can only occur if the amount of fissile material is above a *critical size*, so that the number of neutrons continues to rise despite some escaping and some hitting nuclei without causing fission. Atomic bomb explosions are uncontrolled chain reactions of this kind. But nuclear fission can be controlled in *nuclear reactors* (q.v.) and used as a source of energy.

Fluorescence The property of some substances to absorb light of one wavelength and emit light of a longer wavelength: e.g. fluorescein, an organ compound whose solution in alkalis glows bright green due to fluorescence. In fluorescent lighting tubes, the electric current causes mercury vapour to emit ultra-violet light, which then excites fluorescent substances on the sides of the tube to emit visible light. Unlike *phosphorescence* (q.v.), fluorescence stops as soon as the original illumination stops.

Force That which makes a body change its state of rest of uniform motion in a straight line. Units are the newton (S.I. system), the dyne (c.g.s. system) and the poundal (f.p.s. system). Force (p), mass (m) and acceleration (f) are related by the equation $p = mf$ (Newton's second law of motion).

Formulae (not dealt with under separate entries, see *Area, Volume, Binomial Theorem*, etc.).

Circumference of circle $= 2\pi r$ (or πd).

Mechanics

Falling bodies

Where g = gravity = 9·8 (in m per sec per sec); u = initial velocity (in m per sec); v = final velocity (in m per sec); h = height (in m); t = time (in sec).

$$v = u + gt$$
$$h = \frac{u + v}{2}t$$
$$h = ut + \tfrac{1}{2}gt^2$$
$$g = \frac{v - u}{t}$$
$$2\,gh = v^2 - u^2$$

Time of swing of pendulum: $t = 2\pi\sqrt{\dfrac{l}{g}}$ where t = time of complete swing (once in each direction) (in sec); l = length of pendulum (in m); g = gravity.

Useful Factors

$(a + b)^2 = a^2 + 2ab + b^2$
$(a - b)^2 = a^2 - 2ab + b^2$
$a^2 - b^2 = (a + b)(a - b)$
$a^3 + b^3 = (a + b)(a^2 - ab + b^2)$
$a^3 - b^3 = (a - b)(a^2 + ab + b^2)$
$x^4 + x^2y^2 + y^4 = (x^2 + xy + y^2)(x^2 - xy + y^2)$
$a^3 + b^3 + c^3 - 3abc =$
$$(a + b + c)(a^2 + b^2 + c^2 - ab - bc - ca)$$
$a^2(b - c) + b^2(c - a) + c^2(a - b) =$
$$-(a - b)(b - c)(c - a)$$

$$bc(b - c) + ca(c - a) + ab(a - b) =$$
$$-(a - b)(b - c)(c - a)$$
$$a(b^2 - c^2) + b(c^2 - a^2) + c(a^2 - b^2) =$$
$$(a - b)(b - c)(c - a)$$

Quadratic Equation
$$ax^2 + bx + c = 0. \text{ Solution:}$$
$$\frac{-b \pm \sqrt{b^2 - 4ac}}{2a}$$

Geometrical Progression
pth term $= ar^{p-1}$

Sum to n terms $= a\dfrac{r^n - 1}{r - 1}$ or $a\dfrac{1 - r^n}{1 - r}$

Sum to infinity when $-1 < r < 1 = \dfrac{a}{1 - r}$

Arithmetical Progression
Last term $= a + (n - 1)d$

Sum to n terms $= \dfrac{n}{2}[2a + (n - 1)d]$

Friction The force that resists the movement of one surface over another. It results from the fusing together of high points of contact between the surfaces. To overcome the fusion, force must be used. If F is the frictional force resisting the motion of one body over another and N is the normal force acting between the two bodies, then the coefficient of friction (μ) is given by F/N. Frictional forces always act to slow down a moving body by causing kinetic energy to be dissipated as heat. In many machines this is undesirable as it represents a waste of useful energy and also the heat produced may damage the surfaces in contact. To reduce friction between moving parts, lubricants are used as well as ball- and roller-bearings. Friction can however be extremely useful as in belt drives and brakes. The study of surfaces in contact and lubrication is known as *tribology*.

Fusion (i) The melting of a solid substance (used, for instance, in the term 'latent heat of fusion').

(ii) *Nuclear fusion* is the joining together of the nuclei of two atoms to form a single heavier nucleus. Fusion occurs most readily between nuclei of the lighter elements (e.g. the isotopes of hydrogen—deuterium and tritium) but still requires exceedingly high temperatures (hundreds of millions of degrees) before it can proceed. Fusion reactions are accompanied by a vast release of energy and this is thought to be the source of the energy of the sun and other stars. On earth, uncontrolled fusion reactions occur in hydrogen bombs, but there is much current interest in the problem of controlling nuclear fusion and using it as a source of energy.

Gamma Radiation (Gamma Rays, γ-Rays) Radiation of the same nature as X-rays and light, i.e. electromagnetic radiation, but of much shorter wavelengths. It is emitted by some radioactive substances, e.g. cobalt 60, and is the most penetrating of all radiation.

Gas Laws The combination of *Boyle's Law* (q.v.) and *Charles's Law* (q.v.) into one equation:

$$PV = nRT$$

where P = pressure; V = volume; T = absolute temperature; R = gas constant = $8·314$ joules per degree per mole; n = no. of *moles* (q.v.).

Gene Originally understood to mean a unit of genetic information that gives to the organism carrying it a certain physical characteristic (e.g. blond hair or blue eyes) which can be transmitted from generation to generation.

Today, the gene is understood on the molecular level to be a length of *DNA* (q.v.) coding for one or more *proteins* (q.v.) according to the *genetic code* (q.v.).

Genetic code The code by means of which a particular sequence of bases in a *DNA molecule* (q.v.) is translated into a corresponding sequence of *amino-acids* (q.v.) in a *protein* (q.v.).

The code works by assigning to each possible group of three DNA bases (triplet) a particular amino-acid. Thus a protein chain of, say, 100 amino-acids in length is coded for by a DNA chain of 300 bases in length. From the four different kinds of DNA bases (called A, T, C and G for short) it is possible to make 64 different triplets e.g. AAA, AAT, AGC, CGA ... As there are only 20 different amino-acids found in proteins, some amino-acids are coded for by more than one triplet e.g. the amino-acid glycine is coded for by the four triplets GGG, GGA, GGT and GGC.

The genetic code is found to be the same for all living organisms, a strong argument for the common origin of all life forms.

Genetic engineering The artificial manipulation of the genetic material of an organism by deletion, insertion or modification of *genes* (q.v.). A typical application is the insertion of the gene for a particular *protein* (q.v.) from one organism into the *DNA* (q.v.) of another organism, often a *bacterium* (q.v.) or yeast, which then becomes capable of making the protein. Such a process is possible because naturally occurring *restriction enzymes* are available to cut DNA at very specific places, thus enabling individual genes to be isolated. Other *enzymes* (q.v.) are used to join the isolated gene into carrier molecules of DNA (called *vectors*), which can then be incorporated in the organism to be modified. Then by ordinary cell division it is possible to grow colonies of modified organisms each carrying the extra gene, a process known as *cloning*. In this way bacteria have been engineered to produce for example human insulin and human growth hormone.

The techniques of genetic engineering (sometimes called *recombinant DNA*) are extremely powerful tools in fundamental research in *molecular biology* (q.v.) and in understanding the origin of diseases. The enormous potential opened up by genetic engineering is also the basis for the current interest in *biotechnology*. Not only can naturally occurring proteins useful in medicine and industry be produced in large amounts, but in the future it will be possible to design and make new proteins with desired functions. Similarly, organisms can be engineered to have desired properties: e.g. bacteria can be made to break down oil slicks; or the genes present in certain bacteria in the roots of plants such as clover, which enable them to use atmospheric nitrogen, can be transferred to bacteria found associated with the roots of wheat, say, thus eliminating the need for nitrogen fertilisers.

Glass A hard, brittle, usually transparent material. Most everyday glass is made by fusing together sand, limestone and soda ash (sodium carbonate) and has composition 70% silica (SiO_2), 15% sodium oxide (Na_2O), 10% calcium oxide (CaO) and 5% other metal oxides. Pyrex is a particularly heat and shock-resistant glass in which some of the silica has been replaced by boron oxide (B_2O_3). Solid glass is formed by cooling molten glass in such a way that it does not have time to form *crystals* (q.v.). It therefore has an amorphous (disordered) structure.

Glass was in use in Ancient Egypt, but is continually being

found in new applications: e.g. very fine glass fibres carrying beams of light are being used to transmit information such as telephone messages, computer data and television programmes.

Gram–Atom The weight in grams equivalent to the *atomic weight* (q.v.). For example, the atomic weight of oxygen is 16, so a gram–atom of oxygen is 16 grams.

Gram-equivalent The weight in grams of a substance equal to the *equivalent weight* (q.v.).

Gram-molecule The weight in grams equal to the molecular weight of an element or compound. For example, the molecular weight of H_2SO_4 is 98, so a gram-molecule of H_2SO_4 is 98 gm.

Gravity Every object attracts every other object with a force directly proportional to the product of the masses of the objects and inversely as the square of the distance between them. If m_1 is the mass of one object, m_2 the mass of the other, d the distance between them, then the gravitational force $F = \dfrac{Gm_1m_2}{d^2}$, where G is a constant. G = $6 \cdot 67 \times 10^{-11}$ Nm^2kg^{-2}.

For objects on or near the earth, the mass of the earth is very much greater than an object, and so the gravitational force between them makes the object 'fall' towards the earth. The acceleration as it does this is called the acceleration due to gravity. At the earth's surface this is $9 \cdot 8$ m per sec per sec in the SI system and 32 ft per sec per sec in the f.p.s. system.

Hadron Elementary particles which are subject to the strong nuclear force. Hadrons are much more numerous than *leptons* (q.v.) and include stable particles like the proton and neutron as well as the mesons and the most recently discovered (and extremely unstable) psi and upsilon particles. Hadrons are believed to be composed of more fundamental particles called *quarks* (q.v.).

Half-life The time for half the nuclei in a sample of radioactive material to decay. This ranges from a fraction of a second for some man-made radioisotopes to 4,510 million years for Uranium 238. (See *Isotope.*)

Heat Energy possessed by a substance in the form of random motions of the atoms which make up the substance. In a red-hot piece of iron the atoms are vibrating back and forth very fast, and so the iron contains more heat than when it is cold and the atoms are moving much less fast. However, heat must not be confused with *temperature* (q.v.). The adding of heat to a substance usually causes a rise in temperature but the amount of this rise depends on the mass and *specific heat* (q.v.) of the substance. Adding heat to a substance may cause a *change of state* (e.g. a solid melting to a liquid) without a change in temperature (see *Latent heat*). Measured in *joules* (q.v.).

Heavy water Water in which the hydrogen is replaced by the *isotope* (q.v.) deuterium and hence written as D_2O rather than H_2O. The nucleus of ordinary hydrogen is simply one proton, while that of deuterium is one proton and one neutron.

Hologram A photograph taken with the light from a laser which, when even a small part of it is illumined by laser light, re-constitutes the entire picture. The discovery of Professor Denis Gabor of Imperial College, London, for which he was awarded the 1971 Nobel prize for physics.

Indicator A substance added in small quantities to a chemical reaction which shows when the reaction is complete by a sudden change of colour. The most familiar indicators change colour depending on whether a solution is acidic or alkaline: e.g. litmus is red in acids but blue in alkalis, and phenolph-thalein is colourless in acids but purple in alkalis.

Infra-red Light *Electromagnetic waves* (q.v.) with wavelengths longer than those of visible light and in the range 7,500–100,000 angstroms, or 0·75–10 micrometres. Infra-red radiation is invisible to the eye but has a heating effect and can be detected at great distances by modern crystal detectors. Every warm body emits infra-red radiation.

Insulator A material, such as glass, rubber, porcelain, plastics, that has no free electrons, and so will not allow electric current to pass when an e.m.f. is applied.

Interference When *waves* (q.v.) from different sources superimpose they can either reinforce each other (*interfere constructively*) or cancel each other out (*interfere destructively*). In the case of light this can give rise to characteristic dark and light bands called an *interference pattern*.

Interferometer A device in which the phenomenon of *interference* (q.v.) of light or radio waves is used as a tool, e.g. in spectro-scopy and astronomy.

Ion An atom or group of atoms that is electrically charged due to an excess or deficiency of electrons. Negatively charged ions are called *anions*; positive ions are called *cations*.

Ionisation The process by which mobile *ions* (q.v.) are produced from atoms and molecules. This can occur when *electrolytes* (q.v.) become molten or dissolve to form solutions, or when gases are subjected to electrical discharges and become *plasmas* (q.v.).

Familiar radioisotopes		
Name	*Type of radiation*	*Half-life*
Carbon 14	beta	5,600 years
Phosphorus 32	beta	14·3 days
Cobalt 60	beta, gamma	5·3 years
Strontium 90	beta	28 years
Iodine 131	beta, gamma	8 days
Caesium 137	beta, gamma	30 years
Radium 226	alpha, gamma	1,620 years
Uranium 235	alpha	710 million years
Uranium 238	alpha	4,510 million years
Plutonium 239	alpha	24,400 years

Isotope One of two or more forms of the same chemical element, differing from other isotopes only in atomic weight. The difference is due entirely to the addition or subtraction of neutrons from the nucleus. Examples: The hydrogen atom has one proton and one planetary electron. Add a neutron to the nucleus and it becomes twice as heavy. It is heavy hydrogen or deuterium. Add another neutron and it becomes tritium, three times as heavy as the normal hydrogen. All three isotopes are hydrogen so far as the chemistry is concerned. Many elements have several stable isotopes (tin has ten). It is customary to give the mass number of an isotope after the name in order to indicate which isotope is present, e.g. uranium 238, uranium 235, plutonium 239, etc.

Every element can be made to have radioactive isotopes, called *radioisotopes*. Many of these are used in science and industry because they emit radition (alpha, beta or gamma). A few elements have naturally occurring radioisotopes. Tritium is a radioisotope of hydrogen. See *Half-life*.

Joule The SI unit of energy or work. It is the work done when 1 newton acts through 1 metre. Replaces the calorie as the unit of heat energy. 1 joule = 0·239 calories.

Laser A device for producing an intense, narrow beam of light, in which all the waves are in step. The atoms of some gases, if electrically excited, can be persuaded by a 'trigger' pulse of light of a certain wavelength to emit more light of the same wavelength. If such a gas is put into a tube with accurately parallel mirrors at each end, and triggered, the light waves will run up and down, getting stronger as they pass over and re-trigger the atoms of the gas. If some of the light is allowed to escape at one end it emerges in such a narrow beam that a laser can shine a spot only a mile or so across on the moon, and so intense it can burn through steel. An even more interesting possibility is the use of the laser in communications. Since a beam of light has an enormously higher frequency than the shortest radio wave, and since the amount of information a beam can carry is proportional to its frequency, a light beam, if it can be *modulated* (See RADIO AND TELEVISION: modulation), should be able to carry as many as a thousand television channels. (See AIRCRAFT, ROCKETS AND MISSILES: Satellites, Communications.)

Latent heat The latent heat of fusion (vaporisation) is the amount of heat required to turn unit mass of a solid (liquid) into liquid (gas) at the same temperature. The latent heat of fusion of ice is 335 joules per gram; the latent heat of vaporisation of water is 2,257 joules per gram.

Lens A piece of transparent material, usually glass, shaped and polished to have curved surfaces. The commonest are a double-convex lens and a double-concave lens. Every combination of two of the following surfaces is possible: convex, concave, plane.

A single lens like this is known as a thin lens, and simplified

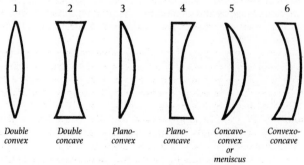

| 1 | 2 | 3 | 4 | 5 | 6 |

Double convex | Double concave | Plano-convex | Plano-concave | Concavo-convex or meniscus | Convexo-concave

1, 3 and 5 are convergent; 2, 4 and 6 are divergent

approximate formulae can be used. The principal focus is then the point where parallel rays parallel to the axis come to a point. The distance from the centre of the lens to the point image is called the focal length.

Lenses are of two sorts whatever their surfaces. One sort makes rays of light *converge* when they pass through the lens; the other sort makes rays of light *diverge*.

The focal length of a convergent lens can be found very simply by getting an image of a distant object and the distance from lens to image is then the focal length.

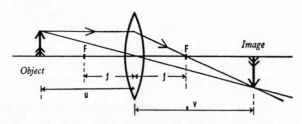

Convergent Lens Formula

The equation of a simple lens, where u = distance of object from centre of lens, v = distance of image from centre, f = focal length, and distances are considered positive when measured *against* the direction the light is travelling, is:

$$\frac{1}{v} - \frac{1}{u} = \frac{1}{f}$$

All measurements are positive when taken from lens to a *real* image or object.

Lepton/Elementary particle (q.v.), distinguished from the generally heavier *hadrons* (q.v.) in not being subject to the strong nuclear force. Only six leptons (and their corresponding anti-particles— see *anti-matter*) have been discovered: the electron, the muon and the tau (in 1975) and their respective neutrinos.

Light Radiation that affects our eyes and we 'see'. It is electromagnetic, and the wavelengths of visible light extend from about 4,000 angstroms (blue) to about 7,000 angstroms (red). It is customary to speak of all electromagnetic radiation of near wavelengths to these as 'light', even though it causes no sensation on the eye.

Magnifying Power The magnifying power of a single convex used with the eye as a magnifying glass equals 1 plus $\frac{25}{f}$, where f equals focal length in centimetres.

The magnifying power of an astronomical telescope or a Galileo-type telescope is the focal length of the objective divided by the focal length of the eyepiece.

Mass The mass of a body is proportional to the amount of matter in it. It is *not* the same as *weight* (q.v.), because $W = M.g$ where g = acceleration due to gravity.

Mathematical signs

Is equal to	$=$	Is approximately equal to	$\doteqdot$
Is not equal to	$\neq$	Is identical to	$\equiv$
The difference between	$\sim$	The sum of	Σ
Greater than	$>$	Varies as	$\propto$
Not greater than	$\not>$	Angle	$\wedge$
Less than	$<$	Infinity	∞
Not less than	$\not<$		

Metals As commonly understood, metals are the substances that are good conductors of heat and electricity, are lustrous when polished and so on. In chemistry, however, a metal is characterised as having a tendency towards losing electrons and thus becoming positively charged. This definition means that only a very few of the elements are not metals. See Periodic Table on pages D38–D39.

Microscope A device for getting a magnified image of very small objects. A single magnifying glass is therefore a simple microscope.

A compound microscope consists of two lenses, one of short focal length, the objective, one of long focal length, the eyepiece. The object is placed in the plane of the principal focus.

The magnifying power is found by multiplying the power of the objective by that of the eyepiece. The power of the objective is the *optical tube length* divided by the focal length of the objective. The optical tube length is taken for modern microscopes as being 18 cm. So if, for example, the focal length of an objective is $0 \cdot 5$ cm, then the magnifying power is 36. An

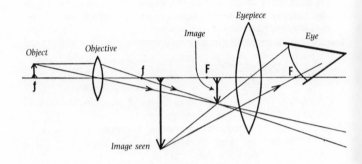

Geometrical Diagram of Microscope

eyepiece with a magnification of 3 will then give a total magnification of 108.

The eyepiece and objective are complex lenses, not simple ones, in order to correct for the various errors that a simple lens inflicts on the image, errors that become more and more important as the magnification is increased.

Microscope, Electron A microscope which substitutes beams of electrons for beams of light to form a very greatly magnified image of an object. With the electron microscope, objects as small as individual molecules can be distinguished.

Mole The amount of substance that contains as many elementary units as there are in 0·012 kg of carbon 12. The number of such units is *Avogadro's number* $= 6·023 \times 10^{23}$.

Molecular biology The study of how living things work at the level of their component molecules: e.g. *proteins* (q.v.) and *nucleic acids* (q.v.).

Molecule The smallest unit of a chemical compound to retain its identity. If split up, the results are the atoms of elements of which it is compounded. A single element can exist in molecular form. For example, hydrogen can be atomic or molecular. In the latter case two atoms of hydrogen are combined into a molecule.

Momentum The product of a body's mass and velocity.

Neutron One of the fundamental particles of nature. Its mass is slightly greater than that of a proton, but the neutron carries no electrical charge. Because of this it is not acted on by the electrical forces in an atom, and so can penetrate more easily. A neutron is therefore a good nuclear projectile. It is the causing agent in nuclear *fission* (q.v.). Neutrons are produced in immense numbers in a *nuclear reactor* (q.v.).

Newton (N) The SI unit of force. It is the force that would give a mass of 1 kg an acceleration of 1 metre per second per second. The force of gravity on a mass of 1 kg is $9 \cdot 8$ N. Replaces the dyne as the unit of force. 1 N $= 10^5$ dynes.

Normal Solution A solution of which 1 litre (1,000 cc) contains one *gram-equivalent* (q.v.) of a substance. Indicated by N, e.g. N-hydrochloric acid means normal hydrochloric acid solution in water. Used for quantitative analysis. A more dilute solution is one-tenth normal, shown by $N/10$.

Normal Temperature and Pressure (NTP) Normal temperature is taken as $0°$ C, normal pressure as 76 cm of mercury. These together give a standard set of conditions for comparing the behaviour of gases.

Nuclear Reactor An apparatus in which a nuclear fuel undergoes *fission* (q.v.) under controlled conditions. The essential parts of a nuclear reactor are: (a) the fuel, which is usually in the form of rods and may be plutonium, natural uranium or enriched uranium (uranium in which the proportion of fissile U-235 to non-fissile U-238 has been made higher than in natural uranium), (b) the *moderator*, which is placed between the fuel rods with the purpose of slowing down the fast neutrons produced during fission so that they produce further fission more readily (moderators commonly used are graphite or *heavy water* (q.v.)), (c) *control rods* (often of cadmium) which absorb neutrons and slow down the rate of fission thus preventing a runaway chain reaction, (d) the *coolant*, which is a fluid (such as carbon dioxide gas or liquid sodium) that is pumped in pipes through the reactor core to remove the vast quantities of heat generated during fission (this heat may be used to generate electricity), (e) a very thick shield of concrete, steel and water to prevent dangerous radiation from escaping from the core. The *fast breeder reactor* is a reactor which 'breeds' more nuclear fuel at the same time as producing energy by fission. This is possible because a fast neutron produced by fission can be absorbed by a non-fissile U-238 nucleus giving a U-239 nucleus which then decays radioactively into fissile plutonium. The reactor at Dounreay, Scotland is of this type. Nuclear reactors will be a very important source of electricity in the future but an outstanding problem is what to do with the dangerous radioactive waste products.

Nucleus Means the centre part of anything. Used chiefly to mean the heavy centre part of an atom. Every atomic nucleus consists of protons and neutrons, with the exception of ordinary hydrogen, the nucleus of which is one proton. Examples: oxygen, 8 protons 8 neutrons; iron, 26 protons 30 neutrons; radium, 88 protons 138 neutrons.

Nucleic Acid Very important biological *polymers* (q.v.) found in all living organisms. There are two major types of nucleic acid: *DNA* (*deoxyribonucleic acid*) and *RNA* (*ribonucleic acid*) (q.v.).

Ohm (Ω) The SI unit of electrical resistance. It is defined by means of *Ohm's Law* (q.v.) i.e. if a conductor carries a current of I amps when the potential difference across it is V volts, then the resistance of the conductor is V/I ohms.

Ohm's Law This states that the current through a conductor is directly proportional to the potential difference across the conductor and inversely proportional to its resistance. Discovered by the German physicist, Georg Ohm, in 1827. See DICTIONARY OF RADIO AND TELEVISION.

Ozone (O_3) is a form of oxygen whose molecules consist of three atoms of oxygen instead of the usual two. It can be obtained by passing an electrical discharge through ordinary oxygen. Ozone occurs in large quantities in the ozone layer of the upper atmosphere, between heights of about 15 and 40 kilometres above the earth. Here it plays a vital role in absorbing a large proportion of the sun's *ultra-violet radiation* (q.v.) which would otherwise be damaging to life on the earth's surface.

Particle Accelerator A machine which accelerates *elementary particles* (q.v.) near to the speed of light by means of electric and magnetic fields. The resulting beams of high energy particles are allowed to hit stationary atomic targets or to meet other beams of particles head on. By observing the products of such collisions, much is learnt about elementary particles and the atomic nucleus.

Periodic Table A table grouping the elements so that certain chemical and physical properties are repeated at regular intervals. It is arranged in horizontal *periods* and vertical *groups*. Elements in one group have similar physical and chemical properties, e.g. fluorine, chlorine, bromine, iodine, all in sub-group *b* of group VII and called the *halogens*. See pages D38 to D39.

Phosphorescence Light emitted by some substances without heating, some as the result of irradiation with ultra-violet light or other light, some as the result of chemical action, e.g. phosphorescent organisms in sea-water and creatures like fireflies and glow-worms. See *Fluorescence*.

Plasma A highly-ionised gas i.e. a gas consisting of charged particles, usually electrons and positive ions. It is the state of matter in which most of the universe exists. In extremely high temperature plasmas (as in the interiors of stars) nuclear *fusion* (q.v.) can occur. Plasma physics is therefore of great importance in the attempt to use controlled nuclear fusion as a source of energy.

Platonic solids The cube is the most familiar of the five Platonic solids, having six faces, each of which is an identical square. There are only four other solid figures of such regularity, i.e. having all their faces as identical regular *polygons* (q.v.). They are the tetrahedron (4 equilateral triangular faces), the octahedron (8 equilateral triangular faces), the dodecahedron (12 regular pentagonal, i.e. 5-sided faces) and the icosahedron (20 equilateral triangular faces).

Polygon In geometry, a plane figure of many sides. A triangle is a 3-sided polygon, a quadrilateral is a 4-sided polygon, a pentagon 5-sided, a hexagon 6-sided, etc. A *regular polygon* has all of its sides the same length: e.g. a square is a regular quadrilateral.

Polymer A compound consisting of a chain of repeated molecular units. It is formed from the individual *monomer* units by the process of polymerisation. Natural polymers include rubber and *proteins* (q.v.), while synthetic polymers include many plastics (e.g. polythene) and artificial fibres (e.g. nylon).

Power The rate of doing work or using energy. The SI unit is the *watt*, equal to 1 joule per second. In electrical circuits the power in watts is found by multiplying the volts by the amperes. The horse-power was formally used in mechanics. 1 horse-power = 746 watts.

Group →	IA	IIA	IIIB	IVB	VB	VIB	VIIB	←
Period ↓	Alkali metals	Alka-line earth metals	←————Transition metals—————					
1	1 • H* 1.008							
2	3 Li 6.939	4 Be 9.012						
3	11 Na 22.990	12 Mg 24.312						
4	19 K 39.102	20 Ca 40.08	21 Sc 44.956	22 Ti 47.90	23 V 50.94	24 Cr 52.00	25 Mn 54.94	26 F 55.
5	37 Rb 85.47	38 Sr 87.62	39 Y 88.905	40 Zr 91.22	41 Nb 92.906	42 Mo 95.94	43 Tc 99	44 R 101
6	55 Cs 132.905	56 Ba 137.34	57 La** 138.91	72 Hf 178.49	73 Ta 180.95	74 W 183.85	75 Re 186.2	76 O 19
7	87 Fr 223	88 Ra 226.05	89 Ac† 227.05					

Metals

• • Semiconductors

• Non-metals

** Lanthanides (rare earth me

	58 Ce 140.12	59 Pr 140.907	60 Nd 144.24	61 P 1

† Actinides

	90 Th 232.12	91 Pa 231.05	92 U 238.07	93 2

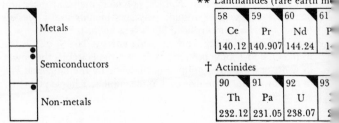

(showing atomic weights)

←VIII→	IB	IIB	IIIA	IVA	VA	VIA	VIIA	O
→	Noble metals						Halo-gens	Inert gases
								2 ● He 4.003
			5 ● B 10.811	6 ● C 12.011	7 ● N 14.007	8 ● O 15.999	9 ● F 18.998	10 ● Ne 20.183
			13 Al 26.982	14 ● Si 28.086	15 ● P 30.974	16 ● S 32.064	17 ● Cl 35.453	18 ● Ar 39.948
28 Ni 93 58.71	29 Cu 63.54	30 Zn 65.37	31 Ga 69.72	32 ● Ge 72.59	33 ● As 74.92	34 ● Se 78.96	35 ● Br 79.909	36 ● Kr 83.80
46 Pd 91 106.4	47 Ag 107.87	48 Cd 112.40	49 In 114.82	50 Sn 118.69	51 Sb 121.75	52 ● Te 127.60	53 ● I 126.904	54 ● Xe 131.30
78 Pt .2 195.09	79 Au 196.97	80 Hg 200.59	81 Tl 204.37	82 Pb 207.19	83 Bi 208.98	84 Po 210	85 ● At 211	86 ● Rn 222

*Hydrogen is sometimes placed above fluorine at the head of group VIIA. It is not included in the alkali metals.

63 Eu 35 151.96	64 Gd 157.25	65 Tb 158.92	66 Dy 162.50	67 Ho 164.93	68 Er 167.26	69 Tm 168.93	70 Yb 173.04	71 Lu 174.97
95 Am 241	96 Cm 242	97 Bk 247	98 Cf 251	99 Es 254	100 Fm 253	101 Md 256	102 No 254	103 Lr, 257

Pressure The force or weight per unit area acting on a surface. Measured in newtons per square metre (SI units), kilograms per sq m or pounds per sq in etc. Atmospheric pressure, that is the weight of air in a column of unit cross-sectional area up to the top of the earth's atmosphere, is roughly 15 lb per sq in. Pressure in gases is also expressed as the height of mercury (or other liquid) that the gas will support. A pressure of 0·76 m (760 mm or 29·921 in) of mercury is equivalent to 33·9 ft of water. This is equivalent to 14·696 lb per sq in or 10,332·3 kg per sq m. To turn kilograms weight to newtons multiply by 9·8, the gravitational acceleration in metres per sec. per sec. A *bar* is equivalent to 100,000 newtons per sq m. High pressures, especially in gases, are measured in kilobars. A *torr* is equivalent to 1 mm of mercury and is used to measure low pressures in gases.

Conversion table of pressures				
Cm of Hg	In of Hg	Millibars	Kg/sq m	Lb/sq in
71·2	28	942	9,650	13·74
73·7	29	976	9,970	14·2
75·5	29·7	1,000	10,220	14·55
76·2	30	1,019	10,400	14·8
78·7	31	1,052	10,750	15·3

Prime number A positive whole number (integer) which has no divisors except itself and 1. The sequence of prime numbers runs 1, 2, 3, 5, 7, 11, 13, 17, 19, 23 . . . . The frequency of prime numbers gets less and less but there is no such thing as the biggest prime number. The largest number so far proved to be prime is $2^{44497} - 1$, an enormous number with 13,395 digits found by using a giant computer in 1979. All non-prime numbers can be expressed as a product of prime numbers (called *prime factors*) e.g. $105 = 7 \times 5 \times 3 \times 1$.

Proteins An extremely important class of biological *polymer* (q.v.) which form a vital part of all living organisms.

Proteins consist of long chains formed by the polymerisation (i.e. linking together) of up to several hundred simpler compounds called *amino-acids* (q.v.). About 20 different amino-acids are found in proteins, different proteins varying in the number of each amino-acid they contain and the order in which they are arranged along the chain. Thus an extremely wide variety of protein structures is possible, each fulfilling a specific function; and, in fact, different organisms produce their own set of proteins. Proteins also vary widely in shape; in some the chain is extended, and in others it is folded into a complicated globular structure.

Many proteins are *enzymes*, that is biological *catalysts* (q.v.), which control the multitude of chemical reactions occurring in living organisms. Most enzymes remain inside the cells producing them, while others pass outside: e.g. the digestive enzymes of animals which are secreted into the alimentary canal to catalyse the breakdown of food into simpler compounds.

Other proteins fulfil the function of transporting substances within an organism: e.g. the protein haemoglobin (which contains iron) is found in red blood cells and transports oxygen from the lungs to all cells of the body. Still other proteins compose the muscles and are responsible for the ability of muscles to contract and produce movement. In bones, skin and tendons, protein fibres (rather like lengths of string) play an essential role as building materials.

Proteins are synthesised (e.g. manufactured), when needed, from their component amino-acids inside all animal, plant and bacterial cells. Viruses, the simplest organisms, have to 'hijack' the protein-making machinery of more complicated cells in order to produce the proteins they need; this is what is happening when viruses *infect* animals and plants. The instructions for the production of each different protein are carried by means of the *genetic code* (q.v.) in the genetic material inside the nucleus of the cell (see *Deoxyribonucleic acid* (DNA)). It is copies of these instructions which are passed on when new cells are formed by cell division, thus enabling the new cells to produce the proteins they require.

Projectile Body thrown or projected. If v is the initial velocity, a the angle of projection, g gravity, the projectile moves in a parabola. The following relationships are true:

$$\text{Total time of flight} = \frac{2v \sin a}{g}$$

$$\text{Maximum height} = \frac{v^2 \sin^2 a}{2g}$$

$$\text{Horizontal range} = \frac{v^2 \sin 2a}{g}$$

Proton The positive heavy particle of the nucleus of an atom; also the nucleus of a normal hydrogen atom.

Pulsar A type of radio star discovered in 1968 which gives out pulses of radio waves at very regular intervals. Believed to be composed of very densely packed neutrons.

Pythagoras Greek mathematician. The theorem of Pythagoras is the one that states that in a right-angled triangle the square on the hypotenuse is equal to the sum of the squares on the other two sides. See *Trigonometry*.

Quark For a long time it has been known that the nuclei of atoms are composed of protons and neutrons. Now it is thought that these nuclear building blocks (and in fact all other *hadrons* (q.v.)) are themselves made up of more fundamental particles called quarks.

Quarks were first proposed in 1963 and until 1974 only three quarks (and their corresponding anti-quarks) were needed to account for all the observed hadrons. These were the 'up' (u), (down) (d) and 'strange' (s) quarks. The proton consists of two up and one down quark (i.e. uud) while the neutron has composition ddu. To get the electric charge of the proton as $+1$ and that of the neutron as 0, it follows that the u quark must have charge $+\frac{2}{3}$ and the d quark charge $-\frac{1}{3}$. The discovery of the psi particle in 1974 and the upsilon in 1977 necessitated the introduction of two more quarks, the 'charmed' quark (c) and the 'bottom' quark (b). It is not known how many quarks there might be. Free quarks have never been observed. Other particles called *gluons* are supposed to keep them bound tightly together in twos or threes.

Quasar (or quasi-stellar source) Much the brightest and most distant type of giant star so far discovered.

Radian A unit of angular measure. One radian is the *angle* (q.v.) made at the centre, O, of any circle when the radius, r, of the circle is drawn round the circle's circumference (see top diagram on facing page).

Since the circumference of a circle has length $2\pi r$, there are 2π radians to a full circle: i.e. 2π radians equals $360°$ or 1 radian equals $57\cdot3°$. A right-angle is equal to $90°$ or $\pi/4$ radians.

Radical A group of atoms that stay together when a compound dissociates but yet not a stable group to qualify as a molecule, e.g. SO_4, NO_3, etc.

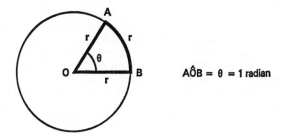

$A\hat{O}B = \theta = 1$ radian

Radioactivity The spontaneous emission of radiation (alpha, beta or gamma) from a material, due to the break-up of the nuclei of the atoms. Materials that are abundantly radioactive are radium and uranium and some artificially made radioisotopes. Many materials, however, are known to have a tiny proportion of a radioactive isotope present, and these materials are everywhere—in food, plants, rocks, etc.

Reaction The correct name for what goes on when chemicals combine or split up.

Reagent Chemicals commonly used in chemical laboratories for experiments and analysis, such as dilute hydrochloric acid, ammonium hydroxide, dilute nitric acid, etc.

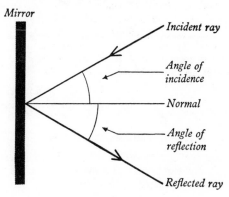

Specular or Mirror Reflection from a Plane Mirror

Reciprocal The reciprocal of a number y is one divided by y and is written $1/y$. E.g. the reciprocal of 4 is $1/4 = 0{\cdot}25$.

Reflection The 'bouncing back' of light rays, heat rays, etc. The simple law of reflection is that the angle between the incoming ray and the perpendicular to the surface is equal to the angle between the reflected ray and the same perpendicular. This is expressed as: The angle of incidence = Angle of reflection. With flat or 'plane' mirrors the perpendicular is easy to draw in diagrams, but with curved reflecting surfaces the perpendiculars have to be arrived at by knowledge of the geometry of circles, parabolas, etc.

Such regular reflection is called mirror or specular reflection. At a roughened surface light is reflected in *all* directions and does not obey the above rules. This is called diffused or scattered reflection.

Refraction The sudden change of direction of light when passing from one transparent substance into another. A ray of light passing from air into water is bent towards the perpendicular, or normal.

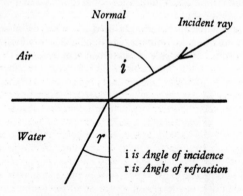

Refraction between Air and Water

If the angle of incidence (i) is taken as that between the incident ray and the normal and the angle of refraction (r) as that between the refracted ray and the normal, then if the less-dense medium is a vacuum $\dfrac{\sin i}{\sin r} = \mu$, the *refractive index* of the

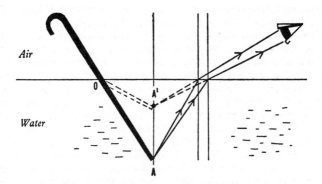

Apparent Bending of Walking-stick in Water Due to Refraction

The point A seems to be at A^1. Similarly with all points on OA so that the part immersed seems to be along OA^1.

substance. In ordinary experiments, as air is so little different from a vacuum for the passage of light, i is measured in air and r in the substance.

Resolving Power The power of an optical instrument or any optical system to deal with fine detail. The resolving power of a telescope is directly proportional to the diameter of the objective. Hence prismatic binoculars 8 × 40 are better than 8 × 25, the first figure being the magnifying power and the second the diameter of the objective in millimetres. The second binocular has the same magnifying power as the first but less resolving power, and so, though objects look just as big, the detail does not show up so well. The resolving power of the human eye is such that two point objects subtending an angle of about 1 minute at the eye can be seen separately, i.e. resolved.

RNA (Ribonucleic acid) A *nucleic acid* (q.v.) similar to *DNA* (q.v.) but differing in the chemical nature of the four bases of which it is composed. RNA plays a vital role in living cells, acting as an intermediary in the production of *proteins* (q.v.) from information coded on DNA by means of the *genetic code* (q.v.).

Root This has two meanings in mathematics. (a) One of several equal factors of a number. Thus the square root $\sqrt{\ }$ or $^2\sqrt{\ }$ is one of two equal factors: e.g. $3 = \sqrt{9}$ (also written $9^{\frac{1}{2}}$) and 3

$\times$ 3 = 9. The cube root is one of three equal factors: e.g. 4 = $\sqrt[3]{64}$ (also written $64^{\frac{1}{3}}$) and 4 $\times$ 4 $\times$ 4 = 64. (b) The root of an equation in an unknown x is a particular value of x that satisfies the equation.

Root-mean-square The average value of a quantity that takes positive and negative values equally (e.g. an alternating current) is zero. If the values are squared, the mean found, and then the square root taken, the non-zero result is called the root-mean-square value.

Salt A salt is the compound formed when the hydrogen in an *acid* (q.v.) is replaced by a metal. Examples of a salt are potassium nitrate and calcium sulphate. Sodium chloride ($NaCl$) is a salt in the chemical sense but is also called common salt in everyday use.

Series In mathematics a series is a sum of many terms each being of the same form so that a general expression can be given for the nth term: e.g. 1 + 1/2 + 1/4 + 1/8 + 1/16 + ... is a series whose nth term is $1/2^{(n-1)}$. *Infinite series* are series in which the number of terms is without limit. Despite having an infinite number of terms, some infinite series sum up to a limiting value. Such series are called *convergent* (e.g. the series given above if continued to infinity adds up to the value 2). Series which are not convergent are called *divergent*.

Set A set is a collection of objects or things that have at least one feature in common. A set may be described by listing all its members (called *elements*) or by specifying the properties that are necessary for membership of the set. To indicate that a, b, c .... are elements of the set A, the usual notation is to write A = {a, b, c ...}. Sets may have finite or infinite numbers of elements. Examples: the set of all people who have reached the summit of Mount Everest, (a finite set); the set E of positive even whole numbers, i.e. E = {2, 4, 6, 8, ...}, (an infinite set). *Set Theory* is an important branch of mathematics which deals with the relationships between sets.

Sine In trigonometry the sine of an angle (other than the right angle) in a right-angled triangle, is the ratio of the side opposite the angle to the hypotenuse. Sin $90°$ = 1, sin $60°$ = 0·866, sin $45°$ = 0·707, sin $30°$ = 0·5. See *Trigonometry*.

SI Units The internationally recommended system of *units* (q.v.) in which the base units are:

Quantity	Name of unit	Symbol
length	metre	m
mass	kilogram	kg
time	second	s
electric current	ampere	A
temperature	kelvin	K
amount of substance	mole	mol
luminous intensity	candela	cd

Other quantities are derived by combining these units e.g. the SI unit of volume is the cubic metre (m^3), that of velocity the metre per second ($m\ s^{-1}$), that of energy the joule ($m^2\ kg\ s^{-2}$) and that of electric charge the coulomb (A. s).

Specific Gravity See *Density*.

Specific Heat The amount of heat in joules that must be added to unit mass of a substance to raise its temperature by $1°$ C. The table gives values for a gram of substance.

Specific heats of common substances

Aluminium . . .	0·846	Alcohol . . . 2·428
Brass	0·384	Chloroform . . . 0·980
Copper. . . .	0·389	Air . . . 1·009[1]
Iron	0·474	Carbon dioxide . 0·846[1]
Rubber	1·675	Oxygen . . . 0·911[1]
Wood	1·675	Water . . . 4·187

[1] At constant pressure.

Squares, Cubes, Square Roots, Cube Roots and Reciprocals See *Root*.

N	N^2	N^3	$\sqrt{N}$	$\sqrt[3]{N}$	$\dfrac{1}{N}$
1	1	1	1·0	1·0	1·0
2	4	8	1·414	1·26	0·5
3	9	27	1·732	1·442	0·3333
4	16	64	2·0	1·587	0·25
5	25	125	2·236	1·71	0·2
6	36	216	2·449	1·817	0·1667
7	49	343	2·646	1·913	0·1429
8	64	512	2·828	2·0	0·125
9	81	729	3·0	2·08	0·1111
10	100	1,000	3·162	2·154	0·1

N	N^2	N^3	$\sqrt{N}$	$\sqrt[3]{N}$	$\dfrac{1}{N}$
11	121	1,331	3·317	2·224	0·0909
12	144	1,728	3·464	2·289	0·0833
13	169	2,197	3·606	2·351	0·0769
14	196	2,744	3·742	2·41	0·0714
15	225	3,375	3·873	2·466	0·0667
16	256	4,096	4·0	2·52	0·0625
17	289	4,913	4·123	2·571	0·0588
18	324	5,832	4·243	2·621	0·0556
19	361	6,859	4·359	2·668	0·0526
20	400	8,000	4·472	2·714	0·05
21	441	9,261	4·583	2·759	0·0476
22	484	10,648	4·69	2·802	0·0455
23	529	12,167	4·796	2·844	0·0435
24	576	13,824	4·899	2·885	0·0417
25	625	15,625	5·0	2·924	0·04
26	676	17,576	5·099	2·962	0·0385
27	729	19,683	5·196	3·0	0·037
28	784	21,952	5·292	3·037	0·0357
29	841	24,389	5·385	3·072	0·0345
30	900	27,000	5·477	3·107	0·0333
31	961	29,791	5·568	3·141	0·0323
32	1,024	32,768	5·657	3·175	0·0313
33	1,089	35,937	5·745	3·208	0·0303
34	1,156	39,304	5·831	3·24	0·0294
35	1,225	42,875	5·916	3·271	0·0286
36	1,296	46,656	6·0	3·302	0·0278
37	1,369	50,653	6·083	3·332	0·027
38	1,444	54,872	6·164	3·362	0·0263
39	1,521	59,319	6·245	3·391	0·0256
40	1,600	64,000	6·325	3·42	0·025
41	1,681	68,921	6·403	3·448	0·024
42	1,764	74,088	6·481	3·476	0·0238
43	1,849	79,507	6·557	3·503	0·0233
44	1,936	85,184	6·633	3·53	0·0227
45	2,025	91,125	6·708	3·557	0·0222
46	2,116	97,336	6·782	3·583	0·0217
47	2,209	103,823	6·856	3·609	0·0213
48	2,304	110,592	6·928	3·634	0·0208
49	2,401	117,649	7·0	3·659	0·0204·
50	2,500	125,000	7·071	3·684	0·02

Superconductivity This is the remarkable property of many metals and alloys to lose all electrical resistance below a certain critical temperature (usually within $20°$ of absolute zero). This means that an electric current can flow in a loop of the metal indefinitely without generating heat or decreasing in strength. Because of the low temperatures required (the metal is usually bathed in liquid helium) superconductivity is expensive to use on a large scale. But superconducting magnets which can produce very high magnetic fields without vast consumption of electrical energy are now quite widely used.

Surface Tension A force acting in the surface of a fluid, whether the surface separates one liquid from another or a liquid from a gas such as air. The effect of the force is to make the liquid surface behave rather like a stretched elastic skin with a tendency to reduce its area. It is surface tension which causes water to climb up a narrow capillary tube and causes water surfaces to be meniscus-shaped. Surface tension also governs the formation and shape of liquid drops and bubbles.

Surface tension is measured in newtons per metre. It varies with the temperature. The surface tension of pure water at $20°$ C is $0·07275$ newtons per metre.

Tangent In geometry a straight line touching (not cutting) a curve at only one point. In trigonometry the tangent of an angle (other than the right angle) in a right-angled triangle is the ratio of the side opposite the angle to the other side that is not the hypotenuse. Tan $0° = 0$, tan $30° = 0·577$, tan $45° = 1·0$, tan $60° = 1·732$, tan $90° = \infty$. See *Trigonometry.*

Telescope An optical device for getting an image of a distant object much bigger than the object appears seen with the naked eye. (The image obtained is really much smaller than the actual object.) There are two simple types: the astronomical telescope and the Galilean telescope. The astronomical telescope has a very long focus convergent lens as objective and a very short focus convergent lens (or system of lenses) as eyepiece. The magnifying power is the focal length of objective divided by the focal length of eyepiece. The bigger the objective in diameter, the greater the resolving power. The image seen is inverted. Prisms can be inserted between the lenses to invert the image and at the same time make the light reflect along paths across and back and across and forward so that the length of the telescope can be short and the optical path long. The result is a prismatic monocular giving the image upright in relation to the object. Two of them make a pair of prismatic binoculars.

The Galilean telescope uses a long-focus convergent lens as objective and a short-focus divergent lens as eyepiece. The image is seen upright. The magnification is again the focal length of objective divided by the focal length of eyepiece, and

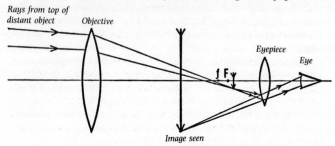

Geometrical Diagram of Astronomical Telescope
F is focus of objective f is focus of eyepiece

Geometrical Diagram of System of
Galileo's Telescope

as the eyepiece has to be placed within the focal length of the objective the length of the telescope is much less than that of the astronomical telescope for the same magnification. There is, however, one disadvantage, which is that the field of view gets very small as the magnifying power is increased, much more so than the comparable change with an astronomical telescope. Galilean telescopes are therefore for use in everyday life, when the field of view needs to be of reasonable size, restricted to a magnifying power of 2 or 3. Two Galilean telescopes side-by-side make a pair of ordinary non-prismatic field or opera glasses.

All the above are refracting telescopes. Sir Isaac Newton designed a reflecting telescope to get over the difficulty of aberrations in the lenses needed for big magnification. All the very big observatory telescopes of today are reflecting ones.

Temperature The state of hotness or coldness of a body or substance. This is not the same as the heat energy of a body or substance, for this depends on the mass and the specific heat.

Thermocouple A kind of *thermometer* (q.v.) made by joining one wire at its two ends to another wire of a different material. If one junction is kept cool and the other heated, an electric current flows and can be used as a measure of the temperature of the hot junction.

Thermodynamics The branch of physics dealing with the laws governing the interconversion of heat with other forms of *energy* (q.v.).

Thermometer An instrument for measuring temperature. The commonest type of thermometer is a glass tube of extremely fine bore and thick walls with a bulb joined at the bottom containing mercury or some other liquid, which also reaches a certain distance up the tube. Warming makes the liquid expand up the tube; cooling makes it contract. A scale of numbers is arrived at by fixing two reference points, usually the melting point of ice and the boiling point of water.

Two temperature scales are in common use. One, called the Fahrenheit scale, has the melting point of ice at $32°$ and the boiling point of water at $212°$. This is in general use in Britain and the USA. The second scale is called Centigrade (Celsius in many European countries) and has the lower point at $0°$ and the upper at $100°$. It is in use generally in many countries, and is international for scientific measurement.

To convert Fahrenheit to Centigrade, first subtract 32 and then multiply the result by $\frac{5}{9}$.

To convert Centigrade to Fahrenheit multiply by $\frac{9}{5}$ and then add 32.

Examples:
(1) $59°$ F, convert to $°$ C
$59 - 32 = 27; 27 \times \frac{5}{9} = 15°$ C

(2) 20° C, convert to ° F

    $20 \times \frac{9}{5} = 36$; $36 + 32 = 68°$ F

To convert °C to the *absolute temperature* scale (q.v.) add 273·15.

Liquid-in-glass thermometers are limited. Mercury freezes at − 39° C; ethyl alcohol boils at 78·3° C. So other devices must be used for very low and very high temperatures. For extreme temperatures a *thermocouple* (q.v.) is frequently used, depending on the electricity generated when two dissimilar metals are joined and the junction heated or cooled. A platinum resistance-thermometer depends on the change of electrical resistance in platinum wire when it is heated. Modern materials called thermistors are also used. The resistance of such materials gets less as it is heated. So an electrical current increases.

Special thermometers of the liquid-in-glass sort are devised to read the minimum or the maximum temperature reached in a certain period of time. A clinical thermometer is a type of maximum thermometer in which the thread of mercury stays put at its highest because of a very narrow constriction at the base of the tube where it joins the mercury-supply bulb.

Trigonometry The branch of mathematics that deals with the properties of *angles* (q.v.). The usual starting-point for trigonometry is the definition of the *sine, cosine* and *tangent* of an angle (all q.v.).

In the diagram *ABC* is a right-angled triangle with $\angle ACB = 90°$ and the angle $\angle BAC$ denoted by θ. Sine θ, cosine θ, and tangent θ (commonly written sin θ, cos θ and tan θ) are defined by the following ratios of lengths:

$$\sin \theta = \frac{BC}{AB}, \quad \cos \theta = \frac{AC}{AB}, \quad \tan \theta = \frac{BC}{AC} = \frac{\sin \theta}{\cos \theta}.$$

It is important to understand that these ratios are independent of the size of the triangle *ABC* and depend only on the magnitude of the angle θ. The numerical values of the sine, cosine and tangent of any angle can be found in books of mathematical tables. Other trigonometrical ratios are defined as follows:

Cosecant θ or cosec $\theta = \dfrac{1}{\sin \theta} = \dfrac{AB}{BC}$

Secant θ or sec $\theta = \dfrac{1}{\cos \theta} = \dfrac{AB}{AC}$

Cotangent θ cot $\theta = \dfrac{1}{\tan \theta} = \dfrac{AC}{BC}$

A useful relationship between $\sin \theta$ and $\cos \theta$ is derived by using *Pythagoras's theorem* (q.v.). According to this theorem, for the right-angled triangle ABC, $AB^2 = AC^2 + BC^2$ and therefore

$$\cos^2 \theta + \sin^2 \theta = \frac{AC^2 + BC^2}{AB^2} = 1.$$

One common use of trigonometric ratios is the calculation of unknown sidelengths and angles of triangles (and other geometrical figures) when only some of them are originally given.

Ultra-violet Light Light that is invisible to human beings and of shorter wavelength than visible light. Sometimes called 'dark light'. It is very active in affecting chemicals and causing *fluorescence* (q.v.). It is present in the light from the sun, but much of it is filtered out by the earth's atmosphere. It is dangerous for the eyes. Range of wavelengths 1,800–4,200 Å. It is also present in mercury-vapour discharge light.

Units All physical quantities can be expressed in terms of five base units: mass (M), length (L), time (T), electric current and temperature. Thus volume = L.L.L, force = (M.L)/(T.T). The magnitude of the base units is set by convention. In the c.g.s. system the base units are the centimetre (L), gram (M) and second (T). In the f.p.s. system they are the foot (L), pound (M) and second (T). The currently accepted system is the Système International d'Unités (see *SI units*).

Vacuum Space which contains no matter. In practice unobtainable since, whatever the walls of the container were made of, the container would evaporate slowly and so destroy the vacuum. Usually very low pressures of air or other gases are called vacuums.

Valency The valency of an element is a number that tells in what proportions the element combines with other elements, and so can be used to work out molecular formulae of compounds. Elements of valency 1 (monovalent elements) include hydrogen, chlorine, silver and sodium; of valency 2 (divalent elements) include oxygen, magnesium and calcium; of valency 3 (trivalent elements) include aluminium and nitrogen; and of valency 4 (tetravalent elements) include carbon.

Oxygen being divalent means that one atom of it will combine with two atoms of monovalent hydrogen (giving water H_2O), or with one atom of divalent magnesium (giving MgO, magnesium oxide), or with 'half' an atom of tetravalent carbon (giving carbon dioxide, CO_2). Three atoms of oxygen combine with two of aluminium to give aluminium oxide Al_2O_3.

Valency is closely related to the theory of the chemical *bond* (q.v.) and is not always as simple as above. Many elements can combine with each other in a number of different ways: e.g. nitrogen and oxygen can give the oxides N_2O, NO, N_2O_3, NO_2, and N_2O_5 and two oxides of copper exist, CuO and Cu_2O.

Vapour Pressure A liquid loses atoms or molecules into its gaseous surround, usually air. When the pressure of these evaporated atoms or molecules is such that as many are returning to the material as are leaving it the vapour is saturated and its pressure is called the vapour pressure of the liquid. It increases with a rise in temperature and depends only on that temperature and the nature of the liquid. A volatile liquid has a high vapour pressure at ordinary temperatures. A liquid that has a low vapour pressure does not evaporate easily. On heating a liquid there comes a temperature at which the vapour pressure equals atmospheric pressure. It then boils.

Vapour pressures of some liquids at 20° C in mm of mercury						
Water .	.	.	. 17·5	Benzene	. . .	74·6
Mercury	.	.	. 0·0013	Chloroform .	. .	161
Acetone	.	.	.185	Ether .	. . .	440
Alcohol	.	.	. 44·5	Carbon Tetrachloride .		91

Velocity In everyday use the same as speed, but in science and mathematics having the extra quality of being negative or positive to show *direction* in relation to any problem.

If u is the starting velocity, f the acceleration, then the velocity v after time t is given by $v = u + ft$. The distance travelled is given by $s = ut + \frac{1}{2}ft^2$. From these can be derived the equation $v^2 = u^2 + 2fs$.

Virus The simplest form of living organism, so small as to be only visible with the aid of the electron *microscope* (q.v.). Viruses are inactive when isolated and can only reproduce by invading a *cell* (q.v.) of a *bacterium* (q.v.), animal or plant and using the more complicated chemical machinery of the host cell. Viruses come in various shapes and sizes (up to a few thousand angstroms in length), but usually a particular kind of virus can only infect one kind of host. Many infectious diseases (such as influenza and smallpox in man) are caused by viruses invading and disrupting their victim's cells (see *proteins*).

Viscosity The internal friction of fluids, i.e. resistance to flow of one part over another. Examples: treacle, a very viscous fluid; ether, a liquid of low viscosity. Viscosity decreases with rise in temperature.

Volt The SI unit of *electromotive force* (*e.m.f.*) (q.v.), potential difference or electrical pressure.

Volume The amount of space occupied by an object, expressed in cubic inches, cubic metres, cubic feet, etc.

Volumes of common shapes

Cube: l^3, where $l =$ length of one side.
Rectangular prism: $l \times b \times d$, where $l =$ length, $b =$ breadth, $d =$ depth.
Sphere: $\frac{4}{3}\pi r^3$, where $r =$ radius.
Cylinder: $\pi r^2 l$, where $r =$ radius of base, $l =$ length of cylinder.
Cone: $\frac{1}{3}\pi r^2 h$, where $r =$ radius of base, $h =$ vertical height.
 $\quad\quad \frac{1}{3}\pi r^2 \sqrt{l^2 - r^2}$, where $l =$ length of sloping side.
Pyramid: $\frac{1}{3}$ area of base $\times h$, where $h =$ vertical height.

Waves Many kinds of disturbance travel from one point to another as waves, for example, ripples on a water surface, pressure variations in air (sound) and electrical and magnetic disturbances (light). The important thing is that the disturbance varies periodically in both space and time. This can be understood by considering a water wave. If a water wave is photographed at

one time it will look as in diagram (a) where the shape of the
wave is repeated regularly and the distance, λ, between successive crests is called the *wavelength*. If the wave is travelling
from left to right with velocity v, at a slightly later time the
picture will look as in (b) which has the earlier wave shape
dotted in (the crest at A having moved to A^1). Moreover if we
remain fixed at B, we have to wait a time T equal to λ/v before
the crest originally at A reaches B. The time T between successive crests arriving at a given point is called the *period*. The
reciprocal $1/T$ is the number of crests passing a point per second
and is called the *frequency*, f. We have shown the important
relationship

$$T = \lambda/v \text{ or } v = f.\lambda$$

which is true for all wave motions. It is important to note that
it is the shape of the wave and the energy carried by it that
moves from A to A' and not the water itself. The water
molecules are actually moving backwards and forwards in the
direction at right angles to the direction the wave is travelling. For this reason, water waves are examples of *transverse*
waves. *Longitudinal* waves, by comparison, are waves in which
the particles are moving back and forth in the same direction
as that in which the wave is moving e.g. sound waves.

All kinds of waves show the characteristic properties of *reflection* (q.v.), *refraction* (q.v.) and *diffraction* (q.v.).

Weight The force of attraction exerted on a body by gravity. See
Mass.

Weights and Measures, Tables of In Great Britain the traditional
Imperial weights and measures (e.g. inches, pounds and pints)
are gradually being replaced by the simpler Metric system (e.g.
centimetres, kilograms and litres) which is based on units of
ten. To get from one system to the other see under *Conversion
table*. See also *SI Units*.

Avoirdupois Weight

16 drams	= 1 ounce (*oz*)
16 ounces	= 1 pound (*lb*)
14 pounds	= 1 stone
28 pounds	= 1 quarter
4 quarters	= 1 hundredweight (*cwt*)
20 hundredweights	= 1 ton
100 pounds	= 1 central, or short hundredweight
2,000 pounds	= 1 short ton
7,000 grains	= 1 pound

Linear Measure		*Land Measure*	
12 inches	= 1 foot	7·92 inches	= 1 link
3 feet	= 1 yard	25 links	= 1 rod
5½ yards	= 1 rod, pole or perch	4 rods or 100 links	= 1 chain
40 poles	= 1 furlong	80 chains	= 1 mile
8 furlongs	= 1 mile		
3 miles	= 1 league		

Square Measure

144 square inches	= 1 square foot
9 square feet	= 1 square yard
30¼ square yards	= 1 square rod, pole or perch
40 square poles	= 1 rood
4 roods	= 1 acre
640 acres	= 1 square mile

Land Square Measure		*Liquid Measure*	
625 square links	= 1 square rod	4 gills	= 1 pint
16 square rods	= 1 square chain	2 pints	= 1 quart
10 square chains	= 1 acre	4 quarts	= 1 gallon

Circular Measure (see also under *radian*)

60 seconds (″)	= 1 minute (′)
60 minutes	= 1 degree (°)
90 degrees	= 1 quadrant (*quad*)
4 quadrants or 360 degrees	= 1 circle (o)

The metric system

Measures of Weight

10 milligrammes (*mg*)	= 1 centigramme (*cg*)
10 centigrammes	= 1 decigramme (*dg*)
10 decigrammes	= 1 gramme (*g*)
10 grammes	= 1 decagramme (*Dg*)
10 decagrammes	= 1 hectogramme (*hg*)
10 hectogrammes	= 1 kilogramme (*kg*)

Linear Measure
10 millimetres (*mm*) = 1 centimetre (*cm*)
10 centimetres   = 1 decimetre (*dm*)
10 decimetres   = 1 metre (*m*)
10 metres   = 1 decametre (*Dm*)
10 decametres   = 1 hectometre (*hm*)
10 hectametres   = 1 kilometre (*km*)

Measures of Capacity
10 millilitres (*ml*) = 1 centilitre (*cl*)
10 centilitres   = 1 decilitre (*dl*)
10 decilitres   = 1 litre (*l*)
10 litres   = 1 decolitre (*Dl*)
10 decolitres   = 1 hectolitre (*hl*)
10 hectolitres   = 1 kilolitre (*kl*)

Land Measure
1 hectare (*ha*) = 10,000 sq metres

X-ray Diffraction A very important technique of *crystallography* (q.v.). The wavelengths of *X-rays* (q.v.) and the size of the repeating units in *crystals* (q.v.) are both of the same magnitude— a few *angstroms* (q.v.). As a result a beam of X-rays incident on a crystal is split up by the process of *diffraction* (q.v.) into a number of secondary beams which leave the crystal in different directions. The intensity and direction of these diffracted beams depend upon the structure of the crystal and can be used by crystallographers to find this structure.

X-Rays Electromagnetic radiation of very short wavelength, ranging from a tenth of an angstrom to 20 angstroms. X-rays affect a photographic plate and cause fluorescence in some chemicals. They penetrate matter according to its density. They are used in medical practice for showing up growths, bone fractures, foreign bodies, etc., in the human body.

A DICTIONARY OF RADIO AND TELEVISION

Some of the terms used in discussing radio and television are general scientific terms (e.g. *ampere, ohm*) and if not found in this section should be looked for in the DICTIONARY OF SCIENCE AND MATHEMATICS. At the same time, a number of terms associated with the high fidelity reproduction of records (discs) and tape cassettes (e.g. *stylus, Dolby system*) are included under the term 'radio', with which this form of hi-fi is so closely integrated.

Abbreviations

A—ampere	kHz—kilohertz
mA—milliampere (milliamp)	MHz—megahertz
μA—microampere	W—Watt
V—volt	kW—kilowatt
mV—millivolt	mW—milliwatt
μV—microvolt	H—henry
Ω—omega (capital) = ohm	mH—millihenry
MΩ—megohm	μH—microhenry
$\mu\Omega$—micro-ohm	AC—alternating current
F—farad	DC—direct current
μF—microfarad	emf—electromotive force
Hz—hertz	RMS—root-mean-square

Note: The above abbreviations are in accordance with the ruling of the British Standards Institution.

LF—low frequency	AF—audio frequency
HF—high frequency	DCC—double cotton covered
VHF—very high frequency	SCC—single cotton covered
RF—radio frequency	N. pole—north pole
SWG—standard wire gauge	S. pole—south pole
DSC—double silk covered ⎫	
DWS—double wound silk ⎭ synonymous terms	

Aerial (Antenna) A conductor that can either send out or pick up radio waves and therefore can be the last stage of a transmitter or the first stage of a receiver. In its simplest form it is a metallic rod or wire but efficient, directional aerials can be of complicated design.

A transmitter operating on long or medium waves has an aerial that is a high wire leading through the transmitter to the ground. For waves as short as, or shorter than, those used for television the antenna is free of any earth connection and the length of rod forming the antenna is related to the wavelength. The commonest relationship is that the antenna is a half the wavelength. The usual design is of two rods in line, each rod just under a quarter wavelength long, the two ends at the middle being where the line joining the antenna to the transmitter or receiver is placed. This is the *half-wave dipole* or Hertzian antenna.

A simple dipole aerial:
$1 = $ approx. $\frac{1}{4}$ wavelength

Feeder

ℓ

$\frac{1}{4}\lambda$

Direction of incoming signal

Director

Reflector   Antenna

A dipole with one reflector and one director

Television video signals are transmitted on various channels of which 57 are available in Britain. Channels 1 to 13 were VHF and were formerly used for the monochrome (black and white) TV service but this has now been discontinued. The channels for colour TV are 21 to 68 on UHF but not all these are used at present. Band VI is on SHF and consists of 20 DBS channels for use in direct broadcasting by satellite. The United Kingdom has been allocated five of these (4, 8, 12, 16, 20).

The audio signals for television are on slightly different frequencies from that of the video signal, so an aerial correctly designed for one will not be accurate for the other. In practice, a compromise is made.

If the electrical component of the electromagnetic wave being transmitted or received is vertical, then the half-wave antenna is vertical. If the electrical component is horizontal the antenna is horizontal. The higher-powered TV stations and some of the relays transmit horizontally polarised signals. Most VHF FM signals are also horizontally polarised although the majority have been, or will be, converted to 'mixed' polarisation for better reception in cars and portables.

Single-dipole antennae transmit and receive in all directions. Another half-wave rod placed exactly a quarter of a wavelength *behind* but unconnected to the transmitter or receiver, enhances the efficiency in the forward direction, and the extra rod is called a reflector. Rods placed in *front* of the operative dipole, and at the correct distance (*not* a quarter wavelength but less), also enhance the directional efficiency and are called directors.

Alternating Current (AC) Electric current which regularly reverses its direction around a circuit. A particular alternating current is usually described by its *frequency* (q.v.) and its *root-mean-square* value (q.v.).

Amateur Radio Certain frequencies in the short-wave bands are allocated internationally for use by amateur radio enthusiasts. Licences are granted by the Home Office subject to the passing of a technical examination and a morse code test. No morse test is required for the Sound Licence 'B' which is limited to telephony only above 144 MHz or for the amateur TV licence.

Amplification This is the electronics and radio term for magnification, and the circuitry that does the amplifying is an amplifier, of which there are several sorts. The radio-frequency or RF amplifier amplifies only signals of high frequencies, whereas the audio-frequency or AF amplifier amplifies signals of frequencies ranging between about 30 and 30,000 Hz in high-fidelity work and to about 8,000 Hz in a good radio receiver. These are very low frequencies compared with radio frequencies, which even on the medium waves are of the order of a million Hz. This enormous difference between the frequencies handled by an AF amplifier and an RF amplifier means a considerable difference in the circuits used.

In radio and electronics and television, amplification involves the use of thermionic valves or transistors. Any one such valve or transistor with its associated circuit of resistors, capacitors and perhaps inductance, is called a *stage*. Each stage except the last in a radio receiver is designed as a voltage amplifier, but the final stage has to deliver power to a loudspeaker or the coils of a cathode-ray tube in a television receiver. This final stage is therefore a power amplifier.

The general principle of amplication is that an input alternating voltage, still at radio frequency if it is RF amplication but at audio frequency if it is AF amplification, is applied between the grid and cathode of a thermionic valve. The output is then taken from the anode circuit. If a transistor is used the input is in most cases (i.e. using common emitter connections) applied between base and emitter and the output taken between collector and emitter. In each case what is taken out is bigger than what is put in. The ratio of output to input is called the *stage gain*.

The stage gain depends on various factors which differ according to whether a valve or transistor amplifier is considered.

Amplitude Modulation The addition of an audio-frequency signal to a carrier in such a way that the carrier amplitude varies in response to the signal. See *modulation*.

Anode The positive electrode of an electrolytic cell or thermionic valve or discharge tube.

Audio Frequency (AF) This means a *frequency* (q.v.) within the range of sound wave frequencies audible to human ears. It can be taken as between 20 hertz and 20,000 hertz, though many people have a much smaller range than this. High-fidelity amplifiers are capable of reproducing from about 30 hertz to 30,000 hertz.

Automatic Gain Control A circuit device which automatically maintains the output of a stage almost constant, even though the input may be varying. It operates by the principle of *feedback* (q.v.), and is used in radio receivers to reduce the effect of *fading* (q.v.).

Bias A voltage applied to transistors and valves to allow them to operate in the most satisfactory manner to avoid distortion. In the case of transistors it may be applied by a battery; but generally it is by an arrangement of resistors.

British Broadcasting Corporation The oldest broadcasting organisation in the world, developing out of a company first formed in 1922.

The BBC broadcasts in sound to countries all over the world

in forty languages beside English. It is organised into two parts, one for the home programmes, with headquarters in Broadcasting House in London, W1, and one for the programmes going overseas—the external services—with headquarters in Bush House, London WC2. Television Centre at White City controls TV services.

The BBC broadcasts in two television services, known as BBC-1 and BBC-2, and in four radio services known as Radio 1, 2, 3 and 4, as well as local radio stations. Radio 1 is the channel for pop music. Radio 2 is the principal channel for more traditional forms of popular music and for sport coverage. Radio 3 is a serious all-music channel during the day but includes items on drama, poetry, the arts, etc., during the evening. Radio 4 is the main channel for up-to-the-moment news and current affairs broadcasting and for plays, documentaries and discussions of more general interest than those found in Radio 3. The radio services are broadcast on medium or low frequencies (MF or LF) and on Very High Frequency (VHF). Details of the frequencies used are printed in *Radio Times* and fuller information is available from the Engineering Information Department, Broadcasting House, London W1A 1AA.

Radio 1 is transmitted on 1,089 and 1,053 kHz; Radio 2 on 909 and 693 kHz and on VHF (although their VHF frequency is often shared with Radio 1); Radio 3 on 1,215 kHz and VHF and Radio 4 is on 200 kHz and VHF. VHF programmes are FM and often in stereo. Radio 2 is to be found between 88–91 MHz, Radio 3 between 90 and 93 and Radio 4 from 92–95 MHz.

There are also numbers of low-powered relays operating on various other frequencies on MF and VHF.

The External Services are mainly broadcast on the higher frequencies in the bands from 25 to 5 MHz, but some of the services to Europe are broadcast on MF and some of the high frequency programmes are relayed on MF from transmitters in Cyprus and other parts of the world.

BBC Television is transmitted on the 625 line standard in the UHF band (band 5). Most programmes are in colour.

An early morning programme called *Breakfast Time* began on 17 January 1983. This is broadcast on BBC 1 UHF channels from Monday to Friday each week.

The BBC has 32 local radio stations, all of which transmit on MF and on VHF. Details of their locations and addresses may be obtained from the BBC. Engineering Information Department.

Capacitance This is the property of a *capacitor* (q.v.) to store electric charge when a voltage is applied across the capacitor plates. The unit of capacitance is the *farad* (F), and a capacitor has a capacitance of one farad if it stores a charge of one coulomb when there is a voltage of one volt across it. The farad is too large for most practical purposes and it is normal to use the microfarad, μF (one millionth of a farad), and the picofarad, pF (one million millionth of a farad).

In understanding how a capacitor behaves in a circuit it is important to remember that electric current is the flow of electric charge. So whenever charge is moving into or out of a capacitor (i.e. the capacitor is *charging* or *discharging*) a current must flow. Also, the charge stored in a capacitor is always equal to the voltage across it times its capacitance.

Suppose a capacitor is connected in a circuit with a battery, a *resistor* (q.v.) and a switch. When the switch is open there is no voltage across the capacitor and therefore no charge stored in it. On closing the switch, current flows for a short time, charging up the capacitor until the voltage across it is equal to that of the battery. The insulating layer in the capacitor then prevents any further current flow. If the battery is now removed from the circuit, the capacitor discharges through the resistor and a current again flows for a short time (but in the opposite direction) until there is no voltage across the capacitor. If the battery is now reconnected, but with positive and negative reversed, the capacitor will again charge up (in the opposite direction to before) and current will again flow. Thus we can see that if we connect a capacitor to an AC generator whose voltage is regularly changing from positive to zero, zero to negative, and negative through zero to positive again, the capacitor will regularly charge up, discharge and recharge in the opposite direction. An alternating current will therefore flow even though there is an insulating layer in the capacitor. The AC is exactly of the same *frequency* (q.v.) as the voltage but the current maxima coincide with the voltage zeros: i.e. the voltage and current are 90° out of *phase* (q.v.). The mag-

nitude of the current is given by V/X_C, where V is the voltage
and X_C is called the *capacitive reactance*. For a capacitor of
capacitance C farads and AC of frequency f, $X_C = 1/2\pi Cf$
ohms.

Capacitor A circuit component which has the property of *capacitance* (q.v.). The simplest form of capacitor is the parallel plate
capacitor which consists of two plates of metal separated by an
insulating material called a *dielectric*. The capacitance C is
given by the formula

$$C = \frac{\varepsilon A}{d} \times \frac{10^{-9}}{36\pi} \text{ farads}$$

where A is the area of the overlapping plates, d is the distance
between the plates and ε is a constant which depends on the
dielectric used and is called the *dielectric constant*. For low
values of capacitance the dielectric may be air ($\varepsilon = 1$). This is
often the case for variable capacitors used in tuning radios.
When the dial is turned, one set of plates interleaves with
another set separated by air gaps and A in the above formula
is increased or decreased. Fixed capacitors of higher values are
made with ceramic, mica, paper, polyester or polystyrene
dielectrics. Very high values are provided by electrolytic
capacitors. Here the dielectric is formed by a thin layer of oxide,
itself formed by the action of an electric current: to retain it,
the capacitor is polarised (i.e. + and − poles).

Carrier Wave Electromagnetic waves of the frequencies of speech
and music cannot be transmitted efficiently over long distances.
So in telecommunications a wave of much higher frequency,
the carrier wave, is used to 'carry' the desired signal by the
technique of *modulation* (q.v.).

Cartridge The operative part which is actuated by the *stylus* (q.v.)
and carried by the *pick-up* (q.v.).

Cassette A compact form of reels of magnetic tape upon which
home recording may be carried out. Alternatively they may
be obtained as professional recordings and are more compact
than the popular disc record.

Cathode The negative electrode of an electrolytic cell or a thermionic valve or discharge tube.

Cathode-ray Tube This device is a glass envelope roughly conical
in shape with a long neck in which a cathode emits electrons

which travel towards a fluorescent screen on the large end of the envelope. A metal electrode in the neck is the anode to attract the electrons and speed them on their way to the screen. The cathode and focusing electrodes and anodes constitute the *electron gun.* When correctly designed a narrow intense beam of electrons travels to the screen and produces a tiny spot of light.

There are several uses for a cathode-ray tube. The most well-known are in television receivers and computer terminals. With extra apparatus they make an oscilloscope, an apparatus that allows waves and oscillations to be seen as visible traces and measured. The electron beam is forced to traverse the screen in lines, each successive line being below the one before it, so that the whole of the working area of the screen is *scanned.* In order to make the beam do this its movements are controlled by electromagnetic coils on the neck. The colour

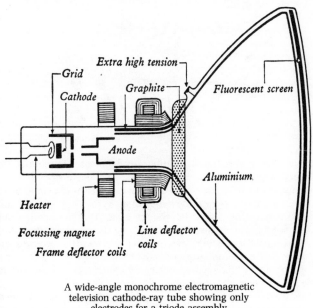

A wide-angle monochrome electromagnetic
television cathode-ray tube showing only
electrodes for a triode assembly

picture tube has three electron guns to provide red, green and blue signals. These combine to form the colour picture.

CB Radio CB Radio or Citizens Band Radio has been legal in USA for some years. A form of radio-telephone, it enables truck drivers and other road users to keep in touch with one another and exchange details of road hazards, etc. Japanese *transceivers* (q.v.) have been imported into UK and illegally used contrary to the Radio Telegraphy Acts. They operated on AM on 27 MHz and caused interference with other apparatus. In 1981 the Government legalised CB Radio with the proviso that FM only could be used and the frequencies allocated are 27 and 934 MHz. A licence fee of £10 is payable annually. Use of AM apparatus remains illegal.

Chip The popular name for an *integrated circuit* (q.v.) derived from silicon chip or micro-chip. It is encapsulated in a small plastic box with connecting lugs on each side.

A silicon chip

Circuit The name given to the arrangement of conductors, capacitors, inductances, valves, etc., that make up the theoretical picture of an electronics device. All these components are shown in diagrams by conventional graphical symbols and the connecting wires by straight lines. The circuit diagram must be distinguished from the wiring diagram, which shows the natural disposition, soldering points, etc., of the real components. The circuit diagram merely tells the theory on which the behaviour of the apparatus is based and can be calculated.

Coil Conducting wire wound on a former and used in AC circuits as a source of *inductance* (q.v.). There may be many or few turns and the core may or may not be of a magnetic material, depending on the application. Coils are widely used in *tuning* (q.v.) circuits and as *chokes* when a high impedance to AC is required.

Colour Code A form of marking by coloured bands or spots to indicate the values of components, different colours being given to the figures 1–10. Usually used for resistors but sometimes applied to capacitors.

Colour Television The first British colour television broadcast was made on 2 July 1967, and the BBC's full colour service on BBC-2 opened on 2 December. Since then both BBC-1 and ITV transmit mainly colour programmes.

Compact Disc As its name implies, a small gramophone record capable of carrying as much information as the conventional record. It is not played by the usual stylus and pick-up but special apparatus enables it to be traversed by a laser beam by which the disc's contents are conveyed to the amplifier. Very fine quality of reproduction is claimed for the system.

Condenser See *capacitor*.

Crystal Detector An early form of rectifier consisting of a thin pointed wire (the 'cat's whisker') in contact with a *semiconductor* (q.v.) crystal. Used as a detector for radio waves prior to the invention of diode valves and *p–n junction* (q.v.) diodes.

Decibel (dB) A unit which compares two levels of *power* (q.v.). To say that two power levels, P_2 and P_1, differ by n dB means that $n = 10 \times \log_{10} P_2/P_1$. Depending upon whether P_2 is greater or less than P_1, n may be positive or negative. If, for example, $P_2 = 2P_1$, then P_2 is $10\log_{10}2$ (about 3) dB up on P_1. In electronics, decibels are often used to compare the output power of a circuit with the input power, i.e. to give a measure of the circuit gain or loss. A bel is ten decibels.

Decibel Table (Based on 1 milliwatt reference)			
Milliwatts	*Decibels*	*Milliwatts*	*Decibels*
1	0	3·981	6
1·259	1	5·012	7
1·585	2	6·310	8
1·995	3	7·943	9
2·512	4	10·000	10
3·162	5	1 watt	30

If it is required to give actual power levels instead of just relative power levels, the *decibel referred to one milliwatt* (dBm) is often used. In this case P_1 is fixed at a reference level of one milliwatt. The table gives the correspondence between power levels measured in milliwatts and dBm.

Decoder Circuitry required to enable stereo broadcasts on VHF to operate a stereo amplifier. It is inserted between the tuner and the stereo amplifier.

Detection (Demodulation) The reverse process to *modulation* (q.v.): i.e. the separation of the original signal from the modulated *carrier wave* (q.v.). This is usually done in radio and television receivers (after changing from a frequency-modulated signal to an amplitude-modulated signal if necessary) by rectifying the high frequency signal to give a direct current varying at audio frequencies. See *rectification.*

Diagrams There are certain standard *graphical symbols* (q.v.) used in electrical, electronic, radio and television circuit diagrams. Straight lines indicate conducting connections (lengths of copper wire when an amateur is wiring up a piece of apparatus).

Digital Electronics It would seem inevitable that two branches of the science known as electronics should ultimately become associated, and digital electronics, which are related to computers and data processing, are becoming increasingly important in the radio field. Details and graphical symbols are outside the scope of this section, but are given in the RSGB *Guide to Amateur Radio* and other literature. (*See* Recommended Reading.)

DIN In general use in Europe as a standard specification. There is an accepted DIN standard for high-fidelity amplifiers and there are DIN plugs and sockets standardised for general use. It derives from Deutscher Industrie Normenausschuss, the German Industrial Standards Board.

Diode This means 'two electrodes' and refers to a component that will allow the passage of an electric current in one direction only and hence can be used for *rectification* (q.v.). The diode may be a thermionic valve with only a cathode and an anode or a semiconductor *p-n junction* (q.v.).

Distortion There are a number of forms of distortion which can affect the reproduction of a radio or other signal by an amplifier. These include noise and hum, but the most prevalent is *harmonic distortion* (q.v.).

Dolby System A system named after the inventor which reduces the hiss which is an undesirable feature of tape recording (particularly cassettes). Also known as DNL (dynamic noise limiter), it enables cassettes to compete with discs as a source of hi-fi recording.

Doping The adding of small quantities of impurities to a *semiconductor* (q.v.). Adding of antimony or arsenic to germanium gives *n-type* germanium. This has a higher conductivity (see *resistivity*) than undoped germanium because the impurity atoms bring extra electrons which are readily available for carrying electricity. Adding aluminium or indium to germanium gives *p-type* germanium. This also has an increased conductivity but due to the presence of positively charged *holes* which, like electrons, can carry electricity. See *p–n junction* and *transistor*.

Early Bird The world's first commercial communications satellite, launched by the United States in the spring of 1965.

Earth A term much used in radio and electronics. For ordinary circuits, including telephone and distribution lines, the earth, being a conductor of electricity, though a poor one, can be used as the return wire to complete the circuit. For circuits involving electromagnetic oscillations and waves the earth is the conductor to which the transmitter or receiver is connected, the antenna being the other. Thus when medium or low frequencies are used the antenna system is a long, high wire or system of wires and the earth connection is a system of wires buried in the ground. For an ordinary receiver the water pipe is a good enough earth. The word 'earth' is also used, however, to mean the common metallic connection to all the circuits, frequently the metal chassis on which everything is mounted. The advantage of an earth connection is that stray currents use the earth as a 'sink' and in receiving weak signals on medium and long waves the signal is increased. Modern receivers frequently need no earth connection at all. Transmission and reception of television signals and any others using dipole antennae make no use of an earth connection.

Electric Field An electric field is a region of space in which an electric charge experiences a force.

Electromagnetic Waves (EM waves) Waves (see DICTIONARY OF
SCIENCE) consisting of both electric and magnetic quantities
varying regularly in space and time and travelling together at
the speed of light.

Diagram (a) gives an instantaneous picture of an EM wave.
The *electric field* (q.v.) is in the x-direction and oscillates between +ve and −ve values as in diagram (b). The *magnetic
field* (q.v.) is in the y-direction and varies in a similar way. The
whole wave travels in the z-direction at the speed of light so
that at a later time the electric field will vary as shown dotted
in (b). The wavelength, λ, is the distance between one crest

(a) Simplified diagram of an   (b) Diagram showing how
    electromagnetic wave   the electric field varies

and the next. The frequency, f, is the number of oscillations
per second at a given point. These are related to the speed of
light, c, by the equation

$$c = f.\lambda$$

The value of c for EM waves in free space, c_0, is 3×10^8 m per
sec or 186,000 miles per sec. Note that EM waves do not need
a medium through which to travel, unlike sound waves. EM
waves do of course travel through other materials but at a
velocity c_0/μ where μ is the refractive index of the material.

EM waves have very different properties depending on the
wavelength. Different names are given to different ranges of
wavelength, and these make up the *Electromagnetic Spectrum*.
(See DICTIONARY OF SCIENCE for *Gamma rays, Ultra-violet light*,
etc).

Wavelengths and Frequencies

λ	n	λ	n
2,000 m	150 kHz	50 m	6 MHz
1,000 m	300 kHz	10 m	30 MHz
500 m	600 kHz	3 m	100 MHz
300 m	1,000 kHz	1 m	300 MHz
	(1 MHz)	10 cm	3,000 MHz
200 m	1,500 kHz	3 cm	10,000 MHz
100 m	3,000 kHz	1 cm	30,000 MHz
	(3 MHz)	5 mm	60,000 MHz

The Electromagnetic Spectrum

Wavelength	Frequency	Name
0·01 Å	3×10^{14} MHz	} Gamma rays and X-rays
0·1 Å	3×10^{13} MHz	
10 Å	3×10^{11} MHz	
100 Å	3×10^{10} MHz	} Ultra-violet light
4,000 Å	$7·5 \times 10^{8}$ MHz	
		Visible light < violet red
7,500 Å	4×10^{8} MHz	
1,000,000 Å	3×10^{6} MHz	} Infra-red light
(0·01 cm)		
0·1 cm	300,000 MHz	} Radio waves from millimetre
1,000,000 cm	30 kHz	waves to long waves

Fading The variation in strength of a received radio signal. Medium waves suffer from this at night when the ground ray and the sky ray are received together and the sky ray is varying. Short waves suffer from it because of variations in the conditions of the reflecting ionosphere. It can be reduced in a receiver by *automatic gain control* (q.v.).

Farad The SI unit of *capacitance* (q.v.).

Feedback This is the feeding back from a later part of a circuit to an earlier part. The feedback may be negative, in which case it stabilises, reduces amplification and, if it varies according to the input, provides automatic gain control. Negative feedback is usually introduced into audio amplifiers as it reduces most forms of distortion. Positive feedback can cause instability but, if controlled (reaction), will increase amplification.

Ferrite A material made like a ceramic, i.e. by baking at a high temperature. It is made of a number of oxides, including iron oxide, and can be designed so that it has any magnetic properties desired. Moreover, it can be moulded into any shape. The magnetic coils used on the cathode-ray tubes of some television receivers are wound on ferrite cores. A long rod of ferrite inside a coil constitutes a ferrite 'aerial' for a radio receiver.

Filter A circuit device for passing oscillations of only certain desired frequencies, e.g. low-pass filter, high-pass filter, band-pass filter (for passing only a band of frequencies and cutting off everything of higher and lower frequencies).

Low-pass filter: the higher the frequency of the input signal the more easily it is short-circuited. The lower the frequency the more easily it is passed on.

High-pass filter: the higher the frequency of the input signal the more easily it is passed on. The lower the frequency the more easily it is short-circuited.

Quartz crystal or ceramic filters are also used in IF stages: tuned to the IF they increase selectivity.

Frequency An alternating quantity (such as an alternating current or a radio wave) consists of repeated *cycles*, one cycle being the sequence of variation of the quantity from zero to maximum positive, from maximum positive through zero to maximum negative and then back to zero. The number of such cycles per second is called the frequency and is measured in *hertz* (one hertz is the same as one cycle per second).

Frequency Modulation (FM) A special way of making a *carrier wave* (q.v.) take an audio-frequency variation. Instead of the amplitude of the carrier being made to vary, the frequency is made to vary instead. It is done on VHF transmissions by the BBC to give a high-quality signal fairly free of interference by locally-made electrical noise. An FM receiver must have extra circuitry to transform the signal into an amplitude-modulated one for audio-frequency amplification in the usual way. The two stages needed are called the *limiter* and *discriminator*, usually combined into one stage called the *ratio detector*.

Galvanometer An instrument which measures small electric currents.

Ganging The mechanical coupling of variable capacitors or resistors in order to control two or more circuits with one knob.

Graphical Symbols There is a convention for representing in circuit diagrams the many sorts of components involved in electronics, radio and television. Most of these are now standardised, but some still have a few variations.

Graphical Symbols

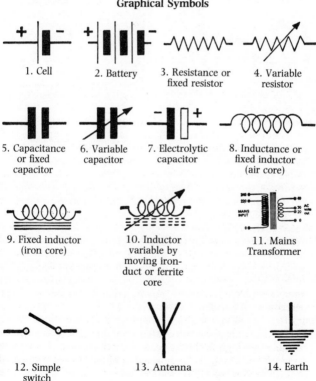

1. Cell
2. Battery
3. Resistance or fixed resistor
4. Variable resistor
5. Capacitance or fixed capacitor
6. Variable capacitor
7. Electrolytic capacitor
8. Inductance or fixed inductor (air core)
9. Fixed inductor (iron core)
10. Inductor variable by moving iron-duct or ferrite core
11. Mains Transformer
12. Simple switch
13. Antenna
14. Earth

15. Rectifier   16. Loudspeaker   17. Mains Triode
                                                    Valve

18. P–N–P Transistor   19. N–P–N Transistor   20. Field Effect
                                                    Transistor

21. Mosfet   22. Integrated Circuit (Micro-chip)

Ground Ray Radio waves on the long and medium wave lengths
are sent out by an earthed antenna and travel along attached
to the ground. This is the ground ray. It provides the commonest and most widespread system of broadcasting. The
range varies according to the power of the transmitter and the
nature of the ground over which it travels. For the sort of
power in use today, the reliable range of a ground ray can be
up to two or three hundred miles.

Half-wave Aerial See *aerial*.

Harmonic Distortion Each fundamental note also has harmonics
which arise at multiples of the original. If an amplifier over-
emphasises the harmonics in relation to the fundamental it
suffers from harmonic distortion. The 'goodness' of an
amplifier is often judged by, among other things, the minimal
percentage of harmonic distortion.

Henry (*H*) The SI unit of *inductance* (q.v.).

Hi-fi An Americanism which is short for, and has been adopted
as meaning, high-fidelity: that is, reproduction of an original
performance exactly as performed without any coloration or
distortion. It is not yet entirely attained, but modern results

are superb (at a price). There is a generally accepted *DIN* (q.v.) specification for Hi-fi which is rather lower than the standard at which many modern amplifiers can now operate.

Hum Continuous, low frequency *noise* (q.v.) in audio equipment usually originating from the mains supply and caused, for example, by inadequate earthing or an unsmoothed power supply.

IBA The Independent Broadcasting Authority (formerly the Independent Television Authority) was set up as the result of the Television Act 1954 to provide a service, additional to that of the BBC, for broadcasting entertainment, disseminating information, religious and educational programmes. The Authority receives no revenue through licence fees but derives its income through advertising. The first transmission started in September 1955.

Programmes are produced by 15 programme companies in 14 separate areas. National news bulletins for all areas are provided by Independent Television News, a non-profit-making company in which all the programme companies are shareholders. The programme companies under contract with the Authority from January 1982 are:

Anglia Television (East of England); Border Television (The Borders and Isle of Man); Central Independent Television (East and West Midlands); Channel Television (Channel Islands); Grampian Television (North Scotland); Granada Television (North-West England); HTV (Wales and West of England); London Weekend Television (London weekends from 7 pm Fridays); Scottish Television (Central Scotland); Television South West (South-West England); Thames Television (London weekdays to 7 pm Fridays); TVS (Television South) (South and South-East England); Tyne Tees Television (North-East England); Ulster Television (Northern Ireland); and Yorkshire Television (Yorkshire).

In addition to the above, Channel 4 TV began operating on 2 November 1982 to cater mainly for minority interests. It is a subsidiary of IBA and the ITV companies pay a subscription towards its running costs. It broadcasts nationally, with the exception of Wales where Channel 4 carries Welsh language programmes emanating from both ITV and BBC.

TV-AM is another new company within the IBA and was

formed to provide early morning programmes both during the week and at weekends. It operates on the ITV channels and began on 1 February 1983.

ILR Independent Local Radio, which comes under the control of IBA. By the end of 1985 fifty local radio stations operating independently of the BBC were broadcasting in the UK. They derive their revenue from advertisements and broadcast popular music and news bulletins. Further information about IBA and ILR is available from IBA Engineering Information Service, Crawley Court, Winchester, Hants SO21 2QA.

Impedance (Z) The word used to represent for AC circuits the equivalent of *resistance* (q.v.) in a DC circuit. The impedance depends on the actual resistance and the *reactance* (q.v.) due to capacitance and inductance. Impedance has the same relationship to emf (E) and current (I) as resistance. So

$$I = \frac{E}{Z}$$

Inductance Whenever a coil has a varying magnetic field through it, an emf is set up in the coil causing a current to flow if the circuit is complete. This is known as *induction* and was discovered by Faraday. Whenever an electric current flows in a coil, a magnetic field is created through the coil. Therefore a varying current in a coil will produce a varying magnetic field through the coil and, by induction, will give rise to an induced current in the coil. However, the induced current is always in a direction which opposes the effect of the original current. This opposition to the passage of a varying current is called *inductive reactance* and depends on (a) the rate of change of current in the coil and (b) the *self inductance* (L) of the coil, which is a quantity that takes into account the diameter of the coil, the number of turns and the nature of the core. L is measured in *henries* and a coil has an inductance of one henry if a current varying at the rate of one ampere per second induces in the coil an emf of one volt. If AC of frequency f flows through a coil of inductance L, the inductive reactance (X_L) is $2\pi f L$ ohms, so that with an applied emf of V volts, the current will be $V/2\pi f L$ amps. By induction it is possible for a varying current in one coil to cause an induced current to flow in another coil. This is known as *mutual inductance* and is the basis of *transformers* (q.v.).

Inductance–Capacitance Circuit (*L–C Circuit*) In an AC circuit the voltage across an inductor leads the current through it by 90° (see *phase*), while that across a capacitor lags the current by 90°. This behaviour leads to interesting effects in both the series *L–C* circuit, in which an inductor is connected in series with a capacitor, and the parallel *L–C* circuit, in which an inductor is connected in parallel with a capacitor. In the series circuit, because the current through each component is the same, the voltage across the capacitor is 180° out of phase with that across the inductor. This means that the two voltages will cancel out if they are of the same magnitude. In the parallel circuit, because the voltage across each component is the same, the current through the capacitor is 180° out of phase with that through the inductor and the currents will tend to cancel each other out. The condition for complete cancellation is the same in each case, namely that the inductive reactance (X_L) equals the capacitive reactance (X_C), where both quantities depend on the frequency f of the electricity.

Now, $X_L = 2\pi f L$ and $X_C = 1/2\pi f C$
so if $X_L = X_C$
then, $2\pi f L = 1/2\pi f C$
$$f^2 = 1/4\pi^2 LC$$
$$f = 1/2\pi\sqrt{LC}$$

This special frequency is called the *resonant frequency*. At the resonant frequency in the series circuit, the combination of inductor and capacitor present no opposition to the current, though resistance in the wires does limit the current. The series *L–C* circuit is known as an acceptor circuit as, at the resonant frequency, the opposition to current is at a minimum. At the resonant frequency in the parallel circuit, the total current is zero. In practice, however, resistance in the wires means that the cancellation is not exact, but the circuit still has a maximum opposition to current at this frequency. It is therefore called a rejector circuit.

Because of this peculiar behaviour of series and parallel *L–C* circuits, they are used in *tuning* (q.v.) and other applications where it is necessary to pick out a particular frequency.

Integrated Circuit (IC) ICs are complete circuit elements (e.g. an amplifier), the individual components (transistors, capacitors and resistors) of which are all together on a single 'chip' of silicon. As individual containers for each component are not required and very little power is needed to make the circuit work, the chip can be made very small (up to 100 components per sq mm).

Intermediate Frequency (IF) This is the fixed frequency that results when an incoming signal is mixed with a locally generated oscillation. The IF in Britain for the *superhet* (q.v.) reception of long waves and medium waves is 470 kHz. The IF for BBC VHF frequency modulation programmes is 10·7 MHz.

Ionosphere High above the earth's surface, starting at 70 miles or so, there are deep layers of gas electrified by the sun's rays. These electrified atoms and molecules affect radio waves and are known under the general term 'ionosphere'. The ionosphere varies daily and seasonally and according to the behaviour of the sun.

Medium waves are reflected from its lowest layers during the day and from higher layers at night (when the lowest layers have disappeared, this giving good intensity of reception some distance away). Short waves are reflected from the ionosphere and enable long-distance communication to take place. Very short waves penetrate the ionosphere and are lost.

Load The purpose of a circuit is to generate a signal or to modify an incoming signal and then to deliver the new signal into another apparatus known as the load. The load takes energy from the circuit that 'drives' it and the nature of the load (e.g. its impedance) alters the behaviour of the circuit. The load for an audio amplifier is usually a loudspeaker, and that for a radio transmitter is an *aerial* (q.v.).

Loudspeaker A device for turning electrical variations into variations of air pressure that reach the ears. There is commercially only one widely-used type—the moving-coil loudspeaker. In this a magnet, usually a permanent magnet, has an annular gap. In this gap floats a tiny light coil of fine wire held in position by a 'spider'. Attached to the coil is a diaphragm, the whole moving in sympathy with current floating through the coil.

For an ordinary commercial loudspeaker the ability of the loudspeaker is usually restricted to about a range of 100–5,000

Hz. By special construction a loudspeaker can be made to cover a wider range than this, and a combination of loudspeakers can be made to cover from 30 to 20,000 Hz.

The loudspeaker is, of course, the final stage of a sound-radio receiver or the audio part of a television receiver.

Magnetic Field A region of space in which a magnet experiences a turning force (couple). Magnetic fields are produced by permanent magnets and electric currents.

Magnetometer An instrument for measuring the intensity of a magnetic field.

Maser A device for the amplification of electromagnetic waves. Used in radioastronomy for amplifying the very small signals received from distant radio galaxies, and for picking up the signals received from communications satellites.

Measuring Instruments To measure current an ammeter (milliammeter, microammeter) is used. For voltage (emf, potential difference) a voltmeter is used. For resistance it is an ohmmeter that is required.

Microelectronics Microelectronics is concerned with the miniaturisation of electronic circuits. This is achieved by use of *integrated circuits* (q.v.) and *printed circuits* (q.v.), which enable complicated circuits (as in computers) to be kept to a very small size.

Microphone An apparatus for changing pressure waves in air (sound) into electrical variations. There are several sorts, such as the crystal microphone, the ribbon microphone, the moving-coil microphone, etc. ˙

Microwaves An electromagnetic wave with a wavelength between fifty and one-fiftieth of a centimetre.

Modulation This is the term for changing a carrier wave in such a way that it has with it the audio-frequency variations corresponding to speech or music. *Amplitude modulation* (q.v.) occurs when a carrier increases and decreases in amplitude. *Frequency modulation* (q.v.) occurs when a carrier varies in *frequency* according to the amplitude of the current from the microphone.

For reception of radio-telephony the modulation must be separated from the carrier. This is usually called *detection* (q.v.), but is sometimes called demodulation.

Molniyas The name given to the first series of Russian communications satellites.

Noise In electronic equipment, noise is unwanted hissing, humming and crackling heard as a background to the wanted signal. Noise may be generated by the equipment itself (for instance due to the random thermal motions of electrons), and this is particularly troublesome in high frequency circuits carrying small signals. An important factor in such circuits is therefore the *signal-to-noise ratio* which needs to be large if the noise is not going to swamp the signal. Noise may also be picked up from outside sources, e.g. mains *hum* (q.v.) and 'atmospherics' in radio receivers. In TV reception, 'noise' can appear as 'snow' on the picture.

Ohm's Law The most important law of simple electrical circuits. It states that the current through a conductor is directly proportional to the potential difference across the conductor and inversely proportional to its resistance. Ohm's Law is directly applicable to most simple DC circuits. By introducing the idea of *impedance* (q.v.), it can be generalised to AC circuits that include capacitors and inductors.

Oscillation An oscillation is one complete cycle of a regularly varying quantity. See *frequency*.

Oscillator An electronic circuit designed to generate continuous *oscillations* (q.v.). This is usually achieved by connecting an *inductance-capacitance circuit* (q.v.) to a valve or transistor amplifier and arranging positive *feedback* (q.v.) to keep the oscillations going. The *frequency* (q.v.) of the oscillations depends on the values of capacitance and inductance in the L–C circuit. Oscillators have numerous uses, e.g. to generate the *carrier wave* (q.v.) needed to transmit radio signals.

PAL Phase Alternative Line, the system of transmission used in Britain for colour TV.

Parallel A method of connecting circuit components. If components have ends ab, a_1b_1, a_2b_2, etc, then they are connected in parallel if all the a's are joined together and all the b's joined together. If electric cells of the same emf are joined in parallel, the total emf is that of any one of them but greater power is available from cells connected in this way. The diagram on page E25 shows how to calculate the resultant resistance (or capacitance) when resistors (or capacitors) are connected in parallel.

Resistors in parallel.

Total given by $\frac{1}{R} = \frac{1}{R_1} + \frac{1}{R_2} + \frac{1}{R_3}$

Capacitors in parallel.

Total $C = C_1 + C_2 + C_3$

Phase This is a term which describes the time relationship of two oscillatory currents or waves of the same *frequency* (q.v.) If both are zero together, increase to their maximum positive together and subsequently remain in step, the two oscillations are said to be *in phase*. If, when oscillation (a) is at its maximum positive, oscillation (b) is zero, then (b) is said to be 90° *out of phase* with (a). The diagram shows the case of (b) *lagging* (a) by 90° (or equivalently (a) *leading* (b) by 90°) because when (a) is at its maximum positive, (b) is zero but increasing towards its maximum positive. If when (a) is at its maximum positive, (b) is at its maximum negative, then (a) and (b) are said to be *180° out of phase* and if combined would cancel each other out completely provided they were of the same magnitude. A phase difference of 360° means that the oscillations are again in phase as an oscillation merely repeats itself every 360°.

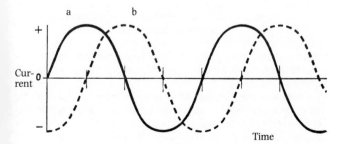

Two oscillations out of phase by 90° or one quarter of a cycle;
(b) 'lags' on (a)

Pick-up The device which carries the cartridge and stylus and enables the latter to follow the grooves of a disc recording. The cartridge it carries may be either magnetic or crystal.

Piezoelectricity Electric current produced by mechanical stimulation of crystals.

p–n junction The boundary between a piece of *n*-type and a piece of *p*-type *semiconductor* (q.v.). (See *doping*). *The p–n* junction has the property of *rectification* (q.v.), and is therefore widely used in *diodes* (q.v.).

Power Power is the rate of doing work or using energy and is measured in *watts*. The rate of work done by an electrical apparatus in watts is equal to the voltage across it (in volts) multiplied by the current through it (in amps).

Pre-amplifier Amplifies the signal input sufficiently to load the main amplifier. Usually contains tone controls.

Prefixes Standard prefixes are:

$p = 1$ million millionth $=$ pica, e.g. 2 picafarads, 2 pF
$n = 1$ thousand millionth $=$ nano, e.g. 4 nanoseconds, 4ns
$\mu = 1$ millionth $=$ micro, e.g. 3 microamperes, $3\mu A$
$m = 1$ thousandth $=$ milli, e.g. 6 milliamperes, 6 mA
$k = 1$ thousand $=$ kilo, e.g. 10 kilovolts, 10 kV
$M = 1$ million $=$ mega, e.g. 10 megahertz, 10 MHz
$G = 10^9 =$ giga, e.g. $11 \cdot 7$ gigahertz, $11 \cdot 7$ GHz

Printed Circuit This is an insulating board with a layer of copper on one side. The copper is dissolved away except along protected paths which then act as connections between components mounted on the board. Photographic methods are often used to scale down the size of printed circuits.

Quadraphony Quadraphonic stereo or 'quad sound' is a system which allows stereo reproduction to be fed into four loudspeakers via four amplifiers, sound coming from each corner of the room.

Radio Receiver The simplest valve radio receiver consisted of the valve and the associated tuning circuit and telephones. The commercial receiver is a *superhet* (q.v.). All modern radio receivers are based on transistor circuits. The controls are normally: on-off, volume, tuning and (sometimes) tone. A wave-change switch is also usually included. The quality of a radio receiver depends, of course, on the circuitry.

The common way of building a receiver was to mount the components on and under a metal chassis, with the control spindles projecting from the front. The chassis technique has been replaced by a board on which connections are printed, i.e. a *printed circuit* (q.v.), but modern practice inclines to the *integrated circuit* (q.v.).

For a beginner a 'crystal set' can still be a satisfactory form of receiver. Fig. 1 is a modern design and uses a germanium diode, either OA91 or OA81. It will need an aerial (the size depending on the distance from the nearest radio transmitter, but 70 cm of wire round the room will often suffice), plus an earth which may be a connection to a metal, water or central-heating pipe (*never* a gas pipe). The coil is wound on a ferrite rod 100–140 mm long and consists of 55 turns of 28 dcc (double cotton-covered) wire wound side by side on a tube formed of cartridge or drawing paper placed round the rod. Taps (by twisting the wire) are taken at the tenth and twenty-fifth turns. A 0·0005 mfd solid dielectric variable capacitor is used for tuning and the circuit is completed by a 1,000 pfd capacitor. Four terminals (or two double terminal blocks) will

To make a simple receiver

Fig. 1

be required, plus a knob. The set can be made up on a 150 mm square of hardboard, with the tuning capacitor in the centre, aerial and earth terminals on one side and phones on the other. The ferrite rod can be fixed by 'sticky tape' at each end. Soldering must be done quickly and cleanly with a hot iron; do not hold the iron on the component being fixed.

The receiver in the second diagram uses the ZN414 IC made by Ferranti. The same coil may be used (but will not need the tap at 10 turns) and possibly an aerial or earth will not be needed. Only $1\frac{1}{2}$ volts is required so that a single cell will be adequate. Both receivers require headphones of 2,000 or 4,000 ohms resistance, but low-resistance phones may be used with a small LS output transformer. A $3\cdot3$ k/ohm resistor across the phone terminals should allow a small crystal earpiece to be tried.

The circuit in Fig. 3 is of an amplifier using a modern IC and this will couple to either of the other receivers to work a small loudspeaker. The best method of constructing this amplifier or the receiver in Fig. 2 is to use a small piece of Veroboard. The chip will clip into it and can be soldered to the Veroboard. The other components can be soldered into the appropriate positions to complete the connections. Components can be purchased from advertisers in radio periodicals or from specialists in 'chip' technology such as Maplin Electronic Supplies Ltd, PO Box 3, Rayleigh, Essex, SS6 8LR.

Fig. 2

Fig. 3

RSGB Radio Society of Great Britain, the national body for British amateur radio enthusiasts, particularly transmitting amateurs, but anyone interested in radio may join. The address of RSGB is Cranborne Road, Potters Bar, Herts EN6 3JN.

Radio Waves in Use

		Names commonly used	
Frequency	*Wave-lengths*	*Wavelength range*	*Frequency range*
Low frequency	Long waves	Above 600 m	Below 500 kHz
Medium frequency	Medium waves	200–600 m	500–1,500 kHz
High frequency	Short waves	10–80 m	3,750 kc/s to 30 MHz
VHF Very-high frequency	Ultra-short waves	Band I 4·41–7·32 m Band II 3–3·43 m Band III 1·39–1·72 m	41–68 MHz 87·5–100 MHz 174–216 MHz
UHF Ultra-high frequency		Band IV 51–63 cm Band V 31–49 cm	475–585 MHz 610–960 MHz
	Micro-waves	7·5 mm–15 cm Divided into several bands—S Band, X Band, J Band, etc.	2,000–40,000 MHz

Reactance (X) This is the term for the effect of capacitance or inductance in cutting down alternating current. It is given the symbol X, usually with suffixes L and C to denote whether it is inductive reactance or capacitative reactance, thus X_L, X_C. It is measured in ohms. It varies with the frequency of the applied alternating current. See *impedance*.

Records Flat round discs, formerly made of a wax/shellac compound, now moulded in plastic material upon which music, etc., is recorded by pressing from a master record. Modern records are 7 in (175 mm) and 12 in (305 mm) in diameter, the former rotating at 45 revolutions per minute and the latter (long playing) at $33\frac{1}{3}$ rpm. *Compact discs* (q.v.) were introduced in 1983.

Rectification Alternating current reverses its direction every half cycle. Rectification is the process by which AC is converted to a direct current which always flows in the same direction. This is achieved by the use of rectifiers or *diodes* (q.v.) which allow current to pass through them in one direction only. In the *half wave* rectifier the $-ve$ half of the cycle is simply suppressed, while in the *full wave* rectifier, the $-ve$ half of the cycle is inverted so as to flow in the desired direction.

Rectification is very important because the mains supply is AC while most electronic circuits need a DC supply. However to be suitable, the rectified supply has to be *smoothed* so that the voltage is nearly constant.

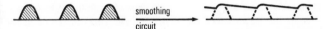

Resistance This is the tendency for all materials to oppose the flow of an electric current and to convert electrical energy into heat. It is measured in ohms and the resistance of a conductor depends, in simple cases, on the *resistivity* (q.v.) of the material and the dimensions of the conductor. A resistance of R ohms carrying a current of I amps converts electrical energy into heat at the rate of I^2R watts.

Resistivity This is the resistance (measured in microhms) of a cubic centimetre of material, and is a measure of how badly the material conducts electricity. The reciprocal of resistivity is *conductivity*, a measure of how well a material conducts electricity. Copper and other metals are good conductors, with a low resistivity which increases with temperature. Glass and plastic are insulators with a very high resistivity. Between these limits lie *semiconductors* (q.v.).

Resistivities

Resistivity in micro-ohm centimetres at room temperature

Aluminium	.	.	2·82	Amber	.	.	.	5×10^{16}
Brass	.	.	About 8	Celluloid	.	.	.	2×10^{10}
Copper	.	.	1·72	Germanium	.	.	46×10^{6}
Iron	.	.	9·8	Graphite	.	.	.	1,375
Magnesium	.	.	4·46	Mica (clear)	.	.	4×10^{16}
Nichrome	.	.	About 100	Paraffin wax	.	.	3×10^{18}
Nickel	.	.	7·24	Plate glass	.	.	2×10^{13}
Steel, hardened	.	About 45	Silicon	.	.	.	10
Tin	.	.	11·4	Sulphur	.	.	.	2×10^{23}

Resistor An electronic component used in a circuit to provide a known *resistance* (q.v.). Both fixed and variable resistors are very widely used.

Resonance When an *inductance–capacitance circuit* (q.v.) responds at a maximum to one frequency only, it is said to be in resonance with a signal of that frequency. *Tuning* (q.v.) consists of selecting the point of resonance.

Root-mean-square (RMS) The average value of a quantity that takes positive and negative values equally (e.g. an alternating current) is zero. If the values are squared, the mean found and then the square root taken, the non-zero result is called the RMS value. Because the heating effect of an electric current depends on the square of the current, the RMS of an AC is equal to the constant DC needed to produce the same heating effect as the AC. The peak value (or amplitude) of an AC is $\sqrt{2} = 1 \cdot 414$ times the RMS value.

Satellite Broadcasting It is anticipated that in a few years' time viewers in UK will be able to view programmes directly received from a satellite. Signals would be beamed towards the satellite and 'bounced' off it back to earth where they would be received on a special aerial system. Refer to the note on page E3 regarding DBS channels.

Scanning The traversing of a scene or screen by a spot of light in an orderly fashion. It is scanning in successive lines in a very short time that allows a scene to be turned into electrical variations by a television camera and then into a pattern of light on a television-receiver screen.

Selectivity The ability of a radio receiver to tune to one radio station without interference from stations with nearby frequencies.

Semiconductor A material whose *resistivity* (q.v.) is much higher than that of metals but much less than that of insulators. E.g. the elements germanium, silicon and selenium and the compounds copper oxide and indium antiminide. Semiconductors have three special electrical properties which make them very useful. (a) Unlike metals, the conductivity of semiconductors can be increased by the addition of small quantities of impurities. This is called *doping* (q.v.), and is the basis behind all modern semiconductor devices such as the *transistor* (q.v.). (b) Some semiconductors (notably selenium) increase their conductivity if light is shined on them. This is useful in photocells and in copying by the process of *xerography*. (c) Over some temperature ranges, semiconductors increase their conductivity very fast with increasing temperature, and can therefore be used where sensitivity to temperature is needed.

Series A method of connecting circuit components such that they are joined end to end. The current through each component is therefore the same, though the voltage across each will differ. The diagram shows how to work out the total resistance (capacitance) when resistors (capacitors) are connected in series. See *parallel*.

Resistors in series. Total $R = R_1 + R_2 + R_3$

Capacitors in series

Total given by $\frac{1}{C} = \frac{1}{C_1} + \frac{1}{C_2} + \frac{1}{C_3}$

Sky Ray Radio waves going out into space and not following the ground.

Sound Sound is the sensation felt when our ears pick up pressure waves (i.e. sound waves) transmitted through a gas or other fluid from a vibrating souce (e.g. a violin string). Sound waves through a gas consist of alternate compressions and rarefactions of the gas travelling along at the speed of sound. This is 332 metres per second or 760 miles an hour in air. The *pitch* of sound heard depends directly on the *frequency* (q.v.) of vibration of the source. Thus the note middle C corresponds to a frequency of vibration 256 cycles per second. The octave higher is always double the frequency.

Music and speech are built up from a large number of simple waves of different frequencies all mixed together. Even a single note played on a violin, say, consists of a lowest frequency which is called the *fundamental* (and corresponds to the pitch of the note), as well as a number of higher frequencies present in lesser strength. These are called *harmonics* and they determine the tone or quality of the note heard. This is why audio equipment sensitive to frequencies up to 15,000 cycles per second is needed for the faithful reproduction of sound.

SSB A modulated carrier wave has two sets of sidebands, lower and upper. Single sideband working is becoming very popular with amateur transmitters and is a system whereby the carrier and one sideband is eliminated and all the transmitter power is concentrated in the remaining (single) sideband. One of its advantages is an improvement in selectivity in the crowded amateur bands.

SSTV Slow scan television, as used by amateur transmitters.

Stereo Stereophonic reproduction is designed to allow each ear to hear sound, speech, etc., correctly from the left or right of the orchestra, studio or other source of transmission. Radio broadcasts on VHF are often in stereo, as are most gramophone discs or tape cassettes. For receiving stereo, two amplifiers (or a twin amplifier) and two loudspeakers are required. The latter should be placed about 6 ft apart.

Stylus The correct name for the 'needle' which is placed in the groove of a disc recording and which transmits its vibrations to the cartridge for amplification and reproduction. The stylus may be made of diamond (the best and longest lasting) or of sapphire or ruby. Standard tip radii are: mono LP or 45's = 0·029 mm and stereo or 'compatible' (i.e. either mono or stereo) = 0·0175 mm by 0·0075 mm, these being the latest elliptical tips.

Superhet The superheterodyne receiver. This is the common

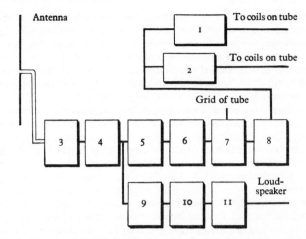

Block Diagram of Superhet Television Receiver: 1. Frame Time Base. 2. Line Time Base. 3. RF Amplifier. 4. Frequency Changer. 5. IF Amplifier. 6. Video Detector. 7. Video Amplifier. 8. Sync. Separator. 9. IF Amplifier. 10. Audio Detector. 11. Audio Amplifier

commercial type for sound and television. It enables high *selectivity* (q.v.) suitable for today's overcrowded air to be obtained without too much loss of quality.

The principle is to mix two oscillations together in a frequency-changer in such a way that no matter what the frequency of the incoming signal is, the outgoing frequency from the frequency-changer is always the same, the *intermediate frequency* (q.v.). At this fixed frequency it is comparatively easy to make satisfactory band-pass filters and transformers.

Symbols For the mathematical treatment of current, emf, etc., symbols in the form of letters are used:

λ = lambda = wavelength
n or f = frequency
v = velocity
R = resistance
I = current
E = emf
R_a = AC resistance of valve

μ = mu = amplification factor of valve, sometimes written m
g = mutual conductance of valve
L = inductance
C = capacitance

Synthesiser An electronic musical instrument which is played by means of a keyboard like a piano. The sounds are produced by oscillations which can be varied to give musical sounds based on orchestral instruments or a variety of noises.

Tape Plastic tape coated with ferromagnetic particles (iron oxide), which can be magnetised by a magnet in a tape head. Varying the force of the magnetisation by feeding audio currents into the tape head enables the tape to record the matter carried by them. Tapes comes in varying widths and narrow ones are fitted into cassettes. Tapes may be wiped clean and used again. For better frequency response and wider range, tape using chromium dioxide particles is coming into more general use. Similar tapes are available for recording television programmes.

Teletext A form of TV newspaper requiring a special receiver on which can be obtained news, weather, train times, etc. The BBC system is called Ceefax and the ITV Oracle.

Telstar The first television satellite, orbited by the United States.

Transformer A device for increasing or decreasing the magnitude of an alternating voltage. A step-up transformer consists of a primary coil of few turns and a secondary coil of a larger number of turns both wound on the same iron core but forming separate circuits. In a step-down transformer the primary has more turns than the secondary. The ratio of the voltage in the secondary to that in the primary is nearly equal to the ratio of the number of turns in the secondary to that in the primary. If the voltage is higher in the secondary than in the primary then the current in the secondary is proportionately lower than that in the primary, so that the power in each coil is the same. Transformers work by means of electromagnetic induction (see *inductance*). The AC in the primary produces a varying magnetic field through the secondary and so induces an emf in the secondary.

Transceiver By special circuit arrangements a set can be switched for use either as a transmitter or a receiver. Generally handheld, has recently come into prominence in *CB Radio* (q.v.). Often called a 'rig' or a 'walkie-talkie'.

Transistor An electronic device consisting of three layers of *semiconductor* (q.v.). The *n–p–n* transistor has two layers of *n*-type semiconductor sandwiching a layer of *p*-type, and the *p-n-p* transistor has two layers of *p*-type sandwiching one of *n*-type (see *doping*). In either case, the middle layer is called the *base* and the outer layers are called the *collector* and *emitter*. The transistor is principally used as an amplifier, since a small current flowing in the base–emitter circuit can be used to control a much larger current in the emitter–collector circuit.

The transistor was invented in 1948 and since then has rapidly been replacing the *valve* (q.v.) in electronic circuits. The advantage of using transistors is that they can be made very small and reliable since they do not require the vacuum tube, the heater or the high voltage power supply necessary for valves.

Triode A thermionic valve with three electrodes—cathode, grid, anode.

Tuner The 'front end' of hi-fi equipment whereby broadcast programmes are received. Usually VHF only, but can include medium and long waves. Some tuners incorporate a *decoder* (q.v.) for stereo.

Tuning In a radio receiver the frequency of the radio station heard is determined by the resonant frequency of an *inductance-capacitance circuit* (q.v.). By varying the capacitance in the circuit, the resonant frequency is changed and so different stations can be selected. See *resonance*.

Valve (Thermionic Valve) Known as 'tube' in USA, this is an evacuated glass bulb containing a cathode, an anode and one or more electrodes called grids. The cathode is heated and emits electrons. Valves are now only used for transmitting and industrial purposes.

Video The word indicating the vision side of a television signal. It is coming by popular usage to mean a video recorder. Recorders are available for the purpose of 'taping' programmes for later viewing or for playing through the TV set commercially produced cassettes of films, etc.

Several different systems are available, Japanese, European and American and they do not necessarily allow interchangeability of cassettes between one another. Portable video recorders are available for use with a video camera to enable production of 'home movies' on cassettes. Libraries and clubs have been established from which tape cassettes of films may be hired for home viewing on TV sets. Video has produced a new branch of the electronics industry and its own vocabulary (see Recommended Reading).

Video Tape A means of recording TV programmes on tape which is simpler and cheaper than recording on film. Most TV programmes are no longer 'live' but 'video-taped'.

Watt (W) The SI unit of electrical *power* (q.v.).

Wavelength From the earliest days of radio, stations have been known by their wavelengths which have been measured in metres. Today the use of frequency, measured in kiloHertz, is preferred but many older sets in the UK are marked in wavelengths. The following formula shows how to calculate a wavelength from a frequency:

$$\frac{300{,}000}{\text{frequency (in kHz)}} = \text{wavelength (in metres)}$$

Conversely, dividing three hundred thousand by the wavelength will give the frequency.

Zener diode A special form of junction diode usually used for voltage regulation or stabilisation.

Recommended Reading

A Dictionary of Electronics (Penguin)
Beginner's Guide to Digital Electronics by I. R. Sinclair (Newnes)
Foundations of Wireless and Electronics by M. G. Scroggie BSc.C.Eng FIEE (Iliffe)
A Guide to Amateur Radio by Pat Hawker G3VA (RSGB)

A DICTIONARY OF AIRCRAFT, ROCKETS AND MISSILES

(WITH A SECTION ON ASTRONOMY)

Abbreviations

AAM	Air-to-air missile
ADF	Automatic direction finding
AEW	Airborne early warning
AFCS	Automatic flight control system
APU	Auxiliary power unit
ASI	Airspeed indicator
ASM	Air-to-surface missile
ASV	Air-to-surface vessel
ASW	Anti-submarine warfare
ATC	Air traffic control
AUW	All-up weight
AWACS	Airborne warning and control system
BCAR	British Civil Airworthiness Requirements
CAA	Civil Aviation Authority (UK)
CAB	Civil Aeronautics Board (USA)
DF	Direction finding
DME	Distance measuring equipment
EAS	Equivalent airspeed
ECCM	Electronic counter-countermeasures
ECM	Electronic countermeasures
EHP	Equivalent horsepower of turboprop
ELINT	Electronic intelligence
EPNdB	Effective perceived noise decibel
ESA	European Space Agency
EVA	Extra-vehicular activity
FAA	Federal Aviation Administration (USA)
FAI	Fédération Aéronautique Internationale
FAR	Federal Aviation Regulations
FBW	Fly by wire
FLIR	Forward-looking infra-red
GCI	Ground-controlled interception
GPU	Ground power unit
GPWS	Ground proximity warning system
HF	High frequency
HUD	Head-up display
IAS	Indicated airspeed
IATA	International Air Transport Association
ICAO	International Civil Aviation Organisation
IFF	Identification friend or foe

IFR	Instrument flight rules
ILS	Instrument landing system
INAS	Integrated nav/attack system
INS	Inertial navigation system
ISA	International Standard Atmosphere
JATO	Jet-assisted take-off
LABS	Low-altitude bombing system
LCN	Load classification number
LLTV	Low-light TV
M	Mach number
MAD	Magnetic anomaly detector
MLS	Microwave landing system
MMO	Maximum operating Mach number
MTBF	Mean time between failures
MTOGW	Maximum take-off gross weight
NASA	National Aeronautics and Space Administration (USA)
NOE	Nap-of-the-Earth low flying
OWE	Operating weight empty
RAE	Royal Aircraft Establishment
RAeC	Royal Aero Club
RAeS	Royal Aeronautical Society
RPV	Remotely piloted vehicle
RVR	Runway visual range
SAC	US Air Force Strategic Air Command
SAR	Search and rescue
SBAC	Society of British Aerospace Companies
SHP	Shaft horsepower
SL	Sea level
SLAR	Sideways-looking airborne radar
SSR	Secondary surveillance radar
STOL	Short take-off and landing
TAS	True airspeed
TBO	Time between overhauls
UHF	Ultra high frequency
VFR	Visual Flight rules
VHF	Very high frequency
VLF	Very low frequency
VNE	Never-exceed speed
VOR	VHF omni-directional range beacon
VTOL	Vertical take-off and landing
ZFW	Zero-fuel weight

Aerofoil The geometry of a section through a wing, rotor blade or tailplane so shaped that it can contribute lift.

Air flow over an aerofoil surface, caused by forward motion of the aerofoil, results in a reduction of pressure above the upper surface and a slight increase of pressure beneath. Thus there is a resultant lift at right-angles to the direction of the air flow.

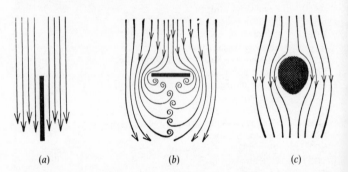

Air action on a flat plate and a stream-lined obstacle. In (a) the plate is edge-on and the air flows smoothly past. In (b) the plate is face-on and a large area of low pressure and turbulence is produced, slowing down the air. In (c) a crudely streamlined object allows the air to flow round the surface.

Afterburning Burning fuel in the jet pipe of a turbojet engine to temporarily increase its thrust. Also sometimes called Reheat.

Action of air on a flat plate drawn forward. If the pressure due to the air is *AB*, this can be resolved into *CB*, at right-angles to the plate, and *DB* along the plate. *CB* can be resolved into *EB at right-angles to the air direction* and *CE* in the same direction as the air. *EB* represents the *lift*, and *CE* the *drag*.

In the same way, an aerofoil inclined at an angle of attack *DBA* to airflow in the direction *AB* will produce lift *EB* which will be additional to the lift already produced by its cambered upper surface.

Aircraft Markings All civil aircraft must be registered and carry their registration markings in prominent external positions. The markings consist of letters/numbers indicating country of origin followed by individual aircraft letters/numbers. Principal national markings are given in the table.

CIVIL AIRCRAFT MARKINGS			
AP	Pakistan	PP/PT	Brazil
A6	United Arab	RP	Philippines
	Emirates	SE	Sweden
B	China	SP	Poland
C	Canada	ST	Sudan
CC	Chile	SU	Egypt
CCCP	Soviet Union	SX	Greece
CN	Morocco	TC	Turkey
CP	Bolivia	TF	Iceland
CR/CS	Portugal	TG	Guatemala
CU	Cuba	TL	Central African
CX	Uruguay		Republic
C5	Gambia	TS	Tunisia

C6	Bahamas	VH	Australia
C9	Mozambique	VP/VQ/	UK colonies and
D	West Germany	VR	protectorates
DM	East Germany	VT	India
EC	Spain	XA/XB/	Mexico
EI/EJ	Ireland	XC	
EP	Iran	XV	Vietnam
ET	Ethiopia	XY/XZ	Burma
F	France	YA	Afghanistan
G	United Kingdom	YI	Iraq
HA	Hungary	YK	Syria
HB	Switzerland	YR	Romania
HC	Ecuador	YU	Yugoslavia
HK	Colombia	YV	Venezuela
HL	Korea, Republic	ZA	Albania
HS	Thailand	ZK/ZL/ZM	New Zealand
HZ	Saudi Arabia	ZS/ZT/ZU	South Africa
I	Italy	4R	Sri Lanka
JA	Japan	4W	Yemen
JY	Jordan	4X	Israel
LN	Norway	5A	Libya
LU/LV	Argentina	5B	Cyprus
LX	Luxembourg	5H	Tanzania
LZ	Bulgaria	5N	Nigeria
N	United States	5X	Uganda
OB	Peru	5Y	Kenya
OD	Lebanon	6Y	Jamaica
OE	Austria	7T	Algeria
OH	Finland	9G	Ghana
OK	Czechoslovakia	9H	Malta
OO	Belgium	9J	Zambia
OY	Denmark	9K	Kuwait
P	Korea, Democratic	9M	Malaysia
	Republic	9O	Zaire
PH	Netherlands	9V	Singapore
PK	Indonesia	9Y	Trinidad and Tobago

Airscrew (Propeller) The device that draws an aircraft through
the air. Its action is similar to the action of a ship's propeller.
It consists of two or more blades inclined at an angle to the
axis. In rotation the speed of the tip of a blade is greater than
that of a part nearer the hub. This makes the resultant

direction of air, due to the combination of forward aircraft speed and propeller rotation, change all the way along the blade. To remedy this to some extent the blade is twisted so that the tip is nearer position (c) in the diagram than the root, which may be in position (d).

(a)   (b)   (c)   (d)

Section of propeller blade end-on, looking towards the hub. The angle between the line of the blade and the transverse axis of the hub is a measure of the pitch. The pitch is coarser in (a) than in (d). In (b) it is coarsest and the propeller is said to be feathered. In (c) there is no pitch at all and the propeller achieves nothing. The arrow in each case indicates the direction in which the blade-section is supposed to be travelling for the hub to be going forward.

As the forward speed of an aircraft changes so does the efficiency of the propeller. The higher the forward speed, the coarser should be the propeller pitch. Propellers are therefore made so that the pitch can be varied by the pilot to suit the conditions and are known as variable-pitch propellers.

Airspeed Indicator Speed through the air increases the pressure due to ram effect. A small tube directed into the air, called a Pitot tube, can be used to direct the airstream to a pressure-measuring device. At the same time a closed tube with holes in its sides can be used to measure the static atmospheric pressure. The difference between the two is an indication of airspeed.

Altimeter The normal height-measuring instrument is an aneroid barometer. As the atmospheric pressure decreases with height above the Earth's surface, the decrease can be used as an indication of height. The drop is approximately 40 mm (1.57 in) on the barometer for 500 m (1,640 ft) up to about 2,000 m (6,560 ft). Such an altimeter measures only height above sea-level, and the zero must be adjusted to suit prevailing conditions.

The radio altimeter relies on the reflection of radio signals to give the true height above the actual ground being flown over.

Anhedral Angle at which a wing is inclined downwards from root to tip as seen from the front.

Apogee The point in an orbit, centred on the Earth, which is furthest from the Earth.

Artificial Horizon An instrument to assist a pilot flying blind to know when he is flying on an even keel. It depends on a gyroscope to maintain a picture of an aircraft in a horizontal position between two horizontal lines. As the aircraft changes its attitude so the picture changes.

Atmosphere The layer of gas round the Earth. It consists chiefly of oxygen and nitrogen, but there are also small quantities of other gases, such as carbon dioxide, argon, helium, etc.

THE STANDARD ATMOSPHERE

Altitude m (ft)		Pressure mmHg (lb/in²)		Temperature (° C)
				Ambient temperature remains constant above 11,000 m (36,000 ft)
30,000	(98,425)	8·790	(0·170)	
25,000	(82,021)	18·834	(0·364)	
20,000	(65,617)	41·065	(0·794)	
15,000	(49,213)	90·342	(1.747)	−56·5
10,000	(32,808)	198.288	(3.834)	−50·0
8,000	(26,247)	267·020	(5·163)	−37·0
5,000	(16,404)	405·182	(7·835)	−17·5
4,000	(13,123)	462·339	(8·940)	−11·0
3,000	(9,843)	525·857	(10·168)	−4·5
2,000	(6,562)	596·263	(11·529)	2·0
1,000	(3,280)	674·114	(13·035)	8·5
Sea-level		760·000	(14·696)	15·0

(mmHg = millimetres of mercury, lb/in² = pounds to the square inch)

The pressure of the atmosphere is greatest at sea-level. It gets less and less the farther one goes away from the Earth, but not in direct proportion to the height. The temperature also gets less with height up to about 11,000 m (36,000 ft), when it reaches $-56\cdot5°$ C and stays at this. This level is called the tropopause. Below it is the troposphere. Above it is the stratosphere.

The atmosphere is not a gas with constant characteristics. So a *standard atmosphere* has been agreed on internationally. Figures for height records, etc., must be reduced to the standard conditions. The pressure at sea-level of this standard atmosphere is 1.03 kg/sq cm (14·7 lb/sq in) or 760 mm (29·75 in) of mercury. The temperature is taken as 15° C or 59° F.

Attack, angle of Angle between the mean chord and free stream direction at which the airflow meets an aerofoil (q.v.).

Autogiro The trade name for a type of rotary-wing aircraft invented by Juan de la Cierva. The wing or rotor is not driven by the engine, but rotates automatically in forward flight.

Automatic Pilot A device whereby an aircraft will fly automatically on an even keel on a prescribed course without the attention of the pilot. Any roll or yaw or pitch or change in direction is indicated by the instruments, and signals are sent to servo mechanisms which make the necessary changes to the control surfaces.

More elaborate automatic pilots can also maintain a rate of climb or descent or a constant height.

Avionics Aviation electronics, including radio, radar, navigation systems and computers.

Ballistic Missiles See *Missiles*.

Boundary Layer The layer of air close to the surface of an aerofoil. It is very thin. The airflow at the leading-edge is usually laminar, i.e. parallel to the surface, but farther back it is broken up and the resulting turbulence produces drag. Several attempts have been made to avoid this, one important one being an arrangement for sucking in air through surface holes in the aerofoil.

British Aircraft Manufacturers The organisations listed here are currently producing complete aircraft on a production basis. Amateur constructors and firms making kits of parts for home construction are not included.

British Aerospace Public Limited Company, Aircraft Group, with factories at Bristol; Brough; Chester; Dunsfold; Greengate; Hamble; Hatfield; Kingston-upon-Thames; Preston; Prestwick; Samlesbury; Warton; Weybridge; and Woodford.

Edgley Aircraft Ltd, Old Sarum Airfield, Salisbury, Wiltshire.

Luscombe Aircraft Ltd, Lympne, Kent.

Nash Aircraft Ltd, Farnham, Surrey.

The Norman Aeroplane Company Ltd, Barry, South Glamorgan.

Pilatus Britten-Norman Ltd, Bembridge, Isle-of-Wight.

Short Brothers PLC, Belfast, Northern Ireland.

Slingsby Aviation Ltd, Kirkbymoorside, North Yorkshire.

Wallis Autogyros Ltd, Rymerston Hall, Norfolk.

Westland Helicopters Ltd, Yeovil, Somerset.

Bypass ratio The ratio between the airflow through the fan and the airflow through the core engine in a bypass turbofan engine.

Chord The distance from the leading-edge to the trailing-edge of an aerofoil surface measured parallel to the longitudinal axis.

Clean In-flight configuration of aircraft with undercarriage, flaps and slats retracted and without external stores.

Control surface Hinged flap at trailing-edge of aerofoil providing control of aircraft movement about its longitudinal, lateral and vertical axes by aileron, elevator and rudder respectively. An elevon combines the functions of elevator and aileron.

Decca Navigator A navigation system used by both ships and aircraft which was developed in the 1950s in Britain with the idea of making it worldwide in scope.

A Decca 'chain' consists of a master transmitter whose low-frequency transmissions (70–130 kHz) are closely related to those of three associated slave transmitters. These slaves transmit so that their signals are each in exact phase with that of the master. The receiver measures the phase of the received signal from each transmitter and displays the phase difference between the master signal and each slave. This can be presented in a number of ways: either numerically, by a coded light system or, in the more advanced receivers, directly on a map, thus giving a precise fix and track information. Each transmitter can be received over a distance of about

1,500 km (950 miles), and a number of chains cover most of Europe, the eastern seaboard of the United States and some other parts of the world, particularly in areas of heavy ship traffic. It is a very accurate aid, fixes of better than one mile accuracy are usual, and it is standard on a number of aircraft, such as the larger helicopters used in North Sea oil exploration. Although it did not gain universal acceptance, it is still being developed and new chains are occasionally opened.

Delta Wing A wing planform which forms the shape of a triangle. It has many of the aerodynamic advantages of a swept-back wing but is structurally more efficient.

Dihedral The angle between the wing and the horizontal, looking head-on at the aircraft. Most aircraft have some dihedral angle which tends to stabilise roll. (See diagram below.)

θ = dihedral angle

Drag The force resisting the motion of an aircraft through the air. It can be broken down into two parts: induced drag caused inevitably with lift (q.v.) by the pressure differences over the wing: and parasitic drag caused by turbulence (q.v.) due to roughness of the skin, interference of airflow round different parts of the aeroplane projections such as aerials, radomes, cockpits.

Drone A pilotless aircraft usually for use as a target.

Escape Velocity The velocity that a body must have to get away from the gravitational pull of Earth. It is given by the equation

$$V = \sqrt{2gR}$$

where R = distance from centre of Earth; g = acceleration due to gravity at distance R.

For ordinary purposes the escape velocity from the Earth is taken as about 11 km a second or 6·8 miles a second. At this velocity a projectile will follow a parabolic course and never return to Earth.

Fail-safe Aircraft structure or system which, if it fails, will not endanger the aircraft.

Feathering Means of setting propeller blades in line with the slipstream so that torque is eliminated and drag is at a minimum. See *Airscrew*.

First flights Some significant first flights of new aircraft made during the period June 1984 to September 1985 inclusive:

June 1984	13	Lockheed P-3 AEW&C Orion
	14	Westland Lynx-3, ZE477
	19	Lockheed HTTB, N 130X
	22	Sikorsky S-76 MkII, N 3123U, first with PT6B-36 engines
July 1984	1	Agusta A129 Mangusta, second prototype, EI902
	3	BAe VC10 K Mk 3, ZA150
	20	Pilatus PC-9, HB-HPB, second prototype
	26	Israel Aircraft Industries 1125 Astra, 4X-WIA, second prototype
	27	Sikorsky S-75 ACAP
	30	BAe Super 748
	30	Rockwell B-1A, 76-174, fourth prototype, after modification as B-1B avionics test bed
August 1984	1	Airbus A310 with enlarged wingtip fences
	4	Edgley EA7 Optica, G-BLFC, first production
	6	Shorts C-23A Sherpa, 83-0512, first for USAF
	12	RFB Fantrainer 600, D-EATR, first production
	14	Gulfstream Aerospace SRA-1, N 47499
	16	ATR 42, F-WEGA
	19	Airbus A300B2, General Electric CF6-80C2 testbed
September 1984	21	Dassault Breguet Mirage 2000H, KF-101, first Indian
	29	Norman Aeroplane Co NAC 1 Freelance, G-NACI
October 1984	5	Agusta A129 Mangusta, third prototype
	12	Warszawa-Okecie PZL-130 Orlik, SP-PCA
	18	Rockwell International B-1B, first production
	31	ATR 42, F-WEGB, second prototype
November 1984	19	Aeritalia/Aermacchi/Embraer AMX, MMX595, second prototype
December 1984	3	Kawasaki C-1 Kai, 78-1021, ECM trainer
	14	Grumman X-29A
	15	Lear Fan Model 2100, third prototype
	28	Enaer T-35 Pillan, 107/CC-EFU, first production

January 1985	28	Aeritalia/Aermacchi/Embraer AMX, MMX596, third prototype
February 1985	4	Grumman C-2A Greyhound, first new production
	13	Panavia Tornado GR Mk 1, first with Alarm missile
March 1985	20	Airbus A300-600, F-WZLR, first with General Electric CF6-80C2 engines
	20	Israel Aircraft Industries Astra, 4X-CUA, first production
April 1985	30	ATR 42, F-WEGC, third aircraft
	30	McDonnell Douglas/BAe Harrier GR Mk 5, ZD318
May 1985	16	Slingsby T67M 200 Firefly
	21	Dassault Breguet Falcon V10F, F-WVPR, all composite material wings
	27	Agusta A129 Mangusta, fourth prototype
June 1985	24	Sikorsky S-76 Shadow, N 765SA
	26	Bell Model 400 Twin Ranger, third prototype
July 1985	8	Airbus A310-300, F-WWCA, Pratt & Whitney JT9D-7R4E engines
	9	Lockheed TriStar K Mk 1, ZD950, first for RAF
	29	Kawasaki XT-4, 56-5601
	31	Airbus A300, Pratt & Whitney PW4000 engine test bed
August 1985	3	Boeing C-135FR, French, CFM-56-2B-1 engines
	7	FMA 1A 63 Pampa, EX-02, second prototype
	30	Bell D292 ACAP
September 1985	6	Airbus A310-300, second with CF6-80C2 engines
	10	Lockheed C-5B Galaxy

Flap Control surface used to provide temporary increase in lift of a wing as in take-off or landing of the aircraft.

Fly-by-wire Flight control system actuated by electrical signalling without mechanical linkage between the pilot's controls and the control surfaces.

Free Fall The state of non-resistance to a gravitational field. This happens with a body falling towards the Earth before it enters the Earth's atmosphere. It happens with a satellite in orbit. A passenger inside a vehicle in free fall has the sensation of being weightless, because the vehicle is not resisting the gravitational field. Anyone falling from a height towards the ground feels the air resistance and so is not exactly in free fall, though nearly so. In the 'weightless' condition a man jumping up will hit the ceiling. He will have no sense of balance. Men can experience this state for a few seconds in an aircraft making an outside loop when the speed is enough for centrifugal force to balance the Earth's gravitational force. Crews have now been weightless for long periods in manned space vehicles.

Fuels For rockets see under *Propellant*.

Petrol is used in piston engines, but gas turbines (turbojet engines, turboprops, turbofans) burn a kerosene or paraffin-based fuel.

g The acceleration due to gravity, which on the surface of the earth is taken as roughly 981 cm per sec per sec or 32 ft per sec per sec. It is also taken as a unit of acceleration for discussions of forces acting on rockets and airmen and astronauts. An airman, for example, flying at 800 km/hr (500 mph) along a curved path of about 1·5 km (1 mile) radius would experience a centrifugal force equivalent to an acceleration of 5 g.

Gas Turbine See *Jet Propulsion*.

Geostationary An Earth satellite which remains permanently above the same point on the Earth. Such an orbit is usually about 35,800 km (22,245 miles) above the Earth's surface. Also called synchronous.

Gravity The force of attraction between bodies according to the law of gravitation, which states that any two bodies in the universe attract each other with a force that is directly proportional to the product of the masses and inversely proportional to the square of the distance between them. That is

$$\text{Force} = \frac{km_1 m_2}{d^2}$$

where k is a gravitational constant $= 6·67 \times 10^{-8}$ in metric units.

Calculation from this shows that the acceleration due to gravity (g) at the Earth's surface is about 981 cm (32 ft) per sec per sec. This varies, however, with geographical position, and gets very much less with height above the Earth's surface.

Guided Missiles See *Missiles*.

Gunship Helicopter designed for battlefield attack.

Gyroscope Used in many navigational instruments in aircraft and ships. It consists essentially of a heavy wheel spun by an electric motor or a turbine and rotating at high speed. It has two properties: (i) if it is supported in frictionless gimbals so that it can rotate freely in all three dimensions, it will remain parallel to its original position, i.e. it has 'rigidity in space': (ii) if it is not supported in gimbals but is made to turn it will *precess* and exert a force proportional to the rate of turn—a measure of the force being a measure of the rate of turn. This is used, for example, to correct gunsights for the movement of the aircraft.

Both these properties can be combined: if a gyro is held in one direction in its gimbals so that it has to turn with the earth it will precess until it points North and the N–S axis of the Earth's rotation is parallel to its own axis. It will then continue to point North, and can be used as a genuine compass.

Heat Barrier Still a major problem in the advance of aircraft speeds. At sufficiently high speeds the kinetic energy of the air flowing past the aircraft is turned into appreciable heat energy, and the temperature of the aircraft skin at Mach 3 can reach the melting point of steel. Aircraft to travel at these speeds therefore must be made of heat-resisting materials, and the crew, passengers and electronic gear must be refrigerated. Spacecraft leave the atmosphere too quickly for kinetic heating to be a problem, but it becomes a major factor during re-entry.

Helicopter This is an aircraft that can rise vertically by the use of rotating wings. These wings, very long and narrow, are aerofoils, and together constitute the rotor. When this is in action the lift provided by the passage of the blades through the air propels the aircraft vertically. The engine-power has to be enough to provide lift for the whole weight of the aircraft.

For forward movement the plane of the rotor is tilted downward in front. This is achieved by altering the pitch of the rotor blades so that as each passes through the rear part of the rotation its pitch is increased and as it passes through the front part of the rotation its pitch is decreased. The unequal thrusts tilt the machine downwards and forwards.

As the helicopter body is free to rotate it tends to go round in the opposite direction to that of the rotor. To overcome this in the classic helicopter type a tail rotor is provided on one side. The pitch of this can be varied to give control for turning the helicopter's direction of flight. Another way of doing it is to have a rotor at the rear rotating in the opposite direction to that of the front rotor, or to have counter-rotating rotors on concentric shafts.

A development of the helicopter is that using normal forward engines as propellers for forward flight, the rotor being used only for lifting. This was the method used in the Fairey Rotodyne, which was designed to go from city-centre to city-centre carrying a load of passengers (the biggest of ordinary helicopters today can carry nearly 50 passengers) at a speed roughly comparable with that of twin-engined airliners current at that time.

Incidence Angle at which the wing mean chord is set in relation to the aircraft's longitudinal axis. This is different from angle-of-attack (q.v.).

Inertial Navigation The only type of airborne navigation which is automatic and independent of outside radio beacons. A system of accelerometers is mounted on a platform which is kept level by a set of gyroscopes. The accelerometers measure the forces in the fore-and-aft, lateral and vertical planes, and from these an onboard computer calculates speed, heading and distance gone. The crew simply tell the computer their latitude and longitude at the start of the flight, and thereafter the inertial system will automatically display navigational information about any required destination. The system can be linked to the autopilot for complete automation, and a wide range of output data is possible. Inertial becomes inaccurate due to mechanical drift in the gyros, but recent advances in gyroscope technology mean that after a transatlantic flight an inertial system will generally show a position within 10 km (5·4 nm) of the true position. This is now virtually the standard long-range navigation system, and developments now being investigated will significantly reduce the present very small errors.

A new form of inertial navigation, commonly known as 'laser inertial', has recently been developed. Based on ring laser gyroscopes, instead of mechanical gyros, laser inertial systems are fitted to the latest generation of airliners and will be standard on the military attack aircraft of the 1990s.

A laser gyro is a small, usually triangular piece of a special material, which has a fine hole running around it, close to the edge. The total length of this hole, known as the path length, varies according to the application, but is typically 43 cm for transport aircraft systems, 20 cm or less for missiles. The longer the path length, the more accurate the navigation.

A beam of laser light is passed around this hole, starting from one corner, being reflected by very highly specialised mirrors at the other two and being received at the start point. Any motion of the block about an axis perpendicular to the plane of the light path will be seen as a change in the phase of the light as detected at the exit receiver, and this phase change is then computed to give acceleration about that axis. Three mutually perpendicular laser gyros give accelerations about all three axes, and from then on the calculation of velocity and distance is just as for a normal mechanical gyro'd system.

Because they are very much simpler mechanically, laser gyros are far more reliable than mechanical ones, and, once certain computing hurdles were overcome by the various companies developing laser gyros, the new systems became more accurate. Laser gyros will become the industry standard in most airborne applications over the next few years. The only benefit of using a mechanical gyro system is that the basic price is less, although reliability factors already make laser gyros cheaper in the long term.

Jet Propulsion The pushing forward of a vehicle by the rapid backwards efflux of a mass of gas. In effect, a rocket is working by jet, but the expression is usually restricted to the gas turbine. The first British jet engine was built by Sir Frank Whittle at the beginning of the last war, and flew in the Gloster E28/39 experimental jet aircraft in 1941.

The gas turbine works by taking air in at the front, compressing it, mixing vaporised fuel—usually kerosene—with it, igniting the mixture, making the burning gases flow through a turbine to drive the compressor by a shaft, and letting them escape in a jet to drive the aircraft. In most large modern gas turbines the compressor and turbine are *axial*: that is, they consist of many small blades set on a drum moving in between stationary blades mounted on a closely-fitted casing. Some small gas turbines have a centrifugal compressor. In a ramjet the forward motion of the engine is used to compress the incoming air sufficiently for combustion to take place. This can happen only at very high speeds—about three times the speed of sound.

TABLE OF FAMOUS JET ENGINES

Manufacturer	Designation	Maximum thrust (kN)	Typical aircraft application
Rolls-Royce	RB211-524D4	236	Boeing 747
	535C	166·4	Boeing 757
	RB163 Civil Spey Mk 512-14DW	55·8	One-Eleven
	RB168 Spey (military) Mk 251	53·3	Nimrod AEW Mk 3
	Viper 600 Series	16·7	BAe 125-600
	Olympus 593	167·7 (dry)	Concorde
	Pegasus 11-F402-RR-404	94·21	AV-8B Harrier II
Turbo-Union	RB199 Mk 103	42·95 (dry)	Tornado
Garrett	TFE 731-3	16·46	BAe 125-700
General Electric	F404-GE-400	71·2	F/A-18A
	CF6-50C	227	Airbus A300B2
	F101-GE-102	133	Rockwell B-1B
Pratt & Whitney	JT8D-17R	77·4	Boeing 727-200
	JT9D-59A	236	Airbus A300B
	F100-PW-100	65·2 (dry)	F-15 Eagle
Kuznetsov	NK-86	127·5	Il-86
Soloviev	D-30KU	108	Il-62M
Tumansky	R-29B	78·45 (dry)	MiG-23/27
	R-31	91·18 (dry)	MiG-25

N.B. To obtain thrust in kg weight multiply kilo Newtons (kN) thrust by 1,000 and divide by g (9·81 m per sec per sec). Thrust (dry) in table refers to unreheated thrust which can be much increased by afterburning.

Lasers Lasers are now commonly used for many industrial and medical applications, but over the past ten years they have become a primary aid to attack-aircraft pilots in delivering their weapons accurately. Low-powered laser beams are also used in a new form of navigation system, the laser inertial navigation system (q.v.).

A laser is a coherent (i.e. single, stable frequency) beam of light, arranged to have a very narrow spread; that is, the beam is pencil-like, and hardly diverges with distance from the source, as does say a conventional torch beam.

In an airborne laser system, the pilot can steer this beam on to the target. Although the beam of light is invisible to the human eye, the direction of the beam can be seen by the pilot as a symbol on a display in front of him (the head-up display). By adjusting the location of this symbol, using a simple hand controller (which is, in fact, connected to the beam's steering mechanism), the beam is positioned on the object of the attack.

In some applications, the aircraft system is both laser transmitter and receiver: so, rather as with radar, by measuring the time taken for a pulse of laser light to travel to and from the target, the aircraft's weapon-aiming computer can accurately calculate the distance; and, since the direction of the beam is also known, the computer can very easily calculate the exact moment to release the weapons so that they hit the target.

In other applications, the laser transmitter might be set up by a ground observer who 'designates' the target: the attacking aircraft detects the laser light reflected from the designated target, which the pilot need never see, and the computer can process that data to give an accurate release point for the weapons. In a third common application, the laser receiver is in the nose of a missile or gun shell; it detects the reflected laser light from the designated target, and the weapon's computer and guidance systems automatically home on to the target accurately.

Since the laser light is invisible, and of a very narrow beam, it is almost impossible for the attacked forces to detect, and therefore attacks are both accurate and without warning.

Lift Vertical force due to the flow of air round an aerofoil. Three-quarters of it, roughly speaking, is composed of suction due to low pressure on the upper surface of the aerofoil: the other quarter is due to pressure underneath. The lift increases with the angle of attack (q.v.) until the aerofoil stalls.

Localiser Equipment giving steering guidance in an instrument landing system (ILS).

Loran Loran is a navigation system which is broadly similar to Decca (q.v.), but the transmissions of master and slaves are not phase-, but time-linked. Each master and slave on a chain emits a short pulse at exactly the same time. The time between the arrival of the pulses from the master and from each of the slaves gives a position fix.

Mach Number A number which relates the speed of an aircraft to the speed of sound in the same conditions. Mach 1, the speed of sound is taken as 333 m (1,094 ft) per sec in air at NTP, so under the same conditions Mach 2 would be 667 m (2,188 ft) per sec and Mach 3, 1,000 m (3,280 ft) per sec, and so on. Mach 1 is 1,225 km/hr (761 mph) at ground level but due to fall in pressure is only 1,062 km/hr (660 mph) at 11,000 m (36,000 ft) (tropopause).

Missiles Missiles are, of course, anything thrown, but today they almost invariably mean the powerful weapons that depend mainly on rocket-engines for their propulsion. They are classified into strategic and tactical; short, medium, intermediate or intercontinental in range; ballistic or guided; use, whether surface-to-air, air-to-air, etc.

Ballistic missiles as weapons are inextricably mixed up with space research, for the same basic missiles, without the warhead and modified electronically, serve to launch satellites.

Ballistic missiles are those that travel most of the way on a trajectory like that of any projectile. Guidance is used at first to set such a missile on course. Then the rocket burns out and the rest of the missile travels a natural course to target. They are classified as ICBM—intercontinental ballistic missile, and IRBM—intermediate-range ballistic missile.

Guided missiles are controlled for all or most of the way to their target. Some are guided all the way by radio signals from the ground. Others are steered by automatic celestial navigation, inertial systems or Doppler radio (which depends on a change of frequency when a source is approaching or receding) or radar. Missiles used for short ranges at moving targets have homing devices, whether radar or the reception of radiation (radio or infra-red) from the target.

One of the latest weapons is the Cruise Missile, armed with a nuclear warhead, which can penetrate enemy defences and streak to targets deep inside enemy territory. By the end of 1983 General Dynamics BGM-109 Tomahawk Ground Launched Cruise Missiles (GLCM) were in their silos at RAF Greenham Common—home of the USAF 501st Tactical Missile

Tomahawk Cruise Missile

Wing—and operational. The UK plans call for 96 Tomahawks to be deployed at Greenham Common and 64 at Molesworth, Cambridgeshire. Others, Pershing IIs, have been delivered in West Germany and eventually Tomahawks are to be deployed in Belgium, Holland, Germany and Italy.

In all these locations, peace movement supporters register their disapproval, and at Greenham Common the peace women camping outside the gates aim now to try to contain the missiles within the airfield perimeter. If it became necessary to use them in war, the missiles would be moved out to woodland firing sites: and it is this, and manoeuvres in which it would be practised, that the peace women say that they would try to prevent, although many practice deployments have been successfully made at night.

The arrival of Tomahawk and Pershing II missiles in Europe is a major element in NATO's modernisation programme, argued as necessary to counter the Soviet deployment of its SS-20 Intermediate Range Ballistic Missiles (IRBMs) in Europe. More than 3,000 Boeing AGM-86B Air Launched Cruise Missiles (ALCMs) are now also in production and would be airlifted to their launch points over non-hostile territory by USAF B-52G bombers.

The Tomahawk GLCM is 6 m long, has a wingspan of 2·5 m and weighs 1,450 kg with its booster. It would take off from its launcher vehicle powered by its solid rocket booster; this falls away after 13 seconds and the GLCM continues to its target at high subsonic speed, powered by a Williams International turbofan. A total of 560 Tomahawks is to be built by 1988.

The number and naming of missiles has reached such a pitch that no list of missiles is worth giving, so soon are so many out of date. Mention may be made, however, of the US Atlas, an ICBM of great range, the booster for many satellite launchings.

Monocoque Aircraft structure deriving its strength from its outer shell and devoid of internal bracing.

Navigation The method by which a vehicle (ship, aircraft, motor car) is steered towards a desired point. For aeronautical use either radio beacons, maps or inertial (q.v.) can be used, while a magnetic compass, or more usually a gyroscopic compass, is used to indicate heading. Radio beacons of types such as VOR or NDB are arranged so that the navigator can calculate a fix from differing bearings, while Decca (q.v.) uses phase-difference and Loran a time-difference between received signals. Inertial navigation uses self-contained sensors to determine position without outside reference.

For basic navigation *dead reckoning* and *astro* (star) navigation are used, as they were used by ancient sailors. The first depends on knowing wind speed and direction accurately so as to compensate the known heading, while the latter relies on tables of the angles of given stars at given times. Neither system is effective in fast-moving aircraft, and computers now perform most of the work.

Omega is a very low frequency navigation aid (10 kHz) originally developed by the US Navy for underwater navigation of its nuclear submarines. However, the eight transmitters located around the world (the last in the network, in Australia, is under construction) give worldwide coverage, and, given the capability of modern airborne navigation computers, accuracies of better than 2 km are generally possible, making Omega the most accurate worldwide navigation aid. It is thus being widely adopted, particularly as a back-up to other systems, such as inertial: the only drawback being that, since it is primarily a military-sponsored tactical navigation aid, it is not guaranteed to be fully operational at all times.

Orbit The name given to the closed path of a satellite round the Earth or any body round any other. The Earth is in orbit round the Sun, the Moon (and many artificial satellites) in orbit round the Earth. Usually an orbit is an ellipse.

Payload That part of the disposable load of an aircraft which can generate revenue (i.e. passengers, freight or weapons in military aircraft).

Perigee The point in an orbit, centred on the Earth, which is nearest to the Earth.

Port The left-hand side of an aircraft as seen by the pilot looking forward. Associated with a red wing-tip light.

Propellant The name given to the materials used in rocket engines. They can be divided into two classes—liquid and solid though the possibilities of ionic propulsion and nuclear propulsion do not come into this division.

Liquid propellants consist mostly of a fuel and an oxidant. The fuel can be paraffin, petrol, alcohol, hydrazine, aniline or other liquid that can be oxidised to form enormous volumes of gas. The oxidant can be liquid oxygen, red fuming nitric acid, hydrogen peroxide, fluorine or others yet to be announced. The V2 used on London during the Second World War was fuelled by liquid oxygen and alcohol.

There are a few single liquid propellants, even though chemically they are mixtures.

There are also solid fuels. The simplest is, of course, gunpowder. There is also cordite. Other solid fuels include: (*a*) JPN, a mixture of nitrocellulose, nitroglycerine, diethyl phthalate, carbamite, potassium sulphate, carbon and wax; (*b*) galcit, a mixture of potassium perchlorate and a fuel such as asphalt; (*c*) NDRC, a mixture of ammonium picrate, sodium nitrate and resin.

Research continues for better and better fuels. Some are naturally kept secret even when discovered.

The 'goodness' of a propellant is measured as *specific impulse*, given by the equation

$$\text{Specific impulse} = \frac{\text{Thrust in kilograms}}{\text{Rate of loss of mass in kilograms}}$$

It is related to the exhaust velocity of gas by the equation

$$\text{Specific impulse} = \frac{\text{Exhaust velocity}}{g}$$

Propeller See *Airscrew*.

Pylon Structure for attaching an external load to an aircraft (e.g. engine nacelle, drop-tank or military store).

Radar Developed during the Second World War, radar is an
electronic system for determining the position of a target
(usually airborne) from a ground station. A large radar aerial
emits extremely high-frequency pulsed radio signals in a beam
only about one degree wide. The aerial rotates at about 5 to
10 r.p.m., thus covering the whole sky with the beam.

Some tiny part of the radar beam may hit an aircraft and
return to the aerial, where it is collected and the time taken
for the two-way passage determined. From this, and the
direction in which the beam was transmitted, a computer determines the position of the aircraft, which is then displayed on a
cathode-ray tube as a fluorescent dot. Techniques have been
evolved to eliminate returns from nearby buildings, or stationary objects some distance away, such as masts. Computers
can calculate such information as aircraft heading and speed
from successive returns and display this information alongside
the radar return on the tube together with the identity of the
aircraft.

Radar is used for many purposes. Virtually all air traffic is
controlled by radar, and its highly accurate position information means it can be used for long-range (up to 400 km
(250 miles)) or short-range control. Around the airfield, aircraft can be brought in to land using either PAR (precision
approach radar) or more commonly GCA (ground controlled
approach) down to one-half mile or less from touchdown.
Aircraft themselves can be equipped with radar for storm
avoidance, when it is used for locating clouds (the beam re-
flects off the rain droplets). Secondary Surveillance Radar (SSR)
is a development of ordinary (primary) radar, and is a back-up
facility for air traffic control. The radar beam has a peculiar
pulse pattern which triggers off a device called the transponder
in an aircraft. But only such transponders as the air traffic
controllers request will be 'on' (i.e. able to be triggered), and
each will be set to one of 4,096 codes as the controllers demand. Once triggered, a transponder emits a radio signal
which is unique to its code. By very advanced computing
techniques on the ground, this coded reply can be correlated
with the primary reply, this giving positive information of each
transponding return. Aircraft height also can be transponded,
and the computer can convert transponder codes into aircraft

call-signs and determine speed and heading.

Recent developments in radar and micro-electronics technology have led to the widespread adoption of radar in airborne applications. Low-level navigation at night is made possible by display of a radar picture of the route ahead to the pilot. This data can also be fed into a terrain-following computer, which then directs the aircraft's autopilot smoothly to avoid the hills ahead, but also to keep low down in the valleys to minimise detection.

Airborne radars which look almost vertically downward can be used for mapping, either for simple cartographic requirements or to detect enemy installations accurately.

The development of high-powered airborne radars has led to the development of airborne early warning (AEW) aircraft, which can detect aircraft, road vehicles or ships up to 350 km away from the platform.

Secondary surveillance radar (SSR) has developed over the past ten years into a primary air-traffic control system. A radar beam, on a specific frequency, is detected by co-operating aircraft, fitted with a transponder. This transponder recognises the incoming radar pulse and returns it, on a different frequency and with a special code embedded in the pulses. This code will have been set by the pilot at the request of the controller, it thus being possible for the controller to have a precise knowledge of each aircraft's identity, or to determine which aircraft are 'friend' (since they will be returning the required code) or 'foe'—those that do not have the code are either not under the controller's particular orders (in a civilian situation) or are enemy forces in a military one. In Europe and America in particular, SSR is now more important an air-traffic control system than is the so-called 'primary' radar.

Radio Beacons As well as the Decca, Consol and Loran (q.v.) beacon systems used for aerial navigation, all airways are defined by a different series of beacons. These basically fall into three types, VOR, NDB and DME.

A VOR (very-high-frequency omni-directional range) transmits in the range 108–118 MHz. An unmodulated reference tone which has the same phase regardless of direction has superimposed on it a second tone whose phase varies as the direction of transmission. A Morse-code identification is superimposed on the transmission. The airborne receiver simply picks up the signal, deciphers the phase of the varying signal and displays the associated bearing.

The older NDB (Non-directional beacon) transmits in the medium-wave band. A constant tone, with Morse-code identification, transmits uniformly in all directions. The airborne receiver interprets the direction from which the signal is coming (by rotating an aerial to give the strongest signal) and displays that relative bearing.

DME (Distance measuring equipment) and its military cousin Tacan (Tactical air-navigation) determine the time taken for a pulse to travel from the beacon to the aircraft; in the aircraft, this is converted into distance. Tacan also gives bearing information.

Range The permissible distance that an aircraft can fly with a specified load, and usually with allowances for diversions, stand-off, etc.

Records Records recognised officially have to be made according to certain fixed rules and all attempts are under the control of the Fédération Aéronautique Internationale (FAI). Unofficially a number of aircraft have flown faster than the official record shows, but not under the permissible conditions.

The official World Records correct to October, 1985, are:

Speed in straight line over 15 to 25 km. Capt. Eldon W. Joersz and Maj. George T. Morgan, Jr. (USAF), at Beale Air Force Base, California, in a Lockheed SR-71A on July 28, 1976, 3,530 km/hr (2,193 mph).

Altitude. Alexander Fedotov, USSR, in an E-266M (MiG-25), 37,650 m (123,523 ft), on August 31, 1977.

Distance in a straight line. Major Clyde P. Evely (USAF), in a Boeing B-52H Stratofortress, on January 10–11, 1962, between Okinawa and Madrid, 20,168·8 km (12,532·3 miles).

Distance in a closed circuit. Captain William M. Stevenson (USAF), in a Boeing B-52H Stratofortress, Seymour Johnson Air Force Base–Bermuda–Sondrestrom (Greenland)–Anchorage (Alaska)–March Air Force Base–Key West–Seymour Johnson Air Force Base, June 6–7, 1962, 18,245 km (11,337 miles).

Altitude in sustained horizontal flight. Capt Robert C. Helt and

Maj Larry A. Elliott (USAF), at Beale Air Force Base, California, in a Lockheed SR-71A on July 28, 1976, 25,929 m (85,069 ft).

Speed in closed circuit. Maj Adolphus H. Bledsoe, Jr., and Maj John T. Fuller (USAF), at Beale Air Force Base, California, in a Lockheed SR-71A over a 1,000 km circuit on July 27, 1976, 3,367 km/hr (2,092 mph).

Re-entry This means re-entry into the Earth's atmosphere. All discussions of space travel depend on the solution of the problem of how a vehicle in orbit at speeds of thousands of miles an hour can get back to Earth safely. This is the problem of losing speed near the ground and of getting through the Earth's atmosphere without burning up.

The problem has long been solved by the USA and Russia. Each has brought space vehicles out of orbit and retrieved them.

The solution of the first stage, the entry into the atmosphere at high speed, has been to have a fairly blunt-nosed vehicle with an outer skin that burns up. In the few minutes of travel such a burn-up of the outside can protect the inside. The solution of the final stage has been the use of parachutes released at a certain height, but the Space Shuttle glides back to Earth.

Reciprocating Engine Another name for piston engine, in which the rotation of a shaft is activated by the in-and-out action of pistons in cylinders. All early aero engines were piston engines.

Rigid rotor A helicopter rotor which has no articulating hinges but does have pitch variation.

Rocket A rocket is a vehicle driven by a type of engine that does not depend on air. It is therefore able to function in outer space.

In a rocket, fuels called propellants are burned to create intense volumes of gas, and this gas is shot out of the only opening in the rocket—the rear. The resultant pressure of the gases is therefore forward. So the rocket travels. The simplest rocket used in fireworks has gunpowder or similar fuel lit by a fuse when on the ground.

As the rocket travels upwards it loses the fuel that is being consumed. So the total weight gets less and the rocket accelerates more and more until all the fuel is spent. The weight at

The propulsion system of a rocket. The fuel burns to form very quickly immense volumes of gas, which expand to press on the surroundings. The only outlet is at the rear. So the resultant pressure, shown by arrows, is forwards.

starting must be great, because all the fuel is there. The ratio of this initial mass to the final mass when the fuel is gone is called the *mass* ratio. The velocity at the end is given by the equation

$$V = c \log_e R$$

where R = mass ratio; c = jet velocity.

Turned into common logarithms, this becomes

$$V = 2 \cdot 3\, c \log_{10} R$$

The bigger the final velocity must be, the more fuel there must be and the bigger (and heavier) must be the casing and rocket-engine apparatus. Consequently the practice has become necessary, for space research, of using rockets in several stages. Then when the first stage, or booster, is burned out its heavy container can be automatically thrown away. The next rocket stage then starts to fire with all the advantages of height and speed reached with the help of the booster. So it can be smaller. Thus a composite rocket of several stages can be built up.

Rockets need an immense amount of engineering and electronics for the many controls needed if they are to achieve anything other than going up in smoke.

The large spacecraft launcher, the American Saturn V, weighs 3,050,000 kg (3,000 tons) at launch and is 110 m (365 ft) high. The five S1C stage Boeing F-1 kerosene engines produce 33,360 kN. (7½ million pounds) thrust, and the five

S2 stage Rocketdyne J-2 liquid hydrogen engines produce 4,450 kN. (1,000,000 lb) thrust.

Safe-life Period during which an aircraft component can be expected to function safely before replacement is required.

Satellites Any body in orbit round a bigger body is a satellite. The Moon is a satellite of the Earth, and the Earth can be described as a satellite of the Sun.

Artificial satellites are man-made objects put into orbit, usually round the Earth.

To get a satellite into orbit round the Earth it must be launched parallel to the Earth's surface, high above the Earth's atmosphere, at sufficient speed. If the speed is too little the intended satellite will fall back to Earth. If the speed is above the escape velocity (q.v.) it will fly off into space. Between a certain minimum velocity, depending on the height, and the escape velocity, there is a range of velocities that will take a satellite into orbit. This range at a height of 480 km (300 miles) is from about 7·9 to 11·1 km/sec (4·9 to 6·9 miles/sec), at 640 km (400 miles) from 7·4 to 10·8 km/sec (4·7 to 6·7 miles/sec), and at 1,610 km (1,000 miles) from 7·15 to 10·1 km/sec (4·45 to 6·3 miles/sec). A vehicle launched at the lower speed would just orbit on a circular orbit, whereas one launched at exactly the higher speed would depart on a parabolic path.

If launched into orbit at a speed between these values (for the correct height) the vehicle would travel on an ellipse, being farthest away from the Earth at one end and nearest at the opposite end.

The satellite must be launched more or less parallel to the Earth. This is done by radioed instructions from the ground. Clearly, enormous rocket power is needed to get a satellite up to the launching height.

Since the successful orbital flight of the Russian Sputnik 1 in October 1957, many thousand successful satellites have been launched; others have been launched secretly. Many of these have since come out of orbit; the time a satellite lasts depends on how deeply it dips into the Earth's atmosphere. At 160 km (100 miles) high a satellite might last a week before air resistance slowed it down and burnt it up; at 1,300 km (808 miles) it could last indefinitely.

The amount of machinery in orbit is getting immense: as well as the existing satellites, there are the same number of last stage boosters, discarded fairings; rockets have blown up in orbit and produced hundreds of fragments. The situation is also complicated by the chattering of the earlier satellites, which, although they have finished their missions, cannot be switched off, and their radio transmitters go on using valuable wavelengths.

Satellites serve several purposes; here is a short guide.

Physical Research—Designed to study electrical and magnetic fields at high altitudes, the emission of atomic particles and X-rays from the Sun.

Navigation—Emit precisely timed radio signals as a navigational aid for submarines and other ships. Satellites are used also for surveying and mapping the positions of the continents on the globe and for geological and other environmental research.

Reconnaissance—USAF Big Bird satellites carry cameras to monitor military activity in hostile countries.

Communications—The first Telstar, launched in 1962, was a failure, but its successors have allowed television viewers to see live events from all over the world. Satellites today carry television, voice and telegraph channels around the world and are an accepted and essential means of communication.

Mancarrying—American and Russian satellites have carried men and women into orbit and safely back. This is the most spectacular feat in space, but from the scientific point of view not necessarily the most valuable. The Russians continued in 1984 to orbit Soyuz manned space vehicles and the successful flights of the Space Shuttle have marked the return of American manned missions in space which were discontinued in 1975.

The explosion and destruction of Shuttle Mission STS 51L on 28 January 1986 during lift off is likely to delay further American Shuttle missions for some months.

Satellites Placed in Orbit during 1984

Satellite	Launcher	Weight kg	Purpose	Country	Date
Cosmos 1522	Skean	40	Military	USSR	5.1.84
Cosmos 1523	Skean	40	Military	USSR	5.1.84
Cosmos 1524	Skean	40	Military	USSR	5.1.84
Cosmos 1525	Skean	40	Military	USSR	5.1.84
Cosmos 1526	Skean	40	Military	USSR	5.1.84
Cosmos 1527	Skean	40	Military	USSR	5.1.84
Cosmos 1528	Skean	40	Military	USSR	5.1.84
Cosmos 1529	Skean	40	Military	USSR	5.1.84
Cosmos 1530	Vostok core	6,300	Reconn	USSR	11.1.84
Cosmos 1531	Skean	700	Nav/SAR?	USSR	11.1.84
Cosmos 1532	Vostok core	6,700	Reconn	USSR	13.1.84
Yuri 2A(BS-2A)	Nu-2	670	Comm (TV)	Japan	23.1.84
Cosmos 1533	Vostok core	6,300	Reconn	USSR	26.1.84
Cosmos 1534	Skean	?	Reconn	USSR	26.1.84
China 14	?	900	Sc	China	29.1.84
DSCS 3-02	Titan 34D	1,043	Failure?	USA	31.1.84
Cosmos 1535	Skean	700	Nav/SAR?	USSR	2.2.84
Westar 6	Space Shuttle Challenger F4	1,100	?	USA	3.2.84
IRT	Space Shuttle Challenger F4	91	Target	USA	3.2.84
Palapa 4	Space Shuttle Challenger F4	1,200	Comm	Indonesia	3.2.84
NOSS 6	Atlas F	64	?	USA	5.2.84
JD1	Atlas F	?	?	USA	5.2.84
JD2	Atlas F	?	?	USA	5.2.84
JD3	Atlas F	?	?	USA	5.2.84
Cosmos 1536	Skean	?	Reconn	USSR	8.2.84
Okzora (EXOS-C)	Mu-3S	?	Sc	Japan	14.2.84
Statsionar-Raduga 14	Proton core	2,000?	Comm	USSR	15.2.84
Cosmos 1537	Vostok core	16,300	Comm	USSR	16.2.84
Progress 19	Vostok core	7,020	Salyut-tanker	USSR	21.2.84
Cosmos 1538	Skean	750	Military	USSR	21.2.84
Cosmos 1539	Vostok core	6,700	Reconn	USSR	28.2.84
Landsat 5(F1tD1)	?	1,938	?	USA	1.3.84
UOSAT 2	?	52	?	USA	1.3.84
Cosmos 1540	Proton core	?	?	USSR	2.3.84
Intelsat 5 F-8	Ariane 1-08	1,928	Comm	France/USA	5.3.84
Cosmos 1541	Vostok core	1,250	Military	USSR	6.3.84
Cosmos 1542	Vostok core	6,300	Comm	USSR	7.3.84
Cosmos 1543	Vostok core	5,700	Sc	USSR	10.3.84
Cosmos 1544	Skean	?	Reconn	USSR	15.3.84
Statsionar-Ekran 12	Proton core	?	Comm	USSR	16.3.84
Molniya 1-60	Vostok core	1,000	Comm	USSR	16.3.84
Cosmos 1545	Vostok core	6,300	Reconn	USSR	21.3.84
Cosmos 1546	Proton core	?	?	USSR	29.3.84
Cosmos 1547	Vostok core	1,250	Military	USSR	4.4.84
LDEF 1	Challenger F5	9,707	Sc	USA	6.4.84
China 15	CZ-3	900	Comm (TV)	China	8.4.84
Cosmos 1548	Vostok core	6,700	Reconn	USSR	10.4.84
IMEWS or DSCS?	Titan 3D	?	Failure?	USA	14.4.84
Progress 20	Vostok core	7,020	Salyut-tanker	USSR	15.4.84
?	Titan 3B-Agena D	3,000	?	USA	17.4.84
Cosmos 1549	Vostok core	6,300	Reconn	USSR	19.4.84
Gorizont 9	Proton core	?	Comm	USSR	22.4.84
Progress 21	Vostok core	7,020	Salyut-tanker	USSR	7.5.84
Cosmos 1550	Skean	700	Nav?	USSR	11.5.84
Cosmos 1551	Vostok core	6,300	Reconn	USSR	11.5.84
Cosmos 1552	Vostok core	6,700	Reconn	USSR	14.5.84
Cosmos 1553	Skean	700	Nav?	USSR	17.5.84

Satellite	Launcher	Weight kg	Purpose	Country	Date
Cosmos 1554	Proton core	?	Triple	USSR	19.5.84
Cosmos 1555	Proton core	?	Glonass	USSR	19.5.84
Cosmos 1556	Proton core	?	Payload	USSR	19.5.84
Cosmos 1557	Vostok core	6,300	Reconn	USSR	22.5.84
Spacenet 1	Ariane 1-09	1,195	?	France	23.5.84
Cosmos 1558	Vostok core	6,700	Reconn	USSR	25.5.84
Progress 22	Vostok core	2,020	Salyut-tanker	USSR	28.5.84
Cosmos 1559	Skean	40	Military	USSR	28.5.84
Cosmos 1560	Skean	40	Military	USSR	28.5.84
Cosmos 1561	Skean	40	Military	USSR	28.5.84
Cosmos 1562	Skean	40	Military	USSR	28.5.84
Cosmos 1563	Skean	40	Military	USSR	28.5.84
Cosmos 1564	Skean	40	Military	USSR	28.5.84
Cosmos 1565	Skean	40	Military	USSR	28.5.84
Cosmos 1566	Skean	40	Military	USSR	28.5.84
Cosmos 1567	Scarp	?	Reconn	USSR	30.5.84
Cosmos 1568	Vostok core	6,300	Reconn	USSR	1.6.84
Cosmos 1569	Vostok core	1,250	Military	USSR	6.6.84
Cosmos 1570	Skean	750	Military	USSR	8.6.84
Intelsat 5 F-9	Atlas Centaur	2,016	Comm	USA	9.6.84
Cosmos 1571	Vostok core	6,300	Reconn	USSR	11.6.84
Navstar 9(USA1)	Atlas E	770	Nav	USA	13.6.84
Cosmos 1572	Vostok core	6,300	Reconn	USSR	15.6.84
Cosmos 1573	Vostok core	6,300	Reconn	USSR	19.6.84
Cosmos 1574 (Cospas 3)	Skean	700	Nav?	USSR	21.6.84
Statsionar-Raduga 15	Proton core	?	Comm	USSR	22.6.84
Cosmos 1575	Vostok core	6,300	Reconn	USSR	22.6.84
USA-2	Titan 34D?	13,300	?	USA	25.6.84
USA-3 capsule	Titan 34D?	60	?	USA	25.6.84
Cosmos 1576	Vostok core	6,700	Reconn	USSR	26.6.84
Cosmos 1577	Skean	700	Nav?	USSR	27.6.84
Cosmos 1578	Skean	550	Military	USSR	28.6.84
Cosmos 1579	Scarp	?	Nuclear?	USSR	29.6.84
Cosmos 1580	Vostok core	6,300	Reconn	USSR	29.6.84
Cosmos 1581	Vostok core	1,250	Military	USSR	3.7.84
Meteor 2-11	Skean	2,750	Weather	USSR	5.7.84
Cosmos 1582	Vostok core	6,300	Reconn	USSR	19.7.84
Cosmos 1583	Vostok core	6,300	Reconn	USSR	24.7.84
Cosmos 1584	Vostok core	6,300	Reconn	USSR	27.7.84
Cosmos 1585	Vostok core	6,700	Reconn	USSR	31.7.84
Gorizont 10	Proton core	?	Comm	USSR	1.8.84
Cosmos 1586	Vostok core	1,250	Military	USSR	2.8.84
Himawari 3 (GMS-3)	Nu-2	670	?	Japan	2.8.84
ECS-2	Ariane 3-01	1,175	Comm	Europe	4.8.84
Telecom 1A	Ariane 3-01	1,185	Comm	France	4.8.84
Cosmos 1587	Vostok core	6,300	Reconn	USSR	6.8.84
Cosmos 1588	Scarp	?	Reconn?	USSR	7.8.84
Cosmos 1589	Skean	?	Reconn	USSR	8.8.84
Molniya 1-61	Vostok core	1,000	Comm	USSR	10.8.84
Progress 23	Vostok core	7,020	Salyut-tanker	USSR	14.8.84
Cosmos 1590	Vostok core	6,300	Reconn	USSR	16.8.84
CCE 1	Thor Delta	242	Sc	USA	16.8.84
IRM 1	Thor Delta	705	Sc	FDR Ger	16.8.84
UKS-1	Thor Delta	77	Sc	UK	16.8.84
Molniya 1-62	Vostok core	1,000	Comm	USSR	24.8.84
Statsionar-Ekran 13	Proton core	?	Comm	USSR	24.8.84
SDS 9 (USA-4)	Titan 3B-AgenaD	?	?	USA	28.8.84
Cosmos 1591	Vostok core	6,300	Reconn	USSR	30.8.84

Satellite	Launcher	Weight kg	Purpose	Country	Date
SBS-4		1,117	?		
Leasat 2	Space shuttle	6,850	Military-comm	USA	30.8.84
(Syncom IV-2)	Discovery F1				
Telstar 3C		1,225	?		
Cosmos 1592	Vostok core	6,300	Reconn	USSR	4.9.84
Cosmos 1593		?	Triple		
Cosmos 1594	Proton core	?	Glonass	USSR	4.9.84
Cosmos 1595		?	Payload		
Cosmos 1596	Vostok core	1,250	Military	USSR	7.9.84
Navstar 10	Atlas F	770	Nav	USA	8.9.84
(USA5)					
China 16	?	3,600	Sc	China	12.9.84
Cosmos 1597	Vostok core	5,900	Reconn	USSR	13.9.84
Capsule 99C		200	?		
Cosmos 1598	Skean	700	Nav?	USSR	13.9.84
Galaxy 3	?	1,218	?	USA	21.9.84
Cosmos 1599	Vostok core	6,700	Reconn	USSR	25.9.84
Cosmos 1600	Vostok core	6,300	Reconn	USSR	27.9.84
Cosmos 1601	Skean	?	Reconn	USSR	27.9.84
Cosmos 1602	Skean	?	Reconn	USSR	28.9.84
Cosmos 1603	Proton core	?	?	USSR	28.9.84
Cosmos 1604	Vostok core	1,250	Military	USSR	4.10.84
ERBS	Challenger F6	2,540	Sc	USA	5.10.84
Cosmos 1605	Skean	700	Nav?	USSR	11.10.84
Nova 2	Scout	165	?	USA	12.10.84
Cosmos 1606	Skean	?	Reconn	USSR	18.10.84
Cosmos 1607	Scarp	?	Reconn?	USSR	31.10.84
Telesat 8	Space shuttle	1,238	Comm	USA	8.11.84
(Anik-D2)	Discovery F2				
Leasat 1		6,850	?		
(Syncom IV-1)					
Spacenet 2	Ariane 3-02	1,195	?	France	10.11.84
Marecs 2		497	Nav?	UK	
NATO 3D	?	720	Military	NATO	14.11.84
Cosmos 1608	Vostok core	6,700	Reconn	USSR	14.11.84
Cosmos 1609	Vostok core	6,300	Reconn	USSR	14.11.84
Cosmos 1610	Skean	700	Nav?	USSR	15.11.84
Cosmos 1611	Vostok core	6,700	Reconn	USSR	21.11.84
Cosmos 1612	Skean	?	Reconn	USSR	27.11.84
Cosmos 1613	Vostok core	6,300	Reconn	USSR	29.11.84
USA-6	Titan 3	13,300	?	USA	4.12.84
NOAA 9	Atlas E	1,712	Nav/SAR	USA	12.12.84
Molniya 1-63	Vostok core	1,000	Comm	USSR	14.12.84
Cosmos 1614	Skean	1,000	Shuttle test	USSR	19.12.84
Cosmos 1615	Skean	?	Reconn	USSR	20.12.84
USA-7	Titan 34D	?	IMEWS or DSCS	USA	22.12.84

Abbreviations: Sc—scientific, and includes a great variety of experiments in cosmic particles, meteorites, light, magnetism, etc.

Comm.—Communications, also abbreviated comsat.

The list above includes all Earth satellites known to have been launched successfully up to 31st December 1984. Details of satellite weight and purpose are often withheld for reasons of military security.

Manned Space Vehicles Launched to December 1984

Name	Orbits or time	Country	Crew	Date
Vostok 1	1 orbit	USSR	Gagarin	12.4.61
Freedom 7	No orbit	USA	Sheppard	5.5.61
Liberty Bell 7	No orbit	USA	Grissom	21.7.61
Vostok 2	17 orbits	USSR	Titov	6.8.61
Friendship 7	3 orbits	USA	Glenn	20.2.62
Mercury Atlas 7	4 hr 56 min	USA	Carpenter	24.5.62
Vostok 3	3 days 22 hrs	USSR	Nikolayev	11.8.62
Vostok 4	2 days 22 hrs	USSR	Popovitch	12.8.62
Mercury Atlas 8	9 hrs 13 min	USA	Schirra	3.9.62
Sigma 7	22 orbits (manually controlled descent after instrument failure)	USA	Cooper	15.5.63
Vostok 5	81 orbits, 5 days	USSR	Bykovsky	14.6.63
Vostok 6	48 orbits	USSR	Valentina Tereshkova*	15.6.63
Voskhod 1	16 orbits, 24 hrs 17 mins	USSR	Komarov, Yegorov, Feoktikov	12.10.63
Voskhod 2	18 orbits	USSR	Belyaev, Leonov[1]	18.3.65
Gemini 3[2]	3 orbits	USA	Grissom, Young	23.3.65
Gemini 4	62 orbits, 97 hrs 50 mins	USA	McDivitt, White[3]	3.6.65
Gemini 5	120 orbits, 190 hrs 56 mins[4]	USA	Cooper, Conrad	21.8.65
Gemini 6 &	26 hours	USA	Schirra, Stafford	15.12.65
Gemini 7[5]	206 orbits, 330 hrs 25 mins	USA	Borman, Lovell	4.12.65
Gemini 8	4 orbits, 10 hrs 18 mins	USA	Armstrong, Scott	16.3.66
Gemini 9	48 orbits, 72 hrs 21 mins	USA	Strafford, Cernan	3.6.66
Gemini 10	44 orbits, 70 hrs 48 mins.	USA	Young, Collins	18.7.66
Gemini 11[6]	48 orbits, 71 hrs 18 mins	USA	Conrad, Gordon	12.9.66
Gemini 12[7]	63 orbits, 84 hrs 26 mins	USA	Aldrin, Lovell	11.11.66
Soyuz 1	17 orbits, 24 hrs 36 mins	USSR	Komarov[8]	23.4.67
Apollo 7	10 days 20 hrs. Live TV, rendezvous with booster	USA	Schirra, Eisele, Cunningham	11.10.68
Soyuz 3	3 days 23 hrs Rendezvous with Soyuz 2, no docking	USSR	Beregovoy	26.10.68
Apollo 8	6 days 3 hrs First manned flight around moon	USA	Borman, Lovell, Anders	21.12.68
Soyuz 4	2 days 23 hrs. Docking target for Soyuz 5	USSR	Shatalov	14.1.69
Soyuz 5	3 days 1 hr. Docked with Soyuz 4. Two cosmonauts transferred for re-entry	USSR	Volynov, Khrunov, Yeliseyev	15.1.69
Apollo 9	10 days 1 hr. LM manned flight for 6 hrs for lunar manoeuvres	USA	McDivitt, Scott, Schweikart	3.3.69
Apollo 10	8 days. LM manned flight for 8 hrs in 60 nm lunar orbit	USA	Stafford, Young, Cernan	18.5.69
Apollo 11	8 days. LM 'Eagle' vehicle for man's first landing on the moon, 20 and 21.7.69	USA	Armstrong, Aldrin, Collins	16.7.69
Soyuz 6	5 days. Rendezvous trials of three Soyuz craft in Earth orbit	USSR	Shonin, Kubasov	11.10.69
Soyuz 7	5 days. Rendezvous trials as above	USSR	Filipchenko, Volkov, Gorbatko	12.10.69

Name	Orbits or time	Country	Crew	Date
Soyuz 8	5 days. Rendezvous trials as above	USSR	Shatalov, Yeliseyev	13.10.69
Apollo 12	10 days. LM 'Intrepid' vehicle on moon 19 and 20.11.69	USA	Conrad, Gordon, Bean	14.11.69
Apollo 13	6 days. LEM 'Aquarius' vehicle used as lifeboat for crippled service module	USA	Lovell, Haise, Swigert	11.4.70
Soyuz 9	17 days long-duration flight. Craft weighed 6,450 kg	USSR	Sevastyanov, Nikolayev	1.6.70
Apollo 14	10 days. Landing in Fra Mauro highlands. Use of wheeled cart. Exploration of Cone Crater	USA	Shepard, Mitchell, Roosa	31.1.71
Soyuz 10	2 days. Docked with Salyut but trouble with hatch prevented transfer	USSR	Rukavishnikov, Thatalov, Yeliseyev	22.4.71
Soyuz 11	24 days. Rendezvous with Salyut. Mission ended with death of cosmonauts	USSR	Dobrovolski, Volkov, Patseyev	6.6.71
Apollo 15	12 days. Landing in Apennines. Use of Lunar Roving Vehicle. Exploration of Hadley Rille	USA	Scott, Worden, Irwin	26.7.71
Apollo 16	11 days. Landing in Descartes highlands 17 mile exploration in LVR2	USA	Young, Duke, Mattingly	16.4.72
Apollo 17	12 days. Landing in Taurus-Littrow area LRV3—found volcanic evidence	USA	Cerman, Evans, Schmitt	7.12.72
Skylab 2	First manned flight to Skylab space station (launched 14.5.73). Deployed sail to reduce temperature and released solar panel. Manned duration 28 days to 22.6.73	USA	Conrad, Kerwin, Weitz	25.5.73
Skylab 3	Second manned flight to Skylab space station. Manned duration 59 days to 25.9.73	USA	Bean, Lousma, Garriott	28.7.73
Soyuz 12	First Soviet manned flight for two years, tested improved Soyuz. Manned duration 2 days to 29.9.73	USSR	Lazarev, Makarov	27.9.73
Skylab 4	Final flight to Skylab space station. Manned duration 84 days to 8.2.74. Skylab space station finally re-entered Earth atmosphere 11.7.79	USA	Carr, Pogue, Gibson	16.11.73
Soyuz 13	Verification of Soyuz modifications and for astronomy. Manned duration 8 days to 26.12.73	USSR	Klimuk, Lebedev	18.12.73

Name	Orbits or time	Country	Crew	Date
Soyuz 14	Rendezvous and docking with Salyut 3 on 4.7.74. Manned duration 15 days to 19.7.74	USSR	Popovich, Artyukhin	3.7.74
Soyuz 15	Overshot Salyut 3 when booster over-burned. Returned in 2 days	USSR	Sarafanov, Demin	26.8.74
Soyuz 16	Successful rehearsal of ASTP mission. Manned duration 6 days to 8.12.74	USSR	Filipchenko, Rukavishnikov	2.12.74
Soyuz 17	Rendezvous and docking with Salyut 4 on 12.1.75. Manned duration 29½ days to 9.2.75	USSR	Gubarev, Grechko	10.1.75
Soyuz 18	Rendezvous and docking with Salyut 4 on 25.5.75. Manned duration 63 days to 26.7.75	USSR	Klimuk, Sevastianov	24.5.75
Soyuz 19	Apollo/Soyuz Test Project (ASTP). Docked with Apollo 18 17.7.75. Astronauts exchanged visits. Manned duration 6 days to 21.7.75	USSR	Leonov, Kubasov	15.7.75
Apollo 18	Apollo/Soyuz Test Project (ASTP). Docked with Soyuz 19 17.7.75. Astronauts exchanged visits. Manned duration 9 days to 24.7.75	USA	Stafford, Slayton, Brand	15.7.75
Soyuz 21	Rendezvous and docking with Salyut 5 on 7.7.76. Scientific and weather experiments. Manned duration 49 days to 24.8.76	USSR	Volynon, Zholobov	6.7.76
Soyuz 22	Carried multi-spectral camera for East German geology survey. Watched Norway NATO exercise. Manned duration 8 days to 23.9.76	USSR	Bykovsky	15.9.76
Soyuz 23	Rendezvous with Salyut 5 on 15.10.76, failed to dock. Manned duration 2 days to 16.10.76	USSR	Vyacheslav, Rozhdestvensky	14.10.76
Soyuz 24	Rendezvous and docking with Salyut 5 on 9.2.77. Manned duration 18 days to 25.2.77	USSR	Gorbatko, Glazhov	7.2.77
Soyuz 25	Rendezvous with Salyut 6 on 9.10.77 but docking unsuccessful. Manned duration 2 days to 11.10.77	USSR	Kovalyonok, Ryumin	9.10.77
Soyuz 26	Rendezvous and docking with Salyut 6 on 10.12.77. Spacecraft returned on 16.1.78	USSR	Romanenko, Grechko (This crew returned in Soyuz 27 after 96 days, on 16.3.78)	10.12.77

Name	Orbits or time	Country	Crew	Date
Soyuz 27	Rendezvous and docking with Salyut 6 on 11.1.78. Spacecraft returned on 16.3.78	USSR	Dzhanibekov, Makarov (This crew returned in Soyuz 26 after 5 days on 16.1.78)	10.1.78
Soyuz 28	Rendezvous and docking with Salyut 6 on 3.3.78. Manned duration 8 days to 10.3.78	USSR	Gubarev, Remek (Czech)	2.3.78
Soyuz 29	Rendezvous and docking with Salyut 6 on 17.6.78. Spacecraft returned on 3.9.78	USSR	Kovalyonok, Ivanchenkov (This crew returned in Soyuz 31 after 140 days on 2.11.78)	15.6.78
Soyuz 30	Rendezvous and docking with Salyut 6 on 27.6.78. Manned duration 6 days to 5.7.78	USSR	Klimuk, Giermaszewski (Polish)	27.6.78
Soyuz 31	Rendezvous and docking with Salyut 6 on 27.8.78. Spacecraft returned on 2.11.78	USSR	Bykovsky, Jähn (E. German) (This crew returned in Soyuz 29 after 7 days on 3.9.78)	26.8.78
Soyuz 32	Rendezvous and docking with Salyut 6 on 25.2.79. Spacecraft returned unmanned 13.6.79	USSR	Lyakhov, Ryumin (This crew returned in Soyuz 34 after 175 days on 19.8.79)	25.2.79
Soyuz 33	Rendezvous with Salyut 6 on 10.4.79, but docking unsuccessful. Manned duration 2 days to 12.4.79	USSR	Rukavishnikov, Ivanov (Bulgarian)	10.4.79
Soyuz 34	(Launched unmanned, see Satellite log. Rendezvous and docking with Salyut 6 on 8.6.79. Returned with Lyakhov and Ryumin on 19.8.79)			
Soyuz 35	Rendezvous and docking with Salyut 6 on 10.4.80. Spacecraft returned on 3.6.80	USSR	Popov, Ryumin (This crew returned in Soyuz 37 after 185 days on 11.10.80)	9.4.80
Soyuz 36	Rendezvous and docking with Salyut 6 on 27.5.80. Spacecraft returned on 31.7.80	USSR	Kubasov, Farkash (Hungarian) (This crew returned in Soyuz 35 after 7 days on 3.6.80)	26.5.80
Soyuz T-2	Rendezvous and docking with Salyut 6 on 6.6.80. Manned duration 4 days to 9.6.80	USSR	Malyshev, Aksenov	5.6.80
Soyuz 37	Rendezvous and docking with Salyut 6 on 24.7.80. Spacecraft returned on 11.10.80	USSR	Gorbatko, Pham Tuan (Vietnamese) (This crew returned in Soyuz 36 after 8 days on 31.7.80)	23.7.80
Soyuz 38	Rendezvous and docking with Salyut 6 on 19.9.80. Manned duration 8 days to 26.9.80	USSR	Romanenko, Mendez (Cuban)	18.9.80
Soyuz T-3	Rendezvous and docking with Salyut 6 on 28.11.80. Manned duration 13 days to 10.12.80	USSR	Kizim, Makarov, Strekalov (First 3-man crew since June 1971)	27.11.80
Soyuz T-4	Rendezvous and docking with Salyut 6 on 13.3.81. Manned duration 75 days to 26.5.81	USSR	Kovalyonok, Savinykh (100th person in space)	12.3.81

Name	Orbits or time	Country	Crew	Date
Soyuz 39	Rendezvous and docking with Salyut 6 on 22.3.81. Manned duration 8 days to 30.3.81	USSR	Dzhanibekov, Gurragcha (Mongolian)	22.3.81
Space Shuttle 'Columbia'	2 days 6 hrs 21 mins. First space vehicle to land back as a winged aircraft and to be reusable	USA	Young, Crippen	12.4.81
Soyuz 40	Rendezvous and docking with Salyut 6 on 15.5.81. Manned duration 8 days to 22.5.81	USSR	Popov, Prunarium (Rumanian)	14.5.81
Space Shuttle 'Columbia' STS 2	2 days 6 hrs 13 mins. Carried Osta-1 scientific experiment which failed to separate. Landed back at Edwards AFB	USA	Engel, Truly	12.11.81
Space Shuttle 'Columbia' STS 3	8 days 0 hrs 5 mins. Carried OSS-1. Extra day in space. Landed back at White Sands, New Mexico	USA	Lousma, Fullerton	22.3.82
Soyuz T-5	Rendezvous and docking with Salyut 7 on 14.5.82. Launched Iskra 2 amateur radio satellite on 17.5.82	USSR	Berezovoy, Lebedev	13.5.82
Soyuz T-6	Rendezvous and docking with Salyut 7 on 25.6.82. Manned duration 8 days to 2.7.82	USSR	Dzanibekov, Ivanchenkov, Chrétien (French)	24.6.82
Space Shuttle 'Columbia' STS 4	7 days 1 hr 9 mins. Landed back at Edwards AFB 4.7.82	USA	Mattingly, Hartsfield	27.6.82
Soyuz T-7	Rendezvous and docking with Salyut 7 on 20.8.82. Manned duration 8 days to 27.8.82	USSR	Popov, Serebrov, Savitskaya (2nd Soviet woman cosmonaut) (This crew returned in Soyuz T-5)	19.8.82
Space Shuttle 'Columbia' STS 5	Deployed SBS-C and Telesat-E. Landed back at Edwards AFB 16.21.82. Manned duration 5 days	USA	Brand, Overmyer, Lenoir, Allen	11.11.82
Space Shuttle 'Challenger' STS 6	Deployed TDRSS-A. Landed back at Edwards AFB 9.4.83. Manned duration 5 days	USA	Weitz, Bobko, Musgrave, Peterson	4.4.83
Soyuz T-8	Failed to dock with Salyut 7 on 21.4.83. Landed safely on 22.4.83. Manned duration 2 days	USSR	Titov, Strekalov, Serebrov	20.4.83
Space Shuttle 'Challenger' STS 7	Deployed Anik C2 (Canada) and Palopa Bl (Indonesia). Released and retrieved Spas Ol. Landed back at Edwards AFB 24.6.83. Manned duration 6 days	USA	Crippen, Hauck, Fabian, Thagaard, Ride (1st US woman astronaut)	18.6.83
Soyuz T-9	Rendezvous and docking with Salyut 7 on 28.6.83. Manned duration 149 days to 23.11.83	USSR	Lyakhov, Alexandrov	27.6.83

Name	Orbits or time	Country	Crew	Date
Space Shuttle 'Challenger' STS8	Deployed Insat 1B (India). Landed back at Edwards AFB 5.9.83. Manned duration 6 days. First night landing	USA	Truly, Brandenstein, Gardner, Bluford, Thornton	30.8.83
Space Shuttle 'Challenger' STS9	First Spacelab mission. Landed back at Edwards AFB 8.12.83. Manned duration 10 days	USA* Germany	Young, Shaw, Parker, Garriott, Lichtenberg, Merbold	28.11.83
Space Shuttle 'Challenger' STS 41B	Deployed Westar 6, IRT and Palapa 4. Landed back at Kennedy Space Centre 11.2.84. Manned duration 8 days	USA* Indonesia	Brand, Gibson, Stewart, McCandless, McNair	3.2.84
Soyuz T-10	Rendezvous and docking with Salyut 7 on 9.2.84. Manned duration 237 days to 2.10.84	USSR	Kazim, Solovyov, Atkov	8.2.84
Soyuz T-11	Rendezvous and docking with Salyut 7 on 4.4.84. Manned duration 7 days to 11.4.84	USSR* India	Malyshev, Strekalov, Sharma (India)	3.4.84
Space Shuttle 'Challenger' STS 41C	Deployed LDEF 1. Landed back at Edwards AFB on 13.4.84. Manned duration 7 days	USA	Crippen, Hart, Van Hoften, Nelson, Scobee	6.4.84
Soyuz T-12	Rendezvous and docking with Salyut 7 on 18.7.84. Manned duration 11 days to 29.7.84	USSR	Dzhanibekov, Savitskaya (1st woman to walk in space), Igor Volk	17.7.84
Space Shuttle 'Discovery' STS 41D	Deployed SBS 4, Leasat 2 (Syncar IV-2) and Telstar 3C. Landed back at Edwards AFB 5.9.84. Manned duration 6 days	USA	Hartsfield, Coats, Resnik, Hawley, Mullane, C. Walker	30.8.84
Space Shuttle 'Challenger' STS 41G	Deployed ERBS. Landed back at Cape Canaveral 13.10.84. Manned duration 8 days	USA/ Canada	Crippen, Sullivan, Leetsma, McBride, Ride, Scully-Power, Garneau (Canada)	5.10.84
Space Shuttle 'Discovery' STS 51A	Deployed Telesat 8 (Anik D2) and Leasat 1 (Syncom IV-1). Landed back at Cape Canaveral 16.11.84. Manned duration 8 days	USA	Allen, Fischer, Gardner, D. Walker, Hauck	8.11.84

* Valentina Tereshkova was the first woman cosmonaut.
[1] Leonov was the first man to leave a spaceship and float freely in outer space.
[2] Gemini 3 was a manoeuvrable spacecraft and changed its flight path three times.
[3] White was the second man and the first American to step out into space.
[4] The approximate time that would be required to fly to the moon, briefly explore and return to earth.
[5] These spacecraft carried out a successful rendezvous in orbit, approaching to within 2 m of each other and flying in formation for more than 2 circuits of the Earth.
[6] First orbit docking achieved.
[7] Docking achieved on third orbit.
[8] Komarov was first in-flight space fatality when parachute shroud lines became entangled.

Shock Wave When air moves over an obstacle faster than the speed of sound it no longer has time to be pushed gradually out of the way. Instead it changes its direction of motion in jumps: the lines along which these jumps occur are called shock waves, and separate regions of different pressure. The boom of an aircraft passing through the sound barrier is simply its shock wave reaching one's ears: the sudden change of pressure is heard as an explosion, or frequently as a double bang.

Space Probe Unmanned vehicle which is launched to escape from Earth orbit and to continue on a voyage of exploration within the Solar system or beyond. About 100 space probes have been launched since the first, Pioneer 1, was put up by the United States in 1958. All have been listed in *Junior Pears Encyclopaedia*.

The first probe to hit the Moon was the Russian Lunik 2 in September 1959 followed by the American Ranger 4 in April 1962. Lunik 3 achieved lunar orbit and photographed the far side of the Moon, unseen previously by Man, in October 1959. The Russians made the first soft landing on the Moon in January 1966 with their Luna 9 probe and obtained pictures of the lunar surface. Surveyor 1, an American probe, followed in May 1966 and transmitted TV pictures from the surface.

Meanwhile the Americans had sent Mariner 2 out on a mission of discovery and it radioed back much information as it passed close to Venus in December 1962. Mariner 4 and the Russian Zond 4 both took photographs of Mars in 1964/65, and Mariner 5 passed within 3,200 km of Venus in 1967.

Russian and American lunar programmes continued with Surveyor 3 finding 15 cm pebbles on the Moon in 1967. The Russians brought back soil samples in Luna 16 in September 1970 and their Luna 17 which landed in the Sea of Rains put the first 8-wheel Lunokhod robot vehicle on the lunar surface.

Pioneer 10 went to Jupiter in 1973, crossed Neptune's orbit on 13 June 1983 and then passed on into deep space beyond the solar system. Russia's Venus 8 probe made a parachute landing on the planet in July 1972. Russia put a Mars 6 capsule on the Martian surface in March 1974 but it failed to transmit any data. The Americans put Viking 1's Mars lander on the surface in July 1976.

Among recent probes have been the Soviet Venus 13 and

14 which made soft landings on that planet in 1982. But perhaps the spectacular success of NASA's Voyager 1 space probe in November 1980 underlines best what can be achieved by space probes. Voyager 1 flew within 4,500 km of Saturn's largest moon Titan and found its atmosphere to be composed of nitrogen—rather than methane as had been supposed. It also flew close to Saturn's rings and sent back superb photographs which revealed they are not made up of broad bands but of hundreds of ringlets, some interwoven. Voyager 2's pictures in August 1981 were even more spectacular.

During 1983 Russia launched its Venus 15 (2.6.83) and Venus 16 (7.6.83) probes which went into orbit around the planet Venus in October 1983 in order to map its surface by radar. Its Vega 1 and Vega 2 probes were launched on 15.12.84 and 27.12.84 respectively. They flew close to Halley's Comet in March 1986.

Space Travel Exploration of other planets by man began in 1969 with the United States' Apollo 11 mission to the Moon. With its complete success the stage was set for other journeys to more remote planets and for more extensive exploration of the Moon itself.

During the remainder of the Project Apollo programme there were a further five successful landings on the Moon. The Lunar Modules carried in all 12 astronauts on to the lunar surface between 1969 and 1972.

The Russians have preferred to send unmanned vehicles to explore the Moon, the most recent was Luna 24 in Aug. 1976.

Specific fuel consumption A measure of engine efficiency based on the rate of fuel consumption divided by the power supplied.

Starboard The right-hand side of an aircraft as seen by the pilot looking forward. Associated with a green wing-tip light.

Supercritical wing Wing of special profile in which lift is generated chordwise over whole upper surface instead of close to leading-edge.

Supersonic Flight Flight at speeds greater than Mach 1. It involves aerodynamic problems that are different from those of subsonic flight. No less troublesome are the problems of having to get from subsonic to supersonic speeds. Some of the adaptations already achieved are the sweptback wing with narrow section and small wing area. See *Shock wave*.

Sweepback Rearwards inclination of aerofoil surface, seen from above, measured relative to longitudinal axis usually at quarter chord line.

Sweepforward Forwards inclination of aerofoil surface, seen from above, measured relative to longitudinal axis usually at quarter chord line. Grumman's forward-swept wing X-29 experimental aircraft, which flew on 14 December 1984, will prove the aerodynamic advantages of this type of layout.

Thermal Imaging A new technology gaining rapid acceptance as an important aid to military aircraft. It enables objects to be detected at night or through cloud or mist, with a clarity far better than even the most advanced radar. The big advantage of thermal imaging systems is that they depend on receiving 'heat' from an object and do not transmit any radio waves themselves. Unlike radar, therefore, the use of a thermal imager is totally undetectable by the opposing forces. Thermal imaging can also be used for mapping, resource surveillance and in numerous land and sea-based applications, both civil and military.

A thermal imager detects the heat being radiated by a body, this radiation being in the form of electro-magnetic waves, of the same nature as light, but, for objects such as the Earth, buildings or vehicles, at a frequency which is invisible to the human eye. The eye only sees such radiation when a body becomes red hot. Advanced thermal imagers can detect differences in temperature as small as $0.5°C$, meaning that a very detailed picture can be built up. If this picture can be presented to the pilot it enables low flying at night, for example: or the picture can be recorded on film for later analysis—to detect enemy installations, troop movements, for example—by intelligence teams.

Because of its passive nature, thermal imaging is taking over many applications previously undertaken by radar, and is becoming of major importance in military aircraft.

Transceiver Radio transmitter/receiver.

Turbofan Development of the jet engine in which a larger amount of air than is needed for combustion is taken in and mixed with the hot exhaust stream. The advantage is that the exhaust stream becomes heavier and slower so that it wastes less energy in turbulence (q.v.), has better fuel consumption and has made possible the new generation of quieter jet engines.

Turbojet Basic jet engine with compressor, combustion chamber, turbine and propulsive nozzle. See *Jet propulsion*.

Turboprop The driving of propellers by gas turbines. This system, vibrationless and powerful, earlier proved successful for civil airliners, notably Viscounts and Britannias.

Turboshaft Gas turbine used to drive a shaft (as opposed to a propeller in the case of a turboprop) which provides power to a helicopter rotor (for instance) via a reduction gearbox.

Turbulence Air moves in two states: laminar flow—that is, in orderly streams; or turbulent flow—that is, in a disorderly mass of small swirls. Under general conditions, whether the flow will be laminar or turbulent depends on the value of the *Reynold's Number*—a dimensionless function of the size of the object, the viscosity and the velocity of flow. Turbulent flow absorbs much more energy than laminar flow, and therefore aircraft designers try to prevent it occurring. It begins in the *boundary layer* (q.v.), a thin skin of relatively stationary air close to the surface of the aeroplane. A promising system for preventing turbulence is to suck this layer away through fine holes in the skin.

Types of Aircraft, Some Outstanding Modern
RUSSIA

An-26 'Curl' Twin turboprop short haul transport. Two AI-2AVT engines. Wing span 29·20 m (95 ft 9½ in). Carries up to 5,500 kg (12,125 lb) of cargo.

Il-62M 'Classic' Long-range jet transport powered by four D-30KU turbofans. Similar layout to VC10. Carries up to 174 passengers. Capable of non-stop flight from Moscow to Havana, Cuba.

Il-86 'Camber' Wide-body airbus powered by four NK-86 turbofans. Wing span 48 m (157 ft). Carries up to 350 passengers.

MiG-25 (E-266) 'Foxbat' Twin jet all-weather fighter, NATO code 'Foxbat'. Two R-31 turbojets each rated at 120 kN (27,010 lb) thrust with afterburning.

Tu-134B 'Crusty' Medium-range transport with rear mounted D-30 turbofans of 66·7 kN (14,990 lb) thrust. Seats for up to 96 passengers.

Tu-154 'Careless' Medium/long-range transport powered by three 93·2 kN (20,950 lb) thrust NK-8-2 turbofans. Carries up to 167 passengers.

Tu-28P 'Fiddler' Supersonic twin jet all-weather interceptor. Carries two large 'Ash' delta wing air-to-air missiles under each wing.

USA

Boeing 747 Four-jet heavy transport known as the 'Jumbo Jet'. Powered by four JT9D, CF6 or RB.211 turbofans. Basic accommodation for 452 passengers, but capable of carrying up to 511 in extended upper deck-300 version.

Boeing 757-200 Short-to-medium range jet transport with two Rolls-Royce 535C, 535E4 or Pratt & Whitney PW2037 turbofans. 178–239 seats.

Boeing 757

General Dynamics F-16A Lightweight air combat fighter. One Pratt & Whitney F100-PW-200 turbofan. Mach 2 +.

Lockheed L-1011 TriStar High density transport powered by three Rolls-Royce RB.211 turbofans. Up to 400 passengers.

Lockheed C-5A Heavy logistics transport. Four US General Electric TF39 turbofans each 183 kN (41,000 lb) thrust. Span 68 m (223 ft). Carries 101,600 kg (100 tons) of payload. Used by USAF Military Airlift Command.

McDonnell Douglas F-4M Phantom RAF version of multi-role supersonic fighter capable of more than Mach 2. Royal Navy Phantom is F-4K. Span 11·75 m (38·55 ft). Two Rolls-Royce Spey RB.168-25R Mk.202 turbofans, 54·5 kN (12,500 lb) thrust each (dry), 70% afterburning.

McDonnell Douglas F-15 Eagle Air superiority fighter. Two

Pratt & Whitney F100-PW-100 turbofans. More than Mach 2.5.

McDonnell Douglas DC-9 Twin turbofan short- to medium-range airliner. Seats for up to 139 tourist class passengers in Series 50 version.

McDonnell Douglas DC-10 High density transport powered by three US General Electric CF6-6 turbofans. Up to 380 passengers.

UNITED KINGDOM
British Aerospace

Concorde Supersonic transport designed and produced in co-operation with Aerospatiale in France. Faster than Mach 2. Four Rolls-Royce Bristol Olympus 593 engines.

BAe 146 Four turbofan short-range transport. Series 200 stretched version in service with Air Wisconsin, seats 109 passengers. Four Avco Lycoming ALF502 turbofan engines.

BAe/Aerospatiale Concorde

Jaguar GR Mk.1 Tactical support aircraft, powered by two Rolls-Royce Turboméca Adour Mk.102 turbofans each of 32·5 kN (7,305 lb) thrust with reheat. Maximum speed Mach 1·5 at 11,000 m (36,000 ft).

One-Eleven Twin-jet short/medium range transport aircraft. Stretched 500 series aircraft seats up to 119 passengers. Rear-mounted Rolls-Royce Spey turbofans. 871 km/hr (541 mph).

Buccaneer Strike aircraft. Mk. 2B version powered by two 49 kN (11,100 lb) thrust Rolls-Royce RB.168 Spey turbofans. Carries variety of weapons, including nuclear, in rotating bomb bay, plus Martel air-to-ground missiles on external pylons.

Harrier GR Mk. 3 V/STOL close support and armed re-connaissance aircraft. Uses two pairs of rotating nozzles which direct thrust downward for lift, or aft for propulsion. Rolls-Royce Bristol Pegasus 103 of 95·6 kN (21,500 lb) thrust. Maximum level speed over 1,186 km/hr (737 mph).

Panavia Tornado Multi-role combat aircraft, powered by two Turbo-Union RB.199-34R-2 turbofans each of 71 kN (16,000 lb) thrust with reheat. Maximum speed 2,337 km/hr (1,320 mph) at altitude. RAF will have 220 Tornado GR Mk. 1 interdictor strike version and 165 Tornado F Mk. 2 air defence variant.

Panavia Tornado

Hawk T Mk. 1 Two-seat basic and advanced jet trainer with capability of air defence and ground attack roles. One Rolls-Royce Turboméca Adour Mk. 151 non-afterburning turbofan of 23·13 kN (5,200 lb) thrust. Maximum level speed 1,038 km/hr (645 mph). The RAF ordered 176 Hawk T Mk. 1s and some of these are in service with the Red Arrows aerobatic team.

Nimrod MR Mk. 2 Maritime reconnaissance aircraft developed from Comet. Four Rolls-Royce Spey Mk. 250 turbofans of 54 kN (12,140 lb) thrust each. Nimrod AEW Mk 3 airborne early warning variant is undergoing trials.

Hawk T Mk. 1

Trident 3B Short/medium-haul three-jet airliner. Aft-mounted 51·5 kN (11,960 lb) thrust Rolls-Royce Spey turbofans plus RB.162 booster. Tourist version has 152 seats.

HS. 125 Srs 800 Twin-jet executive transport powered by 19·13 kN (4,300 lb) thrust Garrett-AiResearch TFE 731-5R-1H turbofans. Seats crew of two and up to eight passengers. Maximum cruising speed 845 km/hr (525 mph).

Pilatus Britten-Norman Ltd.

Islander Twin-engined light transport carrying up to ten passengers, two 194 kW (260 bhp) Lycoming O–540 engines. Speed 274 km/hr (170 mph). Trislander is three-engined version. Turbine Islander has Allison 290 turboprops.

Short Brothers Ltd.

Shorts 330 Widebody commuter airliner. Two 1,020-shp Pratt & Whitney of Canada PT6A-45A turboprops. Standard seating for 30 passengers. Sherpa is civil freighter version and in service with US Air Force in Europe.

Shorts 360 Widebody short-haul airliner. Two Pratt & Whitney PT6A-65R turboprops. Standard seating for 36 passengers.

Skyvan Srs 3 Twin turboprop light transport. Carries 2,085 kg (4,600 lb) of freight or up to 19 passengers. Two Garrett TPE 331-201 of 533 kW (715 shp) each. Maximum cruising speed 327 km/hr (203 mph).

FRANCE

Dassault Mirage III-E long-range fighter-bomber/intruder. One SNECMA Atar 9C turbojet rated at 60·8 kN (15,873 lb) thrust with reheat. Maximum speed Mach 2·2.

Dassault-Breguet Mirage 2,000 Single-seat interceptor and air superiority fighter. One SNECMA M53-5 turbofan rated at 88·3 kN (19,840 lb) thrust with reheat. Maximum speed over Mach 2·3.

A300B Airbus

Dassault Mystère-Falcon 20 Series F Twin turbofan executive transport powered by 20 kN (4,500 lb) thrust US General Electric CF700-2D engines. Seats crew of two and up to 14 passengers. Maximum cruising speed 862 km/hr (536 mph) at 7,620 m (25,000 ft).

Airbus A300B2 Wide-bodied short/medium range airliner. Two US General Electric CF-6-50C turbofans. Seats up to 320 passengers. A310 has shorter cabin for up to 280 passengers; A320 will have increased fuselage cross-section for up to 179 passengers.

HOLLAND

Fokker Fellowship Turbofan successor to turboprop Friendship. Short-haul transport with seats for up to 85 passengers. Two aft-mounted 44 kN (9,900 lb) thrust Rolls-Royce Spey Mk. 555 engines. Maximum cruising speed 843 km/hr (523 mph).

Variable-geometry Aircraft able to greatly alter its configuration in flight, particularly by varying the sweepback of the wings.

Vertical Take-off and Landing (VTOL) A helicopter is a VTOL aircraft. The expression also includes newer devices concerned chiefly with getting fighters quickly off the ground without a long runway. There are several ways of getting vertical lift from jet engines. One is to direct the jets down for take-off and horizontally when airborne as in the British Aerospace Harrier. Another way, used in the Short SC-1, was to have separate engines for the vertical and horizontal thrusts. Designers in several countries are at work on their own ways of solving the problem of VTOL.

Wind Tunnel An experimental device in which a wind is created by fans, and aerofoils and aircraft made accurately to scale are suspended in the wind. Instruments attached to the models measure lift, drag and other parameters at varying wind speeds. Modern high-speed wind tunnels can achieve speeds as high as Mach 3 or Mach 4 in their working sections, but these normally run for only a few seconds and depend on the rapid expansion of compressed air.

Wing loading Aircraft weight divided by wing area.

ASTRONOMY

Astronomical Measures The nearest star (Bungula in Centaurus) is 40,000,000,000,000 km (25,000,000,000,000 miles) away. Measurements as huge as this become meaningless when given in kilometres or miles, so stellar distances (distances between stars) were expressed until a short time ago in light-years. A light-year is the distance light travels in one year. The speed of light is 299,300 km or 186,000 miles per second, so a light-year represents some 9,600,000,000,000 kilometres or 6,000,000,000,000 miles.

A newer astronomical measure of distance is the *parsec*, which is the distance at which the mean radius of the Earth's orbit would subtend an angle of 1 second. A parsec is rather more than 30,600,000,000,000 km (19,000,000,000,000 miles)—or, roughly, 3·25 light-years.

Comet The opportunity to approach closely to Halley's Comet was being seized in 1986, the first time it has been within range of space probes launched from Earth. A comet is a solid nucleus surrounded by luminous space-dust, giving it a characteristic tail. Russian Vega 1 and Vega 2 probes flew by on 6th March and 9th March respectively. Europe's Giotto probe approached within 500 km on 14th March.

Constellations On a cloudless night between 2,000 and 3,000 stars are visible to the unaided eye. With the help of one of the great astronomical telescopes (like the one on Mount Wilson in California) this number is increased to some 50,000,000.

The observable stars are divided into groups or constellations (a word that means 'star-groups').

Magnitude of Stars The classification of stars is according to their brightness as seen from the Earth. The unit of brightness is called the *magnitude*. Stars that can be seen without the help of telescopes are of magnitude 0–6. Magnitude 0 is the brightest; each magnitude that follows is about 2·5 times less bright than the one before it.

There are four stars (given in the list on F46) that, being brighter than magnitude 0, are given minus magnitudes.

The brightness of the Sun in this scale is −26·7; of the Moon −11·2.

THE CONSTELLATIONS

Those in capital letters are invisible from Great Britain

Scientific name	*English name*
Andromeda	The Chained Lady
ANTLIA	The Pump
APUS	The Bird of Paradise
Aquarius	The Water-Pourer
Aquila	The Eagle
ARA	The Altar
ARGO	Jason's Ship Argo
Aries	The Ram
Auriga	The Charioteer
Bootes	The Herdsman
Caelum	The Graving Tool
Camelopardalis	The Giraffe
Cancer	The Crab
Canes Venatici	The Hunting Dogs
Canis Major	The Great Dog
Canis Minor	The Little Dog
Capricornus	The Horned Goat
Cassiopeia	The Lady in the Chair
CENTAURUS	The Centaur
Cepheus	Cassiopeia's Consort
Cetus	The Sea Monster
CHAMAELEON	The Chameleon
CIRCINUS	The Pair of Compasses
Columba	The Dove
Coma Berenices	Berenice's Hair
CORONA AUSTRALIS	The Southern Crown
Corona Borealis	The Northern Crown
Corvus	The Crow
Crater	The Cup
CRUX	The Southern Cross
Cygnus	The Swan
Delphinus	The Dolphin
DORADO	The Goldfish
Draco	The Dragon
Equuleus	The Little Horse
ERIDANUS	The River
Fornax	The Furnace
Gemini	The Twins
GRUS	The Crane
Hercules	The Legendary Strong Man
HOROLOGIUM	The Clock

Scientific name	*English name*
Hydra	The Sea Serpent
HYDRUS	The Water Snake
INDUS	The Indian
Lacerta	The Lizard
Leo	The Lion
Leo Minor	The Little Lion
Lepus	The Hare
Libra	The Balance
LUPUS	The Wolf
Lynx	The Lynx
Lyra	The Lyre
MENSA	The Table Mountain
MICROSCOPIUM	The Microscope
Monoceros	The Unicorn
MUSCA	The Fly
NORMA	The Square
OCTANS	The Octant
Ophiuchus	The Serpent
Orion	The Giant Hunter
PAVO	The Peacock
Pegasus	The Winged Horse
Perseus	The Legendary Hero
PHOENIX	The Phoenix
PICTOR	The Painter's Easel
Pisces	The Fishes
Piscis Austrinus	The Southern Fish
RETICULUM	The Net
Sagitta	The Arrow
Sagittarius	The Archer
Scorpius	The Scorpion
Sculptor	The Sculptor's Workshop
Scutum	The Shield
Serpens	The Serpent
Sextans	The Sextant
Taurus	The Bull
TELESCOPIUM	The Telescope
Triangulum	The Triangle
TRIANGULUM AUSTRALE	The Southern Triangle
TUCANA	The Toucan
Ursa Major	The Great Bear
Ursa Minor	The Little Bear
Virgo	The Maiden
VOLANS	The Flying Fish
Vulpecula	The Fox with the Goose

THE TWENTY BRIGHTEST STARS

Star	Constellation	Magnitude
Sirius	Great Dog	− 1·43
CANOPUS	Jason's Ship Argo	− 0·73
RIGIL KENTAURUS	Centaur	− 0·27
Arcturus	Herdsman	− 0·06
Vega	Lyre	0·04
Capella	Charioteer	0·09
Rigel	The Giant Hunter	0·15
Procyon	Little Dog	0·37
ACHERNAR	The River Eridanus	0·53
Betelgeuse	The Giant Hunter	0·90
AGENA	Centaur	0·66
Altair	Eagle	0·80
Aldebaran	Bull	0·85
ACRUX	Southern Cross	0·87
Antares	Scorpion	0·98
Spica	Maiden	1·00
Fomalhaut	Southern Fish	1·16
Pollux	Twins	1·16
Deneb	Swan	1·26
BETA CRUCIS	Southern Cross	1·31

The Solar System The centre of the Solar System is the Sun, our Earth being one of the planets revolving round it.

THE SUN

Diameter, km/miles	1,390,500/864,000
Mass, reckoning the Earth as 1	330,000
Density, reckoning the Earth as 1	0·25
Volume, reckoning the Earth as 1	1,300,000
Force of gravity on the surface, reckoning the Earth as 1	27·7
Period of rotation on its axis	25·38 days
Speed of rotation at its equator	7,092 km/hr/4,407 mph
Surface area	12,000 times that of Earth
Mass	2,030,073,000,000,000,000,000,000,000 tonnes/ 1,998,000,000,000,000,000,000,000,000 tons
Temperature	c. 5,500° C.
Height of biggest flames from the surface	460,276 km/286,000 miles

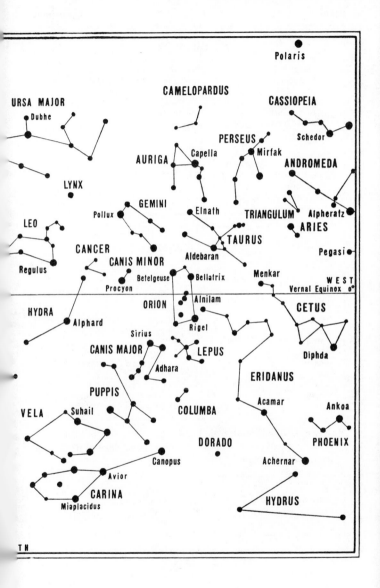

THE MOON

Diameter	3,481 km/2,163 miles
Surface area	37,970,000 sq km/14,660,000 sq miles
Mass	79,252,000,000,000,000,000 tonnes/ 78,000,000,000,000,000,000 tons
Speed in its orbit	3,682 kph/2,288 mph
Estimated temperature, day	+101° C
Estimated temperature, night	−157° C
Force of gravity at surface, reckoning the Earth as 1	4/25
Time of revolution round the Earth	27 days 7 hr 43 min 11 sec
Number of visible craters	30,000

THE PLANETS

	Average distance from the Sun (in millions of miles/km)	Time taken to revolve round Sun	Diameter (in miles/km)
Mercury	36/58	88 days	3,100/4,990
Venus	67/108	224·75 days	7,700/12,390
Earth	93/159	365·25 days	7,927/12,757
Mars	141/227	687 days	4,200/6,760
Jupiter	483/771	11·86 years	88,700/142,750
Saturn	886/1,426	29·46 years	75,100/120,860
Uranus	1,783/2,869	84·01 years	29,300/47,150
Neptune	2,793/4,485	164·79 years	27,700/44,580
Pluto	3,666/5,899	248·43 years	3,600/5,790

Relative Gravitational Pull If the Earth's gravitational pull is reckoned as 100 the relative pull on the surface of the Sun and the other planets is:

Sun	.	.	.	.	2770	Jupiter.	.	.	.	261
Mercury	.	.	.	.	38	Saturn	.	.	.	119
Venus.	.	.	.	.	86	Uranus	.	.	.	88
Mars .	.	.	.	.	38	Neptune	.	.	.	110

MOTOR CARS
MOTORCYCLES, MOPEDS
AND 3-WHEELERS

MOTOR CARS

MOTORCYCLES, MOPEDS, 3-WHEELERS
AND SCOOTERS

HISTORY AND DEVELOPMENT

1876 is perhaps the birth year of the motor car of today. It was then that the internal-combustion engine was developed to a workable form by Otto.

Cugnot Steam Carriage

But the dream of the self-propelled carriage is a very old one. As far back as the sixteenth century, Johann Hautach made a vehicle propelled by coiled springs—a clockwork car. Steam carriages were also developed. The Frenchman Cugnot constructed a workable steam carriage in 1770—a three wheeler. Murdock, Dallery, Symington, Gurney and others all achieved a varying degree of success with steam-propelled carriages during the next fifty years (see models and drawings at the Science Museum). Gurney's steamer could climb Highgate Hill—a long, steep ascent—and in 1831 a Gurney coach ran regularly between Cheltenham and Gloucester at speeds up to 12 m.p.h. At the same time, Ogle and Summers built a car which achieved no less than 35 m.p.h. on the rough roads of that time—a speed greater than Stephenson's 'Rocket' locomotive of the same period, which had the advantage of running on rails.

But on the whole, these were triumphs that led nowhere. Opposition to any new kind of road vehicle was intense, and these early cars were constantly under attack from the highly organised horse-drawn coaching systems. Even more important, the first cars coincided with the almost fantastically rapid growth of Britain's railway systems: men with money chose to invest in railways, not horseless carriages.

Thus when Otto made a workable internal-combustion engine of the sort used in cars today, his achievement was of very little interest to Britain. Cars continued to be thought of as dangerous and unpleasant toys until the turn of the century. In France, however, Panhard and Levassor built a car round the new engine. There was activity in America, too, with petrol-driven cars such as the Duryea. In Germany, Benz constructed a petrol-engined three-wheeler (1885). Daimler made a two-cylinder V engine in 1889. Incidentally, the names Benz and Daimler are still seen on motors today. Meanwhile in Britain what few cars there were had to proceed at walking pace behind a man carrying a red warning flag!

Prescott Steamer, 1903

Benz, 1885

In 1896 this ridiculous law was repealed (the London-Brighton run for Veteran cars celebrates the event each year) and motoring began to be taken more seriously in Britain.

At the turn of the century motorists had a choice of three sorts of self-propelled vehicle: steam, petrol-driven and electric. Electric cars were silent and very easy to manage, but useful only as town carriages. They could not go far without having their batteries recharged—a problem still to be solved.

Steam cars were very numerous. Serpollet, White, Stanley and other manufacturers produced silent, fast and powerful vehicles with hill-climbing power that the petrol cars of the time could not approach. In addition, they involved none of the noisy and difficult gear-changing inseparable from the early petrol-engined cars. An American Stanley Steamer held the world speed record in 1906 at no less than $127\frac{1}{2}$ m.p.h.—an extraordinary speed, for petrol-driven road cars of the same date were not expected to reach more than 30 or 40 m.p.h.

But steam cars had their disadvantages. They were difficult to run. They used a lot of water. They could be very dirty. And it took up to 20 minutes to get steam up.

While the design of the steam car remained static and un-

changing, the petrol car developed very rapidly indeed. Britain
had an extremely advanced design in the Lanchester, a car that
was many years before its time. A host of famous car makes, many
of them still familiar, came into being—Peugeot, Audi, Sunbeam,
Riley, Fiat and Rover among them.

Most important of all, petrol cars were developed that rivalled
steam cars in speed and silence—and beat them in ease of operation and cost. The first Rolls-Royces (1905–10) in particular set
an entirely new standard of refinement, luxury and (from the
owner's point of view) simplicity. They were an example to all
other makers of petrol cars and a clear indication that the days of
the steam car were numbered. Another nail in the steam coffin
was the self-starter—an American invention—which gave the
petrol car an additional lead over the hard-to-start steamers.

Rolls-Royce Silver Ghost

The Rolls-Royce was a craftsman-built car, individually made.
In America Henry Ford started to build cars by mass-production:
that is, in batches of thousands of cars, all made from inter-
changeable parts and assembled by largely unskilled labour. Ford's
contribution to motoring development, although very different
from that of the Rolls-Royce, was just as important. While Rolls-
Royce set a new standard of perfection, Ford made cars available
to people the world over. Motoring for the masses began with
Ford.

By 1914 the car had settled into a pattern that has not changed
very greatly. The engine was a multi-cylinder unit fed with controlled amounts of petrol and air by means of a jet carburettor
(the earliest cars had a wick carburettor). The rear wheels drove
the car and the front wheels steered it. Steering was effected by a
wheel (earlier cars often had tillers) and braking by internal expanding hub brakes—though only on the rear wheels. Electricity

was generally responsible for starting and lighting the most modern cars—and almost invariably responsible for engine ignition. The car's body and chassis were separate, although the first all-steel, 'unit construction' chassis bodies so common today had been produced. Early troubles of quick tyre wear and constant puncturing had been largely overcome.

During the First World War car design was neglected. Engine design advanced rapidly, however. In particular, many new and better metals were developed that allowed higher speeds within the engine and greater power development. It became apparent that the huge, thundering racing cars powered by massive engines were not necessarily the fastest; the comparatively tiny featherweight racing cars of Ettore Bugatti—an immortal name—were beginning to steal the thunder. Smaller, lighter cars of fairly good performance and refinement began to appear. The Peugeot Bébé, designed by Bugatti, was a very early arrival. And in 1923 the first Austin 7 appeared. The Austin 7 and cars like it brought motoring for the masses to Europe just as the Model T Ford brought it to America. Motoring now became world-wide.

By 1925 steam and electric cars had virtually disappeared from the scene. More and more saloon cars were being made. Economy

Model T Ford, 1927

Peugeot Bébé, 1913

Austin 7, 1926

cars of various sorts were successfully produced in huge numbers. Mass-production methods inevitably superseded hand fitting. Motoring was beginning to change people's habits and to expand their horizons.

During the next fifteen years the car finally overthrew the old order. For hundreds of years people had lived their lives within an area of a few square miles. A villager stayed in his village. But now the motor bus took him to other towns, other districts. Charabancs brought visitors to his village. More and more people could afford cars. Road networks covered whole countries and continents. The motor car that had started as a toy had become a near-necessity.

Morris Cowley

Car development was comparatively undramatic during the period 1925–40. Finally cars became much cheaper and shoddier. Sports cars increased their power and speed, but not violently. Racing became a nationally subsidised affair as well as a sport for rich amateurs. Luxury cars were smoother in outline but little else. Towards the end of the period, streamlining made an uneasy appearance as a styling feature, but had little effect on car performance. Citroën, the giant French manufacturer, developed a unit-built car with front-wheel drive that was to remain ahead of its time for twenty years. Other leaders in design were Riley (small,

3-litre Bentley

comfortable, fast sports saloons from 1930 on); Lancia of Italy
(small saloons of very advanced design, including independent
suspension for all four wheels—1937 on); BMW of Germany
(tubular backbone chassis frames, unusually powerful engines);
Fiat of Italy (the tiny 500-c.c. 'Topolino', 1937, the first miniature car to behave like a full-size model); and MG (the sort of
small and inexpensive sports car for which Britain found world
markets).

Riley Falcon, 1937   Fiat 500, 1937

Racing cars saw their peak development in the Mercedes-Benz
and Auto Union machines of Germany, which developed more
than 600 B.H.P.—compared with today's 800+.

Mercedes-Benz Grand Prix racing car, 1937

American cars developed almost exclusively along the lines of
size, comfort and silence. Problems of more power from less fuel—
or of getting more passenger space in a compact vehicle—were of
little interest to American car-owners, who could get all the petrol
(and therefore power) they needed at very low prices.

Which brings the story to World War Two.

SECOND WORLD WAR TO THE PRESENT

After the Second World War, car production was at once resumed on pre-war lines. At first slowly, the designers and makers explored and incorporated new developments. The most important concerned suspension systems (q.v. this section), brakes (particularly discs, q.v.), tyres, luxuries such as radios and heaters, automatic transmissions, better fuels and oils—and new layouts for cars. Another very important development was the rapid rise of the Japanese motor industry, now the world's largest producer of cars.

Today there is no such thing as a typical car. The family motorist can choose between rear-engine, rear-wheel-drive cars; front-engine, front-wheel-drive cars; front-engine, rear-wheel-drive cars. It is generally true to say that present-day cars offer more space, convenience and comforts, performance, mechanical reliability and fuel economy than old models, at the expense of greater complication, shorter life (the modern welded-up integral body/chassis rusts far too quickly) and more difficult, expensive, 'only-the-garage-can-do-it' servicing.

Particularly in this and other technically advanced countries, cars seem suddenly to have become too popular—too 'necessary'

Volkswagen

Fiat 127

Mini

Volkswagen, Mini, Fiat 127—three very different postwar small cars

—too demanding. The worries facing the present-day motorist include the thousands upon thousands of other cars that threaten to bring him to a standstill; the problem (and expense) of finding a parking place; and the sudden realisation, all over the world, that the materials needed to construct and fuel a car are running dangerously short. America now makes 'compact' automobiles. Economy and equipment replace 'performance' as major selling points. And once again, electric cars are being considered.

HOW CARS WORK

ENGINE

The Otto cycle (see History, above) is the name given to the four-stroke cycle of operation by which most car engines work. A very few cars use two-stroke engines.

With a four-stroke engine each cylinder is fired once during each two revolutions of the crankshaft. With a two-stroke engine, a cylinder fires at every revolution. Four-stroke engines use mechanically timed and driven valves to regulate the entrance and exit of gases into the cylinder. The basic two-stroke engine needs no valves; the flow of gases in and out of the cylinder is brought about by pressures within the engine itself.

Four-strokes are generally smoother at low speed, more economical and capable of developing smoother power. And they do their work without the polluting emissions of two-strokes.

Both engines work on a similar principle. One part of petrol is mixed with about 20 parts of air in a carburettor or by measured squirts of fuel (fuel injection). This highly inflammable mixture is compressed by a piston rising within a cylinder. The piston has springy rings to ensure a gastight seal. When the mixture is exploded by the spark plug, the piston is driven down. (Some cars have Diesel engines, which don't need spark plugs.) The piston is attached to a connecting-rod, in turn attached to a journal of the crankshaft. Thus the explosion drives the crankshaft round, and this movement is carried to the driving wheels (see Transmission). The action of the engine is therefore comparable to that of a man's arm cranking a car; the straight, up-and-down movement of his arm (his shoulder is the piston, his arm the connecting-rod)

Two Stroke Cycle

1. Ignition, induction.   2. Exhaust, crankcase charge compressed.   3. Exhaust, fresh charge enters cylinder.   4. Compression, partial vacuum in crankcase.

becomes a rotary or circular movement when applied to the crank.

Most European cars, both medium-sized and large, have four- or six-cylinder four-stroke engines with cylinders in line. Some 'baby' cars have fewer cylinders—the Fiat 126 has two. Three-cylinder and five-cylinder engines are now being produced. Big cars with six, eight or twelve cylinders may have V engines; if they did not, the engines might be too long or their crankshafts too flexible. Some engines have opposing cylinders laid flat.

Four Stroke Cycle

Induction   Compression   Ignition   Exhaust

Four-cylinder, four-stroke engine with cylinders in line

Wankel engine

All the engines described so far are Reciprocating engines—that is, they contain parts that go up and down, driving other parts that go round and round. Many attempts have been and are being made to construct engines with parts that all spin (Rover long ago made a gas-turbine engine, for example). The spinning, rotary engine should, in theory, be smoother and less wasteful.

In fact, the Wankel engine is the only rotary design in international production. The drawing (page G12) shows the Wankel operating cycle. The lobes (shown *a*, *b*, *c*) describe patterns within the casing of the engine that cause pressure/suction areas for the mixture and exhaust. The advantages of the Wankel engine include compactness and astonishing smoothness, but no manufacturer has achieved fuel economy comparable with the piston engine's—economy matters more and more.

Lubrication

Two-stroke engines may be lubricated by a small amount of oil added direct to the petrol. As the mixture must pass through the crankcase as well as to the cylinder, the oil vapour provides enough lubrication for every part. However, modern engines have a positive oil supply from a separate oil tank.

Wankel cycle

Four-stroke engines are elaborately lubricated from a reservoir called the sump. Pure oil is drawn from the sump by an oil pump which passes it under high pressure through channels drilled through such components as the crankshaft, connecting-rods and valve gear.

Cooling

Car engines develop great heat, not only through the explosions within the cylinder but also through friction of the moving parts. This heat must be got rid of, either by cooling with water or air. The VW 'Beetle' was air-cooled.

Most car engines are *water-cooled*. The cylinder-head, where the explosions take place, and also the cylinder block that contains the cylinders, are channelled with water passages. Water is passed through these passages, generally with the aid of a pump driven by the engine itself.

The constantly flowing water in the engine is cooled by the radiator, a grille of small water tubes supported by a lattice of fins. This is joined to the top and bottom of the engine by short lengths of rubber hose so that a loop circuit is formed. The radiator is exposed to the outside air, and may be further cooled by an engine-driven fan. Hot liquids always tend to rise above cool: so the hottest part of the radiator is the top, and the coolest the bottom. The flow of cooling water is thus from bottom to top of the engine and from top to bottom of the radiator.

Air Cooling

The cylinders of an air-cooled car are covered with fins (as on a motorcycle engine) which present a large area of coolable metal to the passing air. The fins are generally supplemented by a powerful engine-driven fan to make sure of a good supply of cooling air even when the car is in heavy traffic.

Flat twin

Air-cooled engines need no cooling water, of course, and this is an advantage, as water may leak or freeze or cause corrosion. Air-cooling disadvantages include extra noise (water is a good sound damper) and the large amount of engine power needed to drive an adequate fan.

Surplus heat from either a water-cooled or air-cooled engine is generally used to warm the car interior.

Engine Power and Capacity

The size of a car engine is described in terms of the amount of water that would be needed to fill all cylinders, with pistons down. In Europe we describe this amount in cubic centimetres (c.c.) or litres—thus 'Daimler 4·2', in which the engine is of approximately 4,200 c.c. (4 litres) capacity. A small 4-seater is about 1·1–1·3 litres; a medium-size family car, 1·5 or 2 litres; an 'executive' saloon, around 3 litres.

The power that an engine develops is described in Brake Horse Power or B.H.P. 'Austin A60' was so called because its engine developed approximately 60 B.H.P.

Capacity and power should not be confused. A racing-car engine of small capacity will develop considerable B.H.P.—more than seven times as much as a family saloon of the same engine size. Both c.c. and B.H.P. must be known to get an idea of a particular engine's characteristics.

Engine power depends on the rate at which it can digest fuel and get rid of the exhaust. Thus, the faster an engine can be made to turn—the more gulps of fuel it can consume—the more power it will deliver. Modern family-car engines often exceed 6,000 revolutions per minute. Modern racing-car engines may turn at 10,000 r.p.m. or more.

To feed a family car with fuel, one carburettor may be enough. Sports and racing engines demand more fuel and therefore more carburettors to mix and deliver it. In more advanced high-performance engines, fuel injectors replace the carburettors. Yet more fuel may be given to the engine by a *supercharger*—a high-speed fan that forcibly feeds air to the carburettor (or mixture to the engine) under pressure; or by *turbocharger*, a high-speed blower using exhaust gases to 'charge' the engine. Turbochargers ('turbos') are now used even on motorcycles.

TRANSMISSION

The power developed by a car's engine must be transmitted to its driving wheels through the clutch, gearbox, various drive shafts and a differential. All these parts are transmission parts.

The Clutch
The clutch is used to join or separate the engine from the rest of the transmission. In starting a car from rest the clutch is 'let in' with a pedal so that the rapidly-turning engine can *gradually* start the driving wheels turning without damage to other transmission parts. Use of clutch also simplifies gear changing.

Friction face

Flywheel   Clutch disc   withdrawal fork

The clutch is made up of three disc-like plates, two joined to the engine and one to the transmission. When the clutch pedal is pushed the plates are separated. When the pedal is released the plates are pushed together by springs so that they join and become one. The plates are lined on their meeting faces with a friction material so that they can tolerate gradual engagement.

The Gearbox

The gearbox allows the driver to match the speed and power of the engine to the road conditions. Car engines work efficiently only when they are turning fast: thus a car with only top gear (highest) working would be unable to climb a hill, as the engine would steadily lose its speed and therefore its power. Exactly the same is true of a small child attempting to climb a steep hill on an adult's bicycle.

Most cars have four gears. A number have five. First is the lowest, used for starting the car from rest or for climbing steep hills. Top is used for easy cruising conditions and for maximum speed. Some cars today are fitted with—

Overdrive, in effect a separate gearbox giving a higher gear. This allows high-speed cruising under easy conditions with the engine turning over slower than it would in direct 'top'.

The majority of cars still make use of a gearbox containing trains of gear-wheels that are engaged by a lever: the clutch helps the operation. But there have always been many other kinds of gearboxes, and recently more and more cars have—

Automatic Gears A car with a fully automatic gearbox has no clutch pedal, and the driver need only set a lever to select the *conditions* under which the car is to be operated. If he selects 'normal driving' he need do nothing further except brake or accelerate. The car itself will do whatever gear-changing is necessary. But although automatic gearboxes simplify driving, they themselves are inevitably complicated, as the basic gearbox must be controlled by electric, hydraulic and vacuum systems that relate engine conditions to the car's needs.

Other kinds of gearing include epicyclic *'preselectors'*, in which the next gear wanted is 'dialled' for in advance; and the *variable-pulley* gearbox, in which belts are driven by two pulleys which change in relative size, and so give the most suitable of an infinite range of gears automatically, as in the old Volvo/Daf.

Computer 'manager'—some makers offer cars and motorcycles whose engine/transmission performance is monitored or controlled by computer.

Differential
When a car turns a corner the inner of the two driven wheels travels a lesser distance than the outer, and therefore turns slower. On a very small and light car this might be acceptable; but on most cars the different speeds of the wheels would lead to excessive tyre wear and dangerous steering effects.

The differential is a mechanism that allows two wheels to turn at different speeds, yet both remain driven.

Drive Shafts and Universal Joints
When the clutch has taken up the engine's power and the gearbox has adjusted it to road conditions there still remains the necessity to take the power to the driving wheels. How this is done depends on the layout of the car. Most cars have the engine at the front and the driving wheels at the back: in this case power is led to the differential, and thence to the driving wheels, through the *propeller shaft*. Generally, this shaft is a simple tube with a universal joint at either end.

Two other shafts, called half-shafts, must then carry power from either side of the differential to each driving wheel. These may be enclosed in a rigid casing. If the car has independent rear suspension (described later) each shaft must have universal joints.

If the car is front-engined and front-wheel driven, or rear-

Propeller shaft between gearbox and rear axle.

engined and rear-wheel driven, then a propeller shaft is unnecessary. The drive can be taken from the differential straight to the rear wheels by two short shafts, each with universal joints.

Some 'workhorse' and high-performance cars have 4-wheel drive.

A universal joint

Universal Joints allow a stiff shaft to transmit power through an angle, or through constantly changing angles.

They must be fitted to a propeller shaft because the rear axle moves up and down on its springs while the gearbox remains stationary.

If the driving wheels are driven direct by shafts from the differential, then universal joints must be provided to allow for the wheels' up-and-down movements.

The most commonly used universal joints are the Hardy-Spicer type, which is comparable to gimbals; and the constant-velocity type, which uses metal balls running within tracks cut into two half-spheres, one cupping another.

Front engine,
front-wheel
drive

Rear engine,
rear-wheel
drive

BRAKES

By the end of the Second World War, the majority of the world's
cars were braked on all four wheels by internal expanding hub
brakes operated by hydraulic power, as above. Hydraulic systems
are preferred to mechanical systems because there are no
mechanical power losses; because hydraulic power is simply
transmitted along flexible pipes instead of by rod or cable systems;
and because each of the four brakes must automatically receive
exactly the same proportion of the power exerted by the driver.

During the Second World War, disc brakes (external contracting
brakes in which brake pads close like pincers on a disc attached
to the road wheel) were successfully developed for aircraft and are
now commonplace equipment for cars and motorcycles.

brake shoe

ON   OFF

A drum brake   A disc brake

Whatever system is used, an additional and separate braking system must also be supplied. This is called the 'parking brake' or 'hand-brake', and is used only to hold the car when at rest or to stop the car in the event of a failure of the main braking system. Hand-brakes are normally mechanically applied to one pair of wheels only.

BODY AND CHASSIS

The chassis of a car is the framework that supports the body, engine and other components. This 'skeleton' is often visible in old sporting cars. However, the majority of present-day mass-produced cars use the body itself as a chassis. The 'Unit Construction' modern car body is an all-metal welded box structure of great rigidity, and no separate chassis is needed. Sometimes additional local strength is given by a small chassis-like structure. Sometimes the engine and perhaps the transmission and driving wheels are mounted on a small separate chassis that may be removed from the body quickly and easily for servicing.

'Unit Construction' is not the only method. Until quite recently, Triumph mass-produced small cars with a separate chassis frame; and luxury-car makers supplied a chassis on which various special-ist coach-builders could fit individual bodywork. Sports and racing

Du Pont, Model G, 1930; its chassis is clearly visible

cars are often built up round a complicated arrangement of tubes called a Space Frame, which gives great rigidity with minimum weight; or with a chassis taking the form of a massive spine with outriggers to hold bodywork, engine, suspension and other components.

Sheet steel is the raw material of bodies for mass-produced cars. It can be formed in huge presses with great speed and economy. Sheet aluminium may also be used for parts that are not highly stressed (boot lids, for example).

Plastics bodies are popular with small-production makers of kit cars, racing cars, etc. The time and space needed to produce the bodies forbid large-scale production. But a major producer tried combining both techniques with a central steel 'cage' to which various plastic front and rear assemblies were attached to provide a range of cars.

Subaru 1800cc 2/4-wheel drive estate

STEERING

Cars are steered by their front wheels: other layouts have been tried, but have never been successful.

A typical steering linkage consists of a steering wheel, whose motion is translated through the steering box to push the drop arm. This is connected by a drag link so that it steers one road wheel. The other road wheel is connected to the first by the track rod.

Steering linkage

ELECTRICAL SYSTEM

The equipment of a car includes a complete electrical generating system, a storage battery to hold the electricity and a variety of systems and mechanisms that use it.

Electricity is supplied by dynamo or the more modern alternator, usually driven by belt from a pulley on the engine's crankshaft. The output of the dynamo or alternator charges the battery (usually 12-volt, but sometimes 6). A voltage regulator or cut-out keeps the output at a suitable level.

The battery stores electric power and passes it on demand. The greatest demand is that of the self-starter motor, which makes the battery supply enough power to turn over the engine quicker and for longer than a man could.

The petrol/air mixture within the cylinders is fired by sparking-plugs. These are supplied by the ignition coil with current stepped up in voltage from the battery's 6 or 12 volts to 6,000–12,000 volts. The coil current is directed by a mechanical or electronic distributor to each sparking-plug in turn.

Electricity from the battery powers a host of other components and accessories. On a modern family car they will certainly include the lighting system, direction indicators, horn and panel lights; and may also include a radio, heater fan, petrol pump, cigar lighter, computer and so on.

The windows or the hood—or both—may be raised and lowered by separate electric motors. The clutch, various panel instruments, gearbox and/or overdrive may also use electricity.

Electricity must complete a circuit to do a job. Thus one wire may be used to take current from the battery to a lamp bulb, and another wire to take current back to the battery. Sometimes, however, the car itself is used as a conductor of current, thus halving the considerable amount of wiring.

SUSPENSION

Suspension is the word used to describe those parts of the car that join the road wheels to the chassis or body.

The traditional method of suspension was by leaf springs supporting an axle, and this method is still quite often used for the rear axle.

Almost invariably today, the front wheels have independent front suspension (i.f.s.): with i.f.s., each wheel is free to behave independently of the other.

Leaf spring

Independent rear suspension (i.r.s.) is also becoming increasingly common and is in any case necessary with a rear-engined car.

Springs
Springs may be in the form of leaves, coils, compressed liquids or torsion bars (bars twisted along their length). Citroën introduced inert gas as a springing medium—rather as if the car were suspended on four interlinked footballs. Others followed.

Ride Controllers and Shock Absorbers
If a car were suspended only on springs it would meet a bump, bounce over it and keep on bouncing. So-called shock absorbers or dampers let the spring do its work but prevent it from bouncing. They control the ride of the car and keep it steady.

Torsion bar   Coil spring for I.F.S.

With most cars, this control is the result of keeping each wheel steady. But ideally, it would be better to control the ride of the car as a whole: Citroën have gone a long way towards achieving this by linking each inert-gas suspension unit to the other by means of a hydraulic mechanism so that the behaviour of any one road wheel affects the behaviour of the others. The car is in fact self-levelling. Some British cars have front and rear wheels collectively sprung by liquid-filled tubes ('Hydrolastic').

Anti-Roll Bars

Anti-roll bars are used to link the behaviour of one road wheel to another. Thus on heavy cornering the heavily loaded outside wheels transfer some of their load to the inside wheels and the car remains more nearly level.

Tyres

Tyres, while not part of the suspension, will affect its behaviour. Over- or under-inflation has drastic effects both on the way a car feels and how it behaves. Attempts have been and are being made to design tyres having renewable treads; and there are tyres that can be run flat for limited distances.

Marlboro McLaren MP 4/2B TAG Turbo F1

RACING CARS

Apart from the fun of it, motor racing has always been of enor-mous value to every motorist. Fuels, metals, oils, tyres, brakes—in fact, nearly every part of the ordinary car—all gain from the high-pressure testing and development that racing gives.

Grand Prix track racing is undertaken only by thoroughbred, out-

and-out 'Formula 1' machines. The World Championship is decided by Grand Prix events all over the world.

Track Racing also includes events for production, sports, 'Enduro', Vintage and Veteran cars.

Road Racing includes the classic Le Mans—a race open to all kinds of sports/racing cars driven over a closed road circuit.

Rallies are typified by the classic, all-Europe Monte Carlo and by the Lombard/RAC Rally of Great Britain—a five-day 2000 + miles event incorporating speed trials and forest stages. The winners of the various classes are those who lose the fewest number of points. Motoring clubs throughout Britain hold Rallies.

Time Trials, Sprints, Hill Climbs, Rallycross, etc., are events that pit the driver 'against the clock'. The winners are those who cover a given distance, climb a certain hill or complete a number of circuits in the shortest time. Many such events are held throughout Britain.

Trials are winter events held over deserted country roads or in muddy fields and up hills. Often no one can complete the course, in which case the team that gets farthest wins. Special cars and skills are needed.

Club Racing takes place all over Britain and the world. In Britain such races are the proving grounds for new drivers. Cars range from true racing machines to Vintage Sports Cars.

Drag Racing. An American motor sport that has invaded Europe. Aim: to achieve the highest speed in a straight line over a short distance.

Peugeot rally car

Formula Track Racing Cars True racing cars are defined by Formulae arrived at by international agreement. At present those in force include:

Formula 1—3-litres unsupercharged or 1½-litres supercharged or turbocharged engines in single-seater bodies. 12 cyls max.

Formula 2—Racing cars with single-seater bodies. Engine capacity up to 2,000 c.c. Carburettor or injector, but not supercharger. 6 cyls max.

Formula 3—2 litre. Limited modifications to engines from cars produced in units of 5,000 or more. There are other such Formulae, mostly aimed at producing cars based on standard components, such as *Formula Ford* (racing cars based on Ford engines) and *Can-Am* (big cars, big engines); and classes for production motor vehicles, such as *Gran Turismo* (fast touring) and *Saloon* cars; also *Sports* cars. The popular *Group 1* is for standard production saloons.

LAND SPEED RECORD

Some important figures (wheel-driven cars):

			mph
1925	Campbell	Sunbeam	150·9
1926	Thomas	Higham Special	171·1
1927	Segrave	Sunbeam	203·8
1932	Campbell	Napier–Campbell Bluebird	254
1935	Campbell	Rolls-Royce–Campbell Bluebird	301·1
1938	Eyston	Eyston Thunderbolt	357·5
1947	Cobb	Railton	394·2
1965	Summers (USA)	Goldenrod	409·6

Not wheel-driven:

1970	Gary Gabelich	Blue Flame	622·4
1983	Richard Noble	Thrust II	633·5

IDENTIFYING CARS

Cars are identified and described in various ways. Engine capacity and power have already been discussed (see Engine). Descriptions such as saloon, convertible or station wagon are well known to you.

But every car also carries a variety of identity marks:

Jaguar XJSC 3·6 Cabriolet

Registration Letters and Numbers (number plates) which are
   allotted to each new car by the County Council concerned. The
   same letters and numbers appear in the car's official registration
   document. However many owners the car may have, its
   number plate never changes.

Chassis and Engine Numbers are among other details appearing
   in the registration document. These are permanently stamped
   on cars of every nationality.

Alfa Romeo 33 1·3—1·5 litre flat four

Lotus Esprit Turbo

Citroën BX, 1,360 and 1,580 c.c.

Volvo 760 GLE Estate

Mercedes-Benz 190E 4-cylinder 2 litre

Toyota MR2

Renault Espace 2000 TSE

Talbot Samba Cabriolet

Panther Kallista (Ford V6 injection or Escort 1600)

Old and new car logos and badges.

Alfa Romeo

Honda

Aston Martin

Bristol

Bugatti

Citroën

DKW

Ferrari

Daimler

Fiat

Ford

Lamborghini

Mazda

Audi

Toyota

Jensen

Lagonda

Lancia HPE Volumex

GROUP MANUFACTURERS

General Motors, the giant American Group, produces various makes of car throughout the world. Vauxhall (England) and Opel (Germany) are GM Companies.

British Leyland—soon to be re-named 'Rover'—produces Austin-Rover, MG and Land-Rover vehicles. The still-familiar cars named Morris, Triumph, Riley, Jaguar and Daimler also belonged to the Group until quite recently.

Sunbeam, Hillman and Humber cars, still seen, belonged to a Group that itself vanished, to be absorbed by Peugeot Talbot.

So a present-day Austin, Vauxhall, Talbot or Rover has nothing to do with 'vintage' cars of the same names.

Chevrolet Cavalier RS Sedan

Further Reading

Autocar Handbook, Motor Manual—and these magazines' annual
    Road Test compilations

The Observer's Book of Automobiles

Picture History of Motoring, L. T. C. Rolt

Which? Magazine's test reports.

About a Motor Car, Puffin Book (Penguin)

Magazines—*Motor, Autocar, Motor Sport, Practical Motorist, Car,
    Motor Cycle,* etc.

Places to Visit

Science Museum, Kensington, London

National Motor Museum, Beaulieu, Hants

Stratford Motor Museum, Gloucester

TVR Tasmin

Matra–Simca Rancher

MOTORCYCLES, MOPEDS, 3-WHEELERS AND SCOOTERS

1911 Zenith Gradua, J.A.P. engine

1922 Matchless twin

HISTORY

The history of the motorcycle begins, like that of the motor car, with the internal combustion engine. Gottlieb Daimler, pioneer of cars, can perhaps be credited with the first motorcycle (1885) although an Englishman, Edward Butler, produced a motor tricycle a year before.

Whatever its origins, the motorcycle took some time to establish itself. The bicycling craze of the 1890s submerged whatever interest there might have been in motorcycles. At the turn of the century, however, social conditions changed radically in every way. Times were ripe for motorisation of any sort—bicycles included.

And indeed the first motorcycles were very similar to the powered bicycles—the mopeds—of today. Like mopeds, they were power-*assisted* vehicles. You pedalled when the motor needed help. Later and more powerful machines remained as simple as mopeds. They had no gears, or only two; there was no kick-starter—you pedalled or ran alongside the machine to get it going. Transmission was by belt (as it still is with some very modern machines). Lighting was by acetylene—a romantic but smelly and time-consuming method.

Suddenly, though, the motorcycle caught on. From 1910 on, design developed fast. During the First World War, the motorcycle came into its own: motorcycle dispatch riders were popular heroes and machines like theirs were greatly coveted when the war ended.

In the 1920s, no fewer than 200 firms produced motorcycles. The pattern of these machines did not change greatly for 20 years. Spring front-forks, electric lighting, greater power, the kick-starter, three or four gears, a pillion—all these features were adopted as standard.

The motorcycle thus emerged as an international form of transport, appealing particularly to those who enjoyed transport for its own sake (and there is still no more exhilarating way of getting about): and to those who wanted personal transport at rock-bottom prices.

1930 Scott Squirrel, water-cooled 2-stroke

1928 Coventry Victor twin

As we have said, the motorcycle began as a moped. Oddly enough this form of the motorcycle more or less disappeared in the 1930s—and the scooter, although it was invented soon after the First World War, was never commercially developed either. Three-wheelers, blending both motorcycle and car features, did make some progress. But the standard motorcycle, often with sidecar, was the most-used vehicle.

Laverda RGS Corsa, 981 c.c. 3-cylinder

SECOND WORLD WAR TO THE PRESENT

Wars leave nations poor. After the Second World War, everyone wanted personal transport and few could afford it. Two-wheelers became popular. The moped, the minimal motorcycle, became, and remains, part of the world transport scene.

Italian companies invented the motor scooter, whose advantages included weather protection, a soft ride and simple controls. The scooter flourished for some years—but the Japanese were busily re-thinking all markets for powered two-wheelers. In the 1960s they launched today's stylish, colourful, fully-sprung, highly developed machines. These killed off traditional British designs; and the scooter fashion too.

The bigger machines have also changed. A liquid-cooled, multi-cylinder motorcycle is today a common sight—and a very handsome one. Common too are imaginative finishes, luggage carriers, self-starters, aerodynamic fairings and the sort of engineering that make oil stains old-fashioned.

The new crises in fuel, money, materials, parking space and public transport have lead to much greater use of all kinds of two-wheelers. Young people may stick to motorcycles instead of turning to cars. Commuters may find it necessary to keep a two-wheeler handy. Shoppers may take to smart little plastic-clad mini scooters. Electrically powered bicycles are promised.

HOW MOTORCYCLES WORK

The Frame

The wheels, engine and other parts of the machine are mounted in or on the frame—typically, a double loop of steel tubing (the 'duplex' frame). Single steel tubes like a bicycle's are sometimes used; but so are complex steel and alloy structures. The engine is sometimes used as part of the frame. All those parts of the motorcycle that help it to roll or steer are called 'cycle' parts.

Engine

Motorcycles and motor cars are very closely related mechanically. To avoid wasting space, we refer you back to the section on **Motor Cars** when talking about common features. Each reference is given like this—(G25)—which means, turn back to that page in the Cars section.

Suzuki RG250 watercooled 2-stroke 2-cylinder

Like cars, motorcycles have either 2-stroke engines (G9, 10). Some turbocharged engines (G14) are in production, even for medium-sized engines.

The advantage of the 2-stroke used to be its mechanical simplicity—it is possible to make a 2-stroke with only three working parts. But today's 2-strokes have some sort of value to admit the fuel mixture and a metered supply of lubricating oil from a separate tank instead of the old petrol-and-oil mix in the fuel tank ('posilube' instead of 'petroil'). So they are complex. In performance, vibration and noise they are roughly comparable with 4-strokes. 2-strokes can be more powerful.

The important advantages of the 4-stroke are considerably better fuel economy; less annoyance from fouled plugs and exhaust systems; and a smokeless exhaust.

Most motorcycle engines are air-cooled (G12, 13) and have fins outside the cylinders. Many 'superbikes' (and even some small-engined bikes) have liquid cooling—look for the radiator. Engine capacity varies from less than 50 c.c. for moped and beginners' machines to over 1,000 c.c. The vast majority of motorcycles have one or two cylinders, but multi-cylinder machines are on the increase—even 6-cylinders.

Motorcycle engines can be made to develop astonishing power for their size. 100 B.H.P. per litre is not uncommon (G13) which means that some of the 500 c.c. motorcycles you see on the road can develop as much power as a small car. A multi-cylinder 250 c.c. racing motorcycle may give as much as 160 B.H.P. per litre. Some racing engines exceed 12,000 rpm (G14).

Above left: 2-stroke single-cylinder engine
Above right: Honda overhead-cam 4-stroke engine and gearbox

Gearboxes

Power from the engine is taken via a multi-plate clutch (G14) to
a gearbox working in much the same way as a car's (G15) and
for the same reasons (G14). Four or five gear ratios are usual, and
six-speed boxes fairly common. A footchange—a lever rocked
down by the toe for downward changes, and up by toe or heel for
changes up—is usual. Automatic and infinitely variable gearboxes
(G15) have been used with success. Scooters and mopeds may
have two-stage or 'stepless' transmissions, self-changing.

Final drive

Almost always, the drive from engine to gearbox—the 'primary'
drive—is by chain. So too is the final drive—although belts are
used on at least a few motorcycles; and are suitable for light-
weights in conjunction with automatic, scooter-type transmissions. A few makers use shaft-drive on expensive and luxurious
machines.

Ignition and Lighting

Larger motorcycles and an increasing number of scooters use car-type electrical equipment (G21).

Smaller, simpler, cheaper machines may get electricity for ignition and lighting from a Magneto—a rotary electric mechanism fitted within the flywheel of the engine.

1 Headlight control switch	9 Rear brake pedal
2 High beam indicator light	10 Foot rests
3 Speedometer	11 Kick starter pedal
4 Tachometer (engine rpm)	12 Clutch lever
5 Front brake lever	13 Turn signal switch
6 Throttle grip	Horn button (below)
7 Emergency switch	14 Fuel tank cap
8 Headlight control switch (above)	15 Gear-change pedal
Starter button (below)	

Controls

Here is a typical enough layout of the controls found on a modern motorcycle. Some machines have rocking, heel-and-toe gear-change levers. Most motorcycles have steering-column locks and quite a number have lockable petrol-tank fillers. Old motorcycles had controls not shown here; decompressors to help starting and so on. Virtually all motorcycles have a petrol tap (not shown) with a position for 'reserve'. Even 50 c.c. machines may have self-starters operated by a tiny button on the handlebars.

Brakes

Drum brakes (G18), mechanically operated by rods or cables, were
general, but today front and rear discs are common.

Suspension

The majority of motorcycles have telescopically-sprung front forks
with dampers (G23) incorporated. Some have sophisticated anti-
dive systems as well. The rear wheel is mounted in a sprung
pivoted fork with a suspension system like a stubby version of the
telescopic front fork; but again, there are sophisticated variations
designed to enhance the drive-line geometry that have only a
single strut supporting the wheel.

Harris Magnum F2 (various engines)

MOTORCYCLE SPORT

Grand Prix Racing Various formulae. International events—the
   World Championship Series (controlled by the FIM)—in a dozen
   European countries and South Africa. 6 classes from 50 c.c. to
   500 c.c. (including turbos); sidecars. Also road-circuit events.

Circuit racing Club, national, and international. Formulae variable—designed to attract entries. Amateurs and club members
   are more likely to start with *Motocross* (125, 250 and 500
   c.c.—also sidecar events) which is virtually the same thing as a
   Scramble—a race over rough territory; *Trials* (mixed territory,
   observed sections, competitors lose marks for each failure); or
   Grass track or *sand* racing. All these events (and similar events

for sidecar machines) are open to anyone who can get his entry accepted at Club, Local, National or International level. *Speedway* schools are held at venues throughout Great Britain. *Drag racing* events are 'against the clock' straight-line speed competitions. *Enduro* events stretch over days. *Schoolboy Sport* covers some of these activities up to age 16.

Honda CR 125 sportster   On/off-road bike

SCOOTERS, LIGHTWEIGHTS, RUNABOUTS

The scooter craze of some twenty years ago opened up motorcycling. Girls flashed by on Vespas and Lambrettas. Young men jazzed up their mounts. Office workers commuted by scooter. But then the Japanese lightweights arrived. They handled and braked safely, gave amazing power from their 100–250 c.c. engines, had 4 to 6 gears, didn't leak oil—and were colourful, fashionable.

Honda Stream 3-wheeler, articulated   Honda Lead 125

The scooter market was swamped not only by the light-weights, but by other Japanese offerings—the sober, quiet, reliable step-throughs; an endless variety of mopeds; and now, bright little mini-scooters with self-starters and shopping bags. These are about to be supplemented by bigger, plastic-shelled machines very like the original scooters.

So, today, you have the choice of 'masculine' or 'feminine' characteristics—big or small wheels—a near-silent 30 mph or a rorty 70 mph.

Suzuki ZR 50L 2-stroke 50 c.c. USA-style

BMW K100RT flat-four 1000 c.c.

SIXTEENERS, LEARNERS

The Law has been drastically changed. L-riders must now pass a two-part test (test-circuit and on-road) before they may drive machines of more than 125 c.c. or 12 bhp (moped riders need pass only Part 2.) Proper instruction becomes almost essential. 16-year-old riders are restricted to machines of not more than 50 c.c. and of a power giving a maximum speed of 35 mph. But the old 'it must have pedals' restriction is dropped.

Harley Davidson Electra-Glide, USA

Moto Guzzi V75 750 c.c. V-twin

THREE-WHEELERS

The aim of the 3-wheeler has always been to give the advantages of the light car with further advantages in terms of tax, fuel economy, first cost and 'garageability'. In this country, however, the importance of these advantages has lessened over the last few years. First cost is too near that of the cheapest four-wheeled cars (which have also increased their operating and economy efficiencies). Three-wheelers do not keep their value well—secondhand prices are low. There can be no doubt that the modern miniature car scores over the 3-wheeler in terms of quietness, comfort, carrying capacity, and, all too often, reliability. On the other hand, the 3-wheeler offers the motorcyclist one enormous advantage: he or she need not pass the car driving test to drive certain 3-wheelers. A motorcycle licence suffices.

There is no 'typical' 3-wheeler. It could be said that there are two main classes—those derived from motorcycles and those derived from motor cars—but even then, there is a great deal of overlap. The 'car' type of 3-wheeler is typified by the Reliant 'Robin' with its water-cooled 4-cylinder engine, or by the dashing little Bond 'Bug'. Both are virtually cars with a wheel missing. The Trojan, Messerschmidt, Peel and many others exemplified the other school—they could be called motorcycles or scooters with a wheel (and bodywork) added.

The Sinclair electric 3-wheeler failed; but could be a pattern for the near future.

Sinclair C5 electric runabout 3-wheeler

RAILWAYS

Locomotion No. 1

THE AGE OF THE TRAIN

Today, for many long-distance journeys and for carrying large numbers of people into city centres to work or for shopping, we take trains for granted. Although many people use cars for trips into town for business or to the country or seaside for holidays, using motorways, and even with buses linking country villages with nearby towns, and serving suburban areas in large cities, the railway is still the best form of transport for mass travel. Much of our freight traffic goes in large juggernaut lorries by road, but railways are far better for bulk traffic: that is, large amounts of material from a single loading point to a single unloading point. This includes coal from mines to power stations, iron ore from mines and quarries to steelworks, clay from clay workings to pottery or china factories, or paper mills, petrol and other fuel from oil refineries to storage depots, and containers carrying general goods all over the country.

On longer journeys of more than about 500 km (or roundly 300 miles) jet airliners are faster than trains. Up to those distances, even though aircraft are faster from airport to airport, the train is often quickest from city centre to city centre because of the added time taken by taxi, bus, or local train to travel between the city centre and the airport at each end.

Thus the modern train in many parts of the world is beating the competition from private cars, buses and long distance coaches, and, in some cases on longer journeys, aircraft as well. Many trains now reach speeds of 200 km/h (125 mph), and in a few cases travel up to 260 km/h (162 mph). They are quiet and comfortable, and many have air conditioning so that the temperature inside is just right for the passengers even though it may be snowing outside, or there might be a heat wave. Above all, railways are far safer than other forms of transport—particularly roads. In four of the last ten years—1976, 1977, 1980 and 1982—not a single passenger was killed in a train accident on British Rail compared with several thousand people killed in car accidents each year.

Today in most countries trains are powered by diesel or electric traction but in a few countries, particularly South Africa, Zimbabwe, India and China, a large number of trains are still hauled by steam locomotives. In Britain and a few other countries there are many tourist railways run with preserved steam locomotives, sometimes with qualified railway enthusiasts helping to work the line in their spare time as a hobby at weekends and holidays.

The steam locomotive was one of man's greatest inventions for, without it, we would not have the industrial world we know today. This is because something more powerful and faster than the horse was needed to speed up journeys and to carry heavier loads. For thousands of years until the early 1800s, movement around Britain and other countries was limited to the speed of the horse: about 30 km/h (roundly 20 mph) for a rider on horseback, and less than half that for the average speed of a horse-drawn coach or wagon. Canals—that is, man-made waterways—had been built in many parts of Britain towards the end of the eighteenth century to allow boats to carry bulk cargoes between inland towns and cities not near the sea or navigable rivers. Although a horse-drawn barge could carry much heavier loads than a horse-drawn wagon on the bad roads of the eighteenth century, speeds were no more than 5 km/h (3 mph).

HOW RAILWAYS BEGAN

(1800–1850)

The railway which has evolved into the modern systems of today has its origins more than 150 years ago in the development of two separate forms of technology. On the one hand was the rail way or guided track, and on the other the steam engine. It was the successful combination of these two that started the great railway expansion from the 1830s.

Nobody knows when the first railway was built. The first

mention of one, in which a special track of wooden rails was used, is found in the sixteenth century. Men had discovered that a cart or wagon ran more easily on a track than on the rough roads of the time. The earliest railways were purely local lines, no more than a few hundred metres long; with the coming of iron works and coal mines, they were used to help move wagon-loads of material. The wagons were pulled by men or horses. One of the oldest mineral railways in the world, the Middleton Railway at Leeds, can trace its origin back to 1758; it survives today and is operated by students of Leeds University.

The first railways to carry merchandise from one town to another were built in the 1800s. The Surrey Iron Railway, from Wandsworth to Croydon, was approved by Parliament in 1801 and opened, for goods only, in 1804, while the first passenger-carrying railway in the world, the Oystermouth Railway from Swansea to Oystermouth (closed as recently as 1959), was opened in 1806. Both lines employed horses. The Stockton & Darlington Railway was opened in 1825, followed in 1830 by the Liverpool & Manchester and Canterbury & Whitstable Railways using steam locomotives.

At the time that the first railways were being built engineers were experimenting with steam locomotives—at first with little success. The development of the stationary steam engine working on low pressure steam and atmospheric pressure by Thomas Newcomen in the early eighteenth century and used for pumping water out of mines, was followed by experiments by other pioneers later in the century. James Watt saw that steam of a higher pressure had power. Richard Trevithick's road steam locomotive, one of the first effective models, was patented in 1802. It was followed a year later by his first rail steam locomotive, built at the Coalbrookdale Iron Works tramway in Shropshire. Little is known about this engine. In 1804 came the more famous Trevithick steam locomotive at the Penydarren Iron Works in South Wales. It was now that George Stephenson, one of the greatest railway engineers of them all, came upon the scene. At the time he was employed at Killingworth Colliery, Northumberland, and by 1815 he had built a type known as the 'Killingworth' locomotive, used on a number of colliery lines. A development of this type was built in 1825 for the Stockton & Darlington Railway by the newly founded firm of R. Stephenson & Co. This was the famous *Locomotion No. 1*, still in existence today.

The Stockton & Darlington was the first public railway in the world to use steam locomotives—though they were used only with goods trains. In quest of suitable locomotives the Liverpool & Manchester Railway held trials in 1829 at Rainhill; the most successful entry was the *Rocket*, built by R. Stephenson & Co.

The Rocket

George Stephenson not only built locomotives but also surveyed, planned and engineered many pioneer railway routes. The first trunk line was the London & Birmingham Railway, engineered by Robert Stephenson, George's son and partner, and completed in 1838. In the same year the Great Western Railway completed the first section of its line between London and Bristol. Railway schemes were now introduced by the hundred. All had to be submitted to Parliament for approval. Many were rejected; but many were approved.

The Battle of the Gauges

From the beginning George Stephenson had had the foresight to realise that lines then only connecting neighbouring towns would one day be joined to form great trunk routes. He therefore standardised a gauge (the distance between the inner edges of the running rails) of 1·435 m (4 ft 8½ in) for all the railways with which he was connected—a familiar gauge to Stephenson, since it was used on some colliery lines in the north-east. Other engineers, however, had their own ideas as to what the gauge should be. Isambard Kingdom Brunel, engineer of the Great Western Railway, adopted a gauge of 2.140 m (7 ft 0¼ in) for the line from London to Bristol, and many lines between London and the West of England and West Midlands were built to this 'Broad Gauge'. Very soon the immense disadvantages of using different gauges for neighbouring lines became obvious. At junction stations where standard and broad tracks met, passengers and goods had to be transferred from one train to another. In the end Parliament decreed that the standard gauge should be used for all main-line railways; and in 1868 the Great Western began to convert its tracks. During the period of change mixed-gauge tracks were used—these having three rails, one of which was common and the other two set to standard and broad gauge respectively; but broad-gauge tracks on the main line from London to Penzance remained until 1892, when the last stretch was converted in one weekend to standard gauge.

But the broad gauge is not lost for ever; the Great Western Society depot at Didcot has a short length reconstructed over 80 years after it was abolished, and a broad gauge locomotive arranged to be fitted with wheels of either 7 ft or 4 ft $8\frac{1}{2}$ in gauge is to be built under the Firefly Project at Bristol and the Science Museum has had a replica GWR broad gauge 4–2–2 built. In 1985 celebrations were held to mark the 150th anniversary since the Great Western Railway was formed, with exhibitions and special steam trains on BR in the West of England.

1850–1900

Gradually the pattern of railway routes became the one we know today. Small local companies soon realised the advantages of amalgamating with other lines to form larger companies.

Meanwhile, more and more railways were built, many of them competing with other railways already in existence. Some companies were on friendly terms with their neighbours, but others were keen rivals and built railways simply in a spirit of competition. This explains why, today, some towns have more than one route to London or other big cities.

During the second half of the nineteenth century, locomotives began to look less like the *Rocket*; boilers were made larger, chimneys shorter and cabs began to appear. By 1870 the locomotive had taken the shape familiar to us now with preserved engines, and coaches had lost their resemblance to wagons.

1900–1980s

By 1900 the main-line railway map was almost complete. The last main line to be built was the Great Central route to London

Main BR Lines

from Nottingham and Leicester, opened in 1899. Apart from underground lines, one or two local lines and the 1983 East Coast main line 14½ mile Selby diversion, building of new railways then almost ceased. From then, in fact, competition from road transport began to take traffic from the railways; first came the electric trams and, later, cars, lorries and buses. Railway companies could no longer afford to compete both against each other and against the new forms of transport, and in 1923 all 123 of them were amalgamated into four groups known as the London, Midland & Scottish, the London & North Eastern, the Great Western and the Southern. The LMS served the country from London to the Midlands, North West, North Wales and part of Scotland, reaching to the far north at Wick. The LNER covered the country from London to the North and East and the remainder of Scotland. The GW's area stretched from London to the West of England, West Midlands and most of Wales. The SR operated from London to the South Coast from Kent to Devonshire and North Cornwall.

On January 1, 1948, together with canals and some road transport, the railways were nationalised and taken over by the nation. Today, there are five BR regions, Eastern, Scottish, London Midland, Western and Southern. In 1963 Britain's railways came under the control of the British Railways Board, with independent boards to manage canals, road transport and transport hotels and catering. The first British Railways Board chairman was Dr Richard (later Lord) Beeching: the present chairman is Sir Robert Reid.

For the last 30 years the railways of Britain have struggled to adapt themselves to the modern world. When he was chairman of British Railways, Dr Beeching found that half the railway system carried about 95 per cent of the traffic while the other half carried the remaining 5 per cent and was losing money. The Beeching Plan called for the closure of a large number of lines. Many branch lines were closed and also some main lines.

During the ten years from 1960 to 1970 the British railway system changed considerably. As we shall see later, steam locomotives finally gave way to diesels and electrics in 1968. Train speeds were higher than ever and 160 km/h (100 mph) became common; new types of signalling were brought into use on a large scale, and new operating methods introduced. In 1974 BR completed the electrification at 25,000 volts a.c. of the West Coast main line over the 645 km (401 miles) between Euston and Glasgow. From 1976, new diesel High Speed Trains known as Inter-City 125 started regular 200 km/h (125 mph) services. But again in the 1980s BR is having to fight against rising costs in running trains. Economies might mean the closure of further lines

which make big losses, and bring a reduction of staff on trains—
some freight trains and short distance passenger trains already
run without guards—to keep the rest of the system intact. Sadly
one of the most scenic main lines, the Settle & Carlisle across the
Pennines between Leeds and Carlisle, is under threat of closure.
But on the positive side is the extension of electrification on the
Kings Cross–Edinburgh main line, the Colchester–Norwich and
Bishops Stortford–Cambridge lines, the Tonbridge–Hastings line,
and around Merseyside.

Railways in other countries

The railway was really Britain's gift to the world. After the success
of the Stockton & Darlington and Liverpool & Manchester railways, businessmen and engineers in other countries soon saw the
advantages of the railway. British engineers were behind the
planning and building of new railways in Europe and North
America. Later, as European countries developed colonies in Africa
and Asia, and Britain opened up the Indian sub-continent, Australia and New Zealand, railways spread to many countries of the
world during the latter part of the nineteenth century. Many
countries by this time had their own engineers who were able to
design railways and supervise construction. Often their ideas were
different from those developed in Britain, particularly in track
gauge. Some, like Brunel, preferred a wider gauge than the 1.435
m (4 ft 8½ in) which was standard in much of Europe and North
America. In countries with hills and mountains, where it would
be difficult to build a straight and easily graded railway, narrower
gauges were used because the smaller narrow-gauge engines and
trains could go round sharper curves and climb steeper gradients
than 1.435 m gauge trains, although at much lower speeds and
with lighter loads. This is why today there are so many different
track gauges in use. Australia for example has three different
gauges—1.067m (3 ft 6 in), 1.435 m (4 ft 8½ in) and 1.600 m
(5 ft 3 in), depending on which State you are in. Nobody thought
about the complications of through-running when the railways
were built in the last century. It was not until the early 1970s
that a 1.435 m gauge route was completed right across Australia
from Sydney to Perth by using existing sections of 1.435 m gauge
and adding a third rail set at 1.435 m gauge to widen or narrow
gauge tracks.

Cecil Rhodes, founder of Rhodesia in the last century (See Section A, A Diary of World Events) dreamed of a through rail route from Cape Town to Cairo for the whole way across Africa from South to North. Alas it did not happen, partly because there were large areas, particularly towards the north of Africa, where railways were never built, and partly because in Central and Southern Africa two different gauges were used, 1.067 m (3 ft 6 in)—'Cape gauge'—in the countries today known as South Africa, Zimbabwe, Zambia, Mozambique, Botswana, Malawi, Zaire and Angola, and 1.000 m (3 ft 3⅜ in) in Kenya, Uganda and Tanzania.

In Europe, where Spain and Portugal use 1.676 m (5 ft 6 in) gauge and the USSR and Finland use 1.524 m (5 ft) gauge, wagons and coaches can run through to the 1.435 m lines used in the rest of Europe by changing the wheel sets or bogies at the frontier stations.

Railways are still being built in some countries, especially developing countries like Zambia where a new railway of 1.067 m gauge was opened throughout in 1976 to give an outlet to the Tanzanian port at Dar es Salaam on the Indian Ocean. In other countries like Japan, France and Italy governments are spending large sums of money in building new high speed railways on straighter routes alongside or parallel to existing lines which may be restricted by curves or traffic congestion. All these new high speed railways are electrified, and many countries have converted to electric operation on their most heavily used routes and diesel operation on the others, and steam locomotives are no longer used in many countries. Just a few countries still have steam locomotives as we have mentioned in the introduction to this section, but in China steam locomotives are still being built, with the workshops at Datong constructing over 200 steam locomotives each year.

Railways in most countries of the world, including Britain, are usually state-owned, since even if they were built by private companies they have been nationalised. Railways are very expensive to build and operate and many now lose money, but without them the life of the country would come to a stop. National governments sometimes help to pay for the losses by giving money called subsidies or grants, which means that the people of the country have to pay for the railways through taxes. In some cases governments pay for new trains, track, or resignalling, or the building of major projects like new tunnels. In Switzerland the government is trying to get people to use trains much more to try to reduce air pollution from car and truck exhausts. As part of a package of measures called 'Rail 2000' the Swiss railways are to run more frequent train services in regular interval timetables which already operate all over the country, with new lines and stations, modern trains and cheaper fares, and all with the help of government subsidies.

Some governments will not pay out as much as others, and the railways have to make do for longer with older equipment. In Britain the government started making payments in 1969 for loss-making local services which have to be kept running, but Inter-City passenger trains and freight trains must make a profit. In recent years the government has tried to make BR run more efficiently with fewer staff and better use of trains.

LOCOMOTIVES

Steam locomotives reigned supreme on the railways of the world for over a century until, in the face of more modern forms of traction powered by diesel engines or electricity, the last steam locomotive was withdrawn from regular service on Britain's main lines in August 1968.

Steam: Some Classic Locomotives of the Past

Steam locomotives were classified according to the 'Whyte' table of wheel arrangements (see H12). In the days when there were 123 different companies the number of locomotive designs ran into hundreds. Yet the same wheel arrangements were adopted by many companies for locomotives on the same type of work. In late Victorian times 2–4–0 and 4–4–0 locomotives were used for passenger duties and 0–6–0 locomotives for goods trains and for shunting. In the first years of the present century locomotive designers began to think in terms of larger locomotives than had been used until then. Some railways built 4–4–2 (Atlantic) locomotives for express duties and others had 4–6–0s. The Great Western built a solitary 4–6–2 (Pacific) locomotive, but it was not very successful and was later rebuilt as a 4–6–0. After the grouping in 1923 designs were standardised and express passenger trains were built right up to the maximum size and weight that the British loading gauge permitted. Some of the most famous

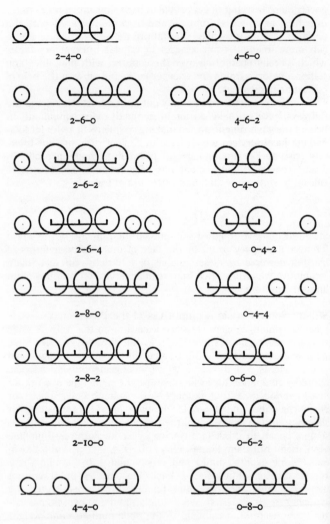

Whyte Classification of Steam Locomotive Wheel Arrangements

express locomotives built during this period were the Great Western 'King' class 4–6–0, most powerful of all 4–6–0 designs; the LNER streamlined 'A4' 4–6–2; the LMS 'Coronation' class 4–6–2, which began as a streamlined engine; and the SR 'Merchant Navy' 4-6-2, a design which appeared in 1941 and was originally partly streamlined.

BR Types
After nationalisation British Railways introduced twelve standard classes of steam locomotives. They were: three types of 4–6–2, for express passenger duties; two types of 4–6–0 for lighter express and intermediate passenger or freight working; three types of 2–6–0 for main-line and branch passenger or freight duties; a 2–6–4 tank for suburban passenger trains; two types of 2–6–2 tank for branch passenger and freight; and a 2–10–0 for heavy express or ordinary freight. Many BR and earlier steam locomotives have been preserved.

The Last of the Line
The very last locomotive built specially for express passenger work, No. 71000 *Duke of Gloucester*, was completed in 1954; but even this engine was withdrawn after a life of only eight years. The last steam locomotive of all, a class '9' 2–10–0 freight engine, No. 92220, was built at Swindon Works for the Western Region in 1960. This engine did not carry the last number, since another batch, Nos. 92221-50, built at Crewe Works, was actually completed first. No. 92220 was specially named *Evening Star*, painted in green livery and given a copper-capped chimney. Both 92220 and 71000 have been preserved.

Modernisation
During the Second World War and the years immediately following the railways were not able to replace old and worn-out equipment. Coal of a quality suitable for steam locomotives was becoming difficult to obtain and very expensive. It was difficult, too, to find men to train as firemen. So when, in 1955, the British Transport Commission announced an immense plan to modernise its locomotives, coaches, signalling and other equipment, part of the plan was that diesel and electric trains should replace steam locomotives, which would gradually disappear. Some trunk routes

and suburban lines would be electrified; on others, diesel locomotives would haul express passenger and freight trains. Trains
with diesel engines built on the coaches themselves (known as
multiple-units) would be used for local and semi-fast journeys.

The multiple-unit system is widely used on BR with both diesel
and electric types. Each unit has its own diesel power plant in the
case of diesel trains, and electric traction motors in the case of
electric trains. Each unit has driving cabs at the outer ends of the
coaches at each end. When two or more units are coupled together, control cables are joined up between them so that all the
diesel engines or all the electric motors can be controlled at the same
time by the one driver from the leading driving cab. Many locomotives on BR can be coupled in pairs and driven from the leading
cab by one man, and are then said to be running 'in multiple'.
Because of different equipment on different classes, not all can work
in multiple; but they can still be coupled and driven separately with
a man on each, and are then said to be running 'in tandem'.

It took only 13 years from the announcement of the modernisation plan in 1955 until the last steam locomotive ran in daily
service on BR in August 1968. Although steam locomotives no
longer run on regular all-year services on BR you can still see and
travel behind steam locomotives on the narrow gauge line run by
BR for tourists, from Aberystwyth, and on the numerous privately-
operated railways in Great Britain which are listed at the end of
the railway section. Moreover, since 1971 BR has allowed a
limited number of steam-hauled excursions to run on selected
secondary main lines. BR itself runs some regular summer season
steam excursions on one or two routes. Among the engines used
are examples of the 'King', 'A3', 'A4', Coronation' and 'Merchant
Navy' classes. The steam locomotives are mostly privately-owned
by preservation societies, but some belong to the National Railway
Museum. They have to be up to the highest standards of maintenance.

Since 1968 new diesel and electric types have been introduced
and some of the first diesel locomotives and multiple-units have
reached the end of their lives and been withdrawn, and a few
preserved. With experts telling us that the world's oil reserves are
limited and with oil now costing much more than coal for the
same power, BR and the government have been looking at possible
longer term electrification, where coal will once again play an

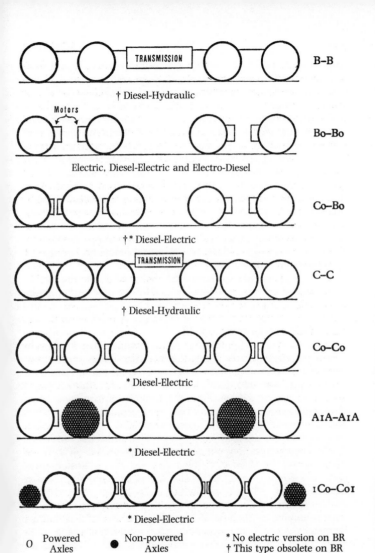

B–B

† Diesel-Hydraulic

Bo–Bo

Electric, Diesel-Electric and Electro-Diesel

Co–Bo

† * Diesel-Electric

C–C

† Diesel-Hydraulic

Co–Co

* Diesel-Electric

AᵢA–AᵢA

* Diesel-Electric

ᵢCo–Coᵢ

* Diesel-Electric

O Powered Axles   ● Non-powered Axles   * No electric version on BR
† This type obsolete on BR

Classification of Diesel and Electric Locomotive
Wheel Arrangements

important part as a power station fuel for electricity generation, alongside nuclear fuel used at some power stations.

Diesel and electric locomotive wheel arrangements are expressed by the Continental system; the Whyte notation for steam locomotives cannot be used, since it does not distinguish clearly between driving wheels and non-driving wheels. In the Continental system the number of axles are counted; driving axles are shown by a letter (A = 1 driving axle, B = 2, C = 3, D = 4) and unpowered axles by a figure. Each bogie or group of wheels is separated from the next by a hyphen. In addition, if in a group of driving axles each has its own driving motor a small suffix 'o' is added after the letter. If several driving axles are driven from one source either by gearing, shaft drive or coupling rods, no suffix is used. For example, if an electric locomotive has two four-wheel bogies with all axles individually powered it would be described as a Bo-Bo. If one motor on each bogie was connected to both driving axles by coupling rods or driving shafts it would become a B-B. Sometimes the suffix 'o' is not included even if separate motors power the axles.

Locomotive numbering on BR

BR diesel and electric locomotives are numbered in a series in which the class number forms the first two figures of the complete number. Shunting locomotives are numbered in classes 01 to 13, main-line diesel locomotives in classes 20 to 59 and electric locomotives from 71 to 91 though with gaps as some classes have been withdrawn. The first locomotive in each class is numbered 001. Thus the lowest numbered locomotive was a shunter 01.001, the medium powered English Electric 160 km/h Co-Co locomotives on the Western Region are 50.001 to 50.050, and the latest electric locomotives on the Euston–Glasgow line 87.001 to 87.035. The Inter-City 125 units are in class 253 and 254 as part of the multiple-unit series 100 to 254, and the APT in class 370. In 1977 BR resumed locomotive-naming with classes 50 and 87 and selected locomotives in classes 33, 47 and 86, and more recently Inter-City 125 units. Preserved steam locomotives have usually kept their BR numbers or in some cases have reverted to older numbers of the pre-BR companies.

Simplified Diagram of British Railways 4-6-2 Express Steam Locomotive

A Smokebox
B Boiler
C Firebox
D Cab
E Coal space
F Water space
G Water tank filler
H Water pick up scoop for taking water at speed from
   troughs
I Firebox stays
J Safety valves
K Regulator valve operated by rodding from regulator lever
   in cab
L Steam pipe taking 'live' steam to cylinders

M Blast pipe for exhausting used steam from the cylinders
   out of the chimney
N Valve chest
O Piston
P Cylinder
Q Valve gear
R Connecting rod
S Coupling rod
T Brick arch
U Tubes carrying superheater elements. 'Wet' steam on its
   way from the regulator to cylinders passes through
   the superheater to dry it and make it more efficient
V Tubes to carry exhaust gases from firebox to smokebox

HOW LOCOMOTIVES WORK

Steam

A steam locomotive has five principal parts—firebox, boiler, smokebox, cylinders and wheels. The firebox is at one end of the boiler, which surrounds it. Tubes from the firebox pass to the front of the boiler and into the smokebox, from which smoke and gases escape through the chimney. A steam pipe leads from the top of the boiler through the regulator valve to the cylinder valves, and from the cylinder valves to the smokebox. A piston inside the cylinder is connected to the driving wheels so that when it moves backwards and forwards the connecting-rods to the driving wheels make them turn. Engines have at least two cylinders, sometimes three or even four.

Coal is burnt in the firebox and heats the water in the boiler, turning it to steam. Because the steam cannot escape, pressure builds up. When the driver opens the regulator valve, steam passes through the pipe leading to the cylinders. Depending on the position of the driver's reversing lever, which operates part of the valve gear, the valves admit steam to one side of the pistons. The steam forces the piston to the opposite end of the cylinder, and the connecting-rods to the wheels push or pull the wheels round. When the steam has made its push the valves let it out of the cylinder into another pipe which leads it to the smokebox. Here, with the smoke and gases from the fire, it is exhausted out of the chimney as a 'puff'. Meanwhile, the valves let in more steam to the other side of the piston, and this pushes the piston back again. So a continuous action is built up, steam pushing first on one side of the piston, then on the other, propelling it backwards and forwards and in turn causing the driving wheels to revolve and the locomotive to move.

As the steam is exhausted out of the chimney it creates a vacuum in the smokebox and draws air through the fire. Thus when the engine is working hard the fire automatically burns fiercely, making a lot of steam. When the engine is eased and steam shut off, the fire dies down and the boiler does not make so much steam—an early form of automation developed by Robert Stephenson nearly 150 years ago. The fireman has to keep the firebox well covered with coal, and the boiler properly filled with water through what is called an injector, a steam-operated device which forces water into the boiler at high speed against the pressure of the steam.

Diesel

The diesel locomotive (or multiple-unit) power equipment is in two parts, the engine and the device for connecting the power output from the engine to the wheels, called the transmission.

The principle of the engine is the same for locomotives and multiple-units, but it is in the methods of transmission that variations occur. There are two of these: mechanical, and electric.

The cylinders are the most important part of a diesel engine. There may be as few as four or as many as sixteen. Each has a piston sliding up and down inside it, connected to a crankshaft. Sometimes the pistons from two banks of cylinders drive a single crankshaft; in others, a cylinder may be open at both ends and have two pistons opposing each other, driving separate crankshafts connected by gearing. The diesel engine works by compression ignition. As the piston moves into the cylinder it compresses the air in the cylinder to a high pressure and to a very high temperature. Just before the piston stroke is completed a minute amount of fuel oil is injected into the cylinder by fuel pump, and the high temperature causes the fuel to ignite and explode, forcing the piston back. Several cylinders and pistons are arranged so that each fires in turn and, as one piston is rising to compress the air, the next will just be firing, the next driven halfway down, another at the end of its power stroke waiting to return to compress the air again. Generally four-stroke engines are used, in which the pistons make two strokes up and down for every one

Diesel Locomotive with Mechanical Transmission

Typical diesel-mechanical shunting locomotive; A is the engine and B the gearbox, from which the torque is transmitted by a jackshaft drive to the road wheels firing movement. The intermediate stroke cleans out the exhaust gas from the previous firing stroke and draws in fresh air for the next one.

The mechanical form of transmission employs a clutch and gearbox to transmit the drive from the output shaft of the engine to the wheels, almost as in a motor-car. Its use in this country is limited to engines of less than about 400 h.p., and on British Rail is confined to some small shunting locomotives and to the multiple-unit rail-car sets, nearly all of which are equipped with this form of transmission, though with a fluid clutch.

In the second system of transmission the diesel engine drives an electric generator which feeds current to electric motors coupled to the locomotive axles. This is the main system used on British Rail locomotives, and it is also in use on some SR and Class 210 diesel multiple-unit trains. The diesel-electric system is used on BR's Inter-City 125 HST units but with alternating current rectified for the d.c. motors. In addition, of course, the diesel generator supplies electricity at lower voltages for the control units worked from the driver's controller, which regulate engine speed and electric power and thus the train speed.

At one time a third transmission system using hydraulics was used on BR and is still used on some diesel types overseas, and one or two diesels in Britain, but it is becoming obsolete.

Electric

Unlike a steam or diesel locomotive, which generates its own power, an electric locomotive or multiple-unit train must obtain its power from some outside source. Electricity is taken from the National Grid and passed to railway sub-stations along the line, where it is transformed (and rectified in many cases) to the correct voltage and fed either to conductor rails or to overhead wires. The electric locomotives and trains collect the current through *shoes* running on the conductor rail or through a device called a *pantograph* which is mounted on the roof and rubs along the underside of the conductor wire. The current then passes through the control system and into the electric traction motors. The return current is generally passed into the running rails. British Rail has standardised electrification at 25,000 volts a.c. with overhead current collection except on the SR where the 750 volts d.c. third rail system is used.

Diesel Locomotive with Electric Transmission

A typical diesel-electric locomotive; A is the diesel engine, which drives
the generator, B, that provides current for C, the electric traction motors

An electric locomotive or train works by passing an electric
current through the traction motors. Speed can be varied by
reducing or increasing the voltage. In simple terms the traction
motor consists of a shaft with many coils of wire wound round
it called the armature, mounted inside an electromagnet. When an
electric current is passed through contacts on the armature shaft,
called the commutator, to the coils of wire in the armature, and also
through the electromagnet, a magnetic attraction is set up which
causes the armature shaft to revolve. As this shaft is geared to the
driving wheels, the process moves the locomotive.

Seven types of a.c. electric locomotive are used on the LMR's
electrified main lines; the first 100 locomotives are sub-divided
into five classes built by different manufacturers. The second 100
are of all one class embodying the best features of the first 100
locomotives. The seventh class of 36 locomotives is much more
powerful than the earlier 200, with 5,100 horse power. Some of
the earlier locomotives dating from the 1960s have been withdrawn. Several locomotives are also being transferred to the ER
for London–Norwich electric services.

Another type of modern locomotive is the electro-diesel, used
on the Southern Region. This works as an electric locomotive when
running on an electrified line but has a diesel engine for running on
non-electrified sidings or lines. This type of locomotive, together
with some of the SR diesel locomotives, can work certain Southern
express trains push–pull fashion, that is with the locomotive at
either end of the train. When the locomotive is pushing, the driver
controls it from a driving cab in the leading coach.

Simplified Diagram of British Rail Main Line Bo-Bo Electric Locomotive Operating on 25,000 Volts Alternating Current from Overhead Contact Wire

A *Cab No. 1*
B *Cab No. 2*
C *Relatively low voltage direct current (about 1,900 volts)*
D *Control equipment*
E *Main rectifier*
F *Relatively low voltage alternating current (about 2,000 volts)*
G *Main transformer*
H *Low voltage alternating current (1000 volts or less)*
I *Other equipment, such as compressor and ejector motors for train brakes, and air-operated*

control apparatus, lighting on locomotive, train heating and control equipment
J *Traction motors*
K *Second pantograph not in use (most locomotives have only one pantograph)*
L *Circuit breaker*
M *Supply from pantograph*
N *Pantograph collecting electricity from overhead wire*
O *High voltage alternating current (25,000 volts)*

BRAKES

If you want to stop a train it's not much good turning off the power alone; a train can coast for several miles, particularly if it is running downhill, without appreciably slowing down.

A train's brakes usually consist of blocks which, when applied, press hard on the treads of the wheels. Latest freight wagons and certain passenger coaches have disc brakes—special brake pads which press against discs on the axle. The means of applying and releasing them is by variations in air pressure. There are two systems in use: one employing a vacuum to hold the brakes off, and opening it to the atmosphere to apply them; and the other using compressed air to do the same thing.

The *vacuum brake* was virtually standard on locomotive-hauled trains on BR until recent years. Throughout every passenger train and many freight trains runs an air-tight pipe flexibly connected between coaches and to the locomotive itself. Connected to this 'train pipe' by a branch pipe on each coach is a cylinder containing a piston. The piston is connected by rodding to the brake blocks. A vacuum pump or ejector on the locomotive draws air out of the system which releases the brake; admission of air to the train pipe by the driver's brake valve applies the brakes. The difference in air pressure above and below the piston causes it to move up or down and in turn the brake blocks press against the wheels or move away.

If a passenger operates the alarm signal or a train becomes uncoupled accidentally and breaks the flexible train pipe between the coaches, air enters the brake system automatically and applies the brakes.

The *compressed-air brake* is more complicated, but works on the principle that the release of compressed air will apply the brakes. All electric trains in Great Britain use the air brake and on most multiple-units this is applied and released electrically—a much quicker process—although there is still automatic application in case of emergency. Air brakes are used on many types of goods train and today are used as the new standard type on most locomotive-hauled passenger trains. The brake system on these trains uses two pipes running throughout the train, one to apply the brakes when the compressed air is let out through the driver's brake valve, the other full of high pressure compressed air to recharge the system to release them. The compressed air brake is much more powerful than the vacuum type.

COACHES

BR main-line coaches built between 1951 and 1966 weigh about 32–34 tonnes each, are 19·660 m (64 ft 6 in) long over the body ends and 2·743 m (9 ft) wide over the body (2·819 m—9 ft 3 in if you count the door handles). Corridor coaches seat 48 or 64 second-class passengers or 42 first-class passengers. The latest coaches are of 'integral' construction in which the coach body is self-supporting without a heavy underframe. Since 1966 all new second class coaches have been of the open pattern, with pairs of seats on each side of a central passageway. BR's latest Mark III coaches, in use on HST trains and on other lines, are $22 \cdot 570$ m (74 ft) long. They weigh 32 tonnes and seat 48 first or 72 second class passengers. Some trains have restaurant or buffet cars so that passengers can eat or drink. The first railway dining car ran in 1879.

In 1971 BR made history by introducing trains with fully air-conditioned coaches on ordinary services; until then they had been used for only a few special luxury expresses on which supplementary fares were charged. On air-conditioned coaches the windows do not open and the air is filtered and heated or cooled before being circulated inside the coach.

FREIGHT SERVICES

Until the 1970s goods wagons on British Rail did not change very much in size from the early days of railways, 150 years or so ago. The normal open wagon or covered goods van was still a four-wheeler nearly 5 m (16 ft) long. One reason for the continuity in size has been the limitation of some goods stations where short loading platforms were designed for only one wagon at a time, and sidings in some places could only be reached by short turntables or traversers.

But these small wagons are not suited to today's high speeds and the operating methods adopted over the last 10 years by the railways. Until a few years ago the normal British goods train was slow moving, with each wagon or group of wagons starting from different stations and terminating at different stations. There were several thousand goods stations which handled all the different types of freight traffic. Very often a wagon would pass through two, three or even more marshalling yards on its journey. Many small stations and goods yards were then closed and freight trains were reorganised to run between main centres without re-marshalling. Lorries collect and deliver freight from factories and shops to the main goods stations.

British Rail developed the Freightliner train for carrying goods. These consist of long flat bogie wagons, able to travel at up to 120 km/h (75 mph) carrying containers. They run as block trains, that is without intermediate remarshalling. Containers are loaded in the factory or warehouse, then taken by lorry to the goods station where the container is lifted on to one of the railway wagons. One wagon can often carry up to three containers. When loaded the train sets off on its journey. At the other end the containers are again taken by road to their destination. Sometimes containers are sent overseas by ship, thus being carried by lorry, train, ship, without the goods being handled.

Coal in special hopper wagons and oil in tank wagons are often taken in block loads, from a colliery or port to a power station or oil storage depot. For today's freight services BR has been developing new types of wagon, longer and carrying heavier loads than the old types. Some are four-wheelers but others, particularly tank wagons, are large bogie types weighing 100 tonnes fully loaded. Some coal trains between collieries and power stations are loaded and unloaded while moving slowly at each end of their journey. They are called merry-go-round trains.

Computers are used by BR in the TOPS (Total Operations Processing System) network to record the movement of every locomotive, coach and wagon. The computer can print out the whereabouts of wagons, or tell operators when a locomotive is due for maintenance, and advise crews of train speed limits.

TRACK

The rails used on early railways were of cast iron and later the stronger wrought iron; but for very many years now the rail has been made of steel. Until the 1950s *bull-head* was used almost exclusively on British railways and is still in use on many lines. This has a cross-section rather like a figure 8 with a square-ish head. It is laid in cast-iron *chairs* and held by wooden blocks or spring steel *keys* wedged between the rail and the side of the chair. The chairs are bolted to wooden sleepers, and the sleepers themselves are held in position by stone ballast, often limestone but sometimes granite.

Since about 1946 the place of bull-head as a standard rail has been taken by what is called *flat-bottomed rail*. This, as its name suggests, has a flat base and is capable of standing upright without support. It is held in position by *baseplates*, and the rail and baseplates are spiked, clipped or bolted to the sleeper.

Rails are normally 18·288 m (60 ft) long and are supported by 24 sleepers to a length: there are 2,112 sleepers in 1·609 km (1 mile) of track. Each length is joined to the next by *fishplates*—lengths of steel plate about 600 mm (2 ft) long bolted through the rail ends with four bolts. When new track is laid, small gaps are left between rail ends to allow for expansion in hot weather. The holes through which the fishplate bolts pass are oval, to allow the rail to expand.

Welded track is now used extensively in Britain. In this type of track the 60 ft lengths of rail are welded together into one piece, sometimes up to $1\frac{1}{2}$ km (1 mile) or more in length without a break. In the previous paragraph we mentioned that gaps allow for the rails to expand in hot weather. If special measures are not taken, continuously-welded rail would be badly distorted when it expands in very hot weather. To overcome this difficulty, welded rail is nearly always carried on concrete sleepers which are so heavy that the rail is held tightly in position. The sleepers are spaced slightly closer at about 26 for every 60 ft. Moreover, soon after it is laid the rail is heated artificially to average summer-time temperatures, starting at one end and working through to the far end. As the rail is heated it expands, and is fastened down tightly in its expanded form. In subsequent hot weather, therefore, it cannot expand any more; in cold weather it tries to contract but since it is rigidly held it is unable to do so. In some ways it is like a piece of elastic which has been stretched a little and fastened down while stretched. The engineers responsible for heating the rail try to fix it in position at a temperature about halfway between the extremes of cold and hot weather. Deep stone ballast also helps to hold the track rigidly. By 1982 more than half BR track was welded.

A new form of track in which sleepers and ballast are replaced by a solid bed of reinforced concrete paving to which the rails are attached is being tried out experimentally by British Railways.

SIGNALLING

First the signals themselves. Most main lines have *colour-light signals* in which powerful coloured lamps, which can be seen by day or night, give the signal indications so that the driver knows whether it safe to proceed at top speed or whether he must slow down or stop. The indications are: red—danger, stop; single yellow—caution, be ready to stop at next signal; double yellow—preliminary caution, be ready to stop at second signal ahead; green—clear, proceed at normal speed. At certain junctions on high speed main lines flashing single or double yellow lights mean that the route ahead is set for a train to take a diverging line and must slow down. At the junction signal itself a row of five white lights pointing to left or right above the main colour indication shows which way the points are set for the divergence.

On some secondary and branch lines old style *semaphore signals*, with an arm about $1\frac{1}{2}$ m (5 ft) long, are still used. *Stop* signals have a red arm with a white vertical stripe near the left end, and at night show a red light for danger and green for clear. *Distant* signals have a yellow arm with a vee notch cut from the left-hand end and a black vee stripe near the end. At night they show a yellow light at caution and green for clear. These signals give the driver an advanced indication of the next stop signals ahead. All semaphore signals have the arm horizontal for danger or caution.

Stop signal at danger   Distant signal at clear   Four aspect colour light signal

British Rail Semaphore and Colour-light Signals

At some signals on high speed routes preceding junctions, the single and double yellow aspects are flashing to show that the train must slow down to turn off the main line at points ahead.

Some signals, nearly all on the Western Region, have the arm lowered at about 60 degrees to show clear, but most semaphore signal arms are inclined 45 degrees above horizontal for clear.

All passenger lines on British Rail are worked on the 'absolute block' system of signalling. In this system each line is divided into sections. With modern colour-light signalling there is usually a signal capable of showing a red aspect at the entrance to each section so that in effect there shall not be more than one train on one line between successive signals. The block system, though, was devised over 100 years ago when all signalling was controlled mechanically. Where mechanical signalling is used there is usually a signalbox where the sections, called 'block sections', meet.

The principle is that there shall never be more than one train in a block section on one line at a time. The signalboxes are equipped with 'block instruments' and bells for each line, so that signalmen in neighbouring boxes can keep each other fully informed about the passage of a train through the sections they control. The block instrument has a dial resembling a clock face but without any figures. The dial is marked with three panels; one says 'line blocked', another 'line clear' and the third 'train on line'. The indications are given by a needle pivoted in the centre which points to the appropriate panel. The needle is deflected by an electro-magnet when the signalman turns a switch on the block instrument to the appropriate position. The indication is electrically repeated by the block instrument applying to the same section in the signalbox at the entry end of the section.

When a signalman wants to signal a train he must carry out the routine laid down by regulations in which he 'offers' the train by coded bell signals to the next signalbox ahead and if the line is clear the signalman there 'accepts' the train by a repetition of the bell signal. Bell signals are exchanged when the train enters and leaves the section of line between the two boxes and indicators show whether the section is clear or occupied by a train.

At one time the safety of trains depended solely on the correct operation of the block system by the signalmen, but today, lines carrying fast, frequent services are equipped with additional safeguards to prevent a signalman from forgetting a train. Many of these devices are worked by the trains themselves from what are known as *track circuits*. A track circuit is an electrically-insulated section of line which has a weak electric current passed through the running rails and connected to an electro-magnetic relay at one end of the section. As the train passes over the line, its wheels short-circuit the current, which is cut off from the relay. The relay arm therefore falls away from the magnet and makes contact with other electrical circuits, which can be used to operate such equipment as locks on signal and point levers and can prevent a signalman from pulling a signal lever to clear a signal when a train is standing on a track circuit ahead of it. Track circuits can also be used to control signals automatically.

The track circuit is in fact the basis of all modern signalling, because it allows the signalman to 'see' trains several miles away. In mechanical signalling, where the signalman works points and signals from levers which operate rods or wires, Government regulations limit mechanical operation of points to no more than 320 m (350 yds) from the signalbox. At big junctions, several signalboxes were often needed to control the layout. But with electric operation of points and signals there is no limit, and signal cabins often work points and signals as much as 80 km (50 miles) away. Track circuits are used to show the signalman the positions of trains by lights on a track diagram in the signal cabin. Track circuits are also used to initiate the operation of barriers at level crossings, the ones in which barriers automatically lower across half the road when a train is coming. Other level crossings with full barriers are often controlled from a signalbox many miles away, the signalman 'seeing' the crossing by closed-circuit television. These types of crossing, which also have flashing lights to stop cars and pedestrians when a train is approaching, are gradually replacing the old type with swing gates. By the way, NEVER try to pass over a crossing when the barriers are down and the red lights flashing. All improvements and developments in railway signalling over the last 150 years have come piece by piece, added on to what was already there so that it could be proved to be absolutely reliable and fail safe. This means that if a piece of equipment breaks down the signals will go to danger and trains will stop.

Modern centralised signal cabins have been introduced on many sections of British Rail as part of the modernisation plan. In some, the signals and points are controlled from the banks of thumb-switches. But in the most recent signalling centres the controlling miniature push-buttons or thumb-switches are placed in their appropriate positions on a diagram which consists of a replica of the track layout. The buttons usually work on the route-setting principle; that is, the operation of two buttons will set up a complete route from signal to signal—the equipment checking first that no other train is on the line concerned, then changing the points needed for the route and finally clearing the signal.

Illustrated is part of a modern signalling panel. To set up a route the signalman turns the thumb-switch at the entrance to a signal section and presses a button at the end of it. When the route is set, white lights are illuminated on his diagram along the track concerned so that he can see the path the train will take. As the train passes along the route, the lights change from white to red to show the signalman the position of the train. After the train has passed the signalman restores the thumb-switch to its normal position until it is needed again and the white lights are extinguished. Where there is a junction, the button he presses determines the route that is set. For example, in the illustration, if he wants to send a train on the up relief line into the up goods lines he will turn switch 4 and press button D. That sets the route from signal 4 to signal 6. He then turns switch 6 and presses button F. The points will be set, signal 6 will clear and the white diagram lights will show the route set as far as signal 8. If instead the train was to continue up the relief line he would turn switch 6 but press button E.

The signalmen in these modern cabins advise each other of approaching trains by the train describer. Usually the describer displays a code of figures and letters indicating the train's classification, its destination area and its number. The code is set up on the describer by the signalman who dials the code on a telephone-type dial or operates push buttons. The code description automatically moves from aperture to aperture along the track diagram in step with the train, so the signalman can see its description at a glance. When the train continues on its way towards the next signal cabin its description is automatically passed to the describer there so that the signalman knows what train is approaching him. He can watch its progress, too, from his track circuit diagram. Usually there are several automatic signal sections controlled solely by track circuits between the areas worked by the push-button panels. Colour-light signals are installed throughout the 645 km (401 miles) between Euston and Glasgow, as part of electrification, mostly controlled from centralised power signalboxes supervising long sections of line. There are only 6 signalboxes between Euston and Nuneaton—a distance of 156 km (97 miles), and over the 354 km (220 miles) from the Warrington area to Glasgow only five signalboxes. Edinburgh signalbox controls more than 320 route kilometres.

Most British Rail main lines, whether equipped with semaphore or colour light signals, are fitted with 'AWS'—the automatic warning system. This device, situated at all semaphore distant signals and nearly all colour-light signals, operates a bell in the driver's cab if the signal is clear; if it is at caution a horn sounds and the brakes are applied automatically unless the driver acknowledges the warning.

More advanced than AWS is a new sophisticated form of signalling in which the signals ahead (if indeed lineside signals are retained) or the condition of the line ahead and the safe running speed are displayed continuously in the driver's cab. This form of signalling is used in some countries for running at over 200 km/h (125 mph). On other railways, Holland for example, cab signalling is being tried on lower speed lines. It can be achieved by pairs of wires laid along the centre of the track which transmit signalling codes to a train passing above by induction—a form of magnetism. If the wires are crossed at, say, 100 metre intervals the transmitted code operates a counter on the train which shows the distance travelled. Another means of transmitting details of line conditions on to a display in the driver's cab is by transponders. These are packages of electronic equipment which are placed between the rails and are normally dead. When a train passes over a transponder an inducted signal from the train is aimed at the transponder, which is energised by it and replies with coded details of its location (for example, distance from London, and such fixed details as permanent speed restrictions or other operating information that applies at that place) for display to the driver. They are being installed between London and Glasgow for the APT (see page H37).

The next stage beyond that is the introduction of automatic speed control. Automatic trains which drive themselves after the train operator has pressed the start button are at work on London's Victoria Line underground route. The trains pick up inducted codes transmitted through the running rails as signalling and safety codes, without which the trains cannot move on their own. Other codes are transmitted to the train to reduce speed and stop within a metre or so of the correct place at stations, all without any action on the part of the train operator. Trains automatically slow down and stop at signal sections if there is another train close ahead, and automatically restart when the line is again clear. At junctions, points are set automatically by programme machines. These have long paper rolls with holes punched in to represent the day's train service and denoting train number, time and route. Feeler arms 'read' the punched holes for each entry and, by switching electrical circuits on and off, act on the normal signalling equipment to set the route, provided the train describer shows that the right train is approaching. The paper roll steps forward line by line for each train as it passes through the junction.

On the Tyne & Wear Metro in Newcastle, although there is a central control office which includes a push-button signalling panel and a diagram showing every track on the system and all the trains as a row of red lights, the trains normally signal themselves through junctions by a different system from that used by London Transport. The driver sets up the train working number and its destination by dials on his control desk which puts a code into a transponder underneath the train. When the train approaches a junction area a loop of wire on the track detects the code on the train and sends this information as electrical impulses to the relay room so that the equipment can set the points and signals automatically if the line is clear.

Computers are used at several modern BR signalboxes to record train movement and operate train describers. In experiments in London and in other countries, computers initiate the route-setting operation automatically when fed from the train describer with the number of a particular train as it approaches within two or three miles of a junction. BR is also trying out computer-controlled radio signalling direct to the driver's cab particularly on remote cross country lines, as for example in the Scottish Highlands and in Wales. The lines concerned have a single track, at passing loops the points are self resetting, there are no signals in the normal sense although there are indicators to show that the points are properly set, and the driver's authority to move out of a passing loop on to the single line is a message displayed on a receiver on the locomotive control desk, transmitted to the train by radio from the control centre many miles away.

UNDERGROUND RAILWAYS

In many cities of the world underground electric railways for many years have helped to move passengers quickly and to avoid street congestion. London underground railways were among the earliest, in the last century, with most of the system built between 1900 and 1910. Now new lines have been built, not only in London with the Jubilee Line, but also in rapid transit form—a cross between a tram and a train—in Newcastle and in other world cities. In Newcastle, which is the first railway of its type in Britain, the trains are lightweight, articulated, two-unit electric cars, which can be coupled in three-car formations. They have open saloon interiors, with plenty of room for standing, and sliding doors. They work from overhead catenary at 1,500 volts d.c. New tunnels have been built under Newcastle city centre, and a new bridge across the River Tyne links existing suburban railways to Whitley Bay and South Shields which are served by the new Tyne & Wear Metro. In Liverpool, new underground lines have been built across the city, and the famous Glasgow Subway has also been modernised.

Other new Light Rapid Transit (LRT) systems are being discussed or planned for Manchester and Birmingham cross-city transport and for a line in London's Dockland. At Birmingham Airport a new form of transport was opened in 1984 in which small cabins without wheels run on a guided way; electro-magnets hold the cars hovering above the track and electric conductors along the track pull the cars by magnetic attraction.

THE RAILWAY SPEED RECORD HOLDERS

Railway speeds in the last few years have increased, but until 1976 British trains did not normally exceed 160 km/h (100 mph), with averages of 130–40 km/h (80–90 mph). The first 160 km/h (100 mph) run by rail ever was claimed for the Great Western's 4-4-0 *City of Truro*, which was said to have reached 164·5 km/h (102·3 mph) on May 9, 1904, with a Plymouth to London mail. LNER 4472 *Flying Scotsman* made the first authentic 160 km/h (100 mph) run in 1934. The world's speed record for steam locomotives is held by Great Britain's No. 60022 *Mallard*, which, in July 1938, reached 202·5 km/h (126 mph) with a test train between Grantham and Peterborough.

Japan was the first country to go beyond the 160 km/h (100 mph) speeds at one time thought to be the practicable limit for trains in daily service, with regular speeds of up to 209 km/h (130 mph) on the New Tokaido line between Tokyo and Osaka, built specially for high-speed running and opened in 1964. During 1972 the Japanese opened a second high-speed railway, the New San Yo line, and more high speed railways are being built. On some, trains run every 15 min. Then, during the late 1960s and

The French TGV

early 1970s Britain, France, Germany and Italy started experiments with trains running at up to 200 km/h (125 mph). In Italy a new line—the Direttissimo—between Rome and Florence is being opened in sections and has a top speed of 250 km/h (155 mph).

But during 1981 French Railways opened the first part of a new high-speed railway between Paris and Lyon which, with trains running day-in day-out at 260 km/h (162 mph), puts the French Railways right at the top in running the fastest trains in the world. The specially-built 10-car trains called TGVs (Train Grande Vitesse) include two electric power cars one at each end, and eight intermediate passenger coaches, two of which next to the power cars each have a motor bogie at one end. The trains are streamlined and are finished in a bright orange-red and white livery. On February 26, 1981 a specially formed TGV train of seven cars, and with an altered gear ratio to the motors, on a test run to check safety limits pushed the world rail speed record to 380 km/h (236·1 mph). This was an increase of 50 km/h (31 mph) over the 330 km/h also held by the French since 1955. The French and Japanese have shown that we can probably think of 320 km/h (200 mph) as the safe limit for everyday trains on conventional railways using steel wheels on steel rails. The Japanese, particularly, and engineers in other countries (including at one time Britain), have been running trials with other forms of guided land transport. The coaches run astride a basically concrete beam but do not touch it since they are held just above it

British Rail's High
Speed Train 'Inter-City 125'

either by an air cushion as in a hovercraft or by the repellent force of magnets under the car and in the track. Linear electrical conductors on the track and on the car propel the car along. Speeds of over 600 km/h (around 400 mph) have been reached on trials.

In Britain new high-speed railways are not considered to be worth the large amount of money they would cost. It was found that by making certain curves less sharp and banking other curves with more superelevation, several existing Inter-City main lines could take trains of normal construction at up to 200 km/h (125 mph). This has allowed the development of the High Speed Train (HST), which consists of fixed formation units of seven Mark III passenger coaches with two 2,250-h.p. diesel-electric streamlined power cars, one at each end, so that there is no locomotive shunting at terminals. In 1985 BR raised the world's speed record for diesel traction from the 227 km/h (141 mph) which it set in 1973 to 231 km/h (144 mph) on the inaugural run of the Inter-City Tees-Tyne Pullman as it ran down Stoke bank between Grantham and Peterborough, the same stretch on which *Mallard* gained the world's speed record for steam in 1938. The main feature of the Tees-Tyne Pullman run was the high average speed, for it ran the 432 km (268½ miles) between Newcastle and London in 2 hours 19 min 37 sec, an average speed for the entire journey of 185 km/h (115.4 mph) itself a world record for a diesel train. Inter-City 125 trains are now running from London

to Bristol, Penzance and South Wales, and with eight intermediate
coaches on the East Coast route between London and Scotland.
During 1982 Inter-City 125 units were also introduced to the
Bristol, Birmingham, Derby line, and to Sheffield–St Pancras
services. Inter-City 125 trains have high-power brakes and stop
in the same distance as ordinary 160 km/h (100 mph) trains.

The train originally designed for running in Britain at 240
km/h (150 mph) on existing track is known as the Advanced
Passenger Train (APT). Practically everything about it is new. The
coach bodies tilt as trains go round curves, and it has special
braking and suspension. The first experimental unit, which was
on trial for several years, was powered by gas turbines; on August
3, 1975, it raised the British rail speed record to 243 km/h (151
mph) on a test run between Reading and Didcot. This train has
finished its trials and is now in the National Railway Museum.
The first of three prototype electric APT units started trials in
1979 between London and Glasgow. The APT concept will not
now be developed any further although individual features will be
adopted. For the East Coast electrification expected to start operation by 1989 and for existing West Coast electrified lines the high
speed trains will be hauled by Class 91 electric locomotives, called
the *Electra* class, and the Mk IV coaches on the West Coast route
are likely to have tilting bodies. It is expected that these trains will

British Rail's Advanced Passenger Train with tilting bodies

run at up to 225 km/h (140 mph), and will be known as Inter-City 225.

By 1993 it is hoped that BR and French Railways will be linked by the Channel Tunnel. Early in 1986 the British and French Governments announced that they supported plans for twin rail tunnels just over 48 km (30 miles) long under the English Channel from a point near Folkestone to just south of Calais. Cars and lorries will be carried on ferry trains.

PRESERVATION

Although British Rail no longer runs daily steam locomotives on main lines, steam locomotives are by no means extinct in Britain. Over the last few years as steam engines have been withdrawn many have been sold to private owners for preservation. Some are not in working order and can be seen only as static exhibits at museums. Others, including several large express locomotives, are kept in working order ready to run on BR main line special trips.

Numerous smaller tank and tender engines can be seen running on standard gauge lines operated by preservation societies or private companies. These branches are all in private ownership and new railway companies have been formed to operate services mainly as tourist attractions. Most employ volunteer railway enthusiasts to help run and maintain the line under the guidance of a few professional engineers and other staff.

In September 1975, the new National Railway Museum was opened at York. It houses the state collection of locomotives, coaches and other relics.

PRINCIPAL LINES RUN BY PRIVATE RAILWAYS WITH STEAM LOCOMOTIVES

Standard gauge 1·435 m

Name	Location
Bluebell	Horsted Keynes–Sheffield Park
Dart Valley	{ Buckfastleigh–Totnes { Paignton–Kingswear
Keighley & Worth Valley	Keighley–Oxenhope

Name	Location
Middleton	Leeds
Severn Valley	Bridgnorth–Kidderminster
Lakeside	Windermere Lakeside–Haverthwaite
North Yorkshire Moors	Grosmont–Pickering
Kent & East Sussex	Tenterden–Bodiam
West Somerset	Minehead–Bishops Lydeard
Nene Valley	Wansford–Peterborough
North Norfolk	Sheringham–Weybourne
Gwili	Bronwydd Arms–Penybont
Mid-Hants	Alresford–Alton
Strathspey	Boat of Garten–Aviemore
Great Central	Loughborough–Rothley
Isle of Wight	Havenstreet
Llangollen	Llangollen–Berwyn
Bo'ness	Bo'ness–Kinneil
Midland Trust	Butterley–Ironville

Narrow gauge

	gauge (mm)	
Festiniog	600	Porthmadog–Blaenau Ffestiniog
Talyllyn	685	Tywyn–Nant Gwernol
Welshpool & Llanfair	762	Llanfair Caereinion–Welshpool
Ravenglass & Eskdale	381	Ravenglass–Eskdale (Dalegarth)
Romney, Hythe & Dymchurch	381	Hythe–Dungeness
Sittingbourne & Kemsley	762	Sittingbourne
Fairbourne	310	Fairbourne
Llanberis Lake	600	Llanberis
Snowdon Mountain	800	Llanberis
Bala Lake	600	Llanuwchllyn–Bala
Vale of Rheidol (BR)	600	Aberystwyth–Devils Bridge
Brecon Mountain	600	Pontsticill–Pant
Leighton Buzzard	600	Pages Park–Vandyke Road
Lincolnshire Coast	600	Humberston
Wells & Walsingham	261	Wells–Walsingham
Mull & W. Highland	261	Craignure

NOTE: Some other lines are attemping to complete arrangements to open services as this edition closed for press. There are also numerous other narrow gauge and miniature railways.

SOME BRITISH RAILWAYS FACTS AND FIGURES

Largest station area: Clapham Junction, 11·23 Ha (27¾ acres)
Largest number of platforms: Waterloo, 21
Busiest station: Clapham Junction, 2,400 trains each 24 hours
Longest platform: Colchester, 603 m (1.980 ft)

Steepest Main-line Gradients:
  Lickey Incline, 1 in 37·7 (nearly 3·2 km/2 miles)
  Exeter (St David's-Central), 1 in 31·3 (150 m/7½ chains)
  Dainton Bank (near summit), 1 in 37 (240m/12 chains)

Highest altitude: Druimuachdar, 448 m (1,484 ft) above sea-level
Longest Bridge: Tay Bridge, 3·551 km (2 miles 364 yd)
Longest Tunnel: Severn Tunnel, 7·011 km (4 miles 628 yd)

  Total number of locomotives in service (April 1985):
  Diesel, 2,467   HST power cars, 197
  Electric, 244   APT power cars, 6
  Narrow gauge steam, 3,

British Rail route open for traffic at the beginning of 1985 (the latest date
  for which figures are available): 16,737 km (10,460 miles)
Route electrified: 3,750 km (2,330 miles)
  (includes 1,964 km/1,220 miles electrified on high-voltage a.c. system;
  1,786 km/1,110 miles d.c. third rail system)
Total track length: 40,412 km/25,111 miles (including sidings)

SOME WORLD RAILWAYS FACTS AND FIGURES

The total length of the world's railway routes is over 1,207,000
km (750,000 miles), of which over 320,000 km (200,000 miles)
is in the USA.

The country with the largest single system is the USSR with
over 136,800 km (85,000 miles) of 1·524 m (5 ft) gauge
railway.

The journey between Moscow and Vladivostok, on the Trans-
Siberian Railway (nearly 9,298 km/5,778 miles, taking 7 days) is
the longest that can be taken without changing trains.

The longest stretch of perfectly straight line in the world runs
for 526 km (328 miles) across the Nullarbor Plain, Australia.

The highest railway station in Europe is 3,454 m (11,333 ft)
above sea-level, on the Jungfrau Railway in Switzerland.

The highest railway in the world is in Peru at La Cima where it reaches 4,818 m (15,806 ft) above sea-level.

Until recently the world's longest rail tunnel (other than underground systems) had been the Simplon No. 2 opened in 1921, 19·823 km (12 miles 559 yd) long, but in 1980 it was exceeded by the 22·2 km (13 miles 1,320 yd) Shimuzu Tunnel on the new Joetsu line in Japan. In 1985 boring of the Seikan Tunnel linking the Japanese islands of Honshu and Hokkaido, was completed. It is 53·9 km (33 miles 1,232 yd) long of which 23·3 km (14 miles 827 yd) is under the sea. Rail services will start running through in 1987.

The fastest trains in the world

Date	Motive power	Location	Maximum speed
3/7/1938	**Steam.** LNER A4 4–6–2 No. 4468 (now 60022) *Mallard*	Grantham–Peterborough	202·5 km/h (126 mph)
27/9/1985	**Diesel** BR Inter-City 125	Grantham–Peterborough	231 km/h (144 mph)*
26/2/1981	**Electric** SNCF (French) TGV special set 16	Courcelles–Fremoy–Dye	380 km/h (236·12 mph)

*Average speed Newcastle–Kings Cross over 432 km (268½ miles) 185 km/h (115·4 mph)

The fastest train in Britain

3/8/1975	Gas Turbine Prototype APT	Reading–Didcot	243 km/h (151 mph)

SHIPS

SAILING SHIPS

What Is a Ship?

An odd question? Well, strictly speaking the word applies only to vessels with three or more masts, all of them *square-rigged*. And a vessel is square-rigged when its main sails are square and are stretched by yards suspended by the middle at right angles to the mast. The other kind of rigging is *fore-and-aft*—that is, the sails are turned so that they run lengthwise of a ship. Look at the picture of sailing-ships: you'll see that one rigged fore-and-aft on the mizzen mast (the mast at the back) is a *barque*. Rig her fore-and-aft on the main mast, too, with only the foremast square-rigged, and she is a *barquentine*. A two-masted vessel with a square rig on both masts and a boom mainsail (you'll see what that is in the picture) is a *brig*; rig the main mast fore-and-aft, and she's a *brigantine*. A vessel rigged entirely fore-and-aft is a schooner; give her a square top sail and she's a *topsail schooner*.

Note: Despite what we've said about the strict meaning of the word 'ship', we shall use it in this section, as everyone in practice does, to mean any sea-going vessel.

SHIP'S FLAGS AND SIGNALS

The International Code

On the sea, with its traffic of ships from all parts of the world, there must be no barriers of language. The International Code enables ships to communicate with one another no matter what tongue is spoken on board.

A set of signal flags consists of 26 alphabetical flags, 10 numeral pennants (a pennant is a flag that's triangular instead of rectangular), 3 substitutes and the answering, or code, pennant.

Now, every ship at sea has signal letters assigned to it. There are four of these in every case, the first letter or first two letters indicating the nationality of the ship. (For example, British ships' signal letters begin with G or M.)

If you want to signal to a particular ship you first hoist the flags that make that ship's signal letters. If you don't do this, it will be understood that you are addressing all ships within signalling distance.

Fore-and-aft Schooner

Topsail Schooner

Brig

Brigantine

Barque

Barquentine

Cutter

Ships receiving a signal have to hoist their answering pennant *at the dip* (that is, about half-way up) when they see each flag hoisted, and *close up* (that is, as high as it will go) when they have understood it. The ship sending the message hoists its own answering pennant to show that the message is completed.

The substitutes are used to repeat a letter. If, for example, one wanted to use the letter A three times in a single group of flags, one would clearly need three complete sets of flags to do it, were it not possible to use the substitutes.

All the signal flags have special meanings when flown alone. For example:

> A—Flown by man-of-war when on full-speed trial.
> B—'I am taking on or discharging explosives.'
> G—'Pilot wanted.'
> H—'Pilot on board.'
> P—Departure flag.
> Q over L—'Infectious disease on board.'
> W—'Medical assistance required.'
> Y—'I am carrying mails.'
> N and C together—SOS.
> C—'Yes.'
> N—'No.'

Sirens

One short blast on a ship's siren means that she is directing her course to starboard, two short blasts to port, three short blasts for engines full-speed astern. In fog one long blast at intervals not longer than two minutes means a ship is under way, two long blasts that she is under way but not moving through the water.

Distress Signals

(*a*) A gun or other explosive signal fired at intervals of about a minute.

(*b*) A continuous sounding of any fog-signal apparatus.

(*c*) Rockets or shells throwing red stars fired one at a time at short intervals.

(*d*) A signal by radio or any other method consisting of the letters SOS in Morse Code.

(*e*) A signal sent by radio consisting of the spoken word 'Mayday' (from the French *m'aidez*, meaning 'help me').

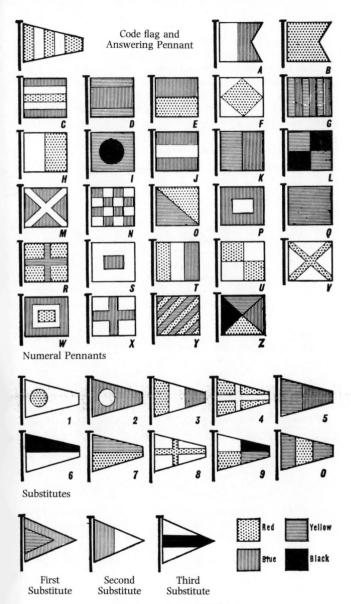

Code flag and Answering Pennant

A B C D E F G H I J K L M N O P Q R S T U V W X Y Z

Numeral Pennants

1 2 3 4 5 6 7 8 9 0

Substitutes

First Substitute

Second Substitute

Third Substitute

Red   Yellow

Blue   Black

International Code of Signals

(*f*) Hoisting of the signal flags NC in the International Code.

(*g*) A signal consisting of a square flag having above or below it a ball or anything resembling a ball.

(*h*) Flames on the ship (as from a burning tar barrel).

(*i*) A rocket parachute flare showing a red light.

The ensign hoisted upside down is generally understood as an unofficial distress signal.

MEASURES OF WIND AND WAVE

The **Beaufort Scale** for measuring the force of winds at sea is used internationally.

Scale No.	Wind force	Mph	Kph
0	Calm	1	1·6
1	Light air	1–3	1·6–4·8
2	Light breeze	4–7	6·4–11·2
3	Gentle breeze	8–12	12·8–19·2
4	Moderate breeze	13–18	20·8–28·8
5	Fresh breeze	19–24	30·4–38·4
6	Strong breeze	25–31	40·0–49·6
7	Near gale	32–38	51·2–60·8
8	Gale	39–46	62·4–73·6
9	Strong gale	47–54	75·2–86·4
10	Storm	55–63	88·0–100·8
11	Violent storm	64–72	102·4–115·2
12	Hurricane	73–82	116·8–131·2
13	Hurricane	83–92	132·8–147·2
14	Hurricane	93–103	148·8–164·8
15	Hurricane	104–114	166·4–182·4
16	Hurricane	115–125	184·0–200·0
17	Hurricane	126–136	201·6–217·6

Wave Scale

		Height of waves, crest to trough (*ft and m*)	
0	Calm		
1	Calm	$\frac{1}{4}$	0·077
2	Smooth	$\frac{1}{2}$–1	0·15–0·30
3	Smooth	2–3	0·61–0·91
4	Slight	3–5	0·91–1·50
5	Moderate	6–8	1·87–2·44
6	Rough	9–13	2·74–3·96
7	Very rough	13–19	3·96–5·79

8	High	18–25	5·49–7·62
9	Very High	23–32	7·01–9·75
10	Very High	29–41	8·84–12·50
11	Phenomenal	37–52	11·28–15·85
12	Phenomenal	45 and over	13·7 and over

Note: the highest sea in the Bay of Biscay is 8.23 m (27 ft). In mid-Atlantic the waves will sometimes top 12·19 m (40 ft).

THE WORLD'S PRINCIPAL MERCHANT FLEETS

Flag	No. of ships	Tons Gross
Liberia	1,934	62,024,700
Japan	10,425	40,358,479
Greece	2,904	35,058,593
Panama	5,499	37,244,233
USSR	7,095	24,492,469
USA	6,441	19,291,868
Norway	2,271	17,662,916
United Kingdom	2,468	15,874,062
China, People's Republic of	1,805	13,259,776
Italy	1,590	9,157,867
France	1,174	8,945,046
Spain	2,529	7,004,852
Singapore	825	6,512,344
Korea (South)	1,799	6,771,402
India	710	6,414,741
Germany, Federal Republic of	1,813	6,242,467
Brazil	706	5,721,821
Denmark	1,101	5,211,262
Netherlands	1,337	4,585,991
Saudi Arabia	422	3,863,272

NAVAL VESSELS

In general

Warships are usually painted grey. Unlike a merchant ship, a warship has no raised deck at the stern. Propulsion is usually by gas turbine, although steam turbines and diesels are still used. Nuclear-powered propulsion is now found in many classes of submarine, and also in some surface warships. It is likely that more surface warships will be nuclear-powered in the future, although it remains an expensive option: hence the very limited use, so far, in merchant ships. Armour plating at water-level and below is generally no longer used in modern warship construction, although aircraft carriers normally have armoured flight decks. Aerial and sensor arrays above the upper deck and superstructure are prone to heavy damage from missile attack, but top-weight and stability factors do not allow heavy armour in these areas. A warship's *standard displacement* is a measurement made when it is ready for sea with ammunition and stores, but omitting fuel and reserve feed water. *Load displacement* refers to the ship ready for sea with all stores, fuel and ammunition.

Cruiser. *Blake*, 1961. 172·2 m (565 ft)

ASW Carriers

These have replaced the former general-purpose warships, fast and heavily armed, called cruisers. The Royal Navy no longer has any of these: HMS *Blake* was finally paid off at the end of 1979, and her silhouette is retained as a reminder of a very important type of Royal Navy vessel. The successors to the cruisers, as far as helicopter platforms are concerned, are the Invincible Class Anti-

Submarine Warfare (ASW) Carriers. There are three of this new class, *Invincible*, *Illustrious* and *Ark Royal*: they carry Sea Harrier VSTOL fixed-wing multi-purpose aircraft as well as Sea King ASW helicopters. The main armament is the Seadart anti-air/anti-surface missile. These ships form the centre-piece of the Royal Navy's future task groups and have the command facilities to exercise control over wide areas above, below and on the surface of the sea.

The Destroyer

A smaller warship, though now the same tonnage as Second World War light cruisers. Can be used for general purposes, but their primary role is anti-missile defence of major units or formations. Destroyers are organised in flotillas, the leader having a black band round the top of the forward funnel. The Royal Navy has some 15 guided missile destroyers (standard displacement, 5,000 tonnes: 158·5 m (520 ft) long: speed, 32 knots: armed with two 4·5-in guns and guided missile launchers, and equipped with a Wessex anti-submarine helicopter). This total includes the one Type 82 destroyer, *Bristol*, the largest destroyer in the Fleet. The latest class is the Type 42, gradually replacing the County class although two of these remain with the Fleet. Type 42 armament is the Seadart missile, but it also carries a Lynx helicopter, Seacast close-defence missiles, and 4·5-in automatic gun and anti-submarine torpedoes.

Frigate. Type 21

The Frigate

Again, a general purpose ship but with a major anti-submarine role. The latest is the Broadsword class (Type 22), all-missile ship, which carries Exocet and Sea Wolf weapon systems and is capable of carrying two Lynx anti-ship and anti-submarine helicopters.

Destroyer. Type 42

(The helicopter has become a major feature in the weapons systems of most modern warships.) There are seven of these. Other modern frigates are from the Type 21 and Leander classes. The Royal Navy has some 39 frigates in the Operational Fleet or engaged in trials and training. A new type of frigate, the Type 23, is to be ordered for the Royal Navy.

Escort vessels

Modern destroyers and frigates are often discussed as escort vessels. Although they can and do operate independently on patrol and in a variety of peacetime roles, their organisation is in the form of mixed flotillas: which enables them, with their complexity of weapon systems and sensors, to afford protection to groups of other ships, whether they be amphibious groups, hunter-killer groups or merchant convoys. They are well prepared for defensive and offensive operations.

Submarine. *Dreadnought*, nuclear propelled. 266 ft

The Submarine

There are three main parts to a submarine. The *pressure hull*, inside which the crew lives and works, is circular in section to balance-out the enormous pressures exerted on the submarine when dived—four 'atmospheres' (4×15 p.s.i.) for every 100 feet of depth. The *casing* is for streamlining and to give the crew something to walk on when the submarine is surfaced. The fin ('sail' in the US Navy) houses the upper sections of five or more retractable masts (e.g. periscopes) and provides a raised platform as a bridge and look-out position.

There are three main types of submarine. The *ballistic-missile* submarine (SSBN) acts as an underwater launching platform extremely difficult to locate and destroy, and is nuclear-reactor-powered; the missiles are usually armed with nuclear warheads. There are two types of *hunter-attack* submarines built to seek out and, if necessary, sink enemy surface ships and other submerged submarines; *Fleet* submarines (SSNs) which are nuclear-reactor-powered, and *Patrol* or *Conventional* submarines (SSKs) which have diesel-electric propulsion. Only the Royal Navy and the US, French and Russian navies have nuclear submarines. The Royal Navy has four SSBNs, the *Resolution*-class (8,500 tons, crew 147) armed with Polaris missiles (to be replaced by Trident in the late 1990s), 14 SSNs and 15 SSKs. The very first SSN was *H.M.S. Dreadnought*, followed by *Valiant, Churchill, Swiftsure* and *Trafalgar* classes—all approximately 3,500 tons, crew 100–120. Many other countries have SSKs. The normal submarine weapon is the torpedo. Some modern types (such as the British *Tigerfish*) have advanced guidance systems. An even newer anti-ship missile is coming into common use: the Royal Navy version is called *Sub-Harpoon*. Fired like a torpedo while submerged, the weapon travels up to the surface, where wings unfold and it flies at its target over long ranges at rocket-powered speed. Nuclear-reactor-powered submarines can remain submerged for many weeks without surfacing, travelling at underwater speeds of 25 knots or more if required. Their undetectability is based not only on 'invisibility', but also on operating as silently as possible so that anti-submarine forces fail to locate them with noise-seeking sonar. Nuclear-powered hunter-attack submarines have been recognised for some years as the capital ships of modern sea-power: even a suspicion that an enemy SSN is in his vicinity can cause the commander of a powerful group of surface warships, including aircraft carriers, to go to the defensive and possibly withdraw. The SSN is also the best weapon for detecting and destroying hostile submarines.

Resolution class Polaris submarine (*SSBN*)

Swiftsure class Fleet submarine (SSN)

Oberon class conventional patrol submarine (SSK)

Other ships in the Operational Fleet include the Royal Navy's two
assault ships, *Fearless* and *Intrepid*, which can carry an Army
battalion and a brigade group HQ, landing craft capable of
carrying heavy tanks, and RAF as well as RN helicopters. There
are also 1 anti-submarine/commando carrier, 1 ice patrol ship
and 45 ships which constitute the Mine Counter-measure Force,
and are divided between minehunters and minesweepers. There
are a number of offshore patrol vessels and 24 support and auxiliary vessels supplying fuel and stores to the Fleet at sea. There
are also some 19 patrol vessels of various kinds, training ships,
numerous vessels for survey purposes, a number of ships in reserve
as support ships, and some 700 vessels forming the Royal Maritime Auxiliary Service.

There are also numerous mooring, salvage and boom vessels, 2
seaward defence boats, 2 fleet maintenance ships, 1 submarine
depot ship, 1 royal yacht/hospital ship, 84 fleet and some support
and auxiliary vessels, ranging from minesweeper support to fleet
replenishment tankers.

Sailing vessel under way

Steam vessel, less than 150 ft (45·75 m) long, under way

Sailing vessel or steam vessel under 150 ft (45·75 m) long, at anchor

Vessel over 150 ft (45·75 m) long, at anchor

Steam vessel, over 150 ft (45·75 m) under way

Lights at sea:
G—Green
R—Red
W—White

Small pulling boat under way

A vessel not under command

Vessel towing another

NAUTICAL TERMS

abaft, behind.

abeam, opposite the centre of the ship's side.

admiral, from the Arabic *Amir-al-Bahr*, Commander of the Seas.

aft, towards the stern.

alee, away from the wind; to put the helm over to the lee side of the boat.

avast, hold fast, stop; from the Italian *basta*, enough.

ballast, weight put in a ship or boat to help keep her stable; nowadays, usually sea-water.

batten down, to fix tarpaulins to the hatches with iron battens and wedges.

beam, the width of a ship at her widest part.

belay, to make a rope fast to a cleat or belaying pin.

bells, are struck to give the time every half-hour, starting anew at each change of watch. 12.30 is one bell; 1, two bells; 1.30, three bells; and so on until 4, which is eight bells; then the pattern is repeated from 4.30, one bell, to 8, eight bells; 8.30 being one bell again, and 12 noon and midnight, eight bells.

bilge, the broadest part of a ship's bottom.

binnacle, the case in which the compass is housed.

boom, a spar for stretching the foot of a sail; any long spar or piece of timber.

bow, the front or forepart of a ship.

bowsprit, a spar projecting from the bow.

bulkhead, a partition dividing a cabin or hold.

bulwark, a ledge round the deck to prevent things falling or being washed overboard.

cable, a sea measure of 100 fathoms: 182·88 m or 600 ft.

cleat, a piece of wood or metal fastened on parts of a ship, and having holes or recesses for fastening ropes.

coaming, the rim of a hatchway, raised to prevent water from entering.

companion, a wooden hood over a hatch.

companion-ladder, steps leading down to a cabin.

coxswain, a petty officer in charge of a boat and crew (a 'cock' was a small rowing boat).

davits, iron fittings that project over a ship's side for hoisting a boat.

Davy Jones' locker, the bottom of the sea. There are three possible explanations for this term:

 1. Davy Jones was a noted pirate, given to putting his victims over the side.
 2. In Negro language 'duffy' or 'davy' is a ghost, and 'Jones' means 'Jonah'.
 3. The Hindu goddess of death is called Deva Lokka.

deadlights, a storm-shutter for a cabin window.

displacement, the quantity of water displaced by a boat afloat.

dog watch, a division of the usual four hour's watch, to make a change of watches; from 4 to 6 and 6 to 8 p.m.

draught, the depth to which a ship sinks in the water.

fathom, a nautical measure of 1·8288 m or 6 ft.

fender, a buffer made of bundles of rope, cork or other material, to prevent a ship from scraping against a pier when moored.

fid, a wooden tool used for separating the strands of a hemp or nylon fibre rope in splicing.

first watch, 8 p.m. till midnight.

flukes, the part of an anchor that hooks into the sea bed.

fore-and-aft, lengthwise of a ship.

forecastle (fo'c'sle), the forepart of the ship under the maindeck, the crew's quarters. The term is a survival from the old days when high wooden castles were built on each end of a fighting ship. The *aftercastle* is a term no longer used, but it is interesting to note that the cleaning gear for the after parts of ships in the Royal Navy is still stamped AX, the old sign for 'aftercastle'.

galley, a ship's kitchen.

grapnel, a small anchor with several claws or arms.

halyards, ropes by which sails are hoisted.

hatch, the cover for a hatchway.

hatchway, the opening in a ship's deck into the hold, or from one deck to another.

hawse, the bows or forward end of a ship.

hawser, a small cable; a large rope.

Jacob's ladder, a ladder with rope sides and wooden treads.

knot, one nautical mile per hour.

lanyard, a short rope used for fastening or stretching.

larboard, the port side: the term was officially banned in 1844, and 'port' substituted, to avoid confusion with 'starboard'.

lee, the sheltered side of a ship.

leeway, the distance a ship is driven to leeward of her true course.

marline spike, an iron tool used for separating the strands of a rope in splicing.

middle watch, from midnight till 4 a.m.

nautical, or sea-mile, one-sixtieth of a degree measured at the equator; 1,853·18 m or 6,080 ft.

offing, to seawards; towards the horizon.

The line and the circle are the original Plimsoll Mark. The top line is the Deck Line. TF = Tropical Fresh Water. F = Fresh Water. TS = Tropical Summer. S = Summer. W = Winter. WNA = Winter North Atlantic. LR = Lloyd's Register. The figures show the amount of water the ship is drawing. They are 15·24 cm (6 in) high and the bottom of the figure represents the foot.

Plimsoll line, a line 45.72 cm (18 in) long running through a ring painted on both sides of a merchant ship. A ship may be safely loaded until this line is awash. It is named after Samuel Plimsoll, who was responsible for bringing it into use.

poop, the raised after-part of a ship.

port, the left side of a ship looking forward.

quarter, a ship's sides near the stern.

quarter-deck, the after end of the upper deck.

ratlines, the rope steps placed across the shrouds to enable sailors to go aloft.

scuppers, holes in a ship's sides for draining water from the decks.

shrouds, very strong wire ropes which support the masts on both sides.

splicing, joining two ropes by weaving together the untwisted strands.

starboard, the right side of a ship looking forward.

stay, a rope supporting the mast or a spar.

stern, the rear end of a ship.

superstructure, the parts of a ship built above the upper deck.

taffrail, the rail on the counter, or projecting stern, of a ship.

tonnage: The gross and net tonnage of a ship are measures of space, not of weight. Gross tonnage is the number of tons enclosed in a ship, 100 cu. ft counting as 1 ton or 1,016 kg. Net tonnage is the amount of space devoted to passengers and cargo. Deadweight tonnage is the number of tons weight that a ship can carry.

1 tonne = 1,000 kg.

topside (or **freeboard**), the part of a ship that is out of the water.

trick, a turn or spell of duty at sea. A trick at the wheel or as look-out lasts for two hours.

truck, the circular cap at the top of a mast.

waist, amidships.

warp, to haul a ship into position with a hawser.

watches, divisions of a ship's crew into two or three sections, one set having charge of the vessel while the others rest. Day and night are divided into watches of four hours each, except the period of 4 p.m. to 8 p.m., which is divided into two dog-watches of two hours each. Men not included in the watches are known as 'Daymen'.

weather side, the side of a ship on which the wind is blowing.

weigh, to heave up the anchor.

yawing, the swinging of a ship's head, first in one direction and then in another, due to bad steering or to a high sea.

NAUTICAL MEASURES

1 nautical mile = 6,080 ft = 1,853.18 m

1 knot = 1 nautical mile per hour = 1·151 mph = 1·853 km/h

THE ENGLISH LANGUAGE

SOME OF THE TECHNICAL TERMS OF LANGUAGE

These are a few of the terms you will meet, and need, when you are thinking or talking about language. It is largely for the sake of those of you who are studying foreign and classical languages that we have included terms like *inflexion*, *gender* and *case*. They are now of little concern to the ordinary user of English; and for this we have to thank William the Conqueror. He brought with him to England not only his capacity for castle-building and strong government but also the French language. This became the official language of England for nearly 300 years. The result was that English for that period escaped from the hands of writers and teachers, who tend to fix a language in all its formality, and passed into the care of the ordinary people, who, by the time it got back into official use, had gaily lopped off nearly all the difficult word-endings, inflexions and marks of gender and case.

affix, a syllable, not a word in itself, which can be added to an existing word in order to change its meaning. See PREFIX and SUFFIX.

alliteration, the use in a phrase or sentence of words that begin with, or contain, the same letter or sound: e.g.

> Lord Lundy from his earliest years
> Was far too freely moved to tears.

anagram, a re-arrangement of the letters of a word or phrase which produces another word or phrase: e.g. 'Florence Nightingale' becomes, 'Flit on, cheering angel'.

antecedent, a word which determines the form of another word coming later in the sentence: e.g. in 'Few boys would say that they enjoy washing behind their ears', *boys* is the antecedent of the pronoun *they*, which therefore must be in the plural.

antithesis, words arranged to stress a contrast: e.g. 'To err is human, to forgive divine.'

antonym, a word whose meaning is directly opposite to that of another word: e.g. *light* and *dark*, *large* and *small*, *clean* and *dirty*.

apposition, a second description of a person or thing placed side by side with the first, the second having grammatically the same value as the first: e.g. 'Jones, *captain of Wales*, scored the final try.'

auxiliary verb, a verb that has no meaning itself but helps to make the meaning of another verb: e.g. *will* in 'I will go', *do* in 'I do see what you mean'.

case, the grammatical function of a noun or pronoun: i.e. whether it is subject, object, genitive, etc. Case has almost vanished from the English language, but it is worth remembering that the *subject* is said to be *nominative*; the *object*, *accusative*; the *indirect object*, *dative*; and the *apostrophe form* of the word (Jean's, Jim's), *genitive*.

clause, a group of words containing subject and predicate but not expressing a complete idea: e.g. 'A marshal *who can rid the town of rustlers*—that's what we want.'

complement, a noun or adjective forming the predicate of a verb that cannot govern a direct object: e.g. 'He is *silly*', 'He became *captain*.'

conjugation, the inflexion (*q.v.*) of verbs.

declension, the inflexion (*q.v.*) of nouns or adjectives.

diaresis, the pronouncing of two successive vowels as separate sounds, often marked by the sign (¨) over the second: e.g. Chloë, aërated.

epigram, a short poem, especially one with a witty twist in it; any sharp, memorable saying.

epithet, an adjective.

etymology, the study of the origin of words.

euphemism, disguising a nasty fact with a nice name: e.g. saying 'he is putting on weight' when you mean 'he's getting fat'.

gender, the distinction of nouns according to sex. (As far as their own language is concerned, lucky Englishmen hardly have to bother about this.)

gerund, a noun formed from a verb by adding *-ing*: e.g. '*Walking* is good for you', '*Parking* is forbidden.'

homonym, a word that looks the same as another word but has a different meaning: e.g. *bear*, meaning 'carry' and 'a shaggy animal'; *peer*, meaning 'a lord' and 'peep'.

hyperbole, use of exaggerated terms for emphasis, as in 'a thousand thanks', 'he's got tons of money'.

indirect object, the person or the thing towards whom an action is directed: e.g. 'I gave *him* a penny.'

inflexion, the change made in the form of words to show what grammatical part they play in a sentence: e.g. *him* is formed by inflexion from *he*.

litotes, deliberate understatement for effect: e.g. saying *not a few* when you mean *a great many*.

malapropism, named after Mrs Malaprop in Sheridan's play, *The Rivals*. 'She's as headstrong as an *allegory* on the banks of the Nile,' said Mrs Malaprop, meaning *alligator*. That is a mala-propism: an attempt to use a difficult word and getting it wrong.

meiosis, general understatement—the opposite of hyperbole: e.g. 'Golly, this is *some* game' (meaning it's a terrific game), 'I *didn't half* enjoy it' (meaning you enjoyed it immensely).

metaphor, a telescoped simile (*q.v.*)—instead of saying something is like something else, you say it *is* that other thing. E.g. not 'Sir Jasper is like a fox', but 'Sir Jasper is a fox'. Language is full of metaphors: the *spine* of a book, a *blind* alley, saw-*teeth*, etc.

metonymy, naming something not by its own name, but by something closely associated with it: e.g. 'The Crown' for 'the Government'.

mixed metaphor, using together metaphors that don't match, with ridiculous results: e.g. 'Well, he's a dark horse, and he can paddle his own canoe.'

onomatopœia, the forming of a word so that it resembles the sound of the thing of which it is the name: e.g. *click, cuckoo, babble*.

oratio obliqua, indirect or reported speech: e.g. a friend says 'I am grateful' and you report this as: 'He said he was grateful.'

oxymoron, using together in one expression words that are contradictory: e.g. *bitter-sweet*, or 'he was a *happy pessimist*'.

palindrome, a word or sentence that reads the same backwards or forwards: e.g. 'Madam, I'm Adam.'

periphrasis, presenting an idea in a roundabout, wordy way.

phrase, any group of words, usually without a predicate.

predicate, the part of a sentence that tells you about, or describes, the subject.

prefix, an affix attached to the beginning of words: e.g. *dis-, un-, in-* in the words 'disappeared', 'uninterested', 'invaluable'.

prosody, the technique of verse—its rhyme, metre, etc.

pun, a play on words, different in meaning but the same in sound, so as to produce an amusing effect: e.g. Tom Hood's

> A cannon-ball took off his legs,
> So he laid down his arms.

(*Note*: A pun can be used seriously; there are several examples in Shakespeare.)

rhetorical question, a question that isn't asked in order to obtain an answer, but as a striking way of suggesting that the answer is obvious: e.g. 'Did you ever see such a rotten bowler as Smith?'

simile, likening one thing to another: e.g. 'The ice was like iron', 'He ran like the wind.'

spoonerism, getting the initial letters of words mixed up: e.g. the statement of the famous Dr Spooner (after whom this error was named) that an undergraduate had 'hissed all his mystery lectures'.

split infinitive, putting a word between the parts of the infinitive: e.g. 'to quickly run', 'to suddenly fall down'. A safe rule is to avoid it if it sounds clumsy, but not if it is the sharpest and neatest way of saying what you want to say.

suffix, an affix attached to the end of a word: e.g. *-ness*, *-ship*, *-able* in the words 'thinness', 'scholarship', 'bearable'.

syllepsis, e.g. 'He was kicking the football with determination and his left foot', 'She lost her spectacles and her temper'.

synecdoche, naming a part when you mean the whole: e.g. 'a fleet of a hundred sail' (meaning ships).

synonyms, words that are much the same in meaning and use: e.g. beautiful, handsome, good-looking; breakable, fragile, frail.

syntax, the part of grammar that deals with the way words are arranged in sentences.

tautology, unnecessary repetition: e.g. 'I have been *all alone by myself* for hours.'

AN EMERGENCY GUIDE TO PUNCTUATION

If you want to feel in a really dangerous, exposed position, sit down to write a simple, brief guide to punctuation—knowing that

H. G. Fowler, in his *Modern English Usage*, devoted 1,000 worried words to the comma alone, and that punctuation is always to some extent an individual matter. However, this section, as warily as possible, sets down such rules as it is safe to pass on. It is meant as a simple, rough-and-ready guide for emergencies.

Remember: punctuation is only a way of helping your reader to understand the sense of what you write. In speech you make your meaning clear by your pauses and by the way your voice rises and falls (e.g. the listener knows when you're asking a question from the way your voice rises at the end of the sentence). Punctuation is simply a collection of devices for getting these pauses and these rises and falls of voice on to paper. (E.g. your rising voice at the end of a question is suggested by the question-mark.)

A. To mark where a sentence ends we use one of three stops:

(i) a **full stop** (.) where the sentence is a statement;
(ii) a **question mark** (?) where the sentence asks a question;
(iii) an **exclamation mark** (!) where the sentence is an exclamation.

B. The **comma** (,) is the stop that stands for the little pauses after single words or groups of words. Read the following sentence aloud (it comes from *Huckleberry Finn*) and note how the commas mark the pauses and the ups and downs of your voice:

We went to a clump of bushes, and Tom made everybody swear to keep the secret, and then showed them a hole in the hill, right in the thickest part of the bushes.

Warning. Alas, it's not always as easy as this. If you've got tangled up in one of the comma's trickier uses, try pp. 96–99 in Eric Partridge's *You Have a Point There*.

C. A more definite pause in the sentence is marked by a **semicolon** (;). For example, you might write:

There was no football this afternoon; the weather was far too wet.

You could say there are two sentences here; but (as has happened in the sentence you're now reading) the sense of each is so closely connected with the sense of the other that they gain from not being separated completely.

D. The **colon** (:) is generally used before a list of things or a quotation. E.g.

> *He told us what he had brought with him: a penknife, a fishing-rod, his lunch and half a pound of worms.*

or

> *Shakespeare wrote: 'To be or not to be, that is the question.'*

But *be warned*: some writers like to use the colon (as we have done in this sentence) where others would use a semi-colon.

E. **Inverted commas** or **quotation marks** (" ") are used (i) to mark off the actual words of a speaker where it is *those actual words* that you are writing down, e.g.

> *"Oh Lord," groaned the reader, "punctuation does seem difficult."*

or (ii) to mark off a quotation that comes inside a sentence: e.g.

> *When he got to "See how they run" he made little running movements with his fingers.*

Note: punctuation marks that don't belong to the quotation come outside the quotation marks. E.g.

> *Did I hear you recite "There was an old man of Kilkenny"?* (not *"There was an old man of Kilkenny?"*).

Warning: There are two kinds of inverted commas, (" ") and (' '). It doesn't matter which you use; but note the following:

> *Tom said, "Did I hear you recite 'There was an old man of Kilkenny'?"*

Where—as here—there's a quotation inside a quotation, use your chosen mark for the main quotation and the other mark for the quotation inside it.

F. **Dashes** (—) or **brackets** () are used to enclose things that are really said *aside*—in other words, they don't belong to the main structure of the sentence. If I say:

> *He's a good boy and—as I was saying to his mother yesterday—his work has been excellent,*

my main sentence is *He's a good boy and his work has been excellent.*

As I was saying to his mother yesterday is said aside, and goes either between dashes or between brackets.

G. The **apostrophe** (') is not so difficult as some people make it (we knew a desperate little boy who'd grasped only that it often accompanies the letter 's', and so put it in front of every letter 's' he wrote, even in the middle of a word). There are two main uses of the apostrophe:

   (i) to show possession: *George's book, Mr Davis's Jaguar*;
   (ii) to mark a missing letter: e.g. *don't (do not), it's (it is)*. (Of course, in *shan't* the apostrophe marks several missing letters. In the eighteenth century it was written *sha'n't*.)

H. An important use of the **hyphen** (-) is to join words where failing to join them would falsify one's meaning. E.g. a *gold nibbed pen* is a pen made of gold with a nib in it; a *gold-nibbed pen* is a pen (of whatever material) that has a gold nib.

Further Reading

You Have a Point There, by Eric Partridge (Hamish Hamilton)
Mind Your Language! by Ivor Brown (Bodley Head)
Words! Words! Words! by Andrew Scotland (Cassell)
Modern English Usage, by H. G. Fowler (Oxford)
Roget's Thesaurus of English Words and Phrases (Penguin) is a very useful book (as well as an entertaining one) for the situation where you want to find a synonym (see L4). As an example, you want another word for 'beautiful': you look it up in the index, are directed to a numbered section, and there find: 'Beautiful, beauteous, handsome, fine, pretty, lovely, graceful, elegant, delicate, refined, fair, personable, comely, seemly, bonny . . .'

A DICTIONARY OF FOREIGN PHRASES AND CLASSICAL QUOTATIONS

It may seem odd to have a collection of words and phrases from other tongues in the middle of a section on THE ENGLISH LANGUAGE. But, rich though our own language is, we still find that certain things have been expressed most strikingly by the old Greeks or

Romans or by modern Frenchmen. In some cases it is not simply that other nations have found a better way of saying something, but that there is a sort of historical flavour about a phrase that disappears if it is translated into English. 'Life is short, art is long' is somehow not quite the same thing as 'Vita brevis, ars longa'. Here, anyway, is a list of such phrases as are still in general use.

Abbreviations: Fr., French; Gr., Greek; Ger., German; It., Italian; L. Latin; Sp. Spanish.

à bas (Fr.), down, down with

ab extra (L.), from without

ab initio (L.), from the beginning

à bon marché (Fr.), good bargain, cheap

ab ovo (L.), from the egg

absit omen (L.), may there be no ill omen

ab uno disce omnes (L.), from one example you may judge the rest

ab urbe condita (L.), from the founding of the city: i.e. Rome, 753 B.C.

à cheval (Fr.), on horseback

à compte (Fr.), on account; in part payment

ad astra (L.), to the stars

ad Calendas Graecas (L.), at the Greek Calends—i.e. never, since the Greek had no Calends

à demi (Fr.), by halves, half

a Deo et rege (L.), from God and the king

à deux (Fr.), of two, between two, two-handed

ad finem (L.), to the end, towards the end

ad hoc (L.), for this purpose

ad hominem (L.), to the man, personal

a die (L.), from that day

ad infinitum (L.), to infinity

ad libitum (L.), at pleasure

ad majorem Dei gloriam (L.), for the greater glory of God

ad nauseam (L.), to the point where one becomes disgusted

ad rem (L.), to the point

ad valorem (L.), according to value

advocatus diaboli (L.), devil's advocate

aetatis suae (L.), of his (or her) age

affaire de coeur (Fr.), an affair of the heart

affaire d'honneur (Fr.), an affair of honour
a fortiori (L.), with stronger reason
à haute voix (Fr.), aloud
à jamais (Fr.), for ever
à la bonne heure (Fr.), in good time; all right; as you please
à la mode (Fr.), in fashion
à la mort (Fr.), to the death
al fresco (It.), in the open air
allez vous en! (Fr.), away with you!
alma mater (L.), benign mother—applied by old students to their
  university
alter ego (L.), one's second self
à merveille (Fr.), wonderfully
à moitié (Fr.), half, by halves
amor vincit omnia (L.), love conquers all
ancien régime (Fr.), the old order of things
anno Domini (L.), in the year of our Lord
anno mundi (L.), in the year of the world
annus mirabilis (L.), year of wonders
ante bellum (L.), before the war
ante meridiem (L.), before noon
à outrance (Fr.), to the bitter end
à pied (Fr.), on foot
à propos de bottes (Fr.), apropos of boots—i.e. beside the point
à propos de rien (Fr.), apropos of nothing
aqua vitae (L.), water of life
à quoi bon? (Fr.), what's the good of it?
arrière pensée (Fr.), a mental reservation
ars est celare artem (L.), true art is to conceal art
ars longa, vita brevis (L.), art is long, life is short
à tout prix (Fr.), at any price
au contraire (Fr.), on the contrary
au courant (Fr.), fully acquainted with
audi alterem partem (L.), hear the other side
au fait (Fr.), well acquainted with; expert
au fond (Fr.), at bottom
au grand sérieux (Fr.), in all seriousness
au naturel (Fr.), in the natural state
au pied de la lettre (Fr.), close to the letter; quite literally
au revoir (Fr.), goodbye; till we meet again

autres temps, autres moeurs (Fr.), other times, other manners
aux armes! (Fr.), to arms!
ave atque vale (L.), hail and farewell
à volonté (Fr.), at pleasure
basta! (It.), enough!
beau monde (Fr.), the world of fashion
bête noire (Fr.), a bugbear; your favourite hate
bien entendu (Fr.), of course; to be sure
bis (L.), twice; encore
bon diable (Fr.), good-natured fellow
bon goût (Fr.), good taste
bona fides (L.), good faith
bon mot (Fr.), a witty saying
bonne bouche (L.), a tasty morsel
bon ton (Fr.), the height of fashion
bon vivant (Fr.), one who lives well
bon voyage! (Fr.), a good journey to you!
caput (Ger.), utterly beaten, done for
carpe diem (L.), enjoy the present day
casus belli (L.), that which causes or justifies war
cause célèbre (Fr.), a notable trial
caveat emptor (L.), let the buyer beware
cave canem (L.), beware of the dog
cela va sans dire (Fr.), that goes without saying
c'est-à-dire (Fr.), that is to say
ceteris paribus (L.), other things being equal
chacun son goût (Fr.), every one to his taste
cherchez la femme! (Fr.), look for the woman; there's a woman at
    the bottom of it!
çi-devant (Fr.), before this; former
comme il faut (Fr.), as it should be; correct
compos mentis (L.), of sound mind; sane
compte rendu (Fr.), an account rendered; a report
coram populo (L.), in the presence of the public
cordon sanitaire (Fr.), a line of guards posted to keep contagious
    disease within a certain area
corpus delicti (L.), the substance of the crime or offence
coup d'état (Fr.), a sudden decisive blow in politics
coûte que coûte (Fr.), cost what it may
crême de la crême (Fr.), cream of the cream; the very best

cui bono? (L.), to whose advantage is it? who is the gainer?

cum grano salis (L.), with a grain of salt

de bonne grace (Fr.), with good grace; willingly

de facto (L.), from the fact; actual or actually

de gustibus non est disputandum (L.), there is no arguing about tastes

de haut en bas (Fr.), from top to bottom

dei gratia (L.), by the grace of God

de jure (L.), in law; by right

de mal en pis (Fr.), from bad to worse

de minimis non curat lex (L.), the law does not concern itself with very small matters

de mortuis nil nisi bonum (L.), speak nothing but good of the dead

de novo (L.), anew

deo volente (L.), God willing

de pis en pis (Fr.), worse and worse

de profundis (L.), out of the depths

de rigueur (Fr.), compulsory; indispensable

desunt cetera (L.), the rest is missing

de trop (Fr.), too much, or too many; superfluous

deus ex machina (L.), a god out of the machine; one who puts things right at a critical moment

dies irae (L.), day of wrath; the day of judgement

Dieu et mon droit (Fr.), God and my right

dolce far niente (It.), sweet-doing-nothing; pleasant idleness

Domine dirige nos! (L.), Lord, direct us!

Dominus illuminatio mea (L.), the Lord is my enlightening

double entendre (Fr.), a double meaning; a play on words

dramatis personae (L.), characters of the play

ecce! (L.), behold!

eheu fugaces ... labuntur anni (L.), alas! the fleeting years slip away!

ejusdem generis (L.), of the same kind

embarras de richesses (Fr.), an embarrassment of riches

en avant! (Fr.), forward!

en déshabillé (Fr.), in undress

en famille (Fr.), with one's family

enfant terrible (Fr.), a terrible child; a little terror

en fête (Fr.), festive; keeping holiday

en masse (Fr.), in a body; all together

en passant (Fr.), in passing; by the way

en plein jour (Fr.), in broad day

en rapport (Fr.), in agreement; in sympathy with

en règle (Fr.), in order; according to rules

en route (Fr.), on the way

entente cordiale (Fr.), cordial understanding

en tout cas (Fr.), in any case, at all events

en train (Fr.), in progress

entre nous (Fr.), between ourselves

e pluribus unum (L.), one out of many

errare est humanum (L.), to err is human

esprit de corps (Fr.), the animating spirit of a collective body, such as a regiment, school, etc.

et tu, Brute! (L.), and you, too, Brutus! (said to be Julius Caesar's last words)

Eureka! (Gr.), I have found it!

ex cathedra (L.), from the chair of office

ex curia (L.), out of court

exempli gratia (L.), by way of example

ex gratia (L.), as an act of grace

ex libris (L.), from the books

ex officio (L.), by virtue of his office

experientia docet (L.), experience teaches

experto crede (L.), trust one who has tried

ex post facto (L.), after the deed is done; retrospective

façon de parler (Fr.), way of speaking

fait accompli (Fr.), a thing already done

far niente (It.), doing nothing

faute de mieux (Fr.), for want of better

faux pas (Fr.), a false step; a slip in behaviour

favete linguis (L.), favour me with your tongues, i.e. be silent

felo de se (L.), a suicide

festina lente (L.), hurry slowly

fiat justitia, ruat coelum (L.), let justice be done, though the heavens fall

fiat lux (L.), let there be light

fidei defensor (L.), defender of the faith

flagrante delicto (L.), in the very act

floreat (L.), let it flourish!

fons et origo (L.), the source and origin

force majeure (Fr.), superior power; a force one cannot resist

fortiter in re, suaviter in modo (L.), forcibly in deed, gently in manner

gaudeamus igitur (L.), so let us rejoice!

gloria in excelsis (L.), glory to God in the highest

hic et ubique (L.), here and everywhere

hic jacet (L.), here lies

hinc illae lacrimae (L.), hence (come) those tears

hoc genus omne (L.), and all that sort (of people)

hoi polloi (Gr.), the many; the rabble

homme d'affaires (Fr.), a man of business

homme du monde (Fr.), a man of the world

honi soit qui mal y pense (Fr.), evil to him who evil thinks

honoris causa (L.), for the sake of honour; honorary

hors de combat (Fr.), unfit to fight

hors concours (Fr.), outside the competition

ich dien (Ger.), I serve

idée fixe (Fr.), a fixed idea

idem (L.), the same

id est (L.), that is

in camera (L.), in a (judge's private) room; in secret

index expurgatorius (L.), a list of forbidden books

in excelsis (L.), in the highest

in extenso (L.), at full length

in extremis (L.), at the point of death

infra dignitatem (L.), below one's dignity

in medias res (L.), in the midst of things

in memoriam (L.), in memory; to the memory of

in re (L.), in the matter of

in situ (L.), in its original position

in statu pupillari (L.), in the state of being a ward

integer vitae (L.), blameless of life

inter alia (L.), among other things

in toto (L.), entirely

in vino veritas (L.), there is truth in wine; truth is told by him who has drunk wine

ipse dixit (L.), he himself said it

ipsissima verba (L.), the very words

ipso facto (L.), in the fact itself; by this very fact

je ne sais quoi (Fr.), I know not what

laborare est orare (L.), work is prayer

lapsus linguae (L.), a slip of the tongue

lares et penates (L.), household gods

laudator temporis acti (L.), one who praises past times

laus Deo (L.), praise to God

lèse-majesté (Fr.), high treason

lettre de cachet (Fr.), a sealed letter; a royal warrant for arrest or imprisonment

lex talionis (L.), the law of retaliation

locum tenens (L.), a deputy

magnum opus (L.), a great work

male fide (L.), with bad faith; treacherously

mal à propos (Fr.), ill-timed

mariage de convenance (Fr.), marriage for advantage rather than love

mauvaise honte (Fr.), false modesty

mauvais sujet (Fr.), a worthless fellow

mea culpa (L.), by my own fault

memento mori (L.), remember that you must die

mens sana in corpore sano (L.), a sound mind in a sound body

meo periculo (L.), at my own risk

meum et tuum (L.), mine and thine

modus operandi (L.), plan of working

modus vivendi (L.), a way of living

mot juste (Fr.), exactly the right word

multum in parvo (L.), much in little

mutatis mutandis (L.), with necessary changes

nemo me impune lacessit (L.), no one hurts me with impunity

ne plus ultra (L.), nothing further; perfection

nil admirari (L.), to admire nothing, to be superior and self-satisfied

nil desperandum (L.), never despair

noblesse oblige (Fr.), rank imposes obligations; much is expected from people in high positions

nolens volens (L.), whether he will or not

noli me tangere (L.), don't touch me

nolle prosequi (L.), to be unwilling to prosecute

nom de guerre (Fr.), an assumed name

nom de plume (Fr.), a pen name

non compos mentis (L.), not of sound mind

nosce teipsum (L.), know thyself

nota bene (L.), mark well

nouveaux riches (Fr.), persons who have only recently become rich; upstarts

nulli secundus (L.), second to none

obiit (L.), he, or she, died

obiter dictum (L.), a thing said by the way

ora pro nobis (L.), pray for us

O sancta simplicitas! (L.), O sacred simplicity!

O! si sic omnia! (L.), Oh, would that all (had been done or said) thus!

O tempora! O mores! (L.), O the times! O the manners!

pace (L.), by leave of

panem et circenses (L.), (give us) bread and circuses! (the cry of the Roman populace)

par excellence (Fr.), eminently, by way of ideal

par exemple (Fr.), for example

pari passu (L.), with equal pace; together

peccavi (L.), I have sinned

pièce de résistance (Fr.), the best item

pied-à-terre (Fr.), temporary lodging

pinxit (L.), (he) painted (this)

pis aller (Fr.), the last or worst shift

poste restante (Fr.), to remain in the Post Office till called for

post hoc, propter hoc (L.), after this, therefore because of this (a false reasoning)

post mortem (L.), after death

prima facie (L.), on the first view

primus inter pares (L.), first among equals

proxime accessit (L.), he came next

quis custodiet ipsos custodes? (L.), who will watch the watchers?

qui s'excuse s'accuse (Fr.), he who excuses himself, accuses himself

quod erat demonstrandum (L.), which was to be proved

quod erat faciendum (L.), which was to be done

quot homines, tot sententiae (L.), so many men, so many opinions

rara avis (L.), a rare bird

reculer pour mieux sauter (Fr.), to draw back to take a better leap

reductio ad absurdum (L.), the reducing of a position to a logical absurdity

répondez, s'il vous plait (Fr.), reply, please

requiescat in pace (L.), may he (or she) rest in peace

revenons à nos moutons (Fr.), let us return to our sheep; let us return to our subject

ruat coelum (L.), let the heavens fall

rus in urbe (L.), the country in the town

sans peur et sans reproche (Fr.), without fear and without reproach

sans souci (Fr.), without care

satis verborum (L.), enough of words

sauve qui peut (Fr.), save himself who can

semper idem (L.), always the same

sic transit gloria mundi (L.), so passes away earthly glory

sic vis pacem, para bellum (L.), if you want peace, prepare war

sine die (L.), without a day being appointed

sine qua non (L.), without which, not; an indispensable condition

sotto voce (It.), in an undertone

status quo (L.), the state in which: things as they now are

stet (L.), let it stand; do not delete

sub judice (L.), under consideration

sub poena (L.), under a penalty

sub rosa (L.), under the rose; privately

sub specie (L.), under the appearance of

succès d'estime (Fr.), a success of esteem or approval (if not profit)

suggestio falsi (L.), a suggestion of something false

sui generis (L.), of its own kind; peculiar

summum bonum (L.), the chief good

sursum corda (L.), lift up your hearts

tabula rasa (L.), a blank tablet

tant mieux (Fr.), so much the better

tant pis (Fr.), so much the worse

tempora mutantur, nos et mutamur in illis (L.), the times are changing and we with them

tempus fugit (L.), time flies

terra incognita (L.), an unknown land

tertium quid (L.), a third something

tête-à-tête (Fr.), a private interview, a confidential conversation

tour de force (Fr.), a feat of strength or skill

tout à fait (Fr.), entirely
tout à l'heure (Fr.), instantly
tout de suite (Fr.), immediately
tu quoque (L.), you too
ubique (L.), everywhere
ultima Thule (L.), the utmost limit
ultra vires (L.), beyond one's powers
veni, vidi, vici (L.), I came, I saw, I conquered
verbum sat sapienti (L.), a word is enough for a wise man
via media (L.), a middle course
vice versa (L.), the terms being reversed
videlicet (L.), that is to say; namely
vi et armis (L.), by force and arms
virginibus puerisque (L.), for girls and boys
vis-à-vis (Fr.), opposite
viva voce (L.), by the living voice; orally
vogue la galère (Fr.), come what may!
voilà tout (Fr.), that's all
vox et praeterea nihil (L.), a voice and nothing more
vox populi, vox Dei (L.), the voice of the people is the voice of God

A SHORT LIST OF AMERICAN WORDS AND PHRASES

The Americans, of course, speak English. But their English is no longer quite the English that is spoken in the British Isles: and sometimes the differences between the two can cause great puzzlement—especially when (as in *biscuit*) the word is the same but the meanings no longer match. This is a list of common words and phrases that are most likely to give rise to difficulties. Some of them, of course, find their way across the Atlantic every year; and it might be interesting to guess which ones, as they become familiar, will have to come out of this list in later editions.

aluminum, aluminium
attorney, lawyer
baggage-check, luggage-ticket
barkeep, barman
baseball park, a baseball playing-field

battery, the pitcher and catcher together in a baseball team
bill, banknote
billboard, hoarding
billion, 1,000,000,000 (as compared with the English billion, which is 1,000,000,000,000. This is said to be the only example of something bigger in English than in American)
cracker, biscuit
biscuit, a soft cake rather like a scone, never sweet, and served hot with butter
bit, 12½ cents
bone up, to swot up
boner, a howler
bootlegger, an illicit seller of liquor
bouncer, chucker-out
box, the rectangular space in which the pitcher stands at baseball
boxcar, a freight-car on the railway, enclosed and covered
brakeman, guard on a freight train
bug, any insect
bully, first-rate
bumper, railway buffers
bureau, dressing-table
buzz saw, circular saw
caboose, brake van on a goods train
cage, the special enclosure in which batting practice for baseball is carried on
cake, cake; but in the plural (**cakes**) it always means a kind of pancake
candy, sweets
candy-store, confectioners
car, a railway carriage or coach; sometimes the cage of a lift
cars (the), a train
carousel, roundabout
casket, coffin
check, cheque
check-room, cloakroom
checkers, draughts
chuckwagon, a wagon carrying food supplies for cowboys, pioneers, etc
clerk, sometimes a shop assistant

comfort station, public convenience
composition book, exercise book
conductor, guard on a passenger train
construction gang, gang of navvies on the railway
davenport, couch
depot, railway station (this use is now dying out)
derby (pronounced as spelt), a bowler hat
diamond, baseball field
dinner-pail, the container for a workman's or a schoolchild's
    midday meal
dirt wagon, dust cart
district attorney, public prosecutor
dooryard, backyard or back garden
doughboy, an infantry soldier
dove, dived
downtown, the business district in an American city (see **uptown**)
dresser, chest of drawers or dressing table
drug store, chemist's shop (soft drinks are sold there, too)
dry goods, articles of drapery, haberdashery, etc
duster, light overcoat or wrap
El, the elevator railway
engineer, engine driver
faucet, tap
fender, bumper of a car
first floor, ground floor
fixings, the garnishings of a meal
fraternity, an organisation of male students, usually designated
    by two or more Greek letters (e.g. the Phi Beta Kappa). See
    sorority
garbage can, dustbin
gas (short for **gasoline**), petrol
get next to, get wise to
given name, Christian name
gondola, railway wagon without sides or with very low sides
grab bag, lucky dip
grade, a division in American schools, similar to the English 'year';
    also a mark in examinations
greenbacks, paper money
gridiron, a football field
guard, prison warder

haberdashery, articles for men's wear

hard sledding, a difficult task

hayseed, a yokel

highball, whisky and soda with broken ice in a tall glass

high-toned, stylish, superior

hogpen, a pig sty

home plate, base at first corner of the diamond in baseball; also the base at which the batter stands to bat

home run, or **homer**, a hit that allows the batter in baseball to make a circuit of all the bases without an error being made in handling the ball

homely, plain, ugly

homestead, a piece of land allotted under an Act of 1862 which gave possession of the land to any head of family who had lived on it for five years and had paid a small fee

homesteader, owner of a homestead

hood, the bonnet of a car

hundredweight, 100 lbs

inaugural, the address made by a new President of the US on the day he takes office (**inauguration day**)

in short order, in no time, immediately

intermission, a school break

intersection, a street crossing

jag, a load (especially a load of liquor, more than the drinker can carry)

jail delivery, a mass escape from prison

janitor, a caretaker

jay, a simpleton

jug-handled, one-sided, unfair

jumping-rope, a skipping rope

keyman, a telegraphist

knock, to find fault with

line, a queue, a boundary

log-rolling, an agreement among politicians each to vote for some item of legislation desired by the others

longshoreman, a docker

lot, a plot of ground

luggage, empty baggage

lunch, a light snack taken at any time in the day

major, to specialise in a subject: an American student is said to

major in the subject or subjects to which he gives most of his
attention

make out, get along, manage

mean, seedy ('I feel mean tonight'): troublesome, inconvenient,
unpleasant ('It was a mean, dirty job')

monkeyshines, capers

mortician, an undertaker

muslin, calico

name for, name after ('John was named for his uncle, Senator
John Smith')

newsy, newsboy

night robes, night clothes

night stick, a policeman's truncheon

nine, a baseball team (compare the English 'cricket **eleven**')

nip and tuck, neck and neck, a close thing

notion department, the haberdashery section of an American
department store

of, used in American in the sense of **before** a particular hour, e.g.
'At ten minutes of seven I got up'

Old Colony, Massachusetts

Old Dominion, Virginia

Old Glory, the American flag

overly, excessively

owl train, a train running in the small hours of the night

paddle to spank, to smack

panhandle, a narrow strip of land within the boundaries of a state
but projecting from the main body of that state. (Look at West
Virginia in the atlas: this is called **the Panhandle State**)

pass up, to refuse, decline

patrolman, a policeman

patrol wagon, a prison van, Black Maria

pavement, roadway

pay dirt, the earth in which a miner finds gold

peek-a-boo, hide and seek

penny a one-cent piece

pie, tart. (The English **pie** is sometimes called in America a **deep
pie**.)

pilot, a cowcatcher on a train

pint, 16 fl oz (as compared with the English pint of 20 fl oz)

pitcher, the player in baseball who throws the ball to the batter;

he tries to 'strike' the batter out, or to 'fan' him, i.e. to cause him to fail in three attempts to hit the ball

platform, one of the projecting ends of a railway car on which passengers step when entering a train. (American railway stations usually have no platforms in the English sense of the word.)

plug-hat, a silk hat

pocket-book, a purse

point, a nib

porch, a verandah on a house

porch climber, a cat burglar

precinct, a division of a city for police or electoral purposes

prison warden, a prison governor

push-pin, a drawing pin

pussyfoot, to attempt to achieve one's aims by concealing what one is up to

quarter, a 25-cent piece

quitter, a shirker

railroad, to get something done in a rush

realtor, an estate agent

river, this word in American is always behind the name of the river, never in front (e.g. Hudson River, Mississippi River)

robin, a red-breasted thrush

rock, a stone of any size

root for, to encourage a team by cheering it on

round-trip ticket, return ticket

roundabout, a short jacket worn by a boy

roundsman, a policeman

rubber, to crane one's neck in order to see or hear

rubberneck, someone standing and staring

rubbers, overshoes

sand, courage, grit

schedule, timetable (the **ch** is pronounced as a **k**)

scratch-pad, scribbling block

section, district of a town or city

sedan, a saloon car

sherbet, a kind of water ice

shingle, the signboard of a professional man

shower party, a party at which the hostess is showered with presents from her friends

sidewalk, a pavement
side-wheeler, a paddle-boat
slingshot, a catapult
sociable, a social gathering
socialize, to get together socially
sorority, an organisation of female students (see **fraternity**)
sourdough, a person who has spent one or more winters in Alaska
spark guard, a fire guard
spat, a slight quarrel
speakeasy, an illegal drinking-place
spool, a cotton reel
spur line, a branch railway line
stand, a witness box
stand pat, to sit tight
station agent, a stationmaster
station house, a police station
stem-winder, a keyless watch
stock-holder, shareholder
stoop, the platform at the top of a flight of steps leading to the front door of a house
stop over, to break a journey
street car, a tram
string, a shoelace
subway, an underground railway
sulky, a light two-wheeled one-horse carriage for one person
suspenders, braces
switch-tower, a signal-box
switchyard, a shunting yard
tag day, a flag day
tape needle, a bodkin
Thanksgiving dinner, a dinner eaten on Thanksgiving Day, the last Thursday in November. (Thanksgiving originated among the early American settlers, as an expression of their gratitude for their preservation.)
through; 'Monday through Friday', means from Monday to Friday inclusive
thumb tack, drawing pin
tightwad, a miser
ton, 20 cwt but 2,000 lb

toss and catch, pitch and toss
towerman, a railway signalman
truck, a lorry or van
tube, a wireless valve
uptown, the residential district in an American city (see **downtown**)
vest, waistcoat
vestibule train, a corridor train
vine, any creeping plant
wad, a sheaf of bank notes
waist, a blouse
washroom, a lavatory
wash rag, a face flannel
way station, an unimportant railway station
well-fixed, well-to-do
windshield, a wind screen
World Series, the most important series of competitions among American baseball teams

A DICTIONARY OF WRITERS

This is a list of only the most famous of our writers, giving their dates, saying for which kind of writing they are most famous (as poet, novelist, dramatist or whatever it may be) and giving the name of their best-known work. The list was compiled by someone who would greatly have enjoyed saying more. ('Don't miss the *Canterbury Tales*. They're warm, funny, grave, full of unforgettable people and phrases, and, though it's worth getting used to the not-too-difficult Middle English of the original, there's a good modern translation by Nevill Coghill.' That sort of thing.) But this is a list purely for reference—by, the compiler hopes, readers who are busy acquiring for themselves the desire to say more about a writer than that his dates were this or that, and his best-known work was that or this.

Addison, Joseph (1672–1719), essayist and dramatist.
Arnold, Matthew (1822–88), poet and critic. *The Scholar Gipsy*.
Auden, W. H. (1907–1973), poet.

Austen, Jane (1775–1817), novelist. *Pride and Prejudice.*

Bacon, Francis (1561–1621), essayist.

Barrie, Sir J. M. (1860–1937), novelist, playwright. *Peter Pan.*

Beaumont, Francis (1584–1616), dramatist, collaborated with **John Fletcher** (1579–1625). *Knight of the Burning Pestle.*

Beerbohm, Sir Max (1872–1956), essayist and critic.

Belloc, Hilaire (1870–1953), poet, essayist, historian and novelist. *Cautionary Tales.*

Bennett, Arnold (1867–1931), novelist. *Old Wives' Tale.*

Blake, William (1757–1828), poet. *Songs of Innocence* and *Songs of Experience.*

Borrow, George (1803–81), chronicler of gipsy life. *Lavengro.*

Boswell, James (1740–95), biographer, diarist. *Life of Dr Johnson.*

Bridges, Robert (1844–1930), poet. *Testament of Beauty.*

Brontë, Charlotte (1816–55), novelist. *Jane Eyre.*

Brontë, Emily (1818–48), novelist. *Wuthering Heights.*

Browne, Sir Thomas (1605–82), essayist. *Religio Medici.*

Browning, Robert (1812–89), poetry. *The Ring and the Book.*

Browning, Elizabeth Barrett (1806–61), poet. *Sonnets from the Portuguese.*

Buchan, John (1875–1940), novelist, historian. *Thirty Nine Steps.*

Bunyan, John (1628–88), author of *Pilgrim's Progress.*

Burns, Robert (1759–96), poet.

Butler, Samuel (1612–80), poet. *Hudibras.*

Butler, Samuel (1835–1902), novelist. *The Way of All Flesh.*

Byron, Lord (1788–1824), poet. *Don Juan.*

Campion, Thomas (1567?–1619), poet.

Carlyle, Thomas (1795–1881), historian and essayist. *The French Revolution.*

Carroll, Lewis (Charles Lutwidge Dodgson) (1832–98), author of *Alice in Wonderland.*

Chaucer, Geoffrey (1340?–1400), poet. *Canterbury Tales.*

Chesterton, G. K. (1874–1936), poet, essayist and novelist. The *Father Brown* stories.

Clare, John (1793–1864), poet.

Cobbett, William (1762–1835), essayist and social critic. *Rural Rides.*

Coleridge, Samuel Taylor (1772–1834), poet and critic. *Rime of the Ancient Mariner.*

Collins, Wilkie (1824–89), novelist. *The Moonstone.*

Collins, William (1721–59), poet.

Congreve, William (1670–1729), dramatist. *Way of the World.*

Conrad, Joseph (1857–1924), novelist. *Lord Jim.*

Cowley, Abraham (1618–67), poet.

Cowper, William (1731–1800), poet. *The Task.*

Crabbe, George (1754–1832), poet. *The Borough.*

Defoe, Daniel (1661?–1731), novelist. *Robinson Crusoe.*

Dekker, Thomas (1570?1641?), dramatist.

De la Mare, Walter (1873–1956), poet and novelist.

De Quincey, Thomas (1785–1859), essayist and critic. *Confessions of an Opium-Eater.*

Dickens, Charles (1812–70), novelist. *David Copperfield.*

Donne, John (1573–1631), poet.

Doyle, Sir A. Conan (1859–1930), novelist. *Hound of the Baskervilles.*

Drayton, Michael (1563–1631), poet. *The Ballad of Agincourt.*

Dryden, John (1631–1700), poet and dramatist. *Absalom and Achitophel.*

Eliot, George (Mary Ann Evans) (1819–80), novelist. *Mill on the Floss.*

Eliot, T. S. (1888–1965), poet. *The Waste Land.*

Evelyn, John (1620–1706), diarist.

Fielding, Henry (1707–54), dramatist and novelist. *Tom Jones.*

Fitzgerald, Edward (1809–83), poet. *Rubaiyat of Omar Khayyam.*

Forster, E. M. (1879–1970), novelist. *Passage to India.*

Galsworthy, John (1869–1933), novelist. *The Forsyte Saga.*

Gaskell, Elizabeth Cleghorn (1810–65), novelist. *Cranford.*

Gay, John (1685–1732), poet. *The Beggar's Opera.*

Gibbon, Edward (1737–94), historian. *Decline and Fall of the Roman Empire.*

Gilbert, Sir W. S. (1837–1911), playwright and humorous poet. *The Bab Ballads.*

Gissing, George (1857–1903), novelist. *The Private Papers of Henry Ryecroft.*

Golding, William (b. 1911), novelist. *Lord of the Flies.*

Goldsmith, Oliver (1728–74), poet, essayist and playwright. *Vicar of Wakefield.*

Graves, Robert (1895–1985), poet and novelist.

Gray, Thomas (1716–71), poet. *Elegy in a Country Churchyard.*

Greene, Graham (b. 1904), novelist. *The Power and the Glory.*

Hardy, Thomas (1840–1928), poet and novelist. *Tess of the D'Urbervilles.*

Hazlitt, William (1778–1830), critic and essayist.

Herbert, George (1593–1633), poet.

Herrick, Robert (1591–1674), poet.

Hobbes, Thomas (1588–1679), philosopher. *Leviathan.*

Hood, Thomas (1799–1845), poet. *Song of a Shirt.*

Hopkins, Gerard Manley (1844–89), poet.

Housman, A. E. (1859–1936), poet. *A Shropshire Lad.*

Hudson, W. H. (1841–1922), novelist and naturalist. *Green Mansions.*

Hunt, Leigh (1784–1859), poet and essayist.

Jacobs, W. W. (1863–1943), novelist and short-story writer.

James, Henry (1843–1916), novelist. *Daisy Miller.*

Jefferies, Richard (1848–87), essayist and novelist. *Bevis.*

Johnson, Dr Samuel (1709–84), poet, critic and dictionary-maker. *Vanity of Human Wishes.*

Jonson, Ben (1573?–1637), poet and dramatist. *The Alchemist.*

Joyce, James (1882–1941), novelist. *Ulysses.*

Keats, John (1795–1821), poet. *Endymion.*

Kingsley, Charles (1819–75), novelist. *The Water Babies.*

Kipling, Rudyard (1865–1936), poet and novelist. *Jungle Tales.*

Lamb, Charles ('Elia') (1775–1834), essayist.

Landor, Walter Savage (1775–1864), poet.

Langland, William (1330?–1400?), poet. *Piers Plowman.*

Larkin, Philip (1922–85), poet.

Lawrence, D. H. (1885–1930), poet and novelist. *Sons and Lovers.*

Lear, Edward (1812–88), poet. *The Owl and the Pussycat.*

Lovelace, Richard (1618–58), poet.

Lytton, Lord (1831–91), novelist. *Last Days of Pompeii.*

Macaulay, T. B. (1800–59), historian. *History of England.*

Malory, Sir Thomas (*c.* 1470), author of *Morte d'Arthur.*

Marlowe, Christopher (1564–93), poet and dramatist. *Dr Faustus.*

Marryat, Frederick (1792–1848), novelist. *Children of the New Forest.*

Marvell, Andrew (1621–78), poet.

Masefield, John (1876–1967), poet and novelist. *Dauber.*

Massinger, Philip (1583–1640), dramatist. *New Way to Pay Old Debts.*

Meredith, George (1828–1909), novelist. *The Egoist.*
Milton, John (1608–74), poet. *Paradise Lost.*
Moore, George (1857–1933), novelist. *Esther Waters.*
Moore, Thomas (1779–1852), poet.
More, Sir Thomas (1478–1535), author of *Utopia.*
Morris, William (1834–96), poet. *The Earthly Paradise.*
O'Casey, Sean (1883–1964), dramatist. *Juno and the Paycock.*
Orwell, George (1903–50), essayist and novelist. *Animal Farm.*
Owen, Wilfred (1893–1918), poet.
Peacock, Thomas Love (1785–1866), poet and novelist.
Pepys, Samuel (1633–1703), diarist.
Pope, Alexander (1688–1744), poet. *Rape of the Lock.*
Raleigh, Sir Walter (1552–1618), poet.
Reade, Charles (1814–84), novelist. *Cloister on the Hearth.*
Richardson, Samuel (1689–1761), novelist. *Clarissa Harlowe.*
Rossetti, Christina (1830–94), poet. *Goblin Market.*
Rossetti, Dante Gabriel (1828–82), poet.
Ruskin, John (1819–1900), writer on art. *Stones of Venice.*
Scott, Sir Walter (1771–1832), poet and novelist. The *Waverley* novels.
Shakespeare, William (1564–1616), poet and dramatist. *Hamlet.*
Shaw, George Bernard (1856–1950), dramatist and critic. *St Joan.*
Shelley, Percy Bysshe (1792–1822), poet. *The Revolt of Islam.*
Sheridan, Richard Brinsley (1751–1816), dramatist. *The Rivals.*
Sidney, Sir Philip (1554–86), poet.
Skelton, John (1460?–1529), poet.
Smollett, Tobias (1721–71), novelist. *Roderick Random.*
Southey, Robert (1774–1843), poet and historian. *Life of Nelson.*
Spenser, Edmund (1552?–1599), poet. *Faerie Queene.*
Steele, Sir Richard (1672–1729), essayist.
Sterne, Laurence (1713–68), novelist. *A Sentimental Journey.*
Stevenson, Robert Louis (1850–94), poet and novelist. *Treasure Island.*
Suckling, Sir John (1609–42), poet.
Swift, Jonathan (1667–1745), author of *Gulliver's Travels.*
Swinburne, Algernon Charles (1837–1909), poet.
Synge, J. M. (1871–1909), dramatist. *Playboy of the Western World.*
Tennyson, Alfred, Lord (1809–92), poet. *Idylls of the King.*
Thackeray, William Makepiece (1811–63), novelist. *Vanity Fair.*

Thomas, Dylan (1914–53), poet. *Under Milk Wood.*
Thomas, Edward (1878–1917), poet.
Thompson, Francis (1859–1907), poet. *The Hound of Heaven.*
Thomson, James (1700–48), poet. *The Seasons.*
Tolkien, J. R. R. (1892–1973), novelist. *The Lord of the Rings.*
Trollope, Anthony (1815–82), novelist. *The Warden.*
Vaughan, Henry (1622–95), poet.
Webster, John (1580?–1625?), dramatist. *Duchess of Malfi.*
Wells, H. G. (1866–1946), novelist. *Kipps.*
White, Gilbert (1720–93), naturalist. *Natural History of Selborne.*
Wilde, Oscar (1856–1900), poet, critic and dramatist. *Importance of Being Earnest.*
Woolf, Virginia (1882–1941), novelist, critic. *To the Lighthouse.*
Wordsworth, William (1770–1850), poet. *Lyrical Ballads.*
Wycherley, William (1640?–1716), dramatist. *The Country Wife.*
Yeats, William Butler (1865–1939), poet.

MUSIC AND THE ARTS

MUSIC

Very probably, music is historically the first of all the arts. After all, one often hears of babies who sing before they say their first word and who beat out rhythms before they sing. So it is easy to imagine a caveman grunting out some sort of music in an age when even speech—let alone writing—was unknown, and before the first cave paintings adorned the walls of his home.

There is another way in which music can claim to be the first of the arts. One writer put it this way: 'all other arts aspire to the condition of music'. By this, the writer meant that music is the freest of the arts. A writer must say what he means in precise words; a painter must make us a picture of something we recognise; a sculptor must present us with a form that has meaning. Or so it was until very recently. The musician, though, has never had to follow these rules because music has no meaning. He plays a fast tune on a trumpet and we all find it 'lively' or 'stirring'. He plays a slow tune on a violin and we all find it 'melancholy' or 'sad'. We even talk of 'pastoral' music—music that suggests green fields and blue skies. Yet music (as the musician would agree) has no meaning other than the meaning we agree to give it. The astonishing thing is that we all agree about its meaning!

Music, then, is free of the rules that bind the other arts. But there are several rules that apply to music. For instance: the basic recipe for all music includes Melody, Harmony and Rhythm.

Rhythm

Rhythm is the cornerstone of music. To prove this, try humming a very well-known tune (*Pop Goes The Weasel* will do) in a way that has all the notes of the melody in the right order, but with the rhythm deliberately distorted. Most people will find it impossible to recognise the tune. It will have lost its identity with its rhythm. Just the same thing happens when you break up the rhythm of a sentence. For example, you can take these words:

'To let a firework off, blue paper must be lit'

and by altering the rhythm, change their sense into:

'To let: a firework. Off-blue paper. Must be lit.'

Melody is the tune. Some melodies—*Greensleeves*, for instance—

are so powerful that even drastic rhythm changes cannot conceal them.

Harmony is the structure of notes and chords that fill out the melody and add to its meaning. You could call harmonies the adjectives and adverbs of music. So if the melody is the noun 'cat', it is the harmonies that make the cat happy or sad, black or tortoiseshell.

Most tunes can be given a variety of harmonies. Yet musically gifted people generally agree on what is the right set of harmonies for a given tune—and they will certainly agree in disliking any wrong harmony or false chord they hear.

All the music we hear contains some—usually all—of the elements of rhythm, melody and harmony. One way of classifying musical instruments is to arrange them under the headings of Rhythm, Melody, Harmony. For instance, a drum is a Rhythm instrument; a flute is a Melody instrument; a guitar is a Harmony instrument because it plays chords. Put these three instruments together and you would have a band that could play many kinds of music.

If you are thinking of taking up a musical instrument, you will be wise to find out which sort suits your natural talents best— Melody, Harmony or Rhythm.

MUSIC HISTORY

Wherever history is recorded it is usual to find some record of music. A mural in the tomb of Rameses (about 1150 B.C.) shows players with large, elaborate harps. Another mural in Thebes shows a girl lute player. There is an Assyrian relief in the British Museum picturing a mixed orchestra of players. All these random examples take us well back before the birth of Christ.

Going further afield and still further back to 2500 B.C., we know of a Chinese scholar called Ling Lun who codified the five tones of oriental music then in use and named each tone. Some tones, according to Ling Lun, were upper class and even royal; others were mere peasants! Oddly enough, this idea of naming tones by social qualities, degrees of nobility and so on, is found quite frequently in various periods and countries.

Moving nearer to our own age, there are endless references in fact and fiction establishing the unchanging importance of music throughout history. Everyone knows about David playing his harp to Saul—about the Pied Piper of Hamelin—about Red Indian war chants. Not everyone knows that the rich Romans had water organs; when people came to dinner, the water organ (*hydraulus*) played. Some people hated the noise and wrote peevish comments about it. Rather the same thing happens today with record players!

The tragedy is that although we know that there has always been music, we cannot hear the music itself. We know exactly how the Egyptians, say, looked and dressed. We can read their writings, study their religions, see their own models and paintings and tools in the museums. But we cannot know how their music *sounded*. In fact we can make no sense at all even of some of the earliest written music. We can roughly trace a melodic thread, but we do not know the rhythms or tones; or harmonies, if any. Ancient music is a mystery without a key.

Because of the lack of clearly written music, we can go back only comparatively few centuries to recapture the sound of old music. True, some melodies heard today are truly ancient, even ageless—the chants of Jewish temples, certain Indian pieces and the Catholic Church's Georgian chants—but our sort of music is possibly an invention of the middle ages.

Written Music

Our music is in the main based on the Diatonic scale which can be sung as Doh, Re, Mi, Fa, Sol, La, Ti, Doh. The notes are each a tone apart excepting Mi-Fa and Ti-Doh, which are a semitone (half tone) apart. Doh is the Tonic or 'home' note defining the music's key. Countless simple tunes (e.g., *Three Blind Mice*) employ only the 'natural' tones of the major Diatonic scale (there are minor scales too). Semitones enlarge the scale to 12 notes. Music not restricted to a key may be expressed by the Chromatic scale of 12 semitones.

Several ways of naming notes and writing music have been tried, of course. The simplest were based on sketching a tune like this:

Sing this sketch and with luck you will hear *God Save the Queen*.

To reduce the luck element, notes were named from A to G. Four or more 'stave' lines were added to align the written notes (today we use five, as shown below). This system was developed to its present-day form—an unsatisfactory form, incidentally, for our music uses 12 notes and five into twelve won't go.

A glance above will show you the result of this bad division. The middle C is the only note the two clefs have in common. If you look for any other note—A, for instance—it will occupy one position in the treble clef and a different position in the bass clef.

This system also forces us to use a variety of complicated correction signs. As you can see, our alphabet of notes runs only from A to G—which makes seven notes; but as already pointed out, ours is a 12-note music. To insert the other five notes in written music, we have to make use of signs for sharps—♯, flats—♭ and naturals—♮. But even then it does not work out. Our scale includes notes that could be called either sharp or flat! Here is an octave of notes from a piano:

* Is this note both B and C flat? † Is the black note F sharp or G flat? And for that matter, is there any real difference between D

sharp and E flat? There is not on the piano, naturally. But is there on a violin?

Fortunately we can ask the questions without answering them here. It is enough to say that we live with our musical notation because the cure—introducing a new system—would be worse than the disease! Musicians are used to it, just as typists are used to their typewriter keyboard's layout.

Music's Development From now on we almost ignore all forms of music but our own European and American kinds—that is, the 12-note forms played in various arrangements of melody, harmony and rhythm.

As far as we know (we cannot be sure) this music first took a wide hold of Europe from, say, the tenth century A.D. on. Hucbald, a monk who lived until A.D. 930, describes a raw-sounding two-voice harmony running in fifths (such as C and G, D and A, etc). The effect of playing only in fifths is very crude indeed.

John Cotton (A.D. 1130) wrote of music 'by at least two singers in such a manner that, while one sounds the main melody, the other colours it with other tones'. This suggests that polyphonic (many-voiced) music was only just beginning. Otherwise, why did Cotton bother to explain it?

Polyphonic music developed fairly rapidly. By the fifteenth and sixteenth centuries minstrels' chants freed music of strict, almost mathematical forms and modes. New rhythms became acceptable. Harmonies were used for emotional as well as formal effects. Opera was reborn in Italy in about 1600. Instruments developed fast. Music schools were established. *Some important composers of the period: Monteverdi (opera), Byrd, Palestrina.*

In the seventeenth century, music almost began again with Bach, who developed past forms to an excellence that is still unsurpassed and also reached forward into the future both with his music and instruments (he virtually re-designed the organ, for example). Bach's impact on music is comparable with that of photography on graphic art—but Bach was also the age's supreme artist as well! *Important composers: Purcell, Handel, Bach.*

In the late eighteenth century, the modern symphony orchestra and its music came into being. Music began to move from so-called 'Classical' forms (that is, formal variations-on-a-set-theme forms) into more free and spacious 'Romantic' forms. In our century, painting has received a very similar liberation: the

painter of today need no longer draw to an academic formula—
he can make his own rules and effects. *Typical 'classical' composers:
Mozart, Gluck, Haydn.*

The rest of the story is probably best told by the names of nine-
teenth-century composers such as Beethoven, Mendelssohn, Berlioz, Schubert, Tchaikovsky, Brahms and others. All these are
'Romantic' composers in that they exploited and developed all
that had gone before along their own individual lines; and also
constantly strove to enlarge the range of effects and feelings that
music and musical instruments convey. The restrictions put upon
them, if any, were all self-imposed. They did not follow the Rules
of the Game that existed in earlier centuries. They tried rather to
change the game.

In our century, music has yet again started afresh. The very
nature of 12-note music is in question. Why not a limitless scale?
Or a number of different scales? Why follow any recognised form?
Why accept the instruments of the orchestra as the only instruments—could not music be made electronically, without
human instrumentalists—or even human composers?

Like painting, music need no longer be representational; it need
no longer attempt to establish definite mind-pictures, as it generally did 70 years ago. Anything and everything that the listener
agrees to accept as music—including arrangements of electronic
noises—is now within the composer's scope.

Jazz

When Pepys, the diarist, invited friends to his house for a musical
evening 300 years ago, music was still at its formal stage. The
Rules of the Game were known and followed. Thus the evening's
music could be improvised on a formal theme understood by all
the players present.

As music became more complicated, improvisation became less
likely and less satisfactory. The written notes offered a more
assured performance of more exciting and advanced music. Improvisation therefore slowly died.

It was revived by jazz players early in this century. The jazz
player takes as his basis a set of harmonies that he and the others
are familiar with—the chord structure of *Tea for Two*, for instance—and improvises melodies and counter melodies that fit
those chords. Almost invariably, the improvisation is solidly

supported by a firm and unchanging rhythm that locks the players together as they perform. This basis of firm harmonies and solid rhythm leaves the jazzman an enormous amount of freedom: and he makes the most of it. He plays round the melody. He adopts new instruments or alters old ones to fit his needs. He welcomes new sounds and ideas—indeed he will go out of his way to surprise his listeners.

The effect of jazz on other musical forms is already felt and felt strongly. Many modern 'classical' composers introduce jazz phrases and passages but seldom with success (the attempts of jazz musicians to use 'classical' forms and methods are equally poor). However, the sheer vitality, inventiveness and virtuosity of the best jazz musicians are heavily infectious. It is very probable that the jazz and 'classical' compositions of the future will move along tracks that meet here and there; and already, both schools are making similar experiments for similar purposes.

Popular Music

Dance, 'pop', 'rock' and most other forms of popular music owe a lot to jazz. 'Folk' music, for instance, is often given jazz elements. However, pop is finding its own, unique 'voices' as the range of (particularly electronic) instruments and sound sources increases. Again, pop musicians are discarding the old recipes for making a tune and reaching out for new freedoms. A pop song of the 1930s had 32 bars, the modern pop song has any number.

No one can predict the future of popular music—but then, the whole idea of pop is that it should please now, this moment.

THE INSTRUMENTS

Instruments can be split into families and groups in various ways, most of them a little vague. For instance, the Flute is a Woodwind instrument—but most modern flutes are made of metal. However, here are some customary groupings:

Strings

Bowed The violin family, particularly the violin—viola—cello—string bass. But also the viols, which have frets.

Violin

Cello   Harp

Hand or Plucked The harp. The guitar family—guitar in its 'classical' form with gut or nylon strings plucked with the fingers; or with steel strings plucked with a plectrum. Also banjo, ukelele, lute and many other fretted instruments.

Spanish ('Classic')
Guitar   Venetian Lute

Spinettina: Augsburg, 17th century

Keyboard Piano, harpsichord, klavier, spinet and many others.

Wind

Flute family—flute, piccolo and others, all blown transversely—
   that is, across a hole.

Recorder family The various recorders, small and large; and many
   other instruments that you blow *down*, including the flageolet—a superior penny whistle—and various pipes.

Metal Flute

Piccolo

Flageolet

Tenor Saxophone   Oboe   Recorder

Bagpipes are wind instruments. They consist of a number of pipes blown by the player and also by an air reservoir, the bag. So there is some slight similarity with the—

Organ, which is an arrangement of various kinds of pipes and other sound producers fed air from a chamber that is kept filled by an air pump (but see Electronic instruments, M14).

Reed instruments may have double reeds—oboes and bassoons—or, more commonly, single reeds, as in clarinets, saxophones.

Brass wind instruments

Trumpets, cornets, horns, trombones, bugles. All these can be called **Lip** instruments because the note is formed by the player's lips—not by a reed, or whistle.

All lip instruments are, at heart, a posthorn to which something has been added. A bugle is a simple horn wound into coils. A trumpet is a bugle with valves added to increase the number of notes obtainable. The French horn is a posthorn wound in circles and with valves to increase its range. The

Trumpet

Trumpet Mute

French Horn

Tuba

trombone literally shortens or lengthens itself (thus changing its pitch) when the player operates the slide. Naturally, there are many other differences and the posthorn idea is an over-simplification; but the fact remains that a trumpet with stuck valves or a trombone with a stuck slide reverts to the instrument that founded its family—and that basic instrument is a tapering tube with a mouthpiece, from which about five notes can be produced.

Percussion instruments

This family includes drums, cymbals, bells and other rhythm in-struments—including the tunable kettle drums of the symphony orchestra, the jazz drummer's outfit, and the huge selection used by a Latin-American band.

Jazz Drum Kit

Once again, the classification is a little vague. One could call a piano a percussion instrument—after all, its strings are hit by hammers.

Tympani

Vibes

From the instruments described so far, one could form anything from a symphony orchestra to a folk group. Throughout history and in every country, instruments have always been basically what they are today. Walt Disney once made a short film about the development of music called TOOT, WHISTLE, PLUNK & BOOM (suggest that they show it at your school) which made this point very well. There is really no *basic* difference between a panpipes and a recorder, or a lyre and ukelele. The differences lie only in additions, subtractions and modifications made over many centuries.

During the last hundred years, though, a completely new class of instruments has appeared. So let us have a new heading:

Electric, Electronic instruments (sometimes called Electrophones) produce their sounds either by amplifying sounds produced by ordinary instruments—the electric guitar is the best example— or by creating original sounds electrically, as in the electric organ and Moog Synthesizer. Your local church organ is probably partly electric; its action and air pump may be worked by electricity. But if it is a new instrument, then it is very probably 'electronic'. Its notes and tones have nothing to do with wind and pipes and everything to do with electronic tone-generators, electric amplifiers and so on.

The future of such instruments is limitless. Most of the pop and beat music heard today would be almost inaudible if there

Electric Guitar

Multi-functional keyboard—memory pack, rhythms, eight voices, set or
fingered chords, transpose

were a power failure—most of the sound is made, and all of it
amplified, by electric devices. The modern church organ,
obviously, would be struck dumb if its power supply were cut.
And many musicians are experimenting with *musique con-
crète*—music actually manufactured from sounds of electronic
origin.

SOME MUSICAL TERMS

Many people are not clear about what is meant by the word
'Pitch', what the Conductor actually does and so on. Here are
explanations of a few of these puzzles.

Ballad A song, often sentimental, that tells a story.

Bar Written music is divided into Bars by upright lines. Each bar
contains so many beats. Count the beats and you will know
the rhythm of the music. See MEASURE.

Beat Rhythmic pulse. A waltz has three beats to each bar.

Chamber Music Music for small instrumental groups—music that is best heard in a room, not a hall.

Conductor His function is not simply to make the orchestra play together, but rather to dictate *how* the music should be played. Two separate conductors will produce very different renderings of the same music from an orchestra.

Counterpoint, Contrapuntal Counterpoint is the combining of two or more melodies, played simultaneously. *Contrapuntal* is the adjective.

Fugue A contrapuntal composition for several parts—that is, instruments or voices.

Key Most music is written in the key of the composer's choice. The KEY SIGNATURE indicates to the player which key has been chosen. If the player sees F sharp written at the beginning of the music, he knows that his 'home key' is G—because the major scale of G is distinguished by possessing an F sharp. As the piece may not stick to its 'home key' of G, the composer will have to insert other sharps, flats and naturals as they occur. These are called Accidentals.

Measure A division of music in terms of beats. If there are three beats to the bar, then the writer will draw vertical lines at three-beat intervals and so divide his composition into Measures.

Notation To write a note filling a whole measure, you write a semi-breve, ⚬. A minim, ⲣ, is worth half the time value of the semi-breve and the crotchet, ⲫ, worth half that. And so on to quaver, semi-quaver and demi-semi-quaver, etc.

Pitch The highness or lowness of a musical sound. Middle A is internationally agreed to have a frequency of 440. A note at the top of the piano, well above middle C, has a higher pitch. People with 'absolute pitch' are able to hear a note and name it correctly.

THE ARTS

Imagine a lucky dip of humanity—a pot filled with cavemen and car-workers, ancient-Egyptian washerwomen and Red Indian warriors. You dip your hand in and take out an SP—a Sample Person. You provide it with the basics of life—the materials for food, shelter and clothing. What will the SP do once settled?

It will first provide itself with the practical things it needs (a bird or beetle would do as much). But later it will do something that hardly any other creatures do. It will add to what it needs something it doesn't need—an individual and personal touch of Art. The latest water-pot will be made in an improved shape and given colour and decoration; fringes will be cut in the edges of sleeves; the home will be decorated.

If your particular SP does none of these things you have chanced on a dull and lifeless specimen. Return it to the lucky dip and try again. You are unlikely to have to make too many tries. Mankind has always produced arts and artists. There were cavemen artists and Victorian ladies who painted flower pictures. There were Eskimos carving walrus tusks and Navajo Indians weaving blankets and rugs. Great artists have sprung from primitive peoples: wicked men have produced work of undying beauty: feeble men have shown huge artistic power.

Ah, but wait. What is all this about 'great' art—'beauty'— 'power'? The *Mona Lisa* is only so much rotting pigment. St Paul's Cathedral is simply a large people-container with a useless dome on top. The SP's decorated water-pot holds water no better than the plain one. You can add up the pebbles in a bucketful and get a sure answer—but how do you add up art? Power, beauty, greatness—who says so? How are judgements possible?

One answer is this: you know artistic judgements are possible because you constantly make them yourself. You spend loving hours painting a kit model or getting a garment just right: you become angry with yourself if your achievement falls short of your intention. That is an artistic judgement. You prefer this poster to that—artistic judgement again. Perhaps you are becoming bored with this piece of writing? Then you are making an artistic judgement. There is nothing wrong with the printing or the paper.

How *is* art truly judged? The answer seems to be—time. Quite obviously 'great' art may stem from unusual human powers and mighty themes. But, then, you can see the 'greatness' of an artist in small things. **Leonardo da Vinci**, for example, did working sketches of machines and practice sketches of animals rolling in the grass. There is a quality about the drawings that says, 'The man who made these was a great artist.' There are very small carvings, *netsuke*, made by Japanese craftsmen. Netsuke were merely permanent, solid knots to hold the strings of a purse or pouch together, so no grand intentions or soaring of the spirit were needed in their production: yet in some of these little carvings you may find not only superb craftsmanship but also the work of considerable artists. Time—and the considered opinions of informed and enthusiastic minds—is needed to sort such matters out.

But you have no time. So let us think about—

Your Judgement

'Beauty is in the eye of the beholder.' In other words, you like it, I loathe it, on first sight.

19th-century ivory netsuke

Nevertheless, instant like/loathe decisions are generally worthless. You take the trouble to read the instructions that come with a power tool or dress pattern—to understand how the thing is *meant* to work. The same trouble should be taken with a work of art.

What do you need to know? First, how the thing fits into—or escapes from—its period. What were other artists producing at the time? What were the times like? What rules and conventions governed the artist and his art? Was the artist trying to please himself, or a patron, a customer?

The last question is important. There is a belief that artists are 'free'—they do their own thing, they need satisfy only themselves. This is nonsense, of course. Most artists, including those with the greatest and most revered names, worked to please a patron—the state, the Church, a rich man, a gallery, an agent, a market. Studies, experiments and innovations were private matters. Some artists rebelled against patronage: you may like to look up the fascinating story of James McNeill Whistler. In 1877, he was called a coxcomb who asked 200 guineas 'for flinging a pot of paint in the public's face'. Other artists had to appear in court to speak for or against him. The Court awarded Whistler 'Damages one farthing'. So art *could* be added up then—but the addition did not hold. Today, Whistler is probably considered a 'great' painter. The farthing— or the 200 guineas—must now be multiplied by thousands and hundreds. Yet his work will not surprise *you*, a person living a hundred years later. You will be puzzled by the scandal and outrage caused by an artist determined to please himself.

Once you have understood the motives, methods and 'provenance' (place, time, pedigree) of a work of art, you are in a position to make a judgement. Having made it, look up other judgements, by notable critics. You will probably find that they have seen much more than you have seen.

You will also find that one critic disagrees with another. So your opinion could well be right after all.

A HISTORY

If, as Henry Ford said, 'History is bunk,' then Art History is double bunk, because though most artists are conditioned by the times they live in, many ignore or flout their times yet still emerge as 'significant artists of the period'.

So when you read here that the arts of, say, Ancient Greece were thus-and-thus, take it with a pinch of salt. Imagine, if you like, an Ancient Greek reading the words and saying, 'Well! All I can say is, this writer ought to meet that crazy artist down the road!'

Another point. To avoid getting lost, go back to the first pages of this encyclopaedia—THE WORLD, ITS HISTORY.

Third and most important: there are countless excellently illustrated books about the arts. When something here stirs your curiosity, go to the library and look at the books.

Ancient Times

Farming, home-building, community Man, seems to have started around 7000 B.C. These people left artifacts (things made with tools) and art works all over the world. If you imagine a man of these times to be a shaggy brute with a club for hitting other shaggy brutes, you are probably right: nevertheless, his (or her) cave-drawings are vivid, accomplished and sure. Some we know to be very accurate—for example, we can compare the deer we see today with the deer drawings done all those thousands of years ago and say, 'He got it right.'

Prehistoric cave painting (from Altamira, Spain)

Benin bronze

For wall and ceiling paintings, all kinds of techniques were used—charcoal sticks, scratchings, shallow relief and so on, often with colour. Frequently the irregularities of the surface were picked up to show the shape of the subject. A protruding lump could be the flank of a beast, for example.

Primitive/Savage/Ethnic Art
It is difficult today to know who are the 'savages'—ourselves, the tool-using technocrats so worried by our knowledge: or them, the primitive peoples, who live close to Nature because they must. The same difficulty strikes us in judging their art. It is only fairly recently that African, Eskimo and such arts from remote, wild places have come to be talked of as 'Art'. Similarly, it is only quite recently that the savageries of some of our present-day artists could be discussed in polite society.

Please consult the books and arrive at your own conclusions. At worst you will find something exciting. At best you may find a half-forgotten something that you will recognise with delight, or fear, or wonder. See books about Lascaux, the Dordogne, Altamira, Bardal, Willendorf, etc.

Neolithic/Megalithic Structures

The ancient men carved and sculpted figures from rock, bone, anything at all. They also made huge structures. Stonehenge (about 2000 B.C.) is one of several European stone circles built at a time when people lived in shallow pits with crude roofs over them. Yet Stonehenge is massive. There are various theories about the purpose of Stonehenge (and obelisks, menhirs, dolmens and other great stone structures). Whatever the truth—probably to do with sun worship—Stonehenge is a staggering example of architecture for a purpose.

China

China has 3,000 years of recorded history. Her influence pervaded the whole Far East—Japan, Korea, Tibet, Mongolia, Annam. A thousand years before Christ was born, the Chinese took for granted sophisticated and beautiful personal possessions—jade, lacquer, bronze, silk, strange stones and crystals marvellously worked, paintings and porcelain (invented 4th–5th centuries A.D.).

All other Chinese crafts and arts were secondary to painting and calligraphy—partly because of the supreme elegance of Chinese writing, but also because the brush strokes could express the matter and spirit of the writer and his message. Thus 'Dear Sir' can be written as an insult or compliment.

Look through books on Chinese art and you will find a strange conflict of simplicity (porcelain, scroll painting, calligraphy, etc.) and outrageous embellishment (certain buildings, fabrics and in-

Chinese calligraphic characters

terior decorations). But invariably you find supreme, sometimes almost unbelievable, skill.

Wood was the material used for Chinese architecture—thus few ancient buildings survive. Intricate systems of interlinking keys supported the curved, tiled roofs.

A word about dynasties: 'Sun', 'Yuan', 'T'ang' are simply the names of ruling families, used to describe the period of a work much as we use 'Georgian' or 'Victorian'.

Japan

From the 7th century A.D. the Japanese adopted China's arts and crafts. From 10th century A.D. on, when China's civilisation was falling apart, the Japanese went their own way, developing un-rivalled skills with lacquer, ivory, pottery, glass and almost any other material—particularly multi-plate colour printing from wood blocks. See books showing *suzuribake* (writing cabinets), *netsuke* (drawstring toggles), *inrō* (little boxes for pills, etc.)—and even bamboo, which was and is the material for anything from plumbing systems to the most delicate craft objects. Sword-making was regarded as a fine art for very good reasons.

Architecture: look up the many Buddhist temples; and Shōsōin (the Imperial Treasure House, 8th century A.D.). The traditional Japanese domestic interior is particularly interesting in its re-finement and simplicity.

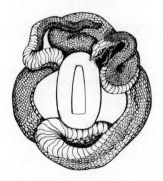

Japanese sword guard: brass, gold,
and silver

India

Great styles of art and architecture had flowered before the birth of Christ. Monasteries, sanctuaries, temples were covered with figures representing innumerable deities. India was, and is, a continent of many faiths and nations—and with an artistic history extending over some 2,000 years. Enough here to say that the golden age of Buddhist art lasted some 300 years, until about A.D. 600 (consult books for examples); that sculpture and architecture are wonderfully mixed—the buildings seem to writhe with figures; and that over the centuries, exquisite works in all materials were produced by artists who found, in their religions, fantastic sources.

Queen Nefertiti (Egypt, 1360 B.C.)

Egypt

The ancient Egyptian civilisations date from about 3000 B.C. The reigning Pharaoh, or king, was regarded as divine. The main function of the artist and the architect was to immortalise him— to record his deeds, to preserve his body and possessions, for all time. Thus architecture and sculpture were monumental (the Pyramids—the Sphinx—the temple of Abu Simbel) and carried out on a staggering scale.

About 2250 B.C., the God/King concept was replaced by that of a heavenly being, Osiris. Now ordinary people could have monumental tombstones and memorials. Because of the Egyptian obsession with death and afterlife, those who could afford it were embalmed, mummified and securely entombed. Today, discoveries are still reported of arts and crafts from the distant past—of works in ivory, wood, glass, gold, precious stones; and, of course, portraiture to commemorate the dead. The painter or stone-carver used his art to report and record as literally as possible—but within certain conventions: an important person was shown large, a less important person small; the side and front of the face could be shown simultaneously; set postures and gestures denoted agreed characteristics and powers (similarly, in Christian art, a halo denoted divine characteristics).

The influence of Egyptian architecture is still to be seen in anything from cinemas to railway bridges and factories. Look up the Egyptian swollen columns and lotus-flower capitals, etc., and see how many echoes you can spot in your district's buildings.

Islam

The Islamic world included Arab, Persian, Syrian and Egyptian peoples who followed the Moslem faith. Islamic art is distinct in that no human and animal figures are represented. The arts were centred on weaving, calligraphy (copying the Koran was a virtuous act), work in precious metals, often inlaid; and in pottery, glass, bronze, enamels. It was largely decorative art: plant forms and geometrical patterns, piercings and curlicues. Thus the term 'arabesque', meaning a curlicue or interlinked decoration.

About a thousand years ago Islam became disunited. Eventually Moslem and Hindu worked together to evolve Mogul art.

An Arabesque

The Taj Mahal

Architecture: Look up in books the Alhambra of Caliph Abd-el-Walid (14th century); mosques, particularly Suleimaniyeh (1550); the Taj Mahal. The pointed arch—from which we derive our Gothic arches and vaulting—was an Islamic innovation.

Ancient Greece

Rhythm, discipline, order, humanity, harmony, balance—these seem to be the themes of Greek art and architecture. Quite certainly we still follow Greek traditions and find echoes of the Greek in every age that followed. We still describe as 'Classical' (meaning Greek) certain European painters of recent centuries. And we still like to see ideal representations of the human body. We feel at home in public buildings on the Greek scale, with classical Greek decorations. The Greek tradition is probably only a bus ride distant from you as you read.

Greek artists and sculptors tried to express, through the human body, a concept of beauty: see the *Discobolos* (Discus Thrower) by **Myron**, 480–445 B.C. Greek architects sought logical rules and harmonies that could shape a disciplined structure: see for example the Parthenon.

The Greeks were masters of pottery, both in form and decoration; of monumental sculpture in stone and bronze; and of perspective and light-and-shade drawings (q.v.). The Grecian civilisations lasted more than a thousand years and were affected by

Greek vase

various religions, scientific advances and philosophies. In the end, it could be said that their greatest achievements were humanistic; for most certainly their art was.

The Parthenon (restored)

Roman

The Greek civilisation gave way to the all-conquering Romans, who respected and adopted Greek artistic thinking and methods. But the Romans were not Greeks: thrusting, practical, empire-minded and brilliant engineers, their ideas were less 'human' and their ambitions more grandiose. They enjoyed dreams of glory and their art and architecture showed it. The Pantheon (A.D. 120) and the Colosseum (A.D. 70) are vast structures. A bronze statue of Emperor Nero stood 34 metres high. Their temples, unlike the Greeks', held great congregations. Their villas were centrally heated, lavishly furnished and decorated with wall paintings, mosaic floors and works of art and craft from any corner of their world (which was the whole known world, excluding only China and the Far East). You will find it very easy to discover more in libraries, by visiting the Roman Palace at Fishbourne, Sussex, or simply by reading newspaper stories about Pompeii, the latest 'finds', and so on.

The Pont Du Gard Aqueduct

The Colosseum (restored)

   Etruscan art is often linked with Roman. The Etruscans once dominated Italy and were eventually absorbed by the Romans.

European Art

Western art—the art of Europe, of Europeans in the United States of America and like-minded civilisations—took the forms familiar to us in a comparatively short time: less than a thousand years. When Rome was sacked, Constantinople became the centre of Imperial Roman and Christian culture in northern Europe. A distinct pattern of thought emerged between A.D. 1100 and 1500—the *Gothic* period; you can capture the flavour of this time by visiting Westminster Abbey, the cathedrals of Lincoln and Salisbury and the Keep of the Tower of London. In York Minster

A section of the Bayeux tapestry

you can follow a whole progression of architectural styles and
building methods. There are fragments of Roman times, and
demonstrations of 'Norman', 'Early English', 'Decorated', 'Perpendicular' developments in the handling of windows, buttresses,
vaultings, structures and surfaces. Putting it briefly: what started
as massive, thick and round-arched ended as lofty, delicate, airy
and filigree. The changes took place over some 300 years.

You can also find traces (here we are working backwards) of
the arts and sciences of the 'Dark Ages' and Mediaeval times. You
can see how the simple pointed arch or the ribbed vault was
developed, enlarged and elaborated. You can even see—for instance in the Bayeux tapestry or in stained-glass windows—how
people living in the 11th century (the time of William the Conqueror) saw themselves; and judge how important Church and
State were in the choice of the subjects the artist might draw
from.

St. Sophia

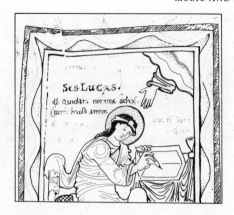

Section of an illuminated Saxon manuscript

Gothic Art was mainly northern European. In the Byzantine Empire (the Christian, Near East area of Constantinople), great underground burial places, the catacombs, were decorated with paintings on the ceilings and elsewhere. The paintings—like the decorations on lamps and glass objects—were almost always simple representations of Christian doctrines and figures. Great basilicas with lavishly decorated domes were built (Hagia Sophia, Istanbul, A.D. 530). Fine work was done in mosaics, ivories, books, jewellery, enamel and wire-work.

Stained-glass window (York Minister)

Renaissance

The word means Rebirth. The new beginning spread through Italy, eventually to affect the whole of Europe, during the 14th-16th centuries. The works of such artists as **Giotto, Martini** and **Andrea Pisano** hint clearly enough at what was to come.

The Renaissance was one result of a chain-explosion of events, possibilities and attitudes. Links in the chain include the conquest of Constantinople by the Turks (which sent many Greek scholars to Italy); scientific research; voyages of exploration; the spread of printing; the nature of Italy itself—it was then a conglomeration of small city-states ruled by sophisticated families; and perhaps above all, a feeling of personal freedom, very different from that which produced the often strait-jacketed figures seen in, say, old stained-glass windows and sacred statues.

In this climate, the artist could find new aims and bring science to aid his eye and craft. Talent found recognition and genius, acclaim. Sculptured figures came alive. Painted figures appeared to have roundness and flesh—and to inhabit landscapes painted in depth (see *Perspective, Modelling* below). The very buildings, while keeping the symmetries of ancient Greece, became ornate, colourful, even frivolous—like the new clothes.

The Italian sun slowly thawed even the northern parts of Europe (though here and there, there were dark matters of church and state to keep out the light). By the end of the period, as later artists complained, the Italians seemed to have accomplished everything: colour, perspective, landscape, the use of human figures to express emotion, 'classical' symmetry, 'modern' adventurousness. Looking at the works of **Botticelli, Michelangelo, Giorgione, Titian** and the architect **Palladio**, you say to yourself, 'Only a superb mind could have thought of that. And only a superb hand could have done it!' (e.g., *The Creation of Adam*, a detail from **Michelangelo's** ceiling for the Sistine Chapel. Or **Giorgione's** *Fête Champêtre*. Or **Ghiberti's** bronze doors for the Baptistery, Florence. But really, such lists are pointless because the achievements were endless.)

In countries north of the Alps, the effects of the Renaissance were felt a century later. During the 15th century, a particularly brilliant school of painting arose in the Netherlands (**Hubert** and **Jan van Eyck, van der Weyden, Memling** and others). French architects adopted Italian manners in their architecture and

Madonna and child, Bruges cathedral (Michelangelo)

Supper at Emmaus (Caravaggio)

sculpture. England was undergoing the Reformation and the effects of the Renaissance were minor. Germany, too, had other matters to deal with. Yet, throughout Europe, the Renaissance 'took', if only in terms of buildings, clothes, ornaments, furnishings—and a new sense of possibility. **Dürer** of Germany, for example, travelled extensively: he was a supreme master in his own ways—but must have seen and been influenced by the mastery of the very different minds and hands he encountered.

Perspective and Modelling

Western people take it for granted that a two-dimensional work can suggest, 'This thing is near, that thing is distant' (perspective); and 'This thing is rounded, that thing is flat' (modelling).

In Eastern and many other cultures, these effects are not necessarily attempted. No doubt the problems of achieving 'reality' through perspective and modelling have always been recognized by artists of all places and periods: but generally, the problems were sidestepped by the adoption of conventions. For example, a Chinese scroll must be unrolled and viewed bit by bit, from bottom (Near things) to top (Distant things). Again, while the ancient

Melencolia I (Dürer)

Egyptians gave incised flat surfaces (a rock-face, say) an added
drama and interest by using bas-relief—shallow modelling—for
the figures, they did not bother with perspective. Yet again, you
can see 'parallel perspective' in many eastern drawings and
paintings. The effect is faintly comical to us, as if the whole scene
were slipping off the surface.

Perspective joke drawing
(after Hogarth)

In the West, the huge importance of the problem seems always to have been recognised. You see it solved in Ancient Roman times and earlier. It was not until some 500 years ago, however, that a general onslaught was made by such masters as **Uccello**, **Masaccio**, **Jan van Eyck**, **Dürer** and **da Vinci**. They found, formalised and set down the answers we have accepted ever since. (The illustration above shows what happens if you don't accept them!) With the mysteries solved, western art could and did stride forward and enter new realms of 'reality'.

Printing, reproduction

To western eyes, there is a respectability and importance in 'oil painting' that may seem to diminish the mere graphic arts of drawing, etching, wood engraving, etc. Yet master drawings (see books with such titles) are masterpieces in their own right—and have always been thought so in China and Japan.

In the east, basically linear works embellished with colour have been hand-printed from blocks for centuries. In the west, printing by mechanical presses began much later and has only recently found techniques that satisfactorily render colour; so superb drawings by great masters could lie neglected because there were no means of reproducing them, or because the drawings were

Head of Venus (Botticelli)

seen as only a step towards the 'serious' work, the oil painting.

Yet many great artists and great works were and are linear at heart (see **Botticelli's** *Birth of Venus*) and today it is accepted that a fine artist may be a draughtsman rather than a colourist. See **Brian Steadman's** present-day illustrations for *Alice in Wonderland/Alice Through the Looking Glass*; book illustrations, Victorian and later, by **Rackham, Harry Clarke, Edmund J. Sullivan, Beardsley, Joan Hassall**; 18th century cartoons and illustrations by **Rowlandson, Gillray**; and the numerous works of **Hokusai** (Japan, 19th century). See also the supreme drawings of such masters as **Michelangelo, Titian, Raphael, da Vinci, Dürer**, etc., who will lead you on to, say, **Ingres** (19th century), a 'classical' draughtsman—and so to the experimentalists of later periods and today.

After the Renaissance

Many artists found rich patrons. The royal courts of France and Spain and the Catholic Church, for instance, constantly demanded allegorical, religious and portrait works. The Renaissance skills endured—but not always the conviction, as you may feel when you look at *The Toilet of Venus* (**Guido Reni**). Architects loaded basically classical structures with ornament, statues, pillars, pediments, sweeping stairways. The grandiose styles of, particularly, 17th-century Italy are called *Baroque*. Later, Baroque merged with the still more extravagant *Rococo* manner. The sugar-cake exercises of early 18th-century Rococo are often breath-taking: there may be too much of everything, but how beautifully everything is done! (See paintings by **Bernini**, **Lanfranco**, **Pozzo**, **Fragonard**, **Watteau**. But better—enjoy complete buildings and structures; the Palace of Versailles in France, the Trevi Fountain and much else in Rome. And look at exhibits in the Wallace Collection, London.)

British architects went their own way. They developed a style blended from Classical, Palladian and Renaissance. A very few, like **Inigo Jones**, could be called 'undiluted Classical' (Whitehall, or the Queen's House, Greenwich). **Sir Christopher Wren** and his disciples, however, made endless variations and combinations of classical and baroque themes (e.g., London and City churches, St Paul's Cathedral). Wren's inventiveness and sparkle was, fortunately, echoed by several contemporaries. A great deal of their work stands, though some is hidden or dwarfed by the efforts of present-day architects. St Paul's, for instance, is almost obscured by mean yet massive 20th-century office buildings.

Several 17th-century artists did not follow the trends of the

St Paul's Cathedral

time. **Velasquez** (Spanish) was coolly powerful, darkly dignified. **Rubens** (Flemish) was only incidentally a vivid Baroque painter. The calm, small, glowing interiors of **Jan Vermeer** (Dutch) seem intensely private, where so much painting of the time was public. And of course there was Holland's **Rembrandt**, who would have been considered a giant at any time—among painters.

Eventually the grandeurs and fripperies of Baroque and Rococo were swept away by the French Revolution. Educated tastes now preferred the drier, more severe style of *Neo-Classicism* (at heart, Greek/Roman) typified by the drawings and paintings of, say, **Ingres**—which contrast with the very different approach of the *Romantics*, such as **Delacroix**. In England, **Reynolds** (1723–92) argued a return to the 'Grand Style' of the Renaissance (see his work, and that of his rival, **Gainsborough**). In the Netherlands landscape painting had been highly regarded since the 17th century and in Britain, too, this kind of work found popularity (**Cox**, father and son, watercolourists of 18th–19th centuries; **Constable**, 18th–19th centuries).

Constable represents one of the accepted forms of painting taken to its logical conclusion. There seemed nothing more to say. But then **Turner** (1775–1851) produced—as one of his critics said—'pictures of nothing, and very like'. His stormy handling of paint and extraordinary success in apparently manufacturing light from paint upset the Fine Arts applecart and perhaps led to *Impressionism*. Perhaps not. Certainly his light still shines.

For some time after the French Revolution, artists could depend on the rich, the Church and the State for patronage. From 1800 onwards, most could not. They found themselves in a free market—free to invent, to compete and even to starve. Those painters who did not experiment followed Neo-Classical trends in the main. They produced carefully finished 'painterly' work, obviously worth hard cash. They added a zest and zing by making their work sexier, or more dramatic, or more story-telling, than of old (see the later paintings of **Greuze** [French], a forerunner of the super-sentimentalists of the Victorian age).

In Britain, the architects flourished. During the 18th and early 19th century, they produced some of the most delightful buildings we know. Wren's innovations, it was found, could be adapted to small structures: thus the fine 'Queen Anne' houses, in which various Classical motifs were carried out in brick. The Industrial

Revolution was under way—people were moving into the new, crowded towns—whole strings and squares of housing had to be supplied: even this was done successfully, with a grace that can be admired in cities and towns throughout the country (Edinburgh's New Town; Bath; and in London, see Bedford Square and the other Georgian squares and streets near by). The severely Classical, Inigo Jones manner was carried on by such architects as **Nash**, who not only built, but planned whole areas of cities (go to Regent's Park in London).

Queen Anne, Georgian and Regency styles are at heart ornamented Classical—that is, Ancient Greek/Roman/Palladian/Italian. There were other styles. There was a craze for the 'Gothic Taste', an amazing mixture of castellations, church-y pointed windows, rustic ironwork and twisted chimneys. The craze lasted some seventy years: look for late-Gothic railway stations, lodges, cottages, schools, in your neighbourhood. The date may be shown in bright bricks and will probably be *c.* 1850.

The Prince Regent (later George IV) gave his name to Regency architecture. But his personal interest was in exotic styles— Chinese and Indian and anything else from the East all mixed together. He built Brighton Pavilion. You can go inside this amazing pleasure palace. At the same time (1800 on) the light-hearted, bright, yet formal buildings of Brighton and other seaside resorts and country towns were being built in the Regency style.

Chiswick House—'Classical'

Victorian

In the period 1840–1900 industrialisation, the railways and machines brought changes to all and vast wealth to some; particularly in Britain, the rich and powerful pace-setter. Artists from abroad came to England: native artists prospered. 'Finish'—perfect execution—was one way to the favour of rich patrons. Another was to cram the picture or sculpture with detail and to make it tell a story ('Look, master has died and the dog is sad! See how his eyes glisten!').

Such works were laughed at when the new century arrived— or at any rate, after the First World War. The laughter only recently died down. Victorian craftsmanship was remarkable; and as works of Art—but judge for yourself from, say, *Too early* (**Tissot**); *The Lament for Icarus* (**Draper**); *Derby Day* (**Frith**); *April Love* (**Hughes**). See also the flaming luxury of some of **Lord Leighton's** work; *Pegwell Bay* by **Dyce**; the super-reality of *The Stonebreaker* (**Brett**); and the book illustrations of the period.

There were endless revolts against the fundamentally commercial values of the time. The *pre-Raphaelite Brotherhood* sought to rediscover the purity and truth-to-Nature of an earlier golden age. **Grimshaw** (*Liverpool Quay by Moonlight*) achieved effects that might astonish a present-day colour photographer. There were social realists (*Application for Admission to the Casual Ward*, **Fildes**); and Fairy Painters (**Dadd**, **Paton** and others). Works from China and Japan influenced **Whistler** the impressionist, and **Aubrey Beardsley** the line artist. **William Morris** founded a sort of Mediaeval arts and crafts workshop whose influence is still seen. The French-inspired *Aesthetic Movement* inspired one, as G. S. Gilbert said mockingly, to 'stroll down Piccadilly/With a poppy or a lily/In my mediaeval hand'. (Get a book about *Art Nouveau* to see what happened later on.)

In France the major revolution brewed. *Modern Art* (q.v.) was starting with the realism of **Courbet**, the rapid emotional effects of the *Impressionists*, the deliberately unclassical nudes of **Manet**, the lushness and freedom of **Renoir**, the posters and paintings of **Toulouse-Lautrec**, the painters of light such as **Monet**. *Post-impressionists* like **Cézanne** and **van Gogh** added strength to the new art.

The Victorians loved to display their wealth. A town house or a sideboard had to be florid, 'important', completely covered with decoration. So much Victorian architecture survives that your own eyes are a sufficient guide. Enough here to say that every conceivable style, ornament and tradition of the past were used, sometimes simultaneously, sometimes disastrously, often delightfully. See St Pancras Station, Big Ben, Balmoral, perhaps your own local railway station or town hall or old public house—anything. Look particularly for uses of cast-iron, a key material of the period.

Modern art

Until the arrival of the French Impressionists of the 19th century, the art of painting had been based on Nature in some form or other. 'Those who take as their standard anything other than Nature,' **da Vinci** wrote, 'weary themselves in vain.' **Whistler**, three centuries later, said much the same thing: the job of the painter was 'to pick and choose, as the musician gathers notes and chords,' from Nature.

But then came the Instant-Nature reproducer, the camera—and various machines that appeared more than human in their cleverness and power—and above all a belief that Man could dominate Nature. So the 20th-century architect talked of houses as 'machines for living', the sculptor turned to mechanisms such as mobiles, and the painter to abstract, theoretical, non-representational pictures—and to Isms. Surrealism, vorticism, pointillism, dadaism, expressionism, cubism, futurism . . .

Time has already been unkind to most of the Isms. There is nothing so dated as a 1930s book about Modern Art unless it is a pre-World War One Futurist Manifesto ('HURRAH for motors! HURRAH for speed! HURRAH for draughts!')

Recently, soiled nappies have been displayed in the name of Art—and even naughtier, more shocking articles. 'I admit it's ugly, but is it Art?' is the question we so often have to answer today.

Time will give the answers—and decide which of our present-day artists are truly important, even great. In all periods, innovators have been derided and attacked. Contrariwise, for every old name still remembered, there are a hundred or a thousand forgotten. We wait and see.

Some names: innovators and experimenters who bred modern art include **Cézanne**, **Matisse**, **Rouault** and the Impressionists

Monet, **Renoir**, **Toulouse-Lautrec** and **Degas**. All worked in France, as did **Picasso** (Spanish), the most diverse and prolific of all. Whatever Isms or classifications these artists chose to apply to themselves from time to time, their works are distinct and personal. The same is true of **Paul Klee** (Swiss), **Kandinski** (Russian), **Brancusi** (Rumanian), **Magritte** (Belgian), **Jackson Pollock** (American) and **Henry Moore** or **Graham Sutherland** (English). All are moderns, all produced paintings or sculptures or both that belong to this century and no other. But this is usually their only link.

Younger, present-day artists of note include **Bridget Riley** (fascinating visual conjuring tricks of the Op Art School), **David Hockney** and **Francis Bacon**. A current American school of interest produces super-real paintings—probably a spinoff from *Pop Art*; you may know, from posters, the work of Pop-artist **Roy Lichtenstein** (blow-ups of frames from strip cartoons) and of artists who paint super-real tubes of toothpaste, etc.

Artists who defy classification include **L. S. Lowry** ('naive' industrial landscapes with figures) and an endless list of commercial artists who are coming to be regarded as Fine Artists. But then, the distinction between Fine Arts in a gallery and commercial art on, say, a plastic food pack is becoming blurred.

Sculpture is equally diverse. **Reg Butler's** skeletal structures, **Jacob Epstein's** brutal and massive pieces, the abstract forms of **Barbara Hepworth**, the elongated delicacy of **Giacometti**—all are regarded as important, but so are stacks of bricks and junked cars.

In architecture, in this century, new materials—particularly steel-reinforced concrete—have changed the very nature of buildings and, seemingly, have often directed the architect's hand. Concrete and steel lend themselves to modular production of parts that can be endlessly repeated: thus the massive tower blocks and office complexes that dominate our town and city skylines.

Architecture is the functional art. It provides containers for things or people. The functional worth of modern high-rise buildings designed to house humans is under continuous and heavy attack, as is their 'art' element. It seems that the architects and planners of today's familiar, commonplace buildings and centres will be judged harshly tomorrow.

Adventurous and exciting buildings in the modern idioms exist, of course; see the cathedrals of Liverpool and Coventry; various small buildings—aviary, elephant house, giraffe house—in Regent's Park Zoo, London; buildings for the universities of Essex, Southampton, Leicester.

The pioneers of present-day architecture include **Frank Lloyd Wright** of America, **le Corbusier** of France, **Pier Luigi Nervi** of Italy—and **Walter Gropius** of Germany, a founder of the *Bauhaus*, a German institution that influenced the design of houses and household objects after World War I and through the 1930s.

Photography Much of present-day art is wild, provocative and formless. One of many reasons why is—photography, which was already flourishing a hundred years ago.

Picture a successful Victorian artist. He has spent his adult life mastering his craft and art. A photographer sets up his camera beside the artist's easel. The one goes 'click' and the other paints on. Later they compare results. Perspective, modelling, detail, light and shade, 'truth'—the photograph is as perfect as the painting in everything but colour (and that is soon to come!). What should the artist do? Burn his canvases and buy a camera? Or change the very nature of his art?

The problem was and is a real one. The camera cannot eliminate the unwanted or invent the wanted—but the able photographer can find ways to over-ride these difficulties and produce the effect he desires. He can use the camera 'creatively', choose his subjects and settings 'artistically'. There are already Old Masters of photography.

One effect on the non-photographic artist was to make him tackle his art from a different starting point. The camera can show every leaf and twig? Right, then the artist will become an impressionist. Or he will put a frame round a single leaf and call his picture, *Forest*.

In short—the wilder schools of *modern art* (q.v.) would most probably have emerged anyhow. But photography made quite sure that they did emerge.

Exceptions and rebels

In our history—we warned you at the outset—we may have made it appear that in each period, art and artists followed the general patterns of that period. Probably most artists did just that, just as you talk of television or tennis, not of tatting or tipcat. But there were always exceptions: artists who didn't, wouldn't or couldn't 'belong'. Please look up: the English painters **Turner**, **Samuel Palmer**, **William Blake**, **Lowry**; the works of **Fuseli**, **Hokusai**, **Bosch**, **Henri Rousseau**, **Pieter Breughel**, **el Greco**; the architects **Gaudi**, **Mackintosh**. This short list (you may enjoy extending it) is of artists who have nothing in common but their uncommonness.

Art and Craft

What are they? When does one become the other? A craft can be defined as a high human skill: Art might be defined as a message designed to appeal to the highest human sensibilities. But why cannot a craft object make this appeal? Is a superb pocket watch by **Breguet** craft, or art? Can a pile of tyres (displayed in a recent Art exhibition) truly be art? Is the *Cutty Sark* both a work of art and craft? Can a photograph be art?—and if not, why not?

There are no answers to these old questions. But you must ask them, constantly.

Remarkable books

There are today endless pictorial books about the Arts. Anything you want can be found in libraries and bookshops. Some books, however, are things apart . . .

Homes Sweet Homes; *Pillar to Post*; *Progress at Pelvis Bay*, all by Sir Osbert Lancaster. Architecture, furnishing, period feeling, in words-and-pictures nutshells. Very funny. There are paperback editions, but try to get new or secondhand hardbacks.

First and Last Loves by Sir John Betjeman. Random opinions, enthusiasms, invaluable snippets. Illustrated. Also his *A Pictorial History of English Architecture*.

Particular Pleasures by J. B. Priestley, containing the author's reflections on certain paintings.

Architecture by W. R. Dalzell.

One Hundred Details from Pictures in the National Gallery by Sir Kenneth Clark. Also *The Nude* and other works by this author.

Autobiography of Cellini, describing the work of a 16th-century artist/craftsman.

Drawings and Notebooks of Leonardo da Vinci (1452–1519)—thoughts, sketches, theories of a genius.

The Saturday Book was a handsome gift annual for grown-ups. It appeared for more than twenty years. Many beautiful and odd things, expert texts.

SPORT

At the beginning of this section, sports are arranged alphabetically; under each heading are given details of governing bodies, championships and records. These are followed by a list of those results of the 1984 Olympics not recorded under particular sports. Finally, under 'Personalities', brief notes are given on some of the sportsmen and women who have made the greatest impression on the British scene in the 1980s.

ARCHERY

Governing body: Grand National Archery Society, National Agricultural Centre, Stoneleigh, Kenilworth, Warks., CV8 2LG.

Olympic Games 1984		
Men	D. Pace (USA)	2,616 pts.
Women	S. Hyang-Soon (S. Korea)	2,568 pts.
33rd World Target Archery Championships 1985		
Men (individual)	R. McKinney (USA)	2,601 pts.
Men (team)	USA	
Women (individual)	S. Irina (USSR)	2,595 pts.
Women (team)	USSR	
United Kingdom Target Archery Championships 1985		
Men	S. Hallard	
Women	S. Harris	

ASSOCIATION FOOTBALL

The Football Association was founded in 1863 and the FA Cup competition was first held in 1871/72. Official international matches have been played since 1872.

Governing bodies: Football Association (England), 16 Lancaster Gate, London W2 3LW; Football Association (Scotland), 6 Park Gardens, Glasgow G3 7YE; Football Association (Irish), 20 Windsor Avenue, Belfast BT9 6EG; Football Association (Eire), 80 Merrion Square South, Dublin, 2; Football Association (Wales), 3 Fairy Road, Wrexham, LL13 7PS.

LEAGUE CHAMPIONS

1889	Preston North End	1900	Aston Villa
1890	Preston North End	1901	Liverpool
1891	Everton	1902	Sunderland
1892	Sunderland	1903	Sheffield Wednesday
1893	Sunderland	1904	Sheffield Wednesday
1894	Aston Villa	1905	Newcastle United
1895	Sunderland	1906	Liverpool
1896	Aston Villa	1907	Newcastle United
1897	Aston Villa	1908	Manchester United
1898	Sheffield United	1909	Newcastle United
1899	Aston Villa	1910	Aston Villa

1911	Manchester United	1955	Chelsea
1912	Blackburn Rovers	1956	Manchester United
1913	Sunderland	1957	Manchester United
1914	Blackburn Rovers	1958	Wolverhampton Wanderers
1915	Everton		
1920	West Bromwich Albion	1959	Wolverhampton Wanderers
1921	Burnley		
1922	Liverpool	1960	Burnley
1923	Liverpool	1961	Tottenham Hotspur
1924	Huddersfield Town	1962	Ipswich Town
1925	Huddersfield Town	1963	Everton
1926	Huddersfield Town	1964	Liverpool
1927	Newcastle United	1965	Manchester United
1928	Everton	1966	Liverpool
1929	Sheffield Wednesday	1967	Manchester United
1930	Sheffield Wednesday	1968	Manchester City
1931	Arsenal	1969	Leeds United
1932	Everton	1970	Everton
1933	Arsenal	1971	Arsenal
1934	Arsenal	1972	Derby County
1935	Arsenal	1973	Liverpool
1936	Sunderland	1974	Leeds United
1937	Manchester City	1975	Derby County
1938	Arsenal	1976	Liverpool
1939	Everton	1977	Liverpool
1947	Liverpool	1978	Nottingham Forest
1948	Arsenal	1979	Liverpool
1949	Portsmouth	1980	Liverpool
1950	Portsmouth	1981	Aston Villa
1951	Tottenham Hotspur	1982	Liverpool
1952	Manchester United	1983	Liverpool
1953	Arsenal	1984	Liverpool
1954	Wolverhampton Wanderers	1985	Everton
		1986	Liverpool

FA CUP

1872	Wanderers	1878	Wanderers
1873	Wanderers	1879	Old Etonians
1874	Oxford University	1880	Clapham Rovers
1875	Royal Engineers	1881	Old Carthusians
1876	Wanderers	1882	Old Etonians
1877	Wanderers	1883	Blackburn Olympic

1884	Blackburn Rovers	1929	Bolton Wanderers
1885	Blackburn Rovers	1930	Arsenal
1886	Blackburn Rovers	1931	West Bromwich Albion
1887	Aston Villa	1932	Newcastle United
1888	West Bromwich Albion	1933	Everton
1889	Preston North End	1934	Manchester City
1890	Blackburn Rovers	1935	Sheffield Wednesday
1891	Blackburn Rovers	1936	Arsenal
1892	West Bromwich Albion	1937	Sunderland
1893	Wolverhampton Wanderers	1938	Preston North End
		1939	Portsmouth
1894	Notts County	1946	Derby County
1895	Aston Villa	1947	Charlton Athletic
1896	Sheffield Wednesday	1948	Manchester United
1897	Aston Villa	1949	Wolverhampton Wanderers
1898	Nottingham Forest		
1899	Sheffield United	1950	Arsenal
1900	Bury	1951	Newcastle United
1901	Tottenham Hotspur	1952	Newcastle United
1902	Sheffield United	1953	Blackpool
1903	Bury	1954	West Bromwich Albion
1904	Manchester City	1955	Newcastle United
1905	Aston Villa	1956	Manchester City
1906	Everton	1957	Aston Villa
1907	Sheffield Wednesday	1958	Bolton Wanderers
1908	Wolverhampton Wanderers	1959	Nottingham Forest
		1960	Wolverhampton Wanderers
1909	Manchester United		
1910	Newcastle United	1961	Tottenham Hotspur
1911	Bradford City	1962	Tottenham Hotspur
1912	Barnsley	1963	Manchester United
1913	Aston Villa	1964	West Ham
1914	Burnley	1965	Liverpool
1915	Sheffield United	1966	Everton
1920	Aston Villa	1967	Tottenham Hotspur
1921	Tottenham Hotspur	1968	West Bromwich Albion
1922	Huddersfield Town	1969	Manchester City
1923	Bolton Wanderers	1970	Chelsea
1924	Newcastle United	1971	Arsenal
1925	Sheffield United	1972	Leeds United
1926	Bolton Wanderers	1973	Sunderland
1927	Cardiff City	1974	Liverpool
1928	Blackburn Rovers	1975	West Ham

1976	Southampton	1982	Tottenham Hotspur
1977	Manchester United	1983	Manchester United
1978	Ipswich	1984	Everton
1979	Arsenal	1985	Manchester United
1980	West Ham	1986	Liverpool
1981	Tottenham Hotspur		

MILK CUP

1961	Aston Villa		Wanderers
1962	Norwich City	1975	Aston Villa
1963	Birmingham City	1976	Manchester City
1964	Leicester City	1977	Aston Villa
1965	Chelsea	1978	Nottingham Forest
1966	West Bromwich Albion	1979	Nottingham Forest
1967	Queen's Park Rangers	1980	Wolverhampton
1968	Leeds United		Wanderers
1969	Swindon Town	1981	Liverpool
1970	Manchester City	1982	Liverpool
1971	Tottenham Hotspur	1983	Liverpool
1972	Stoke City	1984	Liverpool
1973	Tottenham Hotspur	1985	Norwich City
1974	Wolverhampton	1986	Oxford United

SCOTTISH CUP

1954	Celtic	1971	Celtic
1955	Clyde	1972	Celtic
1956	Heart of Midlothian	1973	Rangers
1957	Falkirk	1974	Celtic
1958	Clyde	1975	Celtic
1959	St Mirren	1976	Rangers
1960	Rangers	1977	Celtic
1961	Dunfermline	1978	Rangers
1962	Rangers	1979	Rangers
1963	Rangers	1980	Celtic
1964	Rangers	1981	Rangers
1965	Celtic	1982	Aberdeen
1966	Rangers	1983	Aberdeen
1967	Celtic	1984	Aberdeen
1968	Dunfermline	1985	Celtic
1969	Celtic	1986	Aberdeen
1970	Aberdeen		

EUROPEAN CUP

1957	Real Madrid	1972	Ajax
1958	Real Madrid	1973	Ajax
1959	Real Madrid	1974	Bayern Munich
1960	Real Madrid	1975	Bayern Munich
1961	Benfica	1976	Bayern Munich
1962	Benfica	1977	Liverpool
1963	AC Milan	1978	Liverpool
1964	Inter Milan	1979	Nottingham Forest
1965	Inter Milan	1980	Nottingham Forest
1966	Real Madrid	1981	Liverpool
1967	Celtic	1982	Aston Villa
1968	Manchester United	1983	SV Hamburg
1969	AC Milan	1984	Liverpool
1970	Feyenoord	1985	Juventus
1971	Ajax	1986	Steaua Bucharest

EUROPEAN CUP WINNERS' CUP

1961	AC Fiorentina	1974	FC Magdeburg
1962	Atletico Madrid	1975	Dynamo Kiev
1963	Tottenham Hotspur	1976	Anderlecht
1964	Sporting Club, Lisbon	1977	SV Hamburg
1965	West Ham United	1978	Anderlecht
1966	Borussia Dortmund	1979	Barcelona
1967	Bayern Munich	1980	Valencia
1968	AC Milan	1981	Dynamo Tbilisi
1969	Slovan Bratislava	1982	Barcelona
1970	Manchester City	1983	Aberdeen
1971	Chelsea	1984	Juventus
1972	Glasgow Rangers	1985	Everton
1973	AC Milan	1986	Dinamo Kiev

WORLD CUP

1930	Uruguay	1966	England
1934	Italy	1970	Brazil
1938	Italy	1974	West Germany
1950	Uruguay	1978	Argentina
1954	West Germany	1982	Italy
1958	Brazil	1986	Argentina
1962	Brazil		

OLYMPIC GAMES

1908	United Kingdom	1956	USSR
1912	United Kingdom	1960	Yugoslavia
1920	Belgium	1964	Hungary
1924	Uruguay	1968	Hungary
1928	Uruguay	1972	Poland
1932	No competition	1976	East Germany
1936	Italy	1980	Czechoslovakia
1948	Sweden	1984	France
1952	Hungary		

RECORDS

Championship wins: Liverpool sixteen times; Arsenal eight times; Everton and Manchester United seven times; Aston Villa and Sunderland six times.

Highest score in FA Cup: Preston North End 26, Hyde 0 (1887)

Highest score in Cup Final: Bury 6, Derby County 0 (1903)

Highest score by one man in League game: 10 goals, J. Payne for Luton Town v Bristol Rovers (1936)

Highest score by one man in Division I: 7 goals, E. Drake for Arsenal v Aston Villa (1935)

Highest score by one man in a full international: 6 goals, G. J. Bambrick for Ireland v Wales (1930)

Most goals during career: 550, by James McGrory (Glasgow Celtic), 1922–38. **English record:** 434, by A. Rowley (West Bromwich Albion, Fulham, Leicester City and Shrewsbury Town)

Most caps won by amateur: 62, by R. Haider (Kingstonian and Hendon), 1966–73

Most caps won by a professional: Bobby Moore (West Ham United), 108 for England

Most Welsh caps: I. Allchurch (Newcastle United, Cardiff City and Swansea Town), 1950–66, 68

Most Scottish caps: K. Dalglish (Celtic and Liverpool), 1972–82, 90

Most Irish caps: P. Jennings (Watford, Tottenham Hotspur and Arsenal) 1963–82, 96

ATHLETICS

Governing bodies: Amateur Athletic Association, Francis House, Francis Street, London SW1P 1DL; Women's Amateur Athletic Association, Francis House, Francis Street, London SW1P 1DL.

WORLD AND UNITED KINGDOM RECORDS

(The records given here are those that have been officially ratified as at 31st December 1985; they are for fully-automatic timing for distances up to and including 400 metres)

Men

	World	United Kingdom
100 metres	9·93 sec C. Smith (USA)	10·11 sec A. Wells
200 metres	19·72 sec P. Mennea (Italy)	20·21 sec A. Wells
400 metres	43·86 sec L. Evans (USA)	44.82 sec D. Redmond
800 metres	1 min 41·73 sec S. Coe (GB)	1 min 41·73 sec S. Coe
1,000 metres	2 min 12·18 sec S. Coe (GB)	2 min 12·18 sec S. Coe
1,500 metres	3 min 29·46 sec S. Aouita (Mor)	3 min 29·67 sec S. Cram
1 mile	3 min 46·32 sec S. Cram (GB)	3 min 46·32 sec S. Cram
2 kilometres	4 min 51·39 sec S. Cram (GB)	4 min 51·39 sec S. Cram
3 kilometres	7 min 32·1 sec H. Rono (Kenya)	7 min 32·79 sec D. Moorcroft
2 miles	8 min 13·51 sec S. Ovett (GB)	8 min 13·51 sec S. Ovett
5 kilometres	13 min 00·40 sec S. Aouita (Mor)	13 min 0·41 sec D. Moorcroft
10 kilometres	27 min 13·81 sec F. Mamede (Por)	27 min 30·3 sec B. Foster
Marathon	2 hrs 07 min 12 sec C. Lopes (Por)	2 hrs 07 min 13 sec S. Jones
110 metres hurdles	12·93 sec R. Nehemiah (USA)	13·43 sec M. Holtom
400 metres hurdles	47·02 sec E. Moses (USA)	48·12 sec D. Hemery
3,000 metres steeplechase	8 min 05·04 sec H. Rono (Kenya)	8 min 13·59 sec C. Reitz
High jump	2·41 metres I. Paklin (Sov)	2·26 metres G. Parsons

Pole vault	6·00 metres	5·65 metres
	S. Bubka (Sov)	K. Stock
Long jump	8·90 metres	8·23 metres
	R. Beamon (USA)	L. Davies
Triple jump	17·97 metres	17·57 metres
	W. Banks (USA)	K. Connor
Shot-putt	22·62 metres	21·68 metres
	U. Timmerman (EG)	G. Capes
Discus-throw	71·86 metres	65·16 metres
	Y. Dunchev (Sov)	R. Slaney
Hammer-throw	86·34 metres	77·54 metres
	Y. Sedykh (Sov)	M. Girvan
Javelin-throw	104·80 metres	91·40 metres
	U. Hohn (EG)	R. Bradstock
Decathlon	8,798/8,832 pts.	8,796/8,847 pts
	J. Hingsen (WG)	D. Thompson

Women

100 metres	10·76 sec	11·10 sec
	E. Ashford (USA)	K. Smallwood
200 metres	21·71 sec	22·10 sec
	M. Koch (EG)	K. Cook
400 metres	47·60 sec	49·33 sec
	M. Koch (EG)	K. Cook
800 metres	1 min 53·28 sec	1 min 57·42 sec
	J. Kratochvilova (Czech)	K. McDermott
1,500 metres	3 min 52·47 sec	3 min 59·96 sec
	T. Kazankina (Sov)	Z. Budd
1 mile	4 min 16·71 sec	4 min 17·57 sec
	M. Slaney (USA)	Z. Budd
3 kilometres	8 min 22·62 sec	8 min 28·83 sec
	T. Kazankina (Sov)	Z. Budd
5 kilometres	14 min 48·07 sec	14 min 48·07 sec
	Z. Budd (GB)	Z. Budd
10 kilometres	30 min 59·42 sec	32 min 57·17 sec
	I. Kristiansen (Nor)	K. Binns
Marathon	2 hrs 21 min 06 sec	2 hrs 28 min 04 sec
	I. Kristiansen (Nor)	V. Marot
100 metres hurdles	12·36 sec	12·87 sec
	G. Rabsztyn (Pol)	S. Strong
400 metres hurdles	53·56 sec	56·04 sec
	S. Busch (EG)	S. Morley
High jump	2·07 metres	1·95 metres
	L. Andonova (Bul)	D. Elliott

	World	United Kingdom
Long jump	7·44 metres	6·90 metres
	H. Dreschler (EG)	B. Kinch
Shot-putt	22·53 metres	18·99 metres
	N. Lisovskaya (Sov)	M. Ritchie
Discus-throw	74·56 metres	67·48 metres
	Z. Silhava (Czech)	M. Ritchie
Javelin-throw	75·40 metres	73·58 metres
	P. Felke (EG)	T. Sanderson
Heptathlon	6,867/6,946 pts	6,353/6,347 pts
	S. Paetz (EG)	J. Livermore

THE MILE RECORD

1884	George (GB)	4 min 12·75 sec
1915	Taber (USA)	4 min 12·6 sec
1923	Nurmi (Finland)	4 min 10·4 sec
1931	Ladoumègue (France)	4 min 9·2 sec
1933	Lovelock (New Zealand)	4 min 7·6 sec
1934	Cunningham (USA)	4 min 6·8 sec
1937	Wooderson (GB)	4 min 6·4 sec
1942	Hägg (Sweden)	4 min 6·2 sec
1942	Andersson (Sweden)	4 min 6·2 sec
1942	Hägg (Sweden)	4 min 4·6 sec
1943	Andersson (Sweden)	4 min 2·6 sec
1944	Andersson (Sweden)	4 min 1·6 sec
1945	Hägg (Sweden)	4 min 1·3 sec
1954	Bannister (GB)	3 min 59·4 sec
1954	Landy (Australia)	3 min 57·9 sec
1957	Ibbotson (GB)	3 min 57·2 sec
1958	Elliott (Australia)	3 min 54·5 sec
1962	Snell (New Zealand)	3 min 54·4 sec
1964	Snell (New Zealand)	3 min 54·1 sec
1965	Jazy (France)	3 min 53·6 sec
1966	Ryun (USA)	3 min 51·3 sec
1967	Ryun (USA)	3 min 51·1 sec
1975	Bayi (Tanzania)	3 min 51·0 sec
1975	Walker (New Zealand)	3 min 49·4 sec
1979	Coe (GB)	3 min 49·0 sec
1980	Ovett (GB)	3 min 48·8 sec
1981	Coe (GB)	3 min 48·53 sec
1981	Ovett (GB)	3 min 48·40 sec
1981	Coe (GB)	3 min 47·43 sec
1985	Cram (GB)	3 min 46·32 sec

OLYMPIC GAMES (LOS ANGELES 1984)
Men

100 metres	C. Lewis (USA)	9·99 sec
200 metres	C. Lewis (USA)	19·80 sec O.R.
400 metres	A. Babers (USA)	44·27 sec
800 metres	J. Cruz (Brazil)	1 min 43·0 sec
1,500 metres	S. Coe (GB)	3 min 32·53 sec
5,000 metres	S. Aouita (Mor)	13 min 5·59 sec
10,000 metres	A. Cova (Italy)	27 min 47·54 sec
Marathon	C. Lopes (Portugal)	2 hr 9 min 20·42 sec
110 metres hurdles	R. Kingdom (USA)	13·2 sec
400 metres hurdles	E. Moses (USA)	47·75 sec
3,000 metres steeplechase	J. Korir (Kenya)	8 min 11·8 sec
20 km walk	E. Canto (Mexico)	1 hr 23·13 sec
50 km walk	R. Gonzalez (Mexico)	3 hr 47 min 26 sec
4 × 100 metres relay	USA	37·83 sec W.R.
4 × 400 metres relay	USA	2 min 57·91 sec
High jump	D. Mögenburg (WG)	2·35 metres
Pole vault	P. Quinon (France)	5·75 metres
Long jump	C. Lewis (USA)	8·54 metres
Triple jump	A. Joyner (USA)	17·26 metres
Shot putt	A. Andrei (Italy)	21·26 metres
Discus	R. Danneberg (WG)	66·6 metres
Hammer	J. Tiainen (Finland)	78·08 metres
Javelin	B. Haerkoenen (Finland)	86·76 metres
Decathlon	D. Thompson (GB)	8,797 pts O.R.

Women

100 metres	E. Ashford (USA)	10·97 sec
200 metres	V. Brisco-Hooks (USA)	21·81 sec
400 metres	V. Brisco-Hooks (USA)	48·83 sec
800 metres	D. Melinte (Romania)	1 min 57·6 sec.
1,500 metres	G. Dorio (Italy)	4 min 3·25 sec
3,000 metres	N. Puica (Romania)	8 min 35·96 sec
Marathon	J. Benoit (USA)	2 hr 24 min 52 sec
100 metres hurdles	B. Fitzgerald-Brown (USA)	12·84 sec
400 metres hurdles	N. El Moutawakel (Mor)	54·62 sec O.R.

4 × 100 metres relay	USA	41·65 sec
4 × 400 metres relay	USA	3 min 18·29 sec
High jump	U. Meyfarth (WG)	2·02 metres
Long jump	A. Stanciu (Romania)	6·96 metres
Shot putt	C. Losch (WG)	20·48 metres
Discus	R. Stalman (Netherlands)	65·36 metres
Javelin	T. Sanderson (GB)	69·56 metres
Heptathlon	G. Nunn (Australia)	6,390 pts

BADMINTON

Governing body: Badminton Association of England, Bradwell Road, Milton Keynes, MK8 9LA.

THOMAS CUP
(Men's International Championship)

		Venue
1964	Indonesia beat Denmark	Tokyo
1967	Malaysia beat Indonesia	Djakarta
1970	Indonesia beat Malaysia	Kuala Lumpur
1973	Indonesia beat Denmark	Djakarta
1976	Indonesia beat Malaysia	Djakarta
1979	Indonesia beat Denmark	Djakarta
1982	China beat Indonesia	London
1984	Indonesia beat China	Kuala Lumpur

ALL-ENGLAND CHAMPIONSHIPS
(Men's singles)

1964	K. A. Nielsen	1979	Lim Swie-king
1965	Erland Kops	1980	P. Prakash
1966	T. Huang	1981	Lim Swie-king
1967	Erland Kops	1982	M. Frost
1968–74	R. Hartono	1983	Luan Jin
1975	S. Pri	1984	M. Frost
1976	R. Hartono	1985	Z. Jianhua
1977	F. Delfs	1986	M. Frost
1978	Lim Swie-king		

UBER CUP
(Women's International Championship)

		Venue
1963	USA beat England	Wilmington
1966	Japan beat USA	Wellington
1969	Japan beat Indonesia	Tokyo
1972	Japan beat Indonesia	Tokyo
1975	Indonesia beat Japan	Djakarta
1978	Japan beat Indonesia	Djakarta
1981	Japan beat Indonesia	Tokyo
1984	China beat England	Kuala Lumpur

ALL-ENGLAND CHAMPIONSHIPS
(Women's singles)

1964	Mrs. G. C. K. Hashman	1976	G. Gilks
1965	U. Smith	1977	H. Yuki
1966	Mrs. G. C. K. Hashman	1978	Mrs. G. Gilks
1967	Mrs. G. C. K. Hashman	1979	L. Koppen
1968	Mrs. E. Twedberg	1980	C. Köpen
1969	H. Yuki	1981	Sun Ai Hwang
1970	E. Takenaka	1982	Z. Ailing
1971	Mrs. E. Twedberg	1983	Z. Ailing
1972	Mrs. N. Nakayama	1984	Li Lingwei
1973	M. Beck	1985	P. Hanaiping
1974	H. Yuki	1986	K. Yun-Ja
1975	H. Yuki		

INTER-COUNTY CHAMPIONSHIP

1962	Surrey	1980	Lancashire
1963	Surrey	1981	Lancashire
1964	Essex	1982	Surrey
1965–75	Surrey	1983	Surrey
1976	Lancashire	1984	Surrey
1977	Essex	1985	Surrey
1978	Essex	1986	Lancashire
1979	Lancashire		

BASKETBALL

Governing body: English Basket Ball Association, Calomax House, Lupton Avenue, Leeds LS9 7EE.

OLYMPIC GAMES 1984

Men	Women
USA	USA

NATIONAL CHAMPIONSHIP

1979	Crystal Palace	1983	Sunderland
1980	Crystal Palace	1984	Solent Stars
1981	Sunderland	1985	Manchester United
1982	Crystal Palace		

NATIONAL CUP

1979	Doncaster	1983	Solent Stars
1980	Crystal Palace	1984	Solent Stars
1981	Crystal Palace	1985	Kingston
1982	Solent Stars		

NATIONAL LEAGUE

1979	Doncaster	1983	Crystal Palace
1980	Crystal Palace	1984	Solent Stars
1981	Team Fiat	1985	Kingston
1982	Crystal Palace		

NBA CHAMPIONSHIP

1979	Seattle Supersonics	1982	North Carolina State
1980	Los Angeles Lakers	1983	Philadelphia 76ers
1981	North Carolina	1984	Los Angeles Lakers

BOXING

Governing bodies: British Boxing Board of Control, 70 Vauxhall Bridge Road, London SW1V 2RP; Amateur Boxing Association, Francis House, Francis Street, London SW1P 1DE.

OLYMPIC GAMES 1984

Super Heavy	T. Biggs (USA)
Heavy	H. Tillman (USA)
Light Heavy	A. Josipovic (Yugoslavia)
Middle	S. Joon-Sup (S. Korea)
Light Middle	F. Tate (USA)
Welter	M. Breland (USA)
Light Welter	J. Page (USA)
Light	P. Whitaker (USA)
Feather	M. Taylor (USA)
Bantam	M. Stecca (Italy)
Fly	S. McCrory (USA)
Light Fly	P. Gonzales (USA)

WORLD AND EUROPEAN PROFESSIONAL CHAMPIONS as at 31/3/86

Weight	World (WBC)	World (WBA)	Europe
Heavy	Pinklon Thomas (USA)	Tim Witherspoon (USA)	Frank Bruno (Great Britain)
Cruiser	Bernard Benton (USA)	Dwight Braxton (USA)	Not recognised
Light Heavy	J. B. Williamson (USA)	Vacant	Alex Blanchard (Holland)
Middle	Marvin Hagler (USA)	Marvin Hagler (USA)	Herol Graham (Great Britain)
Lightmiddle	Tommy Hearns (USA)	Mike McCallum (Jamaica)	Said Skouma (France)
Welter	Don Curry (USA)	Don Curry (USA)	Lloyd Honeyghan (Great Britain)
Lightwelter	Lonnie Smith (USA)	Ulbado Sacco (Argentina)	Terry Marsh (Great Britain)
Light	Hector Camacho (USA)	Livingstone Bramble (USA)	Gert Bo Jacobson (Holland)
Superfeather	Julio Ceasar Chavez (Mexico)	Wilfred Gomez (Puerto Rico)	Vacant
Feather	Azumah Nelson (Ghana)	Barry McGuigan (Great Britain)	Jim McDonnell (Great Britain)
Superbantam	Samart Payak-Aroom (Thailand)	Victor Calle Jas (Puerto Rico)	Not recognised

Weight	World (WBC)	World (WBA)	Europe
Bantam	Miguel Lora (Columbia)	Ricardo Sandoval (USA)	Ciro de Leva (Italy)
Superfly	Jiro Watanabe (Japan)	Kaosay Galaxi (Thailand)	Not recognised
Fly	Sot Chitalada (Thailand)	Hilario Zapata (Panama)	Charlie Magri (Great Britain)
Lightfly	Jungkoo Chang (Korea)	Myung-Woo Yuh (Korea)	Not recognised

WORLD HEAVYWEIGHT CHAMPIONS

1906	Tommy Burns (Canada)	1952	Rocky Marciano (USA)
1908	Jack Johnson (USA)	1956	Floyd Patterson (USA)
1915	Jess Willard (USA)	1959	Ingemar Johansson (Sweden)
1919	Jack Dempsey (USA)		
1926	Gene Tunney (USA)	1960	Floyd Patterson (USA)
1930	Max Schmeling (Germany)	1962	Sonny Liston (USA)
1932	Jack Sharkey (USA)	1964	Cassius Clay (USA)
1933	Primo Carnera (Italy)	1970	Joe Frazier (USA)
1934	Max Baer (USA)	1973	George Foreman (USA)
1935	James Braddock (USA)	1974	Muhammad Ali (USA)
1937	Joe Louis (USA)	1978	Leon Spinks (USA)
1949	Ezzard Charles (USA)	1979–82	L. Holmes (USA)
1951	Jersey Joe Walcott (USA)	1984	G. Page (USA)

BRITISH PROFESSIONAL CHAMPIONS
as at 31/3/86

Heavy	H. Currie	Light welter	T. Marsh
Cruiser	S. Reeson	Light	T. Willis
Light heavy	D. Andries	Super feather	J. Doherty
Middle	H. Graham	Feather	Vacant
Light middle	C. Pyatt	Bantam	R. Gilbody
Welter	L. Honeyghan	Fly	D. McKenzie

BRITISH AMATEUR CHAMPIONS 1985

Super Heavy	G. Williamson	Light Welter	I. Mustafa
Heavy	H. Hylton	Light	E. McAuley
Light Heavy	J. Beckles	Feather	F. Havard
Middle	D. Cronin	Bantam	S. Murphy
Light Middle	R. Douglas	Fly	P. Clinton
Welter	E. McDonald	Light Fly	M. Epton

RECORDS

Longest reigning world champion: Joe Louis (22nd June 1937–1st March 1949)

Longest reigning British heavyweight champion: Henry Cooper (12th January 1959–13th June 1970)

CRICKET

Governing bodies: The Cricket Council, Lord's Ground, London NW8 8QN; Women's Cricket Association, 16 Upper Woburn Place, London WC1H 0QP.

TEST MATCH RECORDS

England v Australia 1876–1986
The leading records for the series of matches are as follows:

Highest innings totals
903 for 7 dec.   by England, at The Oval, 1938
729 for 6 dec.   by Australia, at Lord's, 1930

Lowest innings totals
36   by Australia, at Birmingham, 1902
45   by England, at Sydney, 1886–87

Highest individual innings
364   L. Hutton, for England, at The Oval, 1938
334   D. G. Bradman, for Australia, at Leeds, 1930
311   R. B. Simpson, for Australia, at Manchester, 1964
307   R. M. Cowper, for Australia, at Melbourne, 1965–66
304   D. G. Bradman, for Australia, at Leeds, 1934

Most runs by a batsman in one series
England in England: 732 (av 81·33) by D. I. Gower, 1985
England in Australia: 905 (av 113·12) by W. R. Hammond, 1928–29
Australia in England: 974 (av 139·14) by D. G. Bradman, 1930
Australia in Australia: 810 (av 90·00) by D. G. Bradman, 1936–37

Batsmen scoring two centuries in a match
136 & 130   W. Bardsley, Australia, The Oval, 1909
176 & 127   H. Sutcliffe, England, Melbourne, 1924–25
119 n.o. & 177   W. R. Hammond, England, Adelaide, 1928–29
147 & 103 n.o.   D. C. S. Compton, England, Adelaide, 1946–47
122 & 124 n.o.   A. R. Morris, Australia, Adelaide, 1946–47

Bowlers taking 9 or 10 wickets in an innings
   10 for 53   J. C. Laker, England, at Manchester (second innings), 1956
    9 for 37   J. C. Laker, England, at Manchester (first innings), 1956
    9 for 121 A. A. Mailey, Australia, at Melbourne, 1920–21

Bowlers taking 15 or more wickets in a match
   19 for 90   J. C. Laker, England, at Manchester, 1956
   16 for 137 R. A. L. Massie, Australia, at Lord's, 1972
   15 for 104 H. Verity, England, at Lord's, 1934
   15 for 124 W. Rhodes, England, at Melbourne, 1903–4

Hat-tricks
  For England   W. Bates, at Melbourne, 1882–83
                J. Briggs, at Sydney, 1891–92
                J. T. Hearne, at Leeds, 1899
  For Australia F. R. Spofforth, at Melbourne, 1878–79
                H. Trumble, at Melbourne, 1901–2
                H. Trumble, at Melbourne, 1903–4

Most wickets taken by a bowler in one series
  England in England: 46 (av 9·60), J. C. Laker, 1956
  England in Australia: 38 (av 23·18), M. W. Tate, 1924–25
  Australia in England: 42 (av 21·26), T. M. Alderman, 1981
  Australia in Australia: 41 (av 12·85), R. M. Hogg, 1978–79

Record partnerships for each wicket – England
    1st 323   J. B. Hobbs & W. Rhodes, at Melbourne, 1911–12
   2nd 382   L. Hutton & M. Leyland, at The Oval, 1938
    3rd 262   W. R. Hammond & D. R. Jardine, at Adelaide, 1928–29
    4th 222   W. R. Hammond & E. Paynter, at Lord's, 1938
    5th 206   E. Paynter & D. C. S. Compton, at Nottingham, 1938
    6th 215   J. Hardstaff jnr & L. Hutton, at The Oval, 1938
          215   G. Boycott & A. P. E. Knott, at Nottingham, 1977
    7th 143   F. E. Woolley & J. Vine, at Sydney, 1911–12
    8th 124   E. P. Hendren & H. Larwood, at Brisbane, 1928–29
    9th 151   W. H. Scotton & W. W. Read, at The Oval, 1884
  10th 130   R. E. Foster & W. Rhodes, at Sydney, 1903–4

Record partnerships for each wicket – Australia
    1st 244   R. B. Simpson & W. M. Lawry, at Adelaide, 1965–66
   2nd 451   D. G. Bradman & W. H. Ponsford, at The Oval, 1934
    3rd 276   D. G. Bradman & A. L. Hassett, at Brisbane, 1946–47
    4th 388   D. G. Bradman & W. H. Ponsford, at Leeds, 1934
    5th 405   D. G. Bradman & S. G. Barnes, at Sydney, 1946–47
    6th 346   D. G. Bradman & J. H. Fingleton, at Melbourne, 1936–37
    7th 165   C. Hill & H. Trumble, at Melbourne, 1897–98

8th 243   C. Hill & R. J. Hartigan, at Adelaide, 1907–8
9th 154   S. E. Gregory & J. McC. Blackham, at Sydney, 1894–95
10th 127   J. M. Taylor & A. A. Mailey, at Sydney, 1924–25

TEST CRICKET 1877–1986
Summarised results of series completed by 31 March 1986

ENGLAND v	W	D	L	AUSTRALIA v	W	D	L
Australia	86	75	96	England	96	75	86
South Africa	46	38	18	South Africa	29	13	11
West Indies	21	34	30	West Indies	27	15	19
India	30	33	9	New Zealand	9	7	5
Pakistan	13	23	3	India	20	14	8
New Zealand	30	27	3	Pakistan	11	9	8
Sri Lanka	1	1	0	Sri Lanka	1	0	0

SOUTH AFRICA v	W	D	L	SRI LANKA v	W	D	L
England	18	38	46	England	0	1	1
Australia	11	13	29	Australia	0	0	1
New Zealand	9	6	2	New Zealand	0	1	4
				India	1	3	0
INDIA v	W	D	L	Pakistan	1	3	5
England	9	33	30				
Australia	8	14	20	WEST INDIES v	W	D	L
West Indies	6	32	22	England	30	34	21
New Zealand	10	11	4	Australia	19	15	27
Pakistan	4	25	6	India	22	32	6
Sri Lanka	0	3	1	New Zealand	7	11	3
				Pakistan	7	8	4
NEW ZEALAND v	W	D	L				
England	3	27	30	PAKISTAN v	W	D	L
Australia	5	7	9	England	3	23	13
South Africa	2	6	9	Australia	8	9	11
West Indies	3	11	7	West Indies	4	8	7
India	4	11	10	New Zealand	10	14	3
Sri Lanka	4	1	0	India	6	25	4
Pakistan	3	14	10	Sri Lanka	5	3	1

**Greatest number of appearances in Test Cricket
(series completed by 31 March 1986)**

ENGLAND

M. C. Cowdrey	114	R. Illingworth	61
G. Boycott	108	J. B. Hobbs	61
A. P. E. Knott	95	K. W. R. Fletcher	59
T. G. Evans	91	A. W. Greig	58
R. G. D. Willis	90	W. Rhodes	58
D. L. Underwood	86	R. W. Taylor	57
W. R. Hammond	85	H. Sutcliffe	54
K. F. Barrington	82	F. J. Titmus	53
T. W. Graveney	79	A. V. Bedser	51
L. Hutton	79	E. P. Hendren	51
I. T. Botham	79	D. L. Amiss	50
D. C. S. Compton	78	M. J. K. Smith	50
J. H. Edrich	77	J. A. Snow	49
D. I. Gower	76	G. A. R. Lock	49
J. B. Statham	70	G. A. Gooch	48
F. S. Trueman	67	L. E. G. Ames	47
P. B. H. May	66	D. W. Randall	47
F. E. Woolley	64	J. C. Laker	46
E. R. Dexter	62	C. M. Old	46
T. E. Bailey	61	J. M. Parks	46

AUSTRALIA

R. W. Marsh	96	G. D. McKenzie	60
G. S. Chappell	87	S. E. Gregory	58
A. R. Border	81	K. R. Miller	55
R. N. Harvey	79	W. A. Oldfield	54
I. M. Chappell	75	G. M. Wood	53
K. D. Walters	74	D. G. Bradman	52
K. J. Hughes	70	J. R. Thomson	51
D. K. Lillee	70	A. W. Grout	51
W. M. Lawry	67	W. W. Armstrong	50
I. M. Redpath	66	C. Hill	49
R. Benaud	63	V. Trumper	48
R. B. Simpson	62	C. C. McDonald	47
R. R. Lindwall	61	A. R. Morris	46

SOUTH AFRICA

J. H. B. Waite	50	R. A. McLean	40
A. D. Nourse, sen	45	H. J. Tayfield	37
B. Mitchell	42	D. J. McGlew	34
H. W. Taylor	42	A. D. Nourse, jnr	34
T. L. Goddard	41	E. J. Barlow	30

NEW ZEALAND

R. J. Hadlee	63	G. M. Dowling	39
B. E. Congdon	61	J. M. Parker	36
J. R. Reid	58	B. A. Edgar	36
M. G. Burgess	50	R. O. Collinge	35
G. P. Howarth	47	K. J. Wadsworth	33
J. G. Wright	46	R. C. Motz	32
J. V. Coney	46	V. Pollard	32
B. L. Cairns	43	B. F. Hastings	31
B. Sutcliffe	42	H. J. Howarth	31
G. M. Turner	41	B. R. Taylor	30

WEST INDIES

C. H. Lloyd	110	J. Garner	51
G. S. Sobers	93	F. M. Worrell	51
L. R. Gibbs	79	H. A. Gomes	49
R. B. Kanhai	79	W. W. Hall	48
I. V. A. Richards	77	E. D. Weekes	48
A. I. Kallicharran	66	A. M. E. Roberts	47
C. G. Greenidge	66	B. F. Butcher	44
D. L. Murray	62	C. C. Hunte	44
R. C. Fredericks	59	C. L. Walcott	44
M. A. Holding	55	V. A. Holder	40
D. L. Haynes	54	M. D. Marshall	40

INDIA

S. M. Gavaskar	112	M. B. Amarnath	54
G. R. Viswanath	91	E. A. S. Prasanna	49
S. M. H. Kirmani	88	Mansur Ali Khan	46
D. B. Vengsarkar	82	F. M. Engineer	46
R. N. Kapil Dev	74	V. Mankad	44
B. S. Bedi	67	P. Roy	43
P. R. Umrigar	59	R. G. Nadkarni	41
B. S. Chandrasekhar	58	C. P. S. Chauhan	40
S. Venkataraghavan	57	A. D. Gaekwad	40
C. G. Borde	55	R. J. Shastri	40
V. L. Manjrekar	55		

PAKISTAN

Wasim Bari	81	Mudassar Nazar	58
Zaheer Abbas	78	Imran Khan	57
Javed Miandad	74	Mushtaq Mohammad	57
Majid Khan	63	Wasim Raja	57
Asif Iqbal	58	Hanif Mohammad	55

PAKISTAN (*contd.*)

Sarfraz Nawaz	55	Saeed Ahmed	41
Intikhab Alam	49	Sadiq Mohammad	41
Mohsin Khan	46	Iqbal Qasim	41
Imtiaz Ahmed	41	Abdul Qadir	39

SRI LANKA

S. Wettimuny	20	A. L. F. de Mel	16
L. R. D. Mendis	19	J. R. Ratnayeke	14
R. S. Madugalle	18	D. S. de Silva	12
A. Ranatunga	18	R. J. Ratnayake	11
R. L. Dias	16	P. A. de Silva	10

COUNTY CHAMPIONS
(*since 1946*)

1946	Yorkshire	1966	Yorkshire
1947	Middlesex	1967	Yorkshire
1948	Glamorgan	1968	Yorkshire
1949	Middlesex & Yorkshire	1969	Glamorgan
1950	Lancashire & Surrey	1970	Kent
1951	Warwickshire	1971	Surrey
1952	Surrey	1972	Warwickshire
1953	Surrey	1973	Hampshire
1954	Surrey	1974	Worcestershire
1955	Surrey	1975	Leicestershire
1956	Surrey	1976	Middlesex
1957	Surrey	1977	Middlesex & Kent
1958	Surrey	1978	Kent
1959	Yorkshire	1979	Essex
1960	Yorkshire	1980	Middlesex
1961	Hampshire	1981	Nottinghamshire
1962	Yorkshire	1982	Middlesex
1963	Yorkshire	1983	Essex
1964	Worcestershire	1984	Essex
1965	Worcestershire	1985	Middlesex

Since 1864 the title has been won outright by:

Yorkshire	31	Kent	6
Surrey	18	Essex	3
Nottinghamshire	13	Gloucestershire	3
Middlesex	9	Warwickshire	3
Lancashire	8	Worcestershire	3

| Glamorgan | 2 | Derbyshire | 1 |
| Hampshire | 2 | Leicestershire | 1 |

Eight times it has been shared by:

Nottinghamshire	5	Gloucestershire	1
Lancashire	4	Surrey	1
Yorkshire	2	Kent	1
Middlesex	2		

Northamptonshire, Somerset and Sussex are the only counties never to have been first in the County Championship.

GILLETTE/NATWEST BANK TROPHY
(60-over competition, sponsored initially by Gillette and by NatWest since 1981)

1963	Sussex	1975	Lancashire
1964	Sussex	1976	Northamptonshire
1965	Yorkshire	1977	Middlesex
1966	Warwickshire	1978	Sussex
1967	Kent	1979	Somerset
1968	Warwickshire	1980	Middlesex
1969	Yorkshire	1981	Derbyshire
1970	Lancashire	1982	Surrey
1971	Lancashire	1983	Somerset
1972	Lancashire	1984	Middlesex
1973	Gloucestershire	1985	Essex
1974	Kent		

BENSON & HEDGES CUP
(55-over competition)

1972	Leicestershire	1979	Essex
1973	Kent	1980	Northamptonshire
1974	Surrey	1981	Somerset
1975	Leicestershire	1982	Somerset
1976	Kent	1983	Middlesex
1977	Gloucestershire	1984	Lancashire
1978	Kent	1985	Leicestershire

JOHN PLAYER LEAGUE CHAMPIONS
(40-over Sunday competition)

1969	Lancashire	1978	Hampshire
1970	Lancashire	1979	Somerset
1971	Worcestershire	1980	Warwickshire
1972	Kent	1981	Essex
1973	Kent	1982	Sussex
1974	Leicestershire	1983	Yorkshire
1975	Hampshire	1984	Essex
1976	Kent	1985	Essex
1977	Leicestershire		

WORLD CUP
(60-over competition)

1975	West Indies	(runner-up Australia)
1979	West Indies	(runner-up England)
1983	India	(runner-up West Indies)

the next World Cup will be played in India and Pakistan in 1987

RECORDS

Highest score in first-class cricket: 499 Hanif Mohammad, for Karachi v Bahawalpur, 1958–59

Highest score in test cricket: 365 not out, G. S. Sobers, for West Indies v Pakistan, 1958

Most runs in first-class cricket: 61,237 J. B. Hobbs (Surrey & England), 1905 to 1934

Most runs in a season: 3,816 D. C. S. Compton (Middlesex & England), 1947

Most centuries in a season: 18 D. C. S. Compton, 1947

Fastest recorded century: 100 in 35 minutes P. G. H. Fender, Surrey v Northamptonshire, 1920. S. J. O'Shaughnessy, Lancashire v Leicestershire, 1983

Highest team innings: 1,107 Victoria v New South Wales, 1926–27

Most runs in a day: 721 Australians v Essex, Southend, 1948

Highest partnership: 577 V. S. Hazare & Gul Mahomed, for Baroda v Holkar, 4th wicket, 1946–47

Biggest win: Pakistan Western Railways beat Dera Ismail Khan by an innings and 851 runs, Lahore, Pakistan, 1964–65

Most wickets in a season: 304 A. P. 'Tich' Freeman, 1928

Most wickets in a career: 4,187 W. Rhodes (Yorkshire & England), 1898 to 1930.

Most wickets in a match: 19 J. C. Laker, England v Australia, Manchester, 1956

CROSS-COUNTRY RUNNING

Governing bodies: English Cross-Country Union, 7 Wolsey Way, Cherry Hinton, Cambridge; Women's Cross-Country & Race Walking Association, 10 Anderton Close, Bury, Lancs.

ENGLISH CHAMPIONSHIP

Men

	Individual	*Team*
1980	N. Rose (Bristol H.)	Tipton Harriers
1981	J. Goater (Shaftesbury H.)	Tipton Harriers
1982	D. Clarke (Hercules/Wimbleton)	Tipton Harriers
1983	T. Hutchings (Crawley AC)	Aldershot/Farnham
1984	E. Martin (Basildon)	Aldershot/Farnham
1985	D. Lewis (Rossendale)	Aldershot/Farnham
1986	T. Hutchings (Crawley AC)	Tipton Harriers

Women

	Individual	*Team*
1980	R. Smeegh (Aldershot/Farnham)	Birchfield
1981	W. Smith (Hounslow AC)	Sale Harriers
1982	P. Fudge (Hounslow AC)	Sale Harriers
1983	C. Benning (Southampton/Eastleigh)	Sale Harriers
1984	J. Furniss (Sheffield AC)	Aldershot/Farnham
1985	A. Tooby (Cardiff AAC)	Crawley AC
1986	C. Bradford (Clevedon)	Sale Harriers

INTERNATIONAL CHAMPIONSHIP

Men

	Individual	*Team*	*Venue*
1977	L. Schots (Belgium)	Belgium	Dusseldorf
1978	J. Tracey (Ireland)	France	Glasgow
1979	J. Tracey (Ireland)	England	Limerick
1980	C. Virgin (USA)	England	Paris
1981	C. Virgin (USA)	Ethiopia	Madrid
1982	M. Kedir (Ethiopia)	Ethiopia	Rome
1983	B. Devele (Ethiopia)	Ethiopia	Gateshead
1984	C. Lopez (Portugal)	Ethiopia	New Jersey
1985	C. Lopez (Portugal)	Ethiopia	Lisbon
1986	J. Ngugi (Kenya)	Kenya	Colombier

	Women		
1977	C. Valero (Spain)	USSR	Dusseldorf
1978	G. Waitz (Norway)	Rumania	Glasgow
1979	G. Waitz (Norway)	USA	Limerick
1980	G. Waitz (Norway)	USSR	Paris
1981	G. Waitz (Norway)	USSR	Madrid
1982	M. Puica (Rumania)	USSR	Rome
1983	G. Waitz (Norway)	USA	Gateshead
1984	M. Puica (Rumania)	USA	New Jersey
1985	Z. Budd (England)	USA	Lisbon
1986	Z. Budd (England)	England	Colombier

CYCLING

Governing body: British Cycling Federation, 16 Upper Woburn Place, London WC1H 0QE.

1984 OLYMPIC GAMES WINNERS

Men

1,000 metres sprint	M. Gorski (USA)
1,000 metres time trial	F. Schmidtke (W. Germany)
4,000 metres pursuit	S. Hegg (USA)
4,000 metres team pursuit	Australia
Road race	A. Grewal (USA)
100 km road team time trial	Italy
Individual points race	R. Illegems (Belgium)

Women

Road race	C. Carpenter-Phinney (USA)

1985 WORLD CHAMPIONS

Men

Professional road race	J. Zoetemelk (Holland)
Amateur road race	L. Piasecki (Poland)
Professional sprint	K. Nakano (Japan)
Amateur sprint	L. Hesslich (E. Germany)
Professional 5000 m pursuit	H. Oersted (Denmark)
Amateur 4000 m pursuit	V. Eekimov (USSR)
Amateur 4000 m team pursuit	Italy
Professional 100 km motor-paced	B. Vicino (Italy)

Amateur motor-paced hour	R. Dotti (Italy)
Amateur tandem sprint	{ R. Rehounek (Czechoslovakia) V. Voboril (Czechoslovakia)
Amateur 1 km TT	J. Glücklich (E. Germany)
Amateur 100 km team TT	USSR

Women (all amateur)

Road race	J. Longo (France)
Sprint	I. Nicoloso (France)
Pursuit	R. Twigg (USA)

RECORDS

Men's professional motor-paced 1 hour record: 78 km 809 m, W. Avogardi in Italy, 1975

Men's professional unpaced standing start 1 hour record: 51·151 km, F. Moser in Mexico, 1984

Men's amateur unpaced flying start 1 kilometre: 59·50 sec, S. Wallace 1985

EQUESTRIANISM

Governing bodies: British Horse Society and British Show Jumping Association, National Equestrian Centre, Stoneleigh, Kenilworth, Warwickshire, CV8 2LR.

OLYMPIC GAMES

(Team winners are shown first followed by individual winners)

Date	Showjumping	Horse trials	Dressage
1952	Great Britain	Sweden	Sweden
	P. J. d'Oriola (Fra)	H. G. von Blixen-Finecke (Swe)	Maj. H. St Cyr (Swe)
1956	West Germany	Great Britain	Sweden
	H. G. Winkler (W. Ger)	P. Kastenman (Swe)	Maj. H. St Cyr (Swe)
1960	West Germany	Australia	No team winner
	R. d'Inzeo (Italy)	L. Morgan (Aust)	S. Filatov (USSR)
1964	West Germany	Italy	West Germany
	P. J. d'Oriola (Fra)	M. Checcoli (Ita)	H. Chammartin (Swi)

Date	Showjumping	Horse trials	Dressage
1968	Canada	Great Britain	West Germany
	W. Steinkraus (USA)	J. J. Guyon (Fra)	I. Kizimov (USSR)
1972	West Germany	Great Britain	USSR
	G. Mancinelli (Italy)	R. Meade (GB)	L. Linsenhoff (W. Ger)
1976	France	USA	West Germany
	A. Schockemöhle (W. Ger)	E. Coffin (USA)	C. Stückelberger (Swi)
1984	USA	USA	West Germany
	J. Fargis (USA)	M. Todd (NZ)	R. Klimke (W. Ger)

WORLD CHAMPIONSHIPS

Date	Horse trials	Dressage
1966	Ireland	West Germany
	Capt C. Moratorio (Arg)	J. Neckermann (W. Ger)
1970	Great Britain	USSR
	M. Gordon-Watson (GB)	E. Petuchkova (USSR)
1974	USA	West Germany
	B. Davidson (USA)	R. Klimke (W. Ger)
1978	Canada	West Germany
	B. Davidson (USA)	C. Stückelberger (Swi)
1982	Great Britain	West Germany
	L. Green (GB)	R. Klimke (W. Ger)
1986	Great Britain	
	V. Leng (GB)	

EUROPEAN CHAMPIONSHIPS

Date	Horse trials	Dressage
1965	USSR	West Germany
	M. Babirecki (Pol)	H. Chammartin (Swi)
1967	Great Britain	West Germany
	Maj E. A. Boylan (Ire)	R. Klimke (W. Ger)
1969	Great Britain	West Germany
	M. Gordon-Watson (GB)	L. Linsenhoff (W. Ger)
1971	Great Britain	West Germany
	HRH Princess Anne (GB)	L. Linsenhoff (W. Ger)
1973	West Germany	West Germany
	A. Evdokimov (USSR)	R. Klimke (W. Ger)
1975	USSR	West Germany
	L. Prior-Palmer (GB)	C. Stückelberger (Swi)

1977	Great Britain	West Germany
	L. Prior-Palmer (GB)	C. Stückelberger (Swi)
1979	Ireland	West Germany
	N. Haagensen (Den)	E. Theurer (Aut)
1981	Great Britain	West Germany
	H. Schmutz (Swi)	R. Klimke (W. Ger)
1983	Sweden	West Germany
	R. Bayliss (GB)	A.-G. Jensen (Den)
1985	Great Britain	West Germany
	V. Holgate (GB)	V. Schulten-Baumer (W. Ger)

PRESIDENT'S CUP (SHOWJUMPING)

1970	Great Britain	1978	Great Britain
1971	West Germany	1979	Great Britain
1972	Great Britain	1980	France
1973	Great Britain	1981	West Germany
1974	Great Britain	1982	West Germany
1975	West Germany	1983	Great Britain
1976	West Germany	1984	West Germany
1977	Great Britain	1985	Great Britain

KING GEORGE V GOLD CUP

1970	H. Smith (GB) *Mattie Brown*
1971	G. Wiltfang (Ger) *Askan*
1972	D. Broome (GB) *Sportsman*
1973	P. McMahon (GB) *Pennwood Forge Mill*
1974	F. Chapot (USA) *Main Spring*
1975	A. Schockemöhle (Ger) *Rex the Robber*
1976	M. Saywell (GB) *Chain Bridge*
1977	D. Broome (GB) *Philco*
1978	J. McVean (Aus) *Claret*
1979	R. Smith (GB) *Video*
1980	D. Bowen (GB) *Scorton*
1981	D. Broome (GB) *Mr Ross*
1982	M. Whitaker (GB) *Disney Way*
1983	P. Schockemöhle (Ger) *Deister*
1984	N. Skelton (GB) *St James*
1985	M. Pyrah (GB) *Towerlands Anglezarke*

BRITISH JUMPING DERBY

1970	H. Smith (GB)	*Mattie Brown*
1971	H. Smith (GB)	*Mattie Brown*
1972	H. Snoek (Ger)	*Shirokko*
1973	M. Dawes (GB)	*Mr Banbury*
1974	H. Smith (GB)	*Salvador*
1975	P. Darragh (Ire)	*Pele*
1976	E. Macken (Ire)	*Boomerang*
1977	E. Macken (Ire)	*Boomerang*
1978	E. Macken (Ire)	*Boomerang*
1979	E. Macken (Ire)	*Carroll's Boomerang*
1980	M. Whitaker (GB)	*Owen Gregory*
1981	H. Smith (GB)	*Sanyo Video*
1982	P. Schockemöhle (Ger)	*Deister*
1983	J. Whitaker (GB)	*Ryans Son*
1984	Lt. J. Leddingham (Ire)	*Gahran*
1985	P. Schockemöhle (Ger)	*Lorenzo*

BADMINTON HORSE TRIALS

1970	R. Meade (GB)	*The Poacher*
1971	Lt M. Phillips (GB)	*Great Ovation*
1972	Lt M. Phillips (GB)	*Great Ovation*
1973	L. Prior-Palmer (GB)	*Be Fair*
1974	Capt M. Phillips (GB)	*Columbus*
1975	Cancelled after dressage	
1976	L. Prior-Palmer (GB)	*Wide Awake*
1977	L. Prior-Palmer (GB)	*George*
1978	J. Holderness-Roddam (GB)	*Warrior*
1979	L. Prior-Palmer (GB)	*Killaire*
1980	M. Todd (NZ)	*Southern Comfort*
1981	Capt M. Phillips (GB)	*Lincoln*
1982	R. Meade (GB)	*Speculator III*
1983	L. Green (GB)	*Regal Realm*
1984	L. Green (GB)	*Beagle Bay*
1985	V. Holgate (GB)	*Priceless*
1986	I. Stark (GB)	*Sir Wattie*

FENCING

Governing body: Amateur Fencing Association, The de Beaumont Centre, 83 Perham Road, London W14 9SP.

1984 OLYMPIC CHAMPIONS

Men

Foil	M. Numa (Italy)
Foil team	Italy
Sabre	J. Lamour (France)
Sabre team	Italy
Epee	P. Boisse (France)
Epee team	W. Germany

Women

Foil	J. Luan (China)
Foil team	W. Germany

1985 BRITISH CHAMPIONSHIPS

Men's foil	W. Gosbee (Salle Paul)
Men's foil team	Salle Paul 'B'
Ladies' foil	L. Martin (Salle Paul)
Ladies' foil team	Salle Paul
Men's epee	W. Johnson (Salle Boston)
Men's epee team	Salle Boston
Men's sabre	M. Slade (Hemel Hempstead)
Men's sabre team	Salle Boston

GOLF

Governing bodies: Royal and Ancient Golf Club, St Andrews, Fife, KY16 9JD; Ladies' Golf Union, 12 The Links, St Andrews, Fife, KY16 9JB.

OPEN CHAMPIONS
Since 1946

1946	Sam Snead (USA)	1951	Max Faulkner (unattached)
1947	Fred Daly (Balmoral)		
1948	Henry Cotton (Royal Mid-Surrey)	1952	Bobby Locke (South Africa)
1949	Bobby Locke (South Africa)	1953	Ben Hogan (USA)
		1954	P. Thomson (Australia)
1950	Bobby Locke (South Africa)	1955	P. Thomson (Australia)
		1956	P. Thomson (Australia)

1957	Bobby Locke (South Africa)	1971	L. Trevino (USA)
1958	P. Thomson (Australia)	1972	L. Trevino (USA)
1959	G. Player (South Africa)	1973	T. Weiskopf (USA)
1960	Kel Nagle (Australia)	1974	G. Player (South Africa)
1961	A. Palmer (USA)	1975	T. Watson (USA)
1962	A. Palmer (USA)	1976	J. Miller (USA)
1963	Bob Charles (NZ)	1977	T. Watson (USA)
1964	A. Lema (USA)	1978	J. Nicklaus (USA)
1965	P. Thomson (Australia)	1979	S. Ballesteros (Spain)
1966	J. Nicklaus (USA)	1980	T. Watson (USA)
1967	R. de Vicenzo (Argentine)	1981	W. Rogers (USA)
1968	G. Player (South Africa)	1982	T. Watson (USA)
1969	A. Jacklin (Potters Bar)	1983	T. Watson (USA)
1970	J. Nicklaus (USA)	1984	S. Ballesteros (Spain)
		1985	S. Lyle (GB)

RYDER CUP

1957	Great Britain	1967	USA	1977	USA
1959	USA	1969	Tie	1979	USA
1961	USA	1971	USA	1981	USA
1963	USA	1973	USA	1983	USA
1965	USA	1975	USA	1985	GB and Europe

WALKER CUP

1957	USA	1967	USA	1977	USA
1959	USA	1969	USA	1979	USA
1961	USA	1971	Great Britain	1981	USA
1963	USA	1973	USA	1983	USA
1965	Tie	1975	USA	1985	USA

CURTIS CUP

1956	Great Britain	1966	USA	1976	USA
1958	Great Britain	1968	USA	1978	USA
1960	USA	1970	USA	1980	USA
1962	USA	1972	USA	1982	USA
1964	USA	1974	USA	1984	USA

WORLD CUP

1965	South Africa	1972	Taiwan	1979	USA
1966	USA	1973	USA	1980	Canada
1967	USA	1974	USA	1981	Not held
1968	Canada	1975	USA	1982	Spain
1969	USA	1976	Spain	1983	USA
1970	Australia	1977	Spain	1984	Spain
1971	USA	1978	USA	1985	Canada

LADIES' BRITISH OPEN CHAMPIONSHIPS 1985

Amateur   *Open*
L. Behan (Ireland)   B. King (USA)

LADIES' CLOSE AMATEUR CHAMPIONSHIPS 1985

England:	P. Johnson
Ireland:	C. Hourihane
Scotland:	A. Gemmill
Wales:	V. Thomas

HOCKEY

Governing bodies: Hockey Association of England, 16 Upper Woburn Place, London, WC1H 0QP; All England Women's Hockey Association, 160 Great Portland Street, London W1N 5TB.

OLYMPIC WINNERS

1920	England	1960	Pakistan
1924	No competition	1964	India
1928	India	1968	Pakistan
1932	India	1972	W. Germany
1936	India	1976	New Zealand
1948	India	1980	India
1952	India	1984	Pakistan (men),
1956	India		Netherlands (women)

COUNTY CHAMPIONSHIP

	Men		**Women**
1977	Middlesex	1977	Lancashire
1978	Lancashire	1978	Hertfordshire

1979	Kent	1979	Lancashire
1980	Buckinghamshire	1980	Suffolk drew with Leics.
1981	Middlesex	1981	Staffordshire
1982	Buckinghamshire	1982	Suffolk
1983	Lancashire	1983	Leicestershire
1984	Yorkshire	1984	Middlesex
1985	Worcestershire	1985	Lancashire
1986	Surrey	1986	Middlesex

ICE HOCKEY

Governing body: International Ice Hockey Federation, Prinz Eugenstrasse 12, A 1040 Wien, Austria.

WORLD CHAMPIONSHIPS

1976	Czechoslovakia	1981	USSR
1977	Czechoslovakia	1982	USSR
1978	USSR	1983	USSR
1979	USSR	1984	USSR
1980	USSR	1985	USSR

1984 OLYMPIC WINNERS (SARAJEVO)
USSR

ICE SKATING

Governing body: National Skating Association of Great Britain, 15/27 Gee Street, London, EC1V 3RE.

WORLD RECORDS (as at 31/3/86)

Men

500 metres	E. Kulikov (USSR)	37.00 sec	1975
1,000 metres	E. Heiden (USA)	1 min 13·60 sec	1980
1,500 metres	I. Zhelezovsky (USSR)	1 min 54·26 sec	1983
3,000 metres	D. Ogloblin (USSR)	4 min 04·06 sec	1979
5,000 metres	K. Stenshjemmet (Norway)	6 min 56·90 sec	1977
10,000 metres	V. Leskin (USSR)	14 min 26·71 sec	1980

Ladies

500 metres	S. Young (USA)	40·68 sec	1976
1,000 metres	K. Enke (E. Germany)	1 min 22·37 sec	1984
1,500 metres	K. Enke (E. Germany)	2 min 03·42 sec	1984
3,000 metres	A. Schöne (E. Germany)	4 min 24·79 sec	1984

1984 OLYMPIC GAMES (SARAJEVO)

Figure Skating

Men	S. Hamilton (USA)
Women	K. Witt (E. Germany)
Pairs	E. Valova and O. Vasiliev (USSR)
Ice Dancing	J. Torvill and C. Dean (Great Britain)

Speed Events

Men's 500 metres	S. Fokitchev (USSR)
Men's 1,000 metres	G. Boucher (Canada)
Men's 1,500 metres	G. Boucher (Canada)
Men's 5,000 metres	T. Gustafson (Sweden)
Men's 10,000 metres	I. Malkov (USSR)
Ladies' 500 metres	C. Rothenburger (E. Germany)
Ladies' 1,000 metres	K. Enke (E. Germany)
Ladies' 1,500 metres	K. Enke (E. Germany)
Ladies' 3,000 metres	A. Schöne (E. Germany)

LACROSSE

Governing bodies: English Lacrosse Union, 70 High Road, Rayleigh, Essex, SS6 7AD; All England Ladies' Lacrosse Association, 16 Upper Woburn Place, London WC1H 0QP.

WOMEN'S INTERNATIONAL RESULTS 1986

England v Scotland	Scotland won 9–4
England v Wales	England won 6–2
Scotland v Wales	Scotland won 6–3

IROQUOIS CUP (Men)

1976	Hampstead	1978	Cheadle
1977	Sheffield University	1979	Cheadle

1980	S. Manchester & Wythenshawe	1983	Sheffield University
1981	Cheadle	1984	Cheadle
1982	Sheffield University	1985	Cheadle

LAWN TENNIS

Governing body: The Lawn Tennis Association, Barons Court, London, W14 9EG.

WIMBLEDON CHAMPIONS
Since 1919

Men's Singles

1919	G. L. Patterson	1952	F. A. Sedgman
1920	W. T. Tilden	1953	E. V. Seixas
1921	W. T. Tilden	1954	J. Drobny
1922	G. L. Patterson	1955	M. A. Trabert
1923	W. M. Johnston	1956	L. A. Hoad
1924	J. Borotra	1957	L. A. Hoad
1925	R. Lacoste	1958	A. J. Cooper
1926	J. Borotra	1959	A. Olmedo
1927	H. Cochet	1960	N. Fraser
1928	R. Lacoste	1961	R. Laver
1929	H. Cochet	1962	R. Laver
1930	W. T. Tilden	1963	C. McKinley
1931	S. B. Wood	1964	R. Emerson
1932	H. E. Vines	1965	R. Emerson
1933	J. H. Crawford	1966	M. Santana
1934	F. J. Perry	1967	J. Newcombe
1935	F. J. Perry	1968	R. Laver
1936	F. J. Perry	1969	R. Laver
1937	J. D. Budge	1970	J. Newcombe
1938	J. D. Budge	1971	J. Newcombe
1939	R. L. Riggs	1972	S. Smith
1946	Y. Petra	1973	J. Kodes
1947	J. A. Kramer	1974	J. Connors
1948	R. Falkenburg	1975	A. Ashe
1949	F. R. Schroeder	1976	B. Borg
1950	J. E. Patty	1977	B. Borg
1951	R. Savitt	1978	B. Borg

1979	B. Borg	1983	J. McEnroe
1980	B. Borg	1984	J. McEnroe
1981	J. McEnroe	1985	B. Becker
1982	J. Connors	1986	B. Becker

Women's singles

1919	S. Lenglen	1956	S. Fry
1920	S. Lenglen	1957	A. Gibson
1921	S. Lenglen	1958	A. Gibson
1922	S. Lenglen	1959	M. Bueno
1923	S. Lenglen	1960	M. Bueno
1924	K. McKane	1961	A. Mortimer
1925	S. Lenglen	1962	J. Susman
1926	L. Godfree	1963	M. Smith
1927	H. Wills	1964	M. Bueno
1928	H. Wills	1965	M. Smith
1929	H. Wills	1966	L. W. King
1930	F. Moody	1967	L. W. King
1931	C. Aussem	1968	L. W. King
1932	F. Moody	1969	P. F. Jones
1933	F. Moody	1970	B. M. Court
1934	D. Round	1971	E. Goolagong
1935	F. Moody	1972	L. W. King
1936	H. Jacobs	1973	L. W. King
1937	D. Round	1974	C. Evert
1938	F. Moody	1975	L. W. King
1939	A. Marble	1976	C. Evert
1946	P. Betz	1977	V. Wade
1947	M. Osborne	1978	M. Navrátilova
1948	A. Brough	1979	M. Navrátilova
1949	A. Brough	1980	R. Cawley
1950	A. Brough	1981	J. Lloyd
1951	D. Hart	1982	M. Navrátilova
1952	M. Connolly	1983	M. Navrátilova
1953	M. Connolly	1984	M. Navrátilova
1954	M. Connolly	1985	M. Navrátilova
1955	A. Brough	1986	M. Navrátilova

DAVIS CUP

1951	Australia	1955	Australia
1952	Australia	1956	Australia
1953	Australia	1957	Australia
1954	USA	1958	USA

1959	Australia	1973	Australia
1960	Australia	1974	South Africa
1961	Australia	1975	Sweden
1962	Australia	1976	Italy
1963	USA	1977	Australia
1964	Australia	1978	USA
1965	Australia	1979	USA
1966	Australia	1980	Czechoslovakia
1967	Australia	1981	USA
1968	USA	1982	USA
1969	USA	1983	Australia
1970	USA	1984	Sweden
1971	USA	1985	Sweden
1972	USA		

WIGHTMAN CUP

1951	USA	1969	USA
1952	USA	1970	USA
1953	USA	1971	USA
1954	USA	1972	USA
1955	USA	1973	USA
1956	USA	1974	Great Britain
1957	USA	1975	Great Britain
1958	Great Britain	1976	USA
1959	USA	1977	USA
1960	Great Britain	1978	Great Britain
1961	USA	1979	USA
1962	USA	1980	USA
1963	USA	1981	USA
1964	USA	1982	USA
1965	USA	1983	USA
1966	USA	1984	USA
1967	USA	1985	USA
1968	Great Britain		

RECORDS

Longest match (time): 6 hrs. 32 mins. J. McEnroe (USA) beat M. Wilander (Sweden) at St Louis, USA in Davis Cup match, 1982, 9–7, 6–2, 15–17, 3–6, 8–6 (79 games)

Longest match (number of games): 147. R. Leach and R. Dell (USA) beat L. Schloss and T. Mozur (USA) at Newport Casino, Newport, USA, 1967, 3–6, 49–47, 22–20 (6 hrs 10 mins)

Largest number of games in Davis Cup singles: 100 in 1982 H. Fritz (Canada) beat J. Andrew (Venezuela) 16–14, 11–9, 9–11, 4–6, 11–9
Largest number of games in a Wimbledon singles: 112, when R. Gonzales (USA) beat C. Pasarell (USA), 22–24, 1–6, 16–14, 6–3, 11–9 in 1969
Longest Wimbledon match: 5¼ hours, when Gonzales beat Pasarell
Greatest number of Wimbledon singles wins: William C. Renshaw (GB) 7 titles (1881–2–3–4–5–6–9); Mrs Helen Wills Moody (USA) 8 titles 1927–8–9 1930–2–3–5–8)
Greatest number of Wimbledon titles: Mrs L. W. King (USA) 20 titles (6 singles, 10 doubles and 4 mixed) (1961–79)

MOTOR CYCLING

Governing body: Auto-Cycle Union, Millbuck House, Corporation Street, Rugby, Warwicks CV21 2DN.

WORLD CHAMPIONS		
1981	**1982**	**1983**
Road Racing		
50 cc	R. Tormo	S. Dörflinger	S. Dörflinger
	(Bultaco)	(Krauser)	(Krauser)
125 cc	A. Nieto	A. Nieto	A. Nieto
	(Minarelli)	(Garelli)	(Garelli)
250 cc	A. Mang	J.-L. Tournadre	C. Lavado
	(Kawasaki)	(Yamaha)	(Yamaha)
350 cc	A. Mang	A. Mang	A. Mang
	(Kawasaki)	(Kawasaki)	(Kawasaki)
500 cc	M. Lucchinelli	F. Uncini	F. Spencer
	(Suzuki)	(Suzuki)	(Honda)
Sidecar	R. Biland	W. Schwärzel	R. Biland/
	(Yamaha)	(Yamaha)	K. Waltisberg
			(LCR Yamaha)
Moto Cross		
125 cc	H. Everts	E. Geobers	E. Geobers
	(Suzuki)	(Suzuki)	(Suzuki)
250 cc	N. Hudson	D. Laport	G. Jobe.
	(Yamaha)	(Yamaha)	(Suzuki)
500 cc	A. Mallherbe	B. Lackey	H. Carlqvist
	(Honda)	(Suzuki)	(Yamaha)
Speedway		
	B. Penhall	B. Penhall	E. Muller

	Trials		
	G. Burgat (SWM)	E. Lejeurne	E. Lejeurne

BRITISH CHAMPIONS

Road Racing

Solo (500 cc)	R. Smith (Yamaha)	R. Marshall (Suzuki)	R. Marshall (Honda)
Sidecar	J. Taylor (Yamaha)	B. Ford-Dunn (Yamaha)	B. Ford-Dunn/ A. Pirie (Yamaha)

Moto Cross

Solo	G. Noyce (Honda)	N. Hudson (Yamaha)	D. Thorpe (Honda)
Sidecar	T. Good (Wasp Yamaha)	D. Fox (NRE EML)	T. Good (Wasp Yamaha)

Speedway

	S. Bastaple- Godden	A. Grahame	C. Morton

Trials

	M. Rathmell (Montessa)	Y. Vesterinen	S. Saunders (Armstrong)

RECORD

Winner of most World Championships: Giacomo Agostini (15, in 1966–75)

MOTOR RACING

Governing body: RAC (Motor Sport Division), 31 Belgrave Square, London, SW1 8QH.

World Driving Championship 1984: N. Lauda (Austria), *McLaren*

John Player Special British Grand Prix 1984: N. Lauda (Austria), *McLaren*

Le Mans 24-hrs 1984: H. Pescarolo (France), K. Ludwig (W. Germany), *Porsche 956*

Lombard RAC Rally 1984: A. Vatanen (Finland), *Peugeot 205 Turbo 16*

Monte Carlo Rally 1984: W. Röhrl (W. Germany), *Audi Quattro Sport*

RECORDS

Winner of most World Championships: Juan Manuel Fangio (five, in 1951, 1954, 1955, 1956, 1957)

Winner of most Grand Prix: Jackie Stewart (26)

Winner of most Grand Prix in one year: Jim Clark (seven, in 1963)

NETBALL

Governing body: All England Netball Association Limited, Francis House, Francis Street, London SW1P 1DE.

WORLD CHAMPIONS

1963	Australia beat New Zealand
1967	New Zealand beat Australia
1971	Australia beat New Zealand
1975	Australia beat England
1979	Australia, Trinidad and New Zealand joint champions
1983	Australia beat New Zealand

INTER-COUNTY CHAMPIONSHIP

1975	Essex	1980	Essex	1985	Bedfordshire
1976	Essex	1981	Surrey	1986	Surrey and
1977	Essex	1982	Essex		Hertford-
1978	Essex	1983	Hertfordshire		shire drew
1979	Essex	1984	Bedfordshire		

NATIONAL CLUBS TOURNAMENT

1977	Aquila	1979	Old Plastovians	1982	Wanderers
1978	Blackburn	1980	Linden	1983	OPA
	Independants	1981	New Campbell	1984	Sudbury

ROWING

Governing body: Amateur Rowing Association, 6 Lower Mall, London W6 9DJ.

GRAND CHALLENGE CUP

Between 1839 and 1934 the Cup was won 23 times by Leander, 15 times by London BC, 7 times by Oxford University BC, 4 times by Magdalen College, Oxford, 3 times by Thames RC and once each by Sydney RC and Harvard Athletic Association BC. The winners since 1935 have been:

1935	Pembroke College, Cambridge	1966	TSC Berlin, EG
1936	FC Zurich RC, Switzerland	1967	S. C. Wissenschaft DH f K, Leipzig
1937	R. Wiking, Germany	1968	London University BC
1938	London RC	1969	SC Einheit, Dresden
1939	Harvard University, USA	1970	ASK Vorwärts, Rostock
1946	Leander Club	1971	Tideway Scullers School
1947	Jesus College, Cambridge	1972	WMF Moscow, USSR
1948	Thames RC	1973	Trud Kolomna, USSR
1949	Leander Club	1974	Trud Kolomna, USSR
1950	Harvard University, USA	1975	Leander Club and Thames Tradesmen's RC
1951	Lady Margaret BC, Cambridge	1976	Thames Tradesmen's RC
1952	Leander Club		
1953	Leander Club	1977	University of Washington RC, USA
1954	Club Krylia Sovetov, USSR	1978	Trakia Club, Bulgaria
1955	University of Pennsylvania, USA	1979	Thames Tradesmen's RC and London RC
1956	Centre Sportif des Forces de l'Armée, France	1980	Charles River Rowing Assn, USA
1957	Cornell University, USA	1981	Oxford University BC and Thames Tradesmen's RC
1958	Trud Club, Leningrad, USSR		
1959	Harvard University, USA	1982	Leander Club and London RC
1960	Molesey BC		
1961	USSR Navy	1983	London RC and University of London BC
1962	USSR Navy		
1963	London University	1984	Leander Club and London RC
1964	USSR		
1965	Ratzeburger, WG	1985	Harvard University, USA

DIAMOND SCULLS
First rowed 1844. Winners since 1955:

1955	T. Kocerka (Poland)	1969	H.-J. Böhmer (DDR)
1956	T. Kocerka (Poland)	1970	J. Meissner (W. Germany)
1957	S. A. Mackenzie (Australia)	1971	A. Demiddi (Argentina)
1958	S. A. Mackenzie (Australia)	1972	A. Timoschinin (USSR)
1959	S. A. Mackenzie (Australia)	1973	S. Drea (Eire)
		1974	S. Drea (Eire)
1960	S. A. Mackenzie (Australia)	1975	S. Drea (Eire)
		1976	E. O. Hale (Australia)
1961	S. A. Mackenzie (Australia)	1977	T. J. Crooks (Leander)
		1978	T. J. Crooks (Leander)
1962	S. A. Mackenzie (Australia)	1979	H. Matheson (Nottingham)
1963	G. Kottman (Switzerland)	1980	R. D. Ibarra (Argentina)
1964	S. Cromwell (USA)	1981	C. L. Baillieu (Leander)
1965	D. M. Spero (USA)	1982	C. L. Baillieu (Leander)
1966	A. Hill (Germany)	1983	S. G. Redgrave (Marlow)
1967	M. Studach (Switzerland)	1984	C. L. Baillieu (Leander)
1968	H. A. Wardell-Yerburgh (Eton Vikings)	1985	S. G. Redgrave (Marlow)

UNIVERSITY BOAT RACE
Rowed on the river Thames between Putney and Mortlake (4 miles, 374 yards):

1829	Oxford	1857	Oxford
1836	Cambridge	1858	Cambridge
1839	Cambridge	1859	Oxford
1840	Cambridge	1860	Cambridge
1841	Cambridge	1861	Oxford
1842	Oxford	1862	Oxford
1845	Cambridge	1863	Oxford
1846	Cambridge	1864	Oxford
1848	Cambridge	1865	Oxford
1849	Oxford	1866	Oxford
1852	Oxford	1867	Oxford
1854	Oxford	1868	Oxford
1856	Cambridge	1869	Oxford

1870	Cambridge	1913	Oxford
1871	Cambridge	1914	Cambridge
1872	Cambridge	1920	Cambridge
1873	Cambridge	1921	Cambridge
1874	Cambridge	1922	Cambridge
1875	Oxford	1923	Oxford
1876	Cambridge	1924	Cambridge
1877	Dead heat	1925	Cambridge
1878	Oxford	1926	Cambridge
1879	Cambridge	1927	Cambridge
1880	Oxford	1928	Cambridge
1881	Oxford	1929	Cambridge
1882	Oxford	1930	Cambridge
1883	Oxford	1931	Cambridge
1884	Cambridge	1932	Cambridge
1885	Oxford	1933	Cambridge
1886	Cambridge	1934	Cambridge
1887	Cambridge	1935	Cambridge
1888	Cambridge	1936	Cambridge
1889	Cambridge	1937	Oxford
1890	Oxford	1938	Oxford
1891	Oxford	1939	Cambridge
1892	Oxford	1946	Oxford
1893	Oxford	1947	Cambridge
1894	Oxford	1948	Cambridge
1895	Oxford	1949	Cambridge
1896	Oxford	1950	Cambridge
1897	Oxford	1951	Cambridge
1898	Oxford	1952	Oxford
1899	Cambridge	1953	Cambridge
1900	Cambridge	1954	Oxford
1901	Oxford	1955	Cambridge
1902	Cambridge	1956	Cambridge
1903	Cambridge	1957	Cambridge
1904	Cambridge	1958	Cambridge
1905	Oxford	1959	Oxford
1906	Cambridge	1960	Oxford
1907	Cambridge	1961	Cambridge
1908	Cambridge	1962	Cambridge
1909	Oxford	1963	Oxford
1910	Oxford	1964	Cambridge
1911	Oxford	1965	Oxford
1912	Oxford	1966	Oxford

1967	Oxford	1977	Oxford
1968	Cambridge	1978	Oxford
1969	Cambridge	1979	Oxford
1970	Cambridge	1980	Oxford
1971	Cambridge	1981	Oxford
1972	Cambridge	1982	Oxford
1973	Cambridge	1983	Oxford
1974	Oxford	1984	Oxford
1975	Cambridge	1985	Oxford
1976	Oxford	1986	Cambridge

Cambridge have won 69 times, Oxford 62 times, with one dead heat.

OLYMPIC GAMES, 1984
Men

Single sculls	P. Karppinen (Finland)
Double sculls	USA
Quadruple sculls	W. Germany
Coxless pairs	Romania
Coxless fours	New Zealand
Coxed pairs	Italy
Coxed fours	Great Britain
Eights	Canada

Women

Single sculls	V. Racila (Romania)
Coxless pairs	Romania
Double sculls	Romania
Coxed fours	Romania
Quadruple sculls	Romania
Eights	USA

RUGBY LEAGUE FOOTBALL

Governing body: The Rugby Football League, 180 Chapeltown Road, Leeds, LS7 4HT.

CHALLENGE CUP COMPETITION
since 1954:

1954	Warrington	1957	Leeds
1955	Barrow	1958	Wigan
1956	St Helens	1959	Wigan

1960	Wakefield Trinity	1974	Warrington
1961	St Helens	1975	Widnes
1962	Wakefield Trinity	1976	St Helens
1963	Wakefield Trinity	1977	Leeds
1964	Widnes	1978	Leeds
1965	Wigan	1979	Widnes
1966	St Helens	1980	Hull Kingston Rovers
1967	Featherstone Rovers	1981	Widnes
1968	Leeds	1982	Hull
1969	Castleford	1983	Featherstone Rovers
1970	Castleford	1984	Widnes
1971	Leigh	1985	Wigan
1972	St Helens	1986	Castleford
1973	Featherstone Rovers		

RUGBY UNION FOOTBALL

Governing body: Rugby Football Union, Twickenham, Middlesex, TW2 7RQ.

FIVE NATIONS CHAMPIONSHIP
since 1920

1920	England, Scotland and Wales, tie	1935	Ireland
1921	England	1936	Wales
1922	Wales	1937	England
1923	England	1938	Scotland
1924	England	1939	England, Wales and Ireland, tie
1925	Scotland	1947	Wales and England, tie
1926	Ireland and Scotland, tie	1948	Ireland
1927	Ireland and Scotland, tie	1949	Ireland
1928	England	1950	Wales
1929	Scotland	1951	Ireland
1930	England	1952	Wales
1931	Wales	1953	England
1932	England, Wales and Ireland, tie	1954	England, France and Wales, tie
1933	Scotland	1955	Wales and France, tie
1934	England	1956	Wales
		1957	England
		1958	England

1959	France	1974	Ireland
1960	England and France, tie	1975	Wales
1961	France	1976	Wales
1962	France	1977	France
1963	England	1978	Wales
1964	Scotland and Wales, tie	1979	Wales
1965	Wales	1980	England
1966	Wales	1981	France
1967	France	1982	Ireland
1968	France	1983	France and Ireland, tie
1969	Wales	1984	Scotland
1970	France and Wales, tie	1985	Ireland
1971	Wales	1986	France and Scotland, tie
1972	series not completed		
1973	5-way tie		

COUNTY CHAMPIONSHIP
since 1961

1961	Cheshire	1974	Gloucestershire
1962	Warwickshire	1975	Gloucestershire
1963	Warwickshire	1976	Gloucestershire
1964	Warwickshire	1977	Lancashire
1965	Warwickshire	1978	North Midlands
1966	Middlesex	1979	Middlesex
1967	Surrey and Durham	1980	Lancashire
1968	Middlesex	1981	Northumberland
1969	Lancashire	1982	Lancashire
1970	Staffordshire	1983	Gloucestershire
1971	Surrey	1984	Gloucestershire
1972	Gloucestershire	1985	Middlesex
1973	Lancashire	1986	Warwickshire

VARSITY MATCH
since 1960

1960	Cambridge	1967	Cambridge
1961	Cambridge	1968	Cambridge
1962	Cambridge	1969	Cambridge
1963	Cambridge	1970	Oxford
1964	Oxford	1971	Oxford
1965	Drawn	1972	Cambridge
1966	Oxford	1973	Cambridge

1974	Cambridge	1980	Cambridge
1975	Cambridge	1981	Cambridge
1976	Cambridge	1982	Cambridge
1977	Oxford	1983	Cambridge
1978	Cambridge	1984	Cambridge
1979	Oxford	1985	Cambridge

MIDDLESEX SEVEN-A-SIDE TOURNAMENT
since 1951

1951	Richmond II	1969	St Luke's, Exeter I
1952	Wasps	1970	Loughborough Colleges I
1953	Richmond I	1971	London Welsh I
1954	Rosslyn Park I	1972	London Welsh I
1955	Richmond I	1973	London Welsh I
1956	London Welsh I	1974	Richmond I
1957	St Luke's College, Exeter	1975	Richmond I
1958	Blackheath	1976	Loughborough Colleges I
1959	Loughborough College	1977	Richmond I
1960	London Scottish	1978	Harlequins I
1961	London Scottish I	1979	Richmond I
1962	London Scottish I	1980	Richmond I
1963	London Scottish I	1981	Rosslyn Park
1964	Loughborough Colleges I	1982	Stewart's Melville FP
1965	London Scottish I	1983	Richmond I
1966	Loughborough Colleges I	1984	London Welsh
1967	Harlequins I	1985	Wasps
1968	London Welsh I	1986	Harlequins

RECORDS (as at 31/5/86)

Most Caps: C. M. H. Gibson (Ireland), 67; J. P. R. Williams (Wales), 54; A. B. Carmichael (Scotland), 50; A. Neary (England), 43

Highest international score: Wales beat France 49–14, 1910

Greatest winning margin: S. Africa beat France 55–6, 1906

Place kick record: 100 yd., at Richmond Athletic Ground, 1906, by D. F. T. Morkel in an unsuccessful kick for S. Africa v Middlesex. 67 yd., successful by Don Clarke in a club match at Roturua

Longest dropped goal: 90 yd at Twickenham in 1932, by G. Brand for South Africa v England

SHOOTING

Governing bodies: National Rifle Association, Bisley Camp, Brookwood, Woking, Surrey GU24 OPB; National Smallbore Rifle Association (Address as above).

QUEEN'S PRIZE

1975	C. M. Y. Trotter (Guernsey RC)
1976	Major W. H. Magnay (North London RC)
1977	D. A. Friend (Hurstpierpoint)
1978	R. Graham (Australia)
1979	A. St G. Tucker (Bootham RC)
1980	A. Marion (Canada)
1981	E. M. Ayling (Australia)
1982	L. Peden (Oxford & Cambridge RC)
1983	A. Marion (Canada)
1984	D. F. P. Richards (Manydown RC)
1985	J. T. S. Bloomfields (North London RC)

OLYMPIC GAMES, 1984

Men

Small-bore rifle (prone)	E. Etzel (USA)
Small-bore rifle (three positions)	M. Cooper (GB)
Air rifle	P. Heberie (France)
Free pistol	Haifeng Xu (China)
Rapid-fire pistol	T. Kamachi (Japan)
Running game target	Li Yuwei (China)
Clay pigeon: trap	L. Giovannetti (Italy)
skeet	M. Dryke (USA)

Women

Small-bore rifle (three positions)	Wu Xiaoxuan (China)
Air rifle	P. Spurgin (USA)
Small-bore pistol	L. Thorn (Canada)

SKI-ING

Governing body: National Ski Federation of Great Britain, 118 Eaton Square, London, SW1W 9AF.

1984 OLYMPIC GAMES (SARAJEVO)

Alpine

Men's downhill	B. Johnson (USA)
Men's slalom	P. Mahre (USA)
Men's giant slalom	M. Julen (Switzerland)
Women's downhill	M. Figini (Switzerland)
Women's slalom	P. Magoni (Italy)
Women's giant slalom	D. Armstrong (USA)

Ski jumping

90 metres	M. Nykaenen (Finland)
70 metres	J. Weissflog (E. Germany)

Biathlon

Individual 10 km	E. Kyalfoss (Norway)
Individual 20 km	P. Angerer (W. Germany)
4 × 7·5 km relay	USSR

Nordic

Men's 15 km	G. Swan (Sweden)
Men's 30 km	N. Zimyatov (USSR)
Men's 50 km	T. Wassberg (Sweden)
Men's 4 × 10 km relay	Sweden
Combined event	T. Sandberg (Norway)
Women's 5 km	M.-L. Haemaelainen (Finland)
Women's 10 km	M.-L. Haemaelainen (Finland)
Women's 20 km	M.-L. Haemaelainen (Finland)
Women's 4 × 5 km relay	Norway

BRITISH NATIONAL ALPINE CHAMPIONSHIPS

	Men	Women
1975	S. Fitzsimmons	V. Iliffe
1976	S. Fitzsimmons	V. Iliffe
1977	P. Fuchs	H. Hutcheon
1978	Q. Byrne-Sutton	L. Holmes
1979	S. Fitzsimmons	V. Iliffe
1980	F. Burton	V. Iliffe
1981	M. Bell	M. Langmuir
1982	F. Burton	A. Jochum
1983	R. Duncan	K. Cairns
1984	N. Wilson	L. Beck
1985	F. Burton	L. Beck
1986	M. Bell (after downhill) and giant slalom)	L. Beck

SQUASH RACKETS

Governing bodies: Squash Rackets Association, Francis House, Francis Street, London SW1P 1DE; Women's Squash Rackets Association, 345 Upper Richmond Road, Sheen, London, SW14 8QN.

OPEN CHAMPIONSHIP

1961	Azam Khan (Pakistan)	1969–72	J. Barrington (Ireland)
1962	Mohibullah Khan	1973	G. Hunt (Australia)
	(Pakistan)	1974	G. Hunt (Australia)
1963–65	Abu Taleb (Egypt)	1975	Qamar Zaman (Pakistan)
1966	J. Barrington (amateur)	1976–81	G. Hunt (Australia)
1967	J. Barrington (amateur)	1982–85	Jahangir Khan
1968	G. Hunt (Australia)		(Pakistan)

BRITISH WOMEN'S OPEN CHAMPIONSHIP

1961–64	H. Blundell (Australia)
1965–77	B. McKay (née Blundell) (Australia)
1978	S. Newman (Australia)
1979	B. Wall (Australia)
1980–83	V. Cardwell (née Hoffmann) (Australia)
1984	S. Devoy (New Zealand)
1985	S. Devoy (New Zealand)

AMATEUR CLOSED CHAMPIONSHIP

1974	J. C. A. Leslie	1977	P. S. Kenyon
1975	P. N. Ayton	1978	P. G. Verow
1976	J. C. A. Leslie		

NATIONAL CHAMPIONSHIP

1979	G. P. Briars	1983	P. S. Kenyon
1980	J. P. Barrington	1984	G. Williams
1981	P. S. Kenyon	1985	P. S. Kenyon
1982	G. P. Briars		

WOMEN'S NATIONAL CHAMPIONSHIP

1975	S. Cogswell	1982	A. Cumings
1976	A. Smith	1983	L. Opie
1977–80	S. Cogswell	1984	M. Le Moignan
1981	L. Opie	1985	L. Soutter

SWIMMING AND DIVING

Governing bodies: Amateur Swimming Association, Harold Fern House, Derby Square, Loughborough, Leicestershire LE11 0AL; Channel Swimming Association, 'The Moorings', Alkham Valley Road, Hawkinge, Nr Folkestone, Kent.

SWIMMING RECORDS
(as at 31/12/85)

	Men	
World	*European*	*British*
50 m freestyle	22·52	23·41
	D. Halsall (Switz.)	D. Lowe
100 m freestyle		
48.95	49.58	51·32
M. Biondi (USA)	J. Woithe (GDR)	D. Lowe
200 m freestyle		
1:47.44	1:47·44	1:51·52
M. Gross (FRG)	M. Gross (FRG)	A. Astbury
400 m freestyle		
3:47·80	3:47·80	3:53·29
M. Gross (FRG)	M. Gross (FRG)	A. Astbury
800 m freestyle		
7:52·33	7:52·33	8:12·39
V. Salnikov (USSR)	V. Salnikov (USSR)	D. Stacey
1500 m freestyle		
14:54·76	14:54·76	15:30·10
V. Salnikov (USSR)	V. Salnikov (USSR)	D. Stacey
50 m breaststroke	28·67	29·01
	R. Beab (FRG)	A. Moorhouse
100 m breaststroke		
1:01·65	1:02·84	1:02·93
S. Lundquist (USA)	D. Volkov (USSR)	A. Moorhouse

200 m breaststroke

2:13·34	2:15·11	2:15·11
V. Davis (Canada)	D. Wilkie (GBR)	D. Wilkie

50 m butterfly

	24·77	25·20
	M. Gross (FRG)	A. Jameson

100 m butterfly

53·08	53·08	54·28
M. Gross (FRG)	M. Gross (FRG)	A. Jameson

200 m butterfly

1:56·65	1:56·65	2:00·21
M. Gross (FRG)	M. Gross (FRG)	P. Hubble

50 m backstroke

	26·44	
	D. Richter (GDR)	

100 m backstroke

55·19	55·24	57·72
R. Carey (USA)	I. Polianski (USSR)	G. Abraham

200 m backstroke

1:58·14	1:58·14	2:04·23
I. Polianski (USSR)	I. Polianski (USSR)	D. Campbell

200 m indiv. medley

2:01·42	2:02·48	2:04·13
A. Baumann (Canada)	G. Franceschi (Italy)	R. Brew

400 m indiv. medley

4:17·41	4:18·29	4:25·38
A. Baumann (Canada)	J.-P. Berndt (GDR)	S. Poulter

4 × 100 m freestyle relay

3:19·30	3:20·19	3:23·61
USA national team	USSR national team	national team

4 × 200 m freestyle relay

7:15·69	7:15·73	7:24·78
USA national team	FRG national team	national team

4 × 100 m medley relay

3:29·30	3:42·15	3:47·39
USA national team	USSR national team	national team

Women

World	*European*	*British*
50 m freestyle	25·64	26·48
	A. Verstappen (Holland)	J. Croft

100 m freestyle
54·79   54·79   56·60
B. Krause (GDR)   B. Krause (GDR)   J. Croft

200 m freestyle
1:57·75   1:57·75   1:59·74
K. Otto (GDR)   K. Otto (GDR)   J. Croft

400 m freestyle
4:06·28   4:07·66   4:10·27
T. Wickham (Australia)   A. Strauss (GDR)   S. Hardcastle

800 m freestyle
8:24·62   8:28·36   8:32·57
T. Wickham (Australia)   A. Strauss (GDR)   S. Hardcastle

1500 m freestyle
16:04·49   16:13·55   16:43·95
K. Linehan (USA)   A. Strauss (GDR)   S. Hardcastle

100 m breaststroke
1:08·29   1:08·29   1:11·05
S. Gerasch (GDR)   S. Gerasch (GDR)   S. Brownsdon

200 m breaststroke
2:28·33   2:28·33   2:33·16
S. Horner (GDR)   S. Horner (GDR)   S. Brownsdon

50 m butterfly   28·22
                                                     C. Cooper

100 m butterfly
57·93   59·41   1:01·48
M. Meagher (USA)   T. Kurnikova (USSR)   N. Fibbens

200 m butterfly
2:05·96   2:07·82   2:11·97
M. Meagher (USA)   C. Polit (GDR)   S. Purvis

50 m backstroke   29·16
                          B. Weigang (GDR)

100 m backstroke
1:00·59   1:00·59   1:03·61
I. Kleber (GDR)   I. Kleber (GDR)   B. Rose

200 m backstroke
2:09·91   2:09·91   2:16·00
C. Sirch (GDR)   C. Sirch (GDR)   K. Read

200 m indiv. medley
2:11·73   2:11·73   2:17·31
U. Geweniger (GDR)   U. Geweniger (GDR)   S. Davies

400 m indiv. medley

4:36·10	4:36·10	4:46·83
P. Schneider (GDR)	P. Schneider (GDR)	S. Davies

4 × 100 m freestyle relay

3:42·41	3:42·41	3:50·12
GDR national team	GDR national team	national team

4 × 200 m freestyle relay

8:02·27	8:02·27	8:15·21
GDR national team	GDR national team	national team

4 × 100 m medley relay

4:03·69	4:03·69	4:12·24
GDR national team	GDR national team	national team

OLYMPIC GAMES, 1984

Men

100 m freestyle	R. Gaines (USA)	49·8 sec OR
200 m freestyle	M. Gross (W. Germany)	1 min 47·44 sec WR
400 m freestyle	G. Dicarlo (USA)	3 min 51·23 sec
1500 m freestyle	M. O'Brien (USA)	15 min 5·2 sec
100 m backstroke	R. Carey (USA)	55·79 sec
200 m backstroke	R. Carey (USA)	2 min 0·23 sec
100 m breaststroke	S. Lundquist (USA)	1 min 1·65 sec WR
200 m breaststroke	V. Davis (Canada)	2 min 13·34 sec WR
100 m butterfly	M. Gross (W. Germany)	53·08 sec WR
200 m butterfly	J. Sieben (Australia)	1 min 57·04 sec WR
200 m indiv. medley	A. Baumann (Canada)	2 min 1·42 sec WR
400 m indiv. medley	A. Baumann (Canada)	4 min 17·41 sec WR
4 × 100 m freestyle relay	USA	3 min 19·03 sec WR
4 × 200 m freestyle relay	USA	7 min 15·69 sec WR
4 × 100 m medley relay	USA	3 min 39·3 sec WR
Springboard diving	G. Louganis (USA)	754·41 pts
Highboard diving	G. Louganis (USA)	710·91 pts

	Women	
100 m freestyle	C. Steinseifer (USA) and N. Hogshead (USA)	55·92 sec (tie)
200 m freestyle	M. Wayte (USA)	1 min 59·23 sec
400 m freestyle	T. Cohen (USA)	4 min 07·1 sec
800 m freestyle	T. Cohen (USA)	8 min 24·95 sec
100 m backstroke	T. Andrews (USA)	1 min. 02·55 sec
200 m backstroke	J. De Rover (Netherlands)	2 min 12·38 sec
100 m breaststroke	P. Van Staveren (Netherlands)	1 min 09·83 sec
200 m breaststroke	A. Ottenbrite (Canada)	2 min 30·38 sec
100 m butterfly	T. Meagher (USA)	59·26 sec
200 m butterfly	T. Meagher (USA)	2 min 06·9 sec
200 m indiv. medley	T. Caulkins (USA)	2 min 12·64 sec
400 m indiv. medley	T. Caulkins (USA)	4 min 39·24 sec
4 × 100 m freestyle relay	USA	3 min 43·43 sec
4 × 100 m medley relay	USA	4 min 08·34 sec
Synchronised swimming (solo)	T. Ruiz (USA)	198·467 pts
Synchronised swimming (duet)	C. Costie and T. Ruiz (USA)	195·584 pts
Springboard diving	S. Bernier (Canada)	530·7 pts
Highboard diving	Z. Jihong (China)	435·51 pts

TABLE TENNIS

Governing body: English Table Tennis Association, 21 Claremont, Hastings, Sussex.

WORLD CHAMPIONSHIP			
Men's singles			
1951	J. Leach (England)	1953	F. Sido (Hungary)
1952	H. Satoh (Japan)	1954	I. Ogimura (Japan)

1955	T. Tanaka (Japan)	1971	S. Bengtsson (Sweden)
1956	I. Ogimura (Japan)	1973	J. En-tinh (China)
1957	T. Tanaka (Japan)	1975	I. Jonyer (Hungary)
1959	Jung Kuo-Tuan (China)	1977	M. Kohno (Japan)
1961	Chuang Tse-Tung (China)	1979	Seiji Ono (Japan)
1963	Chuang Tse-Tung (China)	1981	Guo Yeuhua (China)
1965	Chuang Tse-Tung (China)	1983	Guo Yuehua (China)
1967	N. Hasegawa (Japan)	1985	Jiang Jialiang (China)
1969	S. Ito (Japan)		

Women's singles

1951–5	A. Rozeanu (Rumania)	1971	Lin Hui-Ching (China)
1956	T. Okawa (Japan)	1973	H. Yu-lan (China)
1957	F. Eguchi (Japan)	1975	Yung Sun Kim (N. Korea)
1959	K. Matsuzaki (Japan)	1977	P. Yung Sun (N. Korea)
1961	Chiu Chung-Hui (China)	1979	Ge Xinai (China)
1963	K. Matsuzaki (Japan)	1981	Tong Ling (China)
1965	N. Fukazu (Japan)	1983	Cao Yanhua (China)
1967	S. Morisawa (Japan)	1985	Cao Yanhua (China)
1969	T. Kowada (Japan)		

WORLD CUP

1980	G. Yuehua (China)	1983	M. Applegren (Sweden)
1981	T. Klampar (Hungary)	1984	J. Jialiang (China)
1982	G. Yuehua (China)		

SWAYTHLING CUP

1950	Czechoslovakia	1965	China
1951	Czechoslovakia	1967	Japan
1952	Hungary	1969	Japan
1953	England	1971	China
1954	Japan	1973	Sweden
1955	Japan	1975	China
1956	Japan	1977	China
1957	Japan	1979	Hungary
1959	Japan	1981	China
1961	China	1983	China
1963	China	1985	China

CORBILLON CUP

1950	Rumania	1965	China
1951	Rumania	1967	Japan
1952	Japan	1969	USSR
1953	Rumania	1971	Japan
1954	Japan	1973	S. Korea
1955	Rumania	1975	China
1956	Rumania	1977	China
1957	Japan	1979	Japan
1959	Japan	1981	China
1961	Japan	1983	China
1963	Japan	1985	China

ENGLISH OPEN CHAMPIONSHIPS

Men's singles

1974	K. Johansson (Sweden)
1975	A. Strokatov (USSR)
1976	S. Bengtsson (Sweden)
1977	S. Gomozkov (USSR)
1978	Li Chen-shih (China)
1979	K. Yao-hua (China)
1980	D. Douglas (England)
1982	J. Jialiang (China)
1984	D. Douglas (England)
1986	Z. Katinic (Yugoslavia)

Women's singles

1974	Mrs M. Alexandru (Rumania)
1975	Miss E. Antonian (USSR)
1976	Mrs J. Hammersley (England)
1977	Miss C. Knight (England)
1978	Chu Hsiang-yum (China)
1979	Mrs J. Hammersley (England)
1980	Mrs J. Hammersley (England)
1982	Chen Lili (China)
1984	A. Zacharian (USSR)
1986	E. Kovtun (USSR)

VOLLEYBALL

Governing body: English Volleyball Association, 128 Melton Road, West Bridgford, Nottingham NG2 6EP

OLYMPIC WINNERS

	Men		Women
1964	USSR	1964	Japan
1968	USSR	1968	USSR
1972	Japan	1972	USSR
1976	Poland	1976	Japan
1980	USSR	1980	USSR
1984	USA	1984	China

WATER POLO

Governing body: Amateur Swimming Association, Harold Fern House, Derby Square, Loughborough, Leicestershire, LE11 0AL.

OLYMPIC WINNERS

1900	Great Britain	1952	Hungary
1904	USA	1956	Hungary
1908	Great Britain	1960	Italy
1912	Great Britain	1964	Hungary
1920	Great Britain	1968	Yugoslavia
1924	France	1972	USSR
1928	Germany	1976	Hungary
1932	Hungary	1980	USSR
1936	Hungary	1984	Yugoslavia
1948	Italy		

YACHTING

Governing body: Royal Ocean Racing Club, 20 St James's Place, London SW1A 1NN.

OLYMPIC GAMES, 1984

Finn	R. Coutts (New Zealand)
Star	W. Buchan (USA)
Flying Dutchman	J. McKee (USA)
Tornado	R. Sellers (New Zealand)
470	L. Doreste (Spain)
Soling	R. Haines (USA)
Boardsailing	S. Van Den Berg (Netherlands)

THE AMERICA'S CUP

Shamrock II lost to *Columbia* in 1901
Shamrock III lost to *Reliance* in 1903
Shamrock IV lost to *Resolute* in 1920
Shamrock V lost to *Enterprise* in 1930
Endeavour lost to *Rainbow* in 1934
Endeavour II lost to *Ranger* in 1937
Sceptre lost to *Columbia* in 1958
Gretel lost to *Weatherly* in 1962
Sovereign lost to *Constellation* in 1964
Dame Pattie lost to *Intrepid* in 1967
Gretel II lost to *Intrepid* in 1970
Southern Cross lost to *Courageous* in 1974
Australia lost to *Courageous* in 1977
Australia lost to *Freedom* in 1980
Liberty lost to *Australia II* in 1983

THE ADMIRAL'S CUP

1969	USA	1979	Australia
1971	Great Britain	1981	Great Britain
1973	Germany	1983	West Germany
1975	Great Britain	1985	West Germany
1977	Great Britain		

OLYMPIC GAMES 1984 (Los Angeles)
(A list of winners not already noted under particular games or sports)

GYMNASTICS

Governing body: British Amateur Gymnastic Association, 95 High Street, Slough SL1 1DH.

Men	
All-round	K. Gushiken (Japan)
Horizontal bars	S. Morisue (Japan)
Parallel bars	B. Conner (USA)
Long horse vault	Lou Yun (China)
Pommel horse	Li Ning (China) and P. Vidmar (USA)

Rings	K. Gushiken (Japan)
Floor exercises	Li Ning (China)
Team combined exercises	USA

Women

All-around	M.-L. Retton (USA)
Pommel horse vault	E. Szabo (Romania)
Asymmetrical bars	J. McNamara (USA) and M. Yanhong (China)
Balance beam	E. Szabo (Romania) and S. Pauca (Romania)
Floor exercises	E. Szabo (Romania)
Rhythmic all-around	L. Fung (China)

MODERN PENTATHLON

Individual	D. Massala (Italy)
Team	Italy

WEIGHTLIFTING

Governing body: British Amateur Weight Lifters' Association, 3 Iffley Turn, Oxford.

Fly	Guoqiang Zeng (China)	235 kg
Bantam	Schude Wu (China)	267.5 kg
Feather	Chen Weiqiang (China)	284·5 kg
Light	Yao Jingyuan (China)	320 kg
Middle	K. Radschinsky (W. Germany)	340 kg
Light heavy	P. Becherv (Romania)	355 kg
Middle heavy	N. Vlad (Romania)	392·5 kg
First heavy	R. Milser (W. Germany)	385 kg
Heavy	N. Oberburger (Italy)	390 kg
Super heavy	D. Lukim (Austria)	412·5 kg

WRESTLING

Governing body: British Amateur Wrestling Association, 2 Huxley Drive, Bramhall, Stockport, Cheshire.

Freestyle

Light fly	R. Weaver (USA)
Fly	S. Trstena (Yugoslavia)
Bantam	W. Tomiyami (Japan)
Feather	R. Lewis (USA)
Light	Y. In-Tak (S. Korea)
Welter	D. Schultz (USA)
Middle	M. Schultz (USA)
Heavy	L. Banach (USA)
Super heavy	B. Baumgartner (USA)

Graeco-Roman

Light fly	V. Maenza (Italy)
Fly	A. Miyahara (Japan)
Bantam	P. Passarelli (W. Germany)
Feather	Weon-Kee Kim (S. Korea)
Light	V. Lisjak (Yugoslavia)
Welter	J. Salomaki (Finland)
Middle	I. Draica (Romania)
Light heavy	S. Fraser (USA)
Heavy	V. Andrei (Romania)
Super heavy	J. Blatnick (USA)

CANOEING

Governing body: The British Canoe Union, Flexel House, 45/47 High Street, Addlestone, Weybridge, Surrey.

Men

500 m kayak singles	I. Ferguson (New Zealand)
1000 m kayak singles	A. Thompson (New Zealand)
500 m kayak pairs	New Zealand
1000 m kayak pairs	Canada
1000 m kayak fours	New Zealand
500 m Canadian singles	L. Cain (Canada)
1000 m Canadian singles	U. Eicke (W. Germany)
500 m Canadian pairs	Yugoslavia
1000 m Canadian pairs	Romania

Women

500 m kayak singles	A. Andersson (Sweden)
500 m kayak pairs	Sweden
500 m kayak fours	Romania

HANDBALL

Men	Women
Yugoslavia	Yugoslavia

JUDO

Governing body: The British Judo Association, 16 Upper Woburn Place, London WC1A 0QP.

Bantam	S. Hosokawa (Japan)
Feather	Y. Matsuoki (Japan)
Light	B.-K. Ahn (S. Korea)
Light middle	F. Wieneke (W. Germany)
Middle	P. Siesenbacher (Austria)
Light heavy	H. Hyoung-Zoo (S. Korea)
Heavy	H. Saito (Japan)
Open	Y. Yamashita (Japan)

WINTER OLYMPICS 1984 (Sarajevo)

BOBSLEIGH	
Two-man	E. Germany
Four-man	E. Germany

LUGE	
Men	P. Hildgartner (Italy)
Two-man	H. Stanggassinger and
	F. Wembacher (W. Germany)
Women	S. Martin (E. Germany)

PERSONALITIES

Ian Terence Botham

Born in Heswall, Cheshire, on 24 November 1955, Ian Botham began his cricketing career by joining the ground staff at Lord's and then was engaged by Somerset. He made his first-class debut in 1974 at the age of 18 and was immediately recognised as a star. In 1976 he was awarded his county cap and a year later he played his first Test match for England. It was against Australia at Nottingham, and he took 5 wickets. By 1982, after only 42 Tests, Botham had reached 2,000 runs and taken 200 wickets in Test cricket and he is now approaching Dennis Lillee's record number of Test wickets, 355.

In 1981 he played some of the most spectacular cricket ever seen for England in Test matches against Australia. He resigned as England's captain after the second Test match, but he hit 149 not out in the third Test, and England, having followed-on 227 runs in arrears, won the match. He took 5 wickets for 11 runs in the Test match at Birmingham and snatched a win for England by 29 runs, and followed this in the fifth Test with 118, his hundred being reached off only 86 deliveries.

In 1985 he hit a record 80 sixes in the season and averaged over 100 for Somerset in the County Championship as well as playing a vital part in England regaining the Ashes by beating Australia 3–1. An enthusiast in all he does, Ian Botham has played League football for Scunthorpe United and raised vast sums of money for leukaemia research by walking from John O'Groats to Land's End.

Steve Cram

Steve was born on 14 October 1960 and is 1·86m tall and married. He first came to prominence when he won the world mile record for his age group in 1978 and gained a place in England's team for the Edmonton Commonwealth Games. At 1500 metres he came eighth in the 1980 Olympics and then in 1982 he won both the European Championship and Commonwealth Games titles. But 1983 was his best year when he won the World Championships in convincing style and also took the European Cup 1500 metres gold. In the 1984 Los Angeles Olympics he won the 1500 metres silver medal, beaten in the run-in by Sebastian Coe. The tables were turned in 1985 when Cram broke the mile record, held by Coe since 1981.

Steve Davis

Born in London on 22 August 1957, Steve Davis has red hair and blue eyes. He started playing snooker when he was on holiday at the age of twelve. He was the Junior English Billiards Champion when he was seventeen and he made his first one hundred snooker break at that age. In September 1977 he achieved his first 147 break and he was undefeated as an English amateur international. In 1978 he won the Lucania National Snooker Tournament and also the Pontins Open. He won the Lucania Pro-Am in 1977, 1978 and 1979. He became a professional in 1978 and in April 1981 he won the world professional snooker title. He lost the title the following year but in February 1982 he won the Benson and Hedges Masters, the only title he had not won. He regained the world professional title in 1983, retained it in 1984, but lost to Dennis Taylor in the final in 1985 and to Joe Johnson in the 1986 final.

Christopher Dean: *see* joint entry with Jayne Torvill.

Jo Durie

Born on 27 July 1960 in Bristol, Jo Durie is ranked No. 1 in Britain and No. 6 in the world. She won her first title in 1972 as British Under 12 Champion and went on to take all the Junior Championships in each age group, culminating in 1976 with a hat-trick of the British Under 18 National Grass Court, Hardcourt and Indoor Championships. From that year she devoted herself full-time to tennis. She was first ranked internationally in 1978 (No. 133 in the world) and in 1979 was chosen to represent Britain in the Wightman Cup. But by the autumn of that year she had back problems that were so severe they could only be cured by a tricky spinal operation. The operation was a success and during 1980 Jo fought her way back into competitive tennis; she was chosen for the Wightman Cup team again in 1981, 82 and 83. She won the British Hardcourt Championship in 1977, 78 and 81. In 1983 she won the National Closed Tournament singles and doubles, with Ann Hobbs. This partnership also won the German Open in 1983, reached the Eastbourne doubles finals and Wimbledon doubles semi-finals. In 1984 Jo had her most successful year in the Wimbledon singles when she reached the quarter-finals.

Michael William Gatting

Born in Kingsbury, Middlesex, on 6 June 1957, Mike Gatting played for England Schools at cricket and made his debut for Middlesex in 1975. He was awarded his county cap two years later. He is a hard-hitting right-handed batsman, a useful medium-pace bowler and an excellent fielder, who first played for England in January 1978 against Pakistan in Karachi. He did not score a century in the County Championship until 1980, but he now has more than thirty first-class hundreds to his credit. He was made captain of Middlesex in 1983 and led his side to success in the Benson and Hedges Cup in his first season and in the NatWest Trophy in 1984. Middlesex also challenged for the County Championship in both seasons and Gatting gained such a reputation as a captain that he was appointed vice-captain of England for the tour of India in 1984–85. He had played thirty Test matches without scoring a century, but in the series against India he scored two centuries, including a top score of 207, and reached 1,000 runs for the tour. He scored two more Test centuries when England beat Australia in the 1985 series and led Middlesex to the County Championship title. He was named as vice-captain of England for the tour to West Indies and then as England captain in 1986 against India.

David Gower

David Ivor Gower was born on 1 April 1957, at Tunbridge Wells, and educated at King's School, Canterbury. It was intended that he should find a career in law, but he decided to try his luck in first-class cricket. His home county, Kent, had so many promising youngsters on their staff that they raised no objection when Leicestershire asked permission to sign him, and David Gower was greatly helped by the former England captain Ray Illingworth as he tried to win a place in the Leicestershire first team. He made his first-class debut in 1975 and received his county cap in 1977. A year later he was in the England side to meet Pakistan at Birmingham. Later the same summer he hit his first Test hundred, 111 against New Zealand at The Oval. The following year he hit a splendid 200 not out against India at Birmingham. He has toured Australia, West Indies, India and Sri Lanka, was vice-captain to Willis in 1982 and in Australia, 1982–83, and led England against Pakistan at Lord's in 1982. He was England's leading batsman in the World Cup in 1983 and hit two centuries in the Test matches against New Zealand later the same summer. In 1984 he went to New Zealand and Pakistan as vice-captain of the England team. He became captain of Leicestershire and in

May 1984 was named England's captain, leading them to success in India 1984–85. Further success came when he led England to regain the Ashes by beating Australia 3–1. His own contribution to the series was a record 732 runs, which included three centuries, one of them an innings of 215 at Nottingham, the highest score of his career. He captained England in the West Indies, 1986 but an unsuccessful tour meant he lost the captaincy at the beginning of the summer season.

Lucinda Green

Lucinda Green, MBE, was born in London on 7 November 1953 and is 1·73m tall. She has fair hair and wears yellow cross-country colours. Her speed and flair across country have made her reputation as Britain's and the world's outstanding event rider and kept her at the forefront of eventing for over a decade. She has won Badminton a record six times – 1973 on *Be Fair*, 1976 on *Wide Awake*, 1977 on *George*, 1979 on *Killaire*, 1983 on *Regal Realm* and 1984 on *Beagle Bay*. Lucinda's first event horse – *Be Fair* – was given to her by her parents as a fifteenth birthday present. This combination competed in the gold-medal-winning British Junior Team in 1971, won Badminton in 1973, competed in Kiev and, when Lucinda was 21, they became European Champions. In 1977 she became the first rider to win Badminton and Burghley in the same year. Her success continued with different horses, culminating in 1982 with the sport's highest prize – the World Championships which she won on *Regal Realm*. Lucinda married Australian event rider David Green in 1981 and their first child, Freddie, was born in April 1985. Later that year Lucinda was a member of the gold-medal-winning British team in the European Championships, but unfortunately *Regal Realm* was lame in 1986 and Lucinda was unable to defend her World Championship title.

Bryan Robson

Manchester United and England captain Bryan Robson has brown hair and brown eyes. He was born on 11 January 1957 in Co. Durham and now lives in Cheshire with his wife and two children. He joined West Bromwich Albion at the age of fifteen when he left school and made headlines by scoring two goals in his first three matches. While he was there WBA were promoted to the

First Division. Eight years later he left to join Manchester United
in a record-breaking £1·5 million transfer. United went on to win
the FA Cup and the Charity Shield. Robson's career has been
beset by injuries and in one season he fought back after three
times breaking a leg. England's first international victory under
Robson was in November 1982 when they beat Greece 3–0. He
has 10 Youth caps, six Under-21 caps, two B caps and over forty
full international caps for England.

Ian Rush

Ian James Rush was born at St Asaph, North Wales, on 20
October 1961. He is 1·8m tall and has black hair and blue eyes.
He now plays for Liverpool FC who signed him up from Chester
for a substantial fee. He spent his first year in the reserve side at
Liverpool, making his first-team debut towards the end of the
1980–81 season. He started scoring goals to such good effect that
he has become one of the League's leading marksmen: by the end
of the 1983–84 season he had scored over 100 goals for Liverpool.
In April 1984 he was named Football Writers' Footballer of the
Year.

Tessa Sanderson

Born in Kingston, Jamaica, on 14 March 1956, Tessa Sanderson
is 1·68m tall. She came to England with her parents when she
was very young. Her javelin-throwing career took off in the mid
1970s when she came fifth in the 1974 Commonwealth Games,
tenth in the 1976 Olympic Games and then in 1977 she took two
bronze medals – in the European Cup and World Cup. The following year she won the silver medal in the European Championships and was set for the 1980 Moscow Olympic Games. But,
disappointingly, she failed to qualify. A serious injury in 1982
kept her out of the European Championships, but in 1983 she
returned to win the Gold in the Commonwealth Games and to
come fourth in the World Championships. The highlight of her
career came at the 1984 Los Angeles Olympic Games where her
Gold Medal in the javelin was popular and deserved.

Daley Thompson

Francis Daley Thompson was born in London on 30 July 1958.
He is 1·85m tall with black hair and brown eyes. He is unmarried

and lives in Crawley and London. He has taken part with outstanding success in athletic events since 1975 when he was the AAA indoor junior champion at 60 m and 200 m and the outdoor champion at 100 m, long jump and decathlon. In 1976 he took part in the Montreal Olympics and was placed eighteenth in the senior decathlon. In 1976 and 1977 he gained the world's junior decathlon record and the British and Commonwealth senior records. In 1977 he was placed third in the world. In 1978 he won a Commonwealth Gold Medal and a European Silver Medal in the decathlon events. In 1980 he went on to win the Olympic Decathlon. 1982 was his best year to date. He won the European Decathlon and in so doing regained the World Record and later went on to retain the Commonwealth title—the first athlete to hold all three major titles plus the world record at the same time. However, in 1983 the world record was taken from him by W. Germany's Jurgen Hingsen, although in the 1984 Los Angeles Olympic Games Daley beat his old rival to take the Decathlon Gold Medal.

Jayne Torvill

Jayne Torvill was born on 7 October 1957 in Nottingham where she still lives. She has brown hair and grey-blue eyes and is single. Her partner Christopher Colin Dean was also born in Nottingham and he was born on 27 July 1958. He is single and has blond hair and green eyes. Christopher started skating when he was eleven and Jayne when she was nine but they have only been skating together for seven years. Their first major success was in the 1977–78 season when they were third in the British Ice Dance Championships and they represented Great Britain in the 1978 European and World Championships, gaining ninth and eleventh places respectively. In November 1978 they won the British title for the first time and won it again in 1979, 1980 and 1981. In the 1980 European Championships they gained fourth place, fifth place in the Olympic Games and fourth place in the World Championships. In 1981 they were first in the European Championships and retained their title in 1982 and 83. In March 1981 they won the World Ice Dancing Championship and retained this title in 1982, 83 and 84. Their greatest triumph came at the 1984 Olympics in Sarajevo when they took the ice dancing gold medal, having sealed their victory with an unprecedented number

of sixes for their Bolero free dance: they gained three sixes and six
5·9s for technical merit and a perfect nine sixes for artistic impression. In the World Championships of 1983 they had also
gained nine sixes for their Barnum on Ice, and these are the only
two occasions this has been achieved in ice dancing. After their
outstanding successes together, Jayne Torvill and Christopher
Dean have now turned professional.

COMPUTERS AND INFORMATION TECHNOLOGY

Access time is the time taken for a computer to obtain the data, either from the main *memory* or from the *backing store*. This is measured from the time it takes to issue the instruction until the data is stored in the specified location. The times are in millionths of seconds: thus a typical home micro-computer may take 4 millionths of one second to perform a simple memory access. See *direct access*.

Acoustic coupler This is a device which enables digital signals to be transmitted and received using an ordinary telephone.

Acronym The explosion of computing over the last twenty years has been accompanied by a surge in computing vocabulary. Although acronym is itself not a computing word, it is useful to understand that many computing words are acronyms; they have been derived from a group of letters formed from the initial letters of the words in a name or phrase, e.g. *BASIC* from Beginners All-purpose Symbolic Instruction Code. It often seems that the word is thought of first, and then a cumbersome phrase invented to fit it. Sometimes any letters are chosen, e.g. the word **BIT** comes from **BI**nary digi**T**.

Address This is a memory location in a computer. Also used as a verb meaning to identify a memory location.

ALGOL Acronym for 'ALGOrithmic Language'. A high level computer language, designed for solving scientific and mathematical problems.

Analog (Or **Analogue**) Analog data relates continuously to what is happening. Thus, for example, traditional (analog) watch hands move constantly round the face, when wound up. The winding of the spring could be said to be the input and the movement of the hands the output. This continuous movement is usually contrasted with the stop/go pattern found in digital systems. A digital watch displays its output in steps of separate units of a second or of fractions of a second. It is either one time or another. Conversion devices are called ADCs

(Analog to Digital Converter) and DACs (Digital to Analog Converter). See *digital*.

Application This is the task a computer is being used for, e.g. word processing, games, payroll. Hence an *Application Package* is the set of programs and written instructions which enables the computer to perform a specific task.

Arithmetic and Logic Unit (ALU) That part of a computer's CPU in which calculations and comparisons of values are performed. See *computer*.

ASCII The American Standard Code for Information Inter-change. The most common way of representing characters in binary code.

Assembly language See *low level language*.

Assembler The program which translates assembly language into machine code. The machine 'assembles' the translation in the main memory, awaiting execution. Assemblers are 'machine-oriented' rather than 'problem-oriented' since they only work for that type of machine.

Babbage, Charles A mathematician who was concerned with the inaccuracies in astronomical and mathematical tables. In 1822, he thought of producing a machine he called a 'difference engine', a mechanical device for working out the tables he wanted. He managed to build a machine which would do equations containing x squared to an accuracy of 8 decimal places. In the course of his experiments, Babbage conceived the idea of what he called an 'analytical engine', which was to be a general-purpose calculator, as opposed to the one-purpose machine which his difference machine was. In concept, he had created the 'universal computer', since up to then all machines required human intervention at each stage of the problem, wheels had to be set and so on. Babbage proposed that there should be a store for the data, a mill for processing it (i.e. what we now call a central processing unit), and input and output devices; and that is a specification for a computer which any modern computer designer would recognise.

Backing store Although the largest computers have enormous memories capable of storing several million characters of information, even the largest computers need to store and retrieve data outside the main memory. If one does not have backing storage, then each time the computer is used the program has to be typed in. Backing storage can be held on magnetic tape, discs and drums, and still, in some cases, punched cards and paper tape. An essential feature of backing store is that the information and programs can be both read from, and written onto, the store.

Bar codes These are a series of alternating lines and spaces printed closely together, often to be found on groceries. The pattern contains information about the product: e.g. its price and product number. A *bar code reader* is an input device used to scan the line patterns. The advantage of bar codes and bar code readers is that as a way of obtaining information and sending it to a computer as data it is much faster than other methods, e.g. keying in on a shop till.

ISBN 0-7207-1666-7

BASIC BASIC stands for Beginners All-purpose Symbolic Instruction Code and is a programming language. Developed in the United States in 1964 as a simple beginner's language, it has, over the years, established itself as the world's most popular learning language. It has always been the most common language available on microcomputers, partly because it has a low memory requirement. Unlike most high level languages it runs in conjunction with an interpreter which executes and runs one BASIC statement at a time. A single statement can make the computer immediately respond; thus BASIC is said to be interactive. Another feature of BASIC compared to other languages is that it uses line numbers. Although easy to use there are a number of drawbacks to BASIC. One arises out of its very ability to respond and be added to; this tends to lead to unstructured ('spaghetti') programming. There have been many attempts to improve BASIC, a notable recent example being that of BBC BASIC.

Binary The binary numbering system is the simplest possible as it uses only two numbers, 0 (zero) and 1 (one). Binary readily represents the actual electrical switching of pulses—0 signifies no pulse and 1 a pulse. All data put into a digital computer is transformed into binary signals for storage or processing. In the decimal system each place represents ten times that on its right. In the binary system, each place is worth twice that on its right. The first place on the right is the number of ones, the next the numbers of twos, the next the number of fours (2 × 2), and so on.

BIT An acronym of BInary DigiT. A bit is a binary number only one digit long. A bit must be a 0 or a 1. It is the smallest bit of storage. There are 8 bits in a byte. See *Byte* and *Binary*.

Boole, George A logician, who in 1854 perfected a way of writing down 'logical operations'. He was concerned with a branch of philosophy called symbolic logic, which tackles problems like, 'If statement A is true and B is true, is statement C also true?' Boole found a shorthand way of writing this which became known as Boolean algebra. This algebra was particularly appropriate to electrical switching, which formed the basis of the binary system and how computers work.

Boot Jargon for starting a computer: from the expression 'to pull yourself up by your own bootstraps'. Hence a **Bootstrap Program** is a program which starts the computer working.

Bus The common pathway linking components inside the computer along which information travels.

Bug Originally slang, a bug is a mistake or malfunction in a computer program or equipment. Like living bugs they may be easy to detect, but not to remove. The term originates from the moths that damaged the valves on the early ENIAC computer.

Byte A group of 8 bits. Derived from bit 'by eight'. One byte holds one character of information. Take, for example, the letter B. B coded as *ASCII* binary occupies one byte, and is represented as 01000010 requiring 8 binary bits. The decimal equivalent is 66. A byte is the smallest addressable unit of memory.

CAD This stands for Computer Aided Design. See *Graphics*.

Ceefax Televised information service put out by the BBC, its name deriving from 'see facts'. See *teletext*.

Central Processing Unit (CPU) Sometimes called central processor, or the processor. The device at the heart of the computer, it is the part that does the actual computing, controlling the activities of the computer and carrying out arithmetical and other logical operations. For a fuller explanation see *computer*.

Character A letter, digit, punctuation mark or space.

Chip This is the popular name for a wafer-thin slice of silicon onto which integrated electronic circuits have been chemically etched. They are usually, but not always, made from silicon. Most integrated circuits occupy an area less than half that of the nail on a small finger. A chip this size may house as many as sixty-five thousand separate components. The circuits are solid state. There are no moving parts, so reducing the likelihood of mechanical breakdown.

The development of integrated circuits gave birth to third-generation computers. Chip-based systems are a thousand times cheaper than the discrete-component ones of fifteen years ago, and tens of thousands of times more compact than systems based on valves or *transistors*. One particular development of chips (not all chips are microprocessors) has meant that all sorts of equipment can be fitted with *microprocessors* ranging from washing machines to toys, and also, the whole range of micro-computers. See *Computer Generations*.

Chips are often confused with their casings; the chips are embedded in black plastic rectangles with perhaps 8 or 16 or more metal connectors or 'legs' down the longer sides. The casing is sometimes called a 'beatle'.

COBOL Common Business Orientated Language. A high level computer language that was developed for commercial use. COBOL is very good at handling large files of data, and is by far the most commonly used language in larger computer installations. Cobol is not widely used in micro-computers at present because of the memory requirements.

Compact disc High quality music recordings are increasingly being done on compact discs. These are small silver discs which store digital information. This information is read optically, by laser. The discs are capable of holding 600 megabytes of information: roughly the equivalent of a hundred million words of text, or 2,000 novels. Sections of the computer industry are looking into compact disc systems as a means of accessing large amounts of data quickly. It is intended that compact disc memory be accessed as ROM, hence the development of CD-ROM's (Compact Disc—Read Only Memories). Compact discs can only be 'read from'; unlike magnetic discs, they cannot be written to. See *Magnetic disc, ROM, RAM*.

Compiler A program which translates from a high level language such as *COBOL* or *FORTRAN* into machine code. As instructions in high level languages are complex it is nearly always necessary for each source statement to be broken down into a number of machine code instructions. The original language is known as the source code. Compilers and other items of *system software* provide facilities which help the programmer to debug the code. The set of instructions once compiled is known as the object code. When compilation is complete it is the compiled program which is run. During the process of compilation, errors are identified and listings produced. Contrast with an *interpreter*.

Computer A machine that accepts, processes and stores data according to the user's set of instructions. These instructions are known as a program, which has been stored in the computer.

They are calculating machines, but differ from old mechanical (pre-electronic) machines in three ways: their speed of operation; their large memories; and the fact that, by comparing data, they can make decisions which affect the place in the program to which they go next.

Computers are not 'thinking machines'; they are machines which can carry out arithmetic at great speed. (Strictly speaking computers can never make 'value judgements'.)

All program instructions are processed by the *central processing unit* (CPU). The clock, the control unit and arithmetic/logic unit (ALU) together make up the CPU. The CPU co-ordinates the subsystems of the computer. It is the part that does the actual computing, controlling its activities and carrying out arithmetical and other logical operations. The central clock synchronises all the pulses. Once the program is loaded, the CPU will call up the data and process it according to the program instructions.

On mainframe computers the central processor used to occupy the size of a large cabinet. On micro-computers the *microprocessor* may occupy only one chip.

Computer generations Different generations of computers are often referred to. The first generation machines (1940–52) used vacuum tubes (electronic valves). See *ENIAC*. The second generation machines (1952–64) used transistors and still required air-conditioning and maintenance. The many thousands of separate components still had to be assembled by hand. The third generation used integrated circuits (ICs) as the basic components. At first about ten components could be integrated into an area about 5 mm square. The equipment became more reliable. Much less labour and power was required, and as a result less heat was generated. The process of packing components in a small area continued, and by 1971 Large-Scale-Integration (LSI) chips were being marketed. The micro-processor chip was in production and being used in fourth generation micro-computers. Although not as powerful as the third generation, they were far more compact, robust and versatile. The fourth generation is that which uses LSI circuits, which have now been adopted by the whole range of computers. The next generation, the fifth, is predicted for the 1990s. Not surprisingly, it is based upon further miniaturisation of circuitry and increasingly sophisticated software. It is expected that by 1990 one million components will be packed into a chip. Inspired by Japanese designers, the aim of the fifth generation is to have very large main memories, extremely fast processing times and improved input/output with voice and touch interactions. See *expert systems*, *supercomputer*, *transputer*.

CP/M Control Program Monitor. The most commonly used operating system for micro-computers, based upon those which utilise the Z80 microprocessor chip.

Cursor A movable marker on a screen which shows where the next character will appear.

Daisywheel See *printer*.

Data Data is whatever has been successfully input into the computer. This data can be processed by the program; the resulting product is not data. See *Information*.

Database A large collection of data, such as local history records, from which particular information can be retrieved using a computer. In essence it is a comprehensive filing system using a collection of organised data for a particular purpose. See *file*. The use of computers allows a flexible approach to work which would be very cumbersome to do manually. Take, for example, a database of records each containing surnames, first names, telephone numbers, dates of birth and number of children. Searching for a name using only a telephone number becomes easy. It is possible to re-sort the records by first name or by date of birth. Calculations can generate the total and average number of children. Data needs only to be recorded once. A key feature of a database is that it contains as little repeated information as possible. The structure of the data is independent of what is to be done with it. Thus the same database may be used for a wide variety of applications.

Data Processing (DP) This can be defined as the conversion of raw facts into useful information. A computer is a general purpose data processor; it always processes data. The main use of the phrase 'data processing' arises from use in business organisations; e.g. for payroll, statistical returns, marketing etc. Thus the computer departments within businesses are often called DP departments.

Deadly embrace A condition which arises when all the processes going on in a computer system compete for the same resources and the whole system seizes up.

Digit A single component of a number. Two is a one digit number, 27 is a two digit number, etc.

Direct access Direct access is a method of organising data files. If a file is organised in this way, then individual items (records) can be brought from backing store into main memory, updated and written back to their place in the file. Sometimes direct access is called **random access** but, strictly speaking, random access should refer only to accessing the computer's main store. Disc backing store can be used for direct access or sequential access files. *Sequential access* means that each item has to be read until the required item is reached. Files held on magnetic tape have to be sequential and can only be updated by rewriting the file.

Disc See *magnetic disc*.

Disc drive A machine with a high speed motor which rotates the disc and a head which reads and writes information to and from the *magnetic disc.*

Dot matrix See *printer.*

Electronic mail This is the use of computer systems to transfer messages between users. A variety of input and output equipment can be used; for example, telex, word processors, video terminals and facsimile machines.

ENIAC This is an acronym for Electronic Numeral Integrator and Calculator. ENIAC was the first modern computer by virtue of its ability to switch tasks. The breakthrough was made by storing the program inside the computer, and not building a machine to do a specific task (e.g. Colossus which was used to de-cipher German codes in the Second World War). ENIAC consumed 150 kilowatts of power and contained 18,000 thermionic valves. These are the sort of glass 'bulbs', about 50 mm high, which can be found in old radios.

ENIAC could do additions at amazing speeds, 5,000 per second, although it rarely worked for more than half an hour without a valve going. This section of JUNIOR PEARS is being written with the aid of a micro-computer. In principle it is very little different from ENIAC. But in practice it takes up 30,000 times less space, is forty times faster, has a larger memory, consumes the power of an electric light bulb and is about 20,000 times cheaper.

EPROM An 'Erasable PROgrammable Memory' chip which can have its contents erased, using ultra-violet light, and have new programs fed into it. Thus the EPROM is sometimes said to have been 'cooked'. (See *PROM.*)

Expert Systems These are computer programs which capture a human expert's knowledge of a particular subject, usually by creating some rules which cover probabilities and approximations. Complex and mammoth amounts of data can be analysed and evaluated until a conclusion is reached.

The first serious expert system—MYCIN—was developed in the mid-1970s to help doctors diagnose meningitis. Until now, the major applications have been where there are a lot of experts—as in medical diagnosis and law. Although there has been much discussion about expert systems, artificial intelligence (see *Turing*), the much-predicted technical breakthroughs are still in the early stages. See *fifth generation computers, transputer*.

Facsimile System (FAX) Transmission of printed words and other images so that the receiver gets an exact copy of the original. A scanner converts the original into electrical signals, which are transmitted by cable or airwaves and printed at the receiving end.

Fibre Optical See *optical fibre*.

File A collection of related **records**. Information on each record is divided into separate categories, under the same headings. A **field** is one item of information within a record. Thus the membership secretary of a computer club may have one file containing all the membership details. There will be an individual record for each member. Within each record there will be details about name, address, and so on. Each of these items is an example of a field.

FORTRAN FORmula TRANslation. A high-level computer language for scientific and technical use.

GIGO Acronym for 'Garbage In, Garbage Out'—a useful reminder that what comes out is only as good as the programs and data put in.

Graphics The creation of non-written text (e.g. pictures, displays and graphs) is an important feature of computers, both on micros (e.g. games, educational programs) and on larger computers (e.g. Computer Aided Design (CAD)). The use of colour has an added impact. In high-resolution graphics, the programmer aims at controlling the individual phospor dots on the display monitor. The only limitation is the memory size of the computer. That unit of the screen addressed by the computer is known as the *Pixel*. In low-resolution graphics, individual shapes, or 'characters', are already constructed and can be built up into an image. These can be conveniently generated by using the keyboard. Each shape is formed by a block, typically eight rows by eight columns.

Hard copy Data printed onto paper generated by the computer.

Hardware All the physical equipment in a computer system, e.g. the keyboard, the screen, floppy disc, etc. If it can be kicked, it's hardware. Contrast with *software*.

High level languages Programming languages developed to be intelligible and as close as possible to the problem to be solved.

These are easier for human beings to use but require a great deal of translation into machine code instructions before they can be executed by the central processing unit of a computer. There are hundreds of high level languages, which can be divided into four classes: scientific (e.g. ALGOL and FORTRAN), business (e.g. COBOL), specialised (e.g. ADA) and interactive (e.g. BASIC and APL).

Hollerith, Dr Hermann In the late 1880s, the U.S. census bureau had a problem. It was still counting the results from the 1880 census, and had another to deal with in 1890. Hollerith, a census statistician, saw that the only answer was mechanisation. He realised that much of the information being processed could be represented by the presence or absence of holes in paper cards and that the sorting could be done by electrical means, since a contact could be made or broken by the card. This led to the idea of feeding calculating machines with punched cards. The firm Hollerith founded to exploit his invention, the Computing Tabulating Recording Company, later became the International Business Machines Corporation: IBM.

Informatics This comes from the French word *l'informatique*, and is said to be the science of information handling. The term is useful in so far as it emphasises the importance of information.

Information Information is derived from data. *Data* in itself is meaningless unless it is interpreted. It is intelligible data. Take, for example, the number 250646. This could be a date, a telephone number or, for that matter, a reference. The meaning is dependent upon the user. When interpreted it becomes information. Refer to *data*.

Information Technology (IT) This generally refers to the use of microprocessor-based equipment to handle, process and communicate information. There was technology that did this long before the advent of the microprocessor, but the development and powerful coalition of micro-electronics, computers and telecommunications has given rise to the umbrella term 'information technology'. This information is always transmitted in the form of digital data. At its simplest, two computers communicating with each other can be said to be an example of IT. This inter-communication has been crucially enhanced by the development of communication media, e.g. optical fibres and satellites. A particularly important reason for the exploitation of the technology has been the growth of the information sector within modern society. It has been estimated that in the USA, trained office workers spend up to 30 per cent of their time merely hunting for information.

I/O Abbreviation for Input/Output.

Input Anything put into the computer system, such as programs and information, which then becomes data. This is done by means of an *input device*: e.g. a keyboard. Other machines for inputting data include magnetic tape and disc drives, card and paper tape readers, bar-code readers and light pens. Whatever the device, it can accept and decode data and transmit it as digital pulses to the computer.

Integer A whole number with no fractions or decimal places.

Integrated circuit see *Chip*.

Interface This is the circuitry which allows the computer to communicate with one or more *peripheral* devices. Data can be passed from one to the other. The interface translates the differing operating characteristics of the devices.

Interpreter This is a translation program which is called upon whenever a program in a language such as BASIC is executed. It translates one line at a time into machine code. The run will be terminated if the program does not accord with the rules of the programming language—a syntax error occurs—and then the translation process has to start all over again. Contrast with *compiler*.

Kilobytes (K) A measurement of memory capacity. As a kilo refers to a thousand, a Kilobyte generally means a thousand bytes. (It is in fact 2 to the power of 10, which is 1,024 bytes.)

LASER Acronym for 'Light Amplification by Stimulated Emission of Radiation'. A device for producing a concentrated light beam on a single wave length, with many potential applications: e.g. laser beam printers which can print 20,000 lines of print per minute, *compact discs*.

Liquid Crystal Display (LCD) A reflective display, used in digital systems for the presentation of output. The LCD is characterised by its low power consumption. The **Light Emitting Diode (LED)** is an electronic component which conducts in one direction only, when conducting electric light is converted into visible light.

LOGO A high level programming language designed specifically for learning. It was first developed in the late 1960s by Seymour Papert. His philosophy was: 'Why not let the child program the computer instead of the computer programming the child?' LOGO is inter-active (like *BASIC*), and very easy to use. It permits users to build their own vocabulary of instructions. One of LOGO's functions is to control a robotic 'turtle' which can trace its path on the floor with the aid of a pen held between its back legs.

Lovelace, Ada Worked out the method by which *Babbage*'s machine could be programmed. She is generally considered to be the world's first programmer. She was the daughter of the poet Lord Byron.

Low level languages Programming languages that are closer to machine code than high level languages, which take less time for the computer to translate and understand. All **assembly** languages are low level language. Assembler program instructions use symbols, each of which corresponds (usually) to a single *machine code* instruction: e.g. the instruction LDA (**L**oa**D** Accumulator) could have a machine code of 10101001 on the 6502 microprocessor.

Machine code Machine code instructions are the control signals that actually work the machine. They are represented as binary patterns and require no translation. Programs written in other languages must be translated into machine code before the computer can execute them.

Magnetic disc Also spelt disk. A rotable disc which is used to store and read data. The surface is coated with a magnetisable material. Magnetic discs are the commonest way of storing data for direct access. The surface of the disc is subdivided into tracks: i.e. concentric rings. There are a wide variety of discs and disc units used by computers. Microcomputer systems normally use *floppy discs*, holding from 100K to 1000K (a mega-byte) bytes. At present the most common size is $5\frac{1}{4}$ in (130 mm) in diameter, and the cost is less than £2. Larger systems generally use hard discs, usually sealed inside a drive unit. These have a much greater storage capacity and faster access time. A number of hard discs are often combined to form a *disc pack*. The smallest of the hard disc units is the Winchester disc drive, used on some micro-computer systems. One of these can hold 80 megabytes. See *backing store* and *compact disc*.

The principle of operation of a disc pack

Magnetic tape An alternative method of storing data is to use magnetic tape wound on spools or cassettes. Tape can only be accessed sequentially but is still widely used in *data processing* installations to store large files: e.g. payroll and employees' records. It is cheaper but slower than disc storage. Tape files are often used as a disc backup and also for long-term storage of files. See also *access* and *backing store*.

Mainframe, Mini & Micro-computer systems The distinction between these types of computer systems is usually based upon the computing power (memory available and the processing capability), the sophistication of the operating system, the number of *peripherals* and the number of users. Thus mainframes work very quickly and can perform many different tasks at once. They can support hundreds of terminals. Mainframe computers require special environments and skilled operators, whereas a micro-computer is usually an isolated unit dependent upon a microprocessor chip. A microcomputer is normally used by a single user, running only one program at a time. In general a mini-computer is smaller than a mainframe but still very fast and capable of performing several tasks at once.

The distinction according to power is not hard and fast, especially because of the advances in technology. Some of today's micro-computers are more powerful than mini configurations of three years ago. Another rule-of-thumb guide is the cost. Small micros can cost less than £50, minis tens of thousands of pounds and mainframes cost several million pounds.

Memory The program and the data it needs are stored inside the main memory of the computer. Sometimes known as immediate access store because data can be instantly retrieved from any location. See *direct access*. In most computers this memory is known as volatile: i.e. the contents are lost when the power is switched off. Therefore programs and data are stored on *backing storage* when not being used. In micro-computers the internal memory is divided into two parts: **Random Access Memory (RAM)** and **Read Only Memory (ROM)**. The contents of RAM can be stored onto floppy disks or cassette tapes in order to keep it more permanently. ROM is the permanent storage space within the computer, usually containing important information that the computer needs all the time: e.g. the operating system. The user can have access to ROM but cannot change, remove, or add to it without actually adding on chips. See *PROM* and *EPROM*.

Microprocessor A *chip* which contains a timing and control unit, and an arithmetic/logic unit. It performs the function of the central processing unit (CPU) found in a traditional computer system. Many people confuse microprocessors with micro-computers. The microprocessor unit (MPU) is not a complete computer because it lacks memory and input/output devices. The micro-computer is just one application of the micro-processor. The importance of the microprocessor is that it permits greater flexibility. Linked with sensors, measuring and switching devices it can be made to run an industrial process; appropriately programmed, it will work a washing machine, sewing machines, calculator, arcade games or many thousands of other devices.

MODEM This stands for **MO**dulator-**DEM**odulator. The modulator converts computer output for transmitting along communication lines such as a telephone line. The demodulator converts it back.

Monitor The computer display screen which looks like a television set. See *VDU*.

Multi-plexing The use of a single telecommunications link to transmit a number of different signals virtually simultaneously.

Multi-user A computer system where several users can use the same computer simultaneously.

Network The linking together of separate computers is called a network and the interconnected points are known as *nodes*. The network enables any individual computer to draw on the computing power or storage facilities of the others. With a network you can distribute computer power. This is a radical departure from the tradition of large computer systems which are still 'sun and planets systems', with many satellites revolving around a central pivot. Networking of micro-computers often occurs so that resources can be shared: e.g. a Winchester disc drive unit. Some networks allow only the sharing of peripherals, whilst others allow full communication between computers.

Number-crunching This phrase represents the computer's ability to perform—'eat up'—numerical calculations. Thus, for example, the Meteorological Office's massive Control Data Cyber 205 (super) computer, installed in 1982, is capable of

400 million calculations per second. Nearly a trillion calculations are necessary in order to make weather forecasts up to a week in advance. See *supercomputer*.

Numerical Control (NC) In the early fifties the engineering industry started using NC machine tools, which read codes from paper tape, to guide the machines through different stages of cutting. By the 1970s these were being replaced by machines which stored the programs in memory, replacing the paper tape; hence Computer Numerical Control (CNC) machinery.

Operating System The operating system acts as an 'interface' between the computer and the user. It determines how the computer responds when turned on and when instructions are keyed in. The first computers did not communicate via an operating system. Indeed a series of switches had to be set by specialists. Now there is great emphasis upon the 'friendliness' of the computer. This is initially determined by the operating system, which is a collection of programs built into the systems software; it contains all the instructions the computer needs. In a micro-computer this is often placed in ROM and is then called firmware.

Optical fibre Optical fibre cables, made of very pure glass, are replacing copper cables as a means of transmission. Light is used as the carrier of the signals. The signals transmitted are superior to traditional methods; data can be transmitted at the rate of about 140 million bits per sec. There is a much higher carrying capacity. Eight optical 'tubes' can do the work of 4,800 traditional phone cables. The undersea optical fibre cable planned to link Britain with Belgium will carry 12,000 voice circuits. Owing to the immense cost, existing cable networks are not in practice being replaced with optical fibre cables. Optical fibre is being used to supplement existing overloaded networks and to build new ones.

On-line Directly connected to the computer.

Output Anything coming out of a computer. This is either to be communicated to the user in a form that can be read (e.g. results printed onto paper or displayed on the VDU) or output in code for other computers and stored on *backing storage* such as disc or tape. See *input*.

Pascal A much admired general purpose high level computer language, designed to encourage structured programming.

Named after the French mathematician Blaise Pascal (see C24) who, in 1642, constructed one of the earliest calculating machines.

Peripherals All the extra machines that can surround, and are controlled by, the computer itself: e.g. a disc drive, printer, keyboard, monitor, plotter, etc. Their purpose is to provide an information link between the outside world and the computer. See *interface* and *backing storage*.

Pixel The tiny dots or **PIC**ture **EL**ements that make up a computer graphics picture displayed on monitor or a *VDU*. See *graphics*.

Point of Sale (POS) Terminals Cash registers in supermarkets and shops are being replaced by POS terminals. In addition to providing exact change for the customers, they can keep records of sales and monitor the speed of the operator. There are two main types: free-standing and those directly linked to a central computer. The free-standing terminal is a computer in its own right but is also capable of generating data (e.g. using micro-cassette tapes) which can be periodically fed into the central computer. The central computer is able to keep records of sales of particular items and make an instant stock check. Potentially, point of sale (POS) devices can be used for checking on the credit-worthiness of shoppers who offer credit cards, direct debiting of the customer's bank account and direct re-stocking to and from the warehouse.

Printer A machine which prints information sent from the computer onto paper. There are many types. **Dot Matrix** and **Daisywheel** printers are commonly used and relatively inexpensive. Dot matrix use printed characters formed by ink dots. The printer-hammer pattern is created from a rectangular block of needles, typically 9 by 7. Only one block of needles is needed to create any of the characters in the given character set. This is in contrast with pre-formed characters such as are found on typewriters and *daisywheel* printers. A daisywheel is so named because the 'daisy' is a series of 'petals', which rotate. The petals, or spokes, are rotated until the appropriate character is found. Daisywheel print is usually of a higher quality than dot matrix but, because of the fixed set of characters, cannot display a wide range of characters. Daisywheel printers are not, normally, used for graphical output.

Program A set of instructions which tells the computer how to perform any particular task. A computer cannot be useful until it is programmed. These instructions will either be in *machine code* or in a programming language. The program must be capable of being understood and accord to the logic of the language being used by the computer's central processor.

PROM Programmable Read Only Memory. A memory into which data is written after manufacture, but which cannot then be altered. See *EPROM*.

RAM Random Access Memory. See *memory*.

Real time The ability of the system to respond almost immediately, regardless of the number of terminals, as a result of inputting data. When a person withdraws money from a cash till, or when a travel agency keys in a flight enquiry, the computer system responds almost immediately and is said to be 'real time'. The action must be processed quickly enough so that further action may be taken: for example, when the travel agent books a flight seat, the transaction must be processed before any other agents enquire whether seats are still available. Another application of real time is in controlling industrial processes: e.g. in a chemical plant. 'Real time' services can be very expensive, and may not always be required by the users. Alternative computer configurations may utilise batch processing, or time-sharing.

Robot Robots are machines designed to replace human labour. ('Robot' comes from the Czech word meaning 'worker'.) For a long time man has dreamed of machines that can both do the work of man and be like man. A robot should to some extent be able to respond 'intelligently' to changes in its environment. A range of sensors should allow the robot to capture data through touch, hearing and vision, crudely like that of a human. Senses, coupled with micro-computers, give robots so-called 'intelligence'. Many industrial robots do not possess this quality. 'Intelligent' and responsive robots are very expensive and are still under development. In 1983 it was reckoned that there were only 155 robots with visual and tactile sensing in operation in the United States.

ROM Read Only Memory. See *memory*.

Semiconductor A material (e.g. silicon, germanium) which can be made to switch from being a good conductor to being a good insulator. This is done by introducing chemical impurities which can very sensitively alter and control its electrical properties.

Software Programs used by the computer. Although software is usually taken to mean the programs loaded by the user, it also includes the systems programs which can come with the machine. See *operating systems* and *systems software*.

Software package Sets of programs to do particular tasks: e.g. stock-control. Like package holidays, they may not be exactly what is required. See *application*.

Speech recognition In the same way as fingerprints, voice prints can be uniquely identified. However, speech recognition is still presenting a number of problems because of variations in accent, tone and pitch, and also because of the very flexible and versatile nature of language. Once speech recognition is developed it will be useful in a number of different ways. See *computer generations*.

Speech synthesizers Computer-generated speech is already a feature in some applications. Voice output can either be constructed by adding together previously recorded words and phrases or, much more difficult, by assembling words from a range of sounds (phonemes).

Spreadsheets These are programs which allow the user to set up tables in rows and columns of (usually) financial figures. The data may be entered directly, or it may be derived from calculations performed upon other data. Therefore, a monthly total could be defined as the sum of all the spending, minus the income. A particular advantage of these models is that an imaginary situation can be simulated: for example, the doubling of wage costs, and the consequences tested. Often micro-computers were introduced into businesses because of spreadsheet facilities.

String A distinct group of characters used in programs. These characters may be alphanumeric (a mixture of letters and figures): e.g. 'SRJ855X', or numeric: e.g. '210385'.

Supercomputers Some computers are so much more powerful than other mainframe systems that they are called supercomputers. In May, 1985 the world sales of the two main manufacturers of supercomputers (Cray and Control Data) amounted to 130 machines with a projected demand of 50 systems a year. A supercomputer system can cost in the region of £20 million. Supercomputers now available have a performance that is about 3000 times better than that of the Ferranti Atlas computer of the early 1960s—the supercomputer of its day. The latest and fastest is the Cray-2, produced by Seymour Cray. It is only 114 cm (45 in) tall and forms a 300 degrees arc of a circle 134 cm (53 in) in diameter. It has four background processors and a common memory capable of storing 256 million 64 bit words. Its internal state changes every 4.1 billionths of a second. See *number-crunching*.

Systems software These are programs which enable the hardware to be used. They include the *operating system*, editors and translation programs.

Telecommunications Long-distance transmission by cable or radio waves. The developments in this aspect of technology have reflected those in sound and television broadcasting. Now, incorporating elements of light technology (e.g. fibre optics; lasers), it is a vital ingredient of *'information technology'*.

Teletext Both Teletext and **videotext** transmit an information service stored in a large computer database. Access depends on microprocessors. There is a crucial difference between teletext and videotext. Teletext broadcasts information through the air. Teletext uses a part of the same signal which produces the TV picture. The user has a keypad which allows him or her to 'call up' any page of information by number. The microprocessor in the user's television sorts out the correct portion of the signal and displays the information on the screen. The BBC calls it 'Ceefax'; the Independent Television's service is called 'Oracle'. The service is free, once you have bought or hired the device. With Videotext, i.e. **Viewdata**, the written information is transmitted by telephone. Videotext is an interactive system allowing the user to interrogate the database in pursuit of the information needed, following the indexing system adopted by the organisers. The British Post Office's version is *PRESTEL*.

Terminal Any device by which data can be sent to or obtained from a computer.

Transistor These came to be used widely in radios, hence the name 'Transistors'. These were the first portable, 'personal' radios. Fundamentally, computers consist of circuits called bistables, which have two stable states. These are known as flipflops and change state according to the electrical pulses they receive. This switching can be done by transistors. Since transistors are simply layers of one substance on another, unlike valves, which are complicated structures of glass envelopes, coils, pins etc.—they can be made very small, and cheaply.

Transputer The transputer, launched in 1985 by a British micro-chip company called INMOS, is a complete computer—processor, memory and communications—on a single chip. Transputers permit parallel processing, which is the carrying out of many operations simultaneously. This capacity may make it suitable for many *fifth generation* computing applications such as artificial intelligence, natural language recognition and vision.

Turing, Alan A British mathematician who proved, in 1937, that any problem with a logical solution, no matter how complex, can be solved by using a small set of simple instructions. Also the 'Turing Test' of computer 'intelligence' is often referred to. According to Turing a machine can be said to be intelligent if its responses to questions are indistinguishable from those of a human being. See *expert systems*.

Validate and **Verify** Accuracy of data is extremely important in data processing. Data can be checked by entering it twice; this is known as verification. Computer programs can be used to ensure that the data which is entered is valid: i.e. permissible. For example, a National Insurance number always commences with two letters, followed by 6 numbers and then one letter. It is easy for the program to check that any national insurance number entered follows these criteria. However, it is possible for the wrong number, but valid by independent means, to be entered.

Videotext See *teletext*.

Visual Display Unit (VDU). The television-like screen on which a computer displays information. It will often have a keyboard attached to it.

Winchester drive & disc See *disc*.

Wordprocessing When using a manual typewriter, it is not possible to make any drastic changes (e.g. move a paragraph or change margins) without re-typing the whole document. Instead of a sheet of paper, the wordprocessor program uses a VDU screen and computer memory. This allows the user to rearrange layout of text, correct, add to or delete from the text. When the text has been satisfactorily designed, a printout onto paper may be output. Some wordprocessing systems don't even print out onto paper; the desired text is directly transmitted to another computer.

With wordprocessing, standard text (e.g. letters) can be quickly produced with only variations (e.g. names and addresses) having to be typed each time. Wordprocessor programs usually provide many other features, such as the ability to shift blocks of text around and to search for and change particular words. Wordprocessors are having a great effect on office work, and are also an invaluable aid for people who are poor typists. Wordprocessing packages are increasingly popular with home computer users.

Z80 An 8 bit microprocessor used as the CPU in a wide range of micro-computers, e.g. TANDY and SPECTRUM.

Further Reading

The British Computer Society: *A Glossary of Computing Terms: An Introduction*, 4th Edition, 1984 (Cambridge University Press)

Anthony Chandor, John Graham, Robin Williamson: *Dictionary of Computers*, 2nd Edition, 1984 (Penguin)

Roger Hunt and John Shelly: *Computers and Commonsense*, 3rd Edition, 1983 (Prentice/Hall International)

Peter Large: *The Micro Revolution*, 1980 (Fontana)

Ian Reinecke: *Electronic Illusions*, 1984 (Penguin)

Usborne Guide to Computers, 1981

Usborne Guide to Computer Jargon, 1983

Peter Zorkoczy: *Information Technology: An Introduction*, 2nd Edition, 1985 (Pitman)

There are many computer magazines that are essential for the micro-computer enthusiast who wants to keep up-to-date with current developments. Magazines like *Personal Computer World* often have beginner's guides to the jargon. Some national newspapers (e.g. *The Guardian*) regularly run computer features.

SOMETHING TO JOIN

A section on *YOUTH ORGANISATIONS*, with notes on the *MORSE CODE, SEMAPHORE, COMPASS* and *KNOTS*.

ORGANISATIONS TO JOIN
(including some courses to apply for)

This is a list of some of the organisations that are either entirely for young people or have sections open to the young. A few of them provide courses only for those who have been specially recommended by their schools or other authorities. Take particular note of the age limits for membership, which are given in most cases. Note also that, in present conditions, subscriptions might well have increased in the months between preparation and publication of this edition.

Air Training Corps A national organisation sponsored by the Ministry of Defence (RAF) with the aim of promoting and encouraging in young men a practical interest in aviation and the RAF, providing training useful both in Service and civilian life, and developing, through the promotion of sports and pastimes in healthy rivalry, the qualities of leadership and good citizenship.

Amateur Athletic Association Controls athletics in England and Wales, with affiliated clubs throughout the country. Details of clubs, membership open to boys of 11 and over, and of training facilities, instructional booklets and coaching schemes from Francis House, Francis Street, London, SW1P 1DL. This is also the address of the Women's Amateur Athletic Association.

Army Cadet Force The British Army's own voluntary youth organisation. Open to boys, and a percentage of girls, between the ages of 13 and 18. Army Cadet Force Association, Millbank Barracks, John Islip Street, London, SW1P 4RR.

Boys' Brigade Oldest of the national uniformed youth organisations, open to boys from 6 to 18. All BB companies are part of a Christian Church and provide a wide range of activities. For details of the nearest company, write to Brigade House, Parsons Green, London, SW6 4TH: Boys' Brigade House, 168 Bath Street, Glasgow, G2 4TQ: or Boys' Brigade, 14 May Street, Belfast, BT1 4NR.

Brathay Exploration Group Each year the Group mounts about 20 expeditions on which groups of young people can discover more about themselves, the world and its inhabitants through challenging and exciting tasks, projects and themes. Recent expeditions have included ski-trekking across Svalbard's glaciers and filming for the BBC, monitoring Barnacle Geese in the mountains of East Greenland, studying Jamaican farms, caves and ecology, and camel-safaris in Kenya. In the British Isles, expedition teams have studied ancient settlements, plants and birds, trekked across the Scottish Highlands and carried out community projects on remote islands. The Group also runs basic mountain expeditions for beginners and organises leader training courses from its Lake District base on the northern shores of Windermere. National links with the Young Explorers' Trust and the Expedition Advisory Centre, London, enable the Group to maintain a direct involvement with the world of exploration and travel. All expeditions are led by expert voluntary leaders, backed by the resources of the Brathay Hall Trust, a charity involved with leadership and development training, environmental studies and with residential youth training courses. High standards of safety and quality are maintained throughout all activities. Brochure and membership details from: Expeditions Co-ordinator, BEG, Brathay Hall, Ambleside, Cumbria LA22 OHP, England. Tel: Ambleside 33942.

British Red Cross Society Membership is open to boys and girls aged from 5–10/11 (Junior members) and from 10/11 up to 18 years (Youth members). Young people aged 15–18 years have the option to join an adult group. Training is offered in first aid, nursing, child care, rescue, survival, accident prevention, camping, etc. Members help at holidays with handicapped children and undertake a variety of service activities within their community. They are encouraged to make contact with Youth members abroad and to take part in the Society's international work by raising money towards specific overseas projects. Headquarters: 9 Grosvenor Crescent, London SW1X 7EJ.

British Sub-Aqua Club Devoted to underwater exploration, science, sport and safe training. Over 1,000 branches. Minimum age: 14, but special Snorkeller Award Scheme for juniors. Applications to General Manager, British Sub-Aqua Club, 16 Upper Woburn Place, London, WC1H 0QW.

British Trust for Ornithology A national society for all birdwatchers: invites members to take part in varied field investigations into bird biology and distribution, with emphasis on the interactions between man and birds: the common birds census, nest record scheme, Waterways Bird Survey, Birds of Estuaries Enquiry, bird ringing (by special permit only after considerable training and practice), and other special enquiries including regular censuses of species such as the heron. Services to members include the newsletter 'BTO News', national conferences—both general and specialist—regional conferences, local meetings in co-operation with local bird clubs, specialist courses in modern techniques, use of the lending library and the extensive reference library at Tring, grants and awards for research, and the option of subscribing at reduced rates to the journals *Bird Study* and *Ringing and Migration*. Annual subscription £10 p.a. (£4.50 p.a. for members under 21 or up to 25 if in receipt of full-time education). Applications to the Membership Secretary, BTO, Beech Grove, Tring, Herts, HP23 5NR, Tel: Tring 3461.

Camping Club Youth Junior section of the Camping and Caravanning Club. Open to young people aged 12 to 17 inclusive. Annual subscription, £2.50 including entrance fee and VAT. Camping at home and abroad. Instruction given. 11 Lower Grosvenor Place, London, SW1W 0EY.

Concordia Youth Service Volunteers Runs international working camps to help with fruit picking and market gardening in Britain; also with the wine harvest, forestry and construction work on the Continent. Age limits for camps abroad: 18–30. Volunteers pay their own travel expenses. The age limit in British camps is 17–25, and the booking fee is £25 or £20 for tented camps. Applications to the Recruitment Secretary, Concordia, 8 Brunswick Place, Hove, Sussex, BN3 1ET.

Council for British Archaeology Publishes *British Archaeological News* monthly from March until September (with winter editions in November and January) which contains advertisements enabling anyone wishing to take part in excavations to get in touch with directors requiring voluntary helpers. For the over-16s mainly. 1986 subscription to the *Calendar*: £6.50 (UK). CBA, 112 Kennington Road, London, SE11 6RE.

Cyclists' Touring Club A national organisation, founded 1878 to protect and promote the interests of cyclists. Personal benefits include legal aid, third-party insurance, illustrated travel magazine and handbook, local cycle runs, clubrooms, social events, organised holiday tours. Junior membership (under 18): £6.50 a year including VAT. 69 Meadrow, Godalming, Surrey. Tel: 04868-7217.

Field Studies Council Has ten Field Centres distributed over England and Wales. Courses, usually lasting a week, are organised from March to late October and include field work in archaeology, botany, geography, zoology and art. Junior members (under 16) may attend only Family Courses or in groups with their teachers; young people over 16 may join suitable courses individually or in groups. Minimum annual subscription: £3. Applications to Information Office, Preston Montford, Montford Bridge, Shrewsbury SY4 1HW.

Girls' Brigade An international uniformed movement for girls of all ages from five upwards. It has a varied programme with a wide range of activities. The Brigade is a Church-based movement with the motto: 'Seek, serve and follow Christ'. National and International Headquarters: Brigade House, Parsons Green, London SW6 4TH.

Girls Guides Association Sister organisation of the Scouts; UK membership of about three quarters of a million, world membership of nearly 8 million in 108 countries. Commonwealth Headquarters: 17–19 Buckingham Palace Road, London, SW1W 0PT.

Junior Astronomical Society Aims to encourage people of all ages interested in astronomy and space. A quarterly, *Popular Astronomy*, includes articles on aspects of astronomy and spaceflight. Regular meetings are held in London. There are special sections to help observers. Subscription: £6.50 a year. Enrolment Secretary, Miss Barbara Kern, 22 Queensthorpe Road, London, SE26 4PH.

National Federation of Young Farmers' Clubs Open to all young people between the ages of 10 and 26 who are interested in farming and the countryside. Headquarters: YFC Centre, National Agricultural Centre, Kenilworth, Warwickshire, CV8 2LG. Coventry 56131.

Outward Bound Trust Is concerned with personal development and with providing positive aid in developing the personal skills needed in a fast-moving world. Using the outdoors and community services, Outward Bound courses help people to understand and develop their talents, abilities and potential.

They last from one to three weeks: age range, 14–60 years: no previous experience or special equipment required. A non-profit-making registered charity administering five residential centres and City Challenge in the UK, the Outward Bound Trust is the focal point of an international network. Information from The Outward Bound Trust, Chestnut Field, Regent Place, Rugby, CV21 2PJ. Tel: 0788-60423/4/5.

Quaker Workcamps Organise about 20 projects in the UK from July to mid-September lasting from 1 to 3 weeks each, and two or three short camps at Easter and Christmas (1 to 2 weeks). Wide variety of work: manual—decorating and construction; running summer play schemes; residential holidays for mentally handicapped children; entertainment in psychiatric hospitals; and work and study camps. Mixed international teams of 10–20 people. Minimum age 16, although this is raised to 18 in some cases. Handicapped participants are welcome. Volunteers pay their own travel expenses, pocket money and £9 registration fee, but food and accommodation are provided. Volunteers who have taken part in Quaker Workcamps or related activities can apply for work camps abroad to Quaker Workcamps Committee, Friends House, Euston Road, London, NW1 2BJ. Volunteers from other countries should usually apply through a work camp organisation in their own country.

Ramblers' Association Works with the support of some 500 rambling clubs and over 250 local groups throughout the country; publishes *Rucksack* four times a year and *Bed and Breakfast Guide* annually, supplying these free of charge to members. Loans 1/50,000 Ordnance Survey maps for small charge to members. Special rates for juniors and full-time students. Details: 1/5 Wandsworth Road, London, SW8 2XX.

Partner organisation, **Ramblers' Holidays Ltd,** organises walking and mountaineering holidays in Britain and on the Continent: details from 13 Longcroft House, Fretherne Road, Welwyn Garden City, Herts. Welwyn Garden 31133.

St John Ambulance Consists of two branches: the Association and the Brigade. The Association organises training courses for industry and the general public; the Brigade is a uniformed organisation responsible for first aid, nursing and welfare duties where the general public is concerned. It also trains its own members. The Brigade has a junior branch comprising Juniors (aged 8 to

11 years) and Cadets (aged 11 to 16). These youngsters have to qualify in a simplified form of first aid (and, if girls, in nursing), and are encouraged to study and take part in subjects such as adventure training, sailing, canoeing, swimming, life saving, climbing, welfare, crafts and many other hobbies and pursuits. Registrar: St John Ambulance, 1 Grosvenor Crescent, London, SW1X 7EF. 01-235-5231.

Scout Association Training for Cub Scouts (boys, 8–10$\frac{1}{2}$), Scouts (boys, 10$\frac{1}{2}$–15$\frac{1}{2}$), Venture Scouts (young men and women, 15$\frac{1}{2}$–20). Beaver Colonies (boys 6–8) in many places. Outdoor Movement (e.g. camping, hiking, exploring, sailing, climbing, swimming). Community service also important (conservation, help for the needy including Third World projects, etc.). Progress Awards given for achievement. Headquarters: Baden-Powell House, Queen's Gate, London, SW7 5JS.

Sea Cadet Corps A voluntary youth organisation for boys and girls between 12 and 18. Through its discipline and sea training the Corps sets out to help develop the qualities of self discipline, leadership and a sense of responsibility to the community, and to assist those who are considering a career in the Royal or Merchant Navies, the Royal Marines or the WRNS. However, it is not a pre-service organisation, and no cadet is obliged to join the armed forces. Headquarters: Broadway House, Broadway, Wimbledon, London, SW19 1RL.

White Hall Centre for Open Country Pursuits Courses run by the Derbyshire Education Committee in outdoor education, hillcraft, rock climbing, caving, camping, canoeing, sailing and mountain-walking leader training. Open throughout the year. Minimum age: 14. Details from the Principal, White Hall Centre, Long Hill, Buxton, Derbyshire SK17 6SX.

YMCA A world-wide organisation represented in 90 countries in 10,000 YMCAs with some 26 million people, mainly young, men and women, participating in a wide variety of programmes guided by trained leaders. There are some 250 centres in England. Headquarters: 640, Forest Road, London, E17 3DZ.

Young Explorers' Trust (The Association of British Youth Exploration Societies) Membership is open to groups and societies, however small, setting out to organise expeditions involving a significant element of exploration and discovery. The Trust offers an information service and a regional network to provide a local focus for members and those wishing to organise expeditions. Overseas expeditions may apply in December or May for the Trust's approval, and grants are made annually to expeditions that reach the appropriate standard of organisation, safety and field tasks. Details from the Administrative Secretary, Young Explorers' Trust, at the Royal Geographical Society, 1 Kensington Gore, London, SW7 2AR. 01-589-9724.

Young Ornithologists' Club Run by the Royal Society for the Protection of Birds for boys and girls. Runs courses, holds meetings, organises projects, encourages field work: publishes its bi-monthly magazine *Bird Life*. Further details from The Lodge, Sandy, Beds. SG19 2DL (please enclose 2nd class stamp).

Youth Hostels Associations These organisations have the object of helping young people to explore the countryside. In Britain and Ireland alone they maintain about 400 hostels where members are provided with beds and meals at low rates. A number of Adventure Holidays are arranged as introductions to new activities such as pony trekking, sailing, skin-diving, etc. Subscription (England and Wales): 5–15, £1.10 a year; 16–20, £3.30; 21 and over, £5.50. Headquarters: *England and Wales*, Trevelyan House, St Albans, Herts, AL1 2DY. *Scotland*, 7 Glebe Crescent, Stirling. *Northern Ireland*, 56 Bradbury Place, Belfast.

Altogether in the 60 countries where the Youth Hostel movement flourishes there are over 5,000 hostels.

A British membership card (with photograph) is accepted in all countries affiliated to the International Youth Hostel Federation. The YHA's Adventure Centre at 14 Southampton Street, London, WC2E 7HY, sells rucksacks, sleeping bags, tents, camping equipment, climbing kit, maps and guides.

YWCA of Great Britain Affiliated to the World YWCA, active in over 80 countries. Services in UK include accommodation for single young people and older women; clubs and community centres; opportunities to serve others; detached youth work and further education and training. Headquarters: 52 Cornmarket Street, Oxford, OX1 3EJ.

THE MORSE CODE

The Morse code consists of groups of dots and dashes, each group representing a letter or number. You can communicate in Morse by flashing a light, by sound or by using a flag. The dots should be made as short as possible, and the dashes should be three times as long as the dots. **The Morse alphabet** is used to avoid confusion between letters with similar sounds.

A for Alfa	·—	N for November	—·
B Bravo	—···	O Oscar	———
C Charlie	—·—·	P Papa	·——·
D Delta	—··	Q Quebec	——·—
E Echo	·	R Romeo	·—·
F Foxtrot	··—·	S Sierra	···
G Golf	——·	T Tango	—
H Hotel	····	U Uniform	··—
I India	··	V Victor	···—
J Juliet	·———	W Whiskey	·——
K Kilo	—·—	X X-Ray	—··—
L Lima	·—··	Y Yankee	—·——
M Mike	——	Z Zulu	——··

Numerals

1	·————	6	—····
2	··———	7	——···
3	···——	8	———··
4	····—	9	————·
5	·····	10	—————

Full stop (AAA) ·—·—·—
Apostrophe ·————·
Oblique stroke —··—·
Brackets (KK) —·——·—
Short break ····
Beginning (CT) —·—·—
Hyphen —····—
Inverted commas (RR) ·—··—·
Underline (UK) ··——·—
Question (IMI) ··——··
Long break (BT) —···—
Ending (AR) ·—·—·
Finish of transmission for indefinite period (VA) ···—·—

SEMAPHORE

It is immensely important in semaphore signalling that the angles should be clear and the arm and the wrist in a straight line. To ensure this, always press the first finger along the stick of the flag. Choose a position where you can be easily seen and a background that is as far away as possible—the sky being obviously the best.

Rules for Semaphoring

At the end of each word you should drop the arms straight down in front of you—this is known as the 'ready' position—and pause. Should you make a mistake, give the 'annul' sign and begin the word again. ('Annul' means 'rub out', 'cancel'.) Before a number give the 'numeral' sign, and if you are going back to letters give the 'alphabet' sign before you do so.

When you are reading a message, acknowledge each word by making the letter 'A' (the 'general answer' sign). If you are uncertain about a word, make no sign, and the sender will then repeat the word.

THE COMPASS

The magnetic compass is an instrument that enables navigators to steer in any direction required, and also shows the direction of any visible object. It is divided into points, quarter points and degrees.

The Points

The compass circle is divided into thirty-two named points. The four main (or cardinal points, N., E., S. and W.), divide the card into four quadrants or quarters. Half-way between the cardinal points are the quadrantal points, N.E., S.E., S.W. and N.W. Half-way again between the cardinal and quadrantal points are the intermediate (three-letter) points, which are named from the cardinal and quadrantal points between which they lie, the cardinal points being named first; N.N.E., E.N.E., E.S.E., S.S.E., S.S.W., W.S.W., W.N.W., N.N.W. Between all these points are sixteen others (called 'by' points) which take their names from the nearest cardinal and quadrantal points.

For example, in the first quadrant (between N. and E.) the points are:

The cardinal	N.
The by-point next to it	N. by E.
The three-letter point half-way between N. and E.	N.N.E.
The by-point next to the half cardinal	N.E. by N.
The half cardinal	N.E.
The by-point	N.E. by E.
The three-letter point between E. and N. E.	E.N.E.
The by-point	E. by N.
The cardinal point	E.

Degrees

The compass circle is also divided into degrees; it is in degrees (by what is called the **Quadrantal Notation**) that a course is usually given and steered. The card is divided into 360°, but is marked 0° at North and South and 90° at East and West. So N.E. would be given as N. 45° E. Gyro compass cards are marked right round from north through 90° (East), 180° (South), 270° (West) and 360° (North). This is called **Circular Notation**. Gyro compasses are carried in addition to magnetic compasses by most warships and many large merchant and passenger ships. The gyro, controlled by the earth's rotation, consists of a wheel turned at great speed by an electric motor. The points, with their equivalents in circular and quadrantal notation, are shown below.

Point	Circular	Quadrantal	Point	Circular	Quadrantal
N.	0	N.	N.E. by E.	56¼	N. 56¼ E.
N. by E.	11¼	N. 11¼ E.	E.N.E.	67½	N. 67½ E.
N.N.E.	22½	N. 22½ E.	E. by N.	78¾	N. 78¾ E.
N.E. by N.	33¾	N. 33¾ E.	E.	90	E.
N.E.	45	N. 45 E.	E. by S.	101¼	S. 78¾ E.
E.S.E.	112½	S. 67½ E.	S.W. by W.	236¼	S. 56¼ W.
S.E. by E.	123¾	S. 56¼ E.	W.S.W.	247½	S. 67½ W.
S.E.	135	S. 45 E.	W. by S.	258¾	S. 78¾ W.
S.E. by S.	146¼	S. 33¾ E.	W.	270	W.
S.S.E.	157½	S. 22½ E.	W. by N.	281¼	N. 78¾ W.
S. by E.	168¾	S. 11¼ E.	W.N.W.	292½	N. 67½ W.
S.	180	S.	N.W. by W.	303¾	N. 56¼ W.
S. by W.	191¼	S. 11¼ W.	N.W.	315	N. 45 W.
S.S.W.	202½	S. 22½ W.	N.W. by N.	326¼	N. 33¾ W.
S.W. by S.	213¾	S. 33¾ W.	N.N.W.	337½	N. 22½ W.
S.W.	225	S. 45 W.	N. by W.	348¾	N. 11¼ W.

KNOTS

The **Reef Knot** is both the firmest of knots and the quickest to untie. It is used for tying two ropes together.

The **Sheet Bend** is the best knot for tying together ropes of differing thickness. If the end is passed round again the knot becomes a **Double Sheet Bend**, which will neither stick nor jerk undone.

The **Clove Hitch** (an easy knot to make, as the picture shows) is

Figure of Eight

Common Bowline

Sheet Bend

Reef Knot

Sheepshank

Clove Hitch

Half-hitch

Round Turn and Two Half-hitches

Wall Knot

Timber Hitch

used to make one rope fast to a larger one. When fastened to a pole or another rope it will neither slip up nor down.

The **Bowline** (used at sea for making a loop on a rope's end) makes a fixed loop that will never slip after the first grip. It can be safely used for making a halter for leading an animal.

The **Sheepshank** is used for temporarily shortening a rope.

The **Figure of Eight** is used at sea to prevent a rope unreeving through a block.

The **Half-hitch** is used to tie ropes to poles.

The **Round Turn and Two Half-hitches** is used for securing a rope to a ring or a post.

The **Timber Hitch** is used for dragging timber along the ground.

The **Wall Knot** is a way of whipping, or finishing off, a rope that is unravelling. Take strand A and loop it back across the front of the rope; then take strand B and loop it over the end of strand A; finally looping strand C over the end of strand B and tucking its end into the loop formed by strand A. Finish by working the knot tight.

THE ARMED SERVICES, THE POLICE AND FIRE BRIGADES

THE ARMED SERVICES

The present integrated Ministry of Defence was created on April 1, 1964. The head of the Ministry is the Secretary of State for Defence, who is also chairman of the Defence Council—the permanent committee of military and civilian chiefs who determine defence policy. He is assisted by a Minister of State and Under Secretary of State for the Armed Forces; and a Minister of State and Under Secretary of State for Defence Procurement.

THE ROYAL NAVY[1]

There is (since 1981) no single Minister responsible for the Royal Navy (senior of the three Armed Services). Before the creation of the unified Ministry of Defence, the title of the department head was First Lord of the Admiralty. The senior naval member of the Navy Board is the Chief of Naval Staff and First Sea Lord.

HOW THE NAVY IS ORGANISED

Outside the Ministry of Defence, the Navy is under the command of two Commanders-in-Chief: Commander-in-Chief Fleet, who is responsible for all the Navy's ships, and Commander-in-Chief Naval Home Command, who is responsible for all the Navy's shore establishments, units ashore and the training of officers and ratings.

Ships and some submarines are based at three Base Ports, Portsmouth and Plymouth in England and Rosyth in Scotland. The fleet is divided into two flotillas commanded by admirals; submarines are commanded by Flag Officer Submarines: all are responsible to the Commander-in-Chief Fleet. The Dockyard at Chatham has been closed and the appointment FO Medway and Chatham was phased out by the end of 1982.

Under Commander-in-Chief Naval Home Command, establishments in the country are divided into regions which are commanded by admirals located at the three Base Ports and known as Flag Officers Portsmouth, Plymouth, and Scotland and Northern Ireland (Rosyth).

[1] For an account of naval vessels, see the section on *Ships*.

The administration and training of the Fleet Air Arm come under the command of the Flag Officer, Naval Air Command.

| Admiral of the Fleet | Admiral | Vice-Admiral | Rear-Admiral | Commodore |

| Captain | Commander | Lieut-Commander | Lieutenant | Sub-Lieutenant |

The **Corps of Royal Marines** was founded in 1664 to serve on sea and land. Today they provide three commando units. Apart from serving in ships, the Marines are also drawn upon for the crews of landing craft and for other amphibious operations (that is, those carried out partly on sea and partly on land).

| Tactical Communication Rating | Missile Operations Rating | Sonar or Weapons Submarine Rating |

Engineering
Mechanic

Air Engineering Mechanic
M (Mechanical), R (Radio/Radar)
or WL (Weapons Electrical)

Petty Officer   Leading Rating

THE ARMY

The man responsible for the detailed running of the Army is the
Minister of State for the Armed Forces, a Member of Parliament,
who in turn is responsible to the Secretary of State for Defence.
The Minister of State controls the Army through the Army Board
of the Defence Council and obtains expert military advice from
the Chief of the General Staff (CGS), who is the senior military
member of the Board.

PRINCIPAL BRANCHES OF THE ARMY

The **Royal Armoured Corps** (RAC), formed in 1939 by amalgamating the Cavalry and the Royal Tank Corps, man tanks and
armoured cars.

The **Royal Artillery** (RA) (the 'Gunners') man both guns and
missiles in Field and Air Defence roles and locating devices.

The **Royal Engineers** (RE) (called the 'Sappers' from the days when they dug 'saps'—that is, trenches or mines that enabled the troops to advance towards the enemy). In general, their job is to help the Army to move. They make paths through minefields, provide means of crossing obstacles and carry out any necessary demolition and lay minefields in a withdrawal. They produce maps for the Army and the RAF and operate the Army Postal Service.

The **Royal Corps of Signals** (R. Signals) is responsible for the Army's communications.

The **Infantry** is the fighting core of the Army and includes the Foot Guards, Infantry of the Line, the Brigade of Gurkhas, the Parachute Regiment and the Special Air Service Regiment.

The **Army Air Corps** (AAC) operates the Army's helicopters and aircraft.

The **Royal Corps of Transport** (RCT) replaced the Royal Army Service Corps in 1965.

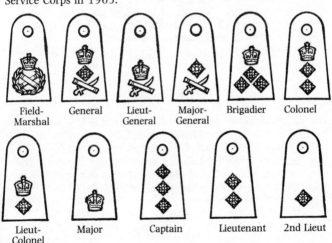

Field-Marshal   General   Lieut-General   Major-General   Brigadier   Colonel

Lieut-Colonel   Major   Captain   Lieutenant   2nd Lieut

The **Royal Army Medical Corps** (RAMC) came into being in 1857, after the Crimean War, as the Army Hospital Corps. Took its present name in 1898.

The **Royal Army Ordnance Corps** (RAOC) is responsible for providing the Army with ammunition, food, equipment and stores.

Also provides clerical staff and mobile bath and laundry units on active service.

The **Royal Electrical and Mechanical Engineers** (REME) was formed in 1942 to meet the needs of mechanised warfare. Maintains and repairs tanks, vehicles, guns, radar, radios, instruments, etc.

The **Intelligence Corps** (Int. Corps) is a small branch consisting of men trained to collect and evaluate intelligence (that is, largely information about an enemy or possible enemy).

The **Corps of Royal Military Police** (RMP), the 'Red Caps'.

The **Royal Army Pay Corps** (RAPC).

The **Royal Army Veterinary Corps** (RAVC) looks after the Army's horses and dogs.

The **Royal Pioneer Corps** (RPC) provides labour for road-building, unloading stores, etc.

The **Royal Army Educational Corps** (RAEC).

The **Army Catering Corps** (ACC), provides the Army's cooks.

Queen Alexandra's Royal Army Nursing Corps (QARANC) provides women nurses for military hospitals.

The **Women's Royal Army Corps** (WRAC), covers a wide range of duties, from cooking and clerical work to driving and signalling.

Sergeant

Corporal

Driver

Armourer

Farrier

Surveyor

Radar Mechanic

Saddler

Parachutist

Signaller   Sniper

HOW THE ARMY IS DIVIDED

The standard formation in the modern Army is the division. In wartime the divisions are grouped to form Corps (two divisions or more), armies (two Corps or more) and army groups (two armies or more).

The fighting infantry unit of the Army is the battalion. Nearly 800 strong, it is divided into a Headquarters, Headquarters' Company, Fire Support Company and three Rifle Companies. It is commanded by a Lieutenant-Colonel.

THE ROYAL AIR FORCE

The Secretary of State for Defence, who is Chairman of the Air Force Board of the Defence Council, has ministerial responsibility for the RAF. The most senior RAF member of the Air Force Board is the Chief of the Air Staff.

HOW THE AIR FORCE IS ORGANISED

The RAF in the United Kingdom is organised into two Commands: Strike and Support. Strike was formed in 1968 when two historic commands, Bomber and Fighter, were merged. The structure of the present Strike Command dates from the early 1970s, when other operational commands were absorbed.

Strike Command, based at High Wycombe, forms the RAF's front-line teeth in the United Kingdom—including nuclear strike, conventional attack, air defence (including fighters and surface-to-air missiles), airborne early warning, strategic and tactical transport, helicopters, air-to-air refuelling, anti-submarine warfare and air support for the Army in the field. The Command is integrated within NATO, and is responsible for the UK Air Defence Region; its fighters regularly intercepting long-range Soviet aircraft. Other roles include search and rescue and regular patrolling of the North Sea oil and gas rigs.

Support Command, based at RAF Brampton, in Cambridgeshire has responsibility for engineering and spares support of front-line units. It also has the job of training officers and airmen to front-line standards. The Central Flying School currently at RAF Leeming trains all flying instructors for the RAF, Royal Navy and Army Air Corps, as well as those of other air forces. It also controls the internationally famous RAF aerobatic team—the Red Arrows.

The RAF Staff College and Headquarters Command and Staff Training are located at Bracknell; and at the Second World War fighter base at Biggin Hill, the Officer and Aircrew Selection Centre assesses all candidates for cadetships, scholarships, commissions and aircrew service. In wartime, Support Command would back the operational commands by providing reinforcement of flying and ground personnel.

RAF GERMANY

RAF Germany's Phantom FGR2 supersonic interceptors assist in policing the northern half of the 30-mile-wide Air Defence Identification Zone—a sort of invisible no-man's-land in the sky running the length of the border with East Germany and designed to prevent infringements by aircraft from either side. But most of RAF Germany's effort goes into providing conventional ground attack, nuclear strike and air defence in support of any NATO land operations. It is responsible for a huge, 60,000-square-mile section from the West German border round to Denmark, over the North Sea, along the Franco-Belgian border to the southern tip of Luxembourg.

In Berlin the RAF maintains the airfield at Gatow and handles all movements in the northern and central air corridors out of the city.

THE RAF REGIMENT

With RAF Police and Fire Service, the RAF Regiment forms the RAF Security Branch. It protects airfields against ground intruders

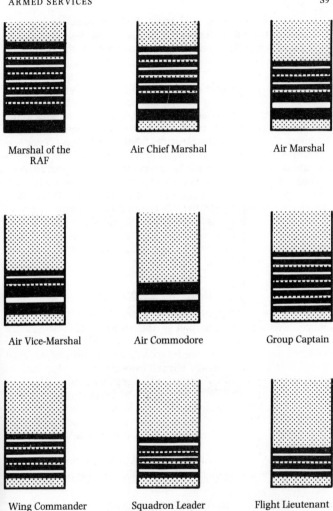

Marshal of the RAF

Air Chief Marshal

Air Marshal

Air Vice-Marshal

Air Commodore

Group Captain

Wing Commander

Squadron Leader

Flight Lieutenant

These are cuff badges worn with No. 1 dress (formal) and mess kit.
Shoulder badges are worn with working dress.

and low-level air attack, and trains RAF personnel in ground defence. Formed into a number of mobile squadrons, it is armed with Rapier missiles and armoured vehicles of the Scorpion Range.

THE WOMEN'S ROYAL AIR FORCE

Today some 500 officers and 4,600 airwomen serve in most general branches and trade groups. A few women serve in the air loadmaster category of the General Duties (GD) Flying Branch.

Women enjoy equal rights in pay and employment and compete on equal terms with men for promotion, appointments and training courses.

Flying Officer   Pilot Officer

Pilot's Wings

RELATIVE RANKS—SEA, LAND AND AIR

(Comparable ranks in the Women's Royal Naval Service and Women's Royal Air Force appear in italics. Commissioned ranks of the Women's Royal Army Corps are named as for the Army, the Director holding the rank of Brigadier.)

Royal Navy	*Army*	*Royal Air Force*
Admiral of the Fleet	Field-Marshal	Marshal of the RAF
Admiral	General	Air Chief Marshal
Vice-Admiral	Lieutenant-General	Air Marshal
Rear-Admiral	Major-General	Air Vice-Marshal
Commodore* (*Commandant*)	Brigadier	Air Commodore (*Air Commandant, WRAF*)
Captain (*Superintendent*)	Colonel	Group Captain (*Group Officer*)
Commander (*Chief Officer*)	Lieutenant-Colonel	Wing Commander (*Wing Officer*)
Lieutenant-Commander (*First Officer*)	Major	Squadron Leader (*Squadron Officer*)
Lieutenant (*Second Officer*)	Captain	Flight-Lieutenant (*Flight Officer*)
Sub-Lieutenant (*Third Officer*)	Lieutenant	Flying Officer (*Flying Officer*)
Acting Sub-Lieutenant	Second Lieutenant	Pilot Officer (*Pilot Officer*)

* Commodore is a title rather than a rank and is attached to certain appointments. Senior Captains equate to Brigadiers and Air Commodores; junior Captains to Colonels and Group Captains.

THE POLICE

There are 43 police forces in England and Wales, administered by the Home Office. In Scotland there are eight police forces administered by the Scottish Home and Health Department. In Northern Ireland the Royal Ulster Constabulary is administered by the Northern Ireland Office.

The main ranks are constable, sergeant, inspector and superintendent. The head of the Metropolitan Police is called the Commissioner; the head of a provincial force is called the Chief Constable.

BRANCHES OF THE POLICE

The CID All police forces have a Criminal Investigation Department. No officer can be recruited to this section until he has served as an ordinary uniformed constable. Ranks in the CID are the same as those in the uniformed police: e.g. detective-constable, detective-sergeant and so on.

In London, where one in every eight policemen belongs to this branch, the CID is controlled by an Assistant Commissioner, with the aid of three Deputy Assistant Commissioners. More than half of the staff of the CID are attached to police stations. The headquarters staff includes Central Office (which deals with national and international crimes), the Criminal Record Office and Fingerprint Bureau, the Special Branch (which in wartime works with the forces in counter-espionage, and is also responsible for protecting important public persons), the Flying Squad and the Fraud Squad (whose job is to detect financial swindles).

The River Police A few forces (e.g. London, Glasgow) have sections of River Police, whose business is to prevent and detect stealing from craft on the river and from waterside premises, to deal with boats found adrift, to help vessels in difficulty, to come to the aid of drowning persons and to retrieve dead bodies, to prevent and detect smuggling and to prevent the pollution of the river.

The Thames Division in London has three river stations—at Wapping, Waterloo Pier and Shepperton.

The Mounted Police These are used mainly for heading processions and controlling crowds.

Special Constables These are part-time unpaid men and women who are employed mainly to help in controlling crowds on special occasions. They have the same powers as full-time constables.

FIRE BRIGADES

During the Second World War the 1,059 fire brigades in England and Wales were amalgamated into a single National Fire Service, and after the war an Act of Parliament created 125 brigades, each administered by the local authority. At the same time the 200 Scottish brigades were regrouped into eleven brigades. The Local Government Act of 1972 made the new county councils responsible for the fire services. In Scotland, the Local Government (Scotland) Act, 1973, which came into effect in 1975, gave responsibility to the nine regions. As a result of the Local Government Act of 1985, which came into force in 1986, the fire services in London and the former six Metropolitan counties are run by joint authorities composed of borough and district councillors.

In big cities the brigades are manned by full-time firemen; elsewhere some or all of the crews are part-timers.

The uniform of the British fireman is of dark-blue serge or cloth, with waterproof leggings and rubber or leather boots. The brass helmet of earlier times has given place to helmets made of leather or leather and rubber, which give much better protection against electric shock.

DECORATIONS AND MEDALS

Victoria Cross (VC) (1856). *Ribbon*, crimson. (Until 1918 it was blue for the Royal Navy.) For conspicuous bravery. By order of Queen Victoria, who instituted the decoration, Victoria Crosses were struck from the metal of guns captured at Sevastopol during the Crimean War (see HISTORY: Diary of Events).

George Cross (GC) (1940). *Ribbon*, dark blue threaded through a bar adorned with laurel leaves. For gallantry. The GC is worn before all other decorations except the VC, and is intended in the first place for civilians. It is awarded to servicemen, however, for actions for which military honours are not usually granted. It is given only for acts of the very greatest heroism.

The Distinguished Service Order (DSO) (1886). *Ribbon*, red with blue edges. Given in recognition of special services in action to commissioned officers in the three services and (since 1942) the Mercantile Marine. A Bar may be awarded for any additional act of service.

Distinguished Service Cross (DSC) (1914), for Warrant Officers and officers in the Royal Navy below the rank of Captain.

Military Cross (MC) (1914), for captains, lieutenants and Class I Warrant Officers in the Army.

Distinguished Flying Cross (DFC) (1918), for officers and warrant officers in the RAF and Fleet Air Arm; awarded for acts of gallantry when flying in active operations against the enemy.

Air Force Cross (AFC) (1918), for acts of courage when flying, though not in active operations against the enemy.

Albert Medal (AM) (1866), for gallantry in saving life at sea or on land.

Medal for Distinguished Conduct in the Field (DCM), for warrant officers, non-commissioned officers and men of the Army and RAF.

Conspicuous Gallantry Medal (GCM), for warrant officers and men of the Royal Navy, Mercantile Marine and RAF.

George Medal (GM) (1940), for acts of gallantry.

Queen's Gallantry Medal (QGM), primarily intended for civilians: but may be granted to all ranks of the Armed Forces for exemplary acts of bravery.

Distinguished Service Medal (DSM), for chief Petty Officers, men and boys of all branches of the Royal Navy, Mercantile Marine and Royal Marines.

Military Medal (MM), for warrant and non-commissioned officers and men and women of the Army.

Distinguished Flying Medal (DFM) (1918) and the **Air Force Medal** (AFM), the equivalent of the DFC and AFC for warrant and non-commissioned officers and men.

King's Police and Fire Services Medal, awarded for distinguished service.

THE LAW

WHAT IS LAW?

The simplest explanation of what law is is to say that it is a body of rules for the regulation of human relationships, in personal and domestic, commercial, industrial and other relationships, which are enforceable by public authority. These rules differ from the rules of manners and morals in that they are made binding and enforceable by the authority of the state, that is, the whole community politically organised. But in subject-matter they frequently coincide with rules of religion or morality, e.g. Thou shalt not steal, or rules of manners or expediency.

The rules take many different forms. Some state what one *may do*, and the consequences of that; thus, if you make a will in proper form, stating what is to happen to your property after your death, the law will ensure that that happens. But you may choose not to make a will; in that case rules of law provide what is to happen to your property. Other rules state what you *must do*, such as pay tax, or debts, and the consequences if you do not. Others again state what you *must not do*, such as commit theft or drive a car recklessly, and what happens to you if you do any of these things.

Law is necessary in any civilised society to avoid or at least minimise conflicts and disputes, to maintain order in society and to ensure that doubtful or disputed claims can be resolved in an orderly way. If there were no system of law, or if it were commonly disregarded, there would be anarchy. Disputes would be settled by force and crime would be unchecked.

Generally speaking, each country in the world, and sometimes distinct parts, states or provinces in a country, have their distinct systems of rules of law. Thus in the United Kingdom there are distinct systems of law in England and Wales, in Scotland and in Northern Ireland. The Isle of Man and the Channel Islands also have distinct systems. The rules of French law, German law and of other countries are different again. Now that the United

Kingdom is a member of the European Communities the system of rules of law of the European Communities is part of the law of the UK and of all of the other (at present twelve) countries which are members. Roughly speaking the laws of England and Wales, Northern Ireland and most English-speaking parts of the Commonwealth and countries originally settled from Britain, such as the USA, have a distinct family similarity. Again the laws of Scotland, South Africa, Quebec and most European countries have a family similarity, because they originated in the system of law developed in the city of Rome and the Roman Empire. It is noteworthy that the laws of England and of Scotland differ in many respects very substantially. The laws of the USSR and countries controlled by governments sympathetic to the USSR also have a family similarity. While these are the three main families of legal systems, there are a number which do not belong to any of these families. The way in which law is made, the actual rules of law, and the way disputes are decided accordingly differs in each country and sometimes within a country, as between England and Scotland or Ontario and Quebec.

The branches of law

The whole body of rules of law of Britain forms a huge mass and for convenience of discovery, study and understanding they are usually grouped under a number of headings, each comprising the rules dealing with particular subjects. The main headings are: *Constitutional law*, dealing with the government of the country, the relations between the government and citizens and the public rights and duties of citizens; *Administrative law*, dealing with the operation of public administration and local government, town planning, new roads, housing and the like; *Social security*, dealing with entitlement to sickness benefit, unemployment benefit and similar payments; *Taxation*, concerned with compulsory payments by persons to the State to defray public expenditure, such as on defence; *Criminal law*, dealing with the kinds of conduct which are treated as punishable, such as murder, theft, reckless driving; *Family law*, concerned with marriage, divorce and children; *Contract*, dealing with agreements and bargains, such as to buy and sell, lease, transport, employ and so on; *Tort* (or, in Scotland, *delict*), concerned with liability for harm done by another, as by injuring in a road accident; *Property*, dealing with rights in land, goods and other things of value; *Trusts*, concerned with persons holding property on behalf of and for others; *Succession*, dealing with wills and the transfer of property when a person dies to those entitled to it. Other branches are sometimes distinguished. There are also important bodies of rules about *Civil and Criminal procedure*, or the steps and stages of actions and prosecutions in court, and *evidence*, dealing with how facts in dispute can be proved.

The making of law in Britain

Rules of law are made in several different ways.

(1) There are the rules contained in regulations, directives and decisions made by the Council and the Commission of the European Communities. These mostly relate to commercial matters and apply in all the countries which are members of the Communities.

(2) Rules are also made by the UK Parliament by passing *Acts of Parliament* or *Statutes*. Proposals are put before Parliament by the Cabinet or by individual MPs in the form of Bills. Bills are discussed and debated and, if passed by each House of Parliament, they are given Royal Assent by the Queen and become Acts. This has been happening for hundreds of years. Every year about 100 Acts are passed in this way; some make new law, some change the existing law in some way.

(3) Parliament frequently authorises Ministers to make rules on matters of detail to give full effect to Acts of Parliament. The rules they make are called *Statutory Instruments*.

(4) In United Kingdom courts it has become accepted that the basic principle underlying a decision of one of the superior courts can lay down a rule regulating future disputes of the same kind. Many such decisions accordingly make new law just as much as Acts of Parliament do. Thus in 1932 the House of Lords decided that if a person was made ill by a poisonous thing in a bottled drink bought for her, the manufacturer of the drink was liable to pay damages (compensation) to her. This had not previously been decided, so that the decision really made new law, and other courts have applied the same rule in similar cases ever since then. Because of this practice the reports of decided cases going back many years have frequently to be examined to see if a court has previously given a ruling which determines a dispute today. This

kind of law is called *case-law*, and a great deal of law in the UK
has been developed by judges in cases.

(5) In early times custom was an important source of law. It is
not now very important and if a judge cannot find guidance from
any of the foregoing kinds of law he may refer to some very authori-
tative textbooks, or the rule developed in another country with a
similar social and legal system, e.g. USA, or in the last resort do
what seems to him right and just.

Deciding legal disputes

Not infrequently people have disputes as to what the law requires
them to do in the circumstances. Thus a car knocks down and
injures a pedestrian; is the pedestrian entitled to damages for his
injuries from the driver? Or was it the pedestrian's own fault? Or
again: one man stabs another after an argument. Is that a criminal assault justifying punishment? Or did he act in self-defence?
Frequently it is uncertain or disputed what rule of law applies,
and what it requires. Frequently the facts are in dispute. How fast
was the car going? Were the street lights lit? Did the driver give
any warning that he was going to stop? And so on. To decide
disputes of various kinds there is a system of courts, staffed by
judges. There are separate sets of courts for England and Wales,
for Scotland and for Northern Ireland, and different courts for
different purposes, dealing with different topics and branches of
the law. In particular, there are different courts for civil, criminal
and some other kinds of disputes.

The European Court

The *Court of Justice of the European Communities* at Luxembourg
consisting of 13 judges drawn from all 12 member-states decides
questions of alleged contraventions of the Treaties establishing
the European Communities by member-states, companies or
individuals. The Treaties and rules made to implement them are
applicable in all the member-states. These mostly concern
commercial problems. Courts in all the member-states may, and
in some cases must, refer disputes to the European Court and its
rulings must be accepted and applied.

The courts of England and Wales

The highest civil court, which hears appeals from all the parts of the United Kingdom, is the House of Lords which, though in theory it is the same body of peers as comprises one of the Houses of Parliament, is for this purpose composed of a number, usually five, out of eleven Lords of Appeal in Ordinary, very experienced lawyers who have been given peerages to enable them to sit and hear appeals.

Below this is the *Court of Appeal, Civil Division*, which consists of the Master of the Rolls and Lords Justices of Appeal. They sit in groups of three and hear appeals from the High Court and County Courts.

The High Court of Justice consists of the Lord Chief Justice of England and a large body of judges, formally called Mr Justice Smith or Mrs Justice Brown. They are grouped in three Divisions, the *Queen's Bench Division*, dealing with contracts, torts and commercial disputes, the *Chancery Division*, dealing with wills and trusts, mortgages, companies and bankruptcy, and the *Family* (formerly Probate, Divorce and Admiralty) *Division*, dealing with family law matters. The judges sit singly, and only very occasionally with a jury. They may sit anywhere in England and Wales, but most of the sittings are at the Royal Courts of Justice in The Strand, London.

The lower English civil court is the County Court. County Courts are held by circuit judges regularly in all the larger towns throughout England and Wales. The procedure is simpler and quicker than in the High Court but they can deal only with claims in most matters not exceeding £5,000.

In criminal cases the highest court is the *House of Lords*. Below it is the *Court of Appeal, Criminal Division*, consisting of the Lord Chief Justice, the Lords Justices of Appeal and the Judges of the Queen's Bench Division, which hears appeals only. Serious criminal cases are tried in the *Crown Court*, which may sit anywhere in England and Wales. The Crown Court consists of a judge of the Queen's Bench Division, or a circuit judge, or a Recorder (who is a lawyer sitting sometimes as a judge), in each case with a jury of 12. Cases are allocated according to seriousness. In London the *Central Criminal Court* (the Old Bailey) is staffed by a number of permanent judges. Sittings of Crown Courts are held regularly in the chief towns of England and Wales. These have replaced the centuries-old system of Assizes. The great majority of criminal cases are heard summarily, i.e. without a jury, by *magistrates' courts,* consisting of a stipendiary magistrate or of three or more justices of the peace who are unpaid, have no training in law, and sit part-time. They are, however, advised by a legally qualified clerk. In serious cases they act as examining justices and decide whether there is a case justifying trial by jury in the Crown Court.

In 1985 a Crown Prosecution Service for England and Wales was established, headed by the Director of Public Prosecutions under the supervision of the Attorney-General, assisted by Chief Crown Prosecutors in areas. The Director and his staff are to take over the conduct of nearly all criminal prosecutions instituted on behalf of a police force by a member of that force or by an ordinary citizen. The staff are to advise the police and to appear for the prosecution in appeals to superior criminal courts.

There are also some *Courts of Special Jurisdiction* which deal only with disputes of particular kinds. Among these are the Employment Appeal Tribunal, consisting of a judge and two laymen, which hears appeals from industrial tribunals, the Lands Tribunal, concerned with compulsory acquisition of land, the Transport Tribunal, the Restrictive Practices Court, and several more. Most of these are composed partly of lawyers, partly of laymen experienced in the particular subject. Coroner's courts seek to determine the cause of death, where a death has taken place suddenly or in suspicious circumstances.

Lastly there is a great complex of tribunals, or bodies, usually of three, of whom frequently only the chairman need have legal training. Among these are *industrial tribunals* which hear claims of unfair dismissal from work, and similar claims, *rent tribunals*, *social security tribunals* and many more.

The courts of Scotland

The highest civil court is again the House of Lords. Below it is the *Court of Session, Inner House,* comprising two Divisions, the First and the Second Division, presided over respectively by the Lord President of the Court of Session and the Lord Justice-Clerk of Scotland, each sitting with three judges. In Scotland all the judges of the Court of Session have the courtesy title of Lord. The two Divisions deal mostly with appeals from the Outer House and the Sheriff Courts. The *Court of Session, Outer House,* comprises the remaining judges of the Court of Session sitting singly, occasionally with a jury, trying civil cases at first instance. The Court of Session sits only in Edinburgh.

The lower Scottish civil court is the *Sheriff Court*. There are 6 sheriffdoms, each having a Sheriff Principal and a number of Sheriffs, all qualified lawyers. They sit singly in all the major towns and may hear practically any kind of civil claim. Appeal lies from a Sheriff to the Sheriff Principal and then to the Court of Session, Inner House, or direct to the Inner House.

In criminal cases no appeal lies from Scotland to the House of Lords. The highest criminal court is the *High Court of Justiciary*, consisting of the same persons as are judges of the Court of Session, but under the titles of Lord Justice-General of Scotland, Lord Justice-Clerk of Scotland and Lords Commissioners of Justiciary. It sits, normally in benches of three, to hear appeals, and individual Lords Commissioners sit with juries of 15 in Edinburgh and other major towns to try cases of serious crime.

The Sheriff Court also tries criminal cases. A Sheriff-Principal or Sheriff with a jury tries cases of medium seriousness and a Sheriff-Principal or Sheriff sitting alone tries summarily lesser offences, such as traffic offences.

The District Court comprises a stipendiary magistrate or Justices of the Peace and deals with petty offences. In Scotland the JPs are much less important than in England and Wales.

A notable feature of the Scottish system is that practically all prosecution in criminal cases is in the High Court by the Lord Advocate and his Deputes and in the sheriff court by the Procurator-fiscal of the Sheriffdom and his deputes. There is, that is, a system of public prosecution. The police never prosecute in Scotland.

Scotland has a variety of courts of special jurisdiction, such as the Scottish Land Court, dealing with agricultural disputes, the Lands Valuation Appeal Court, the Lands Tribunal for Scotland and others. Some courts, such as the Employment Appeal Tribunal, sit also in Scotland. Similarly, it has a range of tribunals generally similar to those in England. There are, however, no Coroner's Courts.

The courts of Northern Ireland
In Northern Ireland the names and powers of the different courts generally follow the English model but there are some variations.

Lawyers

Because law and procedure differ from one country to another, even between the different countries of the UK, lawyers learn and practise the law of a particular country only. In each of the countries of the UK the distinction is drawn between barristers (called advocates in Scotland) and solicitors. Barristers are persons who have been 'called to the Bar' by one of the four Inns of Court in London or by the Inn of Court of Northern Ireland; advocates have been called by the Faculty of Advocates in Scotland. Barristers or advocates are sometimes called 'counsel' and a senior barrister or advocate may be promoted by the Queen to be a Queen's Counsel. The function of counsel is to represent clients in court and argue cases on their behalf. They also do much advisory work. They are the consultants and specialists of the law. Solicitors are persons who have been admitted by the Law Society, the Law Society of Scotland or the Incorporated Law Society of Northern Ireland. They are the general practitioners of the law. They practise from offices, frequently in partnership, and are general legal advisers, drafting wills, dealing with tax problems, winding up the estates of deceased persons, transferring land and houses, and doing much miscellaneous business. Both classes of lawyers have a long and arduous training, normally including study at a University.

The judges of the superior courts are appointed from the senior and experienced barristers or advocates (usually from QCs) and most judges of lower courts are barristers or advocates, though some are solicitors. Many barristers or advocates and solicitors are also employed by Government departments or by local authorities and big companies as legal advisers and to do legal work.

Court procedure

Courts decide cases only when cases are presented to them. In civil cases it is up to the claimant (plaintiff, or in Scotland pursuer) to present his claim against the defendant (or, in Scotland, defender), in the appropriate form. Thereafter a case proceeds through a series of stages, depending largely on its nature and what issues are involved. If there is dispute as to the facts, e.g. whose fault caused the accident, there must be a hearing at which witnesses give evidence of what they heard, saw and so on, and there may be serious dispute as to what conclusions should be reached from the evidence. A layman can present his case himself but in nearly all cases he instructs a solicitor who makes enquiries, collects information and in substantial cases instructs a barrister or advocate to handle the case and appear in court to examine the witnesses and argue the issues of law which arise.

In criminal cases procedure is usually initiated by the police or, in Scotland, the Procurator-fiscal, acting in the public interest. The person accused will again normally instruct a solicitor, who may instruct counsel.

It is generally unwise for a layman to appear unrepresented. The procedure is frequently complicated and sometimes lengthy. The points of law involved may be complex and difficult and the issues of fact may be tangled. It is very easy for the layman to miss important points of fact or of law.

It should not be thought that all legal matters involve disputes. Much legal business does not involve any dispute at all. Thus a man goes to his lawyer to have a will made which will regulate his property after his death, to have a company formed to run a business, to have a charitable trust created, to have a house which he has bought transferred into his name, to arrange for the let of his house and so on. But in all these, and many more, kinds of business, the lawyer has to know what is allowed and what is not, to try to foresee difficulties, to minimise taxation, and to avoid disputes. If disputes arise, the lawyers on each side will try to come to agreement before resorting to a court.

Legal aid and advice
Since getting legal advice and securing representation in court requires the skill and time of highly-skilled professional men and women, it is expensive. To try to ensure that all people who need it can secure legal advice and, where necessary, representation in court there has developed since 1945 a complex system of Legal Aid and Advice.

Enforcement of the law
The civil law is largely enforced by law-abiding persons who apply it and abide by it in their dealings with one another. Even when a dispute has been taken to court one party, having been found by a court liable to do something or to pay money, will frequently then do or pay voluntarily. If he does not, the party holding the

judgment of the court may have to *levy execution* (or in Scotland *do diligence*) against him. Under this, in the last resort, some of his property may be taken and sold and the proceeds paid to the party holding the judgment. Or the creditor may have the debtor adjudicated bankrupt, in which case all his property is taken and sold and the creditors paid from the proceeds of sale.

The criminal law is largely enforced by the police, who may arrest a criminal or suspected criminal and have him tried in a criminal court. If he is found guilty he may be sent to prison, fined or subjected to another form of punishment.

Law Reform

The rules of law require constantly to be revised, to take account of new problems, to be suitable for current social conditions, and to take account of gaps and defects which are found in the rules. Consequently the different legal professional bodies all have committees which regularly propose what they consider desirable or necessary reforms to the government. Organisations such as the CBI, TUC, RAC, BMA and many more do the same. Periodically the government appoints a Royal Commission, a group of about 15 people of experience, to make a thorough investigation of the law on a subject, such as trade unions or gambling, and to report and propose changes. If the government agrees to the proposals it will bring forward a Bill to Parliament to enact the necessary changes.

In 1965 there were created the *Law Commission* and the *Scottish Law Commision*, small permanent bodies charged with keeping the whole of English and Scottish law under review, and bringing forward proposals for reform and improvement. Since 1965 many Acts have been passed giving effect to the proposals of the Commissions.

International law

Quite apart from the rules of law applicable in particular countries there is a body of international law regulating relations between states in the world. It grew up initially from rules proposed by legal scholars in books, but in modern times it is largely made by treaties, conventions and agreements between two or more states. Increasingly too there are international organisations, notably the United Nations Organisation, but also many specialised organisations concerned with particular problems, such as the International Labour Organisation and the World Health Organisation. In the past, international disputes have all too frequently been sought to be solved by force, by making war, but the UNO strives hard to prevent resort to force. Disputes may be taken to the *International Court of Justice* but, differing from the courts in states, states which are parties to disputes cannot in general be compelled to go to the International Court and the means of compelling parties to obey judgments of the Court are limited. International law is growing rapidly in importance and bulk, and steadily playing a larger part in the affairs of states.

Human Rights

The states which are members of the Council of Europe adopted a convention declaring certain Human Rights. Persons who believe that their rights under this convention have been infringed may complain to the Commission on Human Rights and then to the *European Court of Human Rights*. But the convention and the decisions of this Court are not enforceable in the United Kingdom. They are persuasive on the government only: that is, it is free to decide whether they should be given effect to or not.

NATURAL HISTORY

The first thing I do when I get up in the morning is to draw back the curtain and look out through the window at the garden and the new day. If it is a bright summer morning I cannot wait even to get dressed, but go straight downstairs in my dressing-gown. Then I unlock the door and step out into the garden to breathe the fresh morning air 'before many people have used it', as somebody once said. At such times the lawn glitters with beads of dew that glow in different colours, orange, green, turquoise and red, as they reflect separate light waves from the rising sun. A late slug glides towards his shelter, needing to reach it before the sun's heat evaporates the dew and dries the ground. Various flies cluster on sunny patches of the fence to absorb the warming light before they become active, but bumble-bees are already busy at certain flowering shrubs and border flowers, for they are early risers. They set out long before the honey-bees have thought of stirring, and continue to forage later in the evening, sometimes until after sundown. Moreover they fly in light rain or drizzle, which honey-bees never do.

The garden birds, which ceased their singing before sunrise, are now busy collecting food, being hungry after the night. Ladybirds warm their small bodies on sunlit leaves, and a spider circles towards the centre of its orb-web as it spins the last few sticky spirals. Some poppy flowers have split and cast apart their paired sheaths by the delicate pressure of their expanding, crinkly petals—for dawn is their time of opening. I marvel at them, for I can imagine few things so sublimely fresh, or with such a delicately new-born look, as a poppy that has just opened its four satiny, slightly crumpled petals to the rising sun.

So much for a few minutes of sheer enjoyment in my garden at the beginning of the day—but that is what Natural History is about. It is about being aware of the other living things that share this planet with us—the plants that clothe the hills and plains and make them beautiful, and the animals of every shape and size that depend upon the plants for food and shelter. And then, of course, we want to name them, to identify and recognise the many different kinds—but that is not enough. It is not enough to pick a small pink flower by the hedge and say 'This is herb Robert', or to say of a butterfly sunning itself on a bramble in a grassy glade, 'That is a speckled wood', or to point out a jelly-like object on a rock exposed by the ebbing tide and say, 'There is a sea anemone'.

True understanding of Natural History involves enquiry into the whole life of the creatures, their relations with other lives around them, how they feed and reproduce, what are their enemies and by what means they evade them, and how they survive the storms and icy rigours of winter, or the heat and drying winds of summer.

This sort of understanding comes from close contact with living things, and through watching them in the garden, the woods and the open spaces. Books, which contain the accumulated knowledge and observations of devoted men, are of priceless value, of course, and should always be consulted—but nothing can replace the experience of seeing, with your own eyes, the plants and animals in their natural setting. Then there will be other things that you remember, the season and the time of day, the sun that warmed your face, the wind that ruffled your hair, the sudden shower of rain. You will notice how these varying conditions are met, and influence the actions of the creatures that you watch. Thus you will come to know the feel and climate of a creature's life in a direct and personal sense, such as no book alone can ever give you. Then, indeed, you will begin to feel deeply about conserving the wildlife of the earth, and you will want to help in keeping its varied habitats intact and unpolluted for future generations to enjoy.

Now let us return to the subject of gardens, where Nature can be enjoyed simply by stepping out of the back door, or even by gazing through the window. Although gardens are, to a great extent, artificial, man-made habitats, they provide homes and feeding grounds for many wild creatures. In fact, any garden can be enjoyed simply by stepping out of the back door and as countryside gets bulldozed away such private sanctuaries increase enormously in value and importance. Unfortunately, though, there are many kinds of poisons and sprays on the market, and the gardener is urged to use them and to make war on all fronts against aphids, ants, slugs, woodlice, beetles, millipedes, snails and even earthworms, and to scorch and shrivel every kind of weed and wildflower. He is urged to view his garden as a battlefield, where every small creature is a possible threat that must be banished, and where there is little in the way of food for birds.

Millipede and Centipede

Such a gardener is apt to wear a worried look and he can never quite relax. Yet, of all places, a garden should be an environment of peace, where one can sit and enjoy the buzz and flutter of wings, the chorus of bird song, the sudden appearance of a shining beetle on the path, as well as the still beauty of the flowers. Surely the peacock butterfly that comes to sip nectar from the herbaceous border is an added bonus, as lovely as any of the flowers on which it sits—but for its caterpillars to feed, there must be nettles.

THE GARDEN AS A WILDLIFE SANCTUARY

Now let us consider how to make your garden a welcome sanctuary for wildlife. It should have a fairly well-clipped lawn where thrushes and blackbirds can find worms, where starlings can probe for leather-jackets, wireworms, little slugs and other grass-root creatures, and where pied wagtails can run and flutter in pursuit of surface insects. A lawn that has a natural variety of short-turf plants is much more interesting than one that has only grass. And if it is not mown too hard or frequently, their short-stemmed flowers will bloom. So leave some daisies to spangle the lawn in spring, and patches of white clover that will attract bees in summer. The closely-clustered flowers of round-leaved speedwell make fresh and lovely sky-blue patches on my own lawn in late spring, and the small, clover-like heads of black medick dot the ground with yellow brightness where it spreads, flowering throughout the summer. Above all, though, I love to see that little gem among the short-turf flowers, the dove's-foot cranesbill, and I can seldom resist squatting on the grass to gaze at its small pink stars.

Dove's-foot Cranesbill   Poppy

A slenderish kind of tree, planted on the lawn, relieves its flatness, casts an area of shade and gives a feeling of security to smaller birds. They can fly up into its branches if startled while feeding on scattered crumbs. There should also be a fair-sized tree in the garden, for its topmost branches will provide song posts for a song thrush, or perhaps a mistle thrush. Blackbirds tend to sing from lower branches. In fact, the picture that I carry in my mind is of a blackbird singing amid the yellow tassels of a laburnum tree. Nowadays, however, all these birds may choose a television aerial.

A Place for Wild Flowers

I leave an unmown grassy area at the bottom of my garden, where meadow and hedgerow plants can develop freely. Here grasshoppers can live, and their cheerful stridulations enhance my summer days. Here, too, the umbelliferous plants, such as cow parsley and wild carrot, provide feeding platforms for hover-

A small patch of Wild Flower Garden

flies, greenbottles, solitary wasps and pollen-feeding beetles. Greater stitchwort, herb Robert, bird's-foot trefoil, knapweed, ragwort, meadow vetch, mallow, poppy, white deadnettle, spear thistle, ox-tongue and other hedgerow plants may decorate such an area. The flowers of ragwort and knapweed will attract small tortoiseshell and red admiral butterflies, and meadow browns may come to fly floppily over the grasses. The fruiting heads of spear thistle and ox-tongue are likely to give you the joy of seeing goldfinches feeding from them in early autumn.

In this area, too, the underground larvae of swift moths, summer chafers, skipjack beetles and daddy long-legs will thrive, and the close plant cover will shelter such creatures as slow-worms and the larger ground beetles, even, perhaps, a hedge-

hog. One summer, when I was clipping back some of the taller
grasses in my strip of garden meadow, I found a nest of carder-
bees. These smallish, brown bumble-bees had made a soft, snug
nest of woven moss and grass, rather like a bird's nest, with a
covering of moss to protect the cells. Unlike most bumble-bees,
which nest in holes, carder-bees make their nests above ground
at the base of tall grasses and other plants.

A stand of nettles in a corner of your wild strip of garden will
serve as food for the caterpillars of small tortoiseshell, peacock or
red admiral butterflies, and may induce a pair of white-throats to
nest among the tangled stems if you live in a rural district.

Homes for Soil Creatures

A few small boulders, wide rather than deep, and flattish below,
placed in various parts of the garden but not pressed into the soil,
will give daytime shelter to centipedes, slugs, woodlice, beetles
and ground-dwelling spiders, or roof the nests of garden ants.
When you lift such boulders, however, make sure you replace
them with extreme care to avoid harming the sheltering creatures.
A well built-up rock garden varies the terrain with its different
levels. Snails will find homes in crevices between the rocks, while
harvestmen, millipedes, springtails and other creatures lurk beneath the mat-like foliage of aubretia, yellow alyssum, mossy
saxifrage and other low-growing rock plants.

Another way of altering the terrain of your garden is to make a
sand bank. For this, all you have to do is to collect some buckets
of sand from a sandy heath, the beach or a builder's yard, mix it
with soil to make it firm and bank it up in a sunny corner. In

Andrena Bee

spring and summer, if you keep it fairly clear of weeds, it will attract mining bees and digger wasps to make their burrows. The first to arrive in spring will probably be the pretty little Andrena bees, easy to recognise by the rich, orange-brown fur on their bodies. These are the female bees, and each will construct a cell at the bottom of her burrow, which she provides with a paste made from pollen and a little honey. Having completed this after several journeys from the flowers, carrying about half her weight of pollen back each time, she lays an egg on the paste and closes the cell. She then makes a few more cells higher up from the tunnel, constructing, provisioning and closing each in turn. Although her offspring emerge from their pupal skins in late summer, they remain resting in their cells until the following spring. This may seem strange, but if they squandered their little store of energy by flying in the autumn sunshine they would be unable to survive the winter months.

Spider-hunting Wasp

One summer I spent a fascinating half hour watching a spider-hunting wasp dragging her paralysed prey to a burrow she had started, under a stone which jutted from the sand bank in my garden. These wasps always seem to be in a desperate hurry. They make short, darting flights, then scurry about on their long legs, poking into crevices as they search for ground-dwelling spiders. This wasp, having already caught her spider, had paralysed it by stinging the nerve centre at the base of its legs.

When I spotted her—only the female wasps hunt spiders—she was running backwards up the slope, dragging the spider along by one leg, gripped in her jaws. Having to move backwards, she could not see very well where she was going, so after dragging the spider a little way, she would drop it and run up the slope to the stone where her burrow was started, to check that she was backing in the right direction. She did not seem able to return in a straight line to the spider, but ran down the slope to the level where she had left it, then ran to and fro until she found it. On most occasions she dropped the spider on a little ledge of the bank and quickly found it—but twice she dropped the spider on smoothly sloping ground, and it rolled down the bank. Then she would rush feverishly up and down the bank for several minutes, until she finally came across it, and her labours would begin again.

Eventually she made her way up to within a few inches from the stone, dropped the spider for the last time and ran up to complete her burrow. Little jets of sand started to shoot out from under the stone as she dug downwards. I had to wait for about ten minutes before she finally came out to pull the spider up under the stone and into her burrow. There, out of sight, she would lay an egg on the paralysed spider, then fill in the burrow and leave.

When a paralysed spider is left while the wasp explores the terrain or digs her burrow it is liable to be attacked by ants, tiger beetles or other predators. This reminds me of another spider-hunting wasp, of a different species, which I happened to notice while on holiday in Majorca. This wasp had a clever idea. I watched her dragging a spider backwards along the ground. After dragging the spider a little way, she dropped it at the base of a plant stem. Then she ran up the stem, explored its small side-shoots, ran down, gripped the spider, dragged it up the stem and placed it firmly in the fork of a branching side-shoot. Here the spider was fairly safe from attack while the wasp flew off to take her bearings or dig her burrow. Unfortunately I was unable to wait for the wasp's return. The action of this wasp was instinctive rather than thought out—none the less, it was still clever.

Bushes for Birds

Your garden should have some evergreen shrubs or trees, such as laurel, privet, *Euonymus japonica*, yew and holly. These will give protection to small roosting birds through the cold winter months. Holly will also produce some winter food, in the form of berries, for thrushes, blackbirds and starlings—but only if it is a female tree, and only if there is a male tree near by so that its flowers can be pollinated.

Ivy is a very useful evergreen climber if it is allowed to cover part of a garden wall. Spiders of several kinds will spin webs between its leaves, or weave silken traps among its clinging stems. The stick-like caterpillars of the swallow-tailed moth eat its leaves, and in late autumn its rounded clusters of yellow-green flowers provide a last bonanza feast of nectar for wasps, bees, bluebottles, hover-flies, butterflies and many moths, before the cold weather ends their activities. Garden snails will hibernate on the wall between its stems in winter, and wrens may roost behind the shelter of its leaves, while sparrows will sometimes bring dry grass and feathers there, and poke them in their roosts for added shelter. Then, in early summer, the purplish-black berries will be gobbled up by blackbirds, thrushes and even woodpigeons.

Rowan and whitebeam are fine berry-bearing trees to grow in the garden, for they will provide a feast for blackbirds, song thrushes and mistle thrushes in the autumn. Elder bushes will grow anywhere in town or country, and their hanging clusters of shining black berries are quickly cleared by birds. Berberis, pyracantha and cotoneaster are useful ornamental shrubs to have. The oval or cylindrical berries of berberis are rich in vitamins, and the fiery-orange, densely clustered berries of pyracantha make a glorious show in October. These, and the small red berries of cotoneaster, offer a late supply of food for birds when most other berries are over. I have watched blackbirds, thrushes and greenfinches feeding on my cotoneaster bush and one day, to my surprise and joy, a couple of waxwings joined them. The inconspicuous, but nectar-rich, flowers of the cotoneaster cause it to hum with the wings of eager honey-bees in summer.

Waxwing

Flowering Bushes for Insects

You will, of course, want to have some bushes in your garden
that are especially attractive to butterflies and other insects. For
butterflies, buddleia is the bush *par excellence*. In fact, it is also
appropriately known as the butterfly bush. Its long, scented,
mauve or purple flower-clusters bloom from July until September,
when many other shrubs have ceased to blossom. Small tortoiseshells, large whites, red admirals, peacocks, commas and painted
ladies may crowd and jostle each other as they probe the small
flowers for nectar, while sunning themselves, spread-winged, on
the inflorescences.

Red admirals and painted ladies do not survive the winter in
Britain, and those we see in spring and early summer are im-
migrants from the south—red admirals from southern Europe and
painted ladies from North Africa. Both breed in this country. The
caterpillars of red admirals feed on nettles, and those of painted
ladies feed on thistles, and there is now exciting evidence that
some, at least, of the home-bred butterflies migrate south and
attempt the return journey in autumn. Whether or not they
succeed in doing so has yet to be confirmed, but this is more likely
to be the case with the painted lady, which is a rapid and powerful
flyer, occasionally reaching as far as Iceland on its northward
travels.

Painted Lady

Another good bush for your garden is the flowering currant. Its
multitudes of small pink flowers make a beautiful show in spring,
and they are favourites of the big queen bumble-bees. Some years
ago I had a bedroom on the ground floor where I was working.
There was a large flowering currant bush outside my window,

and throughout April I woke each morning to the deep hums and buzzings of the bumble-bees which had been busy among its flowers since dawn. In fact, I always think of the flowering currant as the queen bumble-bee bush. I say 'queen bumble-bee' because bumble-bee colonies are annual affairs, and only the young queens, which have already mated, survive the winter.

Queen Bumble-Bee and Flowering Currant

Thus, after awakening from hibernation, and restoring her energy with the nectar and pollen of spring flowers, the young queen must find a suitable hole for her nest, and start the new colony all on her own. For the first five or six weeks, she must build the wax cells, lay her eggs, forage for nectar and pollen, feed her growing batch of grubs, lay in a store of honey for wet days, make fresh cells and so on, until the first workers hatch and begin to take over. This is a very different situation from that of the queen honey-bee, who never leaves the hive after her mating flight unless accompanied by a swarm of workers, and who is incapable of building cells, foraging or feeding her young, but must, herself be constantly fed and groomed by attendant workers.

Another bush I would recommend is hebe, or veronica, as it is commonly called. It blooms in late summer and the spikes of mauve flowers on my own bushes attract hosts of honey-bees, bumble-bees, hover-flies and silver-Y moths. Most moths fly only after dark, but silver-Y moths are interesting in that they fly in bright sunlight, usually in the afternoon, as well as in the evening and at night. One afternoon, I counted seven of them hovering round the flower-spikes of my veronicas as they probed the small corollas with their tongues. When I came out again at dusk, silver-Y moths were still feeding, impossible to follow as they darted from one veronica bush to the next, but coming suddenly into focus as they hovered, like little swaying ghosts, above the dark foliage. Silver-Y moths do not survive the British winter, but migrants from the Mediterranean regions arrive in late spring, often in great numbers. Their caterpillars feed on various wild and garden plants, and the home-bred moths are believed to make a return flight south in autumn.

Herbaceous Flowers for Insects

Among the summer-flowering herbaceous plants that I grow in my garden, red valerian is one of the best for attracting butterflies, silver-Y moths and others. It is a native of southern Europe, but garden escapes grow wild on railway banks, old walls and cliffs by the sea, at least in the south of England where I live. Red valerian flowers from May throughout the summer, especially if the flower stems are cut right back when the little feathery fruits are forming. Its clustered flowers are great favourites of another immigrant moth from southern Europe and North Africa—the humming-bird hawk-moth. Only recently a friend told me he had seen a humming-bird in his garden, and had called his wife out to have a look. I told him that as all humming-birds are native to America, it must have been the small hawk-moth which flies in bright sunshine and does, indeed, look like a tiny brown and orange bird with a black and white-edged tail tuft. He agreed.

I am always thrilled to see a humming-bird hawk-moth come darting into my garden. I love to watch it flick from flower to

Humming-bird Hawk-moth

flower with marvellously controlled flight, and to see it sway and hover, poised for a magic moment on whirring wings, to probe a nectary with its slender tongue. Indeed, there is no creature that seems to burn with such an intense flame of life as this small hawk-moth, that wings its way over continent and sea, to dart among the flowers of English gardens. Its caterpillars feed on lady's bedstraw, and the generation of moths from these may well make the return flight south.

In late September and October, when the blackbirds feast on blackberries and scatter purple droppings in the nearby scrubby wasteland, the ice plant (*Sedem spectabile*), sometimes called the butterfly plant, attracts small tortoiseshells, peacock butterflies and occasional commas to my garden. These three butterflies hibernate as adults in this country, and continue to fly until they must seek shelter for the winter sleep. They feed and sun themselves on the ice plant's pink, flat heads of glistening flowers, or join the big, bee-mimicking drone-flies on the Michaelmas daisies. Both these plants are 'musts' for your garden sanctuary.

Most of the cultivated daisy-type flowers attract butterflies and other insects, that is to say if they are not the double kind, like those chrysanthemums, dahlias and asters that have lost the central disc of yellow florets through artificial selection. The stand of tall white shasta daisies in my garden attracts a multitude of summer insects, such as bees, hover-flies, drone-flies, greenbottles, ichneumon wasps, hunting wasps, soldier beetles, tiny honey-beetles and delicate green capsid bugs, as well as butterflies. Another daisy-type flower, the sunflower, should be grown especially for birds. Its enormous disc, when left to seed, will certainly attract the tits and finches, and if you live in the country near a wood, then nuthatches may join them.

The Garden Hedge

If you are not lucky enough to have a walled garden there should be a wooden fence or a hedge to give it shelter and a feeling of seclusion. These days most farmers use tractor-drawn mechanical clippers to cut and slash the hedges of their fields, leaving them too low and too narrow to attract nesting birds or shelter other forms of wild life. Thus it has become particularly important that gardens should have well-grown border hedges and plenty of shrubs. Holly, privet, pyracantha, yew and leyland cypress make good evergreen hedges for birds to nest in during spring and summer, and to use as roosts in winter. A pair of song thrushes nested in the privet hedge bordering the front garden of my previous house, and I discovered that the rim of their nest was lined with toffee papers that children had dropped on the pavement after visiting the local shop on their way from school. One day, while lightly clipping the same hedge, I found a young caterpillar of the privet hawk-moth. I reared the caterpillar in a large jam-jar and when it was fully grown and ready to pupate, I released it under the hedge. There it could burrow into the soil, construct an earthen cell and cast its skin to become a chrysalis.

Dunnocks and wrens like to search the ground below the privet hedge for spiders and tiny insects; and in June, its heavily scented, creamy-white flower-clusters attract the honey-bees by day and moths at night.

The Garden Fence
My present garden is fenced but it contains plenty of shrubs. Flies like to sun themselves on the south-facing side, and in April and early May a queen wasp comes to scrape wood from the upright fence posts. She scrapes the surface with her jaws, backing downwards as she works, until she has a little ball of shredded wood. This she carries to her underground nest, and mixes with saliva to make woodpulp for starting the paper nest that will eventually house her first small batch of grubs. Then, in June, the worker wasps arrive, and on throughout the summer they scrape wood-fibre from the fence. They use this to enlarge the paper nest and add cells to the comb, and later to build fresh combs below it and extend the walls around them as the colony expands.

Zebra Spider

The black-and-white zebra spiders hunt flies and other insects on this south-facing fence, each for ever trailing a hardly-visible line of silk. The little spiders run in short, quick jerks, or twist and swivel to survey the surface round them. When a fly is spotted by a zebra spider she cautiously stalks it until within jumping distance. Then she makes a lightning pounce and, with the fly gripped in her legs and jaws, falls from the fence. However, she falls only an inch or two, because the thread, that she had first fixed to the wall, was spun out as she jumped. If the insect she captures is very small, she grips it with her jaws alone, clutching the fence with her legs to save herself from falling.

Protective Coloration

Garden carpet moths and others choose to rest by day on the north-facing fence, where their sleep will not be disturbed by the heat and brightness of the sun. Garden carpets are common even in town gardens, and may be seen in late spring, and throughout the summer and autumn. The moth rests with its wings spread flat against the surface, in the form of a small triangle. Its greyish white wings are marked with dark patches at the edges. These serve to break up and obscure its outline, and thus prevent it from being easily recognised by a bird, as it rests on a fence or tree. This means of protection, known as 'disruptive coloration', is widely used by moths and other vulnerable creatures.

Garden Carpet Moth

Another means of protection, known as 'mimicry', is used by the angle shades moth. This lovely moth is also extremely common in town and country gardens during early summer and again in the autumn. I usually see an angle shades moth resting on the ground at the base of a wall or fence. Its forewings are

Angle Shades Moth

delicately coloured in shades of brown, pink and olive green with angle-shaped markings, and their edges are roughly waved and dented. Thus, as the moth rests by day with wings folded over its back, it strongly resembles a dry and partly withered leaf.

When I am pottering or poking about in the garden I frequently disturb a large yellow underwing. The moth flies rapidly away for a short distance, then drops into a bush or beneath a border plant. It usually rests at the base of plants or low down on the fence where its brown wings, held flat over its back and marked with a few pale lines and darker patches, make it difficult to see. But when the moth flies, its bright yellow hindwings are suddenly displayed, only to vanish as it drops again into the foliage and folds them beneath its forewings. It must be most bewildering to a bird when the yellow-winged moth it was chasing suddenly disappears. The bird may stop to search where the moth plunged, but it continues to look for a yellow moth and misses the concealed brown one. Thus the large yellow underwing is saved from being eaten. This protective device, where vividly marked wings are suddenly displayed in flight, then hidden on alighting, is known as 'flash coloration'.

I have spent several summer holidays abroad in southern Europe. There I like to scramble about among the broom and lavender clumps and pink-flowered cistus bushes on hot, dry, stony hillsides. In such places there are grasshoppers that give very fine displays of flash coloration. The brown, grey or whitish grasshoppers are perfectly camouflaged to match the stony ground where they sit among the sparse dry grasses. As I clamber forwards, they leap up and flutter in front of me, marvellously transformed, and looking like gorgeous butterflies which suddenly vanish as they touch the ground. The broad, gauzy flight-wings of these grasshoppers are brilliant blue or turquoise in some kinds, and vivid red, pink or orange in others, and as the insect alights they suddenly fold like fans beneath its protective forewings. To see them is very well worth toiling up stony tracks, with thorn-scratched arms and legs, in the parching heat of a Mediterranean summer.

Yet another good way to avoid being eaten is to have a nasty taste. However, it is no good being unpalatable if you look much like other creatures that taste nice. You must have distinctive markings that are easily remembered by a predator, and which advertise the fact that you should not be eaten. There are two common garden moths that taste unpleasant, and advertise the fact by means of 'warning coloration'.

One of these is the magpie moth, which I often see resting on bushes in July and August. This attractive moth is very conspicuous. Its body is yellow with black spots, and its broad wings, which are half-spread as it rests, are white with black and yellow spots and marking. When disturbed, it flutters slowly away and settles on the upper surface of a leaf. Not only the moth, but its caterpillar and chrysalis are also distasteful. The caterpillar is marked like the moth, being white with black and yellow spots, and the chrysalis is black with yellow bands. The caterpillars feed on a variety of plants, including the leaves of currant and gooseberry bushes, and I have found them on the euonymus bush in my garden. The chrysalis rests in a very flimsy hammock-like cocoon,which does not hide its yellow-banded form.

The other distasteful moth is the garden tiger. This large and beautiful moth has creamy-white forewings marked with chocolate brown patches, and its hindwings and abdomen are brilliant red with a few black marks. When touched or gently interfered with, the garden tiger does not fly away, but exposes its vivid hindwings and the band of red hairs behind its head. This is its way of saying, 'Leave me alone, I taste nasty.' The furry caterpillar of the garden tiger, commonly known as the 'woolly bear', feeds on dandelions, docks and various other plants.

Garden Tiger Moth

Ladybird Larva

Aphid Predators

Ladybirds are also distasteful, and their bright red, spotted wing-covers advertise the fact to birds. These little beetles and their larvae feed on the aphids that attack the stems and leaves of roses and other cultivated plants; but when the plants are sprayed with poisons the useful ladybirds are killed. Blue tits, willow warblers and other small birds that like to eat aphids, often suffer too, or even die. Nobody can mistake a ladybird, but its larvae are not always recognised. Ladybird larvae look rather like little flattened caterpillars. They are blackish or bluish-grey, with yellow spots and black legs spread out sideways. When the larva is fully grown it turns into a roundish, black-and-yellow pupa, which is fixed by its tail to a plant stem or leaf. So, when you see these little knob-like objects on rose bushes and other plants, remember what they are. One day, when I was at the south coast, I saw hundreds of seven-spot ladybirds on the breakwaters and the promenade, and crawling over the pebbles of the beach. The probable explanation is that they had flown over from the Continent, and were resting before flying inland to settle in gardens and orchards and continue their search for aphids.

In July and August aphids produce winged forms that fly away to start fresh colonies on other plants. As the winged aphids rise into the air, countless numbers are taken by swallows, house martins and swifts. In fact, swifts have been observed to feed their young on round pellets of compressed aphids, taken on the wing and carried home in their throats.

Myriads of winged aphids, too, get trapped in spider webs, sometimes almost covering each sticky spiral with their tiny forms, only to be left untouched by the sickened spiders. However, plenty will survive to start fresh colonies on garden plants; and other enemies, as well as ladybirds, will eat them as they suck the stems and leaves. The loveliest of these is the green lacewing. This insect has a slender, emerald green body, golden eyes and two long pairs of gauzy, iridescent wings, held roof-wise over its back when not engaged in flight. The green lacewing flies chiefly at night, but on a sunny morning, or in the warm light of evening, I often see it fluttering slowly across the garden with a delightful, twinkling motion of its wings.

In late spring and summer you may see tiny, yellowish-green knobs on very slender stalks, that seem to be growing from stems or the underside of leaves. These are the eggs of the green lace-wing. They are laid near aphid colonies, for it is in its larval form that the lacewing feeds on aphids. This little creature, not unlike a ladybird larva in shape, is brownish-yellow, and has a pair of sickle-shaped jaws through which it sucks the captured aphids until only their skins are left. When fully grown and ready to pupate, the larva spins a flattish cocoon of white silk on leaves or the trunks of trees.

In late autumn green lacewings seek shelter, often in houses, where they hibernate in corners near the ceiling. It is at this time that a peculiar thing happens. As the weeks pass, the lacewing loses its lovely green colour and becomes drab yellow or reddish-brown. But months later, when hibernation draws to an end, the yellow or red colour disappears, and the lacewing becomes gradu-ally green, then emerald green once more as it flutters out into the mild spring air.

Green Lacewing

The dainty hover-flies, which are to be seen wherever there is a border of flowers, also lay their eggs near aphid colonies. The yellowish-white or pale green maggot-like larvae which hatch from these are just as avid aphid-eaters as are those of ladybirds or lacewings. The hover-fly larva looks rather like a small, plump caterpillar with suckers instead of legs, but its front part tapers to a very tiny head. When it comes upon an aphid the larva pierces it with its mouth prongs and quickly sucks it dry. The larva then drops the empty skin and pierces another victim. It may consume a dozen or more aphids before taking a short rest to digest its meal. When fully grown the hover-fly larva fixes itself to a leaf or stem and contracts into a little pear-shaped pupa.

If you are an acute observer you may notice a minute insect hovering over a colony of aphids. Keep watching, and you will see it dart down and settle on the colony. This is a braconid wasp, and it is laying an egg in one of the aphids. When the egg hatches, the larva of the braconid wasp will eat its victim from within, until only the empty skin is left. It will then spin a cocoon in the aphid husk and pupate. When ready to emerge, tiny jaws will bite a neat, round hole in the back of the aphid skin, a head will appear, then the little black wasp will struggle out and fly away. However, you need a good pocket lens to watch this happen. I have seen small clusters of aphid skins, still clinging to the stems of plants, each with a round hole in its back where a braconid wasp head left.

Then there is another aphid predator, and a very charming one, that sometimes visits my garden in the autumn. This is the goldcrest, our smallest bird, weighing about six grams or less. I looked out of the front-room window on a dull October morning, and there it was, greenish with a yellow flame along its head, daintily picking aphids from the stems and leaves of my rose bushes. The next day I stood for a quarter of an hour by the sycamore tree in my garden, watching half a dozen goldcrests plucking aphids from the under-surface of the leaves, sometimes hanging on a leaf stalk, or hovering for a few seconds beneath a leaf to do so.

Goldcrest

Well, these are some of the predators of aphids that you may be able to observe in your own garden. One purpose I had in mind in drawing your attention to them, apart from their inherent interest, is to give you some idea of the way a natural balance is maintained by living creatures, preventing any one species from becoming over-numerous. However, where insecticides are used, the predators are killed alongside their prey.

Ants and Aphids

Now let us return once more to the aphid colony. No doubt there is one on a rose bush in your garden, and little black ants are running up and down the stem of the bush between it and their nest. Look closely—you will see ants moving slowly about the colony, tapping or stroking the aphids with their antennae. These ants are inducing the aphids to excrete minute drops of honey-dew, which they greedily lap up. Then with full crops they return to the nest and distribute the liquid, mouth to mouth, among their sister ants. I say 'sister ants' because all worker ants are dwarfed females incapable of mating.

Black garden ants derive much of their food from the honey-dew excreted by aphids. They run up and down the trunk and branches of a sycamore tree in my garden, where their tracks lead to aphid colonies on the leaves. These foraging ants keep closely to invisible tracks, which are really scent trails, laid down and kept fresh by the ants as they travel along. In my previous garden there was a rose bush by the back window. On summer evenings, after sunset, a large toad would come regularly and squat beside the bush. Its tongue would flick out every few seconds and lick up ants from the stem as they ran up and down the track leading to the aphid colonies among the leaves.

Common Toad

Food Chains

A toad and a rose bush—I feel pretty sure that you would never have connected these two things together in your mind. But now you see how a toad may be linked to a rose bush by one item of the food it eats. This sort of who-eats-who linkage is known as a 'food chain'. The rose bush-to-toad food chain may be represented thus: rose bush → aphids → ants → toad. All food chains start with a plant, for only plants can use the sun's energy to trigger the chemical processes that build sugars from the carbon dioxide of air and water from the soil, and only plants can combine the sugars with simple minerals of the same soil water, to make proteins, oils and all the complex matter of their bodies. Thus plants are 'producer organisms', because they produce the food on which all animals depend, whereas animals are 'consumer organisms', for they consume, either directly or indirectly, the various plants. The aphids feed on the rose bush directly, whereas the toad feeds on the rose bush indirectly.

However, rose bushes provide food for mildews, black spot fungi, caterpillars, sawfly larvae, capsid bugs, gall wasps and thrips, as well as aphids, and are themselves nourished by the dead leaves and stems of plants, dead creatures and the droppings of live ones, when these are all consumed and reduced to compost by earthworms, woodlice, millipedes, springtails, mites, soil bacteria and fungi. Aphids may feed on the sap of other bushes, herbs or trees, as well as roses, and are consumed by special predators as you know, besides providing honey-dew for ants. Garden ants feed on seeds, nectar, tiny insects, dead creatures of all kinds and rotting fruit, as well as honey-dew from aphids, and are themselves eaten by various birds. Toads eat earthworms, slugs, newts, young slow-worms, spiders and many other insects besides ants, and may be eaten by grass snakes, tawny owls and herons.

Food Web

I have mentioned all these creatures to show you that food chains are connected up, linking many kinds of plants and animals in an intricate web of inter-dependence. This is called a 'food web'. The plants and animals that compose a food web are in a delicate state of balance, which can easily be upset by breaking the connecting link provided by any one species. For instance, the spraying of bushes with insecticides over a wide area in summer, when the larvae of ladybirds, hover-flies and lacewings are feeding on aphid colonies, may cause a plague of aphids to develop later in the season. The reason for this long-term adverse effect of the spraying is that aphids give birth, without mating or laying eggs, to active female young throughout the summer. Thus those that survive, or are missed by the sprays, are able to reproduce very rapidly and so build up their numbers far in advance of their predators.

I have already mentioned that, especially in late summer, aphids produce winged forms which fly to fresh host-plants and give rise to new colonies of wingless aphids. These winged aphids may be so abundant that you can hardly prevent them from getting into your eyes when you walk outside, and they smear up the wind-screens of cars that travel through the suburbs and along country roads. Now, swifts, being unable to perch or settle on the ground, are entirely dependent on flying insects for their food, and winged aphids form the bulk of their diet. Thus the spraying of trees and bushes with insecticides, when aphid colonies are beginning to produce winged forms, may have a drastic effect on the breeding success of the swifts by forcing them to forage far away from their nesting places.

Mating Swarm of Ants

Winged males and queens of the black garden ant provide swifts with a rich source of food when the ants are swarming. However, the swarms last only for an hour or two on a few days in late summer when the local weather conditions over a stretch of country are just right. The swarms are mating flights, and at three or four o'clock on a warm, sultry afternoon the worker ants construct larger exit holes in their nest and release the males, and the young queens, which are many times their size. The winged ants climb stems and take off, flying slowly up into the sky, where mating occurs between males and queens from nests all over the district.

One afternoon in August I looked out of the window and saw a group of swifts flying to and fro across my garden. I went straight out and down the garden to where winged ants were streaming upwards from a well-stocked nest. Standing beside the nest, I watched the queens ascend like drifting dots diminishing in the sky, and every dot on which I fixed my gaze was engulfed by a swift before it dwindled from sight. It was a fascinating spectacle. A perfectly-aimed swift would hurtle towards a flying ant, and pass straight on with no apparent loss of speed or checking of its flight. It was as if the swift had never seen the flying ant, but simply hurtled through the space it occupied. I half expected to see the drifting speck still there as the swift shot past, but the space it left was empty. The impression was not of the insect being plucked from the air, but of it being instantaneously absorbed into the body of the speeding swift. A likely explanation is that the swift flies with a gaping bill and the ant gets lodged in a pocket of its throat, to be swallowed later.

Swifts

Another August, when the same nest swarmed, I watched a group of black-headed gulls flapping and circling over my garden, but no swifts came. It was easy to see the gulls pick the flying ants from the air, and they made a lovely sight as they flapped, veered and circled overhead. However, their performance was clumsy compared with that of the whirling, dashing, cleanly-aimed swifts that homed with such speed on their targets. In fact, as I stood by the nest I saw two gulls make for the same flying ant. Coming from opposite directions, the gulls almost crashed head-on, just veering at the last split-second, the one that missed the ant giving a sudden scream of frightened protest.

The queen ants that have somehow escaped the swifts, swallows, martins, gulls and starlings in the sky come fluttering down to earth, each with a small male clinging to her abdomen. Having landed, the queen ant pushes off the male, who has now finished mating with her. Then she runs a short distance, stops and with her legs starts scraping at the base of her wings, which break away and fall to the ground. Now she runs off to find a suitable hole or crevice, where she digs a small chamber and blocks the entrance with soil. She will spend the rest of her life underground. Her wing muscles disintegrate, and nourishment from these is fed through her mouth to her first small batch of grubs. When these have pupated and emerge as tiny adult workers they make their way out of the chamber, forage for honey-dew and other food, take over the care of eggs and grubs, and feed and groom the queen. Fresh chambers and connecting tunnels are excavated in the soil, and a new ant colony starts to expand.

Making a Garden Pond

The flourishing ant colony beside which I watched the swifts and gulls is under a large stone near my garden pond. A pond adds enormously to the interest of a garden nature reserve. So why not dig one? Ponds used to be an attractive feature of farmlands and villages, but now most of these have been drained and filled in, and of those still left, many are being poisoned by fertilisers and pesticides that seep in from the surrounding fields, orchards or market gardens. Thus your pond could help, in a small way, to remedy this sad loss. The pond could be rectangular or oval. It does not matter much about the shape, but make it at least half as wide as it is long. For a small pond, four feet by two or two and a half feet would be a suitable size, but it can be as big as you like. Decide on a situation where it gets a fair amount of sunshine, but make sure that it is not too near any tree, or the bottom will soon get clogged with leaves.

A suitable depth for a small pond would be one foot six inches to about two feet, but there is one important point to consider before digging it. This is that you should make one end slope very gradually to the top. It will provide a shallow area where birds can drink and splash in the water. It will also allow little froglets and toadlets to climb out of the water when their tadpole stage is finished. When your pond has been dug and smoothed over, and you have made sure that there are no sharp stones sticking out of the soil, you will be ready to line it with a waterproof material. A sheet of heavy polythene would be suitable for this, but make sure that it is big enough to overlap and spread for at least six inches round the edges. When you have pressed down the sheet as thoroughly as you can, lay flat stones round the overlapping edges to keep it in place—broken pieces of flagstone will do. Now your pond is ready to be filled and stocked with water-plants and creatures.

The Garden Pond

Collecting for the Garden Pond

Collecting for your pond will require an expedition into the country. You may find a suitable pond in a low-lying meadow, yellow with buttercups, but wherever your search takes you, make sure that you have a scribbling pad and pencil, so that you can record the various plants and animals you see. You could note down which plants are in flower, the situations where they grow, what insects are seen visiting them and what other creatures are doing—and of course, you should date your observations and record the weather.

I say 'scribbling pad and pencil' because these are rough notes to be made on the spot, and a pencil is quicker to write with than a pen, and useful for making sketches. The notes can be written out properly with a pen in your neat book when you get home; but never rely on memory, or important details of observation may be lost, and others will become distorted and inaccurate. I stress this point very strongly, because it is the most important thing I have ever learned to do in my studies of Natural History.

Now, supposing you discover a fair-sized pond in a meadow. As you approach the pond you will notice that many of the plants in the marshy ground around the pond are different from those in the rest of the meadow. You will see that the plants at the edge of the water are different from those farther back, that those standing in the shallow water are different still and that in deeper water there are plants with floating leaves and others that are completely submerged. This change in the flora from dry ground towards the centre of the pond is called 'zonation'. The plants are zoned according to the amount of water they require. You will notice, too, that there are some animals not seen farther out in the meadow. There may be a moorhen swimming jerkily on the water, a dragonfly cruising to and fro over the pond and some damselflies fluttering around its edges, and you may see some beetles on the leaves of waterside plants that are not found elsewhere.

Waterside Plants

Now let us consider some of the plants you are likely to see in the different zones. There may be scattered clumps of soft rush. It is easy to recognise the stiff, glossy stems, sharply pointed at the top and two or three feet high, each with a small tuft of tiny brown flowers sprouting from one side. You may also see the jointed

Marsh Horsetail

stems of marsh horsetail standing up from the wet grass, each stem with a whorl of about six slender branches curving upwards from the joints. You will probably find that some of the stems have a brown cone at the tip. The cone contains spores, for horsetails are not flowering plants, and like ferns and mosses, they reproduce by spores, not seeds. A spore is an extremely minute reproductive cell which is dispersed by air movement, whereas a seed, which develops from a fertilised ovule, is composed of very many cells, and contains a complete embryo plant with a store of food to give it a start in life. Horsetails are the only representatives left today of a very ancient group of plants. Some

Kingcups

of these were large trees that grew in the warm, steamy coal forests, a hundred million years before the first dinosaurs or the first flowering plants appeared on earth.

But back to the present and the marshy zone. If it is spring, the pale, four-petalled, lilac-tinted flowers of lady's smock or cuckoo flower will be in bloom. Its narrow fruit will dry as they ripen and suddenly explode, shooting the little seeds to a distance of four or five feet from the parent plant. In this manner the plants get scattered about the marsh and are saved from crowding each other. Nearer the water's edge some gaudy clumps of kingcups, with flowers like giant buttercups, are sure to catch your eye. Unlike buttercups, however, the flowers of kingcups have no petals, and it is the sepals, green in bud, that turn golden-yellow as they open above the glossy, heart-shaped leaves. If it is early summer you may see ragged robin, another plant requiring marshy ground. Its flowers somewhat resemble those of red campion, which belongs to the same plant family, only the petals appear to be torn or shredded—hence its name.

Closer to the margin of the pond, water forget-me-nots will be coming into bloom. The flowers, on slightly curling branches of the stem, are larger than those of the common forget-me-not, and heavenly blue but pink in bud, each open flower with a yellow eye-spot at its centre. Now, too, at the water's edge, the yellow flags will be showing their first big blooms, on stems that may be six feet tall, arising from thick stands of sword-like leaves.

In high summer, meadow-sweet will hold its frothy bunches of cream flowers three feet or so above the marshy ground. Despite its strong, sweet scent, the flowers of meadow-sweet are without nectar, but you may see little pollen-eating beetles crawling over them. Nearer the ground, the water mint will be showing its globular heads of little lilac flowers. Bend down and pinch one of its leaves, and your finger-tips will smell of peppermint.

Water Plants

Now we have come to the shallow-water zone. Here, at one end of the pond, encroaching inwards from its margin, are the tall ranks of reed-mace where a moorhen may be hiding, or sitting on a nest of broken reed stems. Between the spear-shaped leaves you will see dark green, cigar-shaped flower spikes. These are the densely-packed female flowers, and the portion of stem above them

Reed-mace

is yellow with the stamens of the male flowers. Soon the male flowers wither, and the spike turns chocolate brown as the female flowers start fruiting. Unlike the holly, where male and female flowers arise from separate trees, the male and female flowers of reed-mace are on the same plant. In this case the plant itself is hermaphrodite, but not the flowers. Another plant, not so common, but which I have rejoiced to see on two or three occas-

Flowering Rush

ions, is the flowering rush. Despite its name, this plant is not a rush, and its tall stem ends in a bouquet of lovely, rose-pink flowers. The flowers have three petals alternating with three sepals of the same bright colour, and the flower stalks all arise from the top of the stem. The flowering rush is, I think, the most beautiful of all the shallow-water plants. Where the water is fairly open, and the reed-mace has not encroached along its margin, you are likely to see water plantains. Their large, plantain-like leaves rise out of the water, and in summer they surround a flower stem about two feet high. This bears loose clusters of small, three-petalled flowers, pale pink or lilac in colour, which open only in the afternoons.

Now look at the plants floating on the surface of the pond. There is probably an area carpeted with bright green patches of duckweed. The little floating discs of duckweed are really flattened stems, and each bears a tiny root which hangs down in the water. In summer new discs are continually being budded and breaking off from the old ones. This is known as 'vegetative reproduction', and it enables the plants to spread quickly over the surface. An-

Frogbit

other floating plant with roots dangling in the water is frogbit. Its rounded floating leaves look like small waterlily leaves, and in summer you will see its white, three-petalled, male or female flowers raised on short stalks above the water. You are most likely to see frogbit if the pond is based on chalky soil. It spreads along the surface during summer by sending horizontal shoots, called runners, through the water. Each shoot has a bud at the tip, which develops into a new plant and becomes detached as the shoot withers—another case of vegetative reproduction.

Nearer the centre of the pond the gorgeous flowers of the white waterlily form many-petalled floating cups, with wide, polished leaves spread on the water around them. The floating leaves and flowers of the waterlily are carried upwards on long stalks from a thick, horizontal stem, called a rhizome, which is rooted in the mud. The leaves unfurl and the flower buds open only on reaching the water surface.

Water Milfoil

The submerged plants will not be so easy to see, and you may have to wade in and pull up a few specimens to identify them. But before doing so, test the mud with a stick, for what looks like the solid floor of the pond may be a covering of soft mud or silt, and your foot will sink straight through it.

Near the edge of the pond the surface may be studded with small rosettes of leaves like green stars. These are the upper leaves of starwort. The rest of the plant is submerged, with pairs of opposite leaves spaced along its stem. Only at the tip do the leaves grow close to form a floating star. A little farther out, in deeper water, you will see submerged feathery jungles of water milfoil. Pull up a plant, and you will notice that its feather-like leaves are arranged in whorls of four along the stem. In parts of the pond water milfoil may be replaced by even denser growths of Canadian pondweed, which has small leaves in groups of three along its stem. This plant was introduced from North America and has since spread in freshwater all over Britain.

Any of these submerged plants will do for your garden pond, but only put a few specimens in your polythene bags, for they will grow new shoots and spread quickly. Frogbit would be a good floating plant to take home, but not duckweed, for it will spread like a green carpet over the surface.

I have mentioned a few of the typical plants that you may find in and around the pond. There are many other kinds, but what you see depends to some extent on the soil and situation. For instance, in a heathland pond where the soil is peaty and slightly acid, you may find bladderwort in the water, and the beautiful bogbean growing from its shallows, with sphagnum moss, sundew, bog asphodel and cotton grass in the marshy ground around it. Bladderwort and sundew are both carnivorous plants. Bladderwort has little air-filled bladders on its feathery leaves. When minute trigger-hairs on one of the bladders are touched by a water flea or other tiny creature the bladder suddenly fills with water, sucking the creature in, where it is slowly digested. Sundew spreads a rosette of spoon-shaped leaves on the ground. The leaves are covered with long red hairs, each with a drop of sticky fluid at

Sundew

the tip. A fly or other insect, attracted by these glistening globules, gets firmly stuck. The edges of the leaf curl inwards, and the hairs bend over like tentacles to draw the insect to its centre. Here, the soft parts of the insect are gradually digested and absorbed. A possible explanation of this unusual habit is that living, as they do, in places where the soil is poor in mineral salts, the plants evolved an ability to trap and digest animal food. Thus they compensate for deficiencies in the soil; but how the change in structure and behaviour came about is not explained at all, and remains a fascinating mystery.

The Common Frog

Now let us take a look at the animal life of the pond. For collecting the various creatures you will need some screw-top jars and a fine-mesh net with a strong frame. If you visit the pond in March

Common Frog

or early April you may see rounded masses of frog spawn floating in the shallow water at its edges. Pull off a little spawn to take home for your pond, and leave the rest—on no account take the whole mass of eggs. The common frog, which really *was* common in the early part of this century, has now become relatively scarce. Frogs depend on the still water of ponds for breeding, and along with the ponds that get filled in or built on, the frogs are being squeezed out from large areas of the country. Also, the toll taken for school and college Biology classes, where the frog is a standard animal for dissection, must have contributed to its decline. Thus, in taking a little spawn for your garden pond, you will be doing an important practical service in helping to ensure the common frog's survival as a species in this country. In summer, when the little frogs leave your pond, they will know it as their home and return there to breed a few years later. Then it will matter that much less if the pond in which they were spawned gets filled in.

A few days after hatching, the tadpole of the common frog develops external gills which show as little tufts on each side behind its head. A week later the external gills wither and internal gills start to form. For the next six weeks or so the tadpole breathes like a fish. Water, sucked in through its mouth, passes over the gills and out through a small opening called a spiracle on its left side. Limb-buds appear by the base of its tail, then, over the next few weeks, a great change occurs. The hind legs gradually take form and the tadpole develops lungs and swims to the surface at times to gulp air. The hind legs lengthen, become functional and assist in swimming, and the front legs break through the skin. Finally, the tail is slowly reabsorbed, and the little frog climbs out on land. This great change from the larval, tadpole form to the adult shape, is known as 'metamorphosis'.

Prehistoric Lobe-fins

Three hundred million years ago an ancient group of fishes known as lobe-fins, because their paired fins were attached to lobe-like, stumpy legs, lived in freshwater pools, swamps and shallow lakes among the coal-forest trees. These lobe-fins developed lungs to help them to breathe when the water became stagnant and poor in oxygen, owing to the rotting portions of tree-ferns, club-moss trees and giant horsetails that gradually littered the mud of their

Lobe-fin

watery world. Thus, whenever pools became clogged or dried up, the fishes were able to make their way overland, with the help of their lobed fins, to fresh bodies of water. Any modifications that made the overland trip easier would be strongly selected, so in the course of millions of years their limbs developed joints, and their bodies became more flexible. Among the ferns and mosses of the forest floor there were hordes of worms, millipedes, early insects and primitive spiders, so the lobe-fins' descendants learned to feed on these, and spent more of their time on land. Their encumbering fringe-fins disappeared, and fingered feet were formed to grip the soil. So, the first amphibians came into being. In the three months of its development in the pond, the common frog re-enacts this age-long evolutionary process.

Mudskippers

Even today there are small fish called mudskippers that spend most of their time on land. Mudskippers live in the mangrove marshes along tropical seashores. They have limb-like front or pectoral fins, by means of which they can lever themselves over the mud quite quickly, assisted by their tails, or climb up on exposed supporting-roots of mangrove trees. Mudskippers have not developed lungs, but they have large gill-chambers which they fill with water before coming on land. However, the water in their gill-chambers has to be renewed at frequent intervals, and they need to keep their skins moist, so they are not able to travel inland from the

Mudskipper

shore. Mudskippers feed on worms, small crustaceans and insects that they find on the mud flats and the mangrove roots. When disturbed, they go skittering over the mud into the sea.

Lungfish

There are three kinds of fish, however, that do have lungs as well as gills. These are the three kinds of lungfish living today, one in Australia, one in South America and one in Africa, of which there are four species. Lungfish are closely related in kind to the ancient lobe-fins, and are the only survivors of an equally ancient group. The living lungfish inhabit pools, streams or rivers that tend to become stagnant or dry up during the long dry season. They survive these critical periods because they can breathe air. The South American lungfish tunnels in the mud, leaving just a small breathing hole, when its stream dries up; and two species of African lungfish do likewise and secrete slime, which hardens in to a cocoon with a hole at the upper end. In this way they can survive for long periods in mud that has become baked by the sun. This resting state in hot weather is known as 'aestivation'.

African Lungfish

The Australian lungfish, which inhabits rivers in Queensland, and relies more on its gills for breathing, does not aestivate. An interesting point about the African and South American lungfish is that their eggs hatch into larvae with external gills. After a few months their external gill-tufts are absorbed and permanent internal gills develop—a similar change to that we saw in the young frog tadpole. Unlike the lobe-fins, the lungfish, despite their ability to breathe air, were never able to invade the land, and the paired fins of the present-day African and South American kinds are reduced to tentacles.

Development of Toads and Newts

We have travelled a long way in time and space—but now back to the pond. Toads and newts may have spawned in the pond, but their eggs will not be so easy to find. The eggs of the common toad will be in long strings of jelly, tangled round the stems of plants in the deeper water. Newts lay their eggs singly, and stick them on water plants, bending a small leaf round each egg to protect it. The development of toad tadpoles follows a similar pattern to that of frog tadpoles, but newt larvae, which are yellowish in colour, do not grow internal gills. They retain their tufts of external gills until they develop lungs and leave the pond. The front limbs appear first, and their feathery gills are not absorbed until all four legs are well developed.

Newt Larva

External and Internal Fertilisation

When frogs and toads reach the pond in early spring, each male mounts a female and clasps her tightly with his forelegs, so that his hands are pressed beneath her breast. The couple remain together, thus, until the female has laid her eggs. The male fertilises the eggs as soon as they emerge from the female's body, after which he releases his hold and they part to make their separate ways back to land. Fertilisation in frogs and toads is external, as it is in fishes and most other water creatures. By this, we mean that the male reproductive cells, called sperms, are shed into the water near the female reproductive cells, or eggs. Each sperm, which can only be seen through a powerful microscope, has a lashing tail, called a 'flagellum', by means of which it swims towards an egg and fuses with it. The fertile egg cell is then able to develop into a new individual creature. Fertilisation in mammals, birds, reptiles and insects is internal. That is to say, the sperms are shed directly into the female's body, where they fertilise the eggs before these are laid. Internal fertilisation is essentially an adaptation of life on land.

Fertilisation in Flowering Plants

Flowering plants overcome this problem of life on land by using insects or wind to carry pollen from the male organs, or stamens, of one flower, to the female organ, or pistil, of another. The pistil consists usually of three parts—the stigma, which is sticky or feathery to trap the pollen; the ovary, which contains the ovules; and the style, not present in all flowers, which is a stem or neck joining the stigma and ovary. After landing on a stigma, each pollen grain of the right kind germinates and sends a pollen-tube containing a male reproductive cell down through the style and into an ovule, where the male cell fuses with an egg cell, which can then develop into an embryo plant. This, however, is a much simplified account of the process, for flowering plants undergo what is known as 'double fertilisation'. That is to say the pollen tube contains a second male cell which fuses with two other cells in the ovule and causes a food store to develop. This food store, known as the 'endosperm', is used to nourish the embryo plant during its growth.

Hermaphrodites

Most flowering plants are hermaphrodite, that is to say each flower has stamens, and a pistil containing the ovules which, after fertilisation, become seeds. As the seeds develop, the ovary grows into a fruit, such as a berry, pod or capsule. However, some flowering plants, such as holly, are either male, having flowers with stamens but no pistil, or female, having flowers with a pistil but no stamens. Some animals, such as earthworms, slugs and garden snails, are hermaphrodite and contain both male and female organs. This means that each earthworm or snail will lay eggs after mating. Slugs and snails lay clusters of round eggs under stones or logs, but earthworms lay theirs in little oval cocoons which can be found in the soil.

Reproduction of Flowerless Plants

Ferns, horsetails and mosses, as mentioned earlier, are not flowering plants and reproduce by spores—but that is not the whole story. The spores of ferns are produced on the underside of the fronds, and those of horsetails on cones at the top of fertile stems. If, after being released in the air, a spore lands on suitable ground it germinates. However, it does not hatch into a baby fern or horsetail, but into a flat, green, tissue-thin, little plant called a 'prothallus', which lies on the surface and attaches itself by tiny root-like structures. I have seen fern prothalli, which are heart-shaped and about a centimetre long, growing on rotting logs in a wood, and at the base of damp shady walls. The fern prothallus forms minute male and female organs on its underside. Each female organ produces an egg and each male organ produces sperms. The sperms swim through wet soil to the female organs and fertilise the eggs. A fertile egg then develops into a minute embryo which is nourished by the prothallus. Soon the baby fern emerges, sending its own roots into the soil, and the prothallus withers.

Fern Prothalli

Alternation of Generations

Here we see a pattern of life that is in one way similar to that of amphibians, such as frogs and newts. Ferns and horsetails, like amphibians, live on land but depend on water for sexual reproduction. The big difference is that these plants reproduce by spores that do not require fertilisation, and it is their offspring, the prothalli, that produce sperms and eggs. This kind of double life-cycle is known as 'alternation of generations'. It occurs, also, in

mosses, liverworts and most seaweeds, and in a few animals, such
as jellyfish, aphids and certain gall-wasps.

Look at some cushions of moss growing on an old wall in spring.
You will see little green or rust-red capsules at the top of slender,
pin-sized stalks, rising from some of the moss plants. These stalked
capsules are the spore-producing generation of the moss. The moss
plant itself is the sexual generation which develops male and
female organs, each in a little cup of leaves at the top of the stem.
The sperms swim in rain water or dew to the female organs and
fertilise the eggs; and the stalked capsules, which are really separate plants, arise from these. Spores are later shed from the ripe
capsules, after which the stalk and capsule wither and fall away.
Some of the spores will land on suitable ground and germinate,
giving rise to new moss plants.

Moss with Capsules

Now compare this with the life-cycle of a fern, where the spore-
producing generation is the fern plant, and the sexual generation
is the tiny prothallus, which gives rise to a baby fern and soon
withers. But meanwhile the little fern has formed roots in the soil
and become independent. Thus the fern can grow to any size,
according to its kind, and there are ferns in tropical rain forests
that grow into tall trees. In mosses the situation is reversed. Here
the sexual generation is the main plant, but it cannot grow big
because it depends on rain water for reproduction. Its offspring is
the stalked capsule which remains attached to the moss plant, so
cannot grow big either. If only the little stalked capsule had
learned to get down from its mother's knee and stand on its own
feet, so to speak, by forming roots in the soil and growing leaves,
then we might have had spore-producing generations of the moss
plant as tall as trees.

Liverworts have a similar life-history to that of mosses. A
common liverwort is pellia which can be found on the banks of
streams and ditches. It has no leaves, and the plant body, called a

Liverwort with Capsules

thallus, is flat and frond-like with a forked tip and lobes at the sides. The male and female organs are on the upper-surface of the thallus and, in early spring, round black spore-capsules are produced on white stalks. Each capsule splits into four segments to release the spores; so what looked like a round-headed pin, opens out like a tiny four-petalled flower.

The Oak Apple Gall-wasp

An example of alternation of generations in animals is to be seen in the life-history of a little gall-wasp that causes the formation of oak apples on the twigs of oak trees. Oak apples swell rapidly in May, and at that time they are variedly coloured with pale green, yellow and rose pink. As they mature in late June, the galls, for that is what they are, become yellowish-brown suffused with rosy tints and spongy in texture. I collected one of these mature oak apples and placed the twig to which it was fixed in a jar. After covering the top of the jar with a piece of gauze, I placed it on the table in my study and waited. A few mornings later, when I got out of bed and went to my study, I found about three dozen tiny

Oak Apple with
Gall-wasps emerging

gall-wasps flitting about in the jar, and I saw that the oak apple was pitted with their exit holes. In the evening I took the gall-wasps back to their oak tree and shook them from the jar on to one of its lower branches.

An oak apple develops from one of the buds on a twig, and after hatching from the eggs, the minute grubs set up some sort of irritation which causes the bud to produce the abnormal plant tissue of the gall. Each grub lives in a separate cell, feeding on sap produced by the tree, and when fully grown it pupates in the cell. In late June or July the little gall-wasps, which are either all brothers or all sisters—for the two sexes develop in separate oak apples—bite their way out. After a short rest they fly off, eventually meet others of the right sex, and start mating. The fertilised females then make their way into the soil at the base of an oak tree, and lay eggs singly in the tissues of young roots. This results in the formation of root galls, each with a single grub inside. The root galls are about a third of an inch wide when mature, and look like little brown nuts. They take about sixteen months to mature, and the adult gall-wasps emerge in the second winter.

Now comes the surprise. If you visit an oak tree that had oak apples on its twigs, and do so round about Christmas time, you may see a wingless insect that looks rather like a very plump ant, crawling up the trunk or along one of the branches. It is an oak apple gall-wasp, and it is a female, for there are no males in this alternate generation. Moreover, she is larger than the tiny winged forms that emerge from oak apples in summer, and different in appearance. If you are patient enough to watch her movements you will eventually see her start laying her unfertilised, virgin eggs in a bud at the end of one of the twigs. Next summer the bud will become an oak apple, and in it will be little grubs that had a mother but no father.

As in ferns and mosses, the alternate generations are dissimilar—the sexual generation of winged gall-wasps arising from oak apples, and the non-sexual generation of wingless forms arising from root galls. The difference is that in ferns and mosses the non-sexual generation produces spores, whereas in the gall-wasps it produces virgin eggs. These astonishing facts were not known to early naturalists, who called the insects from root galls by one name and those from oak apples by another.

Fertilisation in Newts

So—from my simplified account of reproduction in frogs and
toads, the train of my thoughts has taken me to ferny woods, old
walls, the banks of ditches and the branches of an oak tree. But
now let us return to the pond in early spring. I pointed out that
fertilisation in frogs and toads is external, but in the case of
newts, despite the fact that they must reproduce in water, fertilisation is internal. Moreover, it is accomplished in an unusual
manner, for the sperms from the male are not shed directly into
the body of the female.

Smooth newts, being the commonest of the three British
species, are the most likely to be found in the pond. You will
see them swim to the surface with rapidly beating tails, let go
a bubble of air, breathe in a fresh supply and return to the
shady underwater jungle. It is easy to distinguish male newts
at this season, for they are in full breeding dress. Catch one in
a net and place him in a jar of water. You will see that he has
a tall wavy crest along his back and tail, a similar crest along
the lower edge of his tail and fringes of skin on his hind toes.
He is olive brown with a brilliant orange belly, and his lower
tail-crest has an orange margin with a stripe of bluish or
mother-of-pearl iridescence above it. His body and tail are pat-

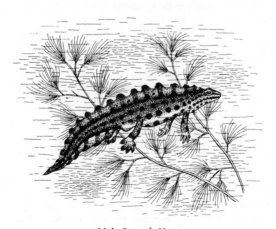

Male Smooth Newt

terned with black spots and there are black lines along his head. Now, having seen what a splendid creature he is, set him free in the pond, for the bright colours and adornments are there to be flaunted and displayed in courtship.

I have watched male newts courting females in ponds, and it is a charming spectacle. The male moves around the female waving his tail, undulating his crest, nudging her with his snout, and pressing or rubbing it gently along her sides. This may go on for hours, then finally he positions himself in front and, facing her, bends his tail double and vibrates it rapidly so that her body is stroked by the vibrations set up in the water. After repeating this performance a few times, the male newt emits a little capsule of sperms, called a 'spermatophore', on the floor of the pond. He then withdraws and the female newt, who has remained still and passive during the courtship, moves forward until the swollen cavity called the 'cloaca', which opens at the base of her tail, is directly over the spermatophore. She then presses her cloaca down on the spermatophore and takes it in. Once inside her body, the capsule dissolves and the released sperms fertilise her eggs. When the breeding season is over the newts climb out on land and move away. The crest and toe-fringes of the male are reabsorbed, and now he looks much like the female.

It will be nice to have a few newts for your garden pond, but it is better not to disturb them in the breeding season. Wait until the newt larvae have hatched and take home a few of these; then you will have the pleasure of watching them grow and develop until their metamorphosis is completed in August or September.

Warm-blooded and Cold-blooded Vertebrates

Newts, frogs, toads and other Amphibians are all backboned animals that have an internal skeleton. Such animals are called vertebrates. There are four other classes of vertebrates besides Amphibians. These are Fishes, Reptiles, Birds and Mammals. Birds and Mammals are said to be 'warm-blooded' vertebrates, which means that they have a constant body temperature. Fishes, Amphibians and Reptiles are said to be 'cold-blooded' vertebrates, which means that their body temperature varies with that of their surroundings. It does not mean that their blood is always cold, and a lizard will have warm blood if it is basking on a rock in full sunshine. Indeed, some reptiles maintain a fairly constant body temperature, but it is controlled by their movements and behaviour, and not from inside, like that of birds and mammals. Take, for instance, the crocodile. When I went on safari in East Africa I saw crocodiles basking with their mouths wide open on the banks of the Victoria Nile. They were not waiting for a meal to walk in, but were regulating their body temperature.

Crocodiles spend the night swimming about and hunting for food in the river. At sunrise they climb out of the water and flop down on a gently sloping beach or a grassy area on top of the bank. As the sun's heat strengthens, they open their mouths wide so that evaporating moisture from the membranes lining the inside of their jaws cools their blood. Around midday, when the sun climbs overhead, they retire into the shade of trees or return to the water, either submerging or lying half out of the water with open mouths. Then for two or three hours in the late afternoon they move back into the sun, and return to the river at sundown. They stay in the water at night to conserve their body

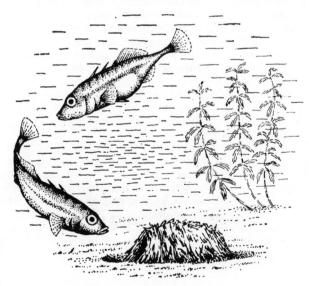

Male Stickleback guiding a female to his nest

heat, because water holds its heat much better than air. By following this sequence of alternating periods in sunshine, in shade and in water, crocodiles are able to maintain a body temperature that varies by only a few degrees.

Back again to our pond in the meadow—the only fish likely to be present is the three-spined stickleback. Take two or three for your garden pond, but do not take too many for they are very voracious. In spring the male three-spined stickleback develops a bright red throat and breast, and his eyes become brilliant blue-green. He scoops out a depression on the floor of the pond and piles bits of weed into this, forming them into a mound with sticky secretions from his body. He then bores a tunnel through the mound and induces females to lay their eggs in it, but drives away all male sticklebacks that enter his territory. He guards and aerates the eggs by fanning water through the nest with his fins, and protects the tiny young for their first few days after hatching.

The other vertebrate inhabiting the pond is the moorhen—a bird with a totally inappropriate name, for moors are one of the few habitats that it invariably avoids. Moorhens usually pair for life, and their nest of dead reeds will normally be on the mud or water, concealed among the stands of yellow flag or reed-mace. However, I have seen a moorhen incubating her eggs in a nest which she had built on the branch of a hawthorn tree over-

Moorhen and Chick

hanging a wide stream. Both parents incubate the eggs, which are whitish with brown speckles, and the black fluffy babies enter the water after hatching, but are fed by their parents for the first three weeks. It is charming to see the parent birds dip under water, emerge with a morsel of food in their beaks and deliver it gently to their chicks. Moorhens feed chiefly on water plants and insects, and there will only be one pair in the pond unless it is a very extensive one, for they are fiercely territorial.

Invertebrate Animals

The vast majority of animals in the world are invertebrates, and the same applies to the pond. Examples of invertebrate animals are insects, spiders, snails and worms. Vertebrate animals are generally big compared with invertebrates—but if you fill a barrel with apples and then pour peas into the barrel, shaking them down so that they lodge in all the spaces, there will be far more peas than apples in the barrel. If, after this, you pour sand into the barrel so that it is filled up with sand, peas and apples, you end up with far more grains of sand than all the peas and apples put together. So it is in any natural environment—there will be far more invertebrate animals than vertebrates, and far more tiny invertebrate animals than there are larger ones.

The peas in the barrel were able to occupy spaces that were not available to the apples, and the sand grains were able to occupy spaces that were not available to the peas. So it is with animals— the smaller they are, the more niches there are in the environment that they can occupy that are not available to larger creatures. The bigger an animal is, the more space it requires to move about in, and the more food it must consume to keep alive. For instance, an African elephant will eat about one and a half hundredweight of vegetation a day, and drink about fifty gallons of water, whereas some chalcid wasps can feed, grow up, pupate and complete their metamorphosis inside the eggs of moths. Thus, a batch of fifty moth eggs, occupying the space of a square centimetre, can supply enough food to nourish fifty chalcid wasps, not for a day but for the whole of their growing lives.

An Invertebrate Phylum

All vertebrate animals are included in one big group or phylum called the 'Chordata', but there are many phyla of invertebrates. I shall describe in brief just one of them which contain familiar animals. This is the phylum 'Arthropoda', which comprises all classes of animals that have segmented bodies, jointed legs and an external skeleton which covers the skin except at the joints and between the body segments. The five main classes of Anthropoda are as follows.

1. *The Crustacea*: With a few exceptions, this class contains all the marine anthropods, and includes crabs, lobsters, shrimps, sandhoppers and water-fleas. It also includes woodlice, which are said to be the only crustaceans able to spend the whole of their lives on land. However, when I was on holiday in Tenerife I found a species of sandhoppers under stones and leaf-litter in the banana plantations well away from the shore.

2. *The Insecta*: This is the only class of invertebrates that have evolved the power of flight. Apart from a few primitive kinds, insects have a larval stage and undergo metamorphosis. They have six legs, and usually two pairs of wings in the adult state.

3. *The Diplopoda*: This is the millipede class. Millipedes feed on fresh and decaying vegetable matter. They are usually long, often cylindrical, and have two pairs of legs on most of their body-segments. The pill-millipedes have short bodies and can curl into tight little balls. They should not be confused with pill-woodlice, which have only seven pairs of legs.

4. *The Chilopoda*: This is the centipede class. Centipedes are carnivorous, and have one pair of legs on most of their body segments, but the front pair take the form of poison-claws and curve round the head. These are used to capture and paralyse their prey. Centipedes are strictly nocturnal creatures, spending the day in hiding and, in some kinds, the mother guards her eggs and the young until they are able to look after themselves. One day in North Africa I turned over a stone, and there was a large centipede, about four inches long, curled round her clutch of nearly white babies. I touched her with a twig, and instead of retreating, she bit at it fiercely, still clutching her group of offspring. In centipedes there is an indirect method of fertilisation similar to that we saw in newts. The male deposits a spermatophore on the soil, which is taken up by the female.

5. *The Arachnida*: This class includes spiders, harvestmen, mites and scorpions. Arachnids have four pairs of legs and are without antennae. All spiders spin silk. Even hunting spiders that do not

spin webs, usually trail a line of silk behind them as they move about, and the females enclose their egg-batches in silk cocoons. Wolf spiders carry their egg-cocoons with them, attached to their spinnerets, and many other spiders guard their cocoons. I was able to testify to one instance of this when I was once in Majorca and found a European black-widow spider with her egg-cocoon under a stone on the waste ground behind my hotel. The egg-cocoon, attached by strong threads to some dry stems on the ground, was exposed to the blazing sunshine when I lifted the stone. To save her eggs, the black-widow started feverishly biting free the threads attaching the cocoon. Soon she had to retreat from the hot sun to cool down in the shadow of the lifted stone, but out she came again to sever a few more threads with frenzied haste before being forced back into the shadows by the heat. Out she came a third time, but I could not torment her any further, so I replaced the stone. The black-widow spider is not aggressive, but she can give an excruciatingly painful, and occasionally dangerous, bite when provoked. However, there is no doubt about her merit as a staunch and devoted guardian of her eggs.

Pond Invertebrates

Most of the invertebrate animals that you catch in the pond will belong to the phylum Anthropoda. But before you start collecting any for your garden pond, just stand or squat quietly at the edge of the water and watch the small creatures come and go. Pond skaters will skim over the surface with backward thrusts of their long middle pair of legs. If you move your arm, those nearest will leap away over the surface-film as if they were on a solid base. They do not even wet their feet, for these are covered with extremely minute, water-resistant hairs. There will also be sociable groups of whirligig beetles twisting, turning, swirling, revolving around each other on the surface. Wave your arm, and they will start gyrating at a frantic pace, yet without ever bumping each other. If you wade into the water they will all dive to the bottom, each with a small bubble of air attached to its rear. Return to the side and stand still for a few minutes—you will see them bob up to the surface, one after another, and twist, swivel and wind around each other as before. As the whirligig beetle swims, the under-surface is immersed, but the shiny upper-surface repels water and remains above it. The middle and hind legs of the whirligig are very short, broad and fringed, to form tiny paddles that are vibrated at speed in swimming. These two insects, the first a bug, the second a beetle, have become adapted to occupy a special niche in the pond community, as surface dwellers that feed on insects which fall into the water.

Pond Skater

Now gaze down into the water itself. Back-swimmer water-boatmen rest back downwards, suspended from the surface-film, or propel themselves with powerful strokes of their long oar-like hindlegs. Lesser water-boatmen swim in rapid jerks over the

Swimming Leech

muddy floor of the pond, and small water-beetles paddle vigorously above the mud, occasionally diving into it and kicking up little puffs of silt as they go by. Larger water-beetles, streamlined and neatly oval, swum up from the submerged jungles of pondweed, tilt themselves head-downwards to break the surface-film with the hind tip of their bodies, pause to renew the air supply beneath their wings, then row themselves smoothly down again. Bright vermilion water-mites, not more than two millimetres long, swim here and there through the water with a rapid running motion of their legs, and a leech swims past with graceful up-and-down undulations of its flattened body.

You will notice creatures moving on the floor of the pond. Water-snails and small black flatworms glide over the mud, and caddis-fly larvae shuffle along in their cases of cut plant stems, leaf sections, small snail-shells or little stones, according to the species. Water-lice crawl over the mud, and freshwater shrimps slither here and there on their sides, or leap up and glide swiftly through the water in a curve that lands them on the mud again. These two crustaceans are scavengers that eat whatever dead or decaying animal or plant material they find. The other pond crustaceans are minute. At the edge of the water milfoil jungle a swarm of water-fleas, or daphnia, floats in mid-water, each tiny unit engaged in a perpetual dance of upward jerks and downward drifts, and little pear-shaped copepods jump through the water with sudden back-whisks of their long antennae. These small crustaceans sift microscopic plant-life from the water. The myriads of microscopic plants form the base, or first link, of many food chains in the pond, for the water-fleas which eat them are eaten by water-mites, damsel-fly nymphs, sticklebacks, newt larvae and small water-beetles.

Now a piece of the mud bottom stirs, and you begin to perceive it for what it really is—the large-eyed head and stout cylindrical body, tapered at the rear, of a two-inch dragonfly nymph. You had not seen it as it rested, alert and watchful, on the mud, for its dingy colours merged with the surroundings. Suddenly the dragonfly nymph's hinged mouth-claw shoots, flash-quick, from beneath its head, and grabs a water-louse. The claw folds back and the nymph's jaws start to munch contentedly.

These are a few of the invertebrate animals that you might see in the pond. If you sweep your net gently to and fro through the thickets of submerged water plants you will find many more that were living among the stems and foliage. Damsel-fly nymphs, mayfly nymphs, smaller caddis-fly larvae with cases of green leaves that make them hard to distinguish among the plants, and water-scorpions. The latter are not scorpions, but predatory water bugs which capture prey with pincer-like front legs. A large, perfectly dry brown spider might turn up in your net. This is the water-spider which, so far as is known, has the distinction of being the only spider in the world that swims and lives permanently under water. The water-spider spins a curved platform of silk among the submerged plants. This is filled with bubbles of air which the spider carries down from the surface and releases under the web. Finally, a silk dome, filled with air, is formed—a diving-bell-home in which the spider rests. When swimming below the surface of the pond the water-spider appears as a living jewel of glittering quicksilver, for its velvety body is enclosed in a sheath of air.

Take home plenty of invertebrate animals for your garden pond, but see that you have far more small invertebrates in your col-

Water-spider with Air-bell

lection than there are larger ones. If you have not already stocked your pond with submergent water plants, fix the stem bases of those you have in small tins of soil, and cover the soil with stones to prevent it from floating out into the water when you lower the plants into your pond. Floating plants like frogbit can be placed straight on the water surface. Do not pour the water creatures from your jars or containers into the pond, but float them out by tilting each jar below the surface and pulling it gently backwards and up.

When the young frogs, toads or newts leave your pond they will find food and shelter in the wild strip of garden. Newts will hide under the large flat-bottomed stones in damp shady parts, and some flower-pots, well concealed and laid on their sides half-buried in the soil, will become permanent day-time shelters for toads throughout the summer months.

Classes and Families

A long, narrow wooden box placed in the shelter of a hedge or large bush in the wild strip, and covered with soil and moss, might tempt a hedgehog to set up home if you fill it loosely with dry grass or hay. Hedgehogs are mammals belonging to the order 'Insectivora', which include the mole and the four kinds of British shrews, one of which is confined to the Scilly Isles. Just as a phylum is split up into separate classes, each containing animals that are more similar to each other than they are to the rest, so each class is split up into separate orders. For instance, dogs, cats, weasels and other flesh-eating mammals that have sharp canine teeth and cutting molars, belong to the order 'Carnivora'. Rats, mice, beavers, squirrels and guinea-pigs belong to the order 'Rodentia', cloven-hoofed mammals such as cattle, sheep, deer, antelopes and giraffes belong to another order, the different kinds of bats to yet another and so on. In the same way, orders are split up into separate families, each containing animals with still closer resemblances. Thus, in the order Carnivora the dog family, 'Canidae', includes wolves, jackals and foxes; the cat family, 'Felidae', includes lions, tigers, leopards and lynxes; and the weasel family 'Mustelidae', includes otters, badgers, polecats and pine martens.

Try to sort out the other orders of mammals, then try to do the same with birds, and then with insects. When you have done your best at this, look them up in books and see how correct you were, and what mistakes you made. Later, try sorting out the orders into separate families. It is a fascinating game to play with a friend, and you will come to understand how different creatures are related to each other and how, in the far distant past, they evolved from common ancestors. Your imagination will be stirred, and you will come to see that by experimenting with different kinds of food, trying out different ways of life and exploring new areas of the environment, the animals were able to avoid competing with each other. Then you will feel an urge to discover all that is known about the processes and pressures, acting over millions of years, that caused the animals to diverge, adapted them to fill new areas of life and initiated the development of structures and behaviour that fitted them for different styles of living.

The Hedgehog

The hedgehog is one of the few wild mammals that most people see sooner or later, even if it is only as a squashed body on the road, for it has adapted well to living in parks and gardens. For millions of years, the hedgehog's one means of defence has been to roll up into a prickly ball and, apart from the motor car, its only enemies in Britain are the fox and the badger, both of which have learned how to force it open with their claws. Young hedgehogs are born in early summer and there are usually five to a litter. The babies are blind at birth and have soft white prickles. About five weeks later the mother starts taking them out on foraging expeditions. At dusk, on a mid-summer evening, you might see her leading a string of young ones from the nest.

Hedgehog

I very often hear a hedgehog before seeing it, for its search for insects, slugs, snails and other creatures is accompanied by snorts, soft grunts and snuffles. If I approach a hedgehog in the open it immediately stops in its tracks and lowers its snout so that the prickles on its neck and head stand upright. Should I come closer, the hedgehog curls into a ball, but if it is beside thick plant cover it usually makes a hasty retreat. One night in late spring I was woken up by a series of loud puffs, hisses and gurgling noises. I thought a hot-water pipe must have burst, so I got up and rushed downstairs; but not being able to find anything wrong inside the house, I went outside to investigate. My flashlight revealed two courting hedgehogs facing each other on the flower bed. After pausing for a moment they made off into the next garden, and I inwardly cursed myself for being so clumsy and missing the chance of watching their behaviour.

In autumn, hedgehogs accumulate layers of fat around the neck and shoulders to supply the small energy demands of hibernation when their bodies cool and their heart and breathing rates slow down to a life-supporting minimum. Then, towards the end of October, each hedgehog seeks out a dry, well-concealed hollow under a thick hedge, the cavity of an old wasp nest or a garden compost heap, and constructs a nest of leaves and moss which are carried home in its mouth. For the first month or two the hedgehog sleeps intermittently, and on mild evenings it may leave the nest or 'hibernaculum', and wander abroad; but by the new year its sleep has become very deep, and it will not stir until it wakes up in the spring.

Another ground-living mammal which uses spines as a means of protection is the echidna or spiny anteater, of which there are two species in Australia. The echidna looks rather like a hedgehog with a thin snout and large claws. Its snout ends in a tiny toothless mouth, and it feeds on termites and ants which are licked up on its long sticky tongue. The echidna's spines offer good protection against dingoes and other predators and, like a hedgehog, it will roll itself into a ball when disturbed. If the ground is soft, however, the echidna can dig itself vertically down, keeping its spines erect until it disappears beneath the surface. Echidnas are egg-laying mammals belonging to the order 'Monotrema', which also contains the duck-billed platypus. Their single eggs are laid in a pouch; when the young hatches, it is carried in the pouch until its spines start to grow. From then on the mother leaves her baby in a safe hiding place returning at intervals to feed it until it has been weaned.

Echidna

Convergence

The echidna somewhat resembles a hedgehog because it lives a similar kind of life and has evolved the same means of protection. When two different kinds of animals have come to bear certain resemblances because they play similar roles in the living community we call this phenomenon 'convergence'. The echidna shows convergence not only with the hedgehog but with the true anteaters of South America which also have thin snouts, small toothless mouths, long sticky tongues and large claws for opening termite nests.

Adaptive Radiation

The mammals with which we are most familiar are known as 'placental' mammals. That is to say, their young develop in the womb or uterus and are nourished through an organ called the 'placenta', which makes extremely close contact with the mother's blood. However, the majority of Australasian mammals belong to the order 'Marsupialia', or pouched mammals. Many of these show convergence with placental mammals of other continents. The reason for this is that the marsupials entered Australia before it became separated from the Asiatic mainland, and before the more successful placental mammals had reached it. Thus the marsupials were able to branch out, diversify and exploit the various habitats and food resources without serious competition. Some became tree dwellers, some grass eaters, some carnivores, some insect eaters and so on.

This branching out process, where a group of related animals becomes variously changed and specialised for different modes of life, is called 'adaptive radiation'. By adaptive radiation the marsupials came to fill similar niches in the environment to those filled by placental mammals in other parts of the world. A 'niche' is the particular role an animal plays in the living community, and where animals fill similar niches they tend to show convergence. The marsupial mole looks remarkably like any other mole, the marsupial mice look like field mice or wood mice everywhere else, the rat kangaroos look like the jerboas of North Africa, the Australian native cat is similar to the civets of southern Asia, the wombat, which has rodent-like front teeth, looks like an oversized marmot, the tree-living possums are similar to lemurs, bush-babies and lorises, the flying phalangers or glider possums show remarkable convergence with flying squirrels, the thylacine or marsupial wolf, so tragically exterminated by the early sheep farmers of Tasmania—or probably so, for the last known wild specimen was shot in 1930—really looked like a wolf or hunting dog, and the kangaroos of the grassy plains have heads resembling those

Thylacine

of gazelles and antelopes that graze the African savannahs. They also have rather similar stomach structures, containing stomach bacteria and protozoans to aid the digestion of leaves and grasses.

Nest Boxes

Now back from the ends of the earth to your garden sanctuary. You have provided a home for a hedgehog, flower-pot shelters for toads and large flat-bottomed stones for newts and for insects and other invetebrates—one of the insects you are likely to shelter will be the handsome violet-bordered ground beetle, the largest of our common garden beetles. You have also established a self-contained habitat for freshwater creatures. The next job will be to put up two or three nest boxes for birds to breed in.

To garden birds, houses with gardens probably appear as inland cliffs and crags scattered among open woodland and scrub. Sparrows and starlings nest in crevices of these crags, and house martins fix their mud cups on the stone surface, in the shelter of eaves and gutters. Blackbirds, thrushes, finches and dunnocks will be happy to nest in the trees, bushes and hedges of this man-made, shrubby woodland, but robins, wrens, tits, nuthatches, wagtails and flycatchers will be ready to accept nest boxes, for there is always a housing problem for hole-nesting birds.

There are two types of nest boxes. One has an open front, boarded up half-way; and robins, flycatchers and wagtails prefer this type. The other is an enclosed box with a round entrance hole, which will suit tits and wrens, and nuthatches if you are fortunate enough to live near an oak wood. For tits and wrens, a hole the size of a ten-penny piece will prevent sparrows from entering and taking over. For nuthatches, the hole must be larger; but the exact size does not matter, for they will reduce it to their requirements by applying mud round the edges and working it in with their bills. Fix the nest boxes to trees, fences or garden sheds and see that they face in a northerly direction. If they face south, the nestlings may get over-heated and die. A little moss, spread on the floor of the boxes will make them more attractive when prospecting birds visit them in spring.

Helping Birds in Winter

You will help the birds through the hard winter months by putting out extra food for them. Net bags, such as those used by green-grocers for carrots or oranges, if filled with peanuts and hung from a branch, will be appreciated by tits and greenfinches. Strings of peanuts in their shells, lumps of fat or meaty bones, hung from branches, will attract tits, and it is delightful to watch these acrobatic little birds swinging upside-down as they peck away at the food. If you want a bird table, all you need is a wooden platform, twelve inches square, screwed down on a post about five feet high; but I prefer to feed the birds on the lawn where I can scatter the food widely. I collect all bread, cake and biscuit crumbs,

Blue Tit on Strung Peanuts

chopped leftovers of cheese, meat scraps, skins of roast chicken, bacon rinds and bread soaked in fat from the frying pan.

The sparrows come first, even before I have finished scattering the crumbs, then a couple of collared doves alight and walk towards the crumbs, one or two blackbirds join them and a song thrush appears in the background. Quickly some starlings arrive, and more flutter down from the sky. The sparrows and collared doves peck away at the bread and cheese, the starlings in a close milling flock gobble everything as rapidly as they can, a blackbird spends half his time chasing off a persistent rival, and this is the song thrush's chance until one of the blackbirds sees him and drives him off, but when the larger mistle thrush comes bounding over the lawn the blackbirds themselves must give way. A robin flies in, picks a morsel of cheese, then returns to a bush but comes back for another, and another, and a few chaffinches and dunnocks feed round the fringes of the scattered crumbs. When all

the other birds have cleared what they can find and flown away
the dunnocks remain for quite a long time, hopping here and
there and flicking their wings almost too rapidly to see, as they
peck up the minutest bits of crumb that only their bills can gather.

Sometimes a magpie alights at the bottom of the lawn and
walks and hops towards the scattered food, alert and wary, with
pauses on his way, and head well up, feathers sleeked, and one
eye on the window so that I have to stand back and keep quite
still. On seeing him the sparrows and small birds scatter into trees
and bushes, the blackbird flies up on to the fence and the starlings
watch the magpie approach, then stand in a row a couple of
yards away, looking very subdued as they wait for him to finish
and fly off. On one occasion, however, a collared dove remained
feeding, then puffed out its chest and went jumping towards the
magpie, driving him off before he reached the crumbs. The magpie
flew on to the fence, but came back, and the collared dove repeated
its aggressive performance, then flew after him and really saw
him off. This was a most surprising piece of behaviour that I
should never have expected from a collared dove.

Collared Dove threatening a Magpie on the lawn

Occasionally some black-headed gulls come circling over the lawn, and then all the small birds scatter. The gulls fly round and round and swoop over the food, but dare not alight or swoop too low. At last one of them swoops down, picks up a piece of bacon rind or chicken skin, slapping the ground with his coral feet as he passes, and swallows the food in flight. The gulls continue to circle over the lawn and then another swoops and grabs some food, a third one follows suit, but none of them dares alight so near the house. Suddenly the gulls fly off, and all the small birds return and flutter down to peck the scattered crumbs.

For the naturalist in the world today, much that he holds most dear seems threatened from all sides. Just as an alpine slope would be bereaved and diminished without its blue gentians, its apollo butterflies, its whistling marmots and its flock of alpine choughs, or as a rock pool would be diminished without its green and scarlet seaweeds, its expanded sea anemones, its starfish and its glass-transparent prawns, so the human species will be bereaved and diminished if it can no longer experience the magic and the pulse of the universe in the clear, sweet trilling of tree-crickets on a warm Mediterranean night, or gasp at the fragile beauty of a wild flower. Natural History is concerned with the quality of life that cannot be registered on the balance sheet of material comforts, for it is about joy and wonder, and the saving and cherishing of this beautiful planet, with its fantastically varied life. In setting up a garden sanctuary, you will be doing something of incalculable value in the world, and come rain, hail or snow, so long as there is a window in your mind and in your house, you will never, never be bored.

Suggestions for Good Books

Rupert Barrington: *The Bird Gardener's Book* (Wolfe)
F. H. Brightman: *The Oxford Book of Flowerless Plants* (OUP)
Michael Chinery: *The Natural History of the Garden* (Collins)
John Clegg: *The Observer's Book of Pond Life* (F. Warne & Co. Ltd)
T. L. Jennings: *Studying Birds in the Garden* (Wheaton)
Arthur Jewell: *The Observer's Book of Mosses and Liverworts* (F. Warne & Co. Ltd)
Jean Mellanby: *Nature Detection and Conservation* (Carousel Books)
David Nichols & John Cooke: *The Oxford Book of Invertebrates* (OUP)

Marion Nixon: *The Oxford Book of Vertebrates* (OUP)
Tony Soper: *The Bird Table Book* (David & Charles Ltd)
Wildlife Begins At Home (David & Charles Ltd)
Hamlyn All-Colour Paperbacks
   Catherine Jarman: *Evolution of Life*
   Sali Money: *The Animal Kingdom*
   Tony Morrison: *Animal Migration*
   John Sparks: *Animals in Danger*
                 Bird Behaviour
   Ian Tribe: *The Plant Kingdom*

Useful Addresses

XYZ Club, Zoological Society, Regent's Park, London NW1
British Naturalists' Association. Branches all over the country.
   Address of local secretary obtainable from Council for Nature,
   Zoological Gardens, Regent's Park, London, NW1
Children's Centre, Natural History Museum, Cromwell Road,
   London SW7

MISCELLANY

However you divide the contents of an encyclopaedia, there are always essential pieces of information left over that seem to go nowhere in particular. It is these that you will find in this final section of JUNIOR PEARS.

Lantern Clock 1688

TIME: CALENDARS AND CLOCKS

THE DAYS OF THE WEEK

The names of the days—Sunday, Monday, Tuesday (Tiw—the God of War), Wednesday (Woden or Odin), Thursday (Thor), Friday (Frig—wife of Odin) and Saturday come from Old English translations of the Roman names (Sol, Luna, Mars, Mercurius, Jupiter, Venus and Saturnius).

HOW THE MONTHS GOT THEIR NAMES

January From Janus, a Roman god. The Anglo-Saxons called it *wulf-monath*—the month of the wolves.

February From a Roman god, Februus. A.S.: *sprote-cal*—the month when the kale, a kind of cabbage, sprouted.

March Originally the first month in the Roman calendar. From Mars, the god of war. A.S.: *hreth-monath*—the rough month.

April From the Latin *Aprilis*. A.S.: *Easter-monath*—month of Easter.

May From Maia, a goddess. A.S.: *tri-milchi*—the month when the cows were milked three times a day.

June From Juno, mother of the gods. A.S.: *sere-monath*—the dry month.

July Named after Julius Caesar. A.S.: *maed-monath*—meadow-month.

August   Named after Augustus Caesar. A.S.: *weod-monath*—the
month of vegetation.

September   The seventh Roman month. From the Latin word
meaning *seven*. A.S.: *haerfest-monath*—harvest month.

October   The eighth Roman month. From Latin word meaning
eight. A.S.: *win-monath*—the month of wine.

November   The ninth Roman month. From Latin word meaning
nine. A.S.: *wind-monath*—month of wind.

December The tenth Roman month. From Latin word meaning
ten. A.S.: *mid-winter monath*—mid-winter month.

THE YEAR

The Equinoctial or **Tropical Year** is the time the earth takes to go
round the sun: 365·422 solar days. The **Calendar Year** consists
of 365 days, but a year of which the date can be divided by 4
without a remainder is called a **Leap Year**, with one day added
to the month of February. The last year of a century is a Leap
Year only if its number can be divided by 400 (e.g. 1900 was
not a Leap Year, but 2000 will be one).

The Longest and Shortest Days   The longest day is the day on
which the Sun is at its greatest distance from the equator; this
is called the **Summer Solstice**. It varies between June 21 and
22.

   The shortest day is the day of the **Winter Solstice**, and in
1986 falls on December 22.

Dog Days   These are the days about the rising of the Dog Star,
the hottest period of the year in the Northern Hemisphere.
Roughly they occur between July 3 and August 25.

St Luke's Summer is a warm period round about St Luke's Day
(October 18).

St Martin's Summer is a warm period round about Martinmas
(November 11).

The Christian Calendar   Until 1582 the calendar used in all Christian countries was the Julian Calendar, in which the last year of
all centuries was a Leap Year. By the sixteenth century this
had caused a difference between the tropical and calendar years
(see **The Year**) of 10 days. In 1582 Pope Gregory ordered that
October 5 should be called October 15, and that of the years at
the end of centuries only every fourth one should be a Leap
Year. This new calendar was called the Gregorian Calendar and

was gradually adopted throughout the Christian world. In Great Britain and her Dominions it came into use in 1752; by then there was a difference of 11 days between tropical and calendar years, and September 3 of that year was reckoned as September 14.

Easter Day can be, at the earliest, March 22; at the latest, April 25.

Whit Sunday can be, at the earliest, May 10; at the latest, June 13.

The Jewish Calendar dates from October 7, 3761 B.C. In 1986 the Jewish New Year (5747) begins on October 4.

The Moslem Calendar dates from the Hejira, or the flight of Mohammed from Mecca to Medina (July 16, A.D. 622 in the Gregorian Calendar). In 1986 the Moslem New Year (1407) falls on September 6.

SUMMER TIME

Summer time—the putting forward of the clock by one hour during the months of summer—was first introduced in the First World War. Its purpose then was to cut down on the use of power for lighting; but in peace-time it was continued so that people might enjoy longer summer evenings.

From February, 1968, summer time was established for a three-year trial period to conform with Central European time. The new title chosen for it was British Standard Time. This experiment was abandoned in October, 1971, when the United Kingdom reverted to Greenwich Mean Time.

Normally British Summer Time is from the day following the third Saturday in March until the day following the fourth Saturday in October.

TIME ALL OVER THE WORLD

This table shows what the time is in the important cities of the world when it is 12 noon at Greenwich. Places in ordinary type are ahead of Greenwich; those in *italics* are behind Greenwich.

Accra, Ghana .	.	12 Noon	Ankara, Turkey .	2.00 p.m.
Adelaide, Australia .		9.30 p.m.	Athens, Greece .	2.00 p.m.
Algiers .	.	1.00 p.m.	Baghdad, Iraq. .	3.00 p.m.
Amsterdam,			*Baltimore, USA* .	7.00 a.m.
Netherlands	.	1.00 p.m.	Bangkok, Thailand .	7.00 p.m.

Belgrade, Yugos-			Madrid, Spain.	1.00 p.m.
lavia .	1.00 p.m.		Mandalay, Burma	6.30 p.m.
Berlin, Germany	1.00 p.m.		Melbourne,	
Berne, Switzerland .	1.00 p.m.		Australia	10.00 p.m.
Bombay, Inda.	5.30 p.m.		Mexico City	6.00 a.m.
Boston, USA .	7.00 a.m.		*Montevideo, Uruguay*	9.00 a.m.
Brisbane, Australia.	10.00 p.m.		*Montreal, Canada*	7.00 a.m.
Brussels, Belgium	1.00 p.m.		Moscow, USSR	3.00 p.m.
Budapest, Hungary.	1.00 p.m.		Nairobi, Kenya	3.00 p.m.
Buenos Aires,			New Delhi, India	5.30 p.m.
Argentina .	9.00 a.m.		*New York*	7.00 a.m.
Cairo, Egypt .	2.00 p.m.		Nicosia, Cyprus	2.00 p.m.
Calcutta, India	5.30 p.m.		Oslo, Norway .	1.00 p.m.
Calgary, Canada	5.00 a.m.		*Ottawa, Canada*	7.00 a.m.
Canberra, Australia	10.00 p.m.		*Panama* .	7.00 a.m.
Cape Town, South			Paris .	1.00 p.m.
Africa .	2.00 p.m.		Peking, China.	8.00 p.m.
Chicago, USA .	6.00 a.m.		Perth, Australia	8.00 p.m.
Colombo, Ceylon	5.30 p.m.		*Port of Spain,*	
Copenhagen,			*Trinidad*	8.00 a.m.
Denmark	1.00 p.m.		Prague, Czecho-	
Darwin, Australia .	9.30 p.m.		slovakia	1.00 p.m.
Detroit, USA .	7.00 a.m.		*Quebec, Canada*	7.00 a.m.
Dublin, Ireland	12 Noon		*Quito, Ecuador*.	7.00 a.m.
Freetown, Sierra			*Reykjavik, Iceland*	11.00 a.m.
Leone.	12 Noon		*Rio de Janeiro* .	9.00 a.m.
Gibraltar.	1.00 p.m.		Rome .	1.00 p.m.
Halifax, Nova			*St John's, New-*	
Scotia .	8.00 a.m.		*foundland*	8.30 a.m.
Hamilton, Bermuda .	8.00 a.m.		*San Francisco, USA* .	4.00 a.m.
Harare, Zimbabwe	2.00 p.m.		*Santiago, Chile*.	8.00 a.m.
Havana, Cuba .	7.00 a.m.		Seoul, Korea .	8.30 p.m.
Helsinki, Finland	2.00 p.m.		Singapore	7.30 p.m.
Hong Kong	8.00 p.m.		Stalingrad, USSR	4.00 p.m.
Honolulu, Hawaii	2.00 p.m.		Stockholm, Sweden.	1.00 p.m.
Jerusalem	2.00 p.m.		Sofia, Bulgaria	2.00 p.m.
Johannesburg,			Suva, Fiji .	12 Midnight
South Africa	2.00 p.m.		Sydney, Australia .	10.00 p.m.
Karachi, Pakistan	5.00 p.m.		Teheran, Iran .	3.30 p.m.
Kingston, Jamaica	7.00 a.m.		Tirana, Albania	1.00 p.m.
Kuala Lumpur,			Tokyo, Japan .	9.00 p.m.
Malaya	7.30 p.m.		*Toronto, Canada*	7.00 a.m.
Lagos, Nigeria.	1.00 p.m.		*Vancouver, Canada* .	4.00 a.m.
Leningrad, USSR	3.00 p.m.		Vienna, Austria	1.00 p.m.
Lima, Peru .	7.00 a.m.		Warsaw, Poland	1.00 p.m.
Lisbon, Portugal	12 Noon		Wellington, New	
Los Angeles, USA	4.00 a.m.		Zealand .	12 Midnight
Luxembourg .	1.00 p.m.		*Winnipeg, Canada*	6.00 a.m.

BRITISH FLAGS

The Union Jack* was adopted in 1606 following the Union of England and Scotland, and took its present form in 1801, when there was the further union with Ireland (see HISTORY). It consists of three heraldic crosses:

> the cross of St Andrew, which forms the blue and white basis;
>
> upon which lies the red and white cross of St Patrick;
>
> upon the whole rests the red and white cross of St George dividing the flag vertically and horizontally.

The Union Jack

The correct manner of flying the flag is with the larger strips of white next to the flagstaff uppermost.

The Royal Standard is the sovereign's personal flag, only to be flown above a building when she is actually present. It is divided into quarters, the 1st and 4th containing the three lions *passant* of England, the 2nd quarter containing the lion *rampant* of Scotland and the 3rd quarter containing the harp of Ireland. (*Passant* and *rampant* are terms in heraldry, see the section on Heraldry that follows.)

The White Ensign, the flag of the Royal Navy, is a white flag bearing the cross of St George, with a small Union Jack in the top corner next to the flagstaff.

---

* Although it has become usual to call this flag the Union Jack on all occasions, it is strictly correct to do so only when the flag is flown at the jackstaff of one of Her Majesty's ships. At all other times it should be called the Union Flag.

The Royal Standard

The Red Ensign (known as 'the red duster'), flag of the Mercantile Marine. It is a plain red flag with the Union Jack in the top corner next to the flagstaff.

The Blue Ensign (similar to the Red Ensign, but with blue background), flag of the Royal Naval Reserve (RNR).

A NOTE ON HERALDRY

Man has always used symbols to decorate his armour; but heraldry as we know it started in Europe in the twelfth century. Knights began to wear helmets which completely covered their wearers' faces, making recognition difficult. So when they met together at tournaments or went on crusades it was necessary that each should have a personal badge. This became known as the knight's **coat-of-arms** because it was worn on his sur-coat over his armour. The most obvious place to put the arms was on the shield. On his helmet a knight sometimes bore another distinguishing badge—the **crest**—which rested on a band of twisted cloth—the **torse**. This held in place a **mantling** to protect the metal from the hot sun. When all these are brought together they form an **achievement of arms** (Fig. 1). Once you have seen them together you are unlikely to make the popular mistake of calling a coat-of-arms a crest.

Because heraldry was formulated so long ago, the language used is a mixture of Norman-French and Latin and English. At first this may seem difficult; but once a few terms are mastered it can be seen to be a very practical language. Describing arms in words is called **blazoning**, and the method is to name the colour or colours of the **field** (the background), then to describe the main

Fig. 1
Achievement of Arms

Per pale gules and
argent, a chief
indented ermine

13th century Knight

charge and its colour, and finally to name the subsidiary charges
with their colours. Only five **tinctures** are commonly used—red,
called **gules**: blue, called **azure**: green, called **vert**: purple, called
purpure: and black, called **sable**. There are two **metals**, gold (**or**)
and silver (**argent**), and these are usually represented by yellow
and white. In addition there are **furs—ermine**, **vaire** and
numerous variations. A basic rule of heraldry is that a coloured
charge should not be placed on a colour nor a metal one on a
metal.

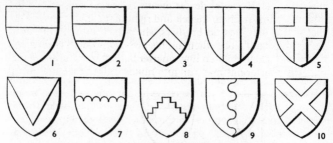

Fig. 2   Some ordinaries and lines of partition

1 Chief: 2 Fess: 3 Chevron: 4 Pale: 5 Cross: 6 Pile: 7 per fess invected:
8 per chevron indented: 9 per pale wavy: 10 Saltire

All items on a shield are known as **charges** and can be anything
and everything from ants to zebras. The main charges are known
as **ordinaries**. Sometimes the field is divided into more than one
colour (as in Fig. 1), and the ordinaries lend their names to these
divisions. The dividing lines can be straight or wavy-shaped or
angular; Fig. 2 shows some of these.

Eldest Son
Label

2nd Son
Crescent

3rd Son
Mullet

4th Son
Martlet

5th Son
Annulet

6th Son
Fleur-de-Lis

7th Son
Rose

8th Son
Cross Moline

Fig. 3

It is possible to tell from a coat of arms to which member of a family it belongs. The head of the family bears plain arms, but his sons must carry a symbol to **difference** his arms from those of his father and his brothers (Fig. 3). Women bear their father's arms on a **lozenge** (a diamond shape), with no difference, and they cannot inherit arms if they have brothers. If a woman marries, her husband **impales** his wife's arms on the **sinister** side of his shield (Fig. 4). (In Latin **dexter** means right and **sinister** left, but in heraldry this refers to the left and right of the man carrying the shield.) If a lady has no brothers, she herself inherits the arms and her husband places them on his own arms on an **escutcheon of pretence**. Their children may **quarter** both parents' arms. Sometimes the quarterings may run into hundreds, but they are not all displayed.

Fig. 4

1 Per pale a chief indented impaling a bend: 2 Per pale a chief indented and on an escutcheon of pretence a bend: 3 Quarterly, 1st and 4th per pale a chief indented 2nd and 3rd a bend. (Note—Colours are omitted in these blazons.)

At first, no doubt, men chose their own symbols; but soon the monarch became the ultimate authority for granting arms. In England this authority is delegated to the Earl Marshal (at present the Duke of Norfolk), who is responsible for arranging great state occasions. To help him he has the College of Arms consisting of the Kings of Arms—Garter, Clarenceux and Norroy and Ulster— six Heralds and four Pursuivants. In Scotland the principal officer is Lord Lyon, who has three Heralds and three Pursuivants.

Heraldry is a living part of our history. Not only is it found in old manuscripts and in churches and castles, but it can be seen on town halls, banks, company offices and advertisements. Look at your school badge and those of your friends. Some are real arms and have been granted to the school; but most are badges based on the arms of the town or a famous man (Fig. 5). Some, alas, may even have been invented by someone with no knowledge of heraldry.

BBC
A gold band of communication surrounding the Earth

National Coal Board
An heraldic pictorial representation of a coal mine

UK Atomic Energy Authority
Pictorial representation of an atomic pile

Barrow Grammar School badge with a bee and arrow from the 'punning' arms of Barrow and the roses of Lancashire

Fig. 5

This is no more than an introduction to the subject and you may want to read more about it. The books listed below are not dry but lively, well-illustrated and in one instance very amusing. Your library may have them. If you want to take your study further, the Secretary of the Heraldry Society, 59 Gordon Square, London, WC1, will be pleased to send you information.

Simple Heraldry, by Iain Moncreiffe and Don Pottinger.
Boutell's Heraldry, revised by C. W. Scott-Giles and J. P. Brooke-Little.

Shield and Crest, by Julian Franklyn.
Discovering Heraldry, by R. H. Wilmott.

NOTES ON COINS

Coins as Weights and Measures A penny weighs 3·564 grams, and has a diameter of 2·0320 cm. The diameter of the 50p coin is 3 cm: of the 20p coin, 2·14 cm. The £1 coin weighs 9·5 grams, and has a diameter of 2·25 cm.

British Coins Our **coppers** are really bronze (97 parts of copper, 2½ parts of zinc and ½ part of tin). The **farthing** (then of silver) was first struck in 1279 and withdrawn at the end of 1960. First **halfpenny** struck, in silver, in 1280: changed to bronze with penny and farthing in 1860: the old halfpenny ceased to exist on August 1, 1969. **Penny** introduced in 8th century: first copper pennies struck in 1797: demonetised on February 15, 1971, when Britain switched to decimal coinage and introduced also the new two pence piece. **Threepence** struck as silver coin in 1551; replaced in 1937 by a twelve-sided brass coin that was demonetised in 1971.

Our **silver** in 1946 became cupro-nickel (75% copper, 25% nickel). The **shilling** (called then a testoon) was first struck as a silver coin by Henry VII: it is now the 5p piece. The **florin** (10p) appeared in 1849, the first step towards putting the English coinage on a decimal basis. (This earlier scheme was abandoned.) The **half-crown** was first struck in the reign of Edward VI: ceased to exist on January 1, 1970. The **sixpence** ceased to be legal tender on June 30, 1980. **The historical portraits** on all bank notes are: £5, Duke of Wellington; £10, Florence Nightingale; £20, William Shakespeare; £50, Sir Christopher Wren.

Legal Tender Bank of England notes and gold dated 1838 onwards are legal tender for any sum. The £1 coin is legal tender to any amount. (The £1 note was withdrawn from circulation during 1985.) Silver (cupro-nickel) coins with values up to and including 10p are legal tender up to £5; 50p and 20p coins up to £10, and bronze up to 20p.

American Coins The word **dime** comes from the French dixième, a tenth part, and is the name given to the silver 10 cent coin, which is a tenth part of a dollar. **Nickel** is the popular name for the five-cent American coin, made of copper and nickel. The probable origin of the **dollar sign** (\$) is that it is an adaptation of the old Spanish method of recording the peseta or piece of eight as a figure eight between sloping lines (/8/).

DISTANCE OF THE HORIZON

The distance to which you can see depends on the height at which you are standing.

At a height of		You can see	
5 ft	(1·52 m)	2·9 miles	(4·64 km)
20 ft	(6·1 m)	5·9 miles	(9·44 km)
50 ft	(15·24 m)	9·3 miles	(14·88 km)
100 ft	(30·48 m)	13·2 miles	(21·3 km)
500 ft	(152·4 m)	29·5 miles	(47·2 km)
1,000 ft	(304·8 m)	41·6 miles	(66·5 km)
2,000 ft	(609·6 m)	58·9 miles	(94·24 km)
3,000 ft	(914·4 m)	72·1 miles	(115·36 km)
4,000 ft	(1,219 m)	83·3 miles	(133·28 km)
5,000 ft	(1,524 m)	93·1 miles	(149 km)
20,000 ft	(6,096 m)	186·2 miles	(298 km)

THE SEVEN WONDERS OF THE ANCIENT WORLD

1. **The Pyramids of Egypt** The oldest is that of Zoser, at Saggara, built about 3000 B.C. The Great Pyramid of Cheops covers more than 4·9 hectares (12 acres) and was originally 146 m (481 ft) high and 230 m (756 ft) square at the base.
2. **The Hanging Gardens of Babylon** Adjoining Nebuchadnezzar's palace near Baghdad. Terraced gardens watered from storage tanks on the highest terrace.
3. **The Temple of Diana at Ephesus** A marble temple erected in honour of the goddess about 480 B.C.
4. **The Colossus of Rhodes** A bronze statue of Apollo (see A DIC-TIONARY OF MYTHOLOGY) with legs astride the harbour entrance of Rhodes. Set up about 280 B.C.
5. **The Tomb of Mausolus** At Halicarnassus, in Asia Minor. Built by the king's widow about 350 B.C. From it comes our word 'mausoleum'.

6. **The Statue of Olympian Zeus** At Olympia in Greece; made of marble inlaid with ivory and gold by the sculptor Phidias, about 430 B.C.

7. **The Pharos of Alexandria** Marble watch tower and lighthouse on the island of Pharos in Alexandria Harbour. Constructed about 250 B.C.

ROMAN NUMERALS

I	.	.	.	.	.	.	1
II	.	.	.	.	.	.	2
III	.	.	.	.	.	.	3
IV	.	.	.	.	.	.	4
V	.	.	.	.	.	.	5
VI	.	.	.	.	.	.	6
VII	.	.	.	.	.	.	7
VIII	.	.	.	.	.	.	8
IX	.	.	.	.	.	.	9
X	.	.	.	.	.	.	10
XI	.	.	.	.	.	.	11
XII	.	.	.	.	.	.	12
XIII	.	.	.	.	.	.	13
XIV	.	.	.	.	.	.	14
XV	.	.	.	.	.	.	15
XVI	.	.	.	.	.	.	16
XVII	.	.	.	.	.	.	17
XVIII	.	.	.	.	.	.	18
XIX	.	.	.	.	.	.	19
XX	.	.	.	.	.	.	20
XXX	.	.	.	.	.	.	30
XL	.	.	.	.	.	.	40
L	.	.	.	.	.	.	50
LV	.	.	.	.	.	.	55

LX	.	.	.	.	.	60
LXX	.	.	.	.	.	70
LXXX	.	.	.	.	.	80
XC	.	.	.	.	.	90
IC	.	.	.	.	.	99
C	.	.	.	.	.	100
CX	.	.	.	.	.	110
CXC	.	.	.	.	.	190
CC	.	.	.	.	.	200
CCC	.	.	.	.	.	300
CD	.	.	.	.	.	400
D	.	.	.	.	.	500
DC	.	.	.	.	.	600
DCC	.	.	.	.	.	700
DCCC	.	.	.	.	.	800
CM	.	.	.	.	.	900
XM	.	.	.	.	.	990
M	.	.	.	.	.	1000
MLXVI	.	.	.	.		1066
MD	.	.	.	.		1500
MDCCC	.	.	.	.		1800
MCMLXXXVI	.	.	.			1986
MM	.	.	.	.		2000

SOME ALPHABETS

Greek

Name	Letter		English equivalent
Alpha	A	α	a
Beta	B	β	b
Gamma	Γ	γ	hard g

Name		Letter	English equivalent
Delta	Δ	δ	d
Epsilon	E	ε	short *e* (as in 'egg')
Zeta	Z	ζ	z, dz
Eta	H	η	long *e* (as in 'bee')
Theta	Θ	θ	th
Iota	I	ι	i
Kappa	K	κ	k or hard *c*
Lambda	Λ	λ	l
Mu	M	μ	m
Nu	N	ν	n
Xi	Ξ	ξ	x
Omicron	O	ο	short *o* (as in 'box')
Pi	Π	π	p
Rho	P	ρ	r
Sigma	Σ	σ, s	s
Tau	T	τ	t
Upsilon	Y	υ	u or y
Phi	Φ	φ	ph, f
Chi	X	χ	kh or hard *ch*
Psi	Ψ	ψ	ps
Omega	Ω	ω	long *o* (as in 'dome')

Russian

Letter	English eq	Letter	English eq
А а	a	Р р	r
Б б	b	С с	s
В в	v	Т т	t
Г г	g	У у	u
Д д	d	Ф ф	f, ph
Е е	yeh	Х х	kh as in 'loch'
Ж ж	zh	Ц ц	ts
З з	z	Ч ч	ch
И ий	e	Ш ш	sh
К к	k	Щ щ	shch
Л л	l	Ы ы	y as in 'did'
М м	m	Э э	e as in 'egg'
Н н	n	Ю ю	yu
О о	o	Я я	ya
Ц ц	p		

The deaf and dumb alphabet

LONGEST AND HIGHEST

HIGHEST BUILDINGS AND OTHER STRUCTURES

	m	ft
KTHI-TV mast, N. Dakota	628	(2,063)
TV Tower, Toronto	550	(1,805)
TV Tower, Oklahoma City	479	(1,572)
Empire State, New York	448	(1,472)
Sears Tower, Chicago	443	(1,454)
ITA TV Masts, Emley Moor (Yorks), Belmont (Lincs)	385	(1,265)
TV Tower, Tokyo	329	(1,082)
Chrysler Building, NY	318	(1,046)
ITA TV Mast, Winter Hill (Lancs)	309	(1,015)
Eiffel Tower, Paris	299	(984¼)
60 Wall Tower, NY	289	(950)
Bank of Manhattan, NY	282	(927)
Rockefeller Centre, NY	259	,(850)
Woolworth Building, NY	241	(792)
Moscow State University	239	(787)
Albert Hertzog Tower, Johannesburg	235	(772)
City Bank, NY	225	(740)
Toronto-Dominion Bank Tower, Toronto	225	(740)
Terminal Tower, Cleveland	215	(708)
Metropolitan Life, NY	213	(700)
TV Mast, Stuttgart	213	(700)
500 Fifth Avenue, NY	212	(697)
Chanin, NY	207	(680)
Lincoln, NY	205	(673)

	m	ft
Husky Tower, Calgary, Canada	190	(626)
GPO Radio Tower London	176	(580)
Chicago Temple	173	(569)
Ulm Cathedral, Germany	161	(529)
Bank of State, São Paulo, Brazil	158	(520)
Blackpool Tower	157	(518)
Cologne Cathedral, Germany	156	(512)
St John the Divine, NY	152	(500)
Strasbourg Cathedral	142	(468)
The Pyramid of Cheops, Egypt	137	(450)
St Peter's, Rome	136	(448)
St Stephen's Cathedral, Vienna	134	(441)
St Joseph's Oratory, Montreal	126	(414)
Salisbury Cathedral	123	(404)
Antwerp Cathedral	121	(397)
Torazzo of Cremona, Italy	121	(397)
The Tower Block, Millbank Development, London	118	(387)
Freiburg Cathedral, Germany	117	(385)
St Paul's Cathedral, London	111	(365)
The Shell Centre, London	106	(351)
St Patrick's Cathedral, Melbourne	103	(340)

LONGEST TUNNELS

	km	Miles		km	Miles
East Finchley to Morden	28	(17½)	Otira, New Zealand .	8	(5)
Golders Green to South			Ronco, Italy . .	8	(5)
Wimbledon . .	25·6	(16)	Hauenstein, Switzer-		
Shimuzu, Japan. .	22·2	(13¾)	land . . .	8	(5)
Simplon, Switzerland to			Colle di Tenda, Italy .	8	(5)
Italy . . .	20	(12½)	Connaught, Canada .	8	(5)
Apennine, Italy. .	18·4	(11½)	Hoosac, USA . .	7·2	(4½)
Furka base, Switzerland	15·4	(9½)	Sainte Marie-aux-		
St Gothard, Switzerland	14·8	(9¼)	Mines, France .	7·2	(4½)
Loetschberg, Switzer-			Rove, France . .	7·2	(4½)
land . . .	14·4	(9)	Severn, England .	6·4	(4)
Mont Cenis, Italy .	13·6	(8½)	Mont d'Or, Switzerland		
Cascade, USA . .	12·4	(7¾)	to France . .	6·4	(4)
Arlberg, Austria .	10	(6¼)	Albula, Switzerland .	6·4	(4)
Moffat, USA . .	9·6	(6)	Boughton to Cedera, S.		
Shimizu, Japan . .	9·6	(6)	Africa . . .	6	(3¾)
Rimutaka, New Zealand	8·8	(5½)	Totley, England. .	5·9	(3½)
Ricken, Switzerland .	8·4	(5¼)	Standedge, England .	4·8	(3)
Grenchenberg, Switzer-			Woodhead, England .	4·8	(3)
land . . .	8·4	(5¼)	Puigcerda to Aix-les-		
Tauern, Austria .	8·4	(5¼)	Thermes, France .	4·8	(3)

LONGEST BRIDGES

	Length of waterway			Length of waterway	
	m	in ft		m	in ft
Oosterscheide, Nether-			Forth Road, Scotland	1,876	(6,156)
lands . . .	5,021	(16,476)	Rio Dulce, Argentina	1,786	(5,860)
Lower Zambesi, Africa	3,450	(11,320)	Hardinge, Bangladesh	1,639	(5,380)
Storsstrom, Denmark	3,200	(10,500)	Victoria Jubilee, Mon-		
Tay, Scotland . .	3,136	(10,290)	treal . . .	1,621	(5,320)
Upper Son, India .	2,999	(9,840)	Moerdijk, Netherlands	1,432	(4,700)
Godavari, India .	2,706	(8,880)	Humber, England .	1,370	(4,626)
Forth Railway,			Verazzano—Narrows,		
Scotland	2,526	(8,290)	New York . .	1,298	(4,260)
Tay Road Scotland .	2,294	(7,365)	Sydney Harbour,		
Rio Salado, Argentina	2,042	(6,700)	NSW . . .	1,255	(4,120)
Golden Gate, San			Jacques Cartier, Mon-		
Francisco . .	1,889	(6,200)	treal . . .	1,185	(3,890)

LONGEST SHIP CANALS

	km	Miles		km	Miles
St Lawrence Seaway,			Kiel . . .	97·6	(61)
Canada (including L.			Volga-Don USSR .	96	(60)
Ontario and Welland			Panama. . .	80	(50)
Canal) . . .	604·8	(378)	Elbe-Trave, Germany	65·6	(41)
Gota, Sweden . .	184	(115)	Manchester . .	56·8	(35½)
Suez . . .	164·8	(103)	Princess Juliana, Neth-		
Volga-Moscow . .	128	(80)	erlands . . .	32·8	(20½)
Albert (Antwerp-Liege)	128	(80)	Amsterdam . .	26·4	(16½)

A GUIDE TO SOME OF THE MOST IMPORTANT MUSEUMS IN GREAT BRITAIN

NATIONAL MUSEUMS

The British Museum, Great Russell Street, London, WC1.
Victoria and Albert Museum, Cromwell Road, London, SW7.
Royal Scottish Museum, Chambers Street, Edinburgh, 1.
National Museum of Wales, Cathays Park, Cardiff.

PREHISTORY AND EARLY CIVILISATION

British Museum, Great Russell Street, London, WC1.
Horniman Museum, London Road, Forest Hill, SE23.
National Museum of Welsh Antiquities, University College of North Wales, College Road, Bangor.
National Museum of Antiquities of Scotland, Queen Street, Edinburgh, 2.
Pitt Rivers Museum, Parks Road, Oxford.
Ashmolean Museum, Beaumont Street, Oxford.
Fitzwilliam Museum, Cambridge.
Yorkshire Museum, Museum Street, York.
Wells Museum, Cathedral Green, Wells, Somerset.
Museum of the Glastonbury Antiquarian Society, Glastonbury.
Verulamium Museum and Roman City, St Albans, Hertfordshire.
Viroconium Museum, Wroxeter, Shropshire.
Reading Municipal Museum, Blagrave Street, Reading.
Bath Roman Museum, Abbey Churchyard, Bath.
Roman Site and Museum, Corbridge, Northumberland.
Legionary Museum, Caerlon, Gwent, Wales.
Avebury Manor, Avebury, Wiltshire.
Segontium Roman Fort Museum, Beddgelert Road, Caernarvon, Gwynedd.
Museum of Sussex Archaeology, Barbican House, Lewes.
Colchester and Essex Museum. The Castle, Colchester.

NATURAL HISTORY AND GEOLOGY

British Museum (Natural History), Cromwell Road, London, SW7.

National Museum of Wales, Cathays Park, Cardiff.

Royal Scottish Museum (Natural History Dept.), Chambers Street, Edinburgh, 1.

Zoological Museum, British Museum, Natural History Dept., Akeman Street, Tring, Hertfordshire.

Oxford University Museum, Parks Road, Oxford.

Cambridge University Museum of Zoology, Downing Street, Cambridge.

Geological Museum, Exhibition Road, London, SW7.

Horniman Museum, London Road, Forest Hill, SE23.

Brooke Museum, Brighton, Sussex.

Robertson Museum and Aquarium, Marine Station, Keppel Pier, Millport, Scotland.

Hancock Museum, Barras Bridge, Newcastle-upon-Tyne, 2.

Marine Biological Station, Aquarium and Fish Hatchery, Port Erin, Isle of Man.

Cannon Hill Museum, Pershore Road, Birmingham.

Royal Botanic Gardens, Kew, London.

Botanic Gardens, Oxford.

University Botanic Gardens, Cambridge.

Zoological Gardens, Regent's Park, London: also in Edinburgh, Manchester and other big cities.

GEOGRAPHY

British Museum (Ethnographical Dept.), Great Russell Street, London, WC1.

Imperial Institute, South Kensington, London, SW7. (For the countries of the Commonwealth.)

Horniman Museum, London Road, London, SE23.

Royal Geographical Society Museum, 1 Kensington Gore, London, W8.

Pitt Rivers Museum, Parks Road, Oxford.

Cambridge University Museum of Archaeology and Ethnology, Downing Street, Cambridge.

Pitt Rivers Museum, Farnham, Blandford, Dorset.

SCIENCE

Science Museum, Exhibition Road, South Kensington, London, SW7.

Museum of the History of Science, Broad Street, Oxford.

Whipple Museum of the History of Science, 14 Corn Exchange Street, Cambridge.

Science and Engineering Museum, Exhibition Park, Great North Road, Newcastle.

Wellcome Historical Medical Museum, 183 Euston Road, London, NW1. (Medical science.)

Anatomical Museum, University New Buildings, Teviot Row, Edinburgh, 8. (Medical science.)

Birmingham City Museum, Dept. of Science and Industry, Newhall Street, Birmingham, 3.

AGRICULTURE

Agricultural Museum, Wye College, Wye, Kent.

Rothamsted Experimental Agricultural Institute, Harpenden, Hertfordshire.

Reading University Dept. of Agriculture Museum, Reading, Berks.

Cambridge Agricultural Institute, Cambridge.

The Curtis Museum, High Street, Alton, Hampshire.

West Yorkshire Folk Museum, Shibden Hall, Halifax, Yorkshire.

TRANSPORT

London Transport Museum, Covent Garden, London, WC2.

MOTOR CARS

Science Museum, Exhibition Road, South Kensington, London, SW7.

Museum of Carriages, Kent County Museum, Chillington, Manor House, Maidstone, Kent.

Museum of Motor Cars, Beaulieu Abbey, Brockenhurst, Hampshire.

SHIPS

Science Museum, Exhibition Road, London, SW7.
National Maritime Museum, Greenwich, London, SE10.
Royal United Service Museum, Whitehall, London, SW1.
Fisheries and Shipping Museum, Pickering Park, Hull.

RAILWAYS

National Railway Museum, Leeman Road, York.
Great Western Railway Museum, Swindon.

AIRCRAFT

Science Museum, London, SW7.
Shuttleworth Collection, Old Warden Aerodrome, Old Warden, Bedfordshire.

PHOTOGRAPHY, FILM AND TELEVISION

National Museum of Photography, Film and Television, Prince's View, Bradford.

PUBLIC SERVICES

Imperial War Museum, Lambeth Road, London, SE1.
Scottish United Service Museum, Crown Square, Edinburgh Castle, Edinburgh.
Royal Military Academy Sandhurst Museum, Camberley, Surrey.
The Armouries, Tower of London, EC3.
Wallace Collection, Hertford House, Manchester Square, London, W1. (Armour.)
Glasgow Museum, Kelvingrove, Glasgow. (Armour.)
Airborne Forces Museum, Maida Barracks, Aldershot, Hampshire.
Chartered Insurance Institute Museum, 20, Aldermanbury, London, EC2. (Firefighting.)
National Army Museum, Royal Hospital Road, SW3.
Royal Air Force Museum, Colindale, Hendon.

SOCIAL AND DOMESTIC HISTORY

Victoria and Albert Museum, Cromwell Road, South Kensington, London, SW7.
Museum of London, Aldersgate Street, EC2.
Cambridge and County Folk Museum, Cambridge.
Welsh Folk Museum, St Fagan's, Glamorgan.
Stranger's Hall Folk Museum, Norwich.
York Castle Museum, Tower Street, York.
Bishop Hooper's Lodging Folk Museum, Gloucester.
Kent County Museum, Chillington Manor House, Maidstone, Kent.
Manx Village Folk Museum, Cregneash, Isle of Man.
Folk Museum, Kinguissie, Inverness.

FURNITURE

Geffrye Museum, Kingsland, London, E2.
Old House, High Town, Hereford.
Georgian House, Great George Street, Bristol.
Ham House, Petersham, Surrey.
Temple Newsam, Leeds.
The Pavilion, Brighton.
Iveagh Bequest, Ken Wood, London, NW3.

COSTUME

Victoria and Albert Museum, Cromwell Road, London, SW7.
Bethnal Green Museum, Cambridge Heath Road, London, E2.
Gallery of English Costume, Platt Hall, Rusholme, Manchester, 14.
Museum of Costume, The Pavilion, Brighton, Sussex.
Canongate Tolbooth, Edinburgh, 8.

CHILDREN'S MUSEUMS

Bethnal Green Museum, London, E2. (Dolls, dolls' houses, toys, model theatres, children's books.)
Tollcross Museum, Tollcross Park, Glasgow.
Museum of Childhood, High Street, Edinburgh.

CRICKET

Imperial Cricket Memorial Gallery, Lord's Cricket Ground, London, NW8.

THE ARTS

National Gallery, Trafalgar Square, London, WC2.
National Portrait Gallery, Trafalgar Square, London, WC2.
Tate Gallery, Millbank, London, SW1. (Modern art.)
Victoria and Albert Museum, Cromwell Road, London, SW7.
Wallace Collection, Hereford House, Manchester Square, London, W1.
Sir John Soane's Museum, 13 Lincoln's Inn Fields, London, WC2. (Architectural drawing.)
Dulwich College Picture Gallery, College Road, London, SE21. (Chiefly seventeenth and eighteenth centuries.)
National Gallery of Scotland, The Mound, Edinburgh, 1.
Scottish National Portrait Gallery, Queen Street, Edinburgh, 2.
National Museum of Wales, Cathays Park, Cardiff.
Fitzwilliam Museum, Cambridge.
Ashmolean Museum, Oxford.
Bowes Museum, Barnard Castle, County Durham.
Walker Art Gallery, Liverpool.
Whitworth Art Gallery, Oxford Road, Manchester.
Norwich Castle Museum, Norwich.
City Museum and Art Gallery, Birmingham.
Barber Institute of Fine Arts, The University, Birmingham, 15.
Graves Art Gallery, Sheffield, 1.
Museum of Eastern Art, Broad Street, Oxford.
Royal College of Music, Donaldson Museum, London, SW7. (Musical instruments.)

MUSEUMS ILLUSTRATING THE LIVES OF FAMOUS PEOPLE

Jane Austen Jane Austen's House, Chawton, Hants.
J. M. Barrie The Birthplace, Kirriemuir, Angus, Scotland.
The Brontës Brontë Parsonage Museum, Haworth, nr. Keighley, Yorkshire.

John Bunyan Bedford Public Library, Bedford.

Robert Burns Alloway Cottage and Museum, Ayrshire.

Lord Byron Newstead Abbey, Nottinghamshire.

Thomas Carlyle Carlyle's House, 24 Cheyne Row, London, SW3.

Sir Winston Churchill Chartwell, Westerham, Kent.

S. T. Coleridge Coleridge's Cottage, Lime Street, Nether Stowey, Somerset.

James Cook Museum of Literary and Philosophical Society, Whitby, Yorkshire.

Charles Darwin Downe House, Downe, Kent.

Charles Dickens Dickens' House, 48 Doughty Street, London, WC1.
Dickens' Birthplace, 393 Commercial Road, Portsmouth.
Bleak House, Broadstairs, Kent.

Francis Drake Buckland Abbey, Plymouth.

Thomas Hardy Dorset County Museum, Dorchester.

Samuel Johnson Dr Johnson's House, Breadmarket Street, Lichfield.
Dr Johnson's House, 17 Gough Square, Fleet Street, London, EC4.

John Keats Keats Memorial House, Wentworth Place, Keats Grove, London, NW3.

David Livingstone Scottish National Memorial to David Livingstone, Blantyre, Scotland.

John Milton Milton's Cottage, Chalfont St Giles, Buckinghamshire.

Horatio Nelson Nelson Museum, New Market Hall, Priory Street, Monmouth.

Isaac Newton The Museum, Grantham.

Cecil Rhodes Rhodes Memorial Museum, Bishop's Stortford.

Capt. Scott Polar Research Institute, Cambridge.

Walter Scott Huntley House Museum, Edinburgh, 8.

William Shakespeare Shakespeare's Birthplace, Stratford-on-Avon.
New Place, Stratford-on-Avon.
Anne Hathaway's Cottage, Shottery, Warwickshire.
Mary Arden's House, Wilmcote, Warwickshire.

George Bernard Shaw Shaw's Corner, Ayot St Lawrence, Hertfordshire.

R. L. Stevenson Memorial House, Howard Place, Edinburgh.

James Watt Watt Institution, 15 Kelly Street, Greenock, Scotland.

Duke of Wellington Wellington Museum, Apsley House, Hyde
  Park Corner, London, W1.

John Wesley Wesley's House, 47 City Road, London, EC1.

William Wilberforce Wilberforce House, Hull.

William Wordsworth Dove Cottage, Grasmere, Westmorland.
  Wordsworth Museum, Grasmere, Westmorland.
  Wordsworth's Birthplace, Cockermouth, Cumberland.

JUNIOR
PEARS
ENCYCLOPAEDIA